Acme Publishing and Engraving Co.

Chicago of To-Day

The metropolis of the West. The nation's choice for the World's Columbian

exposition - 1891

Acme Publishing and Engraving Co.

Chicago of To-Day
The metropolis of the West. The nation's choice for the World's Columbian exposition - 1891

ISBN/EAN: 9783337287368

Printed in Europe, USA, Canada, Australia, Japan

Cover: Foto ©Andreas Hilbeck / pixelio.de

More available books at **www.hansebooks.com**

EARL & WILSON,

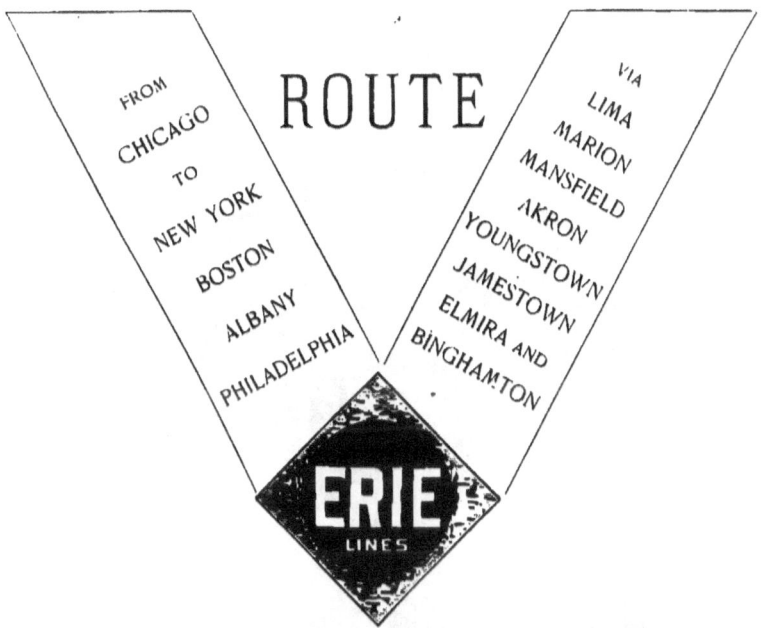

ROUTE

FROM
CHICAGO
TO
NEW YORK
BOSTON
ALBANY
PHILADELPHIA

VIA
LIMA
MARION
MANSFIELD
AKRON
YOUNGSTOWN
JAMESTOWN
ELMIRA AND
BINGHAMTON

ERIE
LINES

Double Daily Service by SOLID EXPRESS TRAINS, carrying Pullman Sleeping Cars (Pullman Dining Cars on Vestibule Limited Trains).

Pullman Sleeping Cars between Chicago and Boston via Binghamton, Albany and the Hoosic Tunnel Route, and to Ashland, Ky., via Marion and Columbus.

W. C. RINEARSON,	A. M. TUCKER,	D. I. ROBERTS,
Gen. Passenger Agent,	Gen. Manager,	Assist. Gen. Pass Agent,
NEW YORK.	CLEVELAND.	CHICAGO.

i

Masonic Temple.

TURNBULL & CULLERTON.

THE necessity of good roofing material, in a climate liable to extremes of heat and cold, is imperative, and this desideratum is found in Turnbull & Cullerton's "Gypsumineral" Cement Roofing, an invention of the utmost value used by men of the most practical type, who have known all the disadvantages of other roofing, and who in this compound have conquered all such difficulties. "Gypsumineral" has had twenty-three years' test; is practically fireproof; can be walked over with less injury than

G. A. TURNBULL.   HON. E. F. CULLERTON.

any other; contracts and expands in sudden changes without injury to roof; contains no injurious matter; does not run in the hottest, nor crack in the coldest weather; is the only cement which can be applied successfully to pitched roofs; will last thirty years, and last, but not least, can be laid on old felt roofing, and be as good as new, and much better than a new resin composition roof. With this as their specialty Messrs. Turnbull & Cullerton have made a success of their business. It was established in 1868 by Messrs. Freutel & Turnbull. In January, 1890, Mr. Freutel retired, and for a short time the firm was known as Turnbull & Co. In March, 1890, Messrs. Turnbull & Cullerton joined their interests, the latter gentleman having been for some time a silent partner. He is an alderman from the ninth ward, and has represented that section of the city in the City Council since 1871, in fact, he is the premier of the Chicago City Council, having been elected twelve consecutive times from three different wards; has been twice acting mayor and ten years the Chairman of Finance Committee, which is really one of the most important offices in the city government. He was also a member of the House of Repre- sentatives of the Twenty-eighth General Assembly of the State of Illinois. He is a native of Chicago. Mr. Cullerton was formerly connected with the car heating and sidewalk ventilation business, and the many who know him give him the credit of being a genial whole-souled business man. Mr. Turnbull is a native of Scotland, but has made his home in Chicago for about a quarter of a century, and is an unassuming, hardworking and successful business man. He is, we are told, a relative of Pittsburgh's most suc- cessful and enterprising iron master, who is also a Scotchman, an author and a public benefactor. The factory of the

and Blue Island avenue, and about fifty a large area of ground They are gen- and sheet steel roofing, as well, Turn- Roofing and Corrugated Iron being the cago Metallic Roofing & Corrugating Col. Egerton Adams (president of Chi- G A. Turnbull vice-president, and E. F. Their success is shown in the wide adop- testimony to the worth of the material, well be quoted here, and fitly conclude cess: "Build not thine house upon a people are employed, the works covering eral manufacturers of corrugated iron bull's Patent Spring-Cap Sheet Steel specialty, under control of the Chi- cago Forge and Bolt Co), is president, Cullerton secretary and treasurer. tion of their roofs and the unvarying so that the motto of the company can this brief notice of its commercial suc- sandy foundation, and keep the waters from intruding into thy dwelling by putting on a Gypsumineral cement roof, then when the floods come thou wilt surely be glad." Among the numerous works in hand or executed by this progressive and prosperous company may be mentioned the roofing of the Frazer & Chalmers Mining Machinery Plant in this city, and which covers an area of over half a million square feet, the roofing of the Grant Locomotive Works, covering an area of 250,000 square feet, besides many other large contracts in and out of Chicago. They roofed J, M. Smyth's new Town Market, and have been working half the summer on the large engine houses and machine shops of the Chicago & Northwestern Railroad Co. along their different lines, in fact, almost wherever large concerns of any class require permanent roofing they call upon Turnbull & Cullerton. Their office is located at 195 La Salle Street.

CHICAGO OF TO-DAY.

THE METROPOLIS OF THE WEST.

THE NATION'S CHOICE FOR THE WORLD'S COLUMBIAN
EXPOSITION.

HANDSOMELY ILLUSTRATED.

1891.

PUBLISHED BY
ACME PUBLISHING AND ENGRAVING CO.,
WASHINGTON BLOCK, CHICAGO, ILL.

INTRODUCTION.

THE compilers of this volume, as a means of introduction, cordially desire to extend to the business men of Chicago their sincere thanks for their kindly assistance in the prosecution of this enterprise. The aim and object of the work are sufficiently apparent in its title,—" Chicago of To-day, the Metropolis of the West,"—and we assume that all will admit that it requires no optimistic pen to record the progressiveness of this mighty city of the prairies. Our duties have been arduous, but have been made much easier by the kind reception with which we have been met, and while our work must necessarily be imperfect in many particulars—absence of proprietors, indifference of merchants, or other untoward circumstances—we hope it will not prove unworthy of the wide distribution which its patrons have already guaranteed, and that it will redound to the future good of the city and the city's trade. We have made many agreeable acquaintances, and wherever our lot may be cast in the future shall always have a pleasant remembrance of the unselfish interest displayed toward this statistical brochure, which is a sufficient guarantee that any legitimate enterprise will have the generous encouragement of the merchants and manufacturers of Chicago. The review, although condensed, will be found to be very complete, covering every material feature of development, yet without any attempt at mere word-painting. The keen perception of capitalists or business men readily discriminates to a characteristic degree between solid merit and glittering pretence, hence we leave this volume for their closest scrutiny. We have endeavored to perform the task to which we assigned ourselves, with due regard to surrounding conditions, without fear or favor, and trust that we have succeeded in portraying the advantages and the business opportunities for the still greater upholding of this colossal commercial and industrial center. It is not claimed, however, that a perfect balance sheet of progress is given. This is prevented by various idiosyncrasies that obtain in almost every community, which render the collection of statistics difficult from the indifference or aversion of individuals furnishing them. It will be noticed that all matter contained in this work, not compiled by the editors, is credited to the authority from which it has been taken, or which has furnished it, and we here take the opportunity of admitting our obligations in this direction to the past historians, the newspaper fraternity, as also Messrs. John J. Flinn, Rufus Blanchard, Colbert and Chamberlain, and other authorities of indisputable reliability. While the work is for the most part couched in our own language, we, of course, have had to secure the early facts and dates from others, and to all who have aided us in any respect we return our sincere thanks. What the future or limits of the city of Chicago may be no man can faintly imagine. Her wealth and trade increase materially day by day; new enterprise is daily drawn to her center, which, combined with the energy and perseverance of her citizens, must more firmly than ever establish and increase the widespread fame and reputation of the " Metropolis of the West."

Very respectfully,

CHICAGO, 1891.   THE PUBLISHERS.

PROMINENT ILLUSTRATIONS.

TABLE OF CONTENTS.

REPRESENTATIVE BUSINESS HOUSES.

xiv   TABLE OF CONTENTS.

Drexel
Fountain

CHICAGO OF TO-DAY
The Metropolis of the West

STRIDING, like some modern Colossus, the southwestern shore of Lake Michigan, Chicago, the capital, the metropolis of the wealth-producing West, rears her stately head, the most remarkable city in the world. Within the past nine decades a swamp, the story of her subsequent rise and progress has no parallel in the whole history of the country. Men and women still live among us who remember when Chicago was, so to speak, in her swaddling-clothes; when there were no mansions and no villas, no huge factories and no mammoth stores; when a ride of half a mile from the site of the Palmer House block was a trip to the country. Beyond that point the region at the time indicated was almost like an unknown portion of the earth. Here and there were a few straggling farmhouses, but in the broad intervals between them lay an arid waste, the scene a veritable swamp, the site of a horrible Indian massacre. To-day look at it! The little handful of citizens, the village of 1831 with its twelve houses, has grown to a mighty population among whom is spoken every civilized language of the globe. Steamers and every description of lake craft ply at the port with the regularity of ferryboats; the news of the Old World is as close to us in point of time as if it came from a neighboring town; while through the telephone we listen to the voices of friends hundreds of miles away. Time and space are practically annihilated; presage and opinion have been at fault; convenience and facility have been potential; and what in the Old World would be deemed but a short lapse of period has sufficed to create a city with over a million inhabitants, replete with the products of the soil, resonant with the hum of manufacture, and abounding with the treasures of art and comfort. Truly has Chicago's march of progress been upward and onward. Great parks, broad avenues and magnificent architecture; schools, colleges, churches, clubs, art galleries, hospitals and public institutions now tell the story of a young race always moving onward toward the achievement of the noblest ends in life! What a contrast! In a little while Chicago will have enlarged her already wide domain by absorbing the surrounding towns and villages; more public improvements will have been carried out, and many notable enterprises will have been inaugurated. In fact, the engineer and capitalist are already at work digging, building, and developing to the utmost our vast possibilities, to the end that Chicago shall be, when the time arrives to celebrate her centennial, one of the greatest, if not the greatest, city on the American continent. And in view of her favorable geographical situation, unrivaled natural advantages and splendid facilities, it requires no great draught on prophetic ken to foresee the realization of this forecast for the Garden City, the Phenix City of America, the Metropolis of the West. While it is not our purpose or mission to enter into minute details concerning the early settlement and history of Chicago, it is proper for us to embody, in a work of this character, a brief sketch of the more notable facts in the development of this populous locality from the trackless waste it once was.

THE CITY'S INCEPTION AND DEVELOPMENT.

The name Chicago is of Indian origin, signifying "wild onion," and is first mentioned by Perrot, a Frenchman, by whom it was visited in 1671. In 1803 a stockade fort was erected near the mouth of the Chicago River, and named Fort Dearborn. When the war with Great Britain broke out in 1812, the government, apprehensive that a post among the Indians so far from the frontier could not be successfully maintained, ordered the commander to abandon it. The Indians destroyed the fort, which was rebuilt in 1816. The town was organized by the election of a Board of Trustees, August 10, 1833. On September 26th of the same year a treaty was made for all their lands with the Pottawattomies, 7,000 of the tribe being present, after which they were removed west of the Mississippi River. Where the Postoffice now stands there was a wolf-hunting in 1832, and in 1833 there were great rejoicings that goods could be transported from New York to St. Louis in the short space of twenty-three days. The charter incorporating the city of Chicago was approved March 4, 1837. The city was first lighted by gas September, 1850. The first railroad in the Northwest was the Galena and Chicago Union, completed to Harlem in 1848, and to Elgin in 1850 The Rock Island Road was opened as far as Joliet in 1851. The Illinois Central Road was chartered in 1851, and communication was established with New York in 1852, by the completion of the Michigan Southern, connecting with the Erie Railroad. Some of the early settlers feared that canals and railroads would ruin the city. To the pioneers of that period, did they survive, a visit to the Chicago of to-day would possess all the merit of a fairy tale. Instead of the insignificant military station, they would now find a solidly-built, wealthy metropolis; the greatest railroad center and primary grain port in the world; the scene of the ceaseless activities of over a million of eager, restless toilers, attracted by its fame from far and near. Fragmentary as our remarks under the semblance of an historical caption may appear, we opine we have said enough of the past. Our business, as the title of this work indicates, is with the present; with living men and their daily occupations and successes; what they are doing for themselves in manufactures, commerce, trade and finance, and in advancing the general prosperity of the community.

LA SALLE ST.
LOOKING
SOUTH.

STATISTICAL.

Chicago received its charter of incorporation in 1841, and has rapidly advanced and increased in population and commercial importance since, the following statement of statistical facts exhibiting in a remarkable degree the great resources, wealth, and condition of this municipality in a local as well as a universal sense. The estimated number of the population in 1835 was 1,000, and the exact number according to census returns was, in 1840, 4,470; 1845, 12,080; 1848, 20,035; 1850, 20,260; 1852, 38,733; 1853, 60,652; 1855, 83,509; 1860, 150,-000; 1867, 187,446; 1870, 298,977; 1875, 410,000; 1880, 503,304—1890 reaching a grand total of 1,098,576.

Chicago (pronounced she-kaw-go) is situated on the southwestern shore of Lake Michigan, at the mouth of the Chicago River, lat. 42° 50' 20" N., long. 87° 37' W.; 854 miles from Baltimore, the nearest point on the Atlantic seaboard, and 2,417 miles from San Francisco. Its mean elevation is 75 feet above Lake Michigan, or 591 feet above mean sea-level. The climate is healthful and invigorating, although the winters are cold and the temperature in summer is liable to great and sudden changes; but an exceptionally well-managed health department succeeds in keeping public health pretty high. The death-rate of 17.48 per 1,000 population (1889) is among the lowest for any city of the size of Chicago on the globe. This is a remarkable fact when the unsanitary site, the rapid growth, and the crowded condition of some of its districts by foreigners are considered. Some years ago, the elevation of the principal streets, also the buildings, were raised from 4 to 10 feet, the object of this gigantic undertaking being to admit of a thorough system of sewerage. The Chicago River and its branches separate the city into three divisions, connected by large tunnels. The main stream, flowing directly west, is about 100 yards wide, and forms one of the best harbors on the lakes. Vessels ascend the river and its branches a distance of 4 miles from its mouth, thus affording nearly 18 miles of wharfage.

Chicago as a manufacturing and commercial center holds a most prominent position, and there is an enormous demand for her products from all parts of the United States and also from foreign countries. Much may be truthfully written of the advantages possessed by an industrial

Douglas Monument.

town as compared with those possessed by a commercial or agricultural community. The last mentioned was first in the order of civilization. Man's first possessions were the direct products of the soil. That people living continuously in one place might possess the various articles resulting in differences in climate and peculiarities of soil, an interchange of productions became necessary, and thus arose commerce. At this stage of the world's progress, owing to the accumulation of nature's products, men first had leisure. With leisure came the cultivation of the intellect, when men began to analyze and compare the various commodities in order to learn what changes in character, forms and combinations of different articles were possible to the end that means might be attained for gratifying the desires and wants of man. Thus mechanical still was quickened into life and activity, and thence arose industry. Agriculture, commerce and industry thus are typical of three grades of civilization, the last mentioned being latest in order of appearance, but *first* in culture and refinement. It is then but the fulfillment of nature's edict that the industrial community is peculiar to modern civilization. With the diffusion of knowledge and the advancement of science came the development of manufactures. No country more forcibly illustrates the truth of our first statement than the United States. Here are the finest types of the manufacturing village or city. Nowhere are there industrial communities possessing so high an intellectual and moral tone. They are the natural outgrowth of our democratic institutions, and are the strongest testimonials to the inestimable benefits conferred upon humanity by our republican form of government. No American city more clearly shows this to be true than the subject of this brief sketch. No one can examine the record of the early and later industries, projects and enterprises of this city of far-reaching influences without feeling that no common type of manhood has exercised the invincible energy, the prophetic foresight, the heroic rectitude, the noble patriotism and the sterling business, and every-day prosaic effort that the annals of Chicago realize. Her miles of streets filled with the incessant roar of industry; her lofty temples, magnificent warehouses and elegant residences; her public institutions of learning; her gigantic commerce; her high degree of civilization—all of which have been attained by older cities after a prolonged struggle with adversity, are here the creations and accumulations for less than two generations, presenting to the eye a great and magnificent city which embodies more perfectly than any other in the world the possibilities of accomplishment of. the Anglo-Saxon race—given its best condition of freedom, independence and intelligence. In a word, to quote from the able compilation of Mr. John J. Flinn on the subject, "Not in the Arabian Nights' entertainments, though bathed in all the glorious colorings of oriental fancy is there a tale which surpasses in wonder the plain, unvarnished history of Chicago."

A FEW FACTS ABOUT A BUSY CITY.

RAILROAD SYSTEM OF CHICAGO.—Whether the city of Chicago has gained in the past from her unrivaled water highways, and whatever she may hope to acquire in the future, is largely influenced by the facilities for railway transportation the city may possess. Historians have styled Chicago "the gateway to the West." With equal force it may be entitled the "*entrepot* to the East."

The location of the city is that of a natural geographical center. Such a position in this era of railroads is of greater or less importance in proportion to its railway facilities. Ability to receive and distribute quickly and cheaply the multiforms of traffic is an all important factor in estimating the value of a location as a point for profitable business investment, and as indicating the possibilities of progress. A map of the railroads of the country shows that the railway system of Chicago is one of great value as a factor in the progress of the city, while its increase in extent bears palpable witness to the natural adaptations of the location as a railroad center. Its geographical position has always rendered it a marked point as combining more advantages than any inland city or town of the limited States. Located midway between an empire of population on the East, and an empire of people on the West, to both of which the products of Chicago, and the consumption thereof are requisites to their own commerce, the city's facilities for railroad communication with either section is direct, comprehensive and well sustained. It would be too great a task to undertake to particularize the various lines of railway that concentrate the business of the Great West at this point. Briefly the fol-

CORNER OF ADAMS AND DEARBORN STS.

lowing are the principal railroads having depots in this city; Baltimore & Ohio Railroad, 122 Michigan Avenue; Chicago & Quincy Railroad depot, foot of Lake Street; Chicago, Danville & Vincennes Railroad depot, Fulton Street, between Morgan and Carpenter; Chicago, Milwaukee & St. Paul Railroad Company, Canal near Madison; Chicago and Northwestern Railroad Depots, corner of Canal and Kinzie and corner of North Wells and Kinzie; Chicago & Pacific Railroad; Illinois Central Railroad; Lake Shore & Michigan Southern Railroad Company, passenger depot Van Buren, head of La Salle; Michigan Railroad, and Pittsburg, Fort Wayne & Chicago Railroad, passenger depot, Canal near Madison. The lines above enumerated embrace those whose trains run directly into the city, although a number of other roads, tapping one or other of these inlets also form important items with the business with which Chicago is connected.

RIVER, LAKES AND SHIPPING.—Although the vast railroad system centering in Chicago is of immense importance as giving easy communication with great commercial centers in every direction, yet it is to her superior advantages as related to facilities for traffic upon the great lakes, that Chicago owes more than to any other cause, the commanding position she holds in the commerce of the country. It is sufficient to say that the means of transportation of every kind of merchandise to and from Chicago and the entire lake region, are ample; that the port has all the facilities for handling this vast business, and that the wisdom and enterprise of her merchants and manufacturers have surrounded her with all the instrumentalities for the perfect utilization of the many advantages offered by her favored location.

STREET RAILROADS.—Chicago possesses one of the most complete systems of street railways in the world, being literally gridironed with their tracks. The three divisions of the city are operated by separate companies. The cars are used by about 200,000 persons a day. The North Chicago City Railway has 63 miles of track, of which 12 miles are operated by cable, and owns 354 cars and 1,823 horses, and several cable engines, aggregating 2,700 horse power. The company operating the West division has 122 miles of track. Its equipment is 1,075 cars and 4,780 horses. Its official title is the West Chicago Street Railroad Company operating the Chicago West Division Railway and the Chicago Passenger Railway. The South side is operated by the Chicago City Railway Company, which has, to a large extent, dispensed with the use of horses by the adoption of the cable system. The first section was opened in 1882, since which time it has been extended through 26 miles of double-tracked streets. Its equipment includes 829 passenger cars, 160 grip cars, 1,659 horses, 3 steam motors of 30-horse power each, and cable engines aggregating 7500 horse power. It might also be added in this connection that in the spring of 1888 a company was formed with a capital of $3,000,-000 for the construction of a system of elevated railroads similar to that in vogue in New York and known as the Lake Street Elevated Railroad Company. The lines are now in course of erection and up to date, the company have expended from $800,000 to $900,000 in obtaining rights of way and in construction.

CHICAGO AS A SEAPORT.—An English syndicate to be known as "The Atlantic and Great Lakes Navigation and Trading Company Limited," proposes to open direct water communication for freight and passenger business between Chicago and Great Britain. The syndicate will build and operate its own vessels, for which purpose a capital of $5,000,000 has been subscribed. Already contracts have been made with the large importers of Chicago, Milwaukee and Detroit, by which contracts the merchants have agreed to ship, and to instruct their agents to ship all goods via this line. The company is expected to begin business with the opening of navigation in 1892.

POSTAL FACILITIES AND MAIL SERVICE.—Of all features that pertain to an enterprising and progressive community, there is not, as it is needless to remark, any more useful or indispensable than the postoffice; and, as a consequence its management, efficiency and service are matters of peculiar importance. For years the postal facilities of Chicago were a reproach to a city of otherwise progressive ideas, but latterly the administration of postal affairs has been so improved, that nothing short of telegraphic communication can equal it. The following excerpt from a recent issue of the "Tribune" tells its own tale: "Chicago handles the largest amount of mail matter of any city in the United States,

New York not even excepted. The report of the registry division for the fiscal year ended June 30th, 1891, was yesterday submitted to Postmaster Sexton. The number of registered letters recorded was 230,737, an increase of 13 per cent. The registered letters sent in for delivery were 680,516 in number, and the number of registered letters in transit, 1,079,180. This amount is equal to about 10 per cent more than was received at the New York office for the same period. The grand total of all registered parcels, letters and packages, is 3,214,598." The force employed consists of about 650 regular carriers, 200 substitute carriers, 687 regular clerks, and sixty substitute clerks, making a total of 1,597 employes. Of this force, eighty carriers, thirty-six horses and thirty-six wagons are employed in the collection of the mail from the street letter boxes.

CITY GOVERNMENT.—It is natural that a city of the status of Chicago should require a carefully studied and elaborate system of municipal government. Chicago has had a corporate existence for the past half century, as already intimated, and during this period its municipal government has seen many changes, and during the violent political vicissitudes of years gone by has undoubtedly been misgoverned by reason of unjust legislation, corrupt administrations, and the lethargy of her representative citizens; yet at the present time probably no municipal government moves more smoothly and effectively than does that of Chicago. Nominally control is vested in mayor and city council. The mayor is elected for two years. Sixty-eight aldermen compose the council, two from each ward. Each serves two years, but one from each ward retires annually, so that the conduct of the whole body is practically passed upon by the public vote each year. Owing to its exceedingly rapid expansion Chicago is by no means an easy city to provide for municipally, and the task of its government has been complicated of late by the wholesale annexation of its suburbs. For the current year the estimated expenditure by the city will be close on $16,000,000, while the revenue will probably be less than $14,000,000. The mayor is assisted in the performance of his duties by heads of departments and bureaus as follows: Comptroller, treasurer and assistants, city clerk, commissioner of public works, city engineer, counsel of corporation, city attorney, prosecuting attorney, general superintendent of police, city marshal of fire department, superintendent of fire alarm telegraph, commissioner of health, city collector, superintendent of special assessment, superintendent of street department, mayor's secretary, mayor's assistant secretary, and mayor's messenger. The police force consists of 1,870 men, and though but one-half the force in New York, life and property seem to be as safe in Chicago as in any city in the world. Chicago's disastrous experience in 1871 sufficiently accounts for the care and money lavished upon her fire department. It numbers 917 officers and men, and is equipped with sixty-five steam engines, twenty-one chemical engines, eighty-seven hose carts, twenty-six hook and ladder trucks, one water tower, three fire boats, 390 horses, ninety apparatus stations and a repair shop.

THE WATER WORKS.—The importance to a city of an ample and effective water supply cannot be over-estimated, and foremost among the public works of Chicago is the costly and unique contrivance by which she draws her supply of water from Lake Michigan. Two miles from the shore there is fixed a substantial floating structure, known for the want of a better name as the "Crib," within which is an iron cylinder nine feet in diameter, going down thirty-one feet below the bottom of the lake and connecting with two distinct tunnels, leading to separate pumping works on shore. The first tunnel constructed communicating with the pumping works at the foot of Chicago Avenue, is five feet in diameter; the second tunnel conveying water to the West side works, at the corner of Blue Island Avenue and Twenty-second Street, is seven feet in diameter, and six miles in length. At the shore of each tunnel the water is forced by enormous engines to the top of a lofty tower, from which its own weight distributes it throughout the city. The water supplied by the works is shown by analysis to be of unexcelled purity, and this fact is an important factor in the healthfulness of the city.

THE RIVER TUNNELS.—The two tunnels under the Chicago River, constitute another of Chicago's engineering feats. These wonderful submarine thoroughfares enable the cable cars to pass under the river, thereby relieving the overcrowded bridges. They have proved so great a success that the day is not far distant when nearly every street will dispose with its clumsy swing bridges, and the long lines of vehicles and pedestrians that now patronize those necessary evils will be able to pass quietly and without delay, under the shipping that renders this river the only counterpart of the Mersey. The Washington Street tunnel, under the south branch, connecting the west and south divisions, was commenced in 1866 and completed in 1868. It formerly comprised a double carriage way, reaching from Franklin Street, on the south, to Clinton Street on the west side, and a footway, with approaches on Market and Canal Streets, on opposite sides of the river, but is now used solely by the cable car system connecting the western and southern divisions of the city. LaSalle Street tunnel, under the main river, connects the north and south divisions of the city. With the experience

MONROE ST. EAST FROM LA SALLE ST.

acquired in the construction of the Washington Street tunnel, this was a more perfect structure. It was begun in 1869 and completed in 1871, being open on the 4th day of July of that year.

SEWERAGE SYSTEM.—It is now some quarter a century ago since the sewerage works of this city were commenced, and there are now completed nearly three hundred miles of sewerage. The extension of the works has been vigorously prosecuted, and the system has, by superior engineering skill and great energy reached a highly satisfactory state of completeness, keeping pace, as nearly as possible, with the rapid growth of the city. The subject indeed is considered one of such momentous importance that the State of Illinois has placed it in the hands of a drainage commission, with powers equal to those exercised by the county or municipal governments. These powers embrace the borrowing of an enormous amount of money upon the credit of people owning property in the district to be affected by the carrying out of the scheme, the con-

State St. NORTH FROM Madison St.

demnation of land, the digging of canals, the construction of dams, dykes, docks, etc., and the general management of the drainage system of the district known as the Desplaines Water Shed. It would require a volume in itself to give a proper review of the drainage question. The chief features can only be treated of here. Connected with the south branch of the river is the Illinois and Michigan Canal, which extends to the Illinois River at LaSalle. Formerly this connection was by means of a lock, but recent improvements have effected a continuous flow of water from the lake through the river to the canal, thence to the Illinois River and into the Mississippi, where Chicago now discharges its entire sewerage. This was a wonderful undertaking, but was necessary to cleanse the currentless river, and was accomplished by an immense outlay of money and three years of labor in enlarging and deepening the canal. At any time during the day the visitor can see, by standing on one of the bridges, the murky stream passing slowly southward on its way to the Gulf of Mexico, bearing the offal of the city away with it—a great sewer the most novel in the world.

MANUFACTURES, COMMERCE, AND FINANCE.

The question has been frequently asked—What can be manufactured in Chicago to the best advantage? The simplest answer and an absolutely true one, is *everything*. Last year there were 3,250 factories in Chicago, whose output was valued at $538,000,000. The capital employed in 1890 was $190,000,000, as against $160,000,000 in 1889. The number of workers employed in manufacturing in Chicago in 1890 was 177,000 against 153,500 in 1889; the wages paid by manufacturers in 1890 amounted to $96,200,000 against $84,600,000 in 1889. We subjoin a brief tabulated statement of Chicago's leading manufactures, but it must be borne in mind there is in these pages no attempt made to present them in enumerated detail. The effort is only made to show the progress of Chicago, and through what resources she has grown to her present eminence and will reach greater prominence; by the leading industries to indicate the ramifications thereof, through which she is, year after year, acquiring new attractions as a continental storehouse of manufactures, and a prominent commercial city as well. One of the marked features of this metropolitan direction is in the segregation of its manufactures into special products, in the same line of business revolutions that occur in the growth of a village to a thriving town, and to a great city. A brief list of the leading industries as they at present appear is here given, and much furthe information will be found in the concluding portion of this work, where reference is made to the leading corporations and firms engaged in the variety of manufactures carried on in this city.

ALIMENTS.—Bakeries, flour mills meal and feed mills, coffee and spice mills, baking powder, extracts, etc., confectionery, preserves and canned goods, vinegar and pickles, sugar refinery.

DRINKS AND TOBACCO.—Breweries, malt-houses, distillers and rectifiers, tobacco and snuff, cigars and cigarettes.

BRASS, COPPER, ETC.—Brass, copper and plumbers' supplies, tin, stamped and sheet metal ware, jewelry manufactures, watch cases and tools, optical goods, telegraph and electrical supplies, smelting, refining and iron and brass work, miscellaneous.

BRICK, STONE, ETC.—Brickyards, cut stone contractors, marble and granite works, gravel roofers, lime kilns, terra cotta, stained glass factories.

IRON AND WOOD COMBINED.—Wagons and carriages, agricultural implements, car and bridge builders, elevators, sewing machines and cases.

CHEMICALS.—Chemical works, white lead and paint, white lead corroders, varnish, axle grease, glue, fertilizers, etc., soap, candles, linseed oil and cake, soda, mineral waters, etc., ink.

IRON MANUFACTURERS.—Rolling mills, foundries, machinery, malleable iron, boiler works, car-wheel works, stoves, furnaces and ranges, steam fitting and heating, galvanized iron, tin, slate roofing, barbed wire, wire works, miscellaneous.

LEATHER.—Farmers and curriers, boot, shoe and slipper manufacturers, saddle and harness manufacturers, trunk manufacturers, hose and leather-belting makers.

PRINTING.—Printing, binding and newspapers, lithographing houses, electrotyping and stereotyping, type foundries, printers' ink factories, printers' supplies and presses, printers' furniture, etc., book binderies.

TEXTILES.—Men's and boys' clothing, colored shirts, overalls,etc., mens' neckwear, white shirts, furs, cloaks and suitings, cloak and dress trimmings, childrens' caps, etc., of lace and plush, millinery.

MISCELLANEOUS.—Toy and bicycle factories,sign makers, brushes, brooms, feather dusters, show-cases, glass, corks, paper boxes, sails, awnings, etc., shipyards, perfumers.

The list of enterprises engaged in production might be further extended, but without any attempt to particularize individual branches, it may be said, that in all the elements of progressiveness and in productive achievement, Chicago holds a place among the leading and most active cities of the Union. While the city has not yet reached the summit of her developement and there is still room for the inauguration of additional industrial enterprises, the progress in the past has been marked and gratifying, each year showing some advance over its predecessor, and an increase in the total of the products of capital and labor.

THE UNION STOCK YARDS.—No reference to Chicago of a statistical nature, even of the most infinitesimal character, would be complete without passing reference at least to the Union Stock Yards and the part they play in the world's economy. The old Bull's Head Stock Yards, situated at the corner of Madison Street and Ogden Avenue,were opened in 1848, and gave to Chicago its first regular live stock market. Subsequently there were various ventures of this kind, but none proved successful until the establishment of the present yards, consisting then of 320 acres, by several well known business men of Chicago at Halsted Street, Town of Lake. The yards were considered quite isolated at the time, but the city has grown so rapidly they have been annexed to it and are now about half way between the limits and the City Hall in a flourishing business district. In the beginning 120 acres were covered with pens but the growth of the business has necessitated an extension of pens to 300 acres and where 2,000 pens accommodated stock at the start, 5,000 are now necessary. From thirty to fifty miles of streets and alleys connect the pens with the loading and unloading chutes of the railroads. Thirty-five thousand cattle, 200,000 hogs, 15,000 sheep and 1,500 horses can be accommodated at one time. The expense of maintaining these yards amounts from $250,000 to $350,-000 annually. Viaducts have been constructed to all the leading packing houses, for the purpose of effecting a ready transfer of stock from one point to another. A system of drainage has been brought to a high state of perfection, and the sanitary condition of the yards insures the health of stock. The yards are also supplied with a complete electric light plant, which is so perfect that business can be done by night as well as by day. Water is supplied from six artesian wells, averaging 1,300 feet in depth, and their capacity is 600,000 gallons per day, affording the very best water for the stock. The convergence of the entire system of railway lines in the West at this point makes this the most accessible place in the country for a great live-stock mart, and these have been pronounced by experts in such matters both in the United States and Europe as the most perfect in plan, details, arrangements and appointments in the world. During the year 1890 there were received at these yards: Cattle, 3,484,280; hogs,7,663,828; sheep, 2,182,687; calves, 175,823; horses, 101,566; number of cars, 311,557.

THE EXCHANGE.—The Exchange Building is situated in the center of the yards, where are the offices of the company and those of some hundred and fifty commission merchants; also telegraph offices and central telephone stations connecting with every part of the city, and with all neighboring cities. The Transit House, a fine five story brick hotel, capable of accommodating six or seven hundred guests, is owned and managed by the company. The Chicago Live Stock Exchange was organized in 1884 by men engaged in breeding, feeding, shipping, selling and slaughtering and packing live stock. Adjacent to the Stock Yard property are the plants of all the great packing establishments, and the facilities for handling stock are unequaled, in their entirety constituting the leading live stock market in the world.

GENERAL COMMERCE.—While for the purpose of the proper classification of the facts, an attempt is made to distinguish the industries having for their object the distribution of goods from those engaged in productive pursuits, the division can only be partially accomplished. Very many of the manufacturing houses of the city sell their products to the trade without the interposition of the jobber, and at the same time very many wholesale firms have added to their selling department the manufacture of special lines of goods connected with their business. The man who can grasp the true import of the fact that the commerce of Chicago last year amounted to $1,380,000,000 must have the very liveliest and finest kind of imagination. The following few items will convey to the most obtuse, some faint idea of Chicago's general commerce. Chicago is the grain center of this country, and its Board of Trade, where the grain business is transacted, makes the prices for the world. In 1890 Chicago received

WABASH AVENUE FROM WASHINGTON ST.

15,133,971 bushels of barley and shipped 9,470,221; received, 81,117,251 bushels of corn and shipped 90,556,109; received 4,358,058 barrels of flour, and shipped 4,410,535; received 13,366,699 bushels of wheat, and shipped 11,975,276; received 64,430,560 bushels of oats and shipped 70,768,222; received 2,946,720 bushels of rye, and shipped 3,280,433; received 6,244,847 bushels of flaxseed and shipped 6,594,581; received 72,102,031 pounds of grass seed, and shipped 59,213,035; received 7,663,828 live hogs and shipped 1,985,700;

RANDOLPH St. WEST FROM CLARK St.

received 77,985 pounds of pork and shipped 397,786; received 147,475,267 pounds of lard, and shipped 471,910,128; received 300,198,241 pounds of cured meats, and shipped 823,801,460; received 109,704,834 pounds of dressed beef and shipped 964,134,807. Last year 2,219,312 cattle and 5,733,082 hogs were slaughtered in Chicago. The grain storage capacity of the city elevators is 28,675,000 bushels. Last year was a booming one in Chicago's lumber trade, the sales of which amounted to 2,050,000,000 feet, of which 1,200,000,000 were consumed in the city and the balance was shipped away. The brewers also broke the record turning out 2,250,000 barrels of beer. While the foregoing represent many of the important articles dealt in by Chicago there are many not enumerated.

Some will be found referred to in connection with manufacturers, while others there are in which the absence of statistics leaves the volume in transactions in them to conjecture.

THE JOBBING TRADES.—The position of Chicago is such that the competition of rail and water routes enables her to lay down freight at low rates; and being the business center of a populous and prosperous region she enjoys a large trade in all staple lines. For purchasers on the lakes there is no cheaper or more accessible market than Chicago. In short, Chicago has ever been the great jobbing center of the country. This trade alone last year aggregated $486,600,000 of which $93,730,000 was in dry goods, groceries coming next with a volume of $56,700,000; boots and shoes $25,000,900; clothing $21,500,000; manufactured iron, $15,580,000; tobacco and cigars $10,580,000; music books and sheet music $22,000,000; stationery and wall paper $25,500,000; pig iron $20,035,009; coal, $2,575,000; hardware and cutlery, $17,500,000; liquors, $13,800,000; jewelry, watches and diamonds $20,400,000, and other lines in smaller proportions—all the necessities of life and all the luxuries of advanced civilization having their representative houses in the great Metropolis of the West.

ORGANIZATIONS FOR THE PROMOTION OF THE BUSINESS INTERESTS OF THE CITY.

Business at this day, although built upon the old standard rules of barter and trade, has become more flexible, and the present generation are more closely allied with each other in the same or kindred departments of activity. Representative men in leading avenues of trade now see the necessity for a closer relationship, a more defined dissemination of trade news, and a more frequent co-mingling of all whose interests are to be benefited by such a condition. The marked change in the conduct in many departments of trade during the past quarter century have been so emphatic, that it is subject of favorable comment, and a matter that has resulted in great profit to all interested. The successful organization of associations and exchanges has been most beneficial, and so universally recognized are these institutions, that they are found embracing nearly all the important channels of commercial activity. In this direction of organized effort in behalf of the improvement of the business resources and facilities of the city, Chicago is in no wise behind the other commercial centers of the country.

BOARD OF TRADE.—This undoubtedly constitutes the leading grain and produce exchange in the world and was the first commercial institution in the country to establish and apply a system of grading to cereal products. The growth of the body from its organization in 1848, with eighty-two members until the present day when its membership roll has fully reached two thousand, is one of the most significant chapters in the history of Chicago. The building is situated at the foot of La Salle, on Jackson Street, and is of immense size and exceptional architectural beauty. It covers an area of 200x174 feet, and is built of gray granite. On the first floor are settling rooms, private offices, telegraph offices, etc. Above is a great exchange hall, some idea of the vastness of which may be obtained from the knowledge that one of the largest five-story blocks in the city could be accommodated within it. Throughout the history of this organization, it has contributed in a material way to the promotion of the interests of trade in Chicago. It formulates rules for the inspection and grading of grain, flour and seeds, fixes the minimum net commissions for the purchase and sale of grain and produce, and adopts regulations calculated to aid business transactions.

BUILDERS' AND TRADERS' EXCHANGE.—Another important business association is the Builders' and Traders' Exchange, which has a large membership, including prominent builders, brick and stone masons, plasterers, carpenters, painters, dealers in building materials, etc.

CHICAGO REAL ESTATE BOARD.—This organization was formed in 1887 and is proving a valuable aid to the real estate business of the city. All persons whose business is the purchase, sale, care and management of real estate, are eligible to membership. One of the greatest results achieved by this organization is the prevention of fraud on the part of dishonest and irresponsible real estate dealers, as also the fixing of a minimum scale of charges for commissions.

CHICAGO STOCK EXCHANGE.—Ranking as the second city of the United States in immensity of Chicago's stock operations are second only to those of Wall Street, New York. The Exchange Building is located at the corner of Dearborn and Monroe Streets, and is devoted almost exclusively to the uses of bankers and brokers, and is peculiarly well adapted in its arrangements for the speedy dispatch of business.

LUMBERMEN'S ASSOCIATION OF CHICAGO.—In 1869 application was made to the legislature, and articles of incorporation were obtained for the "Lumbermen's Exchange of Chicago" of which this association formed during the current year may be styled the successor. This organization is now recognized among the most valuable and influential of those which exercise an influence over the trade and commerce of the nation second only to that which is maintained by the Chicago Board of Trade in its supervision over the grain produce, and provisions of the country.

In addition to these organizations having a more general range, there are a number of others the scope of which is more limited, their business being the facilitating of trade in special branches of industry. It is not possible to make an extended notice of these, but among the more important may be mentioned the Chicago American Horse Exchange, Mining Stock Exchange, Fruit Buyers' Association, Fruit and Vegetable Dealers' Association, Mutual Live Stock Insurance Company, American Live Stock Association, Chicago Coal Exchange, Chicago Anthracite Association, Chicago Flour and Feed Dealers' Association, Chicago Live Stock Exchange, Chicago Milk Exchange, Chicago Open Board of Trade, Commercial Exchange (wholesale grocers) Gravel Roofers' Exchange, Institute of Building Arts, National Association of Lumber Dealers, National Butter, Cheese and Egg Association, National Producers and Shippers' Association, Produce Exchange and Union Stock Yards and Transit Company. Surely an all sufficient voucher for the fact that in all the aids of organization the business men of Chicago are fully alive to the application of the axiom that "in union there is strength" to all business affairs.

BANKS AND BANKING.—Chicago's banking business, National, State and private, is perhaps the strongest support of the manufacturing and mercantile interests of the city, and working in alliance with these interests in all their legitimate phases, each appreciably influences and partakes of the tone and methods of the other. Hence the banks of the city, like her business enterprises, are noted for their sound, energetic, yet conservative management, commanding the entire confidence of business men and capitalists and holding the highest rank among the financial institutions of the country. There are twenty-five National and twenty-one State and Private banking institutions, as follows:

NATIONAL BANKS.—American Exchange National Bank, Atlas National Bank, Calumet National Bank, Chicago National Bank, Columbia National Bank, Commercial National Bank, Continental National Bank, Drovers' National Bank, Englewood National Bank, First National Bank, Fort Dearborn National Bank, Globe National Bank, Hide and Leather National Bank, Home National Bank, Lincoln National Bank, Merchants National Bank, Metropolitan National Bank, National Bank of America, National Bank of Illinois, National Live Stock Bank, Northwestern National Bank, Oaklund National Bank, Union National Bank, United States National Bank, Prairie State National Bank.

STATE AND PRIVATE BANKS.—Adolph Loeb and Bro., American Trust and Savings Bank, Bank of Montreal, Cahn and Strauss, Chas. Henrotin, Chemical Trust and Savings Bank, Chicago Trust and Savings Bank, Corn Exchange Bank, Dime Savings Bank, E. S. Dreyer & Co., Farmers' Trust Company, Foreman Bros., Globe Savings Bank, Greenebaum Sons, Guarantee Company of North America, Hibernian Banking Association, Illinois Trust and Savings Bank, International Bank, Meadowcraft Bros., Merchants' Loan and Trust Company, Northern Trust Company, Paul O. Stensland & Co., Peterson and Bay, Prairie State Savings and Trust Company, Schaffer & Co., Security Loan and Savings Bank, State Banks of Illinois, Union Trust Company, Western Trust and Savings Bank.

A very prominent feature among banks here is the great facility afforded them for the transaction of European business, which is all done by direct exchange, and in this respect Chicago holds exactly the same financ⬛⬛⬛tus with foreign countries as New York, and is, indeed, the only inland city that enjoys these facili⬛⬛⬛ile lack of space precludes any detailed financial statements, a fair criterion of the standi⬛⬛⬛e banks of the Western Metropolis may be gathered from a perusal of the following significant s⬛⬛ment which appeared in a recent issue of the New York *Financier:*—"The bankers of the country think New York's banking business is large, and that the percentage of increase of deposits during the six years preceding this statement is, or ought to be, larger than elsewhere, but this is a mistake so far as the percentage of increase is concerned, for Chicago beats New York by over 125 per cent. on New York's increase. that Chicago's commerce, so far as bank deand one-fourth as fast as New York's. the phenomena of the country so far as its development is concerned, but few are aware of

This is a remarkable difference and means posits show it, is growing, growing twice Everybody knows that Chicago is one of

MADISON ST.

the remarkable speed shown by the figures of our tellers. Even Boston's growth of banking during the six years mentioned is far outstripped by Chicago, and it does look as if the "Hub" is going West. Chicago's percentage of increase exceeds Boston's by 30 per cent. upon Boston's figures, in spite of the big manufactories in New England. Philadelphia, too, whose population is now slightly exceeded by Chicago, is away in the rear of the percentage of increase, as Chicago's figures exceeds Philadelphia's by 44 per cent. On the deposits of its National Banks for 1890, Chicago increased during the past six years 46 per cent. or $50,152,348 upon $108,178,165 deposits; New York increased during the same period about 20 per cent. or nearly $89,000,000 on $431,000,000 deposits; Boston increased about 36½ per cent., or $49,800,000, on nearly $137,000,000 deposits; Philadelphia about 32 per cent. or about $38,500,000 on $90,600,000 deposits."

REAL ESTATE OPERATIONS.—The general outlook for Chicago real estate has never been better than at the present time, the recorded transfers of real estate in 1890 over those of 1889 being astounding and show an increase of 70 per cent. Last year 11,608 buildings were erected in Chicago at a cost of $47,322,100. These buildings have a frontage of 266,284 feet, or over fifty miles. The number of building permits issued during the same year was 11,544, or 3,954 more than in 1889. Many of the new buildings erected were massive and imposing structures. Upon treacherous filled in ground have been reared some of the largest and most massive public and

LAKE ST.

office buildings in the world. In the foundations of these buildings railway iron plays an important part. Their necessities also led Chicago architects to devise the system of steel or iron framed structures which is being so generally adopted throughout the country. Altogether, about ten thousand men are engaged in the real estate business in Chicago in various capacities. Last year the transactions in real property made in Chicago aggregated $227,486,959 or $94,112,010 more than in 1889. Of this grand total $183,878,461 represented property within the city limits and $43,608,498 outside. The real estate business contributes immeasurably to the stability of Chicago's financial position, and the houses referred to in the concluding pages of this work represent some of the most substantial of all kinds of landed interests in the "big city by the lake."

CHICAGO'S GROWING SUBURBS.—An important feature of the real estate interest of Chicago is represented in suburban property, affording as it does special facilities for factory sites and residences, and comprising property that is yearly increasing in value with the development of the city. Evanston is undoubtedly one of the most charming suburbs of Chicago, for here is combined the quiet and repose of the country coupled with the most of the advantages to be derived from a residence in the city. It is situated twelve miles from the city on the Northwestern Railway, and has increased so rapidly in population that it is now counted the wealthiest suburb on this route. *Hyde Park* was the most pretentious suburban town of Chicago, claiming twelve miles from north to south limits, and an average width of five miles. It was merged together in Chicago with Lake View, Jefferson, Cicero and Lake, June 30th, 1890. *Pullman*, another suburban city, may justly be termed the prodigy of America. Such a rapid and substantial building up of a city has not an equal, even in the great commercial center of which it is a part. Mr. George M. Pullman, the palace car inventor, conceived the idea of establishing a manufacturing place for his famous cars, and in 1879 bought a tract of land, consisting of three hundred acres, in the name of the "Pullman Land Association," which has since been increased to 3,500 acres. It is located on the shores of Lake Calumet, a shallow lagoon connected with Lake Michigan by the Calumet River, a narrow but navigable stream similar to the Chicago River. Work on the new town began in May, 1880, and was pushed with extraordinary vigor. In two years from that time a city of nearly twenty thousand people had gathered, making a manufacturing town for workmen such as has not an equal on the continent. Many of the heaviest Western manufacturing concerns have already located here, and many more are arranging to build. Tolleston is another beautiful suburb of Chicago, and is the proposed site of the new stock yards projected by Messrs. Armour, Swift, Morris & Co. Englewood is one of the most popular suburban villages, situated six miles directly south of the city, and accessible by several of the railways running out in this direction. It is practically within the old city, and has long since lost its individuality as a city. Edgewater is one of the prettiest suburbs in the country, and is situated on the north shore of Lake Michigan, 7½ miles from the City Hall. Fernwood, Chicago Lawn, Argyle Park, Dauphin Park, Hermosa, Tracy, Cheltenham, Windsor Park and other places of equal note, are interesting alike to the visitor, the capitalist, the investor, and the skilled mechanic.

OTHER POINTS OF INTEREST IN REFERENCE TO CHICAGO.

Pages might be multiplied until this book would extend to cumbrous proportions in the detailed statement of the industrial advance, the commercial progress and social advantages of the Metropolis of the West. The space at disposal, however, will only admit of a brief and inadequate reference to the leading topics only not covered by the preceding pages.

EDUCATION.—One of the most striking features in the history of the development of Western communities is the attention that has been given to educational matters, and wherever a considerable settlement has been formed, the village school has been one of the first objects   der consideration by the community. In Chicago early attention was paid to this importan   d that this attention has not been allowed to lessen with the increase of population, may be   a glance at the following extraordinary items having a bearing on this subject: Investment   lic schools to date, $50,000,000; pupils attending Chicago public schools, 135,551; teachers in Chicago public school, 2,842; cost of maintaining public schools, $3,787,222; academics and seminaries in Chicago, 341; universities in Chicago, 2; private schools in Chicago, 786; pupils attending academies, seminaries, etc., 62,640; teachers in academies, seminaries, etc., 11,640; number of children of school age in Chicago, 165,621.

THE PUBLIC LIBRARY.—This popular institution occupies, with the exception of the Council Chamber, the entire fourth floor of the City Hall. Its establishment dates from 1872, when, in commemoration of the great fire of October, 1871, a great number of English authors and publishers generously contributed copies of their works. The nucleus thus formed has grown into a magnificent collection of 156,243 volumes, the greater part of which belong to the circulating department. The reading room is supplied with 550,000 periodicals, and was patronized during 1890 by 700,000 visitors.

RELIGION.—There are no less than three hundred and seventeen churches in Chicago, among which almost all denominations of Christians are represented. Among the clergy of the city are some of the most distinguished ornaments of the American pulpit. The most noteworthy buildings are the Roman Catholic churches of the Holy Name and the Holy Family; the former the Cathedral Church of the Catholic Diocese, an ornate Gothic structure at the corner of North State and Superior Streets, and the latter, popularly known as the Jesuit Church, an edifice, the interior of which is extremely rich and beautiful, at the corner of May and West Twelfth Streets, adjoining St. Ignatius' College. Among other fine churches are the cathedral of Sts. Peter and Paul, Grace and Trinity (Episcopal); Second Presbyterian; Plymouth and New England (Congregational); St. Paul's (Universalist); Centenary (Methodist); Unity and the Church of the Messiah (Unitarian). The ecclesiastical edifices are mostly of substantial and enduring proportions, and without exception, the condition of their financial affairs attests the most skillful and conservative direction.

ASYLUMS, HOMES, ETC.—In their increasing struggle for wealth, position and pleasure, it cannot be said that Chicagoans are unmindful of the words of the Great Nazarene—"The poor ye have always with you." They systematize everything, even to their charities, which are on a generously magnificent scale. There are twenty-five hospitals and thirty-four asylums in Chicago. Every year the maintenance of these institutions and other relief to the destitute and helpless calls for the expenditure of about $8,000,000, but this enormous sum is cheerfully provided—$5,000,000 by the city and county, and $3,000,000 by private susbcription.

PARKS.—The providing of breathing places in which to escape from the close atmosphere of the streets is an important requirement of the modern city, and it is one which Chicago has not neglected. Her twelve miles of Lake Front is supplemented by a cordon of splendid parks, extending on the North around the present city limits to the lake shore on the South, all connected by magnificent boulevards, which present the most attractive as well as the most extensive system of alternate resorts and driveways to be found in the world. Of the twenty-three thousand , one hundred and forty acres area of the city, two thousand, three hundred acres are devoted to parks. The system under which Chicago's parks are being developed seems very ingeniously devised to secure the best results. It is hardly a republican system, for it gives the right to spend the people's money to commissions, whose members are not elected by the people. One of these commissions is appointed for each of the three divisions into which the Chicago River divides the city, so that there is thus established a feeling of emulation as to which section shall have the most beautiful parks. Lincoln Park, in the North division, comprises a tract of one hundred and twenty acres, lying along the lake shore from North Avenue northward into the annexed town of Lake View. This is the oldest of the large parks and its improvements have reached the fullest state of development. It is the nearest to the business center of the city, and is probably the most popular as a place of resort. It is about two miles from the Court ▮▮▮▮▮▮ including the magnificent Lake Shore and its zoological collection, it presents many attr▮▮▮▮▮▮ the visitor. West from Lincoln Park some three miles is Humboldt Park, the most nort▮▮▮▮▮▮ the West Park system. This is connected with Lincoln Park by a grand boulevard or driveway. Running south and west from Humboldt Park is Central Boulevard—a very elaborately designed driveway connecting this with Garfield Park. Garfield Park (formerly Central) constituting

State St. South from Lake St.

the center of the West Park system, comprises an area of 185 acres. The improvements in this park, though by no means finished, have reached a state of perfection that affords many attractive features and charming vistas. One of the notable sights here is the "Fire" monument, commemorative of the great conflagration of 1871, and of the world's generosity on that occasion. Douglas Park, the southwestern of the West Park system, comprises an area of one hundred and eighty acres, reaching as far south as Nineteenth Street. The distinctive feature of this park is the extent of its ornamental lake systems, providing ample space for rowing and aquatic sports. The South Park system, under the charge of a distinct Board of Commissioners, comprises South Park proper, with its area of about five hundred acres, extending from Fifty-first Street, on the north, to Sixtieth Street on the south, and lying between Cottage Grove and Kankakee Avenues east, or Jackson Park, with an area of five hundred acres, extending from Fifty-seventh Street on the north ... ixty-seventh Street on the south, and lying between Hyde Park Avenue and the Lake Shore; th... ... plaisance, a water and driveway six hundred feet wide, between Fifty-ninth and Sixtieth S..., connecting the two parks, and Grand and Drexel Boulevards forming the northern approach to South Park. The improvement of the South Park system was not commenced till 1874, but the work since that date has been prosecuted with commendable zeal. Drives, walks, lagoons, lakes, and winding water-ways have been constructed; groves planted and cultivated, and the south and east parks now furnish one of the most beautiful and charming resorts. The most noticeable features of the South Park system are its two magnificent driveways—Grand and Drexel Boulevards. Grand Boulevard, the westernmost of these, runs from Thirty-fifth Street south to Fifty-first Street where it forms the grand entrance to South Park. It is two hundred feet in width, the

Clark St. FROM COR OF Jackson LOOKING NORTH

center, sixty feet, forming a grand driveway for recreation only. On each side of this are grass plats planted with rows of forest trees. Drexel Boulevard runs parallel with Grand, three blocks to the eastward, commencing near Thirty-ninth Street, and runs to the city limits. It is elaborately improvised, and is said to have been modeled after the Avenue l'Impératrice, of Paris, the most beautiful street in the world. Drexel Boulevard is two hundred feet wide throughout its extent. Ninety feet in the center are devoted to the planting of forest trees, shrubbery, flower beds, and winding walks, this central portion being raised considerably above the driveways on each side, which are forty feet in width, outside of which are sidewalks

fifteen feet in width. Grand and Drexel Boulevards are connected at Fortieth Street by Oakwood Boulevard, a beautifully improved driveway bordered by grass plats, outside of which are finely paved sidewalks. This whole volume might easily be filled were a detailed discription of these parks and boulevards to be attempted—no other city on this continent being able to boast of so liberal a provision in this respect as Chicago.

Besides those under the control of the State Commissioners, there are a number of small parks scattered through the city, which are cared for by the municipal authorities. Following are the names of the parks in Chicago, with their area in acres: · Aldine Square, 1.44; Congress Park, .07; Campbell Park, .05; Dearborn Park, 1.43; Douglas Park, 179.79; Lincoln Park, 250:00; Douglas Monument Square, 2.02; Logan Square, 4.25; Ellis Park, 3.38; Midway Plaisance, 80.00; Gage Park, 20.00; Oak Park, 0.25; Garfield Park, 185.87; Sheets Park, 1.00; Groveland Park, 3.4; Union Park, 14.03; Holstein Park, 2.3; Union Square, 0.05; Humboldt Park, 200.62; Vernon Park, 4.00; Jackson Park, 586.00; Washington Park. 371.00; Jackson Park (city), 2.00; Washington Square, 2.23; Jefferson Park (Jefferson) 5.00; Wicker Park, 4.00; Lake Front Park, 41.90; Woodlawn, 3.86; Total, 1,974.61.

DOUGLAS MONUMENT.—In connection with the foregoing casual reference to the parks and boulevards of Chicago, a brief account of the Douglas Monument may hardly be deemed out of place, an excellent reproduction of which has been furnished by our artist on Page 36 of this volume. This stately pile was erected in commemoration of the life and services of Stephen A. Douglas, the eminent patriot and statesman—the citizen whom Illinois for many years delighted to honor. It stands in beautifully improved grounds on the lake front, at the head of Douglas Avenue, in the immediate vicinity of the former home of the statesman, still known as the "Douglas Cottage." The monument consists of an octagonal base coping of limestone seventy feet in diameter. Upon this are three circular bases forming the sub-structure of New England granite, the first of which is a little over forty-two feet in diameter,,the height of the three together being four and one-fourth feet. Upon this is the octagonal tomb, twenty and a quarter feet in diameter and ten feet in height, also of New England granite, within which rest the mortal remains of the great senator, within an iron casket, which is placed in a white marble sarcophagus with lead. They are guarded by a heavy wrought-iron grated door with padlock, and an inner safe door with combination lock. The pedestal is fifteen feet in diameter and nearly nineteen feet high. Upon this sets the base of the column of New England granite, about forty-six and a half feet in height, five and one-sixth feet in diameter at the base, and three feet at the top. The cap of the column, including the ornamental friezes and the statue base, is six and a half feet high. The colossal bronze statue of Douglas surmounts the top, looking eastward over the lake, and is nine feet nine inches high, making the entire height of the monument ninety-five feet nine inches. The four pedestals at the base are occupied by heroic sized bronze statues, representing Illinois, History, Justice and Eloquence in sitting attitudes.

PLACES OF SEPULCHER.—In the matter of burial places, Chicago is well in advance of any of the cities in the country, having within her environs, twenty-eight handsome and well-ordered cemeteries, and the citizens have good grounds for the pride they feel in their magnificent "cities of the dead." There are no old grave yards or " God's acres " such as may be seen in the cities and towns of Europe, or in the older cities of this continent, within the business district. The only remains of a cemetery to be seen in the old city is the tomb of the Couch family which still holds its place in Lincoln Park— a great portion of which covers the site of an old graveyard. Of the Chicago places of sepulcher, Graceland Cemetery is the largest and most beautiful. It is located on North Clark Street, five miles from the City Hall. It extends for a mile along an elevated, handsome ridge, whose natural beauty has been enhanced by every appliance of taste and art. In this " city of the dead " the voices of nature breathe comfort into the hearts of the sorrowful, its entire surroundings combining to make it a desirable and delightful spot in which to place the ashes of our dear departed friends. Rosehill Cemetery, too, is one of the most beautiful places in the vicinity of Chicago, and contains many handsome and costly tombs and monuments. Calvary Cemetery, likewise, located south of and adjoin-

AUDITORIUM BUILDING.

PULLMAN BUILDING.

ing the village of South Evanston, is laid out with great taste. The tombs of the leading Roman Catholic families of Chicago are located here, and a large amount of money has been expended in making it the fitting home for those who "sleep the sleep that knows no waking." In alphabetical order the cemeteries of Chicago are as follows: Anshe Maariv Cemetery, North Clark Street and Belmont Avenue; Austro-Hungarian Cemetery, Waldheim; Beth Hamadrash, Oakwoods; B'nai Abraham Cemetery, Waldheim; B'nai Shilom Cemetery, North Clark Street and Graceland Avenue; Calvary Cemetery; Cemetery of the Congregation of the North Side, Waldheim; Chebra Gemilath Chasadim Ubikar, Cholim Cemetery, North Clark Street; Chebra Kadisha Ubikar Cholim Cemetery, North Clark Street; Concordia Cemetery, Madison Street; Forest Home Cemetery, Madison Street; Free Sons of Israel Cemetery, Waldheim; German Lutheran Cemetery, North Clark Street; Graceland Cemetery; Hebrew Benevolent Society Cemetery; Moses Montefiore Cemetery, Waldheim; Mount Greenwood Cemetery, near Morgan Park; Mount Hope Cemetery (projected) to be located at Washington Heights; Mount Olive Cemetery, Dunning; Mount Olivet Cemetery, near Morgan Park; Oakwoods Cemetery located on Sixty-seventh Street and Cottage Grove Avenue; Ohavey Emunah Cemetery, Waldheim; Ohavey Scholom Cemetery; Rosehill Cemetery; Sinai Congregational Cemetery, Rosehill; St. Boniface Cemetery, North Clark Street and Lawrence Avenue; Waldheim Cemetery, and Zion Congregation Cemetery, located at Rosehill.

PLACES OF AMUSEMENT.—Neither residents of nor visitors to, the great Metropolis of the West need let time hang heavily on their hands. Every section of the city has its theaters, its gardens, concert and lecture halls, and other places of amusement. The plays presented in the theaters are generally of a high order of merit, and the prices of admission are moderate. Many of the theaters make quite a magnificent architectural display (most notably the world famous Auditorium); each has a history of success or failure peculiarly its own; and upon the boards of these houses of entertainment the greatest actors of the past and present, both of our own country and of Europe, have delighted thousands by their delightful representations of the different phases of human life. The newspapers daily announce the class of entertainment to be offered each evening in the leading theaters, concert halls, etc., and these announcements are as keenly watched by amusement seekers as are the lists of marriages and births by the ladies. The following constitute Chicago's leading places of amusement: The Alhambra Theater, corner State Street and Archer Avenue; Auditorium Theater, occupying nearly an entire square fronting on Michigan Avenue, Wabash Avenue, and Congress Street; Battle of Gettysburg Panorama, corner Wabash Avenue and Panorama Place; Central Music Hall, corner Randolph and State Streets; Chicago Opera House, southwest corner Clark and Washington Streets; Columbia Theater, Monroe Street; Criterion Theater, Sedgwick and Division Streets; Eden Musee, Wabash Avenue; Epstean's New Dime Museum, Randolph Street; Freiburg's Opera House, Twenty-second Street; Grand Opera House, Clark Street; Halsted Street Opera House, corner Halsted and Harrison Streets; Havlin's Theater, Wabash Avenue; Haymarket Theater, West Madison Street; Hooley's Theater, Randolph Street; H. R. Jacobs' Academy, South Halsted Street; H. R. Jacobs' Clark Street Theater, North Clark Street; Jacob Litt's Standard Theater, Halsted and Jackson Streets; Kohl and Middleton's South Side Museum, South Clark Street; Kohl and Middleton's West Side Museum, West Madison Street; Libby Prison Museum, Wabash Avenue; Lyceum Theater Desplaines Street; Madison Street Theatre; McVicker's Theater, Madison Street; New Windsor North Clark and Division Streets; **Niagara Falls, Wabash** Avenue; Park Theater, State Street; People's Theater, State Street; Timmerman Opera House, corner Sixty-third Street and Stewart Avenue; Waverly Theater, West Madison Street; Weber Music Hall, Wabash Avenue. When it is considered that, in addition to the above, there are numerous music halls, circuses, lecture halls, gardens, etc., it will be conceded that in the amusements of the people from a dramatic or histrionic standpoint Chicago is a city of great attractions.

HOTELS.—Perhaps no feature contributes more directly to the rapid development of a city than the convenience and comfort of its hotels, and in this respect, Chicago stands pre-eminent among the cities of the world. Her great caravansaries are unsurpassed in extent, magnificence or management. Palatial in style, architecture, design and finish, they would do credit to the oldest and most enlightened cities on this planet. There are at present some fourteen or fifteen hundred hotels in the metropolis of the West, including small and large, and houses of all grades, but excluding lodging houses, boarding houses and distinctively family hotels, where no transients are received. The united capacity of these hotels is estimated at little short of 200,000, and during the great World's Fair of 1893, Chicago will have ample hotel accommodation for 500,000 guests. We append herewith a list of the hotels of prominence and their location: Atlantic Hotel, located on the corner of Van Buren and Sherman Streets; Auditorium Hotel, situated on Michigan Avenue and Congress Street; Briggs House, located on Randolph Street and Fifth Avenue; Burke's European Hotel, located on the south side of Madison, between La Salle and Clark Streets; Clifton House, located on Monroe Street and Wabash Avenue; Commercial Hotel, located on the corner of Lake and Dearborn Streets; Continental Hotel, located on Wabash Avenue and Madison Street; Gault House, located on West Madison and Clinton Streets; Gore's Hotel, located at 266-274 South Clark Street; Grand Pacific Hotel, located on La Salle, Jackson and Clark Streets; Hotel Brevoort, located on the . orth side of Madison, between La Salle and Clark Streets; Hotel Drexel, located at entrance to Washington Park; Hotel Wellington, located on Wabash Avenue and Jackson Street; Hotel Grace, located on Clark and Jackson Streets; Hotel Woodruff, located on Wabash Avenue and Twenty-first Street; Hyde Park Hotel, located at Lake Avenue and Fifty-first Street; Leland Hotel, located on the corner of Michigan Boulevard and Jackson Street; McCoy's European Hotel, located at the corner of Clark and Van Buren Streets; Palmer House, located on the southeast corner of State and Monroe Streets; Richelieu Hotel, located on Michigan Boulevard, between Jackson and Van Buren Streets; Saratoga Hotel, located at 155 to 161 Dearborn Street; Sherman House, located at the northwest corner Clark and Randolph Streets; Southern Hotel, located on Wabash Avenue and Twenty-second Street; Tremont House, located at the southeast corner of Lake and Dearborn Streets; Virginia Hotel, located at 78 Rush Street, North Side.

In addition to the hundreds of first-class hostelries of lesser prominence, there are eating houses or restaurants or cafes, with an estimated feeding capacity of 25,000 persons daily. The city still has no need to boast of the stupendous character of this type of accommodation. It is but the natural outgrowth of Western commercial enterprise, coupled with an intelligent and lively appreciation of the "eternal fitness of things" which here finds its culmination.

CLUBS.—The Clubs, and there are many of them, constitute one of the most characteristic features of Chicago. Some are unique and peculiar in their management and purposes. In these clubs are drawn together the various little groups of people who in a great city are congenial to one another, either through holding relative positions in wealth and station, or from having similar desires in mental, social and physical culture. And while on this subject, it may be added, that in a mixed community such as that of Chicago, society is bound to present many curious features. However, the mingling of peoples and classes has its great advantages. It is destructive of bigotry, illiberalism and provincialism, and productive of the truest democracy. In Chicago, every man, unless he is a new arrival, feels that he is really as good as his neighbors. Some of them no doubt, are very rich, but there is little inherited wealth comparatively in Chicago, and less consequently of plutocratic insolence than is found in other cities. Intelligence is wonderfully diffused, and many public lecturers, great actors, leading musicians and others have remarked upon the critically appreciative character of their receptions in the Western metropolis. Of purely social clubs there are forty-six, the chief of which is the Union League Club. Athletics have a prominent place in the social life of Chicago, and there are all manner of base-ball clubs, both outdoor and indoor, boat and yacht clubs, curling clubs, boxing and fencing clubs, cricket clubs, cycling clubs, hand-ball clubs, racing clubs, fishing and gun clubs, etc. And when the statement is made that these clubs and associations are augmented by no less than six hundred and eighty-seven literary societies, the jibes of the past thrown at the culture of the West will at the present day at least hardly hold water.

SECRET AND BENEVOLENT SOCIETIES.—All the benevolent, philanthropic and secret orders, which

Masonic Temple.

Ottawa Indian Monument

La Salle Statue

Lincoln

Schiller Monument

have been universally recognized as ministering to man's needs and his social interest, have nowhere had earlier establishment or continuing growth in greater variety than in Chicago. In fact every man who belongs to a secret society may be morally sure of meeting brethren and a cordial reception in the Western metropolis. The membership of beneficial orders is immense; their financial condition is good. A number of them have elegant buildings of their own (for example, note our artist's illustration of the Masonic Temple). Nearly all occupy well-furnished halls with fine equipment, and their rank in the respective orders at large is the highest.

MEDICAL SOCIETIES.—The history of the medical faculty has been a very brilliant page in the annals of Chicago, while the kindred profession of dentistry has been represented here by those who have attained national and even world-wide distinction in this modern science. The following associations maintain a high standard of professional life: Chicago Academy of Homœopathic Physicians and Surgeons, Chicago Dental Society, Chicago Eclectic Medical Society, Chicago Gynœcological Society, Chicago Medical Press Association, Chicago Medical Society, Chicago Pathological Society, Clinical Society of the Hahnemann Hospital, Illinois State Board of Dental Examiners, Illinois State Board of Health, Illinois State Board of Pharmacy, Illinois State Dental Society, Illinois State Eclectic Medical Society, Illinois State Medical Society, Post-graduate Polytechnic of Eclectic Medicine and Surgery, Woman's Homœopathic Medical Society, Woman's Physiological Institute.

MUSIC AND OTHER ARTS.—As in every community in which there is a strong infusion of German life and spirit, a decided musical taste and talent have always asserted themselves in Chicago. Besides that which finds expression through the church, private and social organizations, private musical tuition forms the part of the Chicagoan's education, of both sexes, one of the most prominent avenues for which is the Chicago Orchestral Union, which is under the direction of the world-famous Theodore Thomas. Then, again, there are a large number of singing societies, sængerbunds, etc. Schools for instrumental and vocal instruction abound; the advantages of comfortable residences and the charm of elevated social life attract hither teachers and votaries of musical culture; enterprising dealers in instruments, sheet music, etc., provide for all the wants of the trade; and that side of culture which gratifies its taste or finds expression in music, has large opportunities for satisfaction here.

The graphic and plastic arts have due encouragement, and in all the branches of painting, crayon work, and in the highest excellence of photographic skill, Chicago's artists have won wide reputation. Most of the many artistic and graceful monuments to be found in the cemeteries, are the handiwork of those engaged in the local marble yards, which supply every variety of monument and memorial. The elucidation of art in Chicago is chiefly represented in the Art Institute of Chicago, located at Michigan Avenue and Van Buren Street; the Chicago Society of Artists, Athenæum Building, Nos. 16 to 26 Van Buren Street, and the Union League Art Association. Again, the art galleries of the Illinois Club, the Chicago Club, the Marquette Club, the Calumet Club, and especially the Union League Club, are becoming very valuable. * * * Thus in the amenities of social life, the means for the acquirement of knowledge or the pursuit of pleasure, as well as in the arena of business life, Chicago furnishes abundant inducements. The city is not only advancing in material prosperity, but there is no community in the country who have more just local pride in their home place than have the residents of this beautiful, the growing "city by the lake."

THE PRESS.—The place in civilization occupied by the modern newspaper is truly an important one. It is a mirror reflecting the habit of thought, the social customs, the advancement and the progress of the community in which it is issued, and a town which supports good newspapers must necessarily be one in which the standards of intelligence have reached a high plane. The press of Chicago is fully up to the highest grade of modern newspaper enterprise. In all the departments of news gathering, of criticism and of thoughtful discussion, the papers of the city are true representatives of its progress and advancement. It has exerted a powerful influence in promoting the material prosperity of the city, and in producing the results of energy and industry which have culminated in the Chicago of to-day. There are published in Chicago 24 dailies, 260 weeklies, 36 semi-monthlies. 5 bi-monthlies and 14 quarterlies, making a total of 531 daily and periodical newspapers. The following are the leading publications in their alphabetical order:

The Abend Post.—This paper is published at No. 187 Washington Street. It is a one cent German daily, independent in politics, and although the first number but appeared in September, 1889, up to date of January 1, 1891, its circulation has reached upward of 30,000.

Arbeiter Zeitung.—This paper is issued by the Socialistic Publishing Society. August Spies, hanged for complicity in the Haymarket bomb-throwing, was editor of this newspaper at the time of his arrest. A. R. Parsons, also executed, was one of its contributors. Since the execution it has fallen into comparative obscurity, although it still has a large circulation among the anarchists.

The Daily News.—This paper was founded in 1875, is independent in politics, and has three distinct editions daily, the Morning News, the Noon News and the Evening News; circulation daily. 220,000 copies. Nothing can better serve to illustrate the marvelous growth of the Daily News than the statement of the increase of circulation from year to year. In 1877 its daily average was 22,037: in 1878, 33,314; in 1879, 45,194; in 1880, 54,801; in 1881, 75,820; in 1882, 88,723; in 1883, 99,726; in 1884, 125,178; in 1885, 131,992; in 1886, 152,851; in 1887, 165,376; in 1888, 192,577; in 1889. 222,745; in 1890, 213,871. This phenomenal growth may in a great measure be attributed to the intelligent direction and executive management of the talented editor and publisher of the paper, Mr. Victor F. Lawson.

The Evening Journal.—This is the oldest newspaper in Chicago, and is published at No. 161 Dearborn Street. Its pages are a reflex of the eventful years of its publication. Its columns are chronicles of Chicago's progress, and her transition from a village to a great city. W. K. Sullivan, editor; John R. Wilson, publisher.

Freie Presse.—This representative journal was established in 1871 by its present editor, Richard Michaelis. It is the only republican German daily newspaper in Chicago. Five issues are made of the paper daily, as also an interesting weekly and Sunday edition, the latter entitled Daheim.

The Globe.—The Globe was founded in 1887 by Austin L. Pattison, formerly business manager of the Chicago Tribune. In politics the paper is Democratic, but is neither blinded by prejudice or fettered with associations.

Goodall's Daily Sun.—This paper is published at the Union Stock Yards, in the interests of dealers in live stock, by Henry L. Goodall.

The Herald.—The history of the Herald has been the history of a struggle; its success has been the success of merit. The Herald was the first Chicago newspaper to use illustrations extensively, and has branch offices in New York, Washington, Milwaukee and Springfield. The executive staff of the Herald is as follows: Publisher, James W. Scott; managing editor, H. W. Seymour; news editor, William A. Taylor; night editor, T. G. Rae; city editor, Chas. E. Chapin; business manager, A. F. Portman.

The Illinois Staats Zeitung.—The large German population of Illinois affords an important field for newspapers printed in the German language. The Illinois Staats Zeitung is a daily morning newspaper, and was first issued in 1848. It stands to-day second only to the New York Staats Zeitung in wealth and circulation, while in ability it is unsurpassed by any German paper in the United States.

The Inter Ocean.—No newspaper venture in the history of Chicago ever developed into established success with such rapid and unmistakable strides as the Inter Ocean. It was founded March 25, 1872, and is to-day a political power throughout the Northwest. Energetic and intelligent management in every department, from the editor's desk through all intervening steps to the press room. is evident to any one who will scrutinize its columns, or make the tour of its home at the northwest corner of Madison and Dearborn Streets. The spirit of the paper is aptly interpreted in the trite enunciation of its initial number, "Independent in nothing; republican in everything." The present able editor is William Penn Nixon.

The Mail.—One of the most successful of the evening journals of Chicago is the Mail, which had its origin in what is known as the Chicago Press in 1882. It answers to the requirements of busy people by presenting all the news in a condensed form, and is noted for its push and enterprise, and its untiring and argus-eyed energy in news gathering.

The Post.—This paper is the property of the Evening Post Publishing Company, with publication offices at Nos. 164 and 166 Washington Street. It was introduced to the world in 1890, and yet despite a somewhat recent establishment, its circulation exceeds that of almost any other paper in Chicago. It is independent in politics as in all other things, and is a newspaper whose power, influence and ability are recognized by men of all parties and all shades of opinion.

The Times.—Founded in 1854 as a Democratic party paper, it was for years in a so-to-speak moribund condition until in 1887 Mr. James J. West assumed the managerial control, since which

ENTRANCE TO STOCK YARDS.

period it seemed to be revivified. Some two years ago, however, a dispute arose among the stockholders, and the ownership of the Chicago Times Company's property is now in litigation.

The Tribune.—The Tribune, established in 1847, has held for forty years a leading position in the journalism of the Northwest; increasing with the growth of the city, and enjoying great confidence and liberal support. There is no necessity to enlarge on the history of the Tribune; the mere statement of the fact that its circulation climbed from 2,240 in 1855 to 90,000 during the current year, indelibly stamps the hall-mark of good management upon its proprietorship. In a great measure the suggestion of the World's Columbian Exposition is due to the forcible arguments passed in its favor by the present editor-in-chief of the Tribune, Mr. Joseph Medill. The office of publication is located at the southeast corner of Madison and Dearborn Streets, and is equipped with every modern appliance known to the art of reproducing with regularity the daily record of the "map of life" as embodied in the newspaper of to-day.

CHICAGO OF TO-DAY THE METROPOLIS OF THE WEST.

BIRD'S-EYE VIEW OF STOCK YARDS.

In addition to the representatives of daily journalism Chicago has a large number of weekly newspapers and periodicals which afford literary pabulum for all tastes. Religion, politics, science, the professions, the trades, the drama and all interests have their special organs, and the whole list of papers presents a creditable testimonial to the fact that the people of Chicago are a reading, and therefore an intelligent people.

PUBLIC BUILDINGS.—The pride with which the Chicagoan shows the public buildings, and those devoted to art, literature, the drama and education, is not unreasonable. While lack of space forbids our entering into detail, without exaggeration it can be said that no city in the country presents a finer or more substantial class of buildings. The most prominent of these is the Board of Trade Building, the "Rookery," the Phenix Building, the Counselman Building, the Goff Building, the Insurance Exchange Building, the Home Insurance Building, the Calumet Building, the Tacoma Building, the Chamber of Commerce Building, and the City Hall and Court House—all of which may be seen in a walk down La Salle Street, from Randolph to Jackson Streets. The United States Custom House and Post Office occupies the square bounded by Adams, Jackson, Dearborn and Clark Streets, and is second only to the New York office in size and importance. The Cook County Hospital is the next interesting public building, situated on the corner of Wood and Harrison Streets; like other public buildings, it occupies a whole square, and was erected at a cost of nearly $1,000,000. The Criminal Court and Jail are situated on the corner of Illinois Street and Dearborn Avenue, on the North Side. There is probably no other building in Chicago with whose name strangers are so familiar as with that of the structure popularly known as the Chicago Exposition Building, although we are given to understand that it will be removed during the current year. It is the largest building in the world whose roof is unsupported by pillars, being 1,000 feet in length, with an average width of 240 feet. It was built after the model of the famous Exposition Building at Vienna, in the short space of ninety-six days, and has been rendered especially remarkable by the many important purposes for which it has been used. It gives way to the immense exposition buildings now in course of construction for the great World's Fair of 1893, to which we make special reference in another portion of this work. The University of Chicago occupies a beautiful site on Cottage Grove Avenue, between Thirty-third and Thirty-fifth Streets. It was founded by the late Stephen A. Douglas. The University, which has a numerous and learned faculty, possesses, in addition to an extensive library, a museum, rich in geological, zoological and numismatic specimens, and also a herbarium. Connected with it is the Dearborn University, famous for its equatorial refracting telescope, one of the largest in the world, and also other costly astronomical apparatus.

SEMI-PUBLIC BUILDINGS.—Under this head come the theaters, hotels, concert halls, art galleries, etc., of which Chicago boasts a large number of very fine ones. The Auditorium is a magnificent example of modern building. The Capitol at Washington, the State House at Albany and the Municipal buildings, Philadelphia, have in time past been regarded as among the finest distinctive types of American architecture; it does not appear to us superlative to assume that the Auditorium occupies an individual position equally as imposing, majestic in its classic simplicity. The credit for the conception of the splendid structure, and the rapidity with which it was pushed to successful completion was due to the fertile idea and unflagging energy of Mr. Ferdinand W. Peck. The Art Institute Building has been pronounced by critics the finest specimen of modern architecture in Chicago. It is built of brown stone; has a beautiful facade, is splendidly lighted, and though not as massive as some of its neighbors, is one of the attractive edifices of the Lake Front. The Palmer House, Tremont House, Grand Pacific Hotel, and others illustrated in these pages present some of the most attractive features of Chicago, and support her claim to a high place among those communities which place a proper estimate upon and render due reward to taste and talent as exemplified in the arts and progress of the times. It might here be added that the Masonic Temple at the corner of State and Randolph Streets will when completed, prove one of the finest buildings in the world. A glance at our artist's sketch of the Masonic Temple as it will appear when completed, will afford a better criterion of the architectural beauties of the structure than any verbal description.

THE GREAT FIRE OF 1871.—The history of the Chicago great fire is one that brings with it sad reflections, but we should feel that we were derelict in our duty were we not to make some notice of it here. For other pens than our own have touched upon that fearful episode in Chicago's history and writing as we are of the Chicago of to-day we are rather making passing reference to the conflagration as opposed to our remarks on the marvelous upbuilding of this very phœnix of cities in the brief space of eight years subsequent to the holocaust. Tradition has it that to the somewhat prosaic fact that a fractious cow belonging to one Mrs. O'Leary who kicked over a kerosene lamp on the evening of Sunday, October 8th, 1871, is referable the greatest conflagration of modern times,—a conflagration which appalled the world, sweeping over 460 acres, destroying 1600 stores, 28 hotels, 60 manufacturing establishments, and homes of some 22,000 persons. With an imagination worthy of the lurid subject, has Mrs. S. B. Olsen in her poem, the "Fall of Chicago" pictured the scene in the lines:

"A voice is ringing in the air,
A tale is trembling on the wire,
The people shout in wild despair
Chicago is on fire!"

We quote from Messrs. Colbert and Chamberlain's excellent description entitled *Chicago and the Great Conflagration:*

"'Yet so it was. A little after nine o'clock on Sunday evening (October 8th, 1871), the lamp was upset which was to kindle the funeral pyre of Chicago's pristine splendor. The little stable with its contents of hay was soon ablaze. By the time the alarm was sounded at the box several blocks away, two or three other little buildings to the leeward had been ignited, and in five minutes the poor purlieu in the vicinity of De Koven and Jefferson Streets was blazing like a huge bonfire. The spread of the fire, or, rather, the flight it took along with the southwest gale, was very rapid. We suppose the Fire Department was on the ground, partly because it usually turns out at fires and partly because one or two of its engines were found burned up among the ruins next day; but it might as well have been in Kamschatka for anything it was able to do toward arresting the progress of the flames. They marched on until they had devoured the thousand or more shanties, houses, planing mills, in their path on the West Division. They heeded not the marshal and his corps, any more than the bull heeds the fly upon his horn. They heeded not even the broad river, but leaped it easily after marching along northward until all between Jefferson Street and the river had been destroyed, up to the edge of the burnt district of Saturday night. (It might here be added that a fire doing damage to the extent of $1,000,000 occurred the previous night, Saturday, October 7th, 1871, which was described in the journals of the time as the "grandest spectacle thus far seen in Chicago," the writer little doubting that another fire was to sweep over the city compared with which the conflagration of Saturday was but as the "flicker of a farthing candle.") * * * The first vault across the river was made at midnight from Van Buren Street, lighting in a building of the South Division Gas Works on Adams Street. This germ of the main fire was not suppressed, and from that moment the doom of the commercial quarter was sealed, though no man could have foretold that the raging element would make such complete havoc of the proudest and strongest structures of that quarter. The axis of the column, as it had progressed from the starting point in the southwestern purlieus, had varied hardly a point from due northeast. Having gained a foothold on the South Division, its march naturally lay through two or three blocks of pine rookeries, and so on for a considerable space through the abodes of squalor and vice. Through these it set out at double-quick, the main column being flanked by another on each side, and nearly an hour to the rear. That to the right was generated by a separate brand from the western burning; that at the left was probably crea-

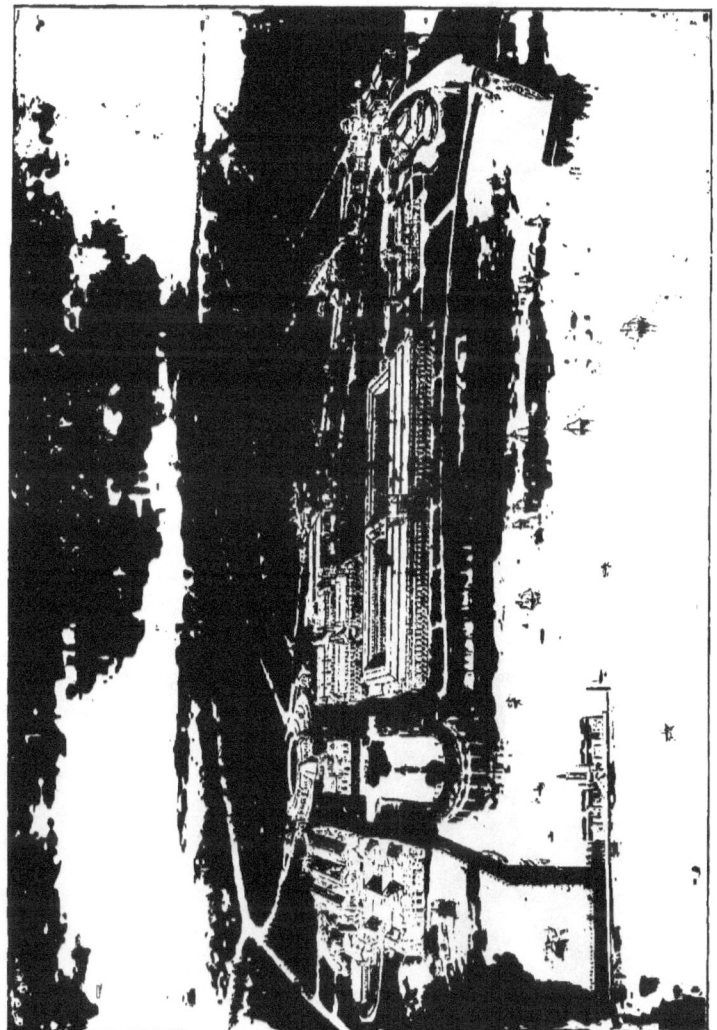

BIRD'S-EYE VIEW OF THE WORLD'S COLUMBIAN EXPOSITION, CHICAGO, 1893.

ted by some of the eddies which were by this time whirling through the streets toward the flame below and from it above. The rookeries were quickly disposed of. Beyond them, however, along LaSalle Street, was a splendid double row of fire proof mercantile buildings, the superior of which did not exist in the land.

WOULD THESE SUCCUMB TO THE SHOWER OF BRANDS

and the triple-heated furnace which had been thrown about them? Alas, yes! One after another they went as the column advanced. And the column was spreading fearfully—debouching to right and left, according as opportunities of conquest offered themselves. It was not long before one o'clock that the Chamber of Commerce was attacked, and fell a prey to the onadvancing force. Soon the Court House was seized upon; but it did not surrender till nearly three o'clock, when the great bell fell down, down, and pealed a farewell dying groan as it went. The hundred and fifty prisoners in the basement story were released to save their lives. They evinced their gratitude by pillaging a jewelry store near by. About the time the Court House was attacked the telegraph operators in the Merchants' Insurance Building opposite, on LaSalle Street, saw the propriety of falling back upon safer ground. The reporter of the Associated Press broke off in the middle of a word his account of the conflagration, and betook himself in General Sheridan's carriage, to a suburban station. From the Court House, the main course of the column seemed to rest eastward, and Hooley's Opera House, the *Times* Building, Crosby's magnificent Opera House (to be reopened that very night) fell rapidly before it; pursuing its way more slowly onward, the fiery worker laid waste some buildings to the northeast, and preparatory to attacking the magnificent at the foot of Randolph Street and the Great Union Depot, joined forces with the other branches of the main column, which had lingered to demolish the Sherman House—a grand seven-story edifice of marble—the Tremont House and the other fine buildings lying between Randolph and Lake Streets. The left column had in the meantime diverged to pass down LaSalle Street and attack all buildings lying to the west of that noble avenue—the Oriental and Mercantile buildings, the Union Bank, the Merchants' Insurance Building, where were General Sherman's headquarters, and the offices of the Western Union Telegraphs, and, in fact, an unbroken row of the stone palaces of trade, which had already made LaSalle Street a monument of Chicago's business architecture, to which her citizens pointed with glowing pride, and of which admiring visitors wrote and published 'warm panegyrics in all quarters of the globe. The column of the left did its mission but to well, however, and by daylight.

SCARCELY A STONE WAS LEFT UPON ANOTHER

in all that stately thoroughfare. But one building was left standing in this division of the city—a large, brick structure with iron shutters, known as Lind's Block. This was saved by its isolated location, being on the shore of the river, and separated by an exceptionally wide street from the seething furnace, which consumed all else in its vicinity. The right column started from a point near the intersection of Van Buren Street and the river, where some buildings were ignited by brands from the West Side, in despite of the efforts of the inhabitants of that quarter to save their homes 'by drenching their premises with water from their hydrants, and we need hardly add, in despite of the desultory though desperate efforts of the Fire Department. The right column also had the advantage of a large area of wooden buildings on which to ration and ram itself for its march of destruction. Thus fed and equipped, it swept down upon the remaining portion of the best built section of the town. It gutted the Michigan Southern Depot and the Grand Pacific Hotel, and the tornado soon left them shapeless ruins It spared not the unfinished building of the Lake Side Publishing Company, which had been already put on a very sightly front, and which had scarcely anything to burn but brick and stone It licked up the fine, new buildings on Dearborn Street, near the Post Office. The Post Office was seized and gutted like the rest.

SOME $2,000,000 OF TREASURE BEING DESTROYED

in its vaults. It swept down upon the new Bigelow House—a massive and elegant hotel which had never been occupied, and demolished that, together with the Honore Block, a magnificent new building, with massive walls adorned with hundreds of stately colonnades of marble. It reached out to the left and took in McVicker's new theater in its grasp for a moment, with the usually fatal result. It assaulted the noble *Tribune* building, which the people had been declaring even up to that terrible hour, would withstand all attacks, being furnished with all known safeguards against destruction by fire; but the enemy was wily as well as strong. It surrounded the fated structure and ruined it too. It threw a red hot brick wall upon the building's weaker side, a shower of brands upon the roof, a subterranean fire under the sidewalk and into the basement, and an atmosphere of furnace heat all around. It conquered and destroyed the *Tribune* building at half-past seven in the evening. It marched on and laid waste Bookseller's Row, the finest row of bookstores in the world. It fell upon Potter Palmer's store of Massachusetts marble, for which Field, Leiter and Company, dry goods importers, were paying the owner $50,000 a year rent. This splendid building with such as had not been removed in wagons, went like all the rest. It deployed to the right, in spite of its ally, the wind, and destroyed the splendid churches and residences which adorned the lower or town end of Wabash and Michigan Avenues. Among these were the First and Second Presbyterian Churches, Trinity Episcopal Church, and the palatial row of residences known as "Terrace Row," in which dwelt, among others, Gov. Bross of the *Tribune*, Jonathan Y. Scammon, the banker and capitalist, and S. C. Griggs, the bookseller. Finally its course southward was stayed at Congress Street by the blowing up of a building. The southern line of the fire was for the most part, however, along Harrison Street, which is one square further to the south. This is a brief sketch of the operations of the fire in the West and South Divisions. It effected a foothold in the North Division as early as half-past three in the morning; and it is remarkable that almost the first building to be attacked on the north side of the river was the engine house of the Water Works; as if the terrible marauder had, with deadly strategy thrown out a swifter brand than all others to cut off the only reliance of his victims, the water supply. The Water Works are nearly a mile from the point where the burning brands must have crossed the river. The denizens of the North Division were standing in their doors and gazing at the blazing splendor of the Court House dome, when they discovered to their horror that the fire was raging behind them, and that

THE WATERWORKS WERE GONE.

A general stampede to the sands of the lake shore, or to the prairies west of the city was the result." In the report of the Chicago Relief and Aid Society we find the following: "And then came the greatest terror of all; the consciousness of the fact that families had been separated; husbands and wives and parents and children were missing. The flight had been so rapid, and in all directions the thoroughfares had been so obstructed, and in some cases utterly impassable, by the crowding of vehicles and masses of people, and the city itself a wave of fire—it is no marvel that under these circumstances thousands for the time were lost sight of, and became lonely wanderers, and that hundreds perished in the flames. The seeds of permanent or temporary disease sown, the bodily suffering and mental agony endured, can never have statistical computation, or adequate description."

COUNTING THE COST.

The amount of property destroyed by the fire, by a careful estimate by Elias Colbert was $192,000,-000. Not more than one-fourth of this was covered by insurance, and of the amount insured not more than fifty per cent. was paid, some insurance companies not paying more than ten per cent. while others paid in full. But then began that marvelous exhibition of human kindness and benevolence for which history furnishes no parallel. From St. Louis, Cincinnati, Detroit,

ADMINISTRATION BUILDING.—THE WORLD'S COLUMBIAN EXPOSITION, CHICAGO, 1893.

New York, Boston and nearly all the large cities of the United States, and from many cities in England, Germany and France came prompt relief. A report for 1874 shows actual cash receipts of $3,000,000, and money and supplies estimated to aggregate over *six millions*, were freely sent to Chicago from all over the world. Before one might say the ashes of this mighty city had time to cool, work was begun for the removal of the debris. No less than forty odd millions were spent on new buildings in the burned district in the first twelve months after the fire, ten years later all traces of the calamity had disappeared, till to-day Chicago as premised in our opening remarks, rears her stately head, the most remarkable city in the world.

THE HAYMARKET MASSACRE.

A brief sketch of the incidents which marked the course of what is known as the "Haymarket Massacre" will serve to show that the responsibility is to be simply allotted to one class, namely the disciples of Anarchy, but there can be little question that the order received its death-blow as far as the western metropolis is corncerned with the execution of the four leading perpetrators of this outrage. Quoting from the able guide and encyclopedia of Chicago compiled by Mr. John J. Flinn, to whom we have to express our acknowledgments for a fund of statistical data, it would seem according to this authority that the term "Haymarket Massacre" as applied to the tragic event of May 4th, 1886, is a misnomer. Mr. Flinn states: The tragedy recalled to mind by the name actually occurred on Desplaines Street, between the Haymarket and the alley which runs east of Desplaines Street, south of Crane Brothers' manufacturing establishment. The wagon from which the anarchist speakers addressed the mob stood directly in front of Crane Brothers' steps about eight feet north of this alley. The bomb was thrown from the mouth of the alley and exploded between the second and third companies of policemen, as the six companies were halting close to the wagon. The bomb thrower unquestionably made his escape through the alley which connects with another opening on Randolph Street, east of the Haymarket. Seven policemen were killed outright, or died shortly afterward of their wounds, as a result of the explosion. A large number of policemen were badly and permanently injured. How many of those in the mob were killed or died afterward of the injuries they received in the police fusillade which followed the explosion has never been known, for their bodies were quietly buried and their wounds concealed by their friends whenever possible. The arrest of the leaders Fielden, Spies, Engel, Lingg, Neebe, Schwab, Fischer, the searching of the *Arbeiter Zeitung* office on the east side of Fifth Avenue, near Washington Street, and the discovery there of a vast supply of dynamite, arms, bombs and infernal machines; the discovery of bombs in different parts of the city, under sidewalks, in lumber yards, at the homes of the anarchists; the sensational surrender of Parsons, who had taken flight on the night of the massacre; the long trial, the speeches, the sentences, the appeal; the refusal of the Supreme Court of the United States to interfere; the efforts made to have the death sentence commuted; the day of execution, the 11th of November, 1887; the shocking suicide of the "tiger anarchist" Lingg, in his cell at the jail; the hanging of Parsons, Spies, Engel and Fischer,, the commutation of the death sentences of Fielden and Schwab to life imprisonment, all contributed toward the popular excitement which followed the fatal 4th of May, and continued until the gallows and the prison had performed the parts assigned them by the law. The executed anarchists are buried at Waldheim Cemetery. The police monument at the intersection of Randolph and Desplaines Streets (Haymarket Square) was erected by the citizens of Chicago in honor of the brave officers who risked or sacrificed their lives in defence of the law and in the commemoration of the death of anarchy in this city.

THE WORLD'S COLUMBIAN EXPOSITION.

Scarcely had the gates closed upon the great Centennial Exposition of 1876, at Philadelphia, than the subject of another great World's Fair to be held in some city of this country upon the four hundredth anniversary of its discovery was broached.

The leaven worked quietly and well; and while the great Paris exposition was in progress, the United States as the representative nation of the New World, began to consider more definitely the propriety of celebrating the anniversary of Columbus' great discovery, by inviting the nations of the Old World to visit our shores.

The closing decade of the most remarkable century in the Christian era, coinciding with the anniversary of an event unequaled in the history of this sphere, suggested the uniting of all mankind in a celebration of peace.

The land where necessity and courage have fostered industry and wealth presents a fitting scene for such a gathering.

Columbia, the youngest among the continents of the civilized world should act the part of hostess at the celebration of her four hundredth birthday by extending to the entire world an invitation to commemorate the event in a display of the material evidences of the progress of the human family and such a commemoration should be called the WORLD'S COLUMBIAN EXPOSITION.

The United States Congress on April 25, 1890, passed an act, which was approved by the President of the United States, declaring it " fit and appropriate that the four hundredth anniversary of the discovery of America be commemorated by an exhibition of the resources of the United States, etc." —further that such an exhibition should be of a national and inter-national character so that not only the people of the Union, and this continent, but those of all nations as well, can participate, and to carry out this purpose, the act of Congress provides "that an exhibition of arts, industries, manufactures, and products of the soil, mine, and sea, shall be inaugurated in the year 1892 in the city of Chicago, U. S. A."

A commission was provided consisting of two commissioners and two alternates from each state and territory in the United Union, and eight commissioners and delegates at large, all of whom were commissioned by the president of the United States of America.

This commission and a corporation organized under the laws of the state of Illinois, are charged jointly with the task of making all preparations for the exposition and conducting it to a successful termination.

The commission is composed of representative citizens of the various states and territories, while the directory of the Illinois corporation embraces some of the wealthiest, best known and most successful business and professional men in the city of Chicago.

These two bodies are working in perfect harmony, and with the common purpose of making the exposition worthy of the great historic event it is designed to commemorate, and a fitting illustration of the world's progress in civilization and in the various lines of human endeavor.

President Harrison issued a proclamation, notifying the world that the EXPOSITION will be held at the time and place named above, and invited all foreign countries to take part in the same.

The Chicago board guaranteed to the national management that a sum not less than ten million dollars would be raised, and expended for the purpose of making the Columbian Exposition a success; five million more came from the city of Chicago and with nearly $200,000 appropriated by the different states for their special exhibits outside of the half million the national government contributes, will make the grandest world's exhibit ever known.

Preparations are under way in every state and territory of the Union looking to a splendid display of its industries and resources.

The appropriations already made exceed $4,000,000, while individual efforts and private contributions will swell the sum to over $7,000,000, making a grand total of state exhibits of over $10,000,000, and many states contemplate the erection of their own separate buildings, all of which will be unique and peculiar in construction and design.

The United States government will have a specially constructed building which will include exhibits from the Executive departments, Smithsonian Institute, United States fish commision and the National museum and such articles and materials as illustrate the function and administrative faculties of the government in times of peace and its RESOURCES IN TIME OF WAR, tending to demonstrate the nature of our people, their institutions and their adaptation to the wants of our people.

MINING BUILDING.—THE WORLD'S COLUMBIAN EXPOSITION, CHICAGO, 1893.

THE ELECTRICAL PALACE — WORLD'S COLUMBIAN EXPOSITION, CHICAGO, 1893.

THE FINANCES.

The exposition is in elegant shape financially and warrants the statement of the exposition managers that all the money necessary to make it a success will be forthcoming.

The Illinois corporation known as the "World's Columbian Exposition" first organized with $5,000,000 capital, was recently increased to $10,000,000; in addition the city of Chicago authorized the issuance of $5,000,000 in bonds and the United States appropriation amounts to $1,500,000 exclusive of the exhibits expenses and buildings by the government.

THE SITE.

After a long and somewhat warmly contested contest a beautiful and suitable site was selected for the exposition, containing fully one thousand acres of land beautifully situated on the shore of Lake Michigan.

The grandest and most imposing location offered was that of Jackson Park in the southern section of the city, and it is intended to use it in its entirety for exposition purposes, leaving the improved parts in their present improved condition while the unimproved parts are being laid out in a manner appropriate to the whole buildings as adopted. In the preparation of the grounds, Jackson Park will be further extended and the inlet on the northern side be made into a large lagoon inclosing the main island with an extensive body of native wood.

This will afford a natural landscape and supply one episode of scenery in refreshing relief to the grandeur of the buildings and through its sylvan qualities to the crowded and busy aspect that will be looked for from every part of the grounds so well and appropriately filled with the world's choicest mechanism. Fom this lagoon so finely formed will continue the waterway southward along the main building and into a large water basin which is to form the center of a great square about which the principal buildings of the exposition will be grouped. Fountains will be in operation in this basin forming a brilliant spectacle in the sunlight, and more brilliant when viewed by the incandescent lights of night illumination.

The banks of these land-locked bodies of water are finished in a manner appropriate to the various localities through which they pass.

The borders in the canal and the basin in the court will all have embankments of stone or brick surmounted by parapets or balustrades of stone, iron, brick or terra-cotta, opening upon steps and landings for the use of boating parties.

A feature of interest to the visiting public will be that all walks and out-door places for assemblages of people will be filled and furnished with out-door seats and resting-places, and will be paved with mosaics of brick, stone or concrete blocks.

The entire grounds will be decorated with shrubs, trees, turf and flowers and no effort lost to display the superior class of garden and lawn decorations known only to the American landscape gardener.

THE BUILDINGS.

Opposite the great square, projects into the great Lake Michigan over 1,500 feet the grand pier to be so constructed as to form a harbor of safety for lake craft.

THE PIER.

The floor of the pier will slope gently from the shore so that visitors will get an unobstructed view of the main court and its surroundings, the handsomely paved beach and its hosts of people and the architectural grandeur of the most imposing and important buildings of the World's Exposition.

GOVERNMENT BUILDING.

The United States government furnishes its own building in which to exhibit its wealth of curios, and the evidences of the world's progress since the United States wore small pants and hadn't learned to whistle or to whittle.

The board of managers has submitted a condensed description of the buildings for the World's Columbian Exposition which from official circles is believed to be absolutely correct, and will be found illustrated in this work. Reference to the plan will show that the general scheme of the grouping is so arranged that while each building is perfect of itself and separate of its kind, each is also an integral part of the grand harmony.

They are two grand courts upon which the main buildings face, and from any point of either of these spaces the principal buildings face, forming a harmonious composition, from one view of which is obtained the all. This is in the ADMINISTRATION BUILDING. This superb building was designed by Richard M. Hunt, the president of the American Institute of Architects.

Its general plan is that of a square composed of four pavilions, and will cover an area of 250 feet square and will rise to a height of 220 feet.

The crown of the structure is a splendid dome ninety feet high, including its base and the general style of the French renaissance.

Externally the height may be divided into three different stages, the first consisting of the four pavilions, corresponding in height with the various buildings grouped about it, which are about sixty-five feet in height. The second stage of the same height is a continuation of the Central Rotunda, 175 feet square, surrounded upon all sides by an open colonnade of noble proportions, being 20 feet wide and forty feet high, with columns four feet in diameter.

This colonnade is reached by staircases and elevators from the four principal halls and is interrupted at the angles by corner pavilions, crowned with domes and groups of statuary. The third stage consists of the base of the great dome thirty feet in size and height and octagonal in form, the dome rising in graceful lines richly ornamented with heavily moulded ribs and sculptured panels to the aerial top.

At each angle of the octagonal base are large eagles, and among the springing lines are panels with rich garlands.

Immediately to the right of this is the PALACE OF MECHANIC ARTS.

The central idea carried out in this building which covers a space of 850 by 500 feet, is that of the railroad train house.

The building is designed according to the Spanish renaissance. It is difficult to assign pre-eminence among such a collection of architectural triumphs, but the richness of the facades of this great palace is unexcelled by any other of the great buildings.

One of the grand features of this triple building will be the use of the three enormous traveling platforms to carry visitors from end to end of the great building, thus affording a complete view of all the machinery in operation without fatigue.

Facing this and on the other side of the administration building are two great buildings, the principal of which is the ELECTRICAL BUILDING which covers a space of 850 by 500 feet, that is to say nearly six acres.

The general design of the building is the Italian renaissance. The motive is very cunningly carried out in the delicate spires and turrets which crown it. At the south end is a great semi-circular arched entrance a marvel of sculptural and colored decorations in the center of which appears a life size and like statue of the great prince of electricity and its first discoverer of usefulness, Benjamin Franklin.

Next to this building is the MINES AND MINING BUILDING. This is of the same dimensions as the Electrical building and is severely classic in its design; the main features are two grand entrances one at the North and South end, which are 100 feet high and thirty-two feet in width and open into vestibules eighty-five feet high, elaborately decorated. At each corner of the building there is a pavilion sixty-eight feet square and ninety feet high, surmounted by dome and flag-staff. A broad balcony sixty feet wide and twenty-five feet high surrounds the building and eight handsome stairways lead to the balcony.

This group of buildings faces upon a T shaped basin and canal toward the lake and the view from the administration building prolonged across the basin between the Liberal Arts building and the Agricultural building, shows the casino situated upon the long pier which rises in capricious but artistic form against the blue waters of the great lake.

AGRICULTURAL BUILDING.—THE WORLD'S COLUMBIAN EXPOSITION, CHICAGO, 1893.

MANUFACTURES AND LIBERAL ARTS BUILDING.—WORLD'S COLUMBIAN EXPOSITION, CHICAGO, 1893.

Next comes the most beautiful of them all, the AGRICULTURAL BUILDING. By architects this is considered second if not the finest building on the ground. It will cover a space 800 by 500 feet almost surrounded by lagoons and canals.

Its design is purely classic and the exterior presents a richness of decoration skillfully handled to produce the most pleasing effect. The grand features of the building are the great center pavilion and those at the corner. The grand entrance is sixty feet wide and leads into a vestibule thirty feet deep and sixty feet wide. Corinthian columns five feet in diameter and forty feet high form this grand entrance and beyond all this is the rotunda 100 feet in diameter, surmounted by a glass dome 130 feet high, under which is a colossal statue of "Ceres" surrounded by other allegorical agricultural characters in most classic groups of statuary. A broad and handsome colonnade connects this building with the palace of mechanical arts, the whole forming one of the many superb architectural groupings which is the pride of the chief architect's heart.

In the Liberal Arts and Manufacturers buildings is included the exhibits which are known as the MAIN BUILDING. This is the largest exposition ever constructed and will cover a space of 1,688 feet in length and 788 feet in width. The principal facade will be toward the lake, and all four sides of its lines are designed on magnificent principles. A central corridor divides the interior of the mammoth building into two great courts, in one of which is erected the $100,000 structure of the Boot and Shoe industry and in the other the equally costly Music pavilion, the architects deeming space too costly to allow those industries to erect special structures on the outside in the 700 acres allotted in the Jackson Park Grant. It would be imposible to give details of this grand central building, a detail of which would include the exhibit of the nations of the earth; suffice it to say it will present a spectacle of varied magnificence impossible to conceive, unseen.

West of this is the most important American industry of the West represented, MINES AND MINING BUILDING, which has been described in brief above and will be a central point for all of our foreign visitors who have heard wild and fictitious tales of the Golconda of the West which in turn have met with the re-actionary results that the gold and silver fields of our Western territory is a myth and an unfounded fable whose base alone is in the fevered imagination of the Wall Street broker or the "Thread the Needle Street" "promoter," a term lately imported.

Then comes the TRANSPORTATION BUILDING which is 960 by 250 feet in size and which is in fact the main entrance which will consist of an immense single arch enriched to an extraordinary degree by carvings, bas-reliefs, and mural paintings, the entire scheme of which will form a rich, beautiful, but quiet climax that will be treated in pure gold leaf and will be known as the GOLDEN DOOR. The general style of this building is on the Romanesque order and from its crowning cupola most striking groups of the great buildings will be seen.

To again direct the sight-seer from a distance, we would say that to the north of the main building, the grand Government building may be seen and beyond this, across the arm of the lagoon, the exquisite FISHERY BUILDING. This peculiar building and one that will probably attract more attention from the thousands of foreign visitors than any other, built upon a curved island is 1,100 feet long and 200 feet wide; the general design is of the Spanish Romanesque with a generally light and pleasing effect. Two polygonal wings are to serve as an aquaria. The three domes of this building will be of the same color and general effect of the Administration building and the artists in charge of the color scheme of the whole exposition have planned to use these two widely separated domes as "accents" of the whole scheme.

Across the lagoon and naturally wooded island from the Government building is the HORTICULTURAL BUILDING which is 1000 by 286 feet in size. The main feature of this building will be that it is most entirely constructed of glass and in it is the great "Crystal Dome" 187 feet in diameter and 113 feet high, in front of which two smaller domes resting upon richly sculptured vases, flank the highly ornate arch main entrance. A broad and rich terrace of the loveliest flowers surrounds the whole building, interrupted only by artificial lakes in which the Victoria Regia and other water plants are in blossom. The management appreciating the fact that American women were an important factor in its growth, intelligence and improvement, made them a special factor in this grand Colum-bian Anniversary and created a board of general lady managers of which the beautiful and talented Mrs. Potter Palmer was made president and her vice-presidents and staff are among the most talented ladies in the nation.

Right at the north of the grand Horticultural building is the WOMAN'S BUILDING 200 by 400 feet in size, the most elegant in the grounds. The general design of this literal gem is of the Italian renaissance with end and center pavilions connected by an open arcade. The design was made by Miss Sophia G. Hayden of Boston and it is under the control of the lady board of managers and will contain exhibits of women's work and be one of the most novel and important features of the great Columbian Exposition.

To the north of these grand central buildings will arise the Illinois State building, and the Art building and its annexes as are designed, and the State and foreign buildings. It is safe to say that the Columbian Exposition will be the greatest International fair the world has ever known. It has had from the very incipiency the official recognition of the National government and the whole United States and the several states and territories by their legislatures have appropriated over $12,000,000 besides what the various corporations and private parties will do to make the exhibition representative and general.

No state, district or county but what will be represented in its best light and the correspondence of the nations show that beyond the seas all will be here. Great Britain, France, Prussia, Austria, Spain and Turkey as well as the smaller powers in the West, have acknowledged the president's kind invitation and are already preparing exhibits. China, Japan, Australia and the powers to the East of the continent and to our West will be with us, and the great plague of the manager's soul is to pro-vide adequate room for all in his space originally allowed.

But Chicago, the grand Phœnix giant who arose sublimely from the ashes of a conflagration second alone to that of Rome and Tyre, will arise proudly and grandly to the occasion and say to the world, "Come! we have room enough for you all."

In this short article it would be impossible to point out the many interesting features of this grand Columbian Exposition. The National government will send their celebrated squadron of "White" to assist in the celebration. A tower higher than Eifel ever dreamed of, will be erected on the grounds. Twenty-five different railroads centering in Chicago will have depots and baggage stations on the grounds. One of the most skilled and best of the Chicago police lieutenants will have charge of the throng and be ably assisted by a well-organized force of the world's "finest." For fire protection there will be a special department chosen from the bravest and best of the best fire department in the world.

Different days wil be set apart for the special observance of every grand organization and body in the Union. Already in all parts of the United States, Mexico, and Canada, "Chicago Clubs" are being formed and weekly deposits made to form a grand treasury to defray expenses in visiting the great Columbian Exposition. Never before in the world's history have foreign powers and people evinced so much interest in the world's grand exhibition. From pole to pole and sun to sun, East, West, North, and South, the world has received our kind invitations and have acted upon it favorably and steps are taken to see that each nation will be represented.

When the project of a great World's Fair was mooted, there were three principal candidates for the honor, consisting of the three principal cities of the Union, New York, Chicago and St. Louis, but in the language of the sublime poet, the progressive Metropolis of the West walked off with the preferred confectionary reposing in its private apparel receptacle. This tribute we pay to Boston and now for ourselves. Chicago is the typical American city, in age, extent and development. Less than sixty years ago what is now Chicago consisted of three log cabins and to-day one million and a quarter of prosperous people proudly call it "Home." Think of it reader, the three log cabins have grown into as many millions and no more progressive city is known than the one selected by the United States Congress, as the fitting place for the great Columbian Exposition.

HORTICULTURAL HALL.—WORLD'S COLUMBIAN EXPOSITION, CHICAGO, 1893.

WOMAN'S BUILDING.—WORLD'S COLUMBIAN EXPOSITION, CHICAGO, 1893.

Twenty years ago the city was devastated by a disastrous fire unequaled in modern history, a conflagration which destroyed nearly twenty thousand buildings and resulted in a loss exceeding $200,000,000 and not a trace of the ruins remains. Its mammoth buildings and great industries recuperated quickly and built from the ashes of Mother O'Leary's lamp a grander city than Aladdin ever depicted in the fabled pages of romance.

To accomodate the great volume of traffic incident to the World's Fair, there are thirty lines of railways entering the city that reach from the Atlantic to the Pacific coasts, from Lake Superior to the Gulf of Mexico and all the great cities of the United States and Canada as well as the borders of Manitoba and Mexico are connected with this grand Metropolis of the West. There are eight Union depots in the city by which a passenger may enter and without leaving his train reach all the principal seaboard cities of the United States, Canada in the North, or Mexico in the South.

Over one thousand exclusively passenger trains arrive and depart in one day and it is estimated that in the usual course of business nearly 200,000 people arrive and depart from Chicago each day. The preparations made by Chicago for the great exposition give promise of its being the greatest the world has ever seen.

The municipality have raised $5,000,000, the people by popular subscription $5,000,000 which represent thoroughly the people of the Western metropolis, its list of 30,000 shareholders, including representatives of every condition of society, trade and profession. The original amount intended to be raised has already been more than subscribed and the directors of the association are confident that another $5,000,000 will be forthcoming, thus giving the exposition $15,000,000 in addition to the $15,000,000 appropriated for the government exhibit and the millions raised by the different states and foreign powers for their exhibits

As provided by Congress, the formal dedication of the exposition, grounds and buildings, will occur October 12, 1892. The president of the United States will take part in the ceremonial, which will be made the occasion of appropriate festivities, including military parades, fire-works displays, public meetings, processions, musical entertainments, tableaux and countless other attractions. The military and naval exhibit of the United States regular and State guards will be a grand feature. The plans of Major-General Schofield have been adopted and all the troops will be under the command of General Nelson A. Miles. More than 10,000 soldiers will participate and those of the National Guard who have the honor to take part, will be crack companies from the different states, those that have shown excellence in drill, discipline and marching being selected and competitive drills to determine which companies shall take part in the great event, are already being held in nearly every state of the Union.

No side shows are to be permitted on the grounds of the exposition. The directory has decided that the entrance fee shall entitle the visitor to see everything within the inclosure. There will, however, be several theaters built and kept running, at which the finest talent in the world will appear and visitors who choose to attend the performance will have to pay an admission fee.

Such sights as "A Street in Cairo" will be free, but natives of Oriental countries in a few cases will be allowed to charge a small fee to special performances of a theatrical nature.

The exposition directory has taken action under which adequate insurance will be placed upon all persons and property during the Fair and it is their intention to place an insurance of about $500,000,000 on the exhibits. Eugene and Paul Champion of Neuilly sur Seime, France, will give a series of electrical fire-works in which neither gunpowder, dynamite or other explosive materials will be used in producing the dazzling effects. An operator will sit at an instrument something like a piano and by a manipulation of the keys, produce designs of the most gorgeous fashion. The principal piece will be a representation of Chicago as a statue of fire, to be surrounded by other figures of flame, each representing a state of the Union.

Chicago will be represented as receiving the homage of all the great powers of the world, each filing past the statues and assembled states, and as they pass Chicago each will halt, bow, and lay down a flag or shield of fire at Chicago's feet, receiving in return, the palm branch of peace. This display will last forty minutes and no less than 40,000 distinct effects will be produced. This and other attractions too numerous to enumerate, will form a part of the grand total that will go to make up the grand ensemble.

The Exposition European committee, embracing Messrs. Butterworth, Handy, Bullock, Lindsay and Peck, have received marked attention from every nation and in every capital and important city in Europe, and have aroused a great degree of interest, insuring extensive participation by all foreign nations. It is expected that most of the potentates and crowned heads of Europe will attend. Among those who have already signified their intentions are the Prince of Wales, Emperor William of Germany, President Carnot of France, the Shah of Persia, and others.

Nearly $10,000,000 of exposition work on the grounds and buildings at the park is now under way, and thousands of workmen and mechanics are shaping in detail the grand effects which will be opened to the public two years hence. One of the grandest and most important departments of the exposition is that devoted to Woman's Work. Mrs. Potter Palmer returned last summer from a visit to Europe, where she awakened the interest of the women of the Old World, and there certainly now exists in all parts of Europe a comprehension and appreciation of the nature and purpose of the board of lady managers of the Columbian Exposition.

Mrs. Potter Palmer, as president of the board, has enlisted the cordial co-operation of the greatest ladies in England, France, Spain and Germany equally with those of the bread winning class.

An organization looking to the interests of women at the great Exposition is organized in London, Paris, Madrid and Berlin under the patronage of the royal families and distinguished ladies. In fact nothing has been overlooked, and no detail, however small, slighted to make this grand Exposition the greatest the world has ever seen and the most representative of the world's progress ever known.

Ample hotel and traffic accommodations are provided and the management offers every convenience to make this a crowning effort to show the world the grandeurs and greatness of the New World, its wonderful resources and advantages, also the great improvements in mechanics, art, literature and general improvements in the lands across the seas. Every nation will be represented that acknowledges any form of government from the greatest to the lowest.

The Continental governments of Europe will view with the splendor of the children of the Orient. The Japanese and Chinese will bring the works of their deft-fingered workers, the Spanish senorita will live with the accomplished mam'oselle or fraulein, and all will form a happy combination of reunion under the flag that makes all people equal. Every country and clime have signified their intention to be represented and add to the greatness of this grand exposition.

To one and all Chicago sends her greeting and in the name of the greatest republic on earth, will give them welcome.

There can be no failure where all is success. A hundred or more of principal attractions have been neglected necessarily in this short resume, but all will be found at the Exposition. All of the work is now in progress and under headway, looking to a completion in the near future.

The trunk lines have offered to transport exhibits at half price, the tariff rates have been suspended by the National government, and every inducement offered by the National and State governments to promote and increase the success of the grand Columbian Exposition. Many of the foreign countries have signified their intention of erecting special buildings for their exhibits, and a special space has been provided for them, as also for various arts and industries calling for a separate and more extensive display.

This will be the occasion of a lifetime, to see the nations of the earth and their wonders in holiday attire. All are invited and all will be made welcome.

SOME DISTINGUISHING FEATURES OF THE GARDEN CITY—THE AGE OF "SKY-SCRAPERS."

Among the distinguishing features of the Garden City in this era of material growth and prosperity is the rage for the erection of mammoth buildings, veritable "sky-scrapers;" and to-day the

THE ROOKERY, ADAMS AND LA SALLE STS.

POST OFFICE, CLARK AND ADAMS ST.

COURT HOUSE, CLARK AND RANDOLPH STS.

Western metropolis can, and will in the future, be able to, boast of having within its confines the "tallest buildings on earth." Especially will this boast savor of a truism when some of the many structures now projected shall have been completed. The introduction of elevators has led to the possibility of constructing, to the monetary advantage of owners, buildings of a height that, a few short years ago, would have been dreaded as standing menaces to limb and life and as monuments of folly if not greed of projectors and owners. But all this has been changed by the operation of new building methods and by the use of steam and other elevators. The latter have made the upper floors of the tallest building in the city almost as easy of access and as accommodating and as useful—and therefore as valuable—as the ground floor. No city in the world can show so many lofty, "sky-kissing" buildings as Chicago can in her principal business section. These are at once the envy and admiration of residents of other cities on the American continent, and notably of New York, which aspires to preserve that lead which Chicago will ere long claim, not only in the vastness and elegance of its business and residential buildings, but in commerce and all that contributes to the creation and maintenance of a nation's commercial metropolis. While to many thoughtful Chicagoans the high-towering edifices do not appear as unmixed blessings, or as possessing an immunity from danger, they yet point to them with pride as evidences of what the city has achieved in her comparatively short history, and particularly since, phœnix-like, she raised herself out of the broad area of ashes to which she was reduced in the memorable year 1871. Little more than half a century ago Chicago's buildings were mere log cabins and wooden sheds. What a contrast between those and the stately, lofty edifices which line the well-paved, well-sewered streets of to-day! There are those yet living among us who have witnessed Chicago's growth from a mere hamlet of a dozen huts or so to the second most populous of cities on the American continent. These old pioneers, these "forefathers of the hamlet," have been made witnesses of incidents in the upbuilding of a mighty city that come under the ken of but few. These old pioneers have their annual gatherings around the festive board, where they, in a few brief hours, recount reminiscences of by-gone times, and live over again, as it were, the scenes of their youth, middle-age and declining years. Year by year the number of old pioneers grows less, but there are yet preserved to us many who are still busy, active, useful citizens, notably such as Mr. John Vogt, who will be found referred to in other pages of this work.

As we have said, if there is one feature of Chicago's phenomenal business enterprise which receives general recognition it is her high buildings, in the erection of which sentiment is mingled with cold business policy. Indeed, the towering office building structures which have been erected during the last five years have brought the city prominently before the investing public all over the country. They have given to what is known as the Chicago style of architecture or Chicago construction an established character. To Chicago more than to any other city is due the development of the revolution in modern buildings, in consequence of which there is practically no limit to the height to which buildings of sufficient foundation area may be carried. Such advances have been made in the adaptability of building materials that the only problems which are to be solved by the builder of a thirty or forty story building are a suitable foundation and an elevator service which will place tenants of all floors in easy communication with the street traffic.

A list of some of the highest structures in the city, and one giving the comparative heights of church steeples, great business blocks and public buildings, was recently published in the *Inter-Ocean*, and this is here given:

Grand Central Passenger Station, corner of Harrison Street and Fifth Avenue, the highest railway depot tower on the continent—200 feet.

Chicago Opera House, corner of Clark and Washington Streets, was the pioneer of the sky-scrapers. The Phœnix Building, corner Jackson and Clark Streets, the Royal Insurance Building on Jackson Street, and the Rialto are about the same height, 140 feet.

Tower on Dearborn Street Passenger Station, noted for its odd shape as well as its height, 160 feet.

Masonic Temple, corner Randolph and State Streets, twenty stories high, now approaching completion. It has but one rival in the city, and very few in the world. The German Opera House on Randolph Street between Clark and Dearborn, and "The Fair" Building, corner Adams and Dearborn Streets, each twenty stories high, will, however, crowd the great temple pretty close—255 feet.

Union Park Congregational Church spire, corner Ashland and Washington Boulevards. This is only one of the 'many tall spires in the city, averaging about the same height—175 feet.

First Presbyterian Church spire, corner Indiana Avenue and Twenty-first Street, the highest in Chicago—180 feet.

The highest steeple on any Catholic Church in the city is that of the Jesuit Cathedral on Twelfth Street, near South Halsted—175 feet.

The tallest elevator chimney is that of the Armour elevator, located on Division Street, on the North Branch of the river—154 feet.

Manhattan Block, Nos. 307 to 321 Dearborn Street, sixteen stories high, is only one of several office buildings of about the same altitude, namely: Cook County Abstract Company's Building, Washington Street, between Clark and Dearborn, seventeen stories; Caxton and Monon Blocks, on Dearborn Street, south of Van Buren, each twelve stories; Unity Building, Dearborn Street, between Washington and Randolph, eighteen stories; Ashland Block, Clark Street, corner Randolph, eighteen stories; the new hotel "Chicago," fourteen stories, and the Monadnock Block, fifteen stories, facing each other on Jackson and Dearborn Streets; the Calumet and Mallers Buildings on La Salle Street, each twelve stories; and Rand–McNally's Building, Adams Street, between La Salle and Fifth Avenue, twelve stories—all of which approach or equal the height of the Manhattan—220 feet.

Douglas Monument, on Thirty-fifth Street, facing Lake Michigan, the highest shaft in the city —140 feet.

Tower of the North Chicago Pumping Station, foot of Chicago Avenue, the tallest water works tower in the city—175 feet.

Board of Trade Tower, one of the most beautiful as well as one of the tallest towers in the world—240 feet.

Chicago Light, the highest beacon in the city, measured from the lake line—85 feet.

The Rookery, twelve stories, corner Adams and La Salle Streets, one of the chief office buildings of Chicago and one of the most ornate structures erected by private enterprise in the world—159 feet.

Tacoma Block, twelve stories high, corner La Salle and Madison Streets, is another of the tall office buildings, and the first of the improved steel frame edifices constructed—164 feet.

Auditorium Tower, the highest building in Chicago. The balcony is 260 feet high, and the observatory tower carries the height up to 275 feet. The flagstaff surmounting this is the highest thing in town—300 feet.

Union League Club House Tower, interesting alike for its beautiful design and because it is the portal of one of the noted club houses of the world—130 feet.

The Inter Ocean Tower, corner Madison and Dearborn Streets—190 feet.

Blatchford & Co.'s Shot Tower, corner Jefferson Street and Milwaukee Avenue, the tallest shot tower in the city—190 feet.

Chicago Sugar Refinery, fourteen stories, corner Twelfth and Canal Streets, the tallest manufacturing plant in the city—167 feet.

Tower of the quaint Owings Building, fourteen stories, corner Adams and Dearborn Streets, unique in design, and a cloud disturber of the first order—225 feet.

Chamber of Commerce building, twelve stories, corner La Salle and Washington Streets, the tallest white stone office building in Chicago and boasting of a wonderful rotunda—200 feet.

Woman's Temple, twelve stories, recently built by the ladies of the Temperance Union as an office building for their own use and for the public, corner Monroe and La Salle Streets. In height it corresponds to the Virginia Hotel, corner Rush and Ohio Streets, and the Pullman and Studebaker Buildings on Michigan Avenue—140 feet.

Labor Temple, twelve stories, erected under the auspices of different trades assemblies—175 feet.

Home Insurance Building, fourteen stories, corner Adams and La Salle Streets, recently enlarged by the addition of several stories—200 feet.

Smoke Stack of the Chicago Sugar Refinery, the highest chimney, with one exception, in the State of Illinois—254 feet.

The Masonic Temple, above referred to, and of which a handsome illustration will be found in these pages, is the first eighteen-story building to be erected in Chicago. It has a frontage of 170 feet on State Street, and 114 feet on Randolph Street. The building will rise to a height of 254 feet. The building in itself without consideration of the value of the land on which it stands, will represent an expenditure of $2,000,000. High gables, which make the structure in reality twenty stories high, rise on all four sides several feet higher than the surface of the roof proper. There will be 9,000 feet of floor space on this roof, and this is to be covered with glass and turned into a roof garden. The main entrance to the building is a splendid arch forty-two feet high and twenty-eight feet wide, opening into a rotunda containing fourteen elevators arranged in a semicircle. The two upper floors of the building will be devoted to lodge rooms and halls for the Masonic fraternity.

The new Fair Building, if completed in accordance with the accepted plans, will be one of the greatest commercial structures in the world. It is a plain building, regular in shape, and will occupy over 16,000,000 cubic feet of space. As planned, it will be eighteen stories high. It has not been decided whether it will be completed to that height before the close of the World's Fair. At present it is being built in sections to a height of eight stories. As a fitting climax to the building enterprise shown during the last five years comes the announcement of the intention of the Odd-Fellows to build a thirty-four story structure, 556 feet in height, and

LINCOLN PARK.

as tall as the Washington Monument.　This will be the highest office building in the world.　The plans have been prepared by Messrs. Adler & Sullivan, architects, and provide for a peculiar-shaped building.　The entire ground space is built up to a height of fourteen stories.　Above this the building extends six stories in the form of a square cross, the four spaces at the angles of the main building being left vacant.　Above this main structure, which is twenty full stories in height, is a tower-shaped structure.　This includes one-tenth of the whole area covered by the building, and is fourteen stories high.　The entire structure is 556 feet in height, while the main portion is to be as high as the Masonic Temple.　The building is severely plain and is suggestive of the Auditorium in its outside appearance.　There are two main arched entrances which open into a Mosaic floored rotunda.　In the four corners of this rotunda will be located the banks of elevators.　The construction will be similar to that of most of the high office buildings in the city with the exception that special arrangements will have

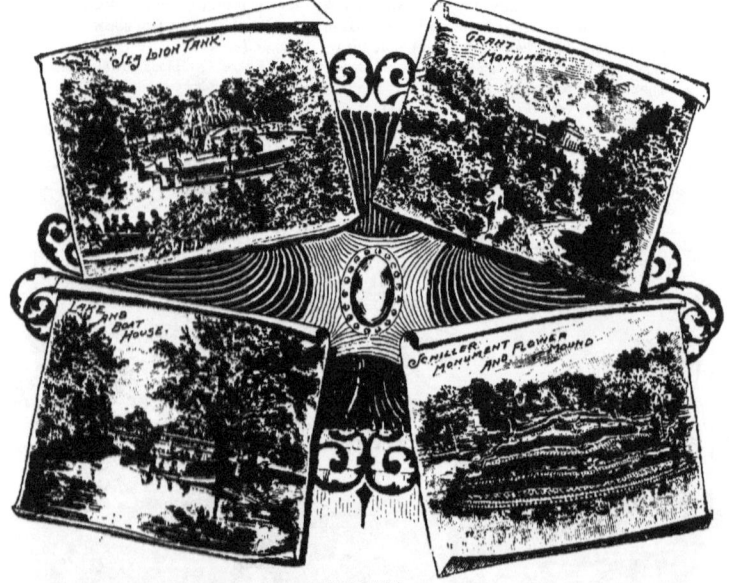

LINCOLN PARK.

to be made for a foundation for the central portion of the building.　It is estimated that $3,500,000 will complete the building without allowing for the land on which it will stand.　The site chosen for this mammoth building is between Monroe Street and Arcade Court, and the building will have one frontage on La Salle Street.

SUMMARY AND REVIEW.—Having sketched, briefly, it is true, the characteristics of Chicago, as shown in her history, her geographical position, natural resources, commercial facilities, by river and rail, we may now bestow a glance on the line of progress and development as it stretches into the immediate future.　Thus we take, for instance, the new city limits.　From an area of less than two square miles (the area of the original town in 1835) Chicago has broadened her limits to 174.1

miles. Such a growth is not simply phenomenal—it is unparalleled in the history of the world. In a little more than half a century, out of a barren and marshy prairie there has sprung a city of 1,000,000 souls. The old town extended exactly one mile north and south of Madison Street, and one mile west of State, with the lake as the eastern boundary. From that small beginning this colossal center of Western commerce has grown. Two years later the future great city had to extend her territory; the southern limits, according to this new addition, became Twenty-second Street; the West Side limits Wood Street, and the North Side limits, North Avenue. Still the city grew. It was during that year the great land boom of 1837 was developed, when land jumped up hundreds of dollars in value in twenty-four hours. The next four or five years following there was a lull, but early in the forties another era of prosperity struck the town, which kept on increasing until, in 1847, the West Side limit became Western Avenue. Six years later, 1853, an extension was made, both north and south; the population which had settled north of North Avenue, between Sedgwick Street and the river, clamored for admission, and the limits were extended to Fullerton Avenue; on the south the extension included all the territory south of Twenty-second Street to the south branch of Halsted, and to Thirty-first east to Halsted Street. A third extension in 1863 squared np things a little more by taking in all of section 31 to the north, and all the territory east of Western Avenue, and north of Thirty-ninth Street to the south. The area of the city then was nearly twenty-five square miles, and in 1869 came the fourth and last extension prior to the great annexation of June, 1890, spoken of in a previous portion of this volume. Such is a brief summary of the transition of Chicago from a swamp to a great city.

THE FUTURE.—Taking Chicago's past for the basis of computation, it seems hazardous to predict to what flights the Western metropolis shall soar in the future. With everything in its favor, it is now growing at a greater ratio than any city in the Union. The enormous resources and facilities at her command have not yet been put to anything like a practical test. The time for that is to come and is not far distant. It is very evident that the people of this wonderfully favored city are now simply *beginning* to estimate its varied capacities, their challenge for the control of the World's Fair being ample evidence of this fact. The sun of Chicago's prosperity is ready to sweep higher above the horizon than ever before. A spirit of local pride and independence has become more universally diffused among her people, and a more aggressive temper moulds and directs her business operations. No one who watches the growth and prosperity of communities, whose soul is enlivened with the progressive ideas which characterize an intelligent and enterprising people, will dispute the fact that here, right here, is located the coming city of the world, and it may be said, even with such broad prophecy, as the Queen of Sheba declared of the wonders of Solomon's kingdom—"The half has not yet been told."

VALEDICTORY REMARKS.

Necessarily, in a volume of the size to which this must be restricted, it is impossible to set forth in detail all the business establishments comprehended in a general view of the prosperity of the city. In the foregoing pages it has been attempted to give the reader unacquainted with the resources and industries of the Western metropolis some idea of their variety as well as their extent. In the following pages some of the leading houses of the city are afforded space to tell their own story, and to set forth more particularly the special features of their own trade—the whole forming an epitome of the commercial and manufacturing activity of one of the busiest, most prosperous and progressive communities on the face of the globe.

CHICAGO OF TO-DAY.

THE METROPOLIS OF THE WEST.

THE pages that follow contain many of the representative houses in Chicago, and in connection with the illustrated portion of the work will be found profitable and interesting.

THE G. H. HAMMOND COMPANY.

The G. H. Hammond Company has achieved a world wide reputation for the progressive enterprise and energy of its management, which has secured for its products, western dressed beef, sheep and hogs, in their various forms, the enviable reputation of being the *finest meats* ever put upon the market, much preferred by the best class of trade everywhere, and resulting in the enormous extension of the company's business, until it is one of the mammoth industrial organizations of the age. The business was established in 1869 by Messrs. Hammond, Plummer & Co., succeeded in 1874 by Messrs. Geo. H. Hammond & Co. Rcpeated enlargements of facilities had been necessitated, and eventually, in 1881, the important interests involved were duly organized and incorporated under the style and title of "The G. H. Hammond Company," with a paid up capital of $1,000,000, which was afterwards gradually increased to $2,500,000. As thus constituted, with its ample resources and sound management, the splendid facilities at command and widespread influential connections, it is unquestionably one of the *world's* representatives in its line, and World's Fair visitors will be astonished at the extent and magnitude of its plant and its operations. The principal plant is centrally located at Hammond, Ind., where are perfect railroad transportation connections to all points. There the company owns about 100 acres, twenty-five of which are covered with buildings, fully equipped with the latest improved machinery and appliances in the various departments of slaughtering, dressing, curing and packing of the meats, the slaughterhouse being considered the most complete and perfect in its appointments of any in the world. This company was the pioneer in the "Chicago fresh dressed beef" trade, now supplying all the large cities and towns in the East with scores of refrigerator carloads daily. One thousand hands are employed in the Hammond packing houses and yards, and the company kills over 400,000 head of cattle annually, besides hogs, sheep and calves. They own and fill numerous large ice houses in

various parts of the country, having a combined capacity of 250,000 tons, and are now operating two immense ice machines with a capacity of over 300 tons of ice daily. They operate a line of 800 refrigerator cars, used exclusively in their own business. The above figures give but a faint idea of the vast ramifications of this giant industry. There is another large plant at Omaha, Neb., where, over 500 hands are employed, killing from 800 to 1,000 hogs, and 300 to 500 head of cattle daily. They are also large manufacturers of pure oleomargarine, having a manufacturing capacity of from 40,000 to 50,000 pounds daily, with the most complete factory in the country. Their celebrated Calumet brand is much sought for, as a perfect equivalent for high grade creamery butter at half the cost. The company maintains large cold-storage warehouses for the distribution of their products in all the principal cities of the Middle and Eastern states, and its meats are universally noted for their exceptional high quality, tender prime cuts from the very pick of the finest cattle on the hoof, as reaching Chicago, and saved from the long and useless journey East, thus enabling the meat to reach its market in prime condition, and having in transit had better care and a more even temperature than is possible in any Eastern slaughterhouse or butcher shop. The Hammond Company is largely instrumental in retaining to Chicago this invaluable trade and also exports from 1,600 to 1,800 carcasses of beef each week by steamships from Boston and New York. The company's officers, who control and guide this enormous traffic are as follows: Mr. A. Comstock, president; Mr. J. C. Melvin, vice-president; Mr. J. P. Lyman, general manager; Mr. Jas. D. Standish, secretary and treasurer. These gentlemen bring to bear special qualifications for the discharge of the onerous duties devolving upon them, and each one has personal charge of a department. Under President Comstock's guidance the company is making remarkable progress, and has fully solved the problem of the meat supply of the future in every section of America and Europe.

E. ROTHSCHILD & BROS.

Chicago's mercantile supremacy is assured as long as she contains such a vast representative clothing manufacturing firm as that of Messrs. E. Rothschild & Bros., Nos. 203 and 205 Monroe street. The character and magnitude of the firm's operations place it in the front rank of American progress and development, and it is proverbial that no eastern manufacturers of clothing can compete with it in the vast territory included within its field of trade. The business was established in 1865 in Davenport, In., by Mr. E. Rothschild, whose success was deservedly so great that in 1871 he decided to enter a much larger field and accordingly removed to this city, where he formed the existing copartnership with his brothers, M. M. & A. M. Rothschild, also experienced in the trade and able and progressive young business men, and engaged in a retail business that at once secured the appreciation of an observant public. In 1865 they decided to devote their attention solely to the wholesale branch of the trade. They at once opened out on Wabash avenue as wholesale manufacturers of fine clothing, subsequently removing to the present immense premises, 203

and 205 Monroe street, in order to secure the needed increase of facilities. Here is the model wholesale manufactory of fine clothing in the United States. The building is a very handsome and substantial structure, five stories and basement in height, and 60x190 feet in dimensions. The premises have been fitted up in the most complete manner, and have all the modern improvements, including steam heat, electric light, telephone and a perfect outfit of cutting machinery, run by steam power. A thorough system of organization is enforced by the copartners, who devote their whole time to the personal supervision of the business, and who produce a stock of fine clothing that is preferred by the best class of trade everywhere. The cutting is all done upon the fifth floor, by machinery run by steam power, over sixty cutters being employed and including the best class of talent. The proprietors select their stock with the utmost care, importing direct from Germany and England all the new shades, patterns and textures of foreign makes, and buying in enormous quantities direct from the principal American mills and commission merchants, all the best class of domestic woolens, cassimeres, cheviots, cloths, etc., All cloth is carefully examined for imperfections and the slightest defect is sufficient for them to throw out the piece, because this firm maintains the highest standard of excellence in the clothing trade. It leads in fashion and style, and all patterns cut, too, are the latest and correct. The work of manufacturing is done in

the most thorough manner and upon an enormous scale of magnitude. Upward of 2,500 tailors are employed in making up outside, while over 100 hands are employed on the premises, and the firm's pay roll averages $45,000 a month and upwards. It is thus one of Chicago's most important and valuable industrial factors. The firm manufacture between five and six thousand garments per week, including full lines of sizes and styles for men, boys and children, in all standard grades, thus most completely meeting the wants of every class of trade. These goods are honestly made from the best materials, trimmed and finished equal to custom made, and wearing better and longer, and giving greater satisfaction than any other stock of ready made clothing upon the market. They carry an enormous stock of seasonable goods on hand, from which buyers can make much more desirable selections than in New York or elsewhere, they being thoroughly conversant with the wants of the western trade, a knowledge gained by twenty-six years' experience with western merchants. Messrs. E. Rothschild & Bros. have ever made a close study of the wants and requirements of the trade of the West, South and Northwest, and offer the best selling clothing that is made at prices that secure a liberal profit to their customers. The Messrs. Rothschild are prominent and respected citizens, public-spirited merchants, loyal to Chicago and her growing interests, and by whose efforts, and prompt, honorable methods has been built up the largest and leading trade of the kind in the West, as creditable to the popular proprietors as it is invaluable to the city.

EARL & WILSON.

Messrs. Earl & Wilson are the only firm in this country who confine themselves to the manufacture of linen collars and cuffs and, as they give their attention to the finest grades only, the trade-mark "E. & W." has become a synonym for the highest excellence. The business was established in 1867, the factory being situated at Troy, N. Y., and salesrooms in New York city. The gentlemen who compose the firm are Messrs. William E. Earl, Washington Wilson, Arthur E. Wilson and E. K. Betts, all men of the highest standing and reputation in that great center. The trade extends to every part of the entire Union and throughout the whole of Canada and Mexico, retail dealers everywhere finding it impossible to

Trade E & W *Mark*

obtain a class of goods elsewhere of the same high quality and style. The facilities of this house are perfect, its resources ample and its connections most extensive and influential, they being always found in the van of progress and the first to adopt the newest shapes and styles which the changes of fashion dictate. The branch in this city was established at 128 Fifth avenue, Sept. 3, 1878, and afterward removed to 174 to 178 Adams street, where it remained several years. Three years ago they removed to their present quarters, which are centrally located at 264 to 270 Fifth avenue. The premises occupy the second floor, 87x160 feet, and are among the most elegant in their appointments in the city. Since the opening of the Chicago branch, in 1878, Mr. J. T. Webber has been connected with the firm as manager of the western branch, having previously occupied a responsible position in their eastern department. Here a very large and varied assortment of collars and cuffs of superior quality, and in the most fashionable shapes, are always in stock, from which the whole of that great section of country, stretching between Ohio and the Pacific coast, is supplied. A large staff of salesmen are continually traversing this part and forwarding daily orders from the most influential retailers in the West. Mr. Webber has ever been a just exponent of those enduring principles of equity which form the basis of the great commercial interests of our country.

GLOBE SAVINGS BANK.

Progress is the order of the day in financial as well as other circles, and it is most gratifying to be able to record that Chicago now possesses such an incentive to thrift and small savings as a duly authorized and powerful savings bank which will receive deposits in such small sums as five cents. We allude to the popular Globe Savings Bank, 225 Dearborn street, which has a paid-up capital of $200,000 as well as a reserve liability of stockholders for an additional $200,000 thus giving its depositors a guaranty fund of $400,000 as security for their deposits. In contrast with the loose banking methods of twenty years ago this institution is incorporated under the State law, which provides that it shall be subject to State inspection at the discretion of the Auditor of Public Accounts of the State of Illinois, in addition to which it is also required to make, annually, four sworn statements of its condition, on dates named by the Auditor. In addition to the foregoing the bank publishes, weekly, a statement of its assets and liabilities, something worthy of remark from the fact that it is the *only* western bank so doing. The bank has the benefit of the wide experience of an eminently capable and responsible board of directors, in the conduct of its affairs, composed of the following gentlemen: C. W. Spalding, J. W. Lanehart, Edward Hayes and Hon. J. P. Altgeld, of Chicago; Hon. John Hayes, Red Oak, Iowa, Ex-Gov. J. A. Weston, Manchester, N. H.; and G. F. Andrews, Nashua, N. H. The officers are as follows: Mr. C. W. Spalding, president; Mr. Edward Hayes, vice-president, Hon. J. P. Altgeld, second vice-president, and Mr. H. S. Derby, cashier. They bring to bear special qualifications for the discharge of the onerous duties devolving upon them, and give that close personal supervision so essential

THE MONADNOCK OFFICE BUILDING.

S. W. CORNER DEARBORN AND JACKSON STREETS.

to the successful operation of such an institution. Mr. Derby was formerly connected with the Illinois Trust and Savings Bank. It is needless to speak of President Spalding; he is one of the most popular and respected of Chicago's capitalists. It its savings department the bank receives deposits of five cents and upward, allowing interest thereon at the rate of four per cent. per annum, payable quarterly. Certificates of deposit, are also issued bearing interest at from two to four per cent. according to time. In this department the bank introduced into Chicago the popular nickel saving stamp system. Commencing with about fifty agents, the system has grown until now more than 250 druggists throughout the city and suburbs have for sale the "Globe Stamps," and thousands daily avail themselves of this method of saving their small amounts of spare money. Books are furnished free by all agents with full

instructions. In the banking department deposits are received subject to check, and no account is "too large and none too small" to receive careful attention. Interest is paid on daily average balances in excess of $500 at the rate of two per cent. per annum. In its bond department a large line of the soundest of income bearing investment securities are carried for sale to customers and others desiring permanent investments of the highest character. The bank is also agent for the Cheque Bank, Limited, of London, England, for the sale of Cheque Bank Cheques, which, as travelers know, are available in all parts of the world. They are safer than currency, more convenient and cheaper than letters of credit. The Globe Savings Bank is known as a colloidal bank. That is to say it loans only on collaterals, bonds and stocks and improved Chicago real estate, and *does not discount commercial paper*, it is therefore not subject to losses by business failures. On account of its conservative policy it already has thousands of depositors and is deservedly the most popular savings bank in the city. In its new quarters the bank will control one of the most magnificent safe depositories in the United States. Boxes will be rented at popular prices. Upon the completion of the magnificent "Monadnock Building," the bank will remove there. In the meantime business is transacted in the Temple Court Building, 225 Dearborn street.

W. P. POWERS.

We give herewith an illustration of one of the most unique and serviceable patents that has been brought to our notice in years, the "Powers' Automatic Temperature Regulator," for regulating steam and hot water heaters and furnaces of all kinds, opening and closing the damper automatically, just when and as much as needed to maintain a uniform temperature. It is operated directly by the temperature of the house, acting upon an ornamental thermostat, of peculiar construction, hung upon the wall of one of the central rooms of the house, which generates an air pressure, and this, being conducted by a concealed tube to the heater, operates the dampers. It is positive in its action, has no batteries or clock work to keep in order, is entirely free from complication, and appears to be very durable. This regulator is the invention of Mr. W. P. Powers, who began its manufacture in La Crosse, Wis., about four years ago, and moved to Chicago in 1889. The regulator is fast coming into general use in all sections of the United States and Canada. It has been eagerly adopted by the hot water heating trade, as, in addition to maintaining a uniform heat in the house, it also closes the dampers just before the boiling point is reached, and so prevents boiling over, a valuable feature which is peculiar to this device. It is manufactured by The Powers' Duplex Regulator Co., whose office and salesroom are at No. 36 Dearborn street. Mr. Powers has invented something of great merit, and is to be congratulated upon his success. He is a native of Wisconsin, and a gentleman in middle life, and is prominent in business circles, being vice-president of the Union Wire Mattress Co., 73 to 83 Erie street, Chicago. His plumbing and steamfitting business in La Crosse, Wis., is still running under the able management of his son, Mr. F. W. Powers, who will in the near future join his father in Chicago and take the position of manager of the Regulator Co. Both father and son are exemplary progressive and industrious business men, who will be found attentive and punctual in the filling of orders, and always desirous to give the fullest satisfaction to patrons.

THE BLAKELY PRINTING COMPANY, GENERAL
PRINTERS.

The business of which the present large and prosperous establishment is the outgrowth, was started in a basement on Fifth avenue, near Washington street, just after the great fire, by Mr. C. F. Blakely, who still conducts their immense business. By close application, hard work and careful attention to the wants and interests of customers, with competent heads of the various departments, it has grown steadily until now it ranks with the largest houses of its kind in the country. The rapid growth of the establishment necessitated a move from Fifth avenue to Dearborn street, and from Dearborn street to their present location, Nos. 184 and 186 Monroe street, the building shown in the illustration, where they have 30,000 square feet of floor surface filled to its utmost capacity with implements and machinery. In the vast composition and job rooms, over two million ems are set weekly. The modern appliances and improvements employed make this the largest and most complete composing room in the city. The facilities for getting out large catalogues and book work, newspapers, railroad and commercial printing, are unsurpassed. The capacity for press work is equally vast. Twenty-five presses, fourteen folding machines, eight stitching machines and eight paper cutters are kept running constantly. Over fifty publications are printed, bound and mailed here, reaching the most distant parts of the civilized world. Over $160,000 in wages are paid out annually to the employes. The establishment consumes over 160 tons (or 16 carloads) of paper per month. The company has never found it necessary to employ canvassers to keep its plant running to its full capacity. Close attention to the wishes of its patrons and efficient service is the motto of this establishment, and the strict observance of the same has enabled it to hold any customers who once place their interests in its hands, many of whom have been with them for over fifteen years. They will take pleasure in furnishing estimates for any kind or style of printing on application.

AUDITORIUM HOTEL.

Of all the locations for a first class hotel in Chicago the magnificent gigantic Auditorium Building presents the best, and here, taking advantage of the splendid opening, those successful and popular hotel proprietors, Mr. James H. Breslin and Mr. Richard H. Southgate, in March, 1890, threw wide open the hospitable doors of the Auditorium hotel, a novelty in every way; as huge a success, and as popular with the best classes of the traveling public, as it is admirably located and luxuriously and completely equipped. The hotel is ten stories and basement in height, and is 190x360 in dimensions. This handsome cut stone building is greatly admired as a wonderful achievement in architecture. The spacious arched main entrances support a row of polished granite pillars, above which towers the vast front of the enormous structure. The hotel fronts on Lake Michigan, with a beautiful park between it and the water, affording guests the charming combination of all the benefits of a summer resort, with close proximity to the business center of the second city in the Union, and directly accessible to railroad depots, steamboat landings, the principal churches and places of amusement, while the Auditorium theater is under the same roof. The proprietors are recognized experts in the modern art of hotel keeping, and in Mr. E. A. Whipple have an experienced and able manager, of soundest judgment. They have spared neither pains nor expense in the fitting up, decorating and furnishing of the hotel. It embodies the highest achievements of the mechanic and scientist, the decorator and the upholsterer, and is the most luxurious and palatial hotel in America to-day. There are five passenger elevators and two freight elevators run by hydraulic power. The hotel is brilliantly illuminated in every part with electric lights. There are no less than 5,500 incandescent lamps, the current being supplied by the proprietors' own dynamos in the basement. The sanitary appliances are of the very highest order. The hotel contains 428 rooms, 90 per cent. of which have outside exposure, and all an abundance of light and air. Many are arranged en suite for the use of families, etc., and have parlor bed-rooms and bath all self contained. The house readily accommodates 650 guests and more on special occasions. There are numerous original features of the most commendable character, such, for instance, as having the main dining hall situated on the top floor, which is as light as day, and which commands pure air and extended views, while the elegant mosaic floor, mirrors and ornamentation are in keeping with the excellence of the service and splendor of the silver and china. This hall is 54 by 186 feet in size and seats 600 people. The grand banquet hall is 44 by 84 feet, and seats 325. On the ground floor are the spacious offices, reading rooms, reception rooms, etc., all having mosaic tile floors and the most artistic decorations. Here is a large restaurant 30 by 90 feet where orders are served at all hours. The bar is replete with the finest and choicest of wines and liquors. All the rooms are richly carpeted and furnished, and each one is provided with electric lights, electric bells, hot and cold water, etc. On the third floor are the magnificent drawing rooms, most luxuriously furnished and complete in every detail of artistic taste in decoration. The hotel is absolutely fireproof, and affords the most complete accommodations on the continent. The proprietors conduct it both on the European and American plans. The rates on the American plan are $4 to $6, and those on the European $2 to $5 per day. These are remarkably moderate considering the attractions of such a place of residence, coupled with a cuisine of the most liberal and varied character. The house employs over 400 servants, and the service is perfect. The names of the proprietors have long been familiar to the public. Mr. Breslin is the proprietor of the Gilsey House, New York, Mr. Southgate of the Hotel Brunswick of New York, two ultra fashionable and prosperous houses, and now, under the skilled and attentive management of Mr. Whipple, the "Auditorium" leads all other hotels in the west. Mr. Whipple, though a young man, is widely experienced, having been the manager of the Grand Pacific Hotel for upward of 13 years, and under his guidance the Auditorium is the favorite stopping place here.

PULLMAN PALACE CAR COMPANY.

Among the countless industries and enterprises of the United States there are none which attracts more universal attention than the Pullman Car Works, and the model city built and owned by them, which forms so delightful a suburb to the city of Chicago, the acknowledged model city of the world. The grand result of all of this gigantic work is due to the inventive genius, fertile brain and wonderful executive power of one man, Mr. George M. Pullman. The idea of constructing a palace car, or one where more comfort could be had in travel than in the very crude cars then in use, was that of Mr. Pullman. In the early spring of 1859 he left his New York home to seek his fortune in the then wild West. Chicago even then promised to become the metropolis of this vast territory, and it was here with limited capital he made the first step, which has resulted in such grand achievements, by remodeling two passenger coaches into sleeping cars. The public was not prepared for such an innovation, and the initial attempt met with but partial success. Mr. Pullman went then to Denver, Colo., and remained four years, when he returned to Chicago. He, by persistent efforts, obtained the permission of the Chicago & Alton railroad to use an old abandoned repair shed on their premises, in which he built the first regular Pullman parlor and sleeping car, costing the then extraordinary price of $18,000, and in this was the foundation of the great institution which proudly bears his name to-day. In April of 1865 this same coach was used as the funeral car of the murdered war heroed president, Abraham Lincoln, whose remains were conveyed in it from the National Capital to their final resting place at Springfield, Ill. From this modest beginning grew the now celebrated Pullman Palace Car Company, which is probably better known to more people than any corporation in the world. The principal works of the company are located at the model city of Pullman, on the west shore of Lake Calumet, fourteen miles south of the Chicago Court House, and ground was broken for their erection on May 25, 1880. The actual amount of capital employed by the company is $50,000,000, which enormous amount makes possible the taking of the most gigantic contracts in their line. The president of the company is the founder, Mr. George M. Pullman; the board of directors consists of Messrs. Marshall Field, J. W. Doane, Norman Williams, O. S. A. Sprague, all of Chicago, and Mr. Henry C. Hulbert of New York and Mr. Henry K. Reed of Boston. Some idea of the magnitude of the Pullman Car Company may be formed when it is learned that they employ in their regular service 2,135 cars, of which 1,849 are standard and 286 tourist, or second-class cars. They have built and placed in service during the past year 101 sleeping, parlor, dining, special and tourist cars, costing $1,365,503.40, or an average of $13,519.83 each per car. Orders have been placed for 119 Pullman cars for the present year, at an estimated cost of $16,500 each, or an aggregate of $1,963,500. The mileage of railways covered by contracts for the operation of the cars of this company is now 120,686 miles, and the number of passengers carried during the past year was 5,023,057, the number of miles run 177,033,116, all of which shows an increase in their different details. The value of the manufactured product of the car plant the past year was $8,105,431.58, and of other industries, including rentals, $2,108,226.52, making a total of $10,213,658.10. The average number of names on the pay rolls at Pullman for the past year was 4,582 and wages paid $2,773,019.27, making an average of nearly $600 for each person employed. The total number of persons in the employ of the company in its manufacturing and operating departments is 12,367, and the wages paid during the past year amounted to $6,249,891.65. Necessarily the amount invested in this vast concern is enormous; the value of the company's real estate, its plant and buildings in the town of Pullman shows on the books for about $8,000,000, but is actually worth very much more. The business of the corporation is not confined to the construction of palace, dining and sleeping cars; they manufacture cars of all descriptions as well, such as passenger coaches, freight cars, street cars and motors, and in this last branch of industry alone employ over 400 men. The company also have large

works at Wilmington, Del., and in their plant include the Union Foundry, Union Car Wheel Works, the Pullman Iron and Steel Works and a brass works, which employ 250 men and which turn out over one-half million dollars' worth of manufactured brass annually. The capacity of the works at Pullman is three sleeping or palace cars, ten ordinary passenger and 240 freight cars per week. In the works at Pullman may be seen the great Corliss 2,500-horse power engine which at the Centennial Exposition was such an attractive feature, and furnished power for running the machinery there. It was purchased by Mr. Pullman after the exposition and required a train of thirty-five cars to bring it to Pullman. It was set up in its present place during the autumn of 1880 and the winter of 1881, and was started at Pullman for the first time April 5, 1881, by Miss Florence Pullman turning the valves which admitted the steam to the cylinders, and great was the enthusiasm as the great fly-wheel began to move, starting the Pullman Car Works, one of the grandest institutions in the world. It was the Pullman Car Company also who built the first vestibuled passenger train, one of the most advanced steps taken in car manufacture or the conveniences of travel. A train which is practically a unit, the several cars being as the rooms of a hotel, access to each being perfect, convenient and safe from the sleeper to the library, smoking car, dining car or buffet. As to the town of Pullman a complete description would be impossible in this limited space. It is situated on the west shore of Lake Calumet, and the surface of the streets are about nine feet above the level of the beautiful little lake. It is the only city in existence built from the foundation on scientific and sanitary principles. Before anything else was done on the flat prairie perfect drainage, sewerage and water supply were provided. The shops, the houses, public buildings, parks, streets and recreation grounds then followed in intelligent creation. The public buildings are very fine, and the grouping them about the open flower-platted spaces is very artistic and effective. Pullman has a population exceeding 15,000, and fully as many more live on its immediate borders. The buildings are all built of stone and brick of handsome and artistic styles of architecture. Through the liberality of the founder they have a handsome public library well stocked with over 6,000 volumes. The Pullman Loan and Savings Bank, which at its last report showed a savings deposit of $392,851.47. The enrollment of their public schools for the last year was 1,167, with a regular staff of twenty-one teachers. They also have several handsome churches, a practical kindergarten on the Froebel plan, a first-class theater with a seating capacity of 1,000 and the finest drop curtain in the west. The Pullman military band is also a feature, which in competition with the best bands in the land captured the prize at the Illinois State Fair at Peoria. Pullman is now a part of Chicago and is in the Thirty-fourth Ward. The health of the city has always been good, the death rate never exceeding 11 per annum of each 1,000 population, less than half the average of American cities. One of the handsomest buildings in the city of Chicago is the Pullman Building, situated at the corner of Michigan avenue and Adams street. It is also the property of the company, and is the home of the city offices. The founder of all we have endeavored to describe, Mr. George M. Pullman, was born in the town of Brocton, Chautauqua County, New York, March 3, 1831, hence has but passed his three score, and in them has confined work fit for an army of workers, although he is remarkably well preserved and still in his prime, his stupendous work having in no way impaired his physical or mental powers. Mr. Pullman was the third oldest in a family of ten, and at fourteen accepted an humble position in a store in his native village. Three years of this work and he joined his older brother inthe cabinet-making business. Force of circumstances compelled him at this time to sell his cabinet shop, and he then accepted a contract of the Erie Canal to remove from its route a large number of houses. Having accomplished this and made some money at it, he started for the West with $6,000 in his pockets when he reached the wind-swept prairies about Chicago. From this time his history has been that of the city of his adoption—energy, industry and prosperity.

ARMOUR & COMPANY.

The enormous growth in financial and commercial enterprises which this century has witnessed in this country, will probably never find a parallel in the pages of history. There is no more striking example of that indomitable, progressive genius which is the principal characteristic of the American people than the great Metropolis of the West. The growth of Chicago during the last twenty years has been the marvel of the world and she stands to-day as the greatest of cosmopolitan centers, into whose borders have gathered the brains and braun of all nations and all creeds. It is a part of the aim of this work to present to the public a brief sketch of some of the most prominent of Chicago's gigantic industries. The great firm of Armour & Company, whose immense trade extends from ocean to ocean, and to every civilized nation on the face of the globe, is a distinctively Chicago institution, and one in which much pride is felt by every resident. The business was first established in 1855 by Plankington and Armour in Milwaukee, but ten years later, appreciating the superior advantages offered in Chicago, it was removed here and has ever since been under the present firm name and style. The members of this immense firm at present are Messrs. P. D. Armour, one of the founders, J. O. Armour, P. D. Armour, Jr., and George H. Webster. The firm connections are H. O. Armour & Co. of New York; the Armour Packing Company of Kansas City, Mo., and The Armour & Co. works in Chicago, dealers in Chicago dressed beef, mutton, hogs, canned meats, lard and provisions, are the largest works in the world. They cover thirty acres in extent, and have 140 acres of floor space. They employ over 7,000 men in their different departments, have forty steam engines and 100 boilers in use, and all of the latest and most perfected style and pattern to facilitate their work. Their cold storage rooms, which have an area of twenty acres, have a capacity of 130,000 tons, an almost incredible amount. Cattle, sheep and hogs, are slaughtered by the thousands, and their sales exceed sixty-five million yearly. Another branch of their industry is their immense glue factory. This factory covers fifteen acres and employs 600 men alone. Their packing industry is immense, and their shipments extend to all parts of the United States, Canada, Mexico, Europe, Australia, and in fact, to the whole civilized world. They deal in pork, beef, mutton, lard, oils, dry salt meats, sweet potted meats, spiced meats, green hams, shoulders, smoked meats, canned meats, extracts, fertilizers, glue, grease, etc., etc. All the members of the firm are prominent members of the Board of Trade, and are connected with many of the leading financial and industrial enterprises of the country, including railroad and steamboat lines, insurance companies, manufactories, buildings and others. The nationality of the members of the firm is decidedly American, and all are prominently identified with the interests of Chicago. Mr. Phillip D. Armour was born in New York State in 1830, and is still as active and enterprising as the youngest member of the firm. He is very popular among his men, and is quite a philanthropist, being the patron of several very deserving charitable institutions in the city, among them being the Armour Mission and the "Creche," where the infants of poor people are taken care of while their mothers are at work. Mr. Webster is a native of Illinois; Mr. J. O. Armour and P. D. Armour, Jr., are both natives of Milwaukee, and have been brought up in the business where they have been of great benefit to their father, the founder of this great enterprise. The main office of the firm occupies the north half of the Home Insurance building at No. 205 La Salle street, and they have branch offices in nearly every large city and town in the United States. The connections and equipments of the firm are necessarily such as to enable them to promptly meet all the demands, whether at home or abroad, with promptness and efficiency. Commanding, as they do, by reason of their extensive trade and vast capital, all the sources of supply in the best grazing sections of the country, they are correspondingly in a position to quote prices for their products, which are out of the range of competing concerns. By sheer merit Armour & Company have won place and power in the commercial world.

MARSHALL FIELD & CO.

Chicago is certainly a city of immense business enterprises, where the history commercially of other cities and nations, pales into insignificance by comparison; and greatest of all these is the world-famed firm of Marshall Field & Co., wholesale and retail dealers in dry goods, carpets and upholstery, and whose name is a household word in every part of this great land. This immense business was originally established thirty-five years ago by Cooley, Wadsworth & Co., and after some changes in style and membership became Field, Leiter & Co., and ten years ago the present style was adopted, and has been maintained ever since. The members of the firm are Messrs. Marshall Field, H. N. Higginbotham, Joseph N. Field, John G. McWilliams, Robt. M. Fair, Thomas Templeton, Lafayette McWilliams and Harry G. Selfridge, all of whom are actively engaged in superintending the mammoth concern of which they are the proprietors. From its very incipiency the firm has taken a leading position, which has increased ever since, until to-day it is the acknowledged leading and largest wholesale and retail dry goods, carpet and upholstery house in the world. The retail stores are located at the corner of State and Washington streets, and are as much identified as to locations for reference as is the most popular park. The retail department occupies the whole of this immense building, 260x150 feet in size and six stories in height with basement, and is one of the handsomest in the city. The firm carry an immense stock of imported and domestic goods, from the cheapest trustworthy goods to the most expensive, in every department. Superb silks, satins and velvet fabrics, hosiery, linens, gentlemen's and ladies' furnishing goods, woolens, shawls, mantles and jackets of every description; cotton and mixed articles of every texture and quality, upholstery, carpets from Axminster to plainest ingrain, and matting, rugs, etc. Fancy notions in endless variety; in fact, everything conceivable that could be classed under these general headings. Over 1,000 clerks and salesladies are employed in the retail department alone, and their prompt and courteous treatment of all customers is proverbial. Buses from all the depots make this store a regular station, so immense is their trade, not only in the city, but with the surrounding country, for no one feels as if they have seen Chicago without visiting the retail store of Marshall Field & Co., the largest retail house in the world. Their wholesale house is a handsome, large brown stone building, 190 x325 feet in size, bounded by Adams, Quincy and Franklin streets and Fifth avenue. It is seven stories in height, not counting the immense basement, and is acknowledged to be the finest wholesale building in the world to-day, fitted and furnished with all the latest improved and most modern inventions for convenience and safety, and is the crowning piece of architecture built by this firm, being fitted with elevators, speaking tubes and all other facilities, and is absolutely fire proof. As the firm were losers to the amount of nearly $3,000,000 in the great fire of 1871, they have neglected no precautions in their new building. The offices of the firm are on the ground floor, and here is Mr. Marshall Field's business home, as well as those of his partners. Over 1,200 hands are employed in this building alone in handling the immense trade of the firm, which extends north, south, east and west to all sections of the United States. They import all of their own foreign goods, and have a corps of European buyers, who are constantly sending them the latest and most stylish goods in their line, and all novelties pertaining to it. The business of Marshall Field & Co. exceeds $40,000,000 annually, and is the largest in the world. Every member of the firm is a practical business man and brings to bear special qualifications for superintending the different departments, each one lending his services to the successful manipulation of the enormous business of this gigantic enterprise. The firm of Marshall Field & Co. certainly stand as one of Chicago's proudest monuments of commercial growth and prosperity and a credit to the American people.

CHAS. LIPPINCOTT & CO.

The Chicago branch office and salesroom of the well-known Philadelphia house of Chas. Lippincott & Co., manufacturers of soda water apparatus, is under the management of Mr. H. Scarborough, and was founded five years ago. At that time an office only was occupied; but the business grew rapidly, necessitating four years ago the occupancy of spacious premises. These are at Nos. 341 and 343 Dearborn street, and here is controlled the western trade of this reliable house. The premises comprise a salesroom, 35x65

tation, and all of which are manufactured in Philadelphia, where the factory is located, and where 500 workmen are permanently employed. Only the very best grade of goods is made. This company use for syrup their own patent porcelain jars with hard rubber faucets, which are acknowledged to be superior to all others. Under the able management of Mr. Scarborough, the business of the Chicago house has been extended throughout the West and Northwest. He was born in Philadelphia, and has been with this firm nearly all his life. He is a

feet in dimensions, stock room in the rear, 20x60 feet in size. The store is handsomely appointed and supplied with all necessary facilities, while eight competent assistants are employed. Here is to be found everything in the line of soda water apparatus, for which this house has secured an enviable repu-

Mason and member of the Knights of Pythias. His assistant and associate is Mr. E. T. Bush, who is becoming widely known, and under the able and energetic management of these gentlemen the business is fast increasing throughout the west.

GORTON & LIDGERWOOD CO.

Many systems have been introduced at different times for heating houses, public buildings, etc., by means of apparatus for the distribution of steam or hot water in the different rooms. The utility of heating by steam or hot water has many advocates in this country on account of the frequent and extreme changes of temperature. Both systems, however, have able and practical exponents in the firm of Messrs.

Gorton, Lidgerwood & Co., manufacturers of the Gorton Side-feed Boilers, whose head office is situated at No. 96 Liberty street, New York, and who have branches at Nos. 201 and 203 Congress street, Boston, and Nos. 34 and 36 W. Monroe street, Chicago. The business was established in 1888, with a capital of $500,000, at Brooklyn, N. Y., where their works are situated, and so great were the improvements introduced by their apparatus that their trade rapidly extended all over the United States and Canada. The principal advantages of their boilers are large heating surface, excellent conveniences for feeding the furnace, economy of fuel and perfect safety. The boilers for steam are provided with an automatic damper regulator, which controls the fire according to the head of steam. This boiler requires absolutely no attention beyond that of filling the reservoirs with coal twice in twenty-four hours, and it is certainly the best for house and office purposes of any in the market. The active officers of the company are: president, Mr. John H. Lidgerwood; vice-president, Mr. Charles Gorton; treasurer, Mr. Walter L. Pierce; secretary, Mr. Joseph A. Gorton; all men of the highest standing in commercial circles. The Chicago branch was opened in 1889, the company being so fortunate as to secure the services of Mr. F. E. Rainier as manager. He occupies two spacious floors, 40x130 feet in dimensions, handsomely fitted up as office and salesroom. Here the company carry a full line of boilers, fixtures, etc., which we strongly recommend our readers to inspect before purchasing, as they will find these productions quite superior, and offered at most reasonable prices. Mr. Rainier is a native of this city, and has been a very important factor in the extension of the business throughout the West. He is a gentleman of great general business ability, active, enterprising, experienced and reliable, and highly esteemed for strict integrity and probity. This system is introduced and used in the following public institutions: The officers' and soldiers' quarters at Fort Sheridan, where about twenty-seven boilers are in use; Brooklyn Navy Yard and Soldiers Home, Marion, Ind. The government indorses the system very strongly.

THE FRED. W. WOLF CO.

It appears that humanity is moving along too swift for "nature," and what the fickle weather clerk refuses us by artificial means we produce. Noticeably is this true of refrigeration and ice making, the great preservatives of perishable goods, done in late years most successfully by artificial means. Chicago boasts of one of the greatest institutions of this kind in the world, the Linde Ice and Refrigerator Machines, which have been awarded the gold medals of excellence in every world's fair held since their introduction in 1880, notably those of Frankfort in 1881, Copenhagen in 1888 and Paris in 1889. The manufacture and patents of this great invention are now controlled by the Fred. W. Wolf Company, whose office is at No. 560 N. Halsted street, with factories at Nos. 302 to 330 Hawthorne avenue. This corporation does not confine itself to one invention, although it makes a specialty of the first named. The extraordinary popularity of the Linde Ice and Refrigerating Machines is shown by their use in 1500 different buildings and establishments in all parts of the world, with a total daily capacity of melting ice of over 39,202 tons per day or 14,308,730 tons per year. The firm of F. W. Wolf was originally established on Lake street, and incorporated in 1887 with a capital stock of $250,000, Mr. Wolf being chosen president and A. A. Wolf as secretary. The succeeding year they built their immense works, with a total cost of plant and machinery, exceeding $250,000, operated by a 100 horse power engine, employing from 150 to 200 men, and consisting of three brick buildings of one story and one of three stories, with a two story brick office, 25x62, for the accommodation of their clerical and business force. Their establishment is one of the most complete in the United States, having every appliance, apparatus and labor-saving machinery to facilitate their work, that they may keep up with their ever increasing orders. In addition to the ice making and refrigerating machinery of Prof. Linde, they make an oil extracting and gas saving apparatus for ice making and refrigerator machinery, valves for steep tanks, attachments for refrigerating pipes, malt kiln floors and mechanical or automatic malt turning machines. They make a specialty of building breweries and malt houses, and are by far the leading architects in the United States, having built 200 breweries and malt houses in the United States, among which are the leading breweries of the land. Mr. F. W. Wolf is the owner of THE LINDE MACHINE patents in the United States of America; these comprise Linde ice making and refrigerating machines. The invention is that of Prof. C. P. Linde, formerly professor of the University of Munich, and is acknowledged to be the most efficient, simple and economical, for the purpose of producing refrigerating effects by the compression and expansion of anhydrous ammonia. It is operated with less power, consumes less cooling water, and is not affected by the ammonia used, is perfectly safe, the ammonia being circulated in small quantities through iron pipes capable of sustaining many times the pressure which they can possibly be subject to. They also make a specialty of the "perfection" malt-kiln floor, composed of steel tiles, also Wolf's patent mechanical malt turner, and the Wolf patent steep tank valve, all of which are standard, practical inventions in use in all parts of the world. The president of the company is also president and treasurer of the Wolf & Lehle Company, engineers and architects, and gives personal attendance to all work done by the company. He is an eminently practical man who understands every detail and particular of his work, having had ten years' practical experience as a machinist. The firm is prosperous, as it deserves to be, and is an institution of which Chicago is justly proud. Mr. Pilsbry is manager of this industry. His connection with the business and intimate knowledge of its every detail make him at once a most valuable adjunct to the successful career of this unique establishment. It stands alone as the most complete and successful business venture in the United States to-day. From the beginning it has been under the most prudent and efficient management, and the management justly prides itself upon the high grade and durability of the concern's manufactures, which have met appreciation whereever they have been introduced. In all respects this is a reliable and progressive concern.

FRANK F. HOLMES & CO.

This popular local underwriting agency was established several years ago by Mr. Holmes, who left adjusting and specially confidential work throughout the Western states with the Royal Insurance Company to go into the local business. A very careful and experienced selection of business has resulted in this agency building up a very large and prosperous class of business. An earnest, systematic, conscientious effort to do the right thing for customers and a pleasing manner of transacting business has made the patrons

FRANK F. HOLMES.

of this agency feel every confidence in the manner Mr. Holmes transacts his business, while the successive profits have been a source of gratification to the large underwriting corporations represented in this agency. Mr. Holmes was born in Illinois, was educated in the public schools of his state and graduated from Knox College of Galesburg, Ill. He ranked high in his class, and was noted for his ability to succeed in what he undertook. His few years in business for himself has surprised his competitors by reason of the great and favorable results that have been accomplished. This agency comprises the Phenix Insurance Company of Brooklyn; the Glens Falls Insurance Company, New York; Oakland Home Insurance Company, California; State Insurance Company of Iowa, and New York Bowery Insurance Company of New York, all sound American corporations. Mr. Holmes' office is at No. 196 La Salle street.

MUTUAL LIFE INSURANCE CO. OF NEW YORK.

The story of the Mutual Life Insurance Company of New York is one of the most astounding and brilliant in the annals of life insurance development. Latterly, when its splendid success has attracted others to the field, it has seemed to shine with more vigor than ever. During the first twenty years of its existence, up to 1862, the Mutual Life showed what was then a phenomenal growth. Its accumulated assets were $9,225,120, and the insurance in force, $39,902,077. And yet so marked has been the advance of the company that the records of the year 1890 alone showed a business more than equal to the whole of its first twenty years, adding on that year, $10,753,633 to its accumulated assets, and $72,276,031, in the latter item almost doubling the twenty years record. The 1890 statement shows total assets of $147,154,961.20; total liability, $838,041,320.46, leaving a surplus for dividends to policyholders of $5,237,462.23. Such, imperfectly stated, is the position of the company, whose mag-

nificent structures in New York, Boston and Philadelphia are the architectural features of those cities. In this brief summary of the Mutual's claim on the public regard it is absolutely necessary to note the fact that these companies are but the monument of the energetic personalities behind them. In the person of Mr. Charles H. Ferguson, of this city, lies much of the success of the Mutual Life, whose Chicago office is in the Tacoma Building. His present position, incomparably superior in point of achievement to any other of its kind, is due entirely to his own intelligent, persistent and conscientious effort. He is a native of Oswego, N. Y., and left school at thirteen. He went west to Milwaukee, and enlisted in the 39th Wisconsin during the war. In 1870 he entered life insurance as solicitor for the Mutual. In 1873 he became the Western general agent at Chicago for the Oswego and Onondaga Fire Insurance Co. of New York. He became connected with the Chicago office of the Mutual as subordinate to the general agents of the company at Detroit. In 1886 he formed a partnership with Mr. H. S. Winston, which continued till 1889. From 1883 to 1886 the new writings of this agency were about a million a year. A result of President McCurdy's personal investigation of the Chicago business was the promotion of Mr. Ferguson to a wider and less restricted field, as general agent for Illinois. This was in June, 1887. Let the figures tell the tale of success. December 31, 1886, there were paid premiums of $606,077; paid policyholders, $310,140; new insurance, $1,700,510, and insurance in force, $20,290,720. Last year the items were: Premiums, $1,025,875, $410,747, $7,324,113 and $31,884,127 respectively. Mr. Ferguson's new writings in 1890 were $2,000,000 more than the amount written in the six states comprising the Northwestern agency, of which Illinois was a part, when he became the agent. It is estimated that 54,125 persons have a direct personal interest in the Illinois department of the Mutual. Mr. Ferguson's fidelity and ability have been warmly recognized, and have met their reward. He enjoys the respect of all, and his friendship is a personal privilege much sought after. He is socially one of the most companionable of men. A member of the Knights Templar, of Thomas Post, No. 5, G. A. R., the Veteran Club, of St. Andrew's and Caledonian Societies, Sons of New York, Mystic Shrine, Royal Arch, member of the Union League and Calumet Clubs and life member of the Second Regiment. In this brief summary of points in Mr. Ferguson's career it should be said as excuse for any omission that a biography of more pretension could best convey the lessons of his life of industry and intelligent skill, which is full of instruction to those who, halt and weary, are inclined to doubt the possibility of success. Like the company he represents, the career of Mr. Ferguson is of value as showing that honesty, capacity and power "to hustle" receive their reward at last and in good measure.

BROWN BROTHERS' COMPANY.

The nursery industry is of great importance, especially at this period of our history, when every real estate owner is alive to the necessity of having his grounds and gardens well filled with trees, flowers and small fruits. What more beautiful sight than to walk through a carefully kept garden filled with flowers, giving forth their delicate odors and trees and bushes bearing in clusters their luscious fruit? The saying that a man can be known by the manner in which he keeps his grounds is a true one. The greatest nursery center of our broad land is without doubt in the vicinity of Rochester, N. Y. No one of our readers is too young to have seen, planted and eaten of the fruit borne by Rochester trees. The soil there is peculiarly adapted to the growth of young trees. The climate is temperate, and not subject to the sudden changes experienced in many parts of our country, so that the young trees are free from disease, and well calculated to be transplanted to any portion of the country. We dare say there are few, if any, bearing orchards in the great West but that the Rochester tree is well represented therein. Above other Eastern nurseries, there is one which has allied itself more closely to the West, and, like the larger part of our inhabitants, came West to grow up with the ever increasing population, and located a branch office in Chicago. Our particular attention was called to this firm of Brown Brothers' Company by seeing them referred to and indorsed for growing the highest grades of stock, not only in their local papers at Rochester, but also in the other large farm journals of the West. Its business in the West had increased to such vast proportions that it was necessary to open an office in Chicago some years ago. This office is under the supervision of Mr. E. C. Morris, secretary of the company, located in rooms 6 and 7, *Times* building. Mr. Morris attends to the trade west of Ohio, all east of that point being controlled by the home office at Rochester. The object in having the office here was to give better satisfaction to the agent and buyer. The distance letters were obliged to travel and the time lost thereby were great hindrances to prompt business transactions in the far West. Their nurseries and green houses are very extensive, covering many hundred acres, which plantings are increased every year. To dispose of their immense amount of stock each season requires the employment of the largest force of agents controlled by any house on the continent. Their shipments to this portion of the country are made in carload lots, from their packing grounds, located on the main tracks of the New York Central Railroad, to a central distributing point, where they are transferred to the various roads, thereby insuring prompt delivery of all goods. The large crops of fruit which have been gathered in the past few years have impressed upon our farm and real estate owners that land will produce more valuable crops of fruit than corn, wheat and oats, and secure for them a larger income. If more would turn their attention to the planting of strong, healthy nursery stock, the bright prospects which we look forward to, of this becoming the great fruit producing section of the country, will be realized. The sale of these articles has become a matter of the highest importance. A leading journal, in commenting on the nursery industry, says: "We cannot agree with our contemporary in the statement that the farmer should be shy of the tree vendor. It is he who sells the farmer the trees that bring the golden shekels. Through him our villages and cities are beautified with flowers and shade trees, and humanity made healthier, happier and more virtuous. His is a noble profession. Poor nursery stock is worse than none at all. It is an abomination on the face of the earth. 'It is a barren fig tree.'"

MORTON, HARRY N. AND MORTON T. CULVER.

Among Chicago's leading real estate men it is safe to say that none enjoy a larger measure of public confidence than the Culvers, father and two sons, whose well-appointed office is at 61 La Salle street. Mr. Morton Culver established the business in 1871, and during the present year took his sons, Harry N. and Morton T. Culver, into partnership. A general real estate and law business is transacted by the firm, including the purchase, sale and transfer of city and suburban real property of every description. Mortgages are negotiated and loans made on approved collateral security, while investments are desirably placed, realty appraised for intending purchasers, and owners' titles searched and everything properly pertaining to real estate and kindred transactions are attended to with ability and fidelity. The Messrs. Culver form syndicates and buy and sell acreage and subdivisions, which are laid out in building lots and sold upon a plan involving small periodical payments, and in this way have disposed of many valuable tracts in the city and immediate vicinity. They have large holdings of North shore lots and other property and are well prepared to offer inducements to those seeking a home or in search of good paying permanent investments. The operations of the firm are extensive and widespread, and connections of the most substantial character have been formed with capitalists and citizens generally. The copartners are all natives of this city. Mr. Morton Culver is well and favorably known in financial and real estate circles, and has always sustained a high reputation in this community. He is a member of the G. A. R., and during the war served in the

134th Infantry. He is a prominent Free Mason of the 32d degree, and has a large circle of friends and acquaintances. Mr. Henry N. Culver and Mr. Morton T. Culver, his sons, are thorough business men, well versed in realty operations and law. The former is a Mason and all are graduates of the Northwestern University law department.

T. C. CUNNINGHAM.

The prosperous and enterprising establishment of T. C. Cunningham, wholesale and retail dealer in stoves and ranges, stove repairs, fire brick, cement, etc., No. 229 Wells street, telephone No. 3711, was founded in May, 1888, by this gentleman, who had had long experience in this line. The intimate and accurate knowledge thus acquired by him of the wants and requirements of the trade has proven of inestimable value to him in enabling him to place before the public goods, the need of which had long been felt. The premises occupied comprise

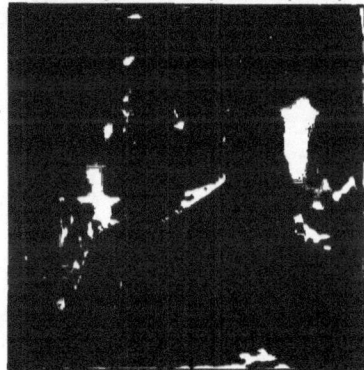

the first floor and double basement of a substantial frame structure, having an area of 24x110 feet, and are admirably arranged for the storage and display of the large stock carried. The line includes all the leading makes in stoves and ranges by the most celebrated manufacturers in the country, also a complete assortment in all the numerous varieties of stove furniture. A specialty is made of stove repairs, and duplicate parts of any stove made may be found here at the lowest market rates. Five to ten assistants are given steady employment at all seasons. Mr. Cunningham, who is a native of Prince Edward County, Ont., Canada, came to Chicago in 1881, furnishes a striking example of what may be accomplished by pluck, energy, and close attention to business. He is in a financial sense, at least, a self-made man. Coming to this city with but one dollar in his pocket, he is now doing an annual business of $40,000 entirely on his own capital. Further comment in this connection is unnecessary. Socially Mr. Cunningham occupies an enviable position. He was one of the founders, and first president of the Washington Lodge, No. 1, Order of Canadian Americans, which has a large and rapidly growing membership, and is the only lodge of the order in the United States. This order was organized in the interests of the large number of Canadians who have made Chicago their home, and who have contributed largely to its growth and prosperity. It was mainly through the efforts of an auxiliary committee appointed by Washington Lodge No. 1, Order Canadian Americans, that the Dominion Government of Canada was induced to participate in the Columbian Exposition. Mr. Cunningham is also a prominent Mason, and belongs to the Royal Arch and Knights Templar.

CHAS. W. GINDELE.

In a work which has for its object a comprehensive review of the leading merchants and manufacturers of the great "Metropolis of the West," it is highly important that special attention should be devoted to those great artisans whose skill and labor have been utilized in the construction of her buildings and public institutions; and foremost among this number is Mr. Charles W. Gindele, who has been closely identified with the rise and progress of Chicago, and whose name will ever be permanently associated with those vast mercantile enterprises that have made Chicago the financial and social center of the west. Mr. Gindele commenced business in Chicago in 1868, when he was admitted as junior partner of the firm of J. G. Gindele & Sons, of which his father, the late J. G. Gindele, was founder and senior member. The firm at this time were the heaviest contractors for cut stone in the city, and the copartnership consisted of J. G. and his sons, F. V., G. A. and C. W. Gindele, and the business was conducted under the firm name of J. G. Gindele & Sons till the spring of 1870, when the firm dissolved. In the spring of 1880 Mr. Gindele established in business for himself as a contractor and builder, and in 1881 the copartnership of Allen, Angus & Gindele was formed. In the spring of 1882 Mr. Allen retired, and the firm style became Angus & Gindele, and so continued until 1886, when Mr. Angus retired, and Mr. Gindele was alone for one year. In the spring of 1887 Mr. Allen again entered the firm and remained till the following year, since which time Mr. Gindele has been alone. The offices are located at 140 Monroe street, in which location Mr. Gindele has been established nine years. He is a native of Bavaria, Germany, but came to Chicago when quite young. Much of his success in business is due to the early training which he received while associated with his revered father. The late John G. Gindele was undoubtedly the oldest and most prominent civil engineer and contractor of his time in Chicago. He was born June 30, 1814, in the city of Rewensberg, Kingdom of Wurtemburg, Germany, and at an early age, although having been educated for the ministry, he showed such a preference for the more congenial occupation of stone-cutting that his father apprenticed him to a skilled master at Lindon, on Lake Constance; and it was here that he laid the foundation of that after career of usefulness and honor. He came to the United States in 1849, and settled in Wisconsin, and in July, 1852, came to Chicago. In 1859 he established in business for himself. During his long residence in this city Mr Gindele occupied many prominent positions of public trust, and at the time of his death, which occurred Jan. 31, 1872, he was county clerk of Cook county. During his business career as a contractor and builder he constructed some of the most important of the city's public works, among them the Washington street tunnel. In Mr. Chas. W. Gindele's office now hangs the original copy of the vote of thanks passed by the City Council, Jan. 6, 1869, to Mr. Gindele, for the thorough and conscientious manner in which he had engineered this important undertaking through to completion. Mr. Gindele's death was a serious loss to the city and county, and as long as honesty and integrity are respected as virtues the name of John G. Gindele will never be mentioned without a tribute to those qualities which he so conspicuously possessed. Mr. Chas. W. Gindele during his long business career has preserved and perpetuated to the public of his adopted city that high standard of integrity which his father so ably exemplified during his long public career, and the pages of this work would be far from complete did they not mention a few of the more prominent buildings and public institutions which he has constructed during the last few years: The *Tribune* building, the Reaper block (Washington and Clark streets), Galbreed's block, Schofield's block, and all the freight and round houses on the "Q" system south of Harrison street and north of Sixteenth street; the Bloomington Court House, McLean Co., Ill., which cost $400,000; the passenger depot of the C. N. & W. R. R. at Milwaukee, Wis.; the Calvary Baptist Church at Kansas City; the Government building at Winona, Minn; the private residence of Potter Palmer, Esq., of this city, and many others, both in Chicago and throughout the West. Mr. Gindele has been president of the Chicago Master Masons' Association for many years, and is at present chairman of the finance committee of the Builders' and Traders' Exchange. He is also a prominent member of the Royal Arcanum. We wish to call especial attention to the fact that Mr. Gindele has been awarded the contract for the construction of the work above the foundation for the naval exhibit at the "World's Columbian Exposition," of which a complete description will be found in another part of this work.

THE COLUMBIA NATIONAL BANK OF CHICAGO.

Chicago as one of the great national cities of financial transactions in the United States has in no branch of business attained such a remarkable degree of development as in the prosperity and usefulness of her banks and fiscal institutions.

The latest and one of the most important additions to the banking facilities of the great western metropolis is "The Columbia National Bank," eligibly located in the Insurance Exchange building, corner La Salle and Quincy streets. This bank opened for business on February 16, 1891, under the National Banking Laws, with a paid up capital of $1,000,000, succeeding to the business of the United States National bank. It solicits the accounts of merchants, corporations, banks, firms and individuals; discounts first-class commercial paper; deals in exchange and government bonds, and transacts a general banking business. It makes a specialty of collections, by means of its numerous correspondents, covering all sections of the United States, Canada and Europe. This bank has a department for the accommodation of ladies, with special

clerical force, teller, etc., for those who wish to open a bank account and who desire banking facilities. Its officials are noted for their courtesy and promptness in the dispatch of business, thoroughly accommodating to patrons and very popular with all who are brought into business relations with them. Mr. L. Everingham, the president, is a prominent member of the Board of Trade of Chicago, and has been the head of the widely known commission house of L. Everingham & Co., which was established in 1865. He is confessedly one of our most capable financiers and an energetic exponent of the soundest principles governing banking and finance. Col. W. G. Bentley, the vice-president, brings into active service a long and successful experience as an attorney and general manager of the Continental Insurance Company of New York, and the high position attained by that company, among insurance circles and business men generally, is largely owing to his breadth of view and conservative policy. Mr. Zimri Dwiggins, the cashier, was the very efficient president of the United States National bank, and, having been engaged in banking and financial organizations from his youth, he possesses, in an eminent degree, every qualification for a successful banker. The bank is to be congratulated in being able to include among its officers a gentleman so favorably known in banking circles, and one of such ability and ripe experience as the custodian of its interests. The Columbia National Bank has been peculiarly fortunate in its selection of directors, the gentlemen composing the directory being widely known in business circles for their executive ability, prudence and integrity. The personal being as follows: Officers—L. Everingham, president; W. G. Bentley, vice-president; Zimri Dwiggins, cashier; J. T. Greene, assistant cashier. Directors—Malcolm McNeil, president McNeil & Higgins Co., wholesale grocers, Chicago; E. S. Conway, secretary W. W. Kimball Co., pianos and organs, Chicago; H. C. Kohn, of Kohn Brothers, wholesale clothiers, Chicago; C. W. Needham, attorney-at-law, Chicago; Peter Kuntz, wholesale lumber merchant, Chicago; J. D. Allen, of Allen, Opdyke & Allen, real estate, Chicago; L. Everingham, of L. Everingham & Co., commission merchants, Chicago; W. G. Bentley, formerly general manager Continental Insurance Co., New York, Chicago; Z. Dwiggins, cashier, Chicago; J. M. Starbuck, banker, Chicago. No bank in this city stands higher in public confidence, and none has a more desirable class of patronage, both as regards depositors and customers. The banking rooms are spacious and handsomely fitted up with all modern conveniences, and the location is an exceedingly eligible one, new accounts continually dropping into them. The remarkable steady, healthy growth of the bank is seen in the following table, the figures being condensed from the official statements made up to the present time in pursuance to the call of the Comptroller of the Currency. This steady advance and large reserve should interest and attract the attention of conservative depositors, and especially of those who contemplate a change in their banking relations, or who may desire to open a bank account. The following is the condensed official statements made to the Comptroller of the Currency, Feb. 26th, May 4th, July 9th and Sept. 25th, 1891:

RESOURCES.

	Feb. 26, '91	May 4, '91	July 9, '91	Sept. 25, '91
Loans and Discounts	$805,018.80	1,141,954.00	1,930,556.82	1,900,820 16
United States Bonds	50,100 00	50,000. 0	50,100 00	50,400.00
Furniture & Fixtures	8 449.50	8,188.70	10,786.55	10,786.55
Expenses Paid	2,718.50	8,716 06	16,423.04	20,502.23
Redemption Fund	2,250.00	2,250.00	2,250.00	2,350.00
Cash and Cash Items	114,484.80	166,625.02	155 192.01	243,787.02
Due from other Banks	529,945.91	480,289 20	428,176.07	478,133.17
Total	$1,567,733.50	1,803,698.98	1,164,096.42	2,109,581.13

LIABILITIES.

Capital Stock Paid in	$1,000,000.00	1,000,000.00	1,000,000.00	1,000,000.00
Surplus, undivided profits	16,872.42	24,893.75	87,178.74	50,369.11
Circulation	45,000 00	45,000.00	45,000 00	45,000.00
Deposits	505 863.08	739,895.21	902,515.68	1,104,218.02
Total	$1,567,733.50	1,808,653 04	1,164,096.42	2,199,581.13

FULLER WARREN CO.

The great representative of progress in the manufacture of stoves and ranges is the Fuller Warren Co,; formerly of Troy, N. Y., but which, in response to the demands of American trade, has made Milwaukee, Wis., its headquarters, and where it has erected the most complete and extensive stove foundries in the United States, located at Thirty-second street and North avenue, in that city. The main buildings are four stories in height, forming one side of a square, while the foundry and molding floors extend around two other sides, being very lofty, light and airy one story buildings, affording exceptional facilities. The company was incorporated in 1890 with a paid up capital of $500,000, as successors to the old firm of Fuller Warren & Co., Mr. Walter P. Warren becoming president, Mr. H. A. Viets, vice-president, Mr. C. W. Jones, secretary, and Mr. J. L. Potter, treasurer. They bring to bear special qualifications for the discharge of the onerous duties devolving upon them, and it is due to their enterprise, energy and ability that the splendid works at Milwaukee have sprung into existence. Here upwards of 900 hands find employment in the manufacture of the "Fuller Warren Co." brand of celebrated stoves, ranges and furnaces. The company's list of styles covers the needs of the public in every section of the Union. They embrace all the improvements and conveniences, new and beautiful styles, perfect in workmanship, finish and operation. The company has wisely decided to make Chicago one of its principal distributing points, and has removed from its old premises on S. Jefferson street to the splendid new buildings centrally located at Nos. 48 and 50 Lake street. It is a five-story and basement brick building, 60x120feet in dimensions, and has all the modern improvements, including elevator, etc. Here is carried an enormous stock of the "Fuller Warren" brand of stoves and ranges, in all styles and sizes, adapted to the varying requirements of the trade. The company has the finest hard and soft coal burning ranges in the market, constructed on correct principles, embodying all the latest improvements, and proving the most economical and reliable of any other make. Similarly in the line of base-burning stoves, the styles shown are not only the most elegant, but the most reliable, securing perfect combustion, with ample ven-

tilation and remarkably powerful heating capacity. Hot air furnaces form another important specialty in which the company leads the trade of the world, and in every branch of its business, live, progressive methods are observable, and the great success achieved reflects the highest credit upon President Warren and his associates.

HUTCHINS' REFRIGERATOR CAR CO.

The vast and ever increasing amount of perishable property constantly in transit to and from all the great business centers throughout the United States imparts to the question of how to preserve the same, in the most superior manner at a minimum cost while in course of shipment, a peculiar interest and importance, and it may be observed in this connection that notable progress has been made in the direction indicated of late years. These remarks apply specially to the peculiar devices with which cars are equipped for the purpose of transporting fruits, early vegetables and kindred products. What, with the discovery in the domain of chemistry, invention and mechanical ingenuity, a high degree of perfection has been obtained in the appliances used for protecting this class of freight referred to, both from heat and cold, in which connection special mention should be made of the products of the Hutchins' Refrigerator

Car Company, whose general offices are 904-916 The Rookery, this city. A large number of the company's cars are engaged in transporting fruits to all eastern points from the Pacific coast, the cars being employed and used exclusively in this traffic by the California Fruit Transportation Co. While various attempts have been made at different times to establish a successful transportation of fruits by refrigeration, it was left to this company to inaugurate the first practical demonstration that all articles of such a perishable nature could be transported from the Pacific to the Atlantic coast without detriment. The perfected car, which this company has developed, combines every improvement which it has been demonstrated by experience that the most tender fruits require in order to be carried successfully. It is a fact that the practical workings of the car enable tender fruits to be carried two or three times as far as it was possible to ship them before, and to keep them as well as fresh picked fruit when unloaded from the cars even in the hottest weather. It is no exaggeration to say that at present over one-half of the entire tonnage of deciduous fruits shipped from the Pacific coast to the Middle and Atlantic States is transported in the refrigerator cars owned and controlled by this company. The surety given the question of transportation in the use of the Hutchins' refrigerator car has opened up a wide range of markets for perishable products where heretofore they have been confined to nearby points. The consumption of fruit by the people of the United States is increasing at a wonderful ratio, and it stands to reason that the healthfulness of this article and its freshness and fine condition are most important factors for consideration. Between six and seven hundred of these cars are at present employed in fruit transportation, and there is every reason to believe that the number will go above a thousand in the near future. Its affairs are managed by its vice-president, Mr. E. R. Hutchins, and Mr. Wm. H. Hubbard, its treasurer. This company was organized a number of years ago, and from its inception the enterprise has proved a distinctly successful venture. It is proper to state in this connection that C. B. Hutchins & Sons of Detroit and Chicago, largely interested in the management and control of the Hutchins' Refrigerator

Car Co., are also the producers of the Hutchins' plastic roof for freight cars. The growth of this concern illustrates very forcibly the well-merited success that any genuine enterprise, backed by sufficient capital and business integrity, can attain in the railroad business world. It is conceded by the larger number of railroads in the United States, in all respects the most perfect, reliable, economical and altogether superior appliances for freight car roofs that is manufactured and placed on the market. The unequivocal indorsement of most of the leading car builders, master mechanics, railroad superintendents and experts all over the country of the Hutchins' plastic roof has been obtained by the well-merited success of this product. The company commenced its operations in this branch about twelve years ago, and their business has grown to such an extent that during the year 1890 the average monthly orders exceeded fifteen hundred. The Hutchins' plastic roof is an absolute insulation against heat and cold, consists of three courses of felt, each of which has undergone a thorough waterproofing process, and then cemented together with two courses of plastic cement; then run through a set of rolls, and pressed into a complete homogeneous sheet. It is made in accordance with exact scientific principles on an entirely improved and new method, and the very best of material available. Its construction is so thorough, and its lasting qualities so excellent, that it will last the lifetime of the ordinary freight car without question. In its adoption and use by some of the leading trunk lines of the country it has been shown that the number of claims filed in claim departments of railroads for injured goods under leaky roofs have decreased in the same ratio as the application of the Hutchins' roof has increased. Its very extensive manufacturing plant is located at Detroit, Mich., and the Chicago office is 904 Rookery, while the business from the Chicago office is under the direction of Mr. Frank S. Woods, general agent of the company.

THE MIDDLETON CAR SPRING CO.

A representative and one of the most reliable concerns in the West, extensively engaged in the manufacture of Combined Spiral Car Springs, is that known as The Middleton Car Spring Company, whose Chicago office is located at 605 Phenix building. This important business was established thirty years ago by Messrs. N. & A. Middleton, who conducted it till 1888, when it was duly incorporated under the laws of Illinois with a paid-up capital of $100,000, its executive officers being Mr Wm. J. Watson, president; Mr. N. Middleton, vice-president; Mr. Wm. F. Bates, secretary and treasurer; and Messrs. G. B. Shaw, J. E. French and John Dupee, directors. The company's works have an area of three acres. The various departments are fully supplied with modern tools, machinery and appliances, operated by three steam engines of 100 horse power. Here 200 skilled hands are employed and the trade of the company now extends, not only throughout the entire United States and Canada, but also to several foreign countries. The company's famous Combined Spiral Car Springs are made of the best materials, and are absolutely unrivaled in America or Europe for strength, durability, workmanship and reliability. These splendid spring are now used largely in the car shops of the leading American railroads, having proved their excellence through long years of use, successfully passing through the severest tests. Orders are carefully filled at competitive prices, while all springs are fully warranted. The officers are able and honorable business men, under whose energetic guidance the prospects of the Middleton Car Spring Company are of the most favorable character. Mr. Watson, the president, is likewise vice-president of the Griffin Car Wheel Co., and is a director of the Metropolitan National Bank and also of the American Trust & Savings Bank. Mr. Middleton, the vice-president is a wealthy capitalist, and a resident of Philadelphia.

THE GREINER PATENT ECONOMICAL CUPOLA COMPANY.

Any one of the foundrymen and steel manufacturers of this country must now be convinced that the Greiner Patent Economical Cupola will take the place of all others if a question of economy is to be taken into consideration, for it has the advantage of splendid results in Europe where more than three hundred are in daily use, in no one of which has the saving of fuel been less than twenty per cent., and in some instances it has reached forty and even as high as fifty per cent. The novelty of the invention consists in a judicious admission of blast into the upper zones of a cupola, whereby the combustible gases are consumed within the cupola, and the heat utilized to preheat the descending charges, thereby effecting a saving in the fuel necessary to melt the iron when it reaches the melting zone. Another point strongly in favor of the Greiner Cupola, and which is very important in most foundries and steel works, is that the application of the Greiner system will increase the melting capacity of the cupola,

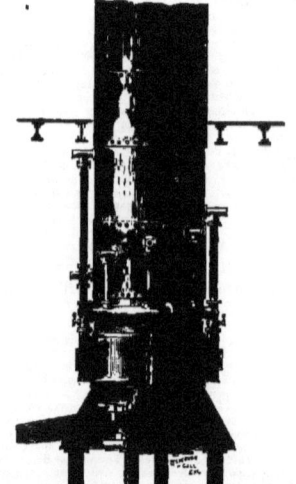

owing to the more rapid melting of the fusion zone, and to the additional room in the cupola that previously was occupied by the extra amount of coke that is not now required. Owing to the more rapid melting, of the metal a purer and better iron is obtained. The system can be adapted to existing cupolas without material alteration being effected, while the only additional fittings necessary generally consist of a circular pipe connected by branches with the main blast box of the cupola, valves to regulate the blast and connecting pipes for the small tuyeres. The patents for the United States are solely controlled by Messrs. Unger & Wigham, whose office is at 301 Phenix Building, at the corner of Jackson and Clark streets, Chicago, Ill., where they recently removed from 219 First National Bank Building. Given the size of the cupola and the conditions under which it is worked, and they are prepared under the patentee's instructions to advise on the proper arrangements for working the Greiner cupola in connection with it. These gentlemen have controlled the patents

since January, 1891, and were formerly located in Philadelphia. Mr. John S. Unger is a native of Germany, and is a mechanical engineer, having been formerly connected with the Iroquois Furnace Co. in building their blast furnaces. Mr. T. A. Wigham is a native of England, and has been in Chicago for four years. Their business interests are widely extended, and the results obtained in several of the most extensive plants in this country, where the patent has been adopted, bespeaks the same success in the United States that it has met with in European countries.

THE CADLER-SEAVER SIGN CO.*

In this age of restless activity and keen competition it is necessary for all who wish to excel in their business enterprises to make known in an attractive manner by signs the wares they have to offer to the public. The business of producing these signs in a tasteful and attractive style is one of great importance. A prominent and reliable concern in this line in Chicago is that known as the Cadler-Seaver Sign Company, whose office is at 1117 Chamber of Commerce, and works are located at 77 Fifth avenue. This company is incorporated with ample capital, and its patronage extends throughout all sections of Chicago and vicinity. The executive officers of the company are Mr. L. G. Cadler, president, and Mr. A. A. Seaver, secretary and treasurer, both of whom are artistic sign writers, who spare no pains to give satisfaction in style and quality of work. They make a specialty of real estate and advertising signs, and have excellent facilities for locating and putting up signs in all parts of the city or suburbs. Prices, which are extremely moderate, are furnished upon application, and the work turned out is unrivaled for elegance, finish and uniform excellence. They occupy three floors, and being 25x65 feet in area, and employ constantly a large force of first-class workmen. Both parties are noted for their integrity and ability, and are very popular in business circles.

JAMES H. BROWN & CO.

Every line of commercial and industrial enterprise is well and ably represented in this city, and in many special branches Chicago supplies the entire Union. Among the leading concerns whose products, by their ingenious device and general excellence, command a large sale wherever introduced, is that of Messrs. J. H. Brown & Company, of No. 22 West Randolph street. Mr. J. H. Brown is the sole proprietor, the "Co." being nominal, and established this business some eleven years ago, from the outset securing a large and widespread trade. He occupies spacious and commodious premises, and is the sole manufacturer of the "Perfect" hog ring, the "Perfect" hog ringer, the "Perfect" stock mark, the "Wet Nurse" calf-feeder, and other novelties. The "Perfect" hog ring has stood the test of years, and his customers are verifying the claim made by him years ago, when he called it the "Perfect." A smooth surface in the flesh is the secret of its staying qualities, as well as the absence of soreness, swelling, or irritation of any sort. The "Perfect" stock mark is comparatively a new article, so constructed as to be kept on sale at the hardware stores, and suited to each customer's needs. This is accomplished by making small discs of a very hard substance equal to hardened steel, and about the size of a quarter, with a raised letter as large as will cover the face. They are attached to the ear by the "Perfect" hog ring, which makes them secure. The "Wet Nurse" calf-feeder can be attached to a pail in one minute, and is made strong enough to last a lifetime. The moment a calf gets its mouth on the nipple, it begins to drink, as the milk comes in instantly. There is no guping, and the calf gets the full benefit of its feed. A heavy stock of these and other novelties is always on hand, and orders can be immediately filled, and at lowest prices. Mr. Brown has built up a trade that extends east to Pittsburgh, Pa., and west to the Pacific. He is an enterprising young man, and is meeting with well-deserved success.

PALMER HOUSE.

The name of the Palmer House in Chicago is synonymous with first-class entertainment. For half a century this well-known house has been known in both continents as the best hotel on the American and European plans that has ever been opened. Our limited space would fail in telling the history of this grand hostelry; enough is to say that the original Palmer House was built on the corner of State and Van Buren streets by Mr. Potter Palmer years ago, when many of its present guests were in their swaddling clothes. When the great fire of 1871 came a new Palmer House was being erected where the present hostlery stands, and this was wrecked in the great conflagration. But scarcely had the ashes cooled around the smoldering ruins, ere Mr. Potter Palmer decided to erect the grandest hotel in the world on the ruins. In 1873 the present grand structure, at the corner of State and Monroe streets, was opened to the public, with every facility and convenience known to the hotel world. The Palmer House is, and has become as much of an institution of the great city as have any of its parks or great public institutions. The grand building alone cost nearly three million dollars; a half million and more was spent in the furniture, and every idea of convenience and luxuriance was added to this model establishment. Additions provided for by the original architect have been and will within a year be made until more than nine hundred guests rooms are open for occupancy. The Palmer is an absolutely fire-proof structure, all of the floors are sheeted, and guarded with the most approved fire-proof devices and appliances. The many different features of excellence in this grand hotel, so well-known at home and abroad, would more than surpass this limited mention in the prominent industries of Chicago. Among the prominent features might be mentioned the grand stairway, in solid marble and iron; the reception rooms and the Egyptian parlors, whose furniture and furnishings are considered among the grandest in the world, where the nobility of the effete east may find a home not less luxuriant than any they have ever seen. The bridal chambers are in receptacles of the gods and goddesses they are to en-shrine, and are marvels of artistic skill and art. The grand dining hall, nearly one hundred feet square, and one-third as high, is a marvel in the corinthian art. Space forbids a deserving description of the ladies' or-dinary and the children's dining rooms, which are rich in their decorations and appointments. The grand ball-room, 50x150 feet, has convenient dressing and toilet rooms, and the grandest of all are the celebrated Palmer House club rooms, which have become a part in the Na-tion's political history, as all prominent political leaders claim a home in the city. The interior and individual appointments of this grand hotel are of the finest and best; no feature has been omitted to make it the grand caravansary of the metropolis of the West. The plumbing and sanitary arrangements are the best, and the crowning work of the finest sanitary engineers in the world, and secure each guest from any unhealthy gases or unpleasant aromas that may arise from unpleasant and imperfect plumbing and sewerage. Every precaution has been taken and this grand hotel is beyond any cavil of doubt *absolutely fire-proof*. To sum up all the advantages of the Palmer House it may safely be said that everything art, capital and science can devise has been utilized for the comfort and safety of its world of guests. The mammoth building is fitted throughout with electrical communications in each seperate room, elevators for passen-gers in each separate floor and suite, electric incandescent lights and every convenience conceivable. The Palmer House club room has long been a matter of history as the rendezvous of the great and exalted of the Nation, where all men may meet and many of the leading statesmen of the world "talk." The Palmer House is conducted under the efficient and ex-perienced management of that prince of hotel men, Copeland

Townsend, who has gathered about him the finest corps of clerks and assistants that can be claimed by any hotel man-agement in the world. Mr. Townsend is at all times ap-proachable, and each guest of this splendid house soon learns to know him as the pleasantest man in the house, who leaves the "sparkling diamonds," so often told of in newspaper stories, to be worn by the clerks, while he forms a genial friendship with all.

N. B. HAYNES CO.

Chicago at all times has good reason to feel pride in the immense business houses in every line that make this magnificent city their home, and among them all none is entitled to more fa-vorable mention than the N. B. Haynes Company, exclusive dealers in ladies' goods, at the corner of Wabash avenue and Madison street. This excellent business was originally established in 1877, and has been located for the past ten years at the present address, the firm name then being N. B. Haynes. On January 1, 1890, the firm was incorporated under the state laws of Illinois, with a paid up capital stock of $100,000, and the following officers: Mr. N. B. Haynes, president; Mr. L. E. Haynes, vice-president; Mr. B. F. Atwood, secretary and treasurer. The firm is one of the strongest in the city, and is the largest concern in the United States dealing exclu-sively in ladies' goods. They occupy a handsome large block, and employ from 200 to 250 people. They are manufacturers' agents for foreign and domestic ladies' goods, making a specialty of French imported goods. A special feature of this concern, and one that will be appreciated by the observing dealer, is that they employ no traveling salesmen, thus saving at least fifteen per cent. in the cost of goods to the retailer. If the retailer desires to make a "leader" of anything in their line, they can secure just what they want, as the N. B. Haynes Company have many odd lots from manufacturers that they de-sire to close regardless of cost. They invite correspondence, assuring prompt replies, and prices that will surely be less than were ever quoted before. The firm has houses in Paris at No. 32 Faubourg Poissoniere; at Lyons, France, No. 18 Rue du d'Argent; Roubaix, St. Etiene-Calais, and at 92 Prince street, New York. The officers of the company are all reliable and experienced business men, who have devoted a lifetime to this especial line, and with their large foreign correspondence and agents keep thoroughly posted on the very latest and best approved styles and fashions.

THE MURPHY SMOKELESS FURNACE AND AUTOMATIC STOKER.

The Murphy Smokeless Furnace and Automatic Stoker has in numerous places been subjected to the severest tests. In every instance it has borne out every claim made for it and given the fullest satisfaction. First, its use secures economy in the use of coal. Second, it rids towns and cities of the annoying smoke nuisance. For once let it be understood by the public as it is by engineers, that smoke represents imperfect and wasteful combustion, and the demand for suppression of the smoke nuisance will be met by an eager desire to effect economy in the use of coal. The Murphy Smokeless Furnace has been established since 1880, and its success has been very marked. The principle of its construction can well remain for more technical description, but the Murphy idea seems to be in non-technical terms to be to feed furnaces in a way other than through the open doors, and to force a supply of air into the fire from as many small openings as possible, rather than one large one, and this in order to make an even distribution for the given fuel. In this way the temperature of the fire is not diminished by the in-rush of a large volume of cold air, nor is the fire hindered by the sudden inroad of a mass of coal it can but imperfectly "digest." Mr. Thomas Murphy began the manufacture of the Murphy Smokeless Furnaces and Grates in 1880, and now retains control of the business he then established. The headquarters of the concern is at Detroit, Mich., and the Chicago office is room 407 Rookery building, corner La Salle and Adams streets. The success of the Murphy patent is attested by the use of the furnaces in many electric light stations, in street railway plants, and in the boiler rooms of large manufacturing concerns, and in some of the largest office buildings in this city, viz., the Chamber of Commerce, the Virginia Flats, the Leiter building, etc. The Murphy Furnace differs essentially from smokeless furnaces,

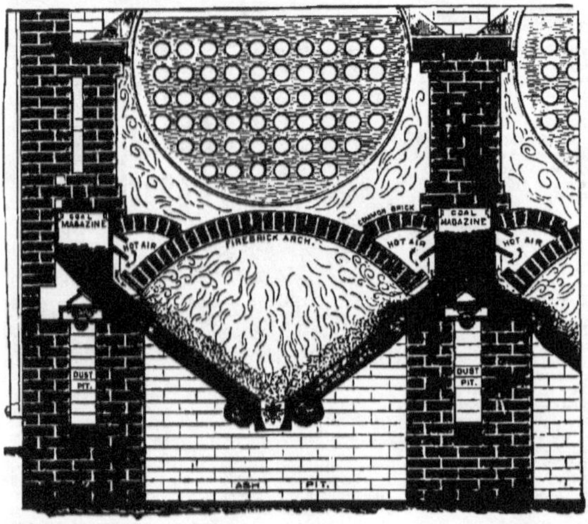

being a mechanical stoker, the coal in this being introduced at either side of the grate and fed toward the center, instead of being put in at the front and carried to the rear. The manner of construction of this furnace is shown in the accompanying illustrations, of which Fig. 1 is a transverse sectional elevation, and Fig. 2 a front view and sectional side elevation. The furnace is especially adapted to the use of slack or small-sized coal, which is put into large hoppers or magazines, these being built into the wall at the side of the furnace proper, as shown clearly in the vertical cross-section, Fig. 1. At the bottom of the magazine is a cast iron plate supporting the upper end of the inclined grates, and known as the coking plate. Resting on this plate is an inverted open box, called the stoker box, and having a rack at each end, meshing with a section of a pinion on a shaft worked from the outside, and by means of which the stoker box is worked back and forth every six, ten, or fifteen minutes, as may be required, and pushing the coal to the edge of the coking plate and onto the grate. The triangular piece shown above the box is moved out and in by a lever from the outside, dividing the coal and helping to bring it down in front of the stoking boxes. Immediately over the coking plates and on the side of each magazine, is an arch plate on which the firebrick arch rests, the brick resting on ribs about an inch apart. Air is admitted in front of the furnace, regulated by a register, passes up through a flue in the brick wall, then over the arch, and there taking up the heat from the brickwork, passes down through the spaces between the ribs on the arch plate to the fresh fuel on the coking plate. The air being introduced in the manner described, at the time it comes in contact with the coal it is sufficiently hot to ignite the gases driven off, thus at once *preventing the formation of smoke.* By the time the coal reaches the grate the bituminous part is consumed, and what remains is in the form of coke. This gets its needed supply of air for combustion through the grates. These, by means of suitable mechanism driven by a small steam engine at one side of the furnace, or battery, as the case may be, are kept constantly in motion, thus keeping them cool, insuring the proper passage of air through them, and preventing the formation of clinkers. As the coke burns it moves down toward the center of the furnace, where the clinker breaker—a heavy shaft armed with spur teeth, and extending the length of the grate—grinds the refuse into the ash pit. The method of driving the stoking apparatus and shaking the grates is clearly shown in Fig. 2 in the front view. An engine of less than one horse power is sufficient for an ordinary battery of boilers. The advantages accruing in the use of these furnaces may be briefly summed up as follows: Freedom from smoke, economy in the use of fuel, great durability, and long life of boilers with them, owing to the fact that the fire doors not being opened to feed or clean the fire, the boiler is not subjected to sudden changes of temperature, and thus one of the most destructive factors in the running

FIG. 1.

of boilers is eliminated. The trade extends from Maine to California—literally from Cape Ann (Gloucester, Mass.) to San Francisco—and from Canada to Texas. The concern has agencies in Pittsburgh, Denver and Cincinnati, and through the Chicago office a brisk business has been built up. Mr. Thomas Murphy, the head of the concern, has a high reputation in mechanical engineering, and his testimony as an expert is often in demand in the courts. He

well adapted to the requirements of the business. A liberal patronage is had, and Mr. Smith is very popular.

LOGAN HOUSE.

One of the most popular and comfortable hotels in this section of Chicago on the American plan is the Logan House, eligibly located at 39 to 45 West Adams street. This hotel

FIG. 2.

has also an extensive wrecking business in Detroit, and is one of its most public spirited citizens.

A. SMITH.

The wholesale and retail tea, coffee and grocery business of Mr. A. Smith merits distinguished mention in this review of the commercial interests of Chicago. The business was established seven years ago by Hemon & Smith, and in 1891 Mr. A. Smith succeeded to the entire interest. Mr. Smith gives close attention to his business interests and in this way has achieved his success. He was born in England, and came to Chicago some years ago; he has, since engaging in business, made many friends by his courteous manner and strict integrity, and is patronized by the best citizens of the district in which his store is located. He has three assistants, who are capable, gentlemanly and favorites with his customers. All goods are delivered free of charge, Mr. Smith keeping several teams for this purpose. The store he occupies is very large and is conveniently and admirably located at 1797 Milwaukee avenue. It is stocked with a complete line of fine staple and fancy groceries of all kinds, canned goods, condiments, meats, pickles, preserves, extracts, baking powders, cheese, household goods, flour, etc., and a very superior selection of fine teas, coffees and spices. In season, all kinds of fruits and vegetables are carried, and a specialty is made of fine dairy products. The building occupied is a two-story frame, and is

has been managed since 1887 by Mrs. E. Loftus, who, previously for twenty-nine years, conducted the Atlantic Hotel, Chatham Square, New York, and the European Hotel, 52 Sherman street, Chicago, from 1876 to 1887. She has had great experience, and is noted for extreme attention to the comfort of her guests. The Logan House contains sixty rooms available for guests, and the rates are only from $1.00 to $2.00 per day, with reasonable reductions to permanent boarders. The rooms are well furnished, ventilated and lighted, while the sanitary arrangements and means of escape in case of fire are perfect. The table is supplied with the choicest and best in the market, and the Logan House is noted for its cleanliness and neatness, and it would be well for Chicago if there were more like it. This hotel had a very small patronage till Mrs. Loftus assumed the management; now she has sixty regular boarders. She has also a boarding house at 271 Jackson boulevard, containing twelve rooms, which are let at very moderate rates. Mrs. Loftus' husband died December, 1880, since which period she has conducted business alone. The Logan House is convenient to the Union Depot, and cars are constantly passing the door to all parts of the city. Mrs. Loftus has won hosts of friends by her integrity and courteous manners, and guests, having once stopped here, are sure to return when visiting the city. She was born in Ireland, and is a relative of Eugene Kelly, the popular New York banker. Most of the children sent by Catholic institutions to this city are sent to be cared for by Mrs. Loftus, she being well recognized by all Sisters of Mercy.

WM. COOK & SONS.

One of the older established sash and door factories of the North side, and one of the best known among the building interests of the city, is that of Messrs. Wm. Cook & Sons of Nos. 53 to 63 North avenue. During the twenty years existence of this firm its style has undergone many changes, although its history has been one long series of successes. The founders were Messrs. Cook & Halleck, afterwards altered to Messrs. Lumas, Cook & Co., Cook, Hallet & Gammon, Cook & Lumas, and in 1891 the present title was adopted. Mr. Wm. Cook, who came to this city from Germany fifty years ago, and to whose wide experience and thorough knowledge of the wants of the best class of American trade the extraordinary prosperity of the firm is mainly due, has admitted his sons, Messrs. W. A. and G. S. Cook to partnership, and is developing the business to proportions never before attained in its long and honorable career. He employs from fifty to sixty skilled hands; his fine brick planing mills are commodious and well equipped with the most modern machinery, driven by a steam engine of eighty horse-power. Railroad sidings are laid on the premises, and every facility exists for the active prosecution of the rapidly growing business in all its various departments. This house commands the permanent patronage of many of the largest and most desirable contractors and builders in the city, and has always maintained the highest reputation for the superiority of its productions. Mr. Wm. Cook is an honored member of the Independent Order of Foresters, and is greatly esteemed and respected by all for his conspicuous ability and honorable methods. His sons are both natives of Illinois, and exhibit the true spirit of American enterprise in all their operations, introducing new methods, and occupying new fields with a zeal and energy that are the best promise for a brilliant future.

F. REICHARDT.

Although the American continent has been productive of many skilled and eminent scientists, whose discoveries have benefited the world at large and relieved suffering humanity of numerous ills, yet there are several forms of disease which can only be successfully combated by the aid of the preparations of European men of genius, which have been tested and never been found wanting. While in many branches, such as dentistry, surgery, and others, we can give pointers to the practitioners of the Old World, yet in others we are still only students, and have to rely upon the chemists of Europe for our preventives and cures. It is, therefore, no matter for surprise that in all parts of this country an extensive demand has grown up for such a well-known and so valuable a preparation as the Dinet & Delfosse Tape Worm Expeller, for the sale of which Mr. F. Reichardt is the sole agent in the United States. For many years this terrible disease, caused by the presence in the intestines of a parasitical worm, of which over two hundred different varieties are known, some of which have been found of the enormous length of 136 feet, was looked upon as incurable. Medical men, chemists, scientists and others sought in vain for some preparation, which, while innocuous to the patient, would dislodge and expel the voracious intruder; but all researches were unavailing until the present specific, manufactured by Messrs. Dinet & Delfosse, was discovered. This is the only successful specific for removing tape-worms completely within one to three hours, without having recourse to any starving or other process. It is manufactured in Darmstadt, Hesse, where extensive works are in continual operation to supply the enormous demand. Mr. Reichardt established his agency in Chicago in 1882, at No. 83 W. Kinzie street, and by his enterprising and judicious methods he has built up a very large trade. He is a courteous and obliging gentleman, and always takes pleasure in supplying any information that may be desired. He is of German birth, and since 1886 a resident of Chicago, where he is held in high esteem by all classes. In all his business relations he is punctual and reliable and merits the confidence reposed in him.

W. S. PATTERSON & CO.

The question of hot water and steam heating in modern buildings is of such importance that it cannot be referred to novices, but calls for the best efforts of experienced and competent engineers. In this line there are none better able to cope with these questions than the well-known firm of W. S. Patterson & Co., engineers and contractors. The business of the house was established in 1885 by Mr. W. S. Patterson, at Appleton, Wis. The business developed rapidly and demanded more central quarters, consequently, in March, 1890, Mr. Patterson moved to Chicago and associated himself with Mr. E. J. McDonough, and continued the business here under the most favorable auspices. They do an engineering and contracting business in steam and hot water heating, making a specialty of Gold's Union Steam and Water Heater. They furnish estimates and specifications upon application. They occupy the ground floor and basement of the premises No. 35 Michigan street, where they have floor space 40x40 feet in dimensions. They employ twenty workmen, and have many contracts for heating apparatus and boilers. The trade is from all parts of the city, suburbs and state, and all parts of the United States. The house maintains a branch at Appleton, Wis., where the proprietors formerly resided. These gentlemen are reliable and energetic, and their business record is of the highest character. They are thus deserving of the large and influential patronage which has been so liberally accorded them.

SMITH & BIRKS.

The business of supplying the necessaries of life must always be one of the leading lines in a large city, and Chicago has numerous houses of high repute in their various spheres contributing to the high standard of excellence for which the city is celebrated. Among the leading houses in the grocery and provision business, the old-established and reliable firm of Smith & Birks is well known and most popular on the west side. The business of the house is conducted in a manner that begets the confidence of customers and constantly increases the liberal patronage. The proprietors are gentlemen who bring long business experience and the highest principles of integrity to bear in order to succeed, and to say that their efforts are appreciated is to say the least that may be said. The business was founded in 1863 by T. M. Smith & Bro., on Milwaukee avenue and continued in that form until 1871, when the firm name was changed to Smith & Mallam. The business was continued by these gentlemen until 1886, when Mr. Mallam retired and Mr. Birks became a partner, since which time the business has been conducted under the present form. The business is located at 1624 and 1626 Milwaukee avenue, where two large stores, 25x75 feet each, are utilized for business demands. The store numbered 1626 is used for the tea, coffee and spice department, and contains a stock of the finest products in those lines, the teas being selected from the finest stocks imported, and are true to color and grade, as well as being sold at most reasonable prices. The coffees and spices are the best obtainable and are guaranteed for strength and quality. The grocery department in No. 1624 contains everything in the line of fancy and staple groceries, both of imported and domestic goods, fine cheese, pure syrups, dried fruits, choice rice, tapioca, farina and prunes, also table delicacies of all kinds, flour, pickles, and, in fact, everything that can be had from any first-class grocery in the land. Provisions of all kinds are carried, and fine fruits may be had in season. This house is favored with an unusually large and select patronage, and does an immense volume of business. Four assistants are employed to attend to the needs of customers, and two teams are used for delivering goods to all parts of the city free of charge to patrons. Mr. Smith is an Englishman of culture and ability. He came to Chicago in 1862, and is well known as a business man of ability and integrity. He is a prominent Free Mason. Mr. Birks has been a resident of Chicago since 1881, and is a young man of sterling worth; he is a member of the British American Association, and is very popular with patrons of the house, as well as in leading social circles.

HALVERSON & BREDSHALL CO.

The Halverson & Bredshall Company, of which John Halverson is president, and John Bredshall, secretary and treasurer, is the successor of the Halverson Furniture Company, and was incorporated January 1, 1890. The latter company was established by Mr. Halver Halverson, brother of John, and for some time conducted a general manufacture of furniture. Of late the company has settled down to the special manufacture of the "Columbia" folding-bed, the demand for which has grown so much of late that the company's resources are taxed to their utmost limit, and it will be necessary to en-

large their capacity to meet the demand. They are the patentees and sole manufacturers of the "Columbia," which has acquired a reputation as wide as the country for efficiency, strength, beauty of form, and adaptability to all the requirements that enter into a folding-bed's equipment. These beautiful and useful articles exhibit in their make-up the highest development, the qualities of convenience which more than a century and a half ago moved the poet Goldsmith to speak of the quarters where

The bed contrived a double debt to pay,
A bed by night, a chest of drawers by day,

The "Columbia" is warmly commended by housekeepers, and is in use in all the large hotels in the country. The Halverson & Bredshall Company occupy the brick building 257-259 N. Green street, 50x125 feet in all, and employ sixty-five men. The firm was incorporated with ample capital for the carrying on of the business on a large scale. Mr. Halver Halverson is a native of Norway, and is about fifty-two years of age. He has been for many years in the furniture business. Mr. Bredshall is also a Norwegian by birth, and came to Chicago when young. Both gentlemen are able and resolute in business affairs, and well deserve the success that the Halverson & Bredshall Co. has achieved. This concern makes a specialty of folding-beds in oak and walnut, in single, three quarters and full sizes, at prices varying from $20 and upwards. Handsome illustrated catalogues will be furnished on application.

R. M. EDDY FOUNDRY CO.

The representative and most successful concern in Chicago extensively engaged in the production of iron castings for boiler fronts, machinery, etc., is that known as the R. M. Eddy Foundry Company, whose foundry is located at 43 to 55 E. Indiana street. This business was founded in 1865 by Mr. R. M. Eddy, who died in 1885, after a successful and honorable career. He was succeeded by the firm of Messrs R. M. Eddy's Sons, and eventually the business was incorporated under the laws of Illinois, with a paid up capital of $100,000, the executive officers being Mr. Geo. D. Eddy, president, and Mr. Albert M. Eddy, secretary and treasurer. The company's plant was built in 1883, and comprises a main four-story brick building, 40x60 feet, and two foundries, one 75x100 feet and the other 30x50 feet in dimensions, with a brick molding room, 40x75 feet in area. The premises have a frontage of 200 feet on Ohio street, and 200 feet on E. Indiana street. The various departments are fully equipped with modern tools, machinery and appliances, while in the yards are large cranes and derricks operated by steam-power for hoisting heavy castings. They turn out in the best possible manner castings for buildings, machinery, boiler fronts, etc., particular attention being paid to heavy work. Only the best pig iron is utilized, and the work produced is unexcelled for finish, reliability and workmanship, while the prices quoted in all cases are exceedingly just and moderate. They do a vast amount of work in the city, and their trade extends throughout all sections of the Middle, Western and Northwestern states. Estimates are promptly furnished for all kinds of light and heavy castings, and 125 men are constantly employed. Both Messrs. George D. and Albert M. Eddy were born in Buffalo, but have resided in Chicago for the last twenty-six years. They are honorable and able business men, whose success in this important industry, is as substantial as it is well deserved. Mr. R. M. Eddy was formerly engaged in business in Buffalo, and was a member of the firm of Eddy & Bingham. The telephone call of the company is 3429, and all communications are given immediate attention, the company being noted for promptitude and integrity.

NORTH CHICAGO ROOFING CO.

In these days of contracting and close competition it is positively necessary that business be done with parties of known integrity and responsibility, in order to insure results that will be at all satisfactory. One of the really responsible roofing companies, with the highest testimonials, of unquestioned reliability and standing, is the North Chicago Roofing Company. The business of this company was established in 1868 by M. F. Freutel on Willow street. In 1885 the present style was adopted and incorporated under the Illinois state laws, with a capital of $5,000. The president and sole manager is Mr. W. L. Springer, a gentleman of long experience and the highest business standing. The business headquarters of the company are at 377 E. North avenue, where they occupy the premises comprising 31x200 feet in dimensions ;completely arranged and equipped yards, having one story sheds for storing all kinds of roofing materials, etc. The company deals in all kinds of roofing materials, building paper, carpet paper and woolen felt; and make felt composition and gravel roofs; they also do jobbing, patching and repairing. This company is prepared to do all kinds of work connected with this business and has a complete equipment, consisting of eight horses, three kettles and from eighteen to twenty employes. The workmen are all experienced, and only the best materials are used. Contracts have been filled for many of the most prominent builders, business men and citizens, and the company has many superior indorsements, among them being the McCormick Harvesting Machine Co.; Harvey Lumber Co.; American Cutlery Co.; St. Nicholas Toy Co.; Western Wheel Works, and others. The business done is extensive and is constantly increasing. Mr. Springer is a native of Cook county, is well known and highly respected in business circles, is a member of the I. O. O. F. the Foresters, Knights of Pythias and Royal League, and is a progressive manager. The company has a high rating, and is noted for its responsibility and reliability for superior work.

H. & M. LEWIS.

Among the active and enterprising business men of Chicago is Mr. H. Lewis, of the well-known firm of H. & M. Lewis, manufacturers of all kinds of mattresses, and general upholsterers and repairers. The firm has acquired an enviable reputation for the superiority of its product, while Mr. Lewis is personally respected as a citizen and noted as a veteran of the late war, who materially contributed to the drill and efficiency of various bodies of troops joining the armies in the field. Mr. Lewis is a native of Farmington, Conn., and was educated at Hartford, for a military life, entering one of the academies, conducted by the famous Captain Parkridge and known as the "England Academy." He made rapid progress, and on graduating was thoroughly grounded in the new system of military tactics and drill, and joined a volunteer military force. When twenty-two years of age he came to Chicago, and subsequently secured a position as traveling agent for several firms, with residence in St. Louis. Upon the breaking out of the War of the Rebellion in 1861, he returned to Chicago, and for one year acted as drill-sergeant of several companies organized in this state. In 1862 he joined General Grant's command and participated in the sanguinary Battle of Shiloh and other severe engagements. Later he was detached and sent to Camp Douglas as drill master, and when he drilled the last three regiments of artillery enlisted in the service. Among them was the celebrated Fifth Independent Battery of Elgin, Illinois, which had six twenty-four pounders, the *heaviest* field guns in the service. For four subsequent years he was actively engaged on special duty in the U. S. Army, finally retiring after a long, honorable and extremely useful military career, serving intelligently, faithfully and valiantly in the cause of the Union. In 1873 he returned to Chicago, and forming the firm of Lewis & Godfrey began the manufacture of mattresses, etc., being originally located on Randolph and

---

Green streets. At the expiration of a year they removed to 838 Madison street, where the business continued for nine years. During this period the copartnership was dissolved, and Mr. Lewis in 1881 made his wife, Mrs. Margaret Lewis, his partner, under the now familiar name and style of "H. & M. Lewis." Mrs. Lewis was a Miss Margaret O'Shea of St. Louis, and was married in 1868. She is a most popular and respected business lady. In 1884 the firm, owing to the steady growth of trade, removed to their present stand, 852 W. Madison street. Here they employ a numerous force of hands in the manufacture of mattresses of all sizes and of all materials, including finest curled South American hair, cotton, husk, wool, moss and excelsior. Quality is their first consideration, and their goods are popular and *preferred* everywhere, being so noted for durability, purity and thorough skilful workmanship. The firm also promptly fill all orders for upholstering and repairing, and carry a large and desirable stock of fine artistic parlor frames and cabinet furniture, which they will upholster to suit. They also have ample storage warehouse accommodations, and in every branch of the business are leaders, fully prepared to promptly execute all orders at moderate prices and give entire satisfaction. They are universally respected and popular, alike socially and in commercial circles, and are well worthy of the substantial success achieved.

JOS. HINTERBERGER.

Among the manufacturing enterprises of this great city, one of the most novel is the making of bungs for barrels. In no place but a metropolis could such an enterprise be sustained, but Mr. Jos. Hinterberger has built up an important trade and does a thriving business in the manufacture of these articles. He occupies the premises located at 83 W. North avenue, where he has a fine plant thoroughly equipped with all the necessary machinery for turning out bungs of all shapes and sizes and vent plugs. He has a complete woodworking plant and is enabled to do turning of all kinds to order. The premises he occupies are 25x75 feet in dimensions and are conveniently arranged. Mr. Hinterberger has been established in business for eighteen years and has been remarkably successful. His wares are used mostly by brewers and oil manufacturers, and with these he does a large business. He employs four workmen constantly and turns out many thousand bungs, his work having a high reputation for excellence among his customers. Mr. Hinterberger was born in Germany and came to Chicago thirty-eight years ago. He is well-known to manufacturers and has numerous friends, by whom he is held in high esteem.

GEO. J. STADLER.

The business of sign painter has been elevated from that of a trade requiring only a certain amount of mechanical skill, to a fine art, in which high talent is necessary to success, Mr. Geo. J. Stadler, of No. 40 West Indiana street, holds a prominent position in the front rank of those whose work has done so much to beautify our streets, his glass and metal signs being marvels of the art, and perfect types of what these signs should be. Mr. Stadler makes a specialty of pictorial painting, and in this department he has done much to elevate and educate the public taste and to create a demand for high class work. He began business in 1885 at No. 261 Larrabee street, but three years later removed to his present eligible position, which is directly central to his large city and suburban trade. He gives constant employment to upward of fifteen hands, and requires two wagons in his steadily expanding business. Mr. Stadler was born in New York, but has resided in this city during the past ten years, and has always been an enthusiastic worker, imbued with an admiration for his art, and executing all its details with thoroughness and accuracy. He is a young, energetic and capable business man, and has a bright and brilliant career before him and by his close application to business is rapidly enlarging his already wide business connection.

WECKLER-PRUSSING BRICK CO.

Chicago's enormous and substantial development has created an active market for the superior grades of brick, and thus has been developed one of the great industries here. Other cities receive their brick, as a rule, from a distance. Chicago, on the other hand, has several of the finest yards in the world, within or near her boundaries. One of the leading concerns of the kind is Weckler-Prussing Brick Company, whose extensive yards are so conveniently situated at Blue Island, Ill. The company was duly incorporated in 1889, with a paid up capital of $50,000, Mr. Adam J. Weckler, the eminent expert in all that concerns brick making, becoming president and treasurer, while Mr. Alexander Prussing became secretary. The company has had deserved success, its product being preferred by the best class of trade everywhere. The grounds cover an area of some 40 acres, while the works are provided with all the latest improved machinery and appliances known to the trade, including two new brick machines. Upward of 100 hands are employed in the yards, turning out an average of 120,000 a day of the finest grade of building brick, and which are found in use all over the city and suburbs. Mr. Adam J. Weckler has long been active as a brick manufacturer. He is a native of St. Jo, Mich., and has lived in Chicago since boyhood. In March, 1879, he began brick manufacturing on his own account, and is still actively operating his large yards at Diversey and Clybourn avenue, which have a capacity of 60,000 bricks daily. The yards are fully 25 acres in extent, and produce a very superior quality of clay. Upward of 60 hands find employment in these yards. Mr. Weckler is likewise president and treasurer of the Weckler Brick Co., which was duly organized in 1885, with a paid up capital of $30,000. Its yards, which cover an area of some 25 acres, are conveniently located at Western and Addison avenues, employing 60 hands, and are fully equipped with the latest improved machinery and appliances. Mr. Wm. H. Weckler, brother of the president, is the company's secretary, and it is one of the most flourishing corporations in the business. Mr. Adam J. Weckler is an active member of the Builders' and Traders' Exchange, and of the Brick Makers' Association. He is a manufacturer and capitalist of the soundest judgment and marked executive capacity, and is specially qualified to guide aright such important interests as these.

ROBERT BERTOLINI & CO..

Among the numerous and varied industries which are actively followed in Chicago are many of an artistic nature, and which greatly contribute to the fostering and developing of the artistic taste of the masses. Prominent among them is that in which is engaged the pushing and prosperous firm whose name heads this sketch, Messrs. Robert Bertolini & Company, manufacturers of statuary and interior decorations in plaster of Paris, etc. The business was founded in 1887 by the present members of the firm, Messrs. Robert Bertolini and J. Bartoli, natives of Lucca, Italy, who have since built up widespread and influential connections, and are now at the head of a rapidly increasing trade. They turn out a class of work of exceptional excellence, and have earned an enviable reputation for the prompt and thoroughly reliable manner in which they execute all contracts and orders. The premises occupied are at No. 149 North Desplaines street; they are spacious and commodious, well appointed and ordered in every respect, and the works are perfectly equipped with all the tools, appliances and paraphernalia requisite for the successful prosecution of the business on an extensive scale. Four skilled and expert assistants are employed, while the partners personally supervise and direct all the operations of the establishment. They are artists of the highest order of merit, and their productions are noted for their originality of conception, breadth of design, and superiority of execution. These include exquisite pieces of statuary of all sizes and descriptions, groups, statuettes, busts, as well as flowers, fruits, etc., etc. The firm also manufacture panels, center pieces, friezes and other interior

decorations. Their warerooms are filled with a choice assortment, and they are at all times prepared to furnish designs, and to produce to order from original drawings, and at lowest prices. They guarantee satisfaction in every instance, while their reputation is an assurance that all contracts will be promptly and faithfully carried out.

W. J. CAMERON.

No department of business in this, as in all other cities, is of more direct value and importance to the community at large than that in which the practical pharmacist brings to bear his professional skill and experience, and among the many Chicago pharmacists who have made a success of their profession is Mr. W. J. Cameron. There are few exponents of this difficult science who bring to its prosecution finer natural aptitudes, supplemented by a better training and experience. Mr. Cameron, who was born in Canada, came to this city in 1890, and a few months later inaugurated his present enterprise. He is a regular licentiate in pharmacy, and has a thorough and intimate knowledge of drugs, their effects upon each other, and the results produced when taken into the system, and is particularly well qualified to fill the important position that he now occupies in the community. His store is located on Wentworth avenue, at the corner of Sixty-second street, and has an area of 20x40 feet. It is well and neatly appointed, its handsome flooring, marble top counters and plate-glass showcases combining to render the pharmacy one of the most attractive in Englewood. Here is always to be found a complete stock of pure, fresh drugs and chemicals, all the reliable and standard medicines and family remedies, together with the latest novelties in perfumery, toilet articles and fancy goods, of both foreign and domestic production. These goods are selected with scrupulous care and experienced judgment, and can be relied upon as the best the market affords. The prescription department is perfect in every particular, being fully supplied with the latest improved apparatus and appliances, and is under the personal supervision of Mr. Cameron, whose experience and ability thoroughly qualify him for compounding physicians' prescriptions and family recipes in a careful and accurate manner. Two assistants are employed. All orders are given prompt attention, and the wants of all classes of patrons are ministered to with eminent success and satisfaction. Mr. Cameron is an accomplished dispensing chemist, and a reliable and responsible business man.

THEODOR HAASE.

An undertaking establishment that holds second place to no other on the west side is that of Mr. Theodor Haase, at 315 W. Chicago avenue, near Noble street. This business was established by Mr. Haase eight years ago at the present place, and during that time his patronage has annually increased, and which seems to be a sufficient recommendation of the orderly and successful manner in which he prosecutes his business. The premises occupied consist of stables, office and show room, all on the ground floor, and quite capacious. He has five horses and furnishes carriages, single and double, for day and night service, for funerals, wedding parties or balls. Mr. Haase is a comparatively young man, and a native of Chicago. He is a member of the Undertakers' Association, also of the Knights of Honor and of the Ancient Order of United Workmen. He carries a full line of coffins, caskets, robes and all necessary undertakers' supplies, and employs skilled assistants and has ample and complete facilities always at hand. Remains are taken in charge at any hour of the day or night and prepared for burial in a superior manner, embalming being performed, when desired, according to the most approved process, and satisfaction guaranteed in every instance. Interments are secured in any of the city or surrounding cemeteries, and funerals are personally directed by Mr. Haase, who gives immediate attention to every detail and furnishes, everything at the lowest figure consistent with first-class service. His telephone call is 4646.

THE HIRAM SIBLEY FIREPROOF WARE- HOUSES.

The rapid delopment of Chicago, as the great central metropolis of the West, has been manifested in numerous ways, but in none more so than in the extended facilities afforded to our merchants for the storage and warehousing of their goods and merchandise. We are led to make these remarks after having paid a visit to the extensive Hiram Sibley Fireproof Warehouses, eligibly located at 210 to 18 N. Clark street, and 164 to 180 N. Water street, These splendid warehouses were erected in 1883 and 1884 by the late Hiram Sibley senior partner in the firm of Hiram Sibley & Co , seedsmen. Mr. Sibley died July, 1888, after an honorable and successful career, and the warehouse business is now under the able and careful management of Mr. F. A. Warren, who is widely known in commercial circles for his ability and sterling integrity. The buildings are located on North Clark street, between the river and the Chicago & Northwestern Railroad. They occupy three city lots and are divided into separate structures by massive party and fire walls, while for convenience

they are known as buildings A, B and C. These warehouses have all modern appliances and safeguards; all elevator shafts are of brick, with iron guide posts for the elevators, and all openings are closed with iron doors and hatches. Besides building for safe keeping against the destroying element of fire, the owner desired to produce an example of strong building as well. The foundations are among the most massive in the city, and easily support the immense weight of ten stories. In fact the Sibley warehouses form a massive structure of pleasing proportions which do great credit to the skill of the builder and the taste and ability of the architect. A general storage, bonded, dockage and forwarding business is transacted, and there are separate fire proof rooms for libraries, works of art, household effects, etc. The rates for storage are the lowest, while insurance is readily granted at a low premium, the fireproof qualities of the structure rendering loss from a conflagration almost impossible. Warehouse certificates are issued, and fifty men are constantly employed. Mr. Warren, the manager, was born in Boston, but was brought up and educated in Chicago. The Hiram Sibley Warehouses have an immense patronage, and include among their permanent customers the leading mercantile houses of the city.

THE ELLISON SIGN MANUFACTORY.

A representative and flourishing concern in this section of the city, whose superior products are to be found in all parts of Chicago and vicinity, is the Ellison sign manufactory, located at Nos. 70 and 72 Milwaukee avenue. This business was founded on February 15, 1890, by Mr. O. M. Ellison, a gentleman of several years' practical experience in this line of business, and who has gained an enviable reputation for the prompt and reliable manner in which he executes all commissions intrusted to him, as well as for the originality and artistic conception of his goods. From the start he built up a large and flourishing business, which each year he has seen steadily grow and develop, and he is to-day the recipient of a widespread and remunerative patronage. His works are in a central location, and have an area of 30 x60 feet. These spacious and commodious premises are well appointed throughout, and are fully equipped with the best improved tools and appliances known to the industry, while every facility is at hand for its successful prosecution on an extensive scale. Mr. Ellison employs ten skilled hands the year around and his output is very large. He manufactures and puts up all kinds of signs, making a specialty of real estate signs. He has had several years' experience in putting up signs, and few men can bring to bear a better knowledge of the most effective way of catching the eye of the public and attracting their attention. He is constantly introducing new styles and designs, and has executed some of the most handsome and attractive advertising signs to be seen in this city and other parts of the country. He promptly executes all commissions satisfactorily and in the highest style of the art, while he quotes the lowest prices. He is a recognized leader in his line, and can furnish anything that may be required, guaranteeing unbounded satisfaction.

OTTO ZEITZ.

There is no more widely known store or one whose stock embraces a line of goods better suited to the location than the one at No. 274 North avenue, which has for the past twenty years been conducted as a first class jewelry establishment by Mr. Otto Zeitz. The store is a marvel of neatness and good taste; the hardwood cases, counters and shelving are artistic, and filled with a fine stock of goods, consisting of diamonds and other precious stones and gems, gold and silver watches, jewelry, ornaments, clocks, silver and plated tableware, and, in fact, everything in the line of jewelers' notions, all of the best and guaranteed to be just as represented. Mr. Zeitz is a practical jeweler and has three competent assistants, and is enabled to do the finest jewelry manufacturing and watch repairing promptly. Mr. Zeitz was born in Germany and has resided in Chicago for twenty-one years, where he has earned a high reputation as a merchant and a gentleman.

WM. KLEMM.

One of the most important and successful industrial enterprises of Chicago, and which secures to this city the most advanced methods and perfect facilities for the manufacture of special and improved machinery of all kinds, is that of Mr. William Klemm, the well known machinist, of No. 196 S. Desplaines street. This gentleman was born in Germany and for the past forty years has been a resident of the United States. He founded this business in 1868, and the history of his house during the past quarter century has been one of continued success and prosperity. He brings to bear upon its every department vast practical experience, perfected facilities, and widespread connections. The premises at first occupied by him at the corner of Fifth avenue and Van Buren street were destroyed in the great fire of 1871, and he has since been located at his present address, where he utilizes an entire floor, 25x125 feet in area. The various departments are fully equipped with the latest improved tools, machinery, and appliances; eight skilled and experienced hands are employed, and the machinery is driven by a 100 horse power engine. Mr. Klemm is an inventor of distinction, and has designed and patented many useful specialties, chief among them being an improved stone jack and windlasses, which in workmanship, efficiency and durability excel all others. These jacks are made as perfect as possible in every detail, the best of care, skill and material are used in their construction, making them the lightest and most powerful jacks ever made. Old jacks are promptly repaired, and fine jobbing in all kinds of machinery is specially attended to. Mr. Klemm is ably assisted by his son, Mr. Wm. Klemm, a young man of marked ability and energy, and thoroughly versed in every detail of the industry. The trade of the house extends over all parts of the continent, the annual sales exceeding $20,000. Mr. Klemm, who is in the neighborhood of sixty years, is an active, hale and hearty gentleman, a practical machinist and mechanical engineer, and is respected and esteemed in industrial circles for his inventive genius and great mechanical ingenuity and skill.

LYONS BROS.

One of the largest, finest and best establishments on the North side is the Lyons Brothers' "China Hall," at No. 366 East Division street. The main store occupies the ground floor and basement. This immense concern was established five years ago by Messrs. John and E. Lyons, and owing to their industry and straightforward dealings has been prosperous from its inception. They carry an immense line of china, glass. crockery and queensware, as well as all the novelties, bric-a-brac, mantel ornaments, etc., in china, majolica and other dainty goods. Their stock of lamps is exceptionally fine, including stand, hanging, piano and banquet lamps of all styles, qualities and designs in endless profusion. Their line of cut glass is also very fine, and will well repay a visit to "China Hall." This is the only house on the North side devoted exclusively to cut glass and queensware, and carries as elegant a stock as any firm in the city. They employ a force of five salesmen and are always prompt and courteous to their trade. Both of the Messrs. Lyons are natives of New York, and have been in Chicago for some years. They are popular in commercial and social circles, and have a rapidly growing trade.

LOUIS A. ANTOINE.

The jewelry business conducted by Mr. Louis A. Antoine at 312 East North avenue is both representative and well established, and, although Mr. Antoine has conducted this enterprise but a short time, he has met with the greatest and most flattering success. The business was established fourteen years ago by Mr. M. B. Essner, who conducted it until 1889, when he was succeeded by Mr. Louis C. Kruezer, who sold out in 1891 to Mr. Antoine, the present proprietor. Mr. Antoine is a practical jeweler and watchmaker. He was born in France, and has resided in Chicago for a number of years. He has an attractive store, well furnished and thoroughly stocked with a fine line of superior goods, consisting of watches of the best makes, diamonds of the best selection and purest water, many being fine matched stones hard to duplicate, jewelry of all kinds, clocks, canes, silverware, etc. A specialty is made of fine watch repairing. Mr. Antoine has a liberal patronage and very large trade. He is popular and has numerous friends, by whom he is held in the highest esteem. There is a manufacturing department connected with the store, in which he employs skilled workmen and is prepared to execute all kinds of orders in the manufacturing jewelry line, and has large and commodious quarters completely furnished with fine showcases, counters, etc. Mr. Antoine will make a great success of the venture, and we bespeak for him the liberal and continued patronage of the citizens of the district.

EMIL JACOB.

The painter's trade is one of the most important in Chicago, and the members of this business manifest great talent, energy and enterprise. One of the best shops on the West side to get any kind of work in this line done neatly and expeditiously, or to purchase supplies in the line of paints, oils, varnishes, wall papers, etc., is that of Mr. Emil Jacob, located at No. 5917 Wentworth avenue. This house was opened by Mr. Jacob during 1890, and through his able and efficient management already enjoys a fair share of the local patronage. The store is 10x40 feet in dimensions, and contains an admirable selection of paints, oils, varnishes, brushes, wall paper, window shades, picture frames, room moulding and kindred commodities. Estimates are likewise furnished and contracts completed for paper hanging, graining, calcimining, glazing and fresco painting, a prominent feature being made of sign and ornamental work. Several skilled hands are employed. Satisfaction is guaranteed in every instance, while charges are uniformly based on a scale of strict moderation. Mr. Jacob is of German nationality, is a thoroughly skilled exponent of the painter's and decorator's craft, and has been a respected resident of Chicago for the past two years.

ZERO MARX.

A genius in the manufacture of beautiful and unique signs is Mr. Zero Marx. He is a native of Germany, and came to Chicago thirteen years ago. Before locating here he began the manufacture of his beautiful signs in St. Louis, and received the highest commendations as well as a most liberal patronage for his work. But considering Chicago a better business center, he located here, and has met with a satisfactory and phenomenal success. Mr. Marx makes the finest signs for banks, offices, breweries, factories, stores, etc., that are made in America. The designs in wood and carved work are novel and beautiful, while the lettering and scenery cannot be anywhere excelled. He has received high commendations wherever his work has been exhibited, and it has only to be seen to be appreciated. At the St. Louis Exhibition of Art, Mr. Marx received the first premium, and diplomas for his work in 1874, 1875, 1876, 1877 and 1878, and from the New Zealand International Exhibition, Australia, he received the gold medal and diploma, first order of merit in 1882. He occupies for the purposes of his business the six-story brick building at 160-162 Superior street. This he erected at a cost of $50,000. It is 50x100 feet in dimensions, and is supplied with every modern convenience and appliance for the successful conduct of the business. The South side office is located at 124 Fifth avenue, the telephone number being 5036. Fifty experienced and skilled artists are kept constantly employed by Mr. Marx in this work, and he has orders always ahead sufficient to keep his force in steady employment. The trade is very large, extending to all portions of the United States, and these signs are becoming more celebrated every year. Mr. Marx is a genius, a gentleman of rare business ability and the highest standing, and is undoubtedly the leading sign-writer to-day in the United States.

B. PENNINGTON & CO.

Though it is true that the West side possesses many fine drug stores, yet it would be difficult to find a more thoroughly representative house, in every sense of the word, than that of Messrs, B. Pennington & Co., at 1056 Milwaukee avenue. It is five years ago since Mr. Pennington first opened the doors of this pharmacy to the public, and during that time he has worthily sustained his reputation for his excellent drugs, and for his reliability and accuracy in compounding and dispensing physicians' prescriptions. The store, 25x65 feet in dimensions, is neat and well appointed and handsomely furnished throughout, possessing all modern improvements, and being equipped with everything that tends to facilitate the successful prosecution of his business. A large soda fountain is a principal feature of the facilities for meeting the requirements of the public. Mr. Pennington is a graduate of the Stockholm College of Pharmacy and a registered member of the Illinois State Board of Pharmacy. He has been in this country for fifteen years, and is a gentleman of high reputation in the community, while his past success and close application to his profession are ample assurances of his continued prosperity. The stock carried comprises a large and varied stock of drugs and pure chemicals, standard proprietary remedies of acknowledged merit, sanitary preparations, herbs, barks, roots, etc., also a full line of toilet articles, perfumes, soaps, sponges, brushes, chamois, fancy goods and everything that comes under that most comprehensive term, druggists' sundries. Physicians' prescriptions are carefully compounded at all hours of the day or night, and Mr. Pennington himself exercises close personal supervision over this department, although he employs duly qualified graduate assistants. The number of the telephone call is 4705, and orders receive prompt attention. This establishment is a representative one in this section of the city.

CHARLES A. MOSES.

Chicago's development upon a scale of such magnificence, and of such elaborate and substantial architectural characteristics, reflects the highest credit upon the building trade, and which is nowhere more ably represented than here. Among the representative members of the trade is Mr. Charles A. Moses, the well-known mason, builder and general contractor, located at 159 La Salle street, room 78, Mr. Moses is a native of New York, who early in life acquired a thorough practical knowledge in every detail of the masons' and builders' trades. He has been actively engaged in building operations in Chicago since 1873, and has taken a creditable part in the rearing of the new city since the great fire. He has had valuable experience in doing the mason and other work on some of the largest and finest buildings ever erected in this city. He is prepared to estimate accurately on any description of work in his line, and quotes lowest rates, commensurate with good, honest work. He adheres rigidly to specifications, employs only skillful reliable journeymen, and exercises close personal supervision over all jobs. Among the hundreds of contracts executed by him, may be mentioned the Ogle County, Ill., Court House; Kane County, Ill., Court House; the handsome building of the Standard Club, Inter Ocean Building, Macon County, Decatur, Ill., Court House, and numerous other government and public buildings, besides hosts of private residences and blocks of stores. Mr. Moses has made a close practical study of every advance made in the science of modern architecture. He is fully conversant with fireproof construction, using only brick, steel and stone, and is prepared to contract to erect all descriptions of fireproof public and private buildings. He is an active member of the Builders' and Traders' Exchange, a popular and public-spirited citizen, and is worthy of the large measure of success achieved in this difficult, yet so vitally essential branch of skilled industry. During the last two years the business has been under the charge of Mr. T. A. Dungan, who at that time assumed the duties of general manager, and it is to his sound judgment and vast experience that much of the success of the business is due. Mr. Dungan has charge of every detail of the business, and is in every respect fully competent to fill the responsible duties of his office. We refer especially to his activity in the construction of the Auditorium, as well as numerous other prominent buildings. Mr. Dungan is a native of Philadelphia, but has been a resident of Chicago ten years, and commands the universal respect of all having business dealings with him.

THE SEARLE & HERETH COMPANY.

No department of commercial enterprise in Chicago is of more direct value and importance to the community at large than that in which the practical manufacturing chemist brings to bear his professional skill and experience. In this connection the attention of our readers is directed to the extensive and representative The Searle & Hereth Company, manufacturers of standard pharmaceutical preparations, whose salesroom and laboratory are located at the northwest corner of Canal and Jackson streets. This business was established in 1887 in Omaha, Neb. Eventually in 1890 it was removed to Chicago, and incorporated with a capital of $150,000, its executive officers being Mr. G. D. Searle, president; Mr. Frank S. Hereth, vice president, and Mr. W. A. Krag, secretary and treasurer. The officers have had long experience, and possess the expert skill requisite for the preparation of their various, highly endorsed, standard pharmaceutical preparations. They occupy a spacious building fully supplied with every convenience. The laboratory is equipped with the latest improved apparatus and appliances necessary for the accurate preparation of their various specialties. A well-disciplined and highly efficient corps of skilled operatives are employed, and the trade of the company extends throughout almost the entire United States. Any preparation bearing the name and stamp of The Searle & Hereth Company is always accepted by The trade as a standard article, and is absolutely unexcelled for purity, quality, strength and uniformity by that of any other house in America or Europe. The officers are highly esteemed in trade circles for their professional ability, and it is their earnest desire to merit by the strictest principles of integrity a continuance of the liberal and influential support already enjoyed. This prominent establishment gives every promise of a long and prosperous future, which a continuance of the present able management will certainly insure it in this valuable industry. Mr. F. S. Hereth, the vice president and chemist, to whom much of the success of this company is due, is a professor of pharmacy in the Chicago College of Pharmacy, and is eminently qualified for that important position. The Searle & Hereth Company is prepared to make preparations according to special or private formulas, and solicits correspondence regarding the same.

T. J. DOUGLAS.

Among those engaged in growing flowers and plants in this city is Mr. T. J. Douglas, whose greenhouses and store are at 241 40th street, corner Langley avenue. Mr. Douglas has probably had a longer experience than any other in this business, having been engaged in it for a period of forty years. He is a native of England, and some years ago went to Australia, where he did an extensive business as a florist. In 1871 he settled in this city, and has since been enjoying a well-merited and deserved success and secured a first-class wholesale and retail trade. He has fine, large greenhouses, which cover half an acre of ground, and grows all kinds of flowers, plants, shrubs, etc., supplying a widespread demand. He makes a specialty of cut flowers and furnishes bouquets, center-pieces for the table, in new and beautiful designs, and memorial emblems for funerals, etc. Mr. Douglas possesses most excellent taste in the arrangement of flowers, and has a splendid custom, which comes from all classes of the community. He also gives his personal attention to laying out and taking care of gardens, and as a florist and horticulturist is pronounced one of the best in the city.

CHAS. V. KUDER.

Among the leading and representative concerns in Chicago engaged in this important line of industrial trade, is the establishment of Mr. Charles V. Kuder, manufacturer of metal cornices, skylights, slate, tin and iron roofing, located at No. 5315 Wentworth avenue. Mr. Kuder has obtained a first-class reputation in his line, and is highly indorsed by builders, architects, property owners and householders, owing to the superiority, finish and durability of his workmanship. Born in Pennsylvania, he removed to Chicago in 1879, and, having acquired a thorough knowledge of this trade in all its branches by years of practical experience, he inaugurated this establishment on his own account in 1883, and from the start has built up a large and influential trade. He is a thoroughly practical and expert galvanized iron worker and roofer, fully acquainted with every detail of this useful industry and the requirements of the most exacting patrons. The premises occupied are conveniently located, having a frontage of 32 by a depth of 50 feet. The spacious and commodious shop is well appointed in every respect, while the workshop is fully equipped with all necessary tools and

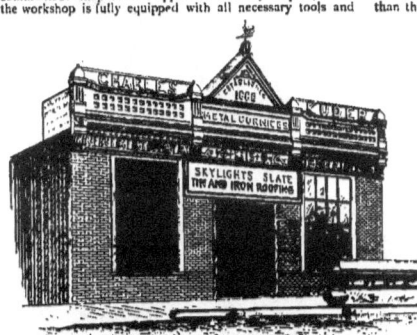

appliances. Here ten skilled workmen are employed under the personal supervision of the proprietor, and the trade of the house extends throughout all sections of the city. Mr. Kuder manufactures to order metallic skylights, galvanized iron cornices, gutters, ventilators, etc., also leaders, tin and iron roofing, and corrugated iron sidings for buildings. His work is unrivaled for finish and uniform excellence, and is highly indorsed by all experts. Estimates are furnished and contracts of any size entered into and executed promptly and satisfactorily. Jobbing is also promptly attended to, while the prices charged are invariably fair and reasonable. Mr. Kuder is highly esteemed in trade circles for his skill, energy and integrity, justly meriting the liberal patronage he has secured.

WEILAND & FREIBERG.

With the great improvement which has been noticeable of late in the quality of the articles demanded by the educated public in every branch of the fine art industries there is, as a consequence, a corresponding improvement in the character of the productions. In the line of fancy ornamental moldings Messrs. Weiland & Freiberg occupy a leading position. They began business in 1890, at No. 103 Fulton street, but in the beginning of the following year were so unfortunate as to lose both stock and premises by fire. This has, however, only served to bring out into prominent relief the characteristic energy of the firm, for they almost immediately re-established themselves in their present elegible quarters.

at 31 and 33 E. Indiana street, and resumed their prosperous career, building up a business which, in this extraordinarily short time, has spread to every important center in the country. They employ a staff of twenty-five most skilful workers, and have at hand all the latest improved machinery known to the trade. Ample steam power is rented with premises, and they have the most perfect facilities for the production of moldings of the most elaborate patterns and designs, in gilt, gold, bronze, ivory, ebony, etc., for all decorative purposes. These goods embody the highest style of art, and reflect the greatest credit on the taste shown by the firm, and their knowledge of the wants of the best class of American trade. Mr. Charles Weiland is a native of Chicago, and Mr. Albin Freiberg, of Germany, the latter gentleman having come to this city fifteen years ago, and both are prominent members of the Masonic Order.

H. J. SCHIRKOWSKY.

There is no more popular style of advertising in existence, than that obtained by good readable signs. No matter what your business may be, you want the world to know it, and where you may be found, to meet your patrons. One of the most extensive sign works in the city, and certainly one of the best, is that of Mr. H. J. Schirkowsky at Nos. 84 and 86 Chicago avenue. Mr. Schirkowsky established his business seven years ago at the same location, where he occupies the main floor and basement, and employs four assistants in caring for his extensive and constantly increasing trade. He is an artist of ability and experience, and does excellent work in signs of all kinds, plain and artistic, and in gold or silver leaf lettering he has no equal in the city. He makes a specialty of brewers' signs, which he makes to order, of any style or in any quantity. Mr. Schirkowsky is a young man of energy and industry, and has a large circle of business and social friends.

GEORGE & MILLER.

There isconsiderable activity in the real estate market in Chicago at the present time, and opportunities are being offered in city and suburban improved and unimproved property, which cannot prove otherwise than profitable to those making investments. Among those who are actively buying and selling realty is the firm of George & Miller, who occupy office 1119 in the Chamber of Commerce building. Mr. T. M. George and Mr H. J. Miller, the co-partners, are well informed as to real estate matters, and they have many valuable building and manufacturing sites for sale or rent, also dwellings in desirable locations in the city and environs. Messrs. George & Miller give their personal attention to the purchase and sale of real estate, the valuation of property and to loans on mortgage and collecting rents, examining titles, and taking charge of estates of absentee owners, etc, They also have some very desirable South side lands to sell at bargains, and can offer the best inducements to those seeking good paying permanent investments. Mr. George was born in Cook county, and has resided in Chicago the past twelve years. Mr. Miller is a native of Worcester, O. For some time he was engaged in the real estate business in Omaha. They both bring a wide range of practical experience to bear upon the real estate business and have formed solid connections with capitalists, investors and property owners and are well equipped to carry through to a successful issue realty operations of any magnitude. Telephone, 2557. Messrs. George & Miller make a specialty of building lots in the addition to Yost, and also to the addition to Harvey, where they are now building half a hundred houses. They also have barguins to offer in acres in various sections of the South side. When desired houses will be erected to suit purchasers of lots, and terms made for payment in monthly or other stated installments.

CHICAGO SPECIALTY BOX CO.

One of the most progressive and reliable concerns in the great western metropolis, actively engaged in the manufacture of skeletons and supplies for wine merchants and liquor dealers, is that known as the Chicago Specialty Box Company, 226 and 228 Kinzie street, of which Messrs. G. Hochstadter and S. Levy are the popular and enterprising proprietors. This business was established in 1889 by Messrs. Hochstadter and

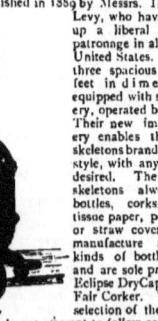

Levy, who have already built up a liberal and influential patronage in all sections of the United States. They occupy three spacious floors, 50x120 feet in d i m e n s i o n s, fully equipped with special machinery, operated by steam power. Their new improved machinery enables them to furnish skeletons branded in the tastiest style, with any name or brand desired. The c o m p a n y 's skeletons always c o n t a i n bottles, corks, caps, labels, tissue paper, patent partitions or straw covers. They also manufacture and import all kinds of bottling machinery, and are sole proprietors of the Eclipse DryCapper and World's Fair Corker. The quality and selection of their goods is the very best, and they do not attempt to follow competition where quality is sacrificed. They only handle and manufacture first-class goods, and their aim is to faithfully serve their customers, thus gaining their entire confidence and permanently enlarging their trade. They will be glad to submit sketches of labels free of charge, and to give estimates on the same. Orders are promptly filled at the lowest possible prices, and complete satisfaction is guaranteed patrons. Both Messrs. Hochstadter and Levy were born in Germany, but have resided in Chicago many years, where they are highly regarded in trade circles for their business ability and integrity. Mr. Hochstadter was formerly distillers' agent and commission merchant, while Mr. Levy was book-keeper for Messrs. Strauss & Hamburgher, wholesale cigars, Lake street. They now employ thirty skilled hands in their factory, and their sales for the past year amounted to over $200,000.

GEO. B. READ & CO.

Mr. Geo. B. Read, the senior partner in the well-known firm of Messrs. Geo. B. Read and Company of No. 963 W. Van Buren street, formerly conducted a high class business in the line of carriage-making, horseshoeing, etc., at Springfield, Mass., for upwards of twenty years, but on the loss of his premises by fire, about twelve years ago, he came to this city. In 1881, finding a suitable opening, he founded the present establishment, admitting Mr. W. B. Read to the partnership, and assuming the style as at present known. Fortune smiled upon the effort, and they have been successful in building up a large and prosperous business among a select and most desirable class of patrons. The senior partner was for a time employed under the War Department, in Springfield, and afterward at Providence, R. I., and New London, Conn., performing his duties with characteristic zeal and ability. He is a practical man, of great experience and ripe judgment, who thoroughly understands every detail of his work. The premises on Van Buren street are spacious and convenient for the interesting work carried on, the blacksmith and paint shops having each a floor space of 800 square feet, while the woodworking apartment contains 400. Carriage-making is done in all its branches, the finished articles being highly reputed for their many excellent qualities of strength, lightness, durability, etc., and the superior finish and style which they exhibit. A very important department is devoted wholly to repairing and paint-

ing, the heads of the firm giving their personal superintendence here, and turning out work that is their best advertisement and recommendation. Horseshoeing is done by experienced and trained assistants, this establishment being the resort of the best racing men, who can nowhere else receive such careful attention in the intricate business of the scientific shoeing of their trotters. Mr. Geo. B. Read was born near Providence, R. I., and has, like so many others who have come West, developed a pre-eminent fitness to meet the exact wants of the Western trade. He is a member of the Masonic Order of the thirty-second degree, of the Royal League, and of the Chicago Carriage Manufacturers' Association, and is widely known and warmly esteemed by a large class, among both commercial and social circles. Both partners are members of Washington Camp No. 1, P. O. S. of A , also of the Commanderies.

SCHULTZ & HIRSCH.

Chicago has become headquarters for the trade in high grade mattresses, bedding, feathers and supplies, largely owing to the ably directed efforts of Messrs. Schultz & Hirsch, leading manufacturers in this line, and the ability and integrity of whose methods is shown by the development of a very large and flourishing trade. Mr. F. Schultz and Mr. J. Hirsch

formed the present copartnership in 1880, and originally located at No. 119 W. Van Buren street, whence they removed to their present site, 260 and 262 S. Desplaines street in 1887, in order to secure the greatly needed increase of facilities. Here they occupy an entire four-story brick building, 60x125 feet in dimensions, and where they employ upwards of seventy-five hands in the manufacture of curled hair, moss, wool, husk and excelsior mattresses, full lines of comforters, pillows, cushions and the finest and heaviest feather beds made anywhere. These are the best feather beds now on the market; all the feathers are pure geese, live picked, most carefully sorted and thoroughly cleansed by the most approved sanitary process. The firm manufacture the *best* hair mattresses, having their own direct importations of South American curled hair, and prepare same in the most careful manner. All work is done thoroughly by expert employes, and their goods are the popular favorites with the best class of trade throughout the United States. The firm deal generally in all descriptions of bedding supplies, and make a prominent specialty of live geese feathers, curled hair, moss, wool, husk, tow, excelsior and ticking of all kinds. They also deal in such novelties as improved cots, cribs, patent springs, etc., and offer the most substantial inducements to mattress makers, dealers in bedding, etc., both as to price and quality. Messrs. Schultz & Hirsch are merchants and manufacturers of soundest judgment and most progressive methods. They are energetic, enterprising and popular, and guarantee entire satisfaction to every customer, and we cannot too strongly recommend this responsible house to the attention and patronage of the trade generally.

C. HILDEBRANDT.

One of the best known business houses on the West Side is that of Mr. C. Hildebrandt, dealer in furniture and upholsterer. Mr. Hildebrandt has had long practical experience in the business, and since 1887 established in his present location, 575 W. Twelfth street. The premises have an area of 25x75 feet, and afford every facility and convenience for the display of the large stock that is always carried, and doing upholstery work, making repairs, etc. The stock displayed embraces parlor and chamber suites in all the new styles: hall, library, dining room and kitchen furniture, also chairs, sofas, lounges, rockers and everything that belongs to the business. The goods are all marked down to the very lowest prices, and customers are assured of the best value in all purchases made at this reliable house. Mr. Hildebrandt's long connection with the business in which he is engaged enables him to obtain the very best strong substantial furniture and to give the best satisfaction to all having dealings with him. As an upholsterer he has a wide reputation and is fully equal to the best in the city. He is prompt in his attention to orders for all work in this direction, and in repairing, repainting and varnishing furniture. He is very moderate in his prices and is doing a splendid flourishing business. Mr. Hildebrandt is a German by birth, and came to Chicago nine years ago. He is a middle-aged gentleman of unquestioned reputation as a business man and citizen, and is a popular member of the Knights of Pythias and Knights of Honor.

JOHN F. ALLES & BRO.

No industry is of such essential importance to every citizen as that of the plumber and gas fitter. There is no security for the health and comfort of the population where the best rules that govern sanitary plumbing have been overlooked, for dread and insidious diseases invariably follow any violation of the principles of hygienic plumbing. Happily Chicago numbers among her enterprising tradesmen and mechanics some of the most reputable and experienced sanitary plumbers in the United States. Among the foremost of these is the well-known and reputable house of John F. Alles & Bro., 233 Lincoln avenue., near Western avenue and Larabee street, who are both natives of this city and who founded their business nine years ago, bringing to bear a wide range of practical experience and skill. They have a well deserved reputation for the thoroughness and excellence of their work, and are patronized by the leading contractors, builders and architects of the city. They occupy the ground floor and basement of the Alles' Block, a building which consists of three stores and fifteen large flats, and is owned and was built by them in 1888 at a cost of $40,000. The premises are 115x75 feet in dimensions, and are elegant in every appointment. The store is 25x85 feet in dimensions, and is filled with a well selected stock of plumbers and gas-fitters' appliances, including lead and iron pipe, gas and steam fixtures, hydrants, pumps, wash basins, bathtubs, water closets, iron sinks, sheet lead, kitchen boilers, faucets and everything pertaining to the business of the plumber and gas-fitter. All kinds of sanitary plumbing, gas fitting and sewerage work is done, and jobbing is promptly attended to. Estimates are furnished and contracts are entered into for the complete plumbing, lighting and heating of buildings of any size. This house has about forty skilled workmen in its employ, and all work is fully guaranteed. Among many large buildings that have been supplied by this house, the Rossville Building 146 S. State street, the Streeter Building, the Crilly Block, the German Hospital and others are samples of the high class of patronage. This house also did the plumbing for the Fourteenth street pumping station. The business done by this house amounts to over $100,000 each year, and is of the most important character. The gentlemen of this firm are young men, and are characterized by their superior energy and ability; they are members of the Master Plumbers' Association. Mr. John F. Alles is a member of the Royal Arcanum and the Mystic Circle ; Mr. Joseph W. Alles is a member of the Knights of Pythias and the Turners' Society. They are both prominent in social circles and widely known as business men of the most stable character.

HENRY WETENKAMP.

Few among the many excellent meat markets that attract the eye along South Desplaines street, have secured a more enduring hold on public favor and confidence than the establishment conducted by Mr. Henry Wetenkamp at 205½ on that busy thoroughfare. It is one of the best equipped stores of the kind in this section of the city, where patrons can always rely upon getting a very superior article, satisfactory treatment and prompt attention. Mr. Wetenkamp established his business here one year ago, and has since conducted it with uninterrupted success. The market, which is of ample dimensions, is clean and neatly kept, and a first-class stock is constantly carried, including choice fresh beef, mutton, lamb, pork and veal, prime butter, lard and provisions, eggs, etc. Several assistants attend to the wants of customers. Mr. Wetenkamp is a native of Wisconsin, is a young man of pleasing manners, and combines push, enterprise and excellent business qualities, and he has before him a promising future.

JOHN KOENIG.

It was ten years and more ago, that Mr. John Koenig now of 494 Larrabee street established tin and hardware business. His business has been a prosperous one from the start, and the excellence of his manufactured goods has been the grand cause of his prosperity. Although his business was originally established at No. 476 Larrabee street, he has been in his present location two years, and his splendid trade has followed him. He occupies the ground floor, 25x60 feet in size, with a complete stock of stoves, heaters and ranges, tinware, hardware, carpenters' tools, builders' hardware, house furnishing goods, cutlery, etc., and employs four men in the manufacture of roofing, guttering, tinware and spouting and all kinds of copper and sheet iron ware, as well as attending promptly to all kinds of jobbing. Mr. Koenig was born in Germany, but came to Chicago in his childhood. He is a prominent member of the Independent Order Foresters, also of the Red Men, and is popular in business and social circles.

JOHN WEPPNER.

With the great number of new buildings going up in Chicago there can be no more important part in their construction than the plumbing and gasfitting and sanitary engineering. One of the most reliable plumbing houses is that of Mr. John Weppner of No 1381 N. Clark street, who does a general business in plumbing and gasfitting, and who contracts for fitting up buildings with all kinds of sanitary and ventilating plumbing. He also carries an elegant line of gas-fixtures and plumbers' supplies of all kinds, having the very latest styles in globes and shades. Mr. Weppner has an immense trade on the North side, which is constantly increasing, and gives employment to a full corps of assistants. The business was established ten years ago by Messrs. Weber & Weppner who continued it up to the past year, when Mr. Weppner became sole proprietor of the store at 1381 N. Clark street. Mr. Weppner was born in Germany, but has been in Chicago many years. Mr J. E. Drendel, the manager of this business during Mr. Weppner's absence, is a young man with great experience, having been in the employ of this gentleman and his late partner for over five years. He is a native of Chicago, and has been identified with the plumbing business for nearly ten years, during which time he has acquired a thorough and intimate acquaintance with its every detail. He is prepared at all times to give estimates and prices and attend to the wants of the numerous customers and patrons.

AUGUST DEHMLOW.

The art of dyeing and cleaning has fully kept pace with the great improvements which have been effected in every branch of trade during recent years. The finest representative western establishment in this interesting line is Mr. August Dehmlow's North Side Steam Dye House at No. 381 Sedgwick strhet, and which occupies the whole space to No. 524 N. Market street, a depth of 204 feet. Mr. Dehmlow began operations here in 1884, and created such a high reputation for the superiority of his work that, in 1889, he was compelled to build the handsome four-story structure which he now occupies, the total cost of this and of the spacious three story addition in the rear being $30,000. Here he has abundant facilities for the active prosecution of the industry, included in the splendid equipment being a fine steam engine of seventy-five horse power, and two large boilers, each of this capacity. The cleansing and dyeing are done by a chemical process, which is much more effective

than the old way, is more expeditious, and does no injury whatever to the material. This is the largest establishment of the kind in the West, requiring the constant services of sixty skilled assistants, and two teams, and having a capacity in the dyeing department of 15,000 pounds of cotton daily. All kinds of fabrics are successfully operated upon here, such as ladies' and gentlemen's garments, silks satins, v e l v e t s, plush, feathers, kid gloves, curtains, laces, etc., the most wonderful renovating and re-coloring effects being produced, causing the articles to assume a fresh and brilliant appearance, quite equal to new. Such a house as this is of great service to the careful housewife, enabling her to transform old-fashioned garments, etc., into the newest shades and tints, thereby effecting a considerable saving in her often limited means. This establishment has five subsidiary branches in the city and suburbs: at No. 2124 Wabash avenue, No. 206 N. State street, No. 277 Lincoln avenue, No. 968 N. Clark street and No. 528 Davis street, Evanston. Mr. Dehmlow is a German by birth, and came to this city to found his present thriving business. He is a gentleman of great capacity, a thorough master of his art, and deservedly merits the esteem in which he is universally held.

D. S. STEVENSON.

Mr. D. S. Stevenson, whose real estate and investment office is in room 407 of the Royal Insurance Building, opposite the Board of Trade, was born in Worcester, England. His father was a large land owner in that county and his estates were managed by his son before the latter came to America. Mr. Stevenson located in Chicago three years ago, selecting this city as the most suitable field for the line of business in which he had such ample experience, and for which he has demonstrated here that he has the most marked ability. He went into business immediately, and his success has been most phenomenal. He is twenty-nine years of age, and probably no other young man has ever come to the city a stranger and received such a large clientage of the best class in so short a time. Mr. Stevenson has not only been successful in business, but has gained a large number of friends in the most exclusive social circles of the city, by whom he is most highly regarded for his many excellent personal qualities. He is also a prominent member of the Royal League here. He conducts a general real estate business, and makes, loans on first mortgages. His office is handsomely fitted up and conveniently arranged for the transaction of business, and has all the modern improvements and conveniences.

LIDELL & WILLIAMS.

One of the representatives of Chicago manufacturing establishments is that of Messrs. Lidell & Williams, the only exclusive manufacturers in the world of base, head and corner blocks. Their skill and enterprise are proverbial, and their product is of such a high standard of excellence and artistic originality, and so much preferred by the best class of trade everywhere, that the firm's facilities are taxed to the utmost, and they are now away behind their orders. The business was established in 1886 by Mr. P. Lidell and Mr. T. Williams, under the existing name and style. Both parties were practical men with a thorough knowledge of the wants of the trade in this line, and early became celebrated for the marked superiority of their work. They have had to enlarge their factory on several occasions, and now occupy, at the corner of Desplaines and Wayman streets, two entire floors, each 120 by 60 feet in dimensions. Here is the finest equipment of machine tools for carving, shaping and finishing base, head and corner blocks in the world. The firm employ over thirty skilled hands, and give the closest personal supervision to the processes of manufacture. Their blocks, unlike many other makes, are made exclusively from choicest kiln-dried lumber, and are genuine carved work, in which the greatest care is given to perfect every detail of the designs, which are all strictly original, of highest artistic conception. New ideas are constantly being introduced, and an inspection of the firm's remarkably handsome illustrated catalogue will abundantly demonstrate that here is the greatest variety to select from, ranging from plain blocks at $5 per 100, up to the magnificent pieces of carving at $210 per 100. Here are hundreds of varieties and styles to select from, enabling the builder to match almost any style of architecture or trim, while the firm are prepared to make blocks of any size or design ordered. They manufacture staple lines in white pine, but are ready to fill orders in any hardwood, including such cabinet woods as walnut, redwood, cherry, oak, etc. They number among their customers the leading builders of the United States, and have achieved an enviable reputation for their work, which is far in advance of any competition. Messrs. Lidell & Williams are both old and respected residents of Chicago, business men of sound and progressive methods, and to them is due the credit of retaining to Chicago the supremacy in this important branch of skilled industry.

HENNESSY BROS.

If any firm in Chicago possesses a monument to its progress it is the firm of Hennessy Bros., contractors and builders, at 23 N. State street, for their name is identified with the erection of some of the noblest structures in this and other cities. This popular and reliable firm was established twenty-eight years ago by P. M. and R. M. Hennessy, and in 1889 Mr. W. F. Evans was admitted to partnership, without, however, changing the style of the firm. They started business originally at 31 N. State street, but the ravages of the big fire in 1871 had no mercy on them and they were completely burned out, and removed to their present quarters, where they have been located for twenty years. Finding their business outside the city required special attention they opened an office in St. Paul, Minn., nine years ago, and over this Mr. P. M. Hennessy presides, while the other partners reside in Chicago and take care of the business here. Their work is conducted on an enormous scale, finding employment for an average of 100 men, and no firm in the country possesses better equipment for the successful and expeditious carrying on of work of this nature. Estimates are furnished from specifications and architects' drawings, and contracts taken for work of any size. Among the most noteworthy of their buildings are the new Wisconsin Central building on E. Harrison street, in this city, which is the finest railroad depot in America, the North side county jail, on Illinois, Dearborn and Michigan streets; the Cathedral of the Holy Name; the West Hotel, Minneapolis; The Ryan Hotel at St. Paul; and the New York Life Insurance building, St. Paul. Both Messrs. Hennessy Bros. were born in Ireland and came to America forty years ago, being men of middle age. They are members of the Builders' and Traders' Exchange. It is hardly necessary to say that their work is all done in a first-class and irreproachable manner, and that they possess the entire confidence of all architects and builders and as being men who would not stoop to do anything that would bear the slightest misinterpretation.

M. G. BROOKS.

The plumbers of Chicago are well-known for their thorough acquaintance with every feature of their business, which often requires the exercise of a great amount of ingenuity in its successful prosecution. They are capable of originating new methods, of suiting their work to the varying conditions always presenting themselves, and of surmounting every obstacle, and solving every problem, which would puzzle many less enterprising business men. Among the representatives in this important line, who fully uphold this reputation is Mr. M. G. Brooks, of No. 1111 Harrison street, an honored member of the Master Plumbers' Association, the Royal Arcanum, and the Patriotic Sons of America, and one of our most respected and honored citizens. The business was begun about nine years ago by Messrs. Brooks Bros., who soon secured a most desirable patronage, and established the trade upon a secure and enduring basis. Upon the dissolution of the partnership in 1888 Mr. M. G. Brooks branched off for himself, and has since enhanced his already great reputation, and added to his large connection, until at the present time he commands a most enviable patronage in all parts of the city and suburban towns. He is prepared to furnish estimates and to take contracts for all work that come within the sphere of his vocation. Gasfitting and and sewer building are branches that receive special attention, Mr. Brooks being a practical expert in this work, his twenty years' experience enabling him to confidently undertake the largest and most difficult jobs. His fine store is filled with an elegant display of gas fixtures and plumbers' supplies of all kinds, at prices which will be found fair and reasonable. Mr. Brooks did the plumbing in the fine residence of C. V. Kasson, Esq., 148 Astor street, also the fine apartment building for Brown & Lindquist, 44 to 58 Oakenwald avenue, and a fine store and flat building for B. Mercil, 945 Madison street, and many stores in

various parts of the city. Mr. Brooks is a licensed plumber of the city of Chicago, and is held in high estimation by a large circle in all classes of society.

HOLTON, SEELYE & MOONEY.

There is great activity at the present time in the Chicago real estate market, and parties buying city and suburban property are obtaining bargains which cannot fall in the near future to pay heavily on the investment. Among those prominent in the activity now prevailing is the firm of Holton, Seelye & Mooney, of 1203 Chamber of Commerce Building. The firm number among their clientele many of the best people of the city. The trio of co-partners are gentlemen of integrity and probity, and careful, shrewd real estate operators, and their advice is sought by those seeking investments, as well as by those having holdings to dispose of. They take charge of and manage estates for resident and non-resident owners, collect rents, negotiate loanson bonds and mortgages and all first class collateral. All the co-partners are well versed in the realty business. Mr. Geo. D. Holton, Mr. Alex. H. Seelye and Mr. Wm. H. Mooney are all widely known in real estate circles, and well equipped to carry through to a successful issue transactions in realty of any magnitude. Mr. Hubbard Parker is associated with them in the down town property and investments; and Z. Squires, Jr., looks after the interests of those desiring homes in the choice "Kenwood" and "Woodlawn." Many of these residences are not found on the sale boards but are exclusively with the above firm. The firm's reputation is unquestioned and they are indorsed and recommended by all having dealings with them. Telephone call, 2435. The office of the firm is neatly and tastefully arranged and fitted up, and is in every sense complete for the transaction of real estate business. To all communications the most prompt and careful attention is given, and everything done to satisfy patrons.

THE JOHN J. CROOKE CO.

Chicago's metropolitan importance is illustrated on every hand. In numerous branches of skilled industry she controls establishments nowhere else found in the West. Such for example is the Tin Foil Factory of the John J. Crooke Company, located at 80 and 82 Illinois street. This industry was originally founded in New York city upward of thirty-four years ago, and for many years thereafter was the only concern of the kind in the United States. The business had a steady growth, necessitating repeated enlargements of facilities, and now it is the largest of its kind in the world, and has the finest equipment in existence. The works are located at the corner of Grand and Mulberry streets in that city, and employ there over 400 hands. In 1880, in response to the rapidly increasing demand of the Western trade, the company opened its Chicago branch, Mr. C. L. Crooke becoming the manager. Under his able and experienced guidance there has been developed here an industry of the most flourishing description. The premises occupied comprise two entire floors, each fifty by 100 feet in dimensions, fully equipped with special machinery run by steam power. Upward of twenty-five hands are here steadily employed in the manufacture of tin foil, bottle caps, etc. The John J. Crooke Co.'s tin foil is too widely and favorably known to require comment here. It is preferred by the best class of trade everywhere, and the company's trade extends all over the Union, while it exports to Canada, Mexico and South America. The Chicago establishment manufactures upward of fifty tons of tin foil monthly. Mr. Crooke is a native of New York, and universally popular and respected as a progressive business man of the soundest judgment and marked executive capacity. He has here developed a great and flourishing industrial establishment, and given to Chicago and the West the same facilities as those enjoyed in New York and the East for securing an abundant supply of tin foil at lowest rates.

STEWART'S "FAIR."

The tendency of the age is toward concentration. The masses flock to the large cities, capital is "pooled" to handle gigantic enterprises, and trusts are formed to govern the product of mines or the great manufacturing interests. So also in mercantile pursuits, the cosmopolitan "fair" has superseded the old notion and general merchandising establishment, and is stocked with everything, from a 'in whistle to a parlor suit. Chicago has several institutions of this kind, one of the most popular being that of Mr. M. L. Stewart, who established the business twelve years ago. Mr. Stewart is a native of France and has resided in Chicago for about twenty years. Energy and progressiveness are his chief characteristics, and he has so developed his natural abilities as to have achieved phenomenal business success. His principal establishment is at 111 and 113 N. Wells street, where he has two stores, connected, 25x60 feet each. Here he carries an immense stock of boots, shoes, hats, caps, clothing, crockery, glassware, tinware, wooden and willow ware, household furniture, etc. The store is splendidly fitted up and furnished, and the stock of goods carried is of a superior quality. In addition to the establishment above mentioned Mr. Stewart also owns and operates two branch stores at numbers 112 and 301 N. Wells street, each being well stocked and liberally patronized. The business conducted by Mr. Stewart is of the most satisfactory character, the customers are numerous, and the patronage is constantly increasing. He employs from twelve to fifteen clerks and is constantly adding to his force and increasing his facilities for business. He is a gentleman of middle age and has an excellent business and social standing. Be sure and look for Stewart's Fair, Nos. 111 and 113?

C. G. WADE, M. E.

The profession of a civil and mechanical engineer is one of great responsibility, requiring superior ability, coupled with thorough practical experience. In this connection we desire to refer, in this commercial review of Chicago, to Mr. C. G. Wade, M. E., civil and mechanical engineer, whose office is situated at 228 La Salle street, room 41. Mr. Wade, after receiving an excellent scientific education and training, located in Milwaukee, Wis., but eventually went to Kansas City, as engineer for the first Cable Railway Company established in that city. He afterwards removed to Denver, Col., in the same capacity during the construction of the first cable railway built there, and, in 1889 came to Chicago, where he is now practising his profession. He is an able and expert engineer, fully conversant with every detail and feature of this valuable and arduous profession. His ability is fully recognized, and he has designed and contracted for the iron work of the A. J Stone nine-story building, corner Madison and Ashland avenues, and has just taken bids for the iron work on a ten-story warehouse, on Quincy and Market streets, for Mr. J. B. Mailers. He makes a specialty of machine designing and structural iron work in bridges and buildings. His work can always be implicitly depended on, and no time, or pains is spared to give entire satisfaction to patrons. Mr. Wade is an honorable and expert engineer, who undertakes any kind of difficult work. He is a graduate of the engineering course of State University of Wisconsin, which institution has since conferred upon him the degree of M.E. He is a popular member of the Western Society of Engineers. One of the most noted feats of engineering skill in Chicago is the recently completed palm house and conservatory for Lincoln park, the engineering work of which was done by Mr. Wade, and which is something unique in the way of iron and glass structures. There are about 130 trusses, nearly all of them curved to one or more arcs of circles, and also containing tangent portions. One prominent feature, from an engineering point, is the many intersections of trusses at oblique angles, hitherto seldom attempted on so large a scale without the use of wood. These trusses differ very greatly, either in size or shape, so that there are nearly as many *kinds* as there are trusses. The palm house portion is fifty feet high. Total area covered by the building, 20,000 square feet.

TOWNSEND, HOSTETTER & CO.

As competition becomes greater there arises a demand for art and advertising novelties, show cards, etc., in order to bring the various productions of our manufacturers prominently before the public. In this connection we desire to refer especially to the progressive and reliable Chicago firm of Messrs. Townsend, Hostetter & Co, manufacturers of chromos, lithographic, iron and glass show cards, whose office and factory are located at 206 and 208 Illinois street. This useful and artistic industry was established in 1887, by Messrs. F. S. Townsend and L. N. Hostetter, both of whom are expert designers and makers of show cards, possessing an intimate knowledge of every detail of the business and the requirements of the most exacting customers. They occupy three spacious floors, 25x125 feet in area, fully equipped with the latest improved tools, machinery and appliances, known to the trade. Here thirty-five skilled hands are employed, and the trade of the firm is by no means confined to the United States and Canada, but extends also to Central and South America and Europe. Two-thirds of this firm's business is done in brewers' iron show cards, and they also produce largely show cards for boot and shoe, clothing and agricultural implement manufacturers. Their work is unrivaled for elegance and originality of design, durability, finish and workmanship, while their prices in all cases are extremely moderate. Orders are carefully filled, and entire satisfaction is guaranteed customers. Mr. Townsend was born in Vermont, while Mr. Hostetter is a native of Philadelphia. They are enterprising and honorable business men, and their show cards are the best yet offered to the public.

EAST CHICAGO FOUNDRY CO.

Chicago, as the great central metropolis of America, can boast of establishments which are the national representatives in their respective branches of skilled industry. Such for example, in the line of iron and steel, is the celebrated East Chicago Foundry Company, with offices in the Rookery building, whose rolls and ingot molds have the preference with the best class of trade everywhere, especially in the West and Southwest. That such a flourishing industry as this should spring up in Chicago, and secure such a magnificent development, must, of necessity, prove a very gratifying subject for consideration in the community. The company was duly organized and incorporated in 1889, with Mr. L. Laflin as president, Mr. John P. Laflin as secretary and treasurer, and under their wise and able executive guidance a business of great magnitude was early developed. In September, 1890, the company had the misfortune to be burned out, and in July, 1891, completed its magnificent new plant, desirably located at East Chicago, Ind., where perfect transportation facilities are secured to every section of the United States and Canada. The foundry and plant cover an area of some eleven acres. The foundry has immense cupolas, a heavy molding floor, immense cranes, and the finest facilities for making and handling the heaviest castings. A specialty is made of these, such as ingot molds for steel mills, rolls for the largest sets of rolls, etc. The company employs a large force of hands, and is turning out the finest work of the kind in America, while the processes of pattern-making, molding, melting, running off, cooling and cleaning up of castings, are all conducted under the direct supervision of eminent experts. The officers are both directly at the executive head of affairs. Mr. L. Laflin is a native of the East, resident here for fully forty years past, and is a capitalist of notably sound judgment and progressive methods. Chicago owes much to him in connection with the development of various enterprises, and under his direction the East Chicago Foundry Co. gives the American public the finest possible facilities for the work of executing heavy castings. He has the valued support of his son, Mr. John P. Laflin, as secretary and treasurer, who was born in Chicago, and is an active and popular young business man. The company, with its reconstructed plant, has better facilities at command than ever, and is sure to retain permanently in Chicago the supremacy in this difficult branch of industry.

ILLINOIS STORAGE CO.

The rapid development of Chicago as the great central metropolis of the United States has been manifested in numerous ways, but in none more so than in the extended facilities afforded to our merchants for the storage and warehousing of their goods. In this connection we desire to refer specially to the reliable Illinois Storage Co., whose warehouse is located at 195 and 197 Michigan street. The company also has railroad and dockage warehouses at 544 to 554 North Water street. This company was incorporated July 1891, with a paid-up capital of $25,000, its ex-

cecutive officers being Mr. W. P. Butler, president and treasurer; Mr. B. A. May, vice-president, pro-tem, and Mr. A. H. C. Prudence, secretary and general manager. Their furniture storage warehouse on Michigan street is a substantial six-story warehouse, 40x100 feet in area, fitted up with

every convenience, elevators, etc. Their general storage warehouse on North Water street is a spacious six-story brick building having an area of 90,000 square feet, having excellent water and railway facilities, while their dock, etc., is 270x150 feet in dimensions. Negotiations are now pending looking to their having an extensive fire-proof general storage warehouse erected, second to none west of New York, in addition to those they now occupy. The company promptly and carefully stores furniture and merchandise of every description, and makes advances on warehouse receipts. The rates for storage are exceedingly moderate, and insurance is readily secured in first-class companies at low figures. Consignments of goods and merchandise are solicited, and every effort is made to give entire satisfaction to customers, all of whom will receive the same

fair and legitimate business treatment, no matter whether located in Chicago, New York, Philadelphia or Europe. The officers are widely known in business circles for their integrity and promptness, and the prospects of the Illinois Storage Co. under their guidance are of the most encouraging and favorable character. The telephone calls of the company are 3390 and 4633; the latter at docks on North Water street, as well as the former, will always receive prompt attention. Special rates for permanent storage can be had at any time.

WM. A. ELMENDORF.

There is no more prosperous concern in the city in proportion to the capital invested than the Varnish Works of Mr. William A. Elmendorf, of Nos. 38 and 40 Larrabee street, on the North side. This business was originally established twenty years ago by Elmendorf, Van Ness & Treat. In 1876 it changed to Elmendorf & Treat, and in 1878 Mr. Elmendorf obtained the entire proprietorship, and has had a very prosperous career. The factory occupies a substantial two-story brick building, 60x140 feet in size, which is fitted out complete with furnaces, kettles, and the latest improved apparatus and appliances for the manufacture of varnishes. The business of the concern exceeds $100,000 annually, and the capacity is over 600 gallons daily. He manufactures exclusively FINE VARNISHES, finishing, rubbing and japans which have a national reputation and sale in nearly every state in the central and western belt. Mr. Elmendorf is a native of New York City, and has been in Chicago since 1850. He is active and energetic, and pays close attention to his business. He was formerly the owner of the Illinois Central Car Lines Sleeping Car business, and sold out to the above company, becoming its manager of the sleeping car department for nearly seven years. He is popular in commercial and social circles, and has a high standing in the financial world. His works are taxed to the utmost to supply his trade, which is constantly increasing, on account of the excellence of his products.

HARALD M. HANSEN.

There is no profession more difficult than that of the architect, or which requires greater natural aptitudes, more study, and a larger practical experience to win success. These essential requisites have been developed in a marked degree in the case of Mr. Harald M. Hansen, the well known architect and superintendent of this city, whose office is located in room 30, at No. 88 La Salle street. This gentleman is a native of Norway, and is a graduate of the Royal Drawing and Art School of Christiana, and of the German Academy of Berlin. In 1870 he settled in Chicago, and became connected with Mr. W. L. B. Jenney, architect. He also accepted the position of professor of drawing in the Architectural School of the Art Institute of Illinois, at Champagne. He, however, soon resigned to embark in the active practice of his profession, and became connected with the house of Mr. Otto Matz, in this city. In 1872 he opened an office on his own account, and quickly gained a fine growing patronage by reason of the superior excellence of his work, and the reliability of his business methods. Mr. Hansen devotes all his time and energy to the practice of his profession, and conscientiously discharges his duty to all favoring him with commissions. His plans are always accurate and complete in every detail, while his estimates and calculations are based on the most practical and comprehensive knowledge of quantities and values. Proofs of his skill are numerous in this city, the buildings designed and erected by him are much admired by experts for their stability and elegance. He has designed and superintended the erection of the block of stores and flats for Mr. Turner, on Wrightwood avenue and N. Clark street, the residence of Dr. Landis, at No. 1115 N. Clark street, the stores, flats and bakery of Mr. H. Piper at Nos. 609 and 617 N. Wells street, the residence of Mr. Geo. Vise at No. 540 N. State street, etc., all of which stand as the best evidence of his skill and ability.

A. BLETTNER.

Owing to the great number of strangers flocking to our city there is more or less slight indisposition, due to the fact that the people are not yet acclimated, and the "corner drug store" is a favorite resort for these, where their trivial complaints may be cured without having recourse to the regular physician. Naturally a person prefers to have his prescriptions compounded by some old and reliable house, such in fact as that at No. 561 W. Twelfth street, at the corner of Loomis street, now known as Blettner's Pharmacy. This store was established more than twenty years ago by Dr. R. C. Knox, since then it has gone through various hands until in 1889 the present proprietor, Mr. A. Blettner, took charge, and retains the well-earned reputation this establishment has so long maintained. The store is one of the neatest in the city,—a blaze of plate glass,—handsome counter and show cases, containing a clean, fresh and well-selected stock of standard drugs and notions that are shown in handsome shape. Mr. Blettner is a native of Chicago, a state licensed pharmacist, and a member of the Illinois State Pharmacuetical Association. He is a young man of integrity, industry and enterprise, and enjoys a very satisfactory trade.

VIRGINIA LIVERY.

The "Virginia Livery" is in every respect, a model establishment, one that reflects the highest credit upon the proprietor, having many advanced improvements and conveniences, while the finest stock and handsome stylish vehicles can always be obtained here. The stables were opened in 1860 by the firm of Wright Brothers, succeeded by Messrs. S. F. Wright & Co., who developed widespread, influential connections, doing the finest livery business in town. In 1889 Mr. William Seymour became proprietor, succeeded in 1890 by K. E. Masterson, under whose exceptionally able and liberal management the stables have won the *preference* with the best classes of the public. The premises are centrally located at No. 250 E. Kinzie street, and comprise a substantial four-story and basement brick building, 150x100 feet in dimensions, having 137 stalls, all light, airy and convenient. At the present time they are crowded, there being 50 livery horses and 87 boarders, but the proprietor, with characteristic enterprise, has determined to give the public the accommodations so much needed, and preparations have been begun to enlarge the number of stalls to 200. It is a pleasure to inspect this well appointed and admirably kept establishment. The basement is devoted to stabling; there also are the wash-room, harness-rooms, and harness-repair shop. On the first floor is the carriage repository, where are full lines of elegant Victoria Cabs, Coupes, Phaetons, etc., ready for service at all hours of the day or night. Here also is a complete blacksmith shop, with facilities for doing all the horse shoeing needed. On this floor also are the handsomely fitted up offices, storerooms, etc., also the veterinary surgeon's office. Mr Oscar Wirth, V. S., gives special attention to the stock stabled here, and brings to bear vast practical experience. He formerly owned one of the largest liveries in England, and had charge of 5,000 horses; he is recognized as remarkably skilful, and gentlemen sending their horses here to board will have the advantage of skilled veterinary attendance. The second floor is devoted to the stabling of carriage and boarding horses, and presents an attractive appearance. On the third floor are the carriage repair and wood working shops, paint shop, etc. Fourth floor is devoted to storage. It is a great advantage to a large livery like this to have all horseshoeing, blacksmithing, repairing, painting and t'mming done upon the premises, where better work is done a 'd always promptly. The stables do all the livery busines : for the famous "Virginia Hotel," the finest on the North side, and has a private connection by wire, thus insuring an immediate response. There are also direct telephone and messenger calls for the use of the general public, and the stables are always open, day and night. Liveried coachmen are furnished on all occasions, and the best of sound, gentle and speedy stock, with elegant, well kept equipages. Ladies and gentlemen can confidently secure their vehicles here, for all purposes, park drives, calls, shopping, theaters, etc., while nowhere is such excellent service given to weddings, parties, balls, funerals, etc. Forty hands are employed, besides fifteen experienced drivers in livery. It is highly creditable to the proprietor's executive methods and abilities that such a model livery exists in Chicago, and K. E. Masterson is universally esteemed and respected, socially is popular, is valued in lending business circles, and to one and all we say, when you want a first-class livery rig, call up the "Virginia Stables."

WM. REINHOLD, M. D.

Dr. William Reinhold is a gentleman who has attained some note on the North side as proprietor of one of the oldest established pharmacies in this section of the city, Dr. William Reinhold is well-known as a naturalist of no small pretensions. The business which he now conducts was established as far back as 1860 by Mr. William Schroeder, and in 1865 he was succeeded by Moench & Reinhold. Mr. Moench retired in 1891, and Dr. Reinhold now conducts it alone. The firm was at one time on Indiana and Clark streets but was burned out at the big fire, and in 1872 removed to the present store at 146 N. Clark street, in the Clarendon Hotel. The store is very handsome and imposing, and is 25x80 feet in dimensions. A full stock of pure drugs is carried, also a great variety of toilet articles, French soaps and perfumes, fancy articles, brushes, combs, etc. He also keeps all the leading proprietary medicines; but it is in the compounding of physicians' prescriptions that Doctor Reinhold makes a specialty, and by virtue of his scientific knowledge the greatest accuracy is assured. His pharmacy and laboratory are in the rear of his store, and are well equipped with every appliance that the delicate nature of his work demands. Indeed, he manufactures all his own tinctures, essences, extracts and preparations, so that purity is assured. His staff includes skilled pharmacists, who are thoroughly well versed in the prescription business. Dr. Reinhold is a native of Germany and came to Chicago in 1863. He graduated at the Rush Medical College in the class of 1866, and is a registered member of the Illinois State Board of Pharmacy. Physicians in his section of the city invariably send their patients to Dr. Reinhold to have their prescriptions filled.

W. H. A. BROWN.

Chicago, as the great distributing center of the products of the fertile fields of the West and Northwest, numbers many merchandise and produce brokers, who are among the most useful members of the commercial world, and prominent among them is the gentleman whose name forms the caption of this sketch. Mr. W. H. A. Brown, whose office is in room 69 of the National Life building, at No. 157 La Salle street, was born in the city of New York, and removed to Chicago some fifteen years ago. He at once founded his present business as a broker and commission dealer in flaxseed, and from the start built up a large patronage. Mr. Brown is a prominent and influential member of the Chicago Board of Trade, and conducts all transactions through its channels. He buys and sells flaxseed on commission, confining his operations to the handling of this staple to the exclusion of all others. He has at his disposal the most satisfactory facilities for filling orders of any magnitude, and for placing consignments to the best advantage. His offices are neatly appointed and handsomely furnished, and are provided with every modern convenience that can facilitate the expeditious transaction of the large business done. Mr. Brown is one of Chicago's pushing and progressive business men, and is deservedly popular, alike in social and mercantile circles. He is a prominent member of the Chicago Athletic Club, and the success he has achieved in his special line of enterprise has been won by commendable merit.

HENRY HEMMELGARN.

There is no more prominent or reliable commission merchant in Chicago than Mr. Henry Hemmelgarn. He has been engaged in business in Chicago since 1865, and has had a successful and prosperous career. The business he now controls was established in 1865 under the firm name of E. Sukel & Co., Mr. Hemmelgarn being a partner. In 1871 he became the sole proprietor of this business and has continued it alone ever since. Mr. Hemmelgarn does an extensive business. He occupies the large building No. 201 East Kinzie Street; which consists of four stories and basement, 30x100 feet in dimensions. Here he carries on a general commission business in grain, produce, seeds, butter, eggs and poultry. He also does a large business in the sale of live stock at the Stock Yards He makes the sale of grain and seeds a speciality, and handles the entire products of the Corner Hill & York Centre creameries, as well as the entire stock and country products of well regulated farms. He has a large warehouse on E. Kinzie street, and utilizes storage for eggs in season outside. Consignments are received from all parts of the country by this house, which it is noted for making liberal advances and prompt returns. The business done is extensive in character, and eleven assistants are employed steadily to handle the trade from day to day. Mr. Hemmelgarn was born in Germany and came to Chicago in 1853. He is well known in leading business, financial and political circles, and is highly esteemed and respected. He was a prominent member of the county board from 1885 to 1887, during which time he was in constant warfare with the boodle members, who were afterward arraigned and some of them imprisoned. During this term Mr. Hemmelgarn did his utmost to unmask these offenders, and deserved great credit for the part taken at that time. He is a genial, amiable gentleman, and is as popular socially as he is successful.

J. P. MILLER & CO.

One of the most noted and successful firms in Chicago, engaged as contractors for boring and sinking artesian, oil and gas wells, is that of Messrs. J P. Miller & Co., whose offices are located at 45 and 47 Michigan street. This business was established in 1869 by Messrs. Spangler & Marrs, who were succeeded in 1871 by Beach & Marrs, in 1874 by Miller & Co., in 1875 by Marrs & Miller, and in 1886 by Mr. J. P. Miller. Eventually in 1890 the present firm of Messrs. J. P. Miller & Co. was organized, the co-partners being Messrs. J. P. Miller, J. Bates and L. Wilson. The partners are able and energetic contractors, who have made a complete study of the geological formations of Illinois and the adjacent states, and are recognized authorities thereon. They promptly contract for the boring and sinking of artesian wells for water, oil and gas, and guarantee entire satisfaction to patrons. The firm employ during the busy season 100 workmen and supply all necessary tools and appliances. They also deal largely in artesian well supplies, and keep a heavy and first-class stock constantly on hand. Orders are carefully attended to, and prices charged for all work are exceedingly just and moderate. The firm have been very successful in their contracts, and refer by permission to the following, viz: Armour & Co., Packers, Chicago, Ill.; M. Brand, Brewer, Chicago, Ill.; Butcher's Association, Dubuque, Iowa; Bohemian Cemetery Co., Irving Park, Ill.; Chicago and N. W R. R. Co., Chicago, Ill.; Chicago Packing Co., Chicago, Ill.; City of Olney. Ill.; City of Pekin, Ill.; City of Barry, Ill.; Sioux City, Iowa: City of Canton, Ill.; City of Mitchell, D. T ; City of East Dubuque, Ill.; City of Keokuk (Round Park), Iowa: City of Geneva (Kane County Court House) Ill.; City of Madison, Wis.; City of Appleton. Wis.; City of Tomah, Wis.; City of DeKalb, Ill.; City of Peoria, Ill.; Judge J. D. Caton, Caton Stock Farms, Ill.; Chicago and Grand Trunk R. R. Co., Chicago, Ill.; Chicago Distilling Co., Chicago, Ill.; F. J. Dewes' Brewing Co.,Chicago, Ill.; M. Engleman, Manistee, Mich.; N. K. Fairbank & Co., Chicago, Ill.; Fowler Bros., Packers, Chicago,Ill.; F. Falk, Brewer, Milwaukee, Wis.; Forest Home Cemetery, Milwaukee, Wis.; Glucose Works, Geneva, Ill ; Gottfried Brewing Co., Chicago, Ill.;

C. Geis, Brewer, Council Bluffs, Iowa; Glucose Manufacturing Co., Davenport, Iowa; Geo. W. Higgins, Packer, Union Stock Yards, Chicago, Ill.; Insane Asylum, Milwaukee, Wis.; Julien House, Dubuque, Iowa; Joliet Prison, Major McClaughry, warden, Joliet, Ill.; Col. Jacobs, Banker, Milwaukee, Wis.; John Johnston, Asst. Cashier, Mitchell's Bank, Milwaukee, Wis.; Sister Joseph, Chicago, Ill.; Lorrimer House, Dubuque, Iowa; N. Morris, Packer, Chicago, Ill.; A. Mitchell, Banker, Milwaukee, Wis.; Michigan City Prison, Michigan City, Ind.; C. Moerlein, Brewer, Cincinnati, Ohio; Milk Condensing Co., Elgin, Ill.; Moline Paper Co., Moline, Ill.; Peter McGeogh, Chas. Mills, Distiller, Covington, Ky.; Powell, Distiller, Chicago, Ill.; Phoenix Distillery, Distillery, Ill.; Ryerson, Hills & Co., Muskegon, Mich.; Racine Hardware Manufacturing Co., Racine, Wis.; M. D. Ringland, Hamilton, Ill.; Chas. Rietz & Bro., Manistee, Mich.; G. W. Robinson, Jr., & Co., Distillers, Cincinnati, Ohio; Soldiers' Home, Milwaukee, Wis.; Steam Supply Co., Dubuque, Iowa: Sterling Water Works Co., Sterling, Ill.; Smelting Works, Chicago, Ill ; Swift & Co., Packers, Chicago, Ill.; H. H. Shnfeldt & Co , Distillers, Chicago, Ill.: Union Stock Yards Co., Chicago, Ill , Water Works Co., Yankton, D. T., and S. M. Wiley Construction Co., Adrian, Mich. Mr. Miller was born in Ohio, Mr. Bates in England, and Mr. Wilson in Michigan. They undertake the most difficult and extensive contracts, and no more reliable and honorable contractors can be found in this important business. The telephone call of the firm is 3620.

DUNLAP SMITH & CO.

No form of investment has become so popular with the conservative, public as judiciously selected real estate, for not only is a permanent source of income assured, but there is a reasonable certainty of increase in values. In no other city on the American continent is this fact more patent than in Chicago, where the rapid development of the real estate market, and the rapidly enhancing values of choice property, render the financial interests involved of immense importance, requiring the retention of the services of a reliable and responsible real estate broker of necessity to those who wish to place their investments in a careful and business like manner. Among the leading representative real estate brokers to whose ably directed efforts the rapid progress of the city is largely due, we can sincerely commend to the attention of our readers Mr. Dunlap Smith, whose offices are situated on the ground floor of the First National Bank building, at the corner of Dearborn and Monroe streets. Mr. Smith founded this business in 1890, under the firm name of Dunlap Smith & Co., and has since conducted it with great ability and success, carrying through to a successful issue many most important transactions. He is locally thoroughly posted, having a complete and intimate knowledge of every section, as well as of the growing suburbs, and those contemplating the purchase of property can fully rely upon his sound judgment and judicious advice to secure the most desirable and remunerative investments. He is deservedly prominent as a real estate and mortgage broker, and his business has been developed by judicious and honorable management to proportions of great and gratifying magnitude. He is doing a general real estate business, buying, selling, renting and exchanging property, negotiating loans on bond and mortgage at favorable rates, and taking full charge of landed estates. His facilities for effecting sales are of a very superior character, and he is at all times able to offer investors a choice from a long list of eligibly situated properties. The firm pay especial attention to North Shore property, and keep thoroughly posted on all matters pertaining thereto. They rent property on a ninety-nine years' lease, and all their investments are considered safe and judicious at West Kenilworth, on the North Shore, fifteen miles from the center of the city, and on the line of the C. & N. W. Mr. Smith is a native of Chicago. He enjoys the highest of reputations for honorable methods and sterling integrity, and is greatly aiding in maintaining that high standard of financial probity which characterizes the real estate market of Chicago. The telephone call of the office is 877.

W. D. GRANT.

A letter, and even a comma, has at times, by misplacement, altered the entire significance of a document, and we doubt not, if this were traced still further, such an error may have directed the destiny of many a human life. So it is of the utmost importance that any commercial documents, which partake in the slightest degree of an official character, should be printed by a firm whose correctness is beyond

BOARD OF TRADE WORK A SPECIALTY.

question, and such a firm is that of W. D. Grant, stationer and printer, room D, Traders' Building, to Pacific avenue, who prints largely the documents and official forms used in connection with the Chicago Board of Trade. W. D. Grant established his business in March, 1889, and brought into it a complete commercial knowledge. He out of the nine years during which he has resided in Chicago was engaged for five and a half years in the responsible position as clerk for two prominent Board of Trade firms. In addition to printing and stationery he keeps every kind of office supplies, does lithographing and engraving, also manufactures blank books. His printing office is at 1060 Claxton Building, Dearborn street, and here he has as complete a modern printing office as can be found in the city for its size. No expense has been spared to introduce every improvement for the purpose of turning out perfect work, and the very fact that Mr. Grant receives so large a share of public patronage shows that his work must be of a superior quality. He is a native of New York state, and since his residence in Chicago has made a large number of valued and influential friends.

H. REINHARDT.

A strictly first-class merchant tailoring establishment, in every sense of the word, is that conducted by Mr. Henry Reinhardt, at No. 406 State street. The building is a four-story brick and stone structure, one of three, which together form a fine block, owned by Mr. Reinhardt. This gentleman is himself a practical cutter and tailor of the highest order. He has been established in the business down town ever since 1863, first on State and afterwards on Clark street. He had a select down-town trade, which would not abandon him and has followed him to his present location, where he moved in 1890. He has made money during the long years he has been engaged in the business, and is now well-to-do. After erecting the fine block, of which he is the owner, he concluded to occupy

one store himself, partly for the satisfaction of being on his own premises and partly because he regarded the rents he was compelled to pay down town extortionately high. It is to these circumstances that the South End is indebted for the presence of an establishment of this high character. A large and elegant stock of materials is carried, including the finest imported goods. Six assistants are employed, all thorough workmen of the best grade, and only first class custom work is done. The store is 25x75 feet in size and affords ample room for a fine, select stock of gents' furnishing goods, which is carried as a side line. Mr. Reinhardt, the proprietor of this elegant establishment, was born in Germany, but has passed the best years of his life in Chicago, where he is an honored and respected citizen, as well as a solid business man. He is a member of the Masonic Order and of the National Union, in both of which organizations his standing is of the best and highest.

EDW. G. BINZ & CO.

One of the most active and enterprising of South side pharmacists is Mr. Edward G. Binz, conducting business under the firm style of Edw. G. Binz & Co., at No. 4259 Wentworth avenue, corner of Forty-third street. The business was established here in 1888, by Mr. Binz, under whose able and efficient management it has enjoyed a continuously prosperous career to date. He occupies a fine and neatly fitted corner store, 15x 30 feet in dimensions, wherein he keeps at all times a well assorted stock of drugs and medicines, chemicals, etc., likewise all the approved proprietary remedies and a miscellaneous assortment of articles in the lines of perfumery, soaps, brushes and other toilet articles. Mr. Binz has built up a first-class local trade, and one which is constantly developing under his close personal attention. He makes a prominent specialty of compounding physicians' prescriptions in the best possible and most accurate manner, and has a large patronage from the neighboring medical fraternity. All orders are promptly filled by day or night, physicians telephoned for free of charge, and no effort on the part of Mr. Binz is spared to please and satisfy each and every one of his patrons, lay and professional. His beef, iron and wine is universally conceded to be one of the best preparations on the market. He is a native of Germany, and a highly respected resident of Chicago for the past twenty-four years.

UNION STEAM BOILER WORKS.

The manufacture and repair of boilers, etc., is rapidly assuming proportions of great magnitude in Chicago, both as regards the number of firms engaged and the immense section of country covered by the trade. One of the most prominent establishments in this line is that of the Union Steam Boiler Works, located at Nos. 36 to 42 East Indiana street, of which Mr. James Leonard is the esteemed proprietor. This gentleman is a master of his trade, being thoroughly expert in all its details and having a long experience that dates back for years beyond the establishment of the works in 1880. He manufactures marine, stationary and locomotive boilers, water towers, lard tanks, coolers and sheet iron work of all kinds. He devotes special attention to repairing, which often requires the exercise of great ingenuity, attending to all orders promptly and executing all commissions with the greatest success. His fine premises, seventy-five by one hundred feet in dimensions, are well equipped with machinery of a modern type, driven by an engine of twenty-five horse power, and he has every facility for the production of the heaviest articles in the highest style of workmanship. Orders are constantly being received from every part of the middle and southern states, and his reputation is extending rapidly to all sections of the country. Mr. Leonard is a native of Columbus, Ohio, but came here in 1876. He is a business man of high ability, a most reliable authority on all matters connected with his line, and a popular citizen, who deservedly enjoys the confidence and respect of a wide and constantly increasing circle.

THE AMERICAN TEA CO.

One of the most enterprising and successful business houses in this busy section of the city is that of Messrs. Langan Bros., importers and dealers in teas, coffees and spices, located at 330 W. Twelfth street between Johnson and Brown streets. This business was established August, 1891, by Messrs. Joseph P. and John M. Langan, who had for five years previously been connected with the great Atlantic and Pacific Tea Co. The premises occupied consist of the ground floor and basement of a fine four-story brown stone building at the number and street indicated in this sketch. The store is 20x120 feet in dimensions, with large plate glass windows on two sides. The interior of the store is finely decorated and tastefully fitted with every convenience necessary for both patrons and proprietors, and the stock carried is the largest and most complete to be found in this vicinity. In teas, coffees and pure spices their store cannot be surpassed, Mr. Joseph P. Langan being an expert buyer of teas and coffees and makes it a special feature of his business to cater to the individual tastes of his customers. Only the choicest selections of Oolong, Ceylon, Congo and Gunpowder teas are kept in stock, while in coffees the line carried is equally choice and full. The spices sold are the purest, and customers can be assured that they contain no adulterations. In addition to the above line of goods Langan Bros. deal in butter, eggs, cheese, dried fruits, canned goods of the best brands and table delicacies and condiments of many varieties. The butter sold at this establishment is of the freshest and choicest "gilt edge" classes, and among them will be found Pure Elgin Creamery, Best Iowa Creamery, Choice Creamery and the best Dairy butter. Messrs. Langan spare no efforts to please their patrons, and all orders are promptly delivered to any part of the city, while orders are called for and delivered in the same prompt manner at the residences of customers, thus insuring a great saving of time and trouble. Messrs. Langan are natives of Ireland. They are young energetic business men, and by their prompt business methods, and their polite attention to those having business relations with them, have won enviable reputations.

AMERICAN COPPER, BRASS & IRON WORKS.

In the manufacture of Brewers', Distillers' and Sugar Refining Apparatus, a representative and progressive concern in Chicago, is that known as the American Copper, Brass & Iron Works, located at Nos. 113 to 119 Michigan street, corner La Salle avenue. This flourishing business was established in 1867 by Mr. C. Kattentidt, who conducted it till 1890, when it was incorporated under the laws of Illinois, with a paid up capital of $25,000, and its trade now extends throughout the entire United States and Canada, also Mexico and South America. The officers of the company are, Mr. Otto Meinshausen, president and treasurer; Mr. H. Meinshausen, secretary, and Mr. C. Kattentidt, superintendent. They occupy a spacious four-story brick building, 80x100 feet in dimensions, which was erected by Mr. Kattentidt in 1878. The various departments are fully supplied with special machinery, tools and appliances, operated by a 35 horse-power steam engine. Here 80 first-class workmen are employed, who turn out in a superior manner all kinds of brewers', distillers' and sugar refining apparatus, confectioners' machinery, in copper, dyers' cylinders, soda fountain apparatus, etc. Their productions are unrivalled for utility, efficiency and reliability, and have no superiors in the market, while the prices quoted in all cases are extremely just and moderate. They are thoroughly practical coppersmiths, brass-founders, finishers and iron tank workers, and spare neither time nor pains to give entire satisfaction to patrons. Orders are carefully attended to, and they have done a large amount of work in the city for leading brewers, maltsters, distillers and confectioners. The officers were all born in Germany, but have resided in Chicago many years. They are honorable and able business men, whose trade is steadily increasing, owing to the intrinsic merits and superiority of their production.

EXCELSIOR ELECTRIC COMPANY.

The truly marvelous progress made in controlling that subtle and mysterious agent, electricity, during the past few decades, and the application thereof to multifarious utilitarian purposes, certainly have no parallel in the domain of the arts and sciences in modern times. The advance made in the direction indicated is one of the distinctly notable features that mark this progressive age in which we live; and the possibilities therein are virtually beyond conception. What with discovery, invention and improvements, something akin to perfection has been attained in electrical apparatus, both for lighting and power purposes, by some of our leading manufacturers, in which connection special mention is due the Excelsior Electric Company (Hochhausen system), main office 115 Broadway, New York, with factory at 216 Willoughby street, Brooklyn, and whose Chicago office, with Herbert Wadsworth, as western manager, is at room 425 in the "Rookery Building." They turn out a class of electrical appliances of a highly meritorious character—of exceptional excellence indeed—and of the superiority of their production, assuredly no more unfailing criterion could be adduced than the widespread sale the same command. They manufacture arc and incandescent lights, arc and incandescent motors, alternating current motors and generators, also electro-plating and depositing machines, and their trade, which is exceedingly large, extends all over the United States. They are prepared to furnish estimates on all classes of work in the line indicated, the construction and equipping of electric lighting and power plant complete being a specialty, and all contracts undertaken by this responsible concern are certain to be performed in the most expeditious, competent and trustworthy manner. The Excelsior Electric Co., of which H. D. Fuller is president, and Wm. Hochhausen, electrician, was organized in 1874, the Chicago office being established at the same time, and from its inception the enterprise has been a highly successful venture, the business rapidly growing and extending. Mr. Wadsworth, the company's representative in this city, is a gentleman of middle age and a native of Maine. He is a thoroughly practical and skilful electrician, as well as a man of energy and excellent business ability, being an expert in his line, and prior to assuming his present position, some two years ago, had been with the Thomson-Houston Co. of this city, for a number of years.

D. H. DICKINSON.

The substantial and elegant manner in which Chicago has been built, together with the artistic effects attempted in all parts of the city, have made this a market of great importance for fine marble of all kinds. The house of Mr. D. H. Dickinson has for many years been known as one of the most important in importing and dealing in American and Italian marble. The business was established in 1870 by Mr. Dickinson, and at the time of the great fire he occupied the premises located at 310 to 316 N. Water street. Here he met with a total loss of building and stock. After the fire he occupied a new building, at the same place, and continued there until 1886, when he removed to his present location. Mr. Dickinson now occupies the two-story, corrugated iron building at 558 to 570 N. Water street. This is a mammoth concern, being 200x125 feet in dimensions, and is equipped with the latest improved machinery and appliances used in handling and working marble. He has two rubbing beds, four gouger saws, eight turning lathes, large steam derrick and other machinery, including the full steam power plant. About sixty experienced workmen are employed and an extensive business is carried on, in supplying the trade with manufactured marble for monumental purposes, as well as rough stock. Mr. Dickinson was born in 1843, is a native of Chatteauguay, near Montreal, Can.; he was reared in Chicago and has been for years identified with her leading business interests. He is a prominent member of the G. A. R. and a thirty-second degree Mason; he served as a sergeant in the 36th Illinois regiment and was afterward quartermaster in the 16th U. S. colored infantry.

HALL SIGNAL CO.

The Hall Signal Co. of 50 Broadway, New York, and 340 The Rookery, Chicago, are manufacturers of all kinds of Electric and Mechanical Signaling apparatus for railroads. The Hall Automatic Electric Block Signal System is in operation on twenty-one of the leading railroads of this country. On the opposite page is shown an application of the Hall highway crossing alarm bell at S. Union street, Chicago. Regarding the Hall highway crossing alarm bell the following letter is of interest:

NEW YORK, NEW HAVEN & HARTFORD RAILROAD CO,
New Haven Station, Sept. 2, 1891.

Gentlemen:—In reply to yours of the 31st ult. regarding the Hall Highway Crossing Bells I would say that we have in use on the different divisions of the N. Y., N. H. & H. R. R., seventy-one highway crossing gate and station bells. The first application of these bells was made in 1883. In all that time they have never failed to perform the service required of them, and the Hall bell has been adopted as the standard bell of this road after a thorough test of all other bells in the market. They are giving entire satisfaction to the officials of our road in every respect, and I take pleasure in recommending them to any road desiring an absolutely reliable highway crossing bell. Very truly,

(Signed)   WINSLOW STEVENS, Electrician.

This company is also the manufacturers of electric distant signals for switches, electric interlocked signals, one with another, the Bezer lock and block system, and the Bezer and Burley interlocking machines.

ACME COPYING CO.

The development of fine arts of recent years has been upon a basis of practical efficiency and enlarged facilities that enables every member of every family in the land to secure an enlarged portrait suitable for framing, and of an accuracy and fidelity to the subject, that previously would have cost hundreds of dollars, now placed at moderate figures, including rich and elegant frames. All the concerns engaged in the copying or enlarging of pictures, are not of equal merit, far from it. On the contrary, the reliable, responsible ones that we can recommend are few in number. The best and most representative concern in the United States, with which to have dealings, is unquestionably the "Acme Copying Company" of 302 and 304 W. Van Buren street. It was established in 1877, and early achieved an enviable reputation for the superiority of its portraits. Eventually, in 1887, the important interests involved were duly incorporated, with Mr. A. D. Lutz, as president; Mr. W. S. Chamberlain, as secretary; and Mr. C. E. Lutz, as treasurer; and under their exceptionally and able equitable management, the company has gone on increasing its business at a rapid ratio, as the following figures demonstrate. Portraits produced and sold in 1886, 25,000; in 1887, 40,000; in 1888, 82,000; in 1889, 85,000; and in 1890, over 100,000, so on annually increasing. A magnificent building has been specially erected by the company, designed in every way to meet the most advanced requirements. The main structure is three stories and basement in height, and 125 feet in depth; adjoining is the studio, considered the best arranged and equipped in the United States. All the goods are made and finished on the premises. The negatives and prints are made by electric light, which can be used on dark and cloudy days as well as on fine days, thus preventing any delay whatsoever. The company's electric light plant is a complete one, having a large number of lamps, and not only provides an abundance of light for photographing, but also for illuminating the building throughout. Their large studios comfortably seat fifty artists, and thirty air brushes are operated, producing the finest grades of portrait work. They employ in and about their establishment over 100 employes. The company promptly fills all orders; it enjoys the best facilities of any house in America; and picture men can rely on always getting

their goods when promised. The company produces all kinds of crayons, pastelles, water colors, etc., and has the largest and most elegant stock of frames to select from. Their "Bonanza" style of portrait has proved the most popular and successful of any ever presented to the American public. It is the best and most profitable for live agents to handle, as they give absolute satisfaction to the most critical. Their celebrated Acme portraits are also deservedly popular, being made of best material and never fading or changing tone. A large variety of styles can be had here, including their beautiful grade "F," the most expensive portrait they make, elegantly hatched, strippled and toned, and a magnificent work of art. To those who seek a very profitable, pleasant and honorable source of employment we would strongly recommend to secure an outfit from this responsible company, and go to work. They cannot fail to do well, and their best references will be their old customers. Mr. A. D. Lutz is especially qualified to successfully guide the company's operations. He and his associates are gentlemen of ability and integrity, and the company is maintained on a plane of efficiency, unapproached by any other concern whatsoever

J. C. BORCHERDT.

The public is becoming more exacting every day as to the service rendered by those whom it intrusts with important functions, and what more valuable and important duty can devolve upon any one than that of dispensing remedies for the ailments of humanity? The pharmacist must conform to the strict and exacting requirements of the statutes before he can practice his calling. He must then prove his fitness for the important work he has set himself to do before the public will implicitly trust him and confidingly swallow his preparations. A singularly happy combination of all the necessary aids to success and preferment;—thorough knowledge of the business, aptness and fitness for the work, long and successful experience as pharmacist and druggist,—are the weighty credentials and indorsements presented by Dr. J. C. Borcherdt, pharmacist. For nearly a quarter of a century Dr. Borcherdt has been before the public as a dispensing druggist, and by conscientious and faithful services has gained his present high station in his calling. His pharmacy at 735 West Madison street is one of the best known institutions in the city. It is completely stocked and equipped, carrying an immense stock of pure standard drugs and chemicals; a fine assortment of surgical instruments and druggists' sundries, toilet and fancy goods; and all the reliable family remedies and proprietary medicines and preparations. The furnishings and appointments of the store are of the most approved modern pattern, and include a fine marble soda fountain for the dispensing of the numerous health-giving summer beverages so popular with the people. There is also kept on hand for the delectation of smokers a fine stock of cigars, choice brands of foreign and domestic production. Dr. Borcherdt prepares a long list of extracts, tinctures and preparations of exceptional value and merit. His chief specialty in this line is the well-known Extract of Malt bearing his name, and which is the oldest and best known malt extract for medicinal purposes on the market. Dr. Borcherdt is the pioneer in the production of medicinal malt extracts, which now hold a high rank in the estimation of the medical profession. Dr. Borcherdt is a native of Buffalo, New York. He has resided in Chicago thirty-eight years, twenty-four of which have been spent in the drug business. He is a registered pharmacist under the Illinois State Board of Pharmacy, a member of the American Pharmaceutical Association and a trustee of the Chicago College of Pharmacy. These facts attest better than words of loftiest import to his exceptional standing and ability in his calling and the profound interest he takes in his chosen calling. Dr. Borcherdt's history would be incomplete without a reference to his military career. He served his country with great credit through the late civil war in the old 49th New York Infantry. He entered the service a private, and rose to the rank of captain. He is an active member of the G. A. R., and is universally respected and esteemed by his fellow men.

HALL SIGNAL CO.

ADOLPH LURIE.

An enormous stock of elegant dry goods, fancy goods, notions, ladies' and gents' furnishing goods, carpets, in fact, of everything that goes to make a palace of trade complete, is presented by the very enterprising house of Adolph Lurie, located at 561 and 563 Blue Island avenue. The spacious establishment occupies the ground floor of a three-story stone building, and covers an area of 3,200 square feet, having a frontage of forty feet on Blue Island avenue. It was established by the present genial proprietor in 1873 on a very elaborate scale, and has since that period constantly grown in proportions. A furtive glance cast into the interior of the neatly arranged store reveals an extensive line of dress goods, comprising henriettas, homespuns, cheviots, korah, moire, and an exceedingly select assortment of imported challies at remarkably low prices. Grenadines, rhadames and India silks are very attractively displayed on well-finished oaken counters. Ladies' challie tea-gowns, tan Stanley capes, sateen and flannel outing suits, ladies' and misses' fine gauge fast black lisle hose, lisle jersey vests, tucks and hamburg edge—these and others, are some of the greatest bargains ever offered for sale. The notion and fancy goods departments are fully and as adequately equipped. It is futile to attempt to do justice to the immense stock and first-class grade of goods that are kept by Adolph Lurie, by mere description. The success of Mr. Lurie's enterprise is attributable in the first place to an innate business tact, secondly to the ability of exactly judging the wants of his patrons, and last, but not least, to his strict attention to business, to his never failing courtesy and to a keen and precise effort to please every one, be they poor or rich, man, woman or child. At the present writing the establishment has sixteen employes, all of which are experienced, capable and accommodating. Mr. Lurie is a native of Germany, but has resided in this city over twenty years. His long experience in business enables him to point back with pleasure to the record and reputation which have, by reason of his own efforts, been made for Lurie's, 561 and 563 Blue Island avenue.

A. E. THOMPSON.

Since the inception of this enterprise in 1884, when it was first opened as a pharmacy by Mr. C. O. Sethness, the store has become one of the most popular centers of trade in the locality, and situated as it is at 1218 Milwaukee avenue, at the corner of Robey street, it is most eligibly located for the control of a first-class patronage. In 1889 the present proprietor, Mr. A. E. Thompson, assumed possession, and by the manner in which he has since conducted the business he has shown his perfect adaptability to the conduct of a first-class drug store. The premises occupied are very large, being 25x75 feet in dimensions, including a well-appointed pharmacy, and laboratory in the rear, and while speaking of the pharmacy we may say that a specialty is made of the compounding of physicians' prescriptions, over which Mr. Thompson himself maintains a complete supervision, and is ably supported by competent graduate assistants. This branch of the business is conducted by day and night. The stock carried is at once attractive and even to the uninitiated shows an unusual display of care in selection. Besides pure drugs and chemicals, it comprises all the proprietary medicines and remedies of standard merit and reputation, toilet accessories, soap, perfumes, sponges, surgical appliances and instruments, sick room needs, mineral waters and pure wines and liquors for medicinal purposes, sanitary preparations, sponges, brushes and combs, chamois, fancy goods, and indeed everything that may rightly be comprehended under the head of druggists' sundries. Mr. Thompson was born in McHenry County, Ill., and has been in Chicago for ten years. He is a graduate of the Chicago College of Pharmacy, class 1886, and was formerly in the employ of J. C. Borcher, and later with R. T. Sill. He is therefore a thoroughly competent pharmacist.

N. J. SANDBERG.

One of the most popular house furnishing establishments on the North side is that of Mr. N. J. Sandberg, who is located at 360, 362 and 364 E. Division street. Mr. Sandberg has been established in this business since 1872, at the same location. He is a native of Sweden, and came to the United States thirty-five years ago. After residing in Milwaukee, Wis., some years, he came to Chicago in 1869, and engaged in business. He built the elegant establishment he occupies in 1886, and has an excellent three-story brick building, 75x125 feet in dimension, of which he uses the ground floor and basement. He has just finished a fine addition in the rear. He has three stone fronts and carries a complete and well selected stock of house furnishing goods of all kinds. Number 360 store is devoted to household goods, crockery and glassware, stoves, tinware, etc. Number 362 is used for carpets, rugs, matting, curtains and all kinds of decorations. Number 364 contains the parlor and chamber suits, fancy goods and upholstered goods. Every department is well stocked with superior goods, and these are sold at the lowest prices for cash or on easy payments. Mr. Sandberg has built up a business of great strength and popularity. He is favored with a large and first-class patronage and finds his business constantly increasing. He employs eight clerks, and utilizes three delivery teams. He is a well-known gentleman in business circles, and is respected everywhere for his uprightness and integrity.

C. H. STRONG & CO.

No book on Chicago's trade would be complete without a prominent allusion to Strong's Arnica Soaps and preparations, and we would urge the thousands who see this notice between now and the World's Fair to become acquainted with these excellent preparations by asking their druggists for them. All of us are familiar with the cards containing a dozen neat little red tin boxes of Strong's Arnica Tooth

soap, which are generally displayed on the counter of a drug store, and in addition to this tooth soap they are the sole manufacturers and proprietors of Strong's arnica jelly, arnica toilet soap, arnica shaving soap, veterinary arnica jelly, Robertson's Infallible corn cure, De Leon's cocoa hair-dressing, etc. These goods are sold only to the drug trade, and the demand is increasing daily. They are absolutely pure and sell themselves. Their flavors are extra strong and they are conveniently packed for traveling, as they cannot break or leak. The business was established in 1875 by C. H. Strong & Co., and in 1883 Mr. Strong retired and Mr. Frank Andrews succeeded him, retaining the name of the old firm. They occupy the fourth floor at 185 to 189 Madison street, and manufacture their specialties there. Its area is about 50x120 so, that they have ample room. Their trade is from the Atlantic to the Pacific and from the lakes to the gulf. They employ traveling men and Mr. Andrews, who is exceedingly popular himself, travels at times. He was born in Ohio and has been in Chicago fourteen years, and has made a name in the druggist specialty line that speaks only praise for him.

JOHN FEATHERSTONE'S SONS.

The present age is undoubtedly one of the greatest progress, and every year witnesses new triumphs in the world of invention. Perfection is rapidly approaching in all kinds of machinery, and nowhere is this more clearly to be seen than in the production of steam engines. In this connection we desire to direct special attention, in this Commercial Review of Chicago, to the representative and successful firm of Messrs. John Featherstone's Sons, iron founders and manufacturers of the famous Corliss steam engines, whose works are located at 2 to 36 Front street, and 354 to 358 N. Halsted street. This extensive business was established in 1870 by Mr. John Featherstone who conducted it till 1888 with great success, when he died after an honorable career. He was succeeded by the present concern of John Featherstone's Sons, which has been duly incorporated under the laws of Illinois with a paid up capital of $600,000, his sons being the executive officers, viz: Mr. Geo. Featherstone president; Mr. John Featherstone, vice-president; and Mr. A. J. Featherstone, treasurer and secretary. Their works have an area of several acres, and have excellent railway and water facilities. The machine shop is a substantial three-story brick building, 200x100 feet, while the foundry is a spacious one-story structure, 200x300 feet in dimensions. The various departments are fully equipped with the latest improved tools, machinery and appliances, operated by a superior 250-horse power steam engine. Here 300 skilled workmen are employed, and the trade of the company, which is steadily increasing, now extends throughout the entire United States and Canada. They make a specialty of the manufacture of the celebrated Corliss steam engines, and also build promptly to order marine engines and special machinery of every description. Jobbing is also promptly attended to, and all descriptions of railroad and general castings of the finest quality are turned out. They have built a number of Corliss engines, and are now largely engaged in the manufacture of the renowned consolidated ice machines for leading breweries, ice companies, etc. They have done work for the following well-known concerns: F. A. Poth Brewing Co., Philadelphia; Peter Doelgers' Brewery, New York; Consumers' Ice Company, New York; Glenn Ice Company, New York; International Packing Co., Chicago; Northwestern Brewery, Chicago; Star Brewing Co., Chicago and the India Wharf Brewing Co., of Brooklyn, New York, for whom they have just furnished a complete refrigerating plant of the latest approved pattern. The engines are unrivaled for efficiency, speed and reliability, and are the embodiments of mechanical workmanship of the highest order of perfection. They are admirably adapted for all kinds of service and have proved their superiority when brought into competition with those of other makers. It will be apparent that the greatest care and scientific researches of years have been exercised to bring these engines to their present point of perfection, and in spite of their superiority the prices quoted for them are exceedingly just and moderate. The officers are all natives of Chicago, where they are highly esteemed in trade circles for their mechanical skill, enterprise and sterling integrity. This company is one of Chicago's most valued factors in the line of skilled industry, and has before it an ever widening career of usefulness.

JARVIS WINE AND BRANDY COMPANY.

The Jarvis Wine and Brandy Company, 39 N. State street, was organized in 1890 under the laws of Illinois by some capitalists of Chicago, for the purpose of carrying a large stock of California wines and brandies, manufactured by the G. M. Jarvis Co., whose headquarters are at Santa Clara, Cal. The Jarvis Wine and Brandy Company carry a very heavy stock of wines and brandies, and by so doing, the stock becomes "aged," and the trade, which is very large, east of Omaha, is supplied in any quantity and with promptness. This business had its origin as far back as 1853, during which year Mr. G. M. Jarvis, president and general manager of the G. M. Jarvis

Company, made a tour of the world, visiting South America, Africa, Australia, Tasmania, New Zealand, Tahita and the Sandwich Islands, and soon after made his home in California. In 1860 Mr. Jarvis planted the now celebrated vineyards at Vine Hill, Santa Cruz County, Cal., and since that time a large coast trade has been supplied from these vineyards. In 1885 the business was incorporated with a capital of $50,000, the main office and distillery being located at Santa Clara, Cal., G. M. Jarvis, president and general manager; Miss Maggie Jarvis, secretary and business manager; Ed. K. Jarvis, distiller and wine maker; Ward M. Jarvis, salesman and outside buyer. The "Jarvis Wine Company" of Omaha, is an offshoot of the home company and is under the management of T. C. Jarvis, who controls the states of Iowa, Nebraska and Colorado, and is doing a good paying and careful business. The capacity of the distillery is 2,000 tons yearly, and while they make all that their eastern branches sell, they also supply a large share of the trade of California and Oregon. The Jarvis Wine and Brandy Company of Chicago, has built up a large and lucrative eastern trade, supplying some three thousand dealers, some of whom are the largest wholesale druggists in the United States, and in their price lists the Jarvis goods are all quoted at the highest price, showing that if their customers want the best they must pay probably a little more for the Jarvis goods, but that they are beyond question the very best on the market. The Jarvis Riesling grape brandy is their specialty, vintage 1877. It has taken many premiums at the California state fairs and district fairs, also won the first premium gold medal at the World's Fair at New Orleans. The eminent surgeon and medical director of the U. S. army, Dr. Basil Morris, says: "While you can supply such pure goods, with such fine quality and flavor, there will be no need of us buying imported brandy." Mr. G. M. Jarvis, the pioneer and starter of this company, and who has always been at the front as president and general manager, is now sixty-three years old, and he has laid the foundation of a grand and remunerative business. J. F. Jarvis is the practical business manager at 39 N. State street, while G. M. Jarvis, jr., a young man of twenty-one, assists in a general way. The business is yearly increasing, and is at present highly satisfactory.

SELLSTROM & KILBY.

In the production and consumption of artistic wearing apparel Chicago is rapidly coming to the front. Our aesthetic cousins down East have for years found endless diversion in poking fun at Chicago's "Wild West" fashions and manners. But that day is long since past, and Chicago's streets will show as many well-dressed men as any of her older and more censorious cities along the Atlantic coast. Great numbers of artistic tailoring establishments are to be found in the business district of the city, and they are well patronized is self-evident. Messrs. Sellstrom and Kilby, Artistic Tailors, 45 Wells street, near C. N. W. R. R. depot, is one of the leading North side establishments in this line. This business was established in 1888 by Nelson & Sellstrom. One year ago Mr. Nelson retired, and Mr. M. E. Kilby was admitted to the firm. This firm does fine custom work only and gives employment to eleven skilful workmen. They are very popular people in their line of trade, and have a very large patronage on their side of the city. Their stock is large and well selected, comprising a fine display of foreign and domestic woolens, including broadcloths of English, French and German looms; diagonals, serges, crepe cloths, cheviots, meltons, tweeds and cassimeres in a great variety of stylish patterns. They are prepared to turn out at short notice first class work in the line of military and band uniforms, also civic society uniforms, in which line of business they have unexcelled facilities and a large experience. Both members of the firm are practical men and thoroughly well posted in their trades. They have an extensive acquaintance throughout the city and are building up a fine trade. Mr. Sellstrom is a native of Sweden and has lived in Chicago nine years. Mr. Kilby is a native of New York state and has spent twelve years in Chicago. Their store is neatly furnished and the goods are tastefully displayed.

FIRNHABER & CO.

The business now conducted by Messrs. Firnhaber & Co. has commended itself to the approval of the public for the last eleven years, when it was established by Mr. J. W. Baker, and in 1882 Mr. Chas. Chamberlain succeeded him. He was in turn succeeded in 1888 by Mr. E. A. Hudson, who gave way to the present firm in 1891. Their yard and storage sheds at 790 and 792 W. Van Buren streets, near Hoyne avenue, cover an area of 37½x93 feet, and in rear of this is their stable. They employ a full force of hands and horses and teams to deliver coal, wood, coke, hay, grain or feed to all parts of the city. Their telephone call is 7188, and orders sent over the wire receive their prompt and instant attention. They make a specialty of baled hay, receiving same in carloads from the producing centers, and therefore are able to sell it at the lowest possible figures. Their coal is all screened and full weight, and they sell it by the ton or carload, and their stock of hard and soft wood is also cut and sawed to any size desired, and will be delivered by the cord or load. The firm consists of Mr. W. R. Firnhaber and Mr. O. W. Schutt, both young men, but full of business life and energy, and trustworthy to a fault. Mr. Firnhaber is a native of Chicago, and a member of the Sons of Veterans. Mr. Schutt is a native of Germany and has been in Chicago eight years. He is a member of the Mutual Protection Association.

FRANK SCHRAGE.

Among the leading druggists of this city, Mr. Frank Schrage occupies an important position. He has been established in the business for twelve years, and at one time managed a store for Gale & Blocki, He is an experienced and practical druggist and chemist, and is very popular with his patrons and the medical profession. He occupies the premises located at the corner of Clark street and Webster avenue, where he has a splendid store, 22x50 feet in dimensions. He carries a full stock of pure drugs and chemicals, together with officinal preparations of his own manufacture, consisting of tinctures, extracts, decoctions, syrups, etc., also toilet articles, perfumes, brushes, sponges, surgeons' supplies, rubber goods and a full line of patent medicines. A large soda fountain graces the store and is popularly patronized. He makes a specialty of compounding physicians' prescriptions, to which he gives his personal attention, the greatest care being exercised to insure accuracy. Mr. Schrage is a native of Wisconsin, has resided in Chicago for sixteen years, and is a prominent business man. He is a member of the Knights of Pythias and is a leader in social circles. He is a regular licensed druggist.

CHICAGO CHAIN WORKS.

Almost every imaginable manufacturing interest is represented in Chicago, and it seems to be the universal opinion that the Garden City is the natural manufacturing center of the country, An important enterprise, and one conferring benefit to any community is the manufacture of wrought iron chains, etc. Such a business is that conducted by the Chicago Chain Works, of which Mr. S. G. Taylor is proprietor. This business has been established for eighteen years, and gives employment to from eighteen to twenty-five workmen. The works are located at 98 and 100 Indiana street, where a one-story brick building, 50x100 feet, is utilized for the purpose of manufacturing all kinds of cables, railroad chains, etc. Their specialty however, is confined to the best dredge and crane chains. The work of welding is all done by hand, and fifteen to twenty forges are used constantly. The chains manufactured by this company have an established reputation for strength and general excellence. They are made in the most careful manner by experienced workmen only. The house has a large trade all over the United States and Canada, and sells annually many thousand dollars worth of goods. The proprietor, Mr. S. G. Taylor, is well-known in business circles; he is rated high commercially, and held in high esteem by all who know him.

HENRY GOETZ.

This house was originally established in 1875 by the present proprietor. Mr. Goetz is a thoroughly educated druggist and gives his personal attention to the compounding of physicians' prescriptions and family recipes, which is always done in a prompt, accurate and satisfactory manner, from pure, fresh drugs. The store, located on the corner of Madison and La Salle streets, is 40x30 feet in dimensions, and is handsomely fitted up and arranged in solid mahogany fixtures. In the store will always be found a complete assortment of chemicals and drugs, and all the leading proprietary medicines of well-known merit; also perfumes, extracts and toilet articles. Mr. Goetz manu-

factures his own extracts, among which are Tacoma Beef, Iron and Wine, cough and cold cures, Tacoma System Regulator and Tacoma Sarsaparilla. Popular prices prevail, and Mr. Goetz is able to offer unsurpassed advantages to his customers. He does an immense soda water business, having the largest and most expensive soda water fountain in the city. It is of marble inlaid with glass, and is estimated to have cost $6,000. Mr. Goetz is a native of Wisconsin, but has been a resident of this city since 1871. He is esteemed as an honorable and public-spirited citizen, and well deserves the widespread favor in which he is held in Chicago.

H. HEDDER.

Mr. H. Hedder's name has been identified with the coal and wood business since 1869, for that was the year he established himself in it at the corner of Van Buren and Clinton streets, and moved to his present yards at 403 W. Chicago avenue, corner of Bickerdike street, in 1872. He owns the yards and sheds, which are very extensive, and cover an area of 50x100 feet Here he has Lehigh, Scranton and Lackawanna and all kinds of anthracite and bituminous coal, also hard and soft wood, cut or sawed to any size by cord or load. He delivers coal and wood free to any part of the city, and always guarantees that it is screened and full weight. Orders by mail receive prompt attention, and are sent out on the day they are received. Mr. Hedder is a native of Germany and has been in Chicago since 1867. His reputation as an honorable dealer has never been questioned, and the purchaser of one ton receives the same consideration as the purchaser of a hundred tons. From the commencement this enterprise has been ably managed and eminently successful, and Mr. Hedder merits his success.

F. M. CROSSMAN.

The name of "Crossman" has long been intimately identified with the livery, carriage, saddle and road horse trade of this city, and with results of a very creditable and satisfactory character, as all who have ever visited Mr. F. M. Crossman's splendid livery stables on W. Randolph street, or his famous "Spring Brook" stock farm will admit. The livery business was begun in 1870, by the firm of Crossman & Co., Mr. Crossman, who is a native of Massachusetts, having in that year settled in Chicago. In 1872 they had to greatly enlarge their facilities, and thus continued without any firm change up to January, 1883. when the old partnership was dissolved, and Mr. Crossman became sole proprietor, but continued under the name of Crossman & Co. until 1891. The stables are conveniently located at Nos. 414, 416 and 418 W. Randolph street, and are the model ones in town. They are brick and frame, 80x190 feet in dimensions, while there is a carrage house, 50x100 feet in size. The premises are splendidly lighted, ventilated and drained, and nowhere in Chicago can such desirable quarters be found for the boarding of high grade track, road, carriage and riding horses. The stables readily accommodate 112, being situated entirely on the ground floor, while Mr. Crossman keeps fifty to seventy-five first-class horses on hand, largely for livery purposes. He is also the principal dealer here in Kentucky and New York saddle, coach and light harness horses, and numbers many of Chicago's leading citizens among his customers. His livery facilities are remarkably extensive. He is prepared to supply coaches, coupes, phaetons, light buggies, carts, road wagons, etc., on shortest notice, with superior, gentle and fast stock that always gives satisfaction. Funerals, wedding parties, social and shopping visits are all specialties with him, and only experienced, sober coachmen are employed, while the tariff is remarkably moderate. The stables are completely and handsomely fitted up and furnished, including waiting rooms, harness rooms, etc. The elegant offices (20x20 feet) are in front and have telephone and all conveniences. Mr. Crossman is the owner of the stables, and offers special low rates for boarding horses or storing vehicles. He gives close personal supervision. All the carriages, broughams and victorias owned by him are built by his order by the famous New Haven, Conn., firm of B. Manville & Co. and C. Stone & Sons, of Chicago. Thus, thisis the place to go to, and test practically any style of carriage or buggy, and get lowest quotations on the most elegant and durable work, offered as the best made, and far ahead of western makes. Mr. Crossman is proprietor of a large stock farm, situated eight miles northwest from the city limits, familiarly known as the "Spring Brook Stock Farm," where he has splendid accommodations for boarding 200 city horses. He is also a large breeder of Holstein cattle, road horses, etc., and there is the headquarters for the famous trotting stallion, "Hay Wilkes," by "Geo. Wilkes." Go to Mr. Crossman's for anything in the livery, horse or carriage line, and rest assured of satisfaction, prompt attention, and courteous, fair and square treatment. Mr. Crossman is universally popular and respected and is noted as one of the best judges of horse flesh in Chicago.

A. HUSSEY & CO.

The name of Hussey has become nationally prominent in the leaf tobacco trade, and is also well known to cigar manufacturers, and it is with the greatest difficulty that they can secure the appropriate grades of stock from the ordinary importers and jobbers. They give the best value for the money of any house in the country, which estimate is proved by the fact that their trade for 1890 nearly doubled in volume, and the causes for this will here briefly be referred to. Mr. A. Hussey the energetic and popular proprietor, established the present business in 1877, with the sole determination to give the manufacturer the benefit of spot cash prices for the choicest assorted leaf tobacco, all strictly as represented. From the start Mr. Hussey made rapid and substantial progress, and repeated enlargements of facilities were necessitated, resulting in 1890 in the opening of the large house in Philadelphia. The Chicago house, situated centrally at Nos. 35 and 37 La Salle street, is in charge of Mr. E. A. Sutter, a well-known expert as to leaf tobaccos, and who has been connected with the concern since 1877. The premises occupied comprise five floors and basement, 60x120 feet in dimensions,and where is carried by far the largest and choicest stock of leaf tobaccos in the United States. Messrs. A. Hussey & Co. employ no traveling man, but instead issue annually a beautifully printed Descriptive Catalogue, known as their "Little Traveller" and which now on its "twenty fifth" trip, frankly, fully and truthfully tells each customer, what the house has to sell. The book is the safest "side partner" for a cigar manufacturer. The house goes personally to the sections and countries where the best tobaccos are grown; and its own direct importations of Sumatra and Havana leaf are recognized by all manufacturers, as being the finest stock to select from. In choicest Sumatra wrappers, and fine old Havana tobaccos, no firm in the world can cope with them, and their "W. C," brand is the favorite. Their lines of binders and fillers are equally reliable and desirable. Another specialty is their domestic wrappers, choicest growths of such tobaccos, as Housatonic, Pennsylvania, Connecticut, New York State, and Wisconsin. The house has always held the lead for its splendid combinations—selections put up in quantities at stated prices per lot and guaranteed to secure the best of results as specified. They are put up under the supervision of an expert manufacturer, and have had a success truly marvelous. It is a fact and a golden one to the manufacturer that with the use of these combinations he is sure to make cigars that give unqualified satisfaction. The firm has large packing houses in Wisconsin, Connecticut, Pennsylvania and in Cuba, and cure and pack the bulk of their own goods, thus knowing what they offer will meet the customer's wants. Mr. Hussey has introduced new and popular methods in the carrying on of an old-time staple business, and the Chicago house, under the management of Mr. Sutter, is the leading exponent in the West and Northwest.

W. H. WARREN.

There is no city in the United States that offers grander opportunities to the contractor, builder, and manufacturer of house builders' material than our own city of Chicago, and one of the leading representatives in this line of business is Mr. W. H. Warren, contractor and builder and manufacturer of fine hardwood, interior house finishings and manufacturer of mantels, banisters, etc., at the corner of Blackhawk and Smith avenue. This business was originally started by Mr. Warren, eight years ago on Pearson street, but his business increased so rapidly he erected his present substantial property, at a cost of $50,000 for the land and building alone. It consists of a substantial five-story brick building, 65x125 feet in dimensions, with an engine room addition, 40x40 feet. This factory is supplied with an 150 horse power engine, and all of the latest improved machinery in his line, some of which was especially designed by Mr. Warren for his particular work. He employs from 125 to 150 hands and does a large and steadily increasing business. He manufactures wood mantels, hardwood interior house finishings, banisters, newel posts, balustrades, and wainscoting, and pays especial attention to custom work in his line of any kind of material. He also contracts for buildings of every description. Mr. Warren's reputation is unsurpassed and he has done work for all the leading architects in all parts of the country. His trade extends to all parts of the country. Mr. Warren is a native of Boston, and was engaged in business there before coming west. He has been in Chicago for ten years and is popular with the builders and business public generally and has made himself known as a gentleman thoroughly understanding his business in every particular.

A. J. AUBERT.

To no class of people is the prosperity of a city due more than to the real estate men. It is their energy and vim that induce capital to invest, and houses spring up under the magic wand of their power in inducing manufacturers to locate. Chicago is particularly under obligations to them, and to none in late years more than to the well-known firm of Mr. A. J. Aubert of No 305 E. North avenue. Mr. Aubert opened his real estate, loan and insurance business six years ago, and has been for three years in his present location. He does a general real estate business, buys and sells on commission, collects

rents, pays taxes, negotiates loans and is a representative of the most reliable companies of fire insurance in the world, among which may be named the "Citizens," of New York; the "Hanover," of New York; "North British and Mercantile," of London and Edenburgh; "Ætna" of Hartford; "German," of Freeport, Ill. and "Milwaukee Mechanics," of Milwaukee, Wis.; "Scottish Union and National," "Fidelity and Casualty Co.," of New York and others. Mr. Aubert is also secretary of the Graylawn Park Land Association, and secretary and trustee of the Lutz Park Land Association addition to Ravenswood. Mr. Aubert handles a number of subdivisions which are well worth the careful consideration of those contemplating purchasing a home. Among the many desirable places of residence which Mr. Aubert offers to the public are Grant Park addition to Chicago, corner Lincoln street and Montrose boulevard. lots, $500 and upward; Aubert's addition to Chicago; corner Lincoln and Sultzer streets; lots, $650 and upward; Leavitt, Sunnyside and Western avenues, $600 and upward; northwest corner Lincoln and Graceland avenues, lots, $550 and upward, $15.00 to $ 25.00 down, six per cent. interest; Graceland avenue, between Oakley avenue and Leavitt street; lots, $500 and upward. In all of these, sidewalks have been laid and streets graded. Lots are sold at acre prices, and abstracts are delivered to purchasers when first payment is made; titles are guaranteed perfect. He handles non-resident property and manages estates and conducts a general real estate business. He is active, energetic and has hosts of friends in business and social circles, and is well liked by all who know him either in a business or social way. Mr. Aubert is not only a whole souled. genial friend and acquaintance, but one of the shrewdest business men of Chicago, one whose judgment in real estate and insurance matters may be relied upon, and to capitalists, if they have money to invest in Chicago realty, we would advise them to consult with Mr. Aubert for we assure them, they can place the utmost confidence in all his transactions.

LAMONTE, O'DONNELL & CO.

In some lines of business the mere mention of the name of a house carries with it the complete idea of strength, reliability and success, and this is especially so with regard to the firm of LaMonte, O'Donnell & Co., printers and bookbinders at 158 and 160 Clark street. The foundation of the business of this house was laid seven years ago, when it was incorporated as the Chicago Printing Co., printers, publishers and bookbinders, but in 1889 the present firm succeeded them and has since conducted the business in an eminently successful manner. The partners are Mr. M LaMonte, a native of New York state, and born on the banks of the Hudson. He is a member of the firm of Spaulding, LaMonte & Co., and has been in Chicago for twenty-five years. He is also a financier of considerable note. Mr. J. J. O'Donnell, a native of Chicago, and a thoroughly practical man, and Mr. Milton George, editor and owner of the *Western Rural*, who only has a financial interest in the business, but does not devote his time to it. Under such favorable auspices the business has grown in extent and reputation until it stands well in the front rank of all the houses in the West. The business premises comprise four floors of a five-story building, which are thoroughly equipped with new and improved machinery and appliances, including no less than nineteen presses, all operated by motor power, having two motors of twenty-five and ten horse power respectively, while employment is given to 260 hands. While devoting prompt and skillful attention to mercantile work of all kinds, the house has made great strides in the direction of the highest class of book work, and makes a specialty of edition work. ' Its methods of business, while recognizing the competition of the hour, do not go to the length of placing its prices at the lowest rate offered by others for inferior work, as they find no opportunity for turning out anything but work of a first-class character. Orders and commissions by telephone or otherwise are given prompt and careful attention. and estimates are furnished for work in any quantity and customers can rest assured of prompt and careful attention.

JOHN MILLER & CO.

A representative and one of the largest commission houses in Chicago, extensively engaged in handling hides, pelts, tallow and grease, is that of Messrs. John Miller & Co., whose offices and salesrooms are situated at 121 to 129 Michigan street. This business was established in 1873 by Messrs. Miller & Klein, who conducted it till 1887, when the present firm was organized, the copartners being Messrs. John Miller and H. W. Schmitt. Both partners have had long experience and possess influential connections and perfect facilities. They own and occupy a spacious and substantial five-story and basement brick building, 60x100 feet in area, fully equipped with every facility for the accommodation of the valuable and well selected stock of hides, tallow, etc. A stock valued at $150,000 is always on hand, and the sales of the firm for the past year amounted to over $1,000,000. The basement at 103 Michigan street, 36x100 feet in dimensions, is also occupied by the firm, and their trade, which is steadily increasing, now extends throughout the entire United States and Canada. Liberal advances are made by this responsible firm on consignments when required, prompt sales and immediate returns being a leading specialty of this concern, while shippers can always rely implicitly on the judgment of the partners with regard to the value and quantity of any lot. Orders for hides, pelts, tallow and grease are promptly filled at the lowest ruling market prices, and entire satisfaction is guaranteed patrons. Mr. Miller was born in Alsace, Germany, but has resided in Chicago many years, while Mr. Schmitt is a native of this city. Having thus briefly sketched the facilities of this house, it only remains to be added that its business has ever been conducted on the enduring principles of equity, and relations entered into with it are certain to become, not only pleasant, but profitable and satisfactory to all concerned.

THE FORSYTH ELECTRIC ELEVATED SUSPENSION RAILROAD.

One of the most vital and absorbing questions of the day in all great cities is, What is the best means of rapid, easy and safe transit from one part to another? The ordinary elevated railway, with its obstruction to and darkening of the streets, its noise and smoke and dust, seems to be universally condemned, and will probably soon give way to some more improved method of conveyance to and from places of business. In New York City they have decided on an underground similiar to the Metropolitan Railroad of London, England, but the conditions are here so different, that it is doubtful if the vitiated air of the tunnel could be endured, with the extreme heat of our summer days superadded. In this connection we desire to call attention to a system which appears to secure the desired rate of speed, usefulness, safety, and freedom from smoke or dust, while causing no obstruction whatever to streets, and giving passengers the greatest amount of comfort possible. We refer to the Forsyth Electric Elevated Suspension Railway, which seems to have solved the puzzling problem of rapid transit, and to be destined to become in the near future the railroad

C. Forsyth on the consummate skill and practical insight displayed in its invention. This system of railway is as applicable to long, as well as to short distances, and while it is claimed that a speed in street travel from twenty-five to thirty miles can be got with ease, there are those sanguine enough to predict that the time is not far distant when Chicagoans will ride in perfect safety at a two-mile-a-minute rate under an easy-running, noiseless and clean roadway in comfortable and not over-crowded cars. The office of the Forsyth Electric Elevated Suspension Railroad is in room 405 Rookery building, La Salle street, and here a model of the railroad may be seen and all information desired obtained.

C. F. CLASS & SON.

The advancement and progress of a city displays itself nowhere more readily than in the elegance of its drug stores, and in the stores of C. F. Class & Son, located at 227 E. Division street, corner of Larrabee street, and at 887 N. Halsted street, near Center street, we find two of those elegant establishments which go to form the beauty of a great city. The business of this well known firm was originally founded

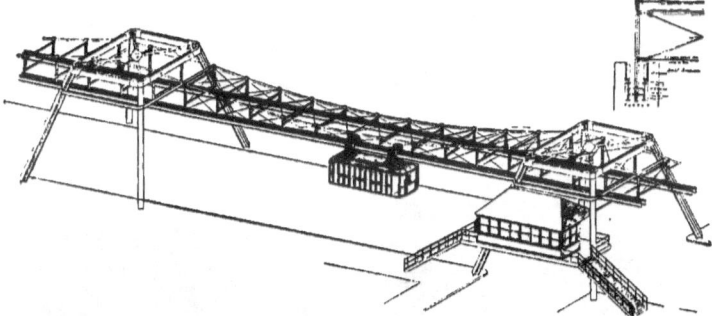

of our streets and suburbs. This means of transporttaion is a radical departure from all others in use at the present time. Its coaches travel below, not above the track, which is supported by cables running over piers at the street crossings, and the motive power is electricity. The construction of these piers will be such as to entirely avoid obstruction to traffic, while securing the greatest possible strength and solidity. The foundations will be within the curbstone lines, and will support four arched columns, whose tops incline toward each other, and are firmly united together by transverse beams. These combine in a marked manner the maximum of strength with the minimum of size and weight. The cables pass over the piers, and are capable of being tightened up to any desired degree, thus securing the required rigidity on the track. The stations will probably be erected in the double arches of the piers at convenient distances apart, and can easily be reached by stairs from the streets below. The great safety of this system will at once be seen, the track being free and unobstructed by ice and snow, and it being absolutely impossible to derail the cars. There are no cinders or oil to annoy pedestrians, no jar, no nothing of the absence of noise and smoke, and there is no obstruction to the passage of light and air into the street. The erection will not injure the value of property, as in the case of the ordinary elevated roads, for it will not darken the streets along which it passes. It is besides most easy of construction and management, and we heartily congratulate Mr. R.

in 1857, and for a long period was located at No. 280 E. Division street. Recently a removal was made from the latter place to No. 227, on the same thoroughfare, where the headquarters of the firm are, the North Halsted street store being a branch establishment. Both stores are spacious and attractive, everything in them being new. The fittings of the Division street Pharmacy are of ash, while the whole is set off by a costly marble soda fountain and the most expensive plate glass show and counter cases. In fact the whole of the interior appointments reflect the greatest possible credit upon the good taste of the proprietors. A full line of pure drugs and chemicals and proprietary medicines of the highest standard reputation are constantly kept in stock in both stores, as well as a great variety of toilet articles, perfumes, soaps, sick room supplies, surgical appliances, fancy goods, cigars, and, in fact, everything that is to be found in drug stores of this high order. But special notice must be made of the prescription departments. In each store is a laboratory and pharmacy fitted with every modern appliance and apparatus to insure accuracy in the compounding of physicians' prescriptions, and here are manufactured tinctures, essences and extracts, so that accuracy and purity are assured, Messrs. Class & Son are natives of Chicago and graduates of the Chicago College of Pharmacy, and are licensed members of the Illinois Pharmaceutical Association. Both father and son are held in high respect, and pay the closest attention to business.

HALL & ROSS HUSKING GLOVE CO.

A branch of industry of a very useful and meritorious character, in this section of Chicago is the manufacture of husking gloves and mittens. In this connection we desire to refer specially, in this commercial review of the Western metropolis to the representative and successful Hall & Ross Husking Glove Company, whose factory is located at 253 to 259 Elston avenue. This industry was founded in 1870 by the Hall Husking Glove Company, which was succeeded in 1881, by the present Hall & Ross Husking Glove Company, the officers being Mr. H. R. Ross, president; Mr. Wm. Hulin, vice-president, and Mr. Ovington Ross, secretary and treasurer. In 1888 they built their present substantial four-story and basement building, which is 75x100 feet in dimensions. The various departments are fully supplied with the latest improved appliances and machinery, operated by a powerful steam engine. Here from 175 to 200 skilled hands are employed, who turn out largely patent husking gloves, husking pins, also goat harvesting, calf and sheep working gloves, and palmed mitts. Only the best materials are utilized, and the goods produced are unsurpassed for finish, durability and workmanship. Orders are filled at the lowest possible prices, and the trade of the company extends throughout the entire United States, Mexico and Canada. Husking gloves are great labor-saving articles; with them twice as much can be husked as by the old way. The company's oil tanned leather gloves are soft and pliable, while their surface is prepared by metal plates, and each pair is provided with steel pins and clamps for tearing the corn from the ears. The officers are popular and honorable business men, who have ever retained the confidence of leading trade circles, and are worthy representatives of this useful industry.

HERMANN BARTH & CO.

The manufacture of furniture is so extensive and diverse in its nature as to require many different departments of manufacture in the general ensemble, and the primary one, the foundation as it were, is the manufacture of the frames on which the work is built. One of the most extensive establishments of this kind is that of Hermann Barth & Co. of Nos. 53 and 55 Dayton street, at the corner of Blackhawk. This extensive business was originally established in 1877, fourteen years ago, on Milwaukee avenue, and the business has so increased, and the demand been so great for their goods, that two years ago they erected the substantial five-story brick block at their present location, 100x150 feet in size, with engine room adjoining, 50x50 feet in size, in which is an immense 125 horse power engine, which furnishes power for the gigantic concern. The factory is equipped with all the latest modern improved machinery appliances and tools necessary in their work; the building alone cost over $25,000, and has grounds, 175x176 feet adjoining, which are used as lumber yards and are filled with hard lumber used in the manufacture of frames. They employ from 100 to 120 skilled mechanics and have an immense trade, which even th's large force has difficulty in supplying. Their trade extends, not only to all the principal furniture companies in Chicago and Illinois, but to all parts of the United States, where the excellence of their work is known and appreciated. Although the firm is known as Hermann Barth & Co., Mr. Barth has no partner and is the exclusive and sole proprietor, manager and director of this immense establishment. He is a native of Germany, and has been a resident of Chicago since 1870. He is well and favorably known in commercial and financial circles in the city as a substantial and progressive business man.

S. H. SINCLAIR CO.

A manufacturing company of high standing, making machines of great merit and extensive use is the S. H. Sinclair Company, of this city. The business conducted by the company was established in 1876 by Mr. H. B. Sinclair, and in 1880 Mr. S. H. Sinclair was admitted to the firm and the style changed to H. B. & S. H. Sinclair. In

1889 Mr. H. B. Sinclair died, and the business was continued by Mr. S. H. Sinclair, who in 1890 also died. In September, 1890, the present company was incorporate to continue the business, with a capital of $25,000. This company has had phenomenal success in the enterprise, and the business is on a firm financial and paying basis. The president and treasurer is Mr. F. A. Walker, who was for five years with H. S. Walker in the boiler and engine business. He is a gentleman of business ability and executive power, and fills the position ably. The secretary is Mrs. M. H. Fithian, who is a capable business woman. The directors are H. S. Walker and Geo. Durry, gentlemen of long experience and high business standing. The business of the company is conducted at 258 Michigan street, where they occupy the third floor, 25x100 feet in dimensions, as office and machine shop. Here they employ thirteen machinists, and a staff of office assistants. They manufacture laundry machinery, making a specialty of shirt, collar and cuff ironing machines. Over five hundred of these machines are in use in Chicago. The trade is all over the United States, and an agency has been established in London, England, under the management of Mr. Isaac Brarthwaite. The San Francisco agents are the Pacific Laundry Machine Company.

THE NATIONAL BREWING CO.

A representative and one of the most popular breweries in Chicago is that of the National Brewing Company, 846 to 856 Eighteenth street, corner Lincoln street. This company was incorporated in 1889, the executive officers being Mr. John D. Raulston, president; Mr. John F. Buehrer, vice-president; and Mr. Walter E. Newberry, secretary, and treasurer. The brewery, malt house, and other buildings, have just been built for the company in the most durable and substantial manner. The buildings are four stories high, the malt house being 50x125 feet, and the brewery and storehouse, 75x125 feet in area. The various depart-

ments are fully equipped with modern appliances, apparatus and machinery operated by a fifty horse power steam engine. There are large cold storage rooms, and the capacity of the brewery is 50,000 barrels per annum. This brewery is noted for its cleanliness, and in this respect has no superior in the country. The lager beer brewed here is made of the best materials, and has no superior for quality, purity, flavor and uniform excellence. It is preferred by thousands, and possesses rare tonic and strengthening properties. Twenty-one men are employed in the brewery, and a number of teams are utilized in filling orders in Chicago and its vicinity. The sales for the past year amounted to over $300,000, and the trade of the company is steadily increasing. The officers are honorable and enterprising business men, under whose careful guidance the prospects of the National Brewing Company are of the most favorable character. The telephone call of the company is 9224.

SILVER ISLET MINING AND MILLING CO.

Mining operations require large capital, great engineering and practical skill and honest management to be successful, the mine being a rich one. If it isn't, then the investment is lost. It is thus a pleasure to direct attention to the "Silver Islet Mining and Milling Company" with offices at 4 Sherman street which owns several of the most valuable claims in the rich mining district of Pitkin, Colo., and as the

result of its careful investments and extensive development work, it is now shipping remarkably rich silver ore. The company was duly incorporated in February, 1890, much of its capital being subscribed by several of Chicago's leading capitalists. The mines cover an area of some 210 acres, embracing two mill sites. The work of development has been done thoroughly, and several very rich leads have been struck, and a carload a day of fine silver ore is being shipped, yielding thus far on an average seventy-one ounces of pure silver to the ton. The average net receipts per car the past year were $625.-95. The company has a fine plant to work the mines and is also about to erect a mill to treat its own ore. The company's officers are as follows: Mr. Frank Drake, president; Mr. L. J. Lamson, vice-president; Mr. C. I. Fowler, secretary; and Mr. John Cudahy, treasurer. These are familiar names. Mr. Drake is well known in the city, having occupied several elective positions and is interested in several mining corporations in Colorado. He is specially qualified to discharge the duties of the presidency, and has the valued support of Mr. Lamson, as vice-president, who is a prominent commission merchant and member of the Board of Trade; Mr. Fowler is also active on 'Change and a leading broker. Mr. Cudahy is too prominently identified with Chicago and its packing interests to require more than mention. Thus the executive is in every way a representative one, and the company has before it prospects of the most favorable character and which are destined to place its stock at a high premium.

E. A. SCHMIDT.

One of the most prominent drug stores in its section of Chicago is the one conducted by Mr. E. A. Schmidt, at 3022 Archer avenue. It was established in the early spring of this year, and has shown already in its youth that it is entitled to a brilliant future. Mr. Schmidt is a popular citizen of Chicago, and his popularity is largely due to his always pleasant manner in waiting on his customers, and his upright and fair dealings. His establishment was originally founded by Mr. Ed. Heller of Chicago, and came subsequently under control of Mr. Schmidt,

who was born in Cincinnati, O., and is a graduate of the Cincinnati College of Pharmacy, class of 1876. Mr. Schmidt had been engaged in a number of prominent drug stores as prescription clerk before embarking on his own account. He has been a resident of Chicago for nine years. Prescriptions are carefully compounded, and patrons of this store have learned to impose implicit reliance on the skill and care with which Mr. Schmidt attends to this important branch of the business. The store is neatly and tastefully appointed with all requisite fittings and conveniences. The stock carried is complete in assortment, and we find shelves filled with drugs of all kinds. This firm carries the usual line of chemicals, sundries, perfumery, toilet goods, mineral waters, etc. A leading specialty is made of filling physicians' prescriptions, and accuracy and purity are guaranteed in each and every instance. If success in business can be judged by a successful beginning, combined with untiring efforts, Mr. E. A. Schmidt is entitled to it.

NORTHWESTERN STEAM CARPET CLEANING AND RENOVATING WORKS.

The Northwestern Steam Carpet Cleaning and Renovating Works, of which Mr. T. Beckert (conducting business under the firm style of T. Beckert & Co.) is the popular proprietor, is located at Nos. 157 and 159 S. Canal street. This enterprise was established by Mr. Beckert in 1889. The premises occupied comprise commodious basement, 50x160 feet in dimensions, supplied with the latest improved machinery for cleaning carpets, rugs, etc., impelled by eight horse power steam engine. The process adopted is such as to thoroughly remove from carpets all dust, to completely disinfect them, to destroy all moths, and to raise and brighten the nap. Carpets are taken up, cleaned and returned the same day without regard to weather, if desired, a special feature being made of refitting and relaying. All orders are promptly attended to and for vouchers, in such connection, as also to satisfactory work, Mr. Beckert refers to the managers of the Chicago Opera House, Lakeside Club, Hotel Bristol, Second Baptist Church, Siegel, Cooper & Co., Secretary E. A. Summers of the A. D. I., and I. Society, Brevoort House, and others. Mr. Beckert is a native of London, England, now resident in Chicago since 1868, and prior to engaging in his present enterprise was for four years fireman on the Chicago and Northwestern Railway.

M. B. LONERGAN.

Of all the arts that have been so greatly improved and widened in their range by discovery, photography is one of the most prominent. The wonderful stride from the work of Duguerre to the beautiful cabinet turned out of the studio of a modern first-class artist photographer is well nigh incomprehensible. The photographer is a necessity to our modern civilization, and when one is found with that rare intelligence and keen eye to the beautiful necessary to success his efforts should deserve the patronage of the intelligent and elite of the community. The spacious gallery of Mr. M. B. Lonergan on the second floor of, Nos. 4134 and 4136 Halsted street, opposite Union Stock Yards, is an elegant affair, delighting the heart of the artist of refined taste. His magnificently carpeted rooms are filled with splendid specimens of high grade art work in oil, crayon, water colors and india ink, as well as photographs of the finest kind, many celebrities being conspicuously noticeable among them. Mr. Lonergan has been established in business since 1880, and has an extensive and very appreciative patronage. He employs only experienced and capable artists and personally supervises all the work done. Mr. Lonergan is an artist indeed, having a cultivated perception of the beautiful in form and feature, and an extraordinary appreciation for the best effects in posing, hence the remarkable attractiveness of his work, which is making its way throughout the city, owing to its superior excellence in every way. His patronage is already extensive and no doubt, as such merit deserves, will be largely augmented.

UNION SWITCH AND SIGNAL CO.

The safety and celerity of railroad travel very largely depends upon the efficiency and perfection of the systems of switches and signals employed. The maze of tracks and switches of frequent trains centered at almost every station along a line necessitates the use of the most approved and absolutely reliable methods for switching and signaling. In this age of extreme competition among railroads, no management can afford to do without the best. Unquestionably the Union Switch and Signal Co. of Pittsburgh owns and controls by far the best and most reliable system viz., "The Westinghouse Pneumatic Interlocking Switch and Signal System," which has now been adopted by all the leading railroads of the United States and Canada. The splendid record of the Westinghouse Air Brake is familiar to all; the record of the Westinghouse Switch and Signal system is making is equally remarkable and gratifying. With it in operation possibilities of accidents, collisions, loss of life and property, delays, etc., are avoided. The utmost confidence can be placed in these unerring signals by night and day, and the amount of benefit they have been to the railroads cannot be over-estimated. The company's general office and works are at Swissvale, near Pittsburgh, where is possessed magnificent manufacturing facilities. The Western branch was opened in Chicago in October, 1883, meeting with assured success from the start. In May, 1885, the offices were removed to the Home Insurance building, in La Salle street, where full working models of the system, as also of the Farmer Mechanical system, can be seen and estimates furnished for complete outfits. Mr. H. H. McDuffee, the manager here, is a native of Rochester, N. H., and has long been actively identified with railroad interests. He is a popular business man of marked executive ability and soundest judgment, and is energetic and progressive. In 1890 this branch did a business of $300,-000, which speaks volumes for the recognized superiority of this system. It is now in general use on all the leading roads running out of Chicago, and we cannot too strongly urge executives of railroad companies to thoroughly investigate its merits. The company also has branch offices in New York and Boston, and offers exceptional facilities to the railroads of America to defend themselves against accident and loss by the introduction of this, the only efficient and reliable, switch and signal system in existence.

GEO. V. HECKER CO.

The use of cereals for food is rapidly growing in favor in this country. In Scotland oatmeal is considered the essential thing for creating "brain and brawn." "More bread and less meat in your diet" is the standard prescription for indigestion and kindred ailments by the best read medical men. The number and variety of cereal foods now before the public makes it an easy thing to meet the requirements of every case and tickle the palates of all classes. Hecker's celebrated cereals have been on the market so long that they are a household word throughout the land. The mills and head offices of the company are located in New York city. Branch offices are established in all the large cities, including Boston, Philadelphia, Charleston, S. C., Savannah, Ga., New Orleans, St. Louis and other leading cities. The Chicago agency of the Hecker Mills is located at 187 Kinzie street, and is under the able management of Mr. William Burrows. The firm was originally established in 1840 as Hecker & Brother, afterward becoming George V. Hecker and Co. In 1890 the firm was incorporated under the laws of the state of New York under the style and title of George V. Hecker Company. The mills are located at 203 Cherry street, corner Pike Slip, New York, and are mammoth concerns, having a daily capacity of 3,500 barrels. This immense output is sold all over the continent. Some of the leading articles of product are: Hecker's Self-Raising Buckwheat, Hecker's Rolled Oats, Hecker's Farina, Hecker's Granules, Hecker's Wheaten Grits, Hecker's Hominy, Self-Raising flour of various kinds, Hecker's Boston Brown

Bread, etc. All wholesale grocers carry these goods, which have a very large sale all over the country. The Chicago agency of the Hecker Company was opened at 41 River street, and moved to the present location about two years ago, and occupies two stories, 70x90 feet. The stock carried is varied and extensive, and is intended for city trade. The general trade is supplied directly from the mills. Mr. Burrows, the Chicago agent, has been connected with the company for twelve years at the New York office. He is a young man of fine business ability, and a native of New York. George V. Hecker Company are going to give a fine practical exhibition of their various manufactures at the Columbia World's Exhibition. The company were awarded the first prize at the Philadelphia Centennial Exposition for their manufactures.

BACH, BECKER & CO.

Representative among leading wholesale Chicago dealers in wool, and exporters of raw furs and skins, is the firm of Messrs. Bach, Becker & Co., whose offices and salesrooms are situated at 103, 105 and 107 Michigan street. The business was established in 1885 by Messrs. Wolf, Becker & Co., who conducted it till 1888, when the present firm

was organized and assumed the management, the co-partners being Messrs. E. Bach and S. M. and A. E. Becker. The partners have had long experience, and possess influential connections and perfect facilities. They occupy four spacious floors, each being 75x100 feet in area, fully equipped with every convenience for the accommodation of the extensive, well-selected stock of wool, furs and skins. Their trade extends throughout the entire United States and Canada, and they also export largely to Great Britain and Europe. Wool growers and shippers throughout the Western, Northwestern, Southwestern and Middle states have always recognized this firm to be prompt and responsible, enabling them to dispose of both grease or second wools at the best rates, and whose immediate returns indicate their determination to forward the best interests of their numerous customers. They make liberal advances when required on consignments of wool and skins, and sell largely to the principal woolen mills in the West and East. They also have most perfect connections in the leading European fur centers, affording them the best and most direct outlets for all kinds of goods. The stock on hand is always valued at over $100,000, and their sales of furs for the past year amounted to $250,000, and of wool to $627,000. The partners were all born in Germany, but have resided in Chicago several years, where they are highly esteemed in trade circles for their business ability and sterling integrity. Mr. Bach was formerly of the firm of Messrs. Frankel, Bach & Co., bankers, of Oskaloosa, Iowa.

LUNDELL, OLSON & CO.

One of the most progressive houses on the North side is the well-known firm of Lundell, Olson & Co. These gentlemen began business ten years ago in this city and by the closest application and industrious efforts have built up a trade that reflects the greatest credit upon them and places them among the prominent dealers of Chicago in their various lines. Mr. J. P. Lundell is a native of Sweden, and came to America nineteen years ago; he has lived in Chicago for eleven years, and has become one of her leading citizens. Mr. R. Olson is also a native of Sweden, and has lived in Chicago for the past fourteen years. He is an excellent business manager, and noted for his practical business experience and ability. Mr. J. M. Lundell came to Chicago twelve years ago, having lived in the country three years previous; he is one of the leading business men of the North side. This firm does a general dry goods, millinery and carpet business, and also manufacture the fine organs bearing their names. Their principal establishment is located at the corner of Oak and Townsend streets, where they do an immense wholesale and retail business in carpets, dry goods of all kinds, imported and domestic, also millinery goods, cloaks, suits, notions, jewelry, boots and shoes, etc. They have a fine establishment, 84x120 feet in dimensions, fronting on both streets, and thoroughly stocked. The Townsend street entrance to this establishment leads into their gents' furnishing goods, boot and shoe, carpet and oilcloth, and the organ department. The Oak street entrance contains dry goods, notions, millinery, cloaks and jewelry. Six courteous and attentive attendants are employed in this store, and the business done is very large. The organ factory is located at 145 Ontario street, where they employ five skilled workmen, and manufacture six styles of organs and two styles of pianos that have an excellent reputation, and have become very popular. The latest machinery is used in this factory, and the workmanship of the employes is of the highest order. The house acts as wholesale dealers in guitars and sewing machines, and sell many goods throughout the country. The house is well known and of high reputation, and the members of the firm are gentlemen of the greatest skill and ability.

THE NELSON & MOLLER CO.

The importance of Chicago, as the great manufacturing center of the United States, is forcibly demonstrated by the existence here of representative establishments in every branch of skilled industry. For instance, in the manufacture of fine parlor furniture, the Nelson & Moller Company has achieved a national reputation. The company began business in 1885, and has already developed a leading position in its line, due to the marked ability and energy of the executive officers, who are recognized as leading authorities in regard to this—the most difficult branch of furniture manufacturing. The factory is conveniently located at Nos. 125 and 127 N. Peoria street, near Austin avenue, easily accessible by the Indiana street cars. It comprises an entire three-story and basement brick building, 40 by 100 feet in dimensions, and completely equipped with the latest improved machinery and appliances. The establishment is a model one in every respect, and is conducted under the close personal supervision of the proprietors. The company makes a specialty of the highest grade of artistic cabinet-finished parlor frames, in the most beautiful and original designs, and affording from their immense and comprehensive stock every facility for selecting to meet the requirements of every line of the trade. The company has developed widespread, influential connections, doing an immense business with eastern and western wholesalers, and also the leading furniture dealers of this city. Messrs. Nelson & Moller are natives of Norway, who have been permanent residents of the city since 1883, and are spoken of in the highest terms, as young business men of soundest judgment, progressive methods, and honorable, equitable policy. Mr. A. Moller is the general manager, and is specially qualified for the discharge of the onerous duties devolving upon him, and under his guidance the product is maintained at the highest standard of excellence. The company offers the most substantial inducements, both as to price and quality, in full lines of parlor furniture, easy chairs, rockers, lounges, etc., and we strongly recommend trade buyers to inspect this stock before placing their orders.

HOWARD & WILSON PUBLISHING CO.

The Howard & Wilson Publishing Co. devote their attention and to publishing first-class agricultural literature and thus contribute to the sum total of Chicago's enterprise the important feature of the contemporary historian, the guide of usefulness. In October, 1885, however, the present company was organized and took hold, and the paper is now a weekly publication, circulated all over the United States, having a circulation of 54,000. It is sent through more than 13,245 post-offices, and 26,000 new subscribers have been added since the new management took hold. Gen. C. H. Howard is the editor; W. B. Lloyd, and O. McG. Howard, associate editors, while Mr. James W. Wilson is the business manager. In the hands of this firm the *Farm, Field and Stockman* has attained a high and influential position. In point of circulation its position is invulnerable; in the far more important feature of its educational and protective influence—if the countingroom will permit the idea that that feature is the more important of the two—the paper has reached the very front. All that appeals to the interests of the field or stock farmer, the agriculturist generally, the *Farm, Field and Stockman* is at the head, in the interest and value. At the same time, the family is by no means lost sight of, entertaining matter for general reading finding full place in its columns, so that it is warmly welcomed wherever it has been permitted to have an introduction. The subscription is $1.00 per year, and its advertising rates are thirty cents per agate line. The success of the paper is shown by the readiness with which wide-awake manufacturers seek the use of its columns. Sample copies are mailed free on application. The offices of the *Farm, Field and Stockman* occupy five large rooms in the building at the northwest corner of Fifth avenue and Washington streets, and are nicely fitted up for its purposes.

ARCHIBALD HAAS.

One of the finest, best equipped, and most patronized pharmacies in this section of the city is that of Mr. Archibald Haas, which was established about three years ago, on the corner of Armitage road and Sheridan street. Mr. Haas has occupied his present premises since November last. Possessed of great professional skill, and a thorough knowledge of the details of the chemist's science, acquired during several years of practical association with medicine, he soon gained a large and influential patronage. The store, located at No. 1046 N. Western avenue, is handsomely and attractively furnished and fitted up. Ornamental fixtures and elegant showcases and cabinets add to the attractiveness of the display made of pure drugs and chemicals, standard proprietary remedies, essences, extracts, herbs, barks, roots, etc. The assortment also includes full lines of fancy and toilet articles. Special attention is given to the compounding of physicians' prescriptions and family recipes, great care being exercised to avoid the possibility of error, and only the purest ingredients being used, while prices charged are fair and equitable. Mr. Haas is a native of Missouri, and is a graduate of the Chicago College of Physicians and Surgeons of the class of '85, and Bennett College, class of '82. He is a member of the Chicago Pharmaceutical Association, and is a regular practicing physician. Mr. Haas is a son of Wm. Haas, who founded the first brewery in Chicago, which was located at the foot of Chicago avenue and the lake shore. Mr. Haas brewed the first glass of ale in Chicago. This was in 1837. The late Wm. B. Ogden was at that time identified with the business.

THE YOUNG & FARREL DIAMOND STONE SAWING CO.

A concern having a well-earned national celebrity is that of the Young & Farrel Diamond Stone Sawing Company, by whose improved methods stone for sidewalks, and cut stone for all purposes, are prepared with expeditious economy and accuracy of finish impossible by any other method. This company was incorporated in 1882, with a paid-up capital of $300,000, and they erected a large and completely equipped manufacturing plant in this city, where a number of Young's famous Diamond saws and planers are in operation. The plant has had to be repeatedly enlarged to cope with the growing demand. The works are located on W. Polk street, fronting on the south branch of the Chicago river, and comprise a series of substantial brick and stone buildings, with large yards for storage. The manufacture of sidewalk stone is one of their specialties, and a large force of men are employed at their quarry at Joliet, Ill., where the stone for this purpose is obtained. They have extensive works there for the planing and sawing of stone, in addition to those in this city. These planed sidewalks are used, not only in Chicago, but are shipped to St. Louis, Kansas City, St. Paul, Minneapolis, Milwaukee, Grand Rapids, etc., and they have even gone as far east as Brooklyn, N. Y. They have no equal for beauty, comfort, strength, cleanliness and durability, and they are put down in such large pieces as to be very attractive and desirable. The company has railroad sidings into their works, both in Chicago and in Joliet, which gives direct railroad connection with the entire country. The company, in addition to its cut stone and sidewalk departments, also deals in rubble, footings, curbing, blocks and sawed stone, and they are sole manufacturers of Young's Diamond saws, planers, cranes, travelers, etc. The president of the company, Mr. Hugh Young, is widely and favorably known in Chicago and in the East. He has long been actively identified with quarrying and stone cutting interests, and his Diamond saws, planers, cranes, etc., are proof of his sound, practical judgment, and his inventive ability. He has the valued support of Mr. F. V. Gindele as treasurer; Mr. Henry Struble as secretary, and Mr. Robert C. Harper as manager; the entire executive being made up of specially qualified men, thoroughly trained and of large experience. The pre-eminence of this company—for it is believed to be unequaled in its class as to scope of business facilities and organization, in this or any other country—is only one among the multitude of illustrations of what opportunities the great west and the great western metropolis, Chicago, afford to character, talent and energy.

HOOLEY'S THEATRE.

Hooley's Theatre has achieved a national celebrity as the most successful and ably conducted playhouse in America. One that has benefited by reason of the exceptional ability and energy of its management, and whose popularity is based upon its annually offering a series of the greatest dramatic attractions available. The present theatre was built shortly after the Chicago fire, by Mr. R. M. Hooley, and who first threw open its doors to the public in 1872. From the start it was the favorite playhouse with Chicagoans, and has had a continuously brilliant series of achievements as regards the superiority of the attractions offered. The present magnificent theater presents the embodiment of every modern improvement, its cost being $150,000. It has an unusually fine orchestra, roomy parquet, and two spacious balconies, giving it a combined seating capacity of 1,550, and though it is one of the smallest first-class theaters devoted exclusively to comedy in Chicago, it is the most profitable, the season of 1890 affording a forcible illustration, the average of business for the forty-seven weeks exceeding $7,000 per week. Among the attractions were Augustin Daly's Company, Mr. and Mrs. Kendal, whose three weeks in January eclipsed in its business any other record of the house, the receipts being nearly $39,000, of which the first week netted $14,125. A. M. Palmer, E. S. Willard, E. H. Sothern, Nat. C. Goodwin, etc., etc., are among the nationally familiar names of companies seen here,

and which will again appear, at the dates assigned, this present season of 1891-92. The house, which has won such an artistic record, and material success, occupies an unusually favorable location on Randolph street, opposite the city court house, and convenient of access from all sections. The premises are 65x125 feet in dimensions, and present a remarkably handsome architectural frontage. The building is heated by steam, lighted by electric light, and is a fireproof structure, with numerous means of exit when required. Mr. R. M. Hooley, whose house has won the most remarkable theatrical success of the age, is a native of New York, resident in Chicago for thirty years past, who has ever led in all measures calculated to advance the city's welfare and development. His theatre is a nucleus and a center for the world's dramatic talent, and the Chicago public have to thank him for securing to them a house fully the equal of the finest in New York, more successful than any there, and one that has before it an ever widening career of prosperity. Mr. Hooley is possessed of shrewdest discrimination and soundest judgment as to the class of plays best adapted to please the refined and intellectual audiences of Chicago, and the public reposes unlimited confidence in his ability and resources to adequately supply the demand in the highest walks of comedy-drama.

CHICAGO FOUNTAIN SODA WATER CO.

The representative and most noted concern in the great Western metropolis, extensively engaged in the manufacture of fountain soda, syrups of all flavors, and marble draught apparatus, is that known as the Chicago Fountain Soda Water Co., whose factory and office are located at 425 and 427 W. Harrison street, in a building owned by Mr. Arthur Christin, the superintendent and treasurer. This company was incorporated in 1886, under the laws of Illinois, with a paid up capital of $100,000, and is a consolidation of three well-known concerns, viz, The Lomax Bottling Co., established in 1850, by J. A. Lomax, Hutchinson & Son's Soda Water Co., founded in 1850, by W. H. Hutchinson, and the A. Christin Soda Water Co., established in 1881, by Arthur Christin. These concerns were consolidated to save expense, and the following gentlemen, widely and favorably known in Chicago's business circles for their integrity and enterprise, are the executive officers and directors, viz.: Chas. G. Hutchinson, president, John A. Lomax, vice-president, Arthur Christin, superintendent and treasurer, George Lomax, secretary. Directors: Arthur Christin, John A. Lomax, Geo. C. Hutchinson, Charles G. Hutchinson and George Lomax. They occupy for offices and warerooms a spacious ground floor, 25x100 feet in area, with a large and well-equipped factory in the rear. Here they carry a large stock of 100 soda water draught apparatus, 2,000 steel tanks for charging soda, all of which they rent to patrons. A heavy stock of syrups of all flavors and fountain soda is always on hand, and twenty-five men and twelve wagons are constantly employed. They supply their fountains to hotel-keepers, druggists, confectioners, etc., in all sections of the city and its vicinity at very moderate prices. Their goods are highly prized by all lovers of pure carbonated waters, on account of their absolute freedom from adulteration, and the great quantity of carbonic acid gas with which they are charged. Their syrups are absolutely unrivaled for purity, flavor and native excellence, and have no superiors in the market. They have several valuable patents on their marble draught apparatus, and their patronage is steadily increasing. Mr. Chas. G. Hutchinson, the president, also carries on a large extract business in Desplaines street, and deals in bottlers' supplies. Mr. J. A. Lomax, the vice-president, is also in the bottling business, at 14 to 18 Charles place, and bottles extensively all kinds of mineral waters. The business of the Chicago Fountain Soda Water Co. is under the immediate personal supervision of Mr. Arthur Christin, the superintendent and treasurer, who is widely known for the prompt and careful manner in which he attends to the wants of customers. The telephone call of the company is 4660, and all orders by that way are attended to as promptly and carefully as by letter or a personal visit could insure.

THE DAVIS SEWING MACHINE COMPANY.

The inventor of the sewing machine has added countless hours to woman's leisure for rest and refinement, and has

NEW SHOPS OF DAVIS SEWING MACHINE CO.

Capacity 400 Machines per Day

FOR TERMS, ETC., ADDRESS

DAVIS SEWING MACHINE CO.

DAYTON, O.   CHICAGO, ILL.

brought numerous comforts within the reach of all, which previously were enjoyed only by the wealthy. In this connection special attention is directed in this commercial review of Chi-

cago, to the representative and successful Davis Sewing Machine Company, manufacturers of the Vertical Feed Sewing Machines, whose office and salesrooms are located at 46 to 50 Jackson street. This company was incorporated 25 years ago with a paid up capital of $600,000, and its trade now extends not only throughout the entire United States and Canada, but also in all parts of the civilized world. The Chicago branch was opened in 1873, and ever since that date has been under the able and energetic management of Mr. A. G. Mason, who handles 20,000 of the company's machines annually. The premises occupied in the Garden City comprise three spacious floors, which are fully stocked with the famous Davis sewing machines, that are offered to customers either for cash or on the installment plan at very moderate prices. In the Chicago branch 40 persons are employed, and the trade of the company is steadily increasing, owing to the superiority and efficiency of its productions. The famous New High Arm Davis can now be purchased with entire confidence. In its construction the company has combined simplicity, durability, speed and excellence of work. The company's new factory is located at Dayton, Ohio. It is the most complete as well as the largest sewing machine plant, except one, in America. Its capacity is 400 finished machines daily, and the company's phenomenal success is solely due to the superior merits of the Davis Vertical Feed Sewing Machine. Mr. Mason has been in the company's employment for the last 22 years, and is widely known for his promptness and just methods. The Davis machine is the perfection of mechanism for hemming, trimming, binding, cording, seaming, braiding, embroidering and other purposes too numerous to particularize, and notwithstanding its remarkable qualities, the price is no higher than is demanded for very inferior machines

W. McGREGOR & CO.

The annually increasing demand for steam power and machinery in the United States necessitates correspondingly large facilities for their production, hence the building of steam engines and boilers constitutes a very important branch of industry. Among the representative and reliable houses in Chicago actively engaged in the manufacture and sale of steam engines, boilers, sawmills, and general machinery, special mention should be made of the widely-known firm of Messrs. W. McGregor & Co, whose salesrooms are located at 53 and 55 South Clinton street and 44 to 48 South Jefferson street. This extensive business was established in 1867 by Mr. Wm. McGregor, who conducted it till 1884 when it was incorporated under the laws of Illinois with large capital, the executive officers being Mr. Wm. McGregor, president, and Mr. Peter Terwilliger, secretary. They occupy three spacious floors, and are now building new works on San Francisco street and Carroll avenue, which have an area of 200x425 feet. Here they will have every convenience for the production of engines, boilers, etc., and they guarantee entire satisfaction to patrons at the lowest possible prices, consistent with first-class workmanship and the best materials. In addition to all kinds of steam engines and boilers, they keep constantly in stock steam pumps, iron lathes, iron planers, wood planers, drill presses, shapers, moulding machines, sawmills, feed mills, shingle mills, feed water heaters, injectors, pulleys, shafting, hangers, leather and rubber belting, iron pipe, iron and brass valves, and everything pertaining to machinery supplies. Only really reliable new and second-hand engines and machinery are handled, and all machines are fully warranted to be exactly as represented. Orders are filled promptly and carefully, and the trade of the house extends throughout all sections of the Western and Northwestern States. Mr. McGregor was born in Scotland, while Mr. Terwilliger is a native of Orange county, New York. They have both resided in Chicago many years, and are highly regarded in trade circles for their mechanical skill, enterprise and integrity. Mr. McGregor is a popular member of the Illinois Club. They issue annually a superior illustrated catalogue and price list, which is forwarded promptly upon application, and which owners of mills and users of machinery should have for reference.

J. A. MACFARLANE & CO.

No class of furniture has come into such general use, or become so popular, as the rattan and reed line, which is by far preferable to any other for cleanliness, durability and appearance. Chicago's principal representative in this line is the well-known firm of J. A. Macfarlane & Co., manufacturers of rattan and reed furniture, iron wagons, tricycles, velocipedes, etc., at Nos. 131 and 133 East Kinzie street. This business was established four years ago by the McFarlane Brothers, at Nos. 141, 143 and 145 East Kinzie street, but their rapidly increasing business compelled them to remove to their present commodious quarters, where they occupy three stories and the basement, 40x100 feet in size. They have their manufactory finely equipped with all the latest and best improved machinery to facilitate their work, and have an improved ten-horse power engine to give them power. The firm is composed of J. A. Macfarlane and his brother, Frederick Macfarlane, natives of Canada, but who have been in Chicago for a number of years, and are thoroughly imbued with the enterprising spirit so infectious in this clime. Their children's carriages, exhibited in different localities from Maine to California, have attracted attention and made sales in nearly every state in the Union, and orders show that the trade is constantly increasing. The firm of J. A. Macfarlane & Co. are the leaders in their line, and the past season they have made a specialty of baby carriages, which they finish in the latest designs as the best sellers and cheapest on the market, warranted in every respect. They finish all goods in XVIth century, bronze, enamel or any shade desired, and show fourteen new designs in chairs, introducing a new braid work in the backs, which is durable and very artistic. Especial attention is paid to their upholstered goods in the standard shades of pea, blue, cardinal, terra cotta, old gold, seal brown, olive and fawn. The gear of the baby carriages is of the best, including the "Acme" and "Novelty," the first being two front "C" springs with heavy "W" coil, or two coil springs in the rear. The "Novelty" gear is two front novelty springs, with two "C" coil springs in the rear, both of which are substantial, comfortable and durable. They make their baby carriages with iron or wood wheels, or with rubber tire and Cowles' patent brake. Both of the proprietors are young men, enterprising and energetic, and are popular in social and business circles.

PORTMAN & PARKER.

To no class of business men is more credit due for the advancement of the interests of Chicago than to the real estate dealers. These gentlemen have advertised the city's advantages and directed the attention of investors and manufacturers to this place until it is to-day the city of greatest possibilities in the Union. A firm engaged in handling real estate, and having a superior reputation, is that known as Portman & Parker, having their office at 268 Wells street. The business was founded by Mr. M. P. Portman about ten years ago, and was continued by him alone until January last, when Mr. J. B. Parker became interested and entered into a partnership. The business is conducted on strict business principles, and the large patronage attests the popularity of the house, as well as the regard held for the members of the firm. A general real estate business is conducted, property is bought and sold on commission, rents are collected, estates managed, taxes and assessments paid and property looked after for non-residents, insurance effected, and loans made on real estate security. All business is done under the direct supervision of the proprietors, who bring experience and business ability to bear to faithfully serve the customers' interests. The house has a liberal patronage, and stands well in business and financial circles, Mr. Portman was born in Germany and came to Chicago twenty-four years ago; he is well known in leading real estate circles and is a member of the Royal Arcanum. Mr. Parker is a native of New York state and has only been in

Chicago a short time, having been for some years in the cattle business in Montana. The firm make a specialty of handling lake shore property, the finest residential locations in the city, some of the finest private residences being located here, among which is that of Potter Palmer, Esq., and many others. Much of the real estate which they handle is owned by themselves, and to those contemplating purchasing either for a home or an investment this firm offers superior inducements, both as to location and price.

A. S. PIPER & CO.

In distributing our gratitude there are few to whom we would all of us be more lavish than to those who contribute to our temporary comfort during the hot weather, and, this being so, the firm of A. S. Piper & Co. would come in for a large share, for they supply the city largely with ice, having houses located at Mount Forest, Ill., on the C. & A. R. R., and water communication by the Illinois & Michigan Canal, and at Little Sturgeon Bay, Wisconsin, with city depots at Ashland avenue and Levee street, and 83 West Twelfth street. But this is only one branch of the business, as in addition they manufacture largely ice tools, wagons, plows and also Nelson's Patent Clearing Tooth which can be attached to any plow. Their workshops are at Bridgeport, Ill. It is not possible within the limits of anything less than a pamphlet itself to do justice to a descriptive account of this enterprise, so we must content ourselves with a mere general notice of the business, which forms a very important page in Chicago's commercial history. The business was established thirty years ago, and the present members of the firm are Mrs. A. S. Piper, Mr. Seth Piper and Mr. Thos. Piper. Mr. N. P. Nelson has been superintendent since 1879, and is the inventor of Nelson's Patent Fifth Wheel, manufactured exclusively by A. S. Piper & Co., and especially adapted for heavy wagons with or without springs. The firm has about thirty ice wagons for city delivery purposes, and employs in summer 175 men, and in winter 400. Their plant at Mt. Forest, Ill., is the most complete in the country, and besides manufacturing the articles above enumerated they make every kind of tool known for the purposes of ice farming, and undertake all kinds of repairing. They furnish ice at wholesale by cargo or car loads to ice dealers, brewers or packers, in any amount desired, and will ship it in any direction on the shortest notice. They have nearly all their varieties of ice tools in stock, and will furnish an illustrated catalogue on application, together with any desired information.

JOHNSON BROS.

We have in the store of Messrs. Johnson Bros., at 1062 West Twelfth street boulevard, a model grocery and meat market, and one which justly does credit to the neighborhood. Nor is this remarkable when we consider the business experience of the proprietors. The store was established on September 12, 1890, by Mr. J. H. and Mr. George D. Johnson, under the style of Johnson Bros. They occupy the ground floor and basement, 25x90 feet, and the place is thoroughly well stocked with every kind of staple and fancy groceries, including a fine assortment of canned goods and some specially fine growths of teas and coffees. They employ an ample force of help and two delivery wagons, and orders are called for and delivered with great promptness, so that customers are saved any trouble. The brothers were born in Ohio and raised in Michigan. Mr. J. H. Johnson has been in Chicago for five years, and was formerly running the electric light plant on the New York & Chicago Pennsylvania limited for the Pullman Palace Car Co. Mr. George D. Johnson was formerly in the clothing business in Buffalo, N. Y., in the store of Mr. J. L. Hudson. They run a meat market in connection with their grocery store, and always carry the choicest fresh and salt meats, which they get daily from the stock yards, as well as a full line of fruits and vegetables in season. It is hardly necessary to say that they pay the closest attention to their business, which is now an assured success.

M. B. SCHMIDT.

The numerous stores and offices of Chicago create a steady demand for fixtures of a superior grade. A house but recently established, yet strong and with the brightest possible future before it, is that of Mr. M. B. Schmidt, manufacturer of and dealer in saloon, store and office fixtures. When Mr. Schmidt started in business he associated a Mr. Nelson with him under the title of Schmidt, Nelson & Co., but this copartnership not being altogether desirable, the firm was dissolved, and the business continued by Mr. Schmidt alone. He occupies the ground floor of the premises 534 N. Wells street for the demands of his business, and has a commodious apartment, 25x60 feet in dimensions, thoroughly stocked with fine hardwood counters, shelving, showcases, etc,, in process of manufacture and complete. Mr. Schmidt employs two experienced cabinetmakers and finishers, and does an excellent business in the finest fixtures of all kinds, He personally superintends the work, thus insuring the best results. Mr. Schmidt is a young man of rare business ability, which he brings to bear on his enterprise. He is developing a good business connection that will be of great power in a short time.

MOYEN BROS.

Chicago has numerous first-class drugstores in all sections of the city, and patrons usually receive most courteous attention, and have their needs supplied intelligently. However, there is always, in each district, some one business house noted for its superiority, and the well known pharmacy of the Moyen Bros., is one of the very best to be found on the West side. The business was established a little less than three years ago by G. F. W. Moyen and F. C. Moyen, young gentlemen who were born and reared in this city. They are thoroughly skilled and experienced druggists and chemists, and are competent to undertake the most delicate analysis or compound the most elaborate prescription. They graduated from the Chicago College of Pharmacy with distinction, and are regularly licensed druggists. They have an elegant drug store on the ground floor of the handsome three-story brick building, at 1595 Milwaukee avenue, corner of Armitage, and have a stock of superior drugs, tinctures, syrups, decoctions and patent medicines, as well as toilet articles, brushes, soaps, rubber goods, physicians' and surgeons' supplies, trusses, bandages, etc.' An elegant soda fountain graces the store and is a place of popular resort, and the finest domestic and imported cigars may be had in many select and popular brands. Physicians' prescriptions are carefully and accurately compounded and only moderate charges are made for services. The gentlemen of this house are well known and highly respected, and are favored with a liberal patronage, which increases constantly, thus attesting the popularity of the house.

J. L. SMITH.

There is no more energetic and progressive hardware dealer in Chicago than Mr. J. L. Smith, who conducts an extensive business at 752 W. North avenue. Mr. Smith was born in Sweden and came to Chicago about twenty-two years ago. He engaged in the enterprise he has made such a success about three years ago on the same street he is now located on, and by his enterprise and close attention to business soon built up a large business. Early in the present year he built the premises he now occupies, at a cost of $5,000, and has a complete establishment with every convenience for properly conducting the business. The building is a three-story brick, 25x75 feet in dimensions. Mr. Smith has his large store on the ground floor stocked with a complete line of the finest hardware, consisting of shelf and builders' hardware, mechanics' tools, axes, tinware, hollow ware, garden tools, nails, locks, hinges, tar paper, sinks, pumps, cutlery, etc. Also a fine line of stoves and ranges, being the agent for the celebrated "Garland" stoves and ranges. He has a number of the leading contractors and builders among his customers, whose trade is of great consequence, and his general trade is very large and constantly increasing. Three persons are employed, and a large business is done in roofing and tin work, also stove repairing. Mr. Smith is characterized by his indomitable energy, and his success is largely due to his untiring efforts and close application.

ULICK BOURKE.

No branch of trade has made greater progress in recent years toward combining the artistic with the useful than that of hand made furniture, the designs, colors and finish being now as elegant, as but a short time ago they were plain and homely. Chicago has many large houses devoted to the business, one of the principal being that of Mr. Ulick Bourke of No. 302 W. Madison street, established as long ago as 1867, and is justly celebrated for the beauty and variety of its stock. Mr. Bourke occupies the whole of a fine building, 36x120 feet in dimensions, five stories in height, and packed with furniture, carpets, stoves, etc., from roof to basement, giving an exceptionally fine choice of complete housekeeping outfits of every style from the mediaeval down to the latest popular modern designs. Their display of parlor and bedroom suites, and dining room and library furniture, is unrivaled, while they keep odd pieces in vast variety, including cabinets, card tables, escritoires, sideboards, easy-chairs, etc., each article a perfect type of the highest progress of the art. Mr. Bourke personally superintends his large force of assistants, averaging over twenty, and requires the constant services of four teams in completing the large orders with which he is favored. Every factor to the highest success is here to be found, resources, facilities and popularity, being all that could be desired by the most sanguine, while there are few men in Chicago to-day who can boast of a more intimate knowledge of the building and furnishing of houses, both in the East and West, than the estimable proprietor of this great emporium. Mr. Bourke is a native of Ireland, but has resided in this country for forty-six years. He is an old and greatly respected citizen of this center, and has merited the confidence of the public by honorable dealing and adherence to correct principles in every phase of life.

A. L. LEUTGERT.

The manufacture of sausages is an industry which now engages the attention of many large and flourishing Chicago firms, among whom a prominent place is due to that of Mr. A. L. Luetgert, whose extensive works are located at Nos. 69 and 71 North avenue. Founded eleven years ago by its present esteemed proprietor, the business has been built up on a sound basis, and has been managed with prudence and wisdom as well as enterprise, until it is now acknowledged to be one of the foremost in its line in the Western states. It requires the constant services of fifty experts assistants, who have all kinds of modern machinery at command, driven by steam power, offering unparalleled facilities for the production of a superior article, which finds its way into the restaurants of every town and city of the United States.' The premises consists of two commodious and substantial brick buildings, four stories in height, whose internal arrangements are models of what the interiors of such structures should be. Mr. Luetgert has established an enviable reputation for the high quality and delicate flavor of his productions. These include summer sausages only, made from the choicest materials, on the very best system known to the trade, and handled and stored in such a careful way as to insure their reaching the consumer in prime condition. Mr. Luetgert is a German by birth, but has, during his residence of a quarter of a century in Chicago, deservedly earned the warm esteem of all who have been thrown into contact with him. His marvelous success in such a short time is sure evidence of his ability and integrity, and should afford encouragement to every struggling merchant to go and do likewise.

CHRIST. JENSEN.

There is no more substantial business house on the North side than that of Mr. Christ. Jensen, importer and wholesale whiskey merchant, at Nos. 234 and 236 Larrabee street. Mr. Jensen established his business sixteen years ago on North Clark street, but his large and increasing trade compelled him, in 1888, to build the large three-story building at his present location, 40x100 feet in size, and at a cost of

$15,000. Mr. Jensen occupies the whole building, which is none too large for his very extensive stock of French, Spanish and German wines, which he imports direct; and brandies, whiskeys, gins, rums and liquors, all of the very best quality. Mr. Jensen is also the manufacturer of the celebrated Malakoff Bitters, and is a rectifier of spirits. His stock is second to none in quality or quantity, and his immense wholesale trade is steadily increasing. Mr. Jensen was born in Germany, but has had his home in Chicago for the past twenty-five years. He is a leading real estate proprietor on the North side, and owns many thousand dollars' worth of ground in his own neighborhood. He is a prominent member of the Knights of Pythias; also of the Plattdeutscher Verein of Chicago, and is popular in all business and social circles. Mr. Frank Strack, the general manager for Mr. Jensen, is a young man well known to the trade, and has made many friends among the customers of this well known house. He is a native of Germany.

DANHEISER & BORG.

The manufacture of chewing gum is an industry to which the greatest care and skill is devoted, as impurity of materials or manufacture might be attended with the most calamitous results. Messrs. Danheiser & Borg have, however, been engaged in the avocation for nearly eight years, and produce the most wholesome plain and fancy chewing gums in the market. They have a wide experience and an intimate knowledge of the wants of the trade. Every suitable and proper appliance is also at hand in their large factory for the purpose, and every one of their fifty or sixty hands has been selected only after the firm have been thoroughly satisfied of their capacity and carefulness. The gums made here can be implicitly relied on and freely used. Messrs. Danheiser & Borg have no less than 15,000 square feet of floor space at Nos. 59 and 61 South Canal street, and transact a business that is co-extensive with the United States, and includes in the great circle of its influence the best and most desirable wholesalers and retailers in every part of the country. The history of this house has been one continuous record of success, and affords a striking instance of what enterprise and perseverance in almost any branch of industry can perform. Mr. Bernard Danheiser is a native of Memphis, Tenn., and Mr. Isaac Borg, of Germany, and both

gentlemen command the respect and esteem of a very wide circle in all grades of life. They are capable business men, honorable and upright, who fully merit the conspicuous success they have achieved.

DAVID TREFRY.

A reliable and responsible house, which by virtue of the extent and importance of its trade has reached the front rank of mercantile establishments in Englewood, is that of Mr. David Trefry, dealer in lamps, glassware, tinware, and all kinds of household goods, at No. 546 Sixty-third street. This business was inaugurated by its present proprietor in 1856, and from its inception it has been the center of a brisk and rapidly increasing trade. Its growth and development have been remarkable, and, to meet its ever increasing requirements, more spacious and commodious quarters have lately been moved into. The premises now utilized comprise the ground floor of a two-story frame building, eligibly located, and having a frontage of 20 feet, by a depth of 40 feet. They are neatly appointed and well ordered in every respect, and are provided with all conveniences and facilities for the storage, display and inspection of the heavy stock always on hand. The assortment is vast and varied, and embraces full lines of household supplies and specialties, such as lamps of all kinds, shapes and sizes, chimneys, burners, globes, wicks, kitchen utensils, tinware, wood and willow ware, copper and sheet iron ware, and a thousand and one various articles, such as are in daily requisition by the housekeeper. These goods are all purchased at first hands from the most reliable sources, and are offered at the lowest prices. They are all warranted to be the finest of their kind in the market, and the house is well and favorably know to handle only the best goods. Petroleum products and the best grades of illuminating oils are also handled. Mr D. Trefry was born in the province of Nova Scotia, and has been a resident of Chicago since 1871. He is a highly esteemed and popular dealer, and has achieved his marked success by dint of energy, enterprise and honorable methods.

G. E. LANGER.

The manufacture of artistic signs has become elevated to the position of an intricate art, in which none can hope to succeed who do not possess a degree of taste and skill considerably above the average. Mr. G. E. Langer of No. 134 E. Kinzie street is one of the most deservedly noted makers in the city. He has introduced many novelties of his own designing, and has done much toward effecting the radical improvements noticeable in this line in recent years. He began business twenty years ago at No. 193 Washington street, and has conducted his affairs upon such a sound and well-balanced basis that he has secured and retained the confidence and patronage of the most desirable establishments of the city. He makes all descriptions of signs for advertising, name plates, street names and numbers, etc., of every conceivable style, size, shape and material. Mr. Langer has achieved his most conspicuous success in glass signs, his productions in this popular department being perfect types of the highest attainment of the art. He is fully prepared to execute the most important commissions for breweries, saloons, hotels, commercial houses, etc., in glass, wood or metal, having a large staff of skilled assistants continually employed, and every facility at hand for the interesting work. He occupies the whole of a handsome three-story brick building with basement, besides a large floor at No. 134 Kinzie street, used for the storage of his immense stock of glass. This well-managed house has influential connections in every part of the United States, and is in constant receipt of large orders from every great center between the Atlantic and Pacific oceans. Mr. Langer is a native of Germany, but has during his thirty-five years' residence in this city become thoroughly western in ideas and sentiments. He is numbered as a member of the Royal Arcanum and of the Turner's Society, and is popular and respected by all classes of the community for his straightforward traits of character in all his business relations as well as in the fulfilment of his duties as a patriotic citizen.

L. EVERINGHAM & CO.

One of the leading grain commission houses of the city, is the well-known firm of L. Everingham & Co. The business of this house was first established in 1865, in Milwaukee, Wis., under the firm name of Bacon & Everingham, and so continued until 1875, when the firm of Bacon & Everingham was dissolved, Mr. Everingham succeeding, and the present business was established in 1880, by the removal of Mr. Everingham to this city to take charge of the same. Mr. Everingham is a member of the Chicago and Milwaukee Board of Trade and the Chicago Stock Exchange. The firm does a general commission business in grain for cash or future delivery, also making a specialty of all kinds of seeds. The market reports sent out by this house are considered as being of the most accurate and reliable character, and their special information indicating the course of the markets is eagerly sought by speculators and dealers all over the country. This house has an established reputation for fair and honorable dealing, and enjoys a most liberal patronage from all of the leading cities, having constant communications with St. Louis, Kansas City, Minneapolis, Duluth, Milwaukee and the most important Eastern points. The volume of business done in grain and provisions for future delivery is simply enormous. The long and successful experience Mr. Everingham has had as an active operator in grain and provisions, enables him to offer special advantages to all who intrust him with their orders, and in addition to his personal supervision of the business, he is amply and ably supported by an efficient corps of assistants who have been with him for a long time, thus giving the firm every facility for intelligent and satisfactory work, where so much depends upon intelligence and promptness. The offices of the firm are in the Royal Insurance building, rooms 200, 201 and 202 being used for the various departments of the trade. Mr. Everingham is a gentleman a little past middle age, and one of the best known in financial and trade circles in the city. He is president of the Columbia National Bank. A gentleman of broad views and a liberal mind, he finds time to give attention to the demands of his religious preferences, being an active officer in one of the leading Protestant churches of Chicago, foremost in charitable and benevolent objects, and always ready to give his substantial support to any measure for advancing the interests of this city. Persons interested in grain and seeds, which form such an important part of the business of the city of Chicago, can find no safer medium for the transaction of their business than this house. Having passed through all the corners, fluctuations in prices, failures on the Board of Trade since 1865 unscathed, with not a check thrown out, and without a suspicion attached to their name, their reputation is widespread, and for their solidity, financial standing and untarnished honor in all of their business relations, they refer to the public at large.

DICKSON & LOTT.

There is no industry in the city of Chicago which takes precedence over that of the live stock commission business. From a small beginning, it has grown to be the largest market in the world for cattle, sheep and hogs. This growth and prosperity is due, in a great measure, to the energy and enterprise of the live stock commission men, who have created this splendid market. Among the most prominent in this line is the well known firm of Dickson & Lott, whose office is in room No. 125 in the Exchange building, at the Union Stock Yards. The present firm was established six years ago, but both members had been connected with other firms in the live stock business for years previous. Mr. W. T. Dickson was born in Illinois, and has been in Chicago for the past twenty-one years, all of which time he has been engaged in the live stock business. Mr. James P. Lott is a native of the "Buckeye" state, and came to seek his fortune in Chicago twenty-one years ago, and has been engaged in the stock business ever since. They do a general live stock commission business, buying and selling cattle, hogs and sheep, paying especial attention to selling. They have perfect facilities for handling and caring for all consignments,

and their large acquaintance enables them to find ready sale for all consignments. Mr. Dickson devotes himself to the cattle department, and Mr. Lott to the hog and sheep business, while the office is in charge of their genial book-keeper, Mr. W. H. Patrick. They employ no salesmen, but do their own selling and give the business their personal attention in all of its details. The firm has established a reputation for their shrewdness, careful attention to their patrons' interests and prompt returns on all consignments. That they are substantial and reliable is attested by the following list of references : National Live Stock Bank of Chicago; Bloomington National Bank, and Funk Bros., of Bloomington, Ill. ; Second National Bank of Monmouth, Ill. ; First National Bank of Paris, Ill. ; First National Bank of Tuscola, Ill. ; the Ringgold County Bank of Mount Ayr, Iowa, and D. C. and E. F. Rankin, Tarkio, Mo. They solicit correspondence, and will quote markets on application by wire or mail.

R. E. POHLE.

One of the foremost industries of Chicago is the manufacture of fine furniture. We desire to call attention to the business in this line of Mr. R. E. Pohle, manufacturer of tables and hall trees. Mr. Pohle has been established in business for seventeen years in Chicago, being a native of the city. He has a large and very complete factory at 316 and 318 S. Clinton street, where he manufactures center, fancy wood top and pillar extension tables, hat racks, hall trees, etc. He gives employment to fifty persons and keeps two teams constantly at work. The factory occupies the large four-story brick building, 40x125, at the above address. Mr. Pohle carries a large and very complete stock of goods of his own manufacture, and issues an annual catalogue of designs offered the trade. By reference to this it is discovered that the tables made at this factory are of every conceivable design, many being quite novel. The goods have all a remarkable degree of freshness and novelty in their design, and are certainly very attractive. The trade of this house extends all over the United States. Mr. Pohle is well known to the business community and is held in the highest esteem. His business is of an extensive and remunerative character and is increasing.

JOHN CARROLL.

When we think of the manner in which funerals were conducted fifty years ago we almost stand aghast with horror, and in probably no business has the march of progress made such wonderful improvements during that time. From a mere trade it has become a dignified profession, just as much so as that of a physician or surgeon, and it exacts from its followers, not only a thorough business training, but a scientific knowledge of a very high character. The leading, oldest established and most popular concern on the North Side is that of Mr. John Carroll, at 199 Wells street, corner of Superior street, whose residence is at 109 Superior street, and telephone call 3475. Twenty-one years ago Mr. Carroll established the business at 171 E. Chicago avenue, in 1871 he was burned out at 61 St. Clair street, and has occupied his present store since 1891. His store and office are comfortably and decorously furnished, and here he carries a full line of caskets and coffins of elegant design, though not necessarily expensive; also robes, and general funeral furnishings. Hearses and carriages are supplied, and funeral directions are attended to by day or night. Remains are met at all depots, and graves opened in any of the neighboring cemeteries. When embalming is desired Mr. Carroll undertakes it on the most improved principle and has met with great success. All work is executed in the most expeditious manner, and everything is done that human nature can do to lessen the distress and alleviate the anxiety of relatives, while Mr. Carroll is at all times most moderate in his charges. He is a native of Ireland and came to Chicago in 1851, being now sixty-five years of age. He is a member of the Chicago Undertakers' Association, and is very popular among his fellow members, while he has hosts of friends.

CRAMER & BURT.

Among the most active, enterprising and popular firms engaged in the metal trade in this great metropolitan center is that of Messrs. Cramer & Burt, with offices most centrally located in the Phoenix building. Mr Ambrose Cramer and Mr. Chas. S. Burt formed the existing copartnership in 1890 to handle the products of leading forges and mills, and with their widespread influential connections have developed a trade of great magnitude. These gentlemen bring to bear special qualifications. Mr. Cramer is a native of Virginia, graduated at the U. S. Naval Academyat Annapolis, Md , and subsequently for eight years was superintendent of the firm of Cramer & Co.,manufacturers of brass and iron fittings, valves, cocks, pipes, etc. Mr. Chas. S. Burt was formerly in the pig iron business in Detroit, with branches at Newberry and Marquette, Mich. He is a graduate of the U. S. Military Academy at West Point, N. Y., and is a post graduate student in chemistry at the Sheffield Scientific School in Yale College. He was formerly the chemist and metallurgist in the Midvale Steel Works, Pa , and has had great experience. Thus it will be seen that the firm are in every respect familiarly conversant with the needs of the trade in the line of metals, and are the representatives here of several leading concerns, being the general Northwestern agents for the Baltimore Copper Smelting and Rolling Co., of Baltimore, Md., representing Mr. Henry H.,Adams of New York, pig iron; Messrs. Geo. H. Hull & Co. of Louisville, Ky., Southern pig iron; Carp River Furnace Co. of Marquette, Mich.; Lone Star Iron Co., Jefferson, Tex. and the Rich Hill Zinc Works, of Rich Hill, Mo. They are also prepared to supply a variety of rich iron ores in any quantity, and to consumers of sheet copper, ingot copper, pig iron, spelter, ores, etc., the firm offer the most substantial inducements, both as to price and quality. It is important to Chicago to have such a progressive and ably conducted house as this is to maintain its supremacy in the metal trade, and the copariners are in every way specially fitted to advise the consumer as to the grades and brands of iron, copper, etc., best adapted to his purposes. Both gentlemen have ever retained the confidence and respect of the commercial world, and have before them the prospects of the most favorable character.

NASH & REA.

It is impossible in connection with the complexities of city life to over estimate the value of first-class plumbers and sewer-builders in keeping that deadly enemy, sewer gas, away from houses. In this connection we desire to refer specially to the progressive and reliable firm of Messrs. Nash & Rea, plumbers, gasfitters and sewer builders, whose store is located at 493 W. Indiana street. They established this business in 1889, and already have built up one of the best trades in the city.. Both Messrs. R. J. Nash and J. T. Rea have had long experience, and are recognized as among the best sanitary engineers and plumbers in Chicago. They employ several first-class plumbers and gasfitters, also from twenty to fifty sewer-builders. During the last six months of 1891 they have done $40,000 worth of sewer work for the city, and are duly licensed sanitary plumbers and sewer builders. They occupy a commodious ground floor and basement, each being 25x50 feet in area, where they keep a large and choice stock of plumbers' and steam gasfitters' supplies, bathtubs, waterclosets, piping, and all kinds of sanitary specialties, which are offered to customers at lowest prices. Everything in the way of plumbing, gasfitting and sewering is done ; contracts are entered into,and the complete fitting up of buildings is satisfactorily executed. Both partners are natives of Chicago, where they are highly esteemed by the community for their mechanical skill, promptness and integrity. The following we listify to the superiority of the work done by Messrs. Nash & Rea : They plumbed the fine two-story flat of Mr. Cook, on Erie, near Lincoln street. Also five flat buildings on the corner of Francisco and Fulton streets, the property of Messrs. Sullivan, McGurn & Kinnare. Also two residences on Walnut

street, near Central Park avenue, the property of Alderman Roth ; also three other residences on Columbia place, belonging to the same gentlemen. Also the two-story flat building on Congress street, west of Kedzie avenue, for Architect Lesher. The firm are highly commended to the public, and those employing them will secure the greatest satisfaction in the thoroughly good manner in which all work will be accomplished. Mr. Nash is a popular member of the Royal Arcanum and of Father Hogan's Total Abstinence and Benevolent Society, while Mr. Rea is also a member of the Royal Arcanum.

H. BEHL.

The essential qualifications to achieve permanent success in the fashionable tailoring trade are combined to perfection by but few out of the hosts of merchant tailors of this great city. One of these few is to be found at No. 724 W Madison street. We refer, of course to Mr. H. Behl, successor to Mr. R. Selle, who established the business twenty years ago and is now the general manager. Both gentlemen are practical expert cutters, of long experience and sound judgment, who have no superiors in the city for securing the most perfect fit and grace of outline. Mr. Behl employs a competent force of skilled operatives, and is fully prepared to meet the heavy run of a fine trade which has been developed here. He displays a comprehensive stock of the freshest seasonable goods, including all the choice fabrics, patterns and textures, from the best foreign and domestic looms. To those who require custom clothing of the highest grade, faultless in every respect, this house commends itself as one that can be implicitly relied on to furnish only such garments as are superior in every respect. Mr. Behl is a German by birth, but came to Chicago no less than forty years ago. He served his adopted country during the war with faithfulness, nobly responding to her call for assistance in maintaining the integrity of the Union. Mr. Selle is also a German, who has resided here for upwards of twenty years. Both are respected and popular in a very wide circle, among all classes of society.

WILLIAM F. PETERSON.

Among the most active and enterprising men engaged in the manufacture of sash, doors, blinds, mouldings, etc., is Mr. William F. Peterson, whose office and factory are located at Nos. 4914-4916 Wentworth avenue. Mr. Peterson is a native of this state, and from early life has been actively identified with this branch of trade, and brings to bear a perfect knowledge of all its branches. He inaugurated his present enterprise in 1890, and, being a practical woodworker of sound judgment and vast experience, able to meet the most exacting requirements of the trade, he at once built up a large and flourishing business, which has since continued to steadily increase and develop. He occupies a frame structure, 20x100 feet in area, where he has every facility for the prompt and satisfactory execution of all orders intrusted to him. His office is neatly appointed and tastefully finished in oak, and is connected by telephone (9515) with all parts of the city and suburbs. The factory is thoroughly equipped with all the best perfected and latest improved machines, tools and appliances known to the woodworking trade, and steady employment is given to twenty skilled hands. He manufactures sashes, doors, blinds, newels, mouldings, banisters, brackets, scroll work and all kinds of mill work from thoroughly seasoned lumber and of the most elaborate finish. He devotes special attention to sash and door work, and has filled many important orders in this line. He always carries a large and fully assorted stock of material on hand, and contractors, builders, architects, etc., will consult their best interests by securing estimates and placing orders with him. Mr. Peterson is a respected member of business circles, and is a worthy representative of this important trade. His success in his enterprise has been won by sheer merit, and the confidence reposed in him by the community is well deserved.

MCMAHON & SCANLON.

The enthusiasm with which Messrs. McMahon & Scanlon commenced their business as wholesale and retail dealers in coal, coke, and wood at 479 W. Lake street, four years ago, has been thoroughly justified by results, for to-day they have one of the most prosperous businesses on the West side, so much so, indeed, that they were recently obliged to open a branch place at 410-418 Ogden avenue, corner of Robey street. Some idea of the extent of their business may be gathered when we mention that they employ a large force of men and eight teams, with which they deliver coal and wood free to all parts of the city. The yard capacity is two thousand tons, and they always have on hand the very choicest shipments of thoroughly screened Lackawanna, Lehigh Valley, Indiana, and other hard and soft varieties of coal. Those desiring it in large lots for manufacturing purposes can have it shipped direct by the carload from the pit mouth, and thus save considerable. Their telephone call is 7009, and all orders so transmitted receive their instant attention. Their local trade is very large and continually increasing, as they have never yet failed to give satisfaction. Both partners are comparatively young men, and untiring in their efforts to please customers. Mr. R. McMahon is a native of Chicago. Mr. M. J. Scanlan is also a native of this city and is town clerk of West Chicago.

his ability in handling this business by the way he has already popularized it, and made it the market for these products in this city.

GUS. ALBERG.

The boot and shoe business has long been one of the leading industries of Chicago, and her products in this line are well known and appreciated. In quality, style and finish this city enjoys an enviable reputation, especially in gents' and ladies' fine shoes, which has been well merited, and is maintained with the most scrupulous care by houses such as that of Messrs. Gus. Alberg & Bro. of No. 5056 Wentworth avenue. This house was established by Messrs. Gus. and John Alberg in 1890, and under their able and energetic management already enjoys a large and lucrative share of the local patronage. The premises occupied comprise a commodious ground floor, 20x50 feet in dimensions, giving ample accommodation for the display of stock and the comfort and convenience of customers. The assortment embraces ladies' and gents' fine foot-wear of every description, goods bearing the trade-mark of the most celebrated manufacturers, and of a quality such as Messrs. Alberg can confidently commend to their customers in point of durability, fit, finish and fabric. Popular prices prevail, too, while special attention is given to every description of repairs. Messrs. Alberg are natives of Germany, now residents for the past seven years of Chicago, where they enjoy the respect and esteem of the community at large.

C. A. CLEMENTSEN.

Among the most promising of recently established houses in this city Messrs. C. A. Clementsen & Co. take a high place. Their line is that of brass founders and finishers, and they are prepared to carry out the largest orders for patterns and models, experimental work, jobbing and brass, bronze, German silver and white metal castings and patented articles, as well as plumbers' specialties. Although the business only dates from the first of January, 1891, yet their foundry is already known throughout the city as a place where the best work is done in the most prompt and accurate manner. They occupy spacious and convenient premises, Nos. 96 and 98 W. Lake street, completely equipped with every necessary appliance, and their resources are taxed to the utmost to keep pace with the large orders that are continually to hand. Mr. Clementsen's resources are ample, his experience great, and his facilities perfect. He employs a large and competent staff of assistants, and closely superintends every detail in the various departments. He has perfected a thorough system of organization in his establishment and is an added element of prosperity, and nothing that can conduce to the transaction of business has been omitted. Mr. Clementsen is a Norwegian by birth, and learned his trade in that country. He has, during his ten years residence here, earned the warm esteem of all classes of society for his ability, uprightness and honorable methods. He has for several years held the responsible position of secretary of the Knights of the White Cross, the oldest Scandinavian society in America, and well deserves the appreciation in which he is held by all classes of the community.

A popular enterprise and one destined to cut an important figure in commercial circles is the California Auction Co., cor. Kinzie and Kingsbury streets. This enterprise has only been established a short time, but is of such meritorious character and of undoubted utility that its success is already assured. The company is incorporated, with a capitalization of $100,-000. Mr. J. C. Macomber is the manager, and is a gentleman of wide experience and great ability in this line. The company occupies a fine two-story brick building at the north end of the C. & N. W. R. R., and have ample room for their business. The building is 50x100 feet in dimensions; the lower story being used as a wareroom, and the second floor as a salesroom. This is fitted up with accommodations for about two hundred, and has an auction platform and seats for dealers. The sales are at 4:30 P.M. each day, when large quantities of California fruits are disposed of. The shipments are received from California direct, daily, and consist of peaches, pears, plums, apricots, grapes, raisins, berries, etc., in fine order and the results of the highest skill in fruit culture. The company handles vast quantities of fruit, having whole train loads consigned to them, and received by the special fast fruit service direct. Six helpers are employed, and Mr. Macomber shows

FRED. NEUSTADT.

The plumber occupies a most important position and one of great responsibility, and it is very necessary that he be a trustworthy and reputable, as well as a skilled artisan, as he has the health and even the life of his patrons depending upon his faithfulness and intelligence. One of the most reputable and skilled plumbers in Chicago is Mr. Fred. Neustadt, who has been established for over sixteen years, and has had many years' experience in the business. For the past three years he has been located at No. 300 North avenue, where he removed from across the street, and occupies an elegant store, 20x60 feet in dimensions, thoroughly equipped and stocked with a fine line of plumbers' supplies, gas fixtures, chandeliers, globes, marble top sinks, baths, porcelain water closets, urinals, sinks, shower baths, hose, pipe, etc. Everything is first-class and of the highest grade. Mr. Neustadt is a regularly licensed sanitary plumber and sewer builder, and employs only experienced and practical workmen, to whom he pays the highest wages. He gives employment to six experienced plumbers, six assistants, two gas-fitters, four sewer builders, one teamster and two clerks. He has an extensive trade in all parts of the city, and has many contracts for the plumbing of large office buildings and fine dwellings, making a specialty of sanitary plumbing for modern dwellings of high class. He numbers among his patrons many leading and well-known citizens, who have had pleasant business and social relations with him for years, and hold him in the highest esteem. Mr. Neustadt is a member of the Master Plumbers' Association, is also a prominent Free Mason and Red Man, a member of the A. O. U. W., the Foresters and the Turner Society, in all of which he is held in the highest esteem. For extensive business, high standing and reputation of the most unexceptional character, there is no plumber occupying a more important place in Chicago than Mr. Neustadt. He is a native of Saxony, and has lived here twenty years.

MOLTER & KRETSCHMER.

Among the leading sanitary plumbers of Chicago the firm of Molter & Kretschmer occupy an inportant place. The business was established in 1888, and has developed rapidly and satisfactorily, until it has become one of the best known and strongest houses in the trade. The members of the firm are Mr. Nicholas P. Molter and Conrad M. Kretschmer, both practical and experienced plumbers, and business men of stability and energy. They occupy the ground floor and basement of No. 426 E. Division street as a store and workshop, and have very convenient and commodious quarters, the dimensions of the premises being 25x80 feet. The store is thoroughly stocked with a complete assortment of plumbers' and gas fitters' goods, including all kinds of bath sinks, closets, faucets, brackets, gas fixtures, chandeliers and other specialties. Everything is of the best class of goods, and the arrangement is of the neatest. Ten competent workmen are employed, and contracts are taken and estimates cheerfully furnished. The house has a liberal patronage and completes many important contracts each year. The members of the firm are regularly licensed plumbers, and handle sanitary specialties for breweries, factories, stores, warehouses and elegant dwellings. Among patrons of the house for whom work has been done and to whom the firm may refer, are the following: Judge Lambert Tree; C. F. Gray, president, Hide & Leather Bank; Kelley & Maus, heavy hardware; T. L. Forrest, cashier of the Hide & Leather Bank; Mechanics' Loan & Trust company; W. H. Colvin, real estate; F. B. Peabody and J. S. Russell, attorneys; F. H. Bremmer, attorney; Edward Furthmann, ex-assistant state attorney; A. F. Stephenson, master in chancery; W. H. Buller and Ernest Slock, real estate, and others. Mr. Molter is a native of Chicago, a member of the Catholic order of Foresters and the Royal League. Mr. Kretschmer is a native of Germany, and came direct to Chicago twenty-two years ago. He is a member of the A. O. U. W. Both gentlemen stand high in leading commercial circles.

CONNELL LEATHER CO.

A progresive and reliable concern in Chicago, engaged in the wholesale trade in leather and findings, is that known as the Connell Leather Co., whose salesrooms are located at 181 W. Monroe street. This company was organized in 1888 with ample capital, and is under the careful and able management of Mr. W. P. Connell, who is fully conversant with every detail of this important industry, and the requirements of the trade. They occupy two commodious floors, fully equipped with every convenience. Here a full stock of leather findings and shoemakers' tools is always on hand, all quoted at extremely low prices. They also manufacture largely boot and shoe uppers, including whole vamps, congress, button and balmorals. Only medium and first-class goods are produced, and the trade of the concern extends thorought the United States. Their low priced boot and shoe uppers are made of good Chicago calf, and the style and workmanship are the same as their other uppers, while nothing but the best silk is used. Orders are carefully and promptly filled, and entire satisfaction is guaranteed. They send out a handsome electrotyped showcard to any shoemaker free of charge, and also solicit consignments of hides, furs, skins, rough and finished leather, tallow, etc., and guarantee quick sales and immediate returns. They issue a comprehensive illustrated catalogue and price list, which is forwarded promptly upon application. The Connell Leather Company makes a specialty of upper fittings for the trade, in which branch it has achieved a substantial success. Mr. W. P. Connell was born in this city, but was brought up in St. Louis and returned to this city about four years ago. He is a young, enterprising business man of good and sound judgment, of sterling integrity and favorably known in social and business circles. The success he has achieved in his enterprise is in every sense fully deserved and he has a bright future before him.

THE WILLARD SONS & BELL COMPANY.

In the manufacture of car and locomotive axles the most progressive and successful concern in Chicago is that known as the Willard Sons & Bell Company, whose office is located at No. 708 Phenix building; while the works are situated at South Chicago. This extensive business was established many years ago by Tynchon, Willard & Co., who were succeeded in 1878 by Messrs. Willard Sons & Bell. Eventually in 1880 it was incorporated under the laws of Illinois with a paid up capital of $105,000, its executive officers being Mr. C. W. Willard president, Mr. H. C. Morton, vice-president, and Mr. F. E. Wilson, secretary and treasurer. The works have an area of five acres, and the various departments are fully equipped with modern appliances and machinery, operated by nine steam engines. Here 250 skilled workmen are employed, who turn out largely car and locomotive axles, boat and mill shafting, wrought iron and steel forgings, etc. The car and locomotive axles and other specialties of this company are unrivaled for strength, quality of materials, workmanship and durability, and have no superiors in this country or Europe. Besides constantly testing the character and quality of all metal used every axle undergoes a rigid inspection in regard to its strength and workmanship before it is allowed to leave the premises. If it shows any defects even in the slightest degree it is at once condemned, and broken up. Orders are filled carefully by the company at the lowest possible prices, and the trade extends throughout all sections of the Middle, Western and Northwestern states. The company's sales for the past year amounted to over $400,000, and the demand for its goods is steadily increasing, owing to their superiority and intrinsic merits. The offices are handsomely equipped, and are supplied with all modern conveniences, electric lights, etc. The standing of the Willard Sons & Bell Company in commercial circles is too well known to need any remarks at our hands, and both as regards integrity and true American enterprise the officers justly merit the high reputation to which they have permanently attained.

WILLIAM DART.

When Cæsar invaded Britain in the year 55 B. C., it is said that he found clocks in use there, though water clocks had been introduced about a century before that time. It almost baffles the imagination to review the improvements that have since been made in clocks and watches, and if we want to see these improvements to perfection, we must visit the store of Mr. William Dart, at 321 W. Madison street. The place is exceedingly spacious and elegant, and glass cases run the whole length of the store, filled with the most beautiful specimens of the goldsmith's and horologer's arts. Mr. Dart also carries a full line of solid and silver-plated ware, suitable for presentations on all occasions, also optical goods, etc. This stock is unusually well selected, and, though the prices of everything range to suit the circumstances of everybody, yet there is not a vulgar or common looking article in the whole store. There will be many thousands who will read this notice and we heartily commend those who contemplate visiting Chicago for the World's Fair to set aside a little memorandum book for addresses, and to put down the address of William Dart, so as to call and take away some suitable souvenir of the place. He intends to import a specially fine line of French and English jewelry for that occasion, and will have novelties that cannot be got elsewhere in the city. He employs an ample force of polite and competent clerks, so that customers need not be subjected to any unnecessary delay. Mr. Dart came to Chicago from England, his native place, in 1873, and was previously engaged for five years in one of the leading jewelry stores in London, and is, therefore, thoroughly well grounded in what is the correct style and fashion, as he is always in communication with the largest English manufacturers.

ISAAC SHILLINGTON.

One of the most convenient and best equipped livery and boarding stables in Chicago is that of Mr. Isaac Shillington, at Nos. 210 and 212 Indiana street. The premises were erected in 1873, one year after the inception of the business, and present every desirable feature necessary to the prosecution of a first-class trade. The stables, which occupy the basement, are well lighted throughout, and thoroughly well ventilated and drained, affording the most perfect accommodation for the score of horses required in the livery department, and for the boarders to the number of forty-five. Five large box stalls are also at hand, and one of the prominent features of the establishment is a splendid granary, capable of holding one carload, supported entirely by iron trusses overhead, thus avoiding the necessity of guarding against the depredations of animals. The first and second floors are devoted to the carriage repository, a large annex in the rear having been recently built to increase the capacity of this crowded department, wash rooms, store rooms and all the necessary conveniences of a first-class livery. Mr. Shillington is fully prepared to execute any commission in his line at the shortest notice, and in the most satisfactory manner. His stylish equipages are the talk of the city, and may be obtained at any hour, the telephone call being No. 3077. He is a native of Belfast, Ireland, and came to this city in 1862. He is a gentleman of great ability and business talent, enterprising and thoroughly upright in all his dealings.

EUGENE PERLICH.

There is no branch of mercantile industry of more importance than that which applies to the daily necessities of the people, and in this connection unquestionably the baker is deserving of prominent mention. A newly established, yet none the less progressive and representative, concern of this type, is that so ably presided over by Mr. Eugene Perlich, at No. 2302 Wentworth avenue. This bakery was opened by Mr. Perlich during the current year and, despite a somewhat recent establishment, already enjoys a fair share of the patronage of the neighborhood. The premises occupied comprise a

neatly appointed ground floor, 10x40 feet in dimensions, its choice fixtures and absolute cleanliness combining to give the place at all times an attractive and inviting appearance. The productions of the house, embracing all kinds of cakes and breadstuffs, have already a standard value in this community, and the widespread patronage, secured in such a comparatively brief period points to a future of pronounced and permanent success. Mr. Perlich is a gentleman of wide experience and has a thorough knowledge of all matters pertaining to his business. He is a native of Germany, and has been a resident of Chicago for the past ten years, where he is widely respected by a large circle of patrons and personal friends.

C. LENZ.

One of the oldest established and most popular boot and shoe establishments on North avenue is that of Mr. C. Lenz. This business was established twenty-three years ago by Mr. Lenz at the present location, 186 North avenue, and his close application to business and fair treatment of customers has brought him a liberal and extensive patronage of the most desirable character. Mr. Lenz was born in Germany, and came to Chicago thirty-one years ago. He is characterized by his progressiveness, liberality and courteous manner and has numerous friends. His store at 186 North Avenue is stocked with a fine line of boots, shoes, gaiters, rubbers, slippers, etc., for ladies', children's, gentlemen's and infants' wear. The stock is well selected, and from the best known manufacturers. Mr. Lenz makes a specialty of fine custom work and has numerous patrons for whom he has made shoes for many years, with unvarying satisfaction. Repairing is neatly done at moderate prices. Mr. Lenz has a good trade of the most desirable kind, many of his customers having traded with him for many years. He employs two assistants, who are courteous and genial and a profit to the business. As a business man, Mr. Lenz has few superiors, and as a friend and companion is unsurpassed. He is a prominent member of the Foresters and is well liked by all who come in contact with him in both a business and social way, and customers can rest assured that goods are as represented.

H. BARTLETT.

A house of importance and high standing in its line is the known as Bartlett, funeral director, undertaker and embalmer. This business is conducted by Mr. W. F. Bartlett, under the style of H. Bartlett, and who is an experienced and skilful embalmer and undertaker. Mr. Bartlett first established in business about thirty-five years ago at Jackson, Mich., and in 1882 moved to Chicago. He has been located at No. 243 N. Clark street for the past ten years, where he has a splendid establishment, supplied with a complete assortment of caskets, coffins, burial cases, etc., in cloth, fine hardwoods, or enamel finish. All kinds of funeral furnishings are carried, and every necessity supplied at the shortest notice. The large room fronting on Clark street is fitted up as a parlor, and is splendidly carpeted and furnished. Mr. Bartlett makes a specialty of embalming, of which he is a skilled master, being a graduate of Professor Clark's school. The office is never closed, and night calls and orders by telephone are promptly attended to, the call being 3056. Mr. Bartlett is a prominent business man and is highly respected. He was born in Gloversville, N. Y., is a member of the Chicago Undertakers' Association, and is a Royal Arch Mason and a member of the Royal Arcanum. The principal and detail of Mr. Bartlett's business are now conducted by Mr. A. E. Branton, who is considered one of the best embalmers and funeral directors in the land. Mr. Branton is a native of England, and has resided in this city for several years. He learned the art of embalming in Rochester, N. Y., and is a graduate of Professor Renard's School of Embalming. Five years ago he came to Chicago and has been with Mr. Bartlett continuously ever since, and now conducts the entire business himself, attending the greater part of the funerals of which he has entire charge.

IOWA LIVE STOCK COMMISSION CO.

One of the largest and most extensive concerns doing a live stock commission business at the Union Stock Yards in this city, is the Iowa Live Stock Commission Company, who occupy convenient offices in room 21, in the Exchange building. This business was incorporated within the past year, according to the laws of Illinois, with a capital of $50,000, and its directors are all active and experienced live-stock men. The presi-

dent of the company is Mr. W. J. Ford, a capitalist of Chicago, while Mr. J. B. Roach is general manager, who, for the past five years, has been a resident of Chicago, and an active live stock commission dealer. Mr. Roach makes a specialty of the cattle business, and superintends that department as salesman. Mr. J. Miller is a native of Utica, N. Y., and for eighteen years has been in business in the Union Stock Yards, and is the manager of the hog department for the company. Mr. S. W. Pryor is also a member of the board of officers, has been for many years in the business, and has charge of the sheep department. The company handles cattle, hogs and sheep on commission, making liberal advances on consignments. Their average receipts are about fifteen cars a day, and they have unexcelled facilities for handling any quantity of stock. They employ six competent assistants, the veteran of them being Mr. Judd E. Illsbey, a native of Cedar Falls, Iowa, but who, for over twenty years, has been engaged with the most prominent live stock men in the Union Stock Yards of this city. Their cattle business is largely from Iowa, the West and Southwest, and is increasing constantly. They furnish market reports free by telegraph on application to any of their customers. They are always in a ready market, and make returns for all consignments on the day of sale. They are a substantial and reliable firm, and offer the National Live Stock Bank of Chicago as reference. Their offices are very central and conveniently furnished and fitted for their staff of assistants to handle their trade.

CHICAGO NICKEL WORKS.

The importance of nickel as a medium of manufacture and plating, with its capability of high finish and polish and untarnishable character, has become a great factor in all metallic work where ornament and taste is sought. One of the most enterprising and substantial institutions of Chicago is the Chicago Nickel Works, located at No. 125 Ontario street, manufacturers of light and heavy hardware, Stearn's hotel and dining-car cooking apparatus; Grout's 'Excelsior jewelers' tools; Goodrich sewing-machine attachment, and general machine work, dies, tools and patterns. This establishment was incorporated under the laws of the State of Illinois some years ago, with ample capital, and has built up a large trade, extending all over the United States and Canada, and which is rapidly increasing and extending. The officers are: Mr. G. L. Reimann, president; J. McGregor, vice-president, and Frank L. Goodrich, secretary and treasurer. Their factory consists of a five-story and basement block, 75x100 feet in size, and is fitted with a 100 horse power engine, and all of the latest and most modern machinery, tools and appliances for their work. They employ from 175 to 200 workmen, and in addition to the above list, do a large business in the manufacture of brass and iron castings, machine work, sheet metal work, polishing and nickel plating, and all other special work incidental to their business. The Chicago Nickel Works are substantial, enterprising works, whose members are well and favorably known

in Chicago business circles, and whose energy and ability to place their establishment in the front ranks of our manufactories. are undoubted.

JOHN J. BLOCK.

One of the most careful and experienced of the stable firms engaged in the general teaming and transferring business is that of Mr. John J. Block, whose office is centrally located at No. 178 Michigan street. The business was founded in 1883, by Messrs. Block Bros., and two years later the present proprietor purchased his brother's interest, conducting it thenceforward on those sound principles which are the chief factors in all enduring success. Mr. Block employs in his responsible work twenty-two horses and eleven men, the latter being specially chosen for their skill and reliability. He does a large teaming business in all parts of the city and suburbs, and has permanent contracts with the leading wholesale houses, who find that nowhere else do their orders receive such prompt attention, or less danger of breakage or loss. Moving of all kinds is done expeditiously, and by the most experienced and careful men, and we recommend our readers to either mail or telephone their orders (call No. 3147), to Mr. John J. Block, who will execute them in the most satisfactory and efficient manner. The stables are located at Nos. 136 and 138 Augustus street (Northwest side), where vans, trucks, etc., light and heavy, for all purposes, are kept continually ready for use. Although a German by birth, Mr. Block has resided here sufficiently long to become intimately acquainted with the requirements of the Western trade. He is a member of the Independent Order of Foresters and of the National Union and is an active member of the Turners' Association. He is an active and enterprising business man, who is deservedly popular and respected. He has built up his large business by sheer merit, and among his customers is spoken of in the most praiseworthy terms. His success in the past answers well for even greater success in the future.

M. A. FRANKLIN & CO.

Among the leading and representative general commission houses doing business in this city is that of Messrs. M. A. Franklin & Company, at No. 163 West Randolph street It was established in 1887 by Mr. Milvern A. Franklin, then and still the sole proprietor of the concern. Bringing to bear all the essential qualifications necessary to insure rapid and permanent success, Mr. Franklin from the outset built up an excellent and prosperous trade, which has since developed until to-day his house stands in the foremost rank. The premises utilized by him comprise two floors and basement, each having an area of 20x120 feet. These spacious quarters are perfectly appointed throughout, and are fitted up with every modern convenience and facility for the storage and preservation as well as the rapid handling of the large stock constantly carried. Mr. Franklin has established valuable connections in all the best producing sections of the country, and is in daily receipt of heavy consignments of country produce of all kinds, from the most reliable sources, such as butter, cheese, eggs, poultry, game, veal, apples, berries, potatoes, etc. His uniformly prosperous career renders him a most desirable medium for the prompt and favorable disposition of consignments, while a notable feature is the promptness with which returns are made to shippers. His trade is immense, extending throughout Illinois, Wisconsin, Iowa, Indiana, Michigan, etc., and is steadily increasing. Liberal advances are made on consignments, if so desired, and the best possible facilities are offered for the prompt disposal of goods. Mr. Franklin makes a specialty of handling car load lots, and to the trade offers the most liberal inducements. Although known to the trade else where, he refers as to his financial standing to the Prairie State National Bank of Chicago, Messrs. Hancisen & Lang of St. Louis, etc. He is a native of Wisconsin, and for eight years has resided in this city, where he has obtained wide popularity and commanding influence in business circles.

E. H. WACHS.

In a great and rapidly developing commercial center like Chicago there is a steadily increasing demand for steam engines, boilers, pumps, etc., which is being supplied by firms whose reputations have reached to all parts of the country. One of the most thoroughly representative of these is that of Mr. E. H. Wachs, whose extensive works are located on the corner of La Salle avenue and Indiana street, in a position directly central to the trade. Mr. Wachs brings to bear a wide experience, and a thorough knowledge of the requirements of the business, and, being himself an expert machinist, he is able to select from the best factories those productions which are most suitable to the wants of his customers, and also to closely supervise his staff of twenty assistants in every detail of their work. He manufactures and carries a large stock of heavy machinery and fittings, such as engines, boilers, pumps, tools, shafting, pulleys, hangers, wrought iron pipe, valves and fittings, of the best material and workmanship, including among his own productions those of the most renowned makers in the country. The trade, both jobbing and retail, will find here a fine selection, which it would be difficult to duplicate elsewhere, and offered at prices which are exceedingly moderate, considering the high quality of the goods. The premises are large, and fitted with every machine and appliance of the most modern type, driven by a forty-horse power steam engine, and giving perfect facilities for filling the largest orders at the shortest notice. Mr. Wachs is a native of Germany, but learned his business in this country, and conducts it in an honorable well-balanced way that is a credit alike to himself and to the commercial circles of the great western metropolis.

RUDOLPH HURT.

A good tailor is a boon to a community and Rudolph Hurt of 594 Blue Island avenue, between Eighteenth and Nineteenth streets, is all that can be desired in a tailor of skill and ideas. He was formerly the head cutter for Mr. J. Goldman, the well-known tailor of Clark street. His success with this house and the solicitation of his many friends induced him to open his establishment about the first of the year. His store is well stocked with the best and latest patterns of woolens, tweeds, corkscrew and broad cloths, serges, cheviots and all fine dress goods. These he makes up in the best and latest styles for his customers, suiting the most critical and fastidious tastes. He makes a specialty of all kinds of uniforms and has an extensive custom in this line. In addition to his fine line of tailorings he also carries a select line of fine furnishing goods, shirts, gloves, etc., also the best and latest styles of hats and caps. Mr. Hurt gives the business of his establishment personal attention. He does all the cutting and fitting himself and employs two experienced tailors in the store as well, as four first-class hands outside, who do the sewing at home. Mr. Hurt occupies for some purposes the ground floor of number 594 Blue Island avenue, being a large and convenient room, 25x50 feet. His patronage is very large and is constantly increasing, his friends and acquaintances highly recommending him to their associates. He is a native of Bohemia, but was only one year old when brought to this country, so that he feels as if he were "to the manor born." He is well known in business and social circles; is a prominent member of the Royal Arcanum and the Gokal Gymnasium Association. Mr. Hurt is a young man and, with his ability, social qualities and hosts of friends, should achieve the most pronounced success.

THE "BELVEDERE."

As the great Western metropolis has grown and expanded in her mercantile and industrial undertakings, and as her enormous wealth is rapidly increasing, so the taste and refinement of her citizens call for a greater outlay, year by year, of money and art upon her hostleries and cafes, and to-day there is no city in the Union that can boast of more elegant and costly hotels, cafes and wine rooms than Chicago. Among the most beautiful and ornate of Chicago's many beautiful wine and lunch rooms is the "Belvedere," centrally located at the corner of Clark and Randolph streets, under the Sherman House, which is one of the most fashionable and widely patronized throughout the city. Mr. S. Freudenburg, the gentlemanly and popular proprietor, was born in Germany, but has been a resident of Chicago twenty-five years. The Belvedere was opened to the public two years ago, and since that time has enjoyed a large and ever increasing patronage, and has in fact become the center and home of good fellowship among the wealthier class of Germans of this city, as well as those visiting Chicago. The interior adornment and furnishings are of the latest, most expensive and beautiful type. The restaurant for ladies and gentlemen is separate from the lunch and bar room, and is 25x100 feet in dimensions, the woodwork throughout being of solid oak, exquisitely carved, and the walls are set with heavy beveled plate glass mirrors; the floors are laid in fancy tiles, and it is luxuriously furnished to correspond in every particular with the lunch and bar room, which is also 25x100 feet. There is nothing in the city to surpass the bar-room of the Belvedere. Everything that the highest grade of artistic talent and the most lavish outlay of money can do has been accomplished here, and the general effect is both striking and in the highest sense of the term beautiful. The bar and fixtures are works of art in themselves, of solid oak, elaborately carved to harmonize with the general *tout ensemble* of the whole; the walls are set with heavy beveled plate glass mirrors, and the furniture is of the richest design, while clusters and arches of incandescent electric lamps are suspended from walls and ceiling, giving the whole interior a most beautiful and brilliant appearance, while all the necessary appurtenances for cooling liquors and preserving edibles are to be found, including an elaborately constructed wine cooler and refrigerator. The cuisine is unsurpassed and is under the direction of a skilled chef, while the choicest delicacies in season are always to be found in the menu. A large stock of the finest imported and domestic wines, liquors and cigars are constantly kept on hand, besides all the leading brands of imported beers, including Pilsener, Werzburger Culmbacher, Munchen, Augustini, Erlanger, Hoffbrau and Kapuziner. This is also a headquarters for the Val Blatz Brewing Company's Vienna beer. Mr. Freudenberg by his long residence in this city has made a host of friends, and is universally esteemed by all who know him as one of the most popular and successful business men o Chicago.

MARTIN BROS.

The business of carriage-making has developed enormously in the past twenty-five years, and the large factories all over the country turn out buggies by machinery, and which are in so many instances unreliable, that it is a comfort to know that there are still some of the old trustworthy firms left. Such a representative firm on the North side is that of Martin Bros., at 47 N. Wells street. This business was established in 1862, by Mr. Robert Martin, sr., father of the present proprietors, but he died in 1890, and his two sons, Mr. Robert and Mr. Frank Martin assumed control under the present style. Their factory is a one-story and basement brick building, and is admirably adapted for their work. They manufacture and deal in all kinds of buggies, business wagons, harness, etc. They repair, paint and fix up second hand work, making it equal to new, also make and repair skids and hand trucks, etc. There is nothing better made in the way of buggies and wagons than they turn out. Their goods are light, but durable, as they use only the very best materials and workmanship. They are also proprietors of the Chicago Iron Bedstead Manufacturing Co., an organization which was started by their father in 1869, having for its object the manufacturing and importing of fancy iron bedsteads, for which they find a ready local trade, and also supply any public institution. The two brothers are natives of Chicago and are comparatively young men, but they are full of push and business energy and well deserve the popular favor and patronage which has remained with them since their father's death.

J. H. WINGER.

The sewing machine is assuredly one of the most important acquisitions which has been laid at our doors in this inventive nineteenth century. It relieves the overworked housewife of much of her hard labor; it has revolutionized the factories where shirts and clothing of all kinds were made by hand, and has raised the whole art of sewing to a higher plane. In this connection we would call especial attention to the beautiful new store of Mr. J. H. Winger, at 257 W. Indiana street. Fifteen years ago Mr. Winger established himself at 253 Indiana street, two doors from his present place, as agent for the Singer Sewing Machines and dealer in supplies, and he has just moved into his spacious new premises, which occupy the ground floor of a new three-story brick building, 25x80 feet in dimensions. The place is elegantly and appropriately fitted up with railings, counters and desks, and contains a fine stock of Singer and other leading makes of sewing machines, as well as silk, oil, spool cotton, needles and attachments, and tailors' supplies. A specialty is made of repairing sewing machines, which is done promptly and at reasonable prices. Machines are also taken in exchange and new ones sold at terms to suit any purchaser. Lessons are given free of charge on all machines. Mr. Winger is a native of Norway and has been in Chicago for twenty-five years. If any man has seen every side of human nature he has, for he can boast of twenty years' experience as a canvasser in this line. His trade extends over Chicago and surrounding territory, and in every instance where a sale has been made he has given entire satisfaction. His house has always borne a reputation for honorable dealing, and Mr. Winger will see that such reputation remains untarnished.

L. M'NAMARA.

The establishment of Mr. L. McNamara is well known and popular as a place of resort to the hundreds of visitors to Lincoln Park, and a review of his business interests is justly deserved on account of his enterprise and progressiveness. The business was established for four years as J. Berry & Co., Mr. McNamara being a member of the firm and manager, and since succeeding to the business he has developed it with great rapidity and ability. The premises have been enlarged and redecorated and are unquestionably the finest ice cream parlors on the North side. Mr. McNamara is a native of Clare County, Ireland, and came to Chicago in 1871. He is a progressive business man and has hosts of friends. The building occupied by Mr. McNamara for business purposes is located at 885 and 887 N. Clark street, and is admirably adapted to the needs of his business. He occupies the ground floor for a store and ice cream parlor and has an elegantly fitted up place of business. The store contains all kinds of confectious made by the house, of pure material, the quality and purity being unsurpassed; also fine cakes, etc. The ice cream parlor is elegantly furnished with fine marble top tables and has a seating capacity of over one hundred. An immense business is done here, the place being a most popular resort for the thousands who visit Lincoln Park. The ice cream m and factured by Mr. McNamara has a high reputation and is in great demand, over one hundred and fifty gallons a day being manufactured and sold in season. A good business is also done in fine confections, which are sold at wholesale in quantities. Five persons are employed, and the business horizon continues to widen each year. Mr. McNamara is held in the highest esteem by his many friends and patrons.

JAS. POOLE.

Chicago has many fine livery establishments, with the best horses and most elegant carriages to be had in any American city. But among them all there is none better managed or equipped than that of Mr. James Poole, whose establishment is located at 270 and 272 Oak street. The busi-

ness at this place was established in 1879. Mr. Poole was born in England, and came to the United States thirty-five years ago. Before coming to America he had charge of H. H. Withers & Co's. stables at Bristol, England, where he broke and trained horses until 1855. Mr. Poole is a thorough horseman; he has no superior as a judge of horseflesh in America; and as a trainer he is careful, painstaking and remarkably successful. Mr. Poole's stables are large, well-lighted and ventilated, and are supplied with every modern convenience. They are equipped with fifty-five stalls and five box stalls, and twenty horses are kept on hand at all times, while thirty are boarded for patrons. A careful and experienced veterinary surgeon is in attendance, Dr. E. I. Quitman, who gives his experience to relieve the suffering animals at the shortest notice. The stables are two stories in height, and 58x125 feet in dimensions. The basement is used for the horses, and the first floor is used as a carriage repository, wash rooms, waiting rooms, office, etc. The second floor is used for storage. The turnouts are all stylish and in first-class order, consisting of carriages, landaus, buggies, hacks, dog carts, phaetons, etc., and the horses have been carefully selected for their speed, reliability and stylish qualities by Mr. Poole personally. Mr. Poole has lately added to his equipment three new victorias, the finest in the city. The stable is kept open for business at all times, and rigs may be had at any time of the day or night, liveried coachmen being furnished when desired. Mr. Poole is well and very favorably known in leading business circles. He owned extensive sales stables at Beloit, Wis., with branch establishment at 37 to 41 W. Forty-fourth street, New York, operating same for over twenty years. He was at one time connected with the New York Cab Co., at Long Branch, N. J., and has a reputation almost national. He is a member of the Liverymen's Association and a prominent Free Mason.

FRANK F. PORTER.

Few, if any, of the various and many branches of commercial activity that contribute to the general aggregate of trade in the city of Chicago are of greater importance than the hardware, range and tool line. A deservedly popular and prosperous house engaged in this business, and one that has always maintained a very enviable reputation for handling only first-class goods and honorable straightforward dealings, is that of Mr. Frank F. Porter, whose well-ordered establishment is eligibly located at No. 317 Sixty-third street, Englewood. Mr. Porter was born in this state and became a permanent resident of this city in 1885, when he inaugurated his present enterprise. He has a thorough knowledge of the business, acquired by long practical experience, and under his able management his house has become the center of a very large and influential patronage, which is each year increasing in volume and importance. He occupies the ground floor and basement of a three-story brick building, 20x70 feet in dimensions, and a three-story storehouse in rear, well adapted for the purposes of the business. His store is admirably arranged and is supplied with every facility for the storage, handling, display and inspection of the heavy stock always carried. The latter is full and complete, and embraces hardware of every description, such as machinists', wheelwrights' and contractors' supplies, builders' hardware of every description in all the very latest and improved styles, mechanics' and artisans' tools, pocket and table cutlery, razors, etc., wrought sleel ranges, furnaces, heaters, the best coal stoves, all of the finest manufacture. These goods are purchased direct from the most reliable makers and are placed before the patrons of the house at prices that defy competition. He also carries a full stock of safety bicycles, ladies' and gents', both medium and high grade, and sells on as easy terms as any house in the city. Four assistants are employed and orders are promptly filled, while satisfaction is in every case guaranteed. Mr. Porter carries only excellent and reliable goods. He conducts his business on the soundest principles of integrity and spares no pains to meet the wants of his patrons. He is an active and enterprising merchant and enjoys the confidence of all with whom he has any dealings.

E. BURKHARDT.

The leading marble and granite works of Chicago are those of which Mr. E. Burkhardt is the experienced and enterprising proprietor. Both as to design, quality and finish his marble mantels are recognized as the finest in the market. The business was established in 1863 by the firm of Messrs. Roach & Burkhardt, first being located on Clark street, and beginning operations on a comparatively small scale. Trade grew and enlarged facilities were necessitated, resulting in the formation of the firm of Messrs. Volk, Feeney, Burkhardt & Roach, with yards on Washington street. In 1871, the great fire burned them out, when Messrs. Feeney & Burkhardt continued the business up to 1882. Then Mr. Feeney retired, and Mr. Burkhardt became the sole proprietor. He has manifested marked energy and enterprise and the soundest judgment in the development of his trade, and his large yards and mill have a desirable location on Kingsbury and Ohio streets, north of Indiana street bridge and the river. The premises are 125 feet by 110 in dimensions, and have all the modern improvements, including two gangs of saws, one rubbing bed, polishing and finishing lathes, etc., run by a fine 25 horse power engine. Mr. Burkhardt employs upward of forty skilled hands here in the manufacture of fine granite and marble cemetery work, headstones, slabs, columns, monuments and statuary, all of the most artistic character. He makes a prominent specialty of high grade marble mantels in the finest of Italian, Vermont and Tennessee marbles, and in every line offers, not only the highest style of workmanship and finish, but also the benefits of manufacturers' prices. He is prominent also as a cut-stone contractor, making a specialty of cut granite for builders' purposes. Mr. Burkhardt has made a close study of every branch of the trade, and is considered to be an authority therein. He is noted as a designer of remarkable skill and ability, and has attained a national distinction in this respect. As an example of his artistic work, it may be stated that he made the designs, and furnished and erected the magnificent soldiers' monuments, built at Elgin, and Rosehill Ill., and every cemetery in this vicinity has numerous examples of his monumental work in marble and granite. Mr. Burkhardt is a native of Erfurt, Germany, and has been a permanent resident of Chicago for the past thirty-five years, permanently respected, and a popular public spirited citizen, influential in political circles, and though frequently solicited, has always declined office. He has won a great success on the basis of merit and honorable effort, and is in every respect a leading representative in his line.

AETNA COPYING COMPANY.

The advances which have been made during recent years in all that appertains to photography is nowhere more noticeable than with regard to what is known as 'photo enlargement. By means of this unique and beautiful art, life-size productions are obtained from the miniature portrait or carte-de-visite, which but a few years ago would have been impossible otherwise than by the hand of the artist and painter. Here in Chicago this industry is represented by the well-known and popular Aetna Copying Co., whose studio is eligibly located at Nos. 349 and 351 W. Van Buren street. This enterprise was established by Messrs. Moyer & Goodwin in 1888, and on the secession of the latter gentleman by the sale of his interest in 1889, the concern was converted to a corporate organization under the present trading title, with an authorized capital of $50,000, and officered as follows: W. D. Moyer, president; M. B. Staley, treasurer; S. F. Staley, secretary. Every variety of enlarging is executed in the highest style of the art, and portraits are exquisitely finished either in oils, water colors, pastel or India ink, constant employment being furnished for a corps of seventeen skilled artists. A business is transacted through traveling and local agents, who take orders on sample, which is broadly distributed throughout the entire United States, and the trade, already large, is annually increasing in volume and value, and constitutes a fitting comment, in our opinion, of the high-class character of the work turned out by this enterprising organization. This concern is in all respects a reliable one and merits public confidence.

H. R. SMILEY.

The manufacture of the finer and more delicate sort of scales is an industry that calls into requisition the highest skill and the most ripe experience. These are possessed in a pre-eminent degree by Mr. H. R. Smiley, of Nos. 77 to 83 North Clinton street, whose reputation has extended to every part of the continent. The business was originated by the late Mr. Lawrence Ambs, whose lamented decease in 1889, deprived Chicago of one of her most talented and able business men. Mr. Smiley succeeded to the proprietorship, having purchased the good will and premises, and has labored assiduously and successfully to build up a solid and prosperous business on the

old principles which secured to his predecessor such a large and influential connection. His elegant scales are classed among the most artistic and exquisite productions that are to be found. They include box and counter scales in ash, cherry, oak, ebony and Italian and Tennessee marble, besides prescription, analytical and hydrometer scales of every variety of shape and design. These articles are guaranteed to be accurate, are made of the very best material throughout, the pivots and bearings being of the best English steel. He also makes block weights of solid rod brass, and nest and aluminum grain weights to suit all purposes. He manufactures any kind of scale to order, for every conceivable purpose, and is continually adding to the long list of his superior articles by the invention of new designs and patterns. Mr. Smiley was born in Boston, of an old Massachusetts family, and has had great experience in the profession, having held for eighteen years a prominent position in connection with the Howe and Fairbanks Scale Co. He is a business man of great ability, and commands the respect and esteem of all.

CHAS. TALLMAN.

No man can lay claim to a closer identity with real estate in Chicago than Mr. Charles Tallman, for he established himself in the business after the great fire in 1871, and was for some time on E. Washington street, though he moved to his present location at 896 W. Twelfth street in December, 1890. His business comprises everything that comes under the head of a legitimate real estate business, such as effecting loans and negotiating mortgages, insurance, collecting rents, paying taxes, superintending repairs, and the general management of property for non-residents. He always has some choice bargains in acre property, and likewise in improved city lots,

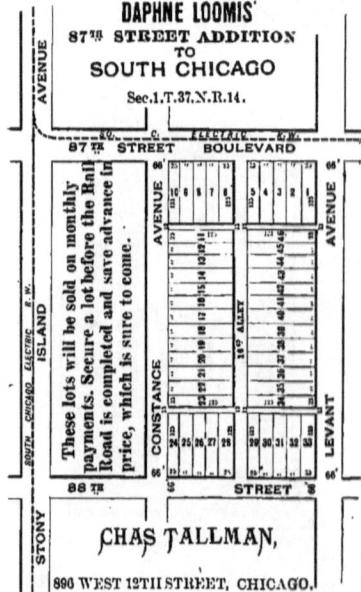

DAPHNE LOOMIS'
87TH STREET ADDITION
TO
SOUTH CHICAGO
Sec.1,T.37,N.R.14.

CHAS TALLMAN,

896 WEST 12TH STREET, CHICAGO.

especially on the West side. He is agent for the E. I. D. Wickes' subdivision, located on Twelfth street boulevard, Lincoln, Robey and Thirteenth streets, which is considered by some to be one of the best investments on the West side. He also represents Daphne Loomis' Eighty-seventh street addition to South Chicago, being a subdivision of five and one-half acres between Eighty-seventh and Eighty-eighth streets, and adjoining the South Chicago Electric Railway. These lots will, in all probability, double in value in a very short time, as they are adjacent to the Lake Shore, B. & O. and Rock Island Railroads. Mr. Tallman represents the Glen Falls Insurance Co. of New York, and can always find an outlet for any kind of risks at good premiums. He follows his business very closely, and is continually in touch with capitalists and influential real estate owners in the city. Mr. Tallman was born in Ogdensburg, N. Y., and came to Chicago in 1853 and has made for himself a name and standing in the trade.

GEO. C. JOHNSON.

The stove and hardware business has many representatives in this city, some of them being leaders in the trade, but none of them of higher standing or reputation than Mr. Geo. C. Johnson, whose place of business is No. 438 W. Chicago avenue. This business has been established for twelve years, and has grown steadily from the very first. Mr. Johnson is a young man of the most industrious habits, and accustomed to applying himself closely to business. He is a native of Chicago, and is one of her most progressive business men. He occupies the commodious store and basement, both 25x85 feet in dimensions, at the above address. Here he carries a complete stock of the leading stoves and ranges, a full line of builders' hardware, and all kinds of tinware and house furnishing goods. He makes a specialty of the celebrated "Acmee" and "Splendid" ranges. His shop, in the basement, is always a busy place, where eight men are constantly employed in the manufacture of tinware, in which Mr. Johnson does a large business. This house has a most liberal patronage, many of the leading builders making all their purchases of hardware through it, and also giving Mr. Johnson contracts for the gutters, heaters, etc. Mr. Johnson stands well in business and financial circles, and is regarded everywhere as a man of honor and integrity.

BLOCK-POLLAK IRON CO.

The trade in old railroad materials has developed to proportions of enormous magnitude and the leading house engaged therein is that of the "Block-Pollak Iron Company," of which Mr. Emil Pollak is president. The business was established a number of years ago, with headquarters in Cincinnati, O., by the firm of Block & Pollak. They early achieved a great success, developing widespread influential connections, and in 1884 opened the Chicago branch, which has become the center of a most important branch of the trade. In July, 1891, the vast interests were duly organized and incorporated under the style and title of the Block-Pollak Iron Co., with a paid up capital of $200,000 and a surplus of $50,000. Thus the new firm is financially strong, and has the benefit of extra experience and soundest judgment in its management. The Company's main offices are in the Commerce Building, 14 Pacific avenue, Chicago, Ill. The offices are centrally located and admirably arranged for the needs of the business. Mr. Emil Pollak is the president of the company and also secretary and treasurer of the Indianapolis Car and Fuel Company, and president of the famous Cincinnati Forge and Iron Company. Mr. Isaac Block, the vice-president, is also a resident of Chicago. Mr. Emil Benjamin, the treasurer, resides in Cincinnati, while Mr. Louis Benjamin, the secretary, is a resident of this city, and devotes close attention to the details of the business. The general manager, Mr. Joseph Block, is a resident of Cincinnati. Mr. Joseph Hyman, the general agent, has had long experience in this branch of trade, and is deservedly popular and respected, while with characteristic energy he is steadily enlarging the business done here. Thus the executive is in every respect responsible and prominent. The company's yards in Chicago extend from Fifty-second to Fifty-fourth streets between Wallace and Desplaines streets, covering an area of some five acres. Here is erected a large warehouse, 82 by 300 feet for storage of materials. The yards are directly connected by switches with several of the principal railroads entering the city. Thus they enjoy every facility for handling material, which they do in carload lots only. In fact the bulk of the company's trade is with the great leading railroads of America, contracting with them for all their old rails, wheels, tires and scrap, and which they last year purchased to the enormous amount of 60,000 tons. While old railroad material is their specialty, yet the company is prepared to buy old iron and steel of any description, in carload lots. It pays prompt cash and highest rates, and is the leading representative concern of the kind in America, managed in such an honorable and equitable manner, as to permanently retain the confidence of the public at large, and the character and magnitude of whose operations is a powerful factor in the wholesale iron trade.

JENKINS & THOMPSEN.

The inhabitants of Chicago are lovers of elegance and refinement, and take the greatest pride in the furnishings of their homes. Possibly there is no city in America where more money has been spent in interior decoration than in Chicago. A prominent house doing business in this line is that known by the name of Jenkins & Thompsen. This business was established in 1885 by Mr. Jenkins, on State street; Mr. Thompsen also being in business elsewhere. In January last the business style was changed to the present form by the retirement of Mr. Moffett and the amalgamation of the business interest of Mr. Thompsen with those of Mr. Jenkins, at 222 N. State street. Here they occupy the ground floor of the handsome four-story building, 30x60 feet in dimensions, and carry a heavy stock of the finest designs in wallpaper; everything in the line of decorative materials, window shades, etc.; also paints, artists' materials, moldings, etc. The paperings and decorations are of handsome and artistic design, and contain many novelties especially selected by the firm. Thirty-five skilled workmen are employed constantly in decorating, frescoing, calcimining, etc., the house never having an unoccupied season. Both members of the firm are practical painters and decorators, and bring to bear the advantages of their long experience in perfecting the finest effects. The house is well patronized, many of the most prominent citizens of the North side being regular customers, and the general trade extends all over the city. The gentlemen at the head of this concern are well known to the business world and are everywhere held in the highest esteem. Mr. Jenkins is a native of Shelby, Ind., and Mr. Thompsen was born in Denmark.

J. S. YOUNG.

In this age of advancement every city, town, village and hamlet has its humane society, and of more benefit and practical use than all of these is the veterinary surgeon. At Nos. 18 and 20 South Ann street, corner of Washington, Dr. J. S. Young has erected a handsome two-story brick building at a cost of $10,000, 50 feet by 180 feet in size, as an infirmary or hospital for all domestic animals, fully equipped to the most minute particular for the treatment of horses, cattle, dogs, cats and domestic animals. The doctor, who is a well-known veterinary, opened in this city in 1875, and has made the diseases and injuries of animals a study ever since, and is considered an authority on all matters in his line. His office and laboratory, which is in the front of his infirmary building, is stocked with a full line of drugs, chemicals, oils and instruments necessary for the proper management of his business. The doctor resides in a handsome home at No. 341 W. Washington street, but has direct telephone communication with his hospital, and responds promptly to all calls, day or night. The capacity of the hospital is forty horses. Dr. Young is a native of England, but has resided in Chicago for the past twenty years.

SHEALY'S STEAM LAUNDRY.

One of the most reliable and popular steam laundries in this section of Chicago is that of Mr. Joe Shealy, eligibly located at 478 Ogden avenue. Mr. Shealy first commenced business on Halsted street in 1882, and eventually in 1887 removed to his present location. He occupies a spacious ground floor, 25x80 feet in area, with boiler house in the rear. The laundry is fully supplied with the latest improved apparatus, appliances and machinery, including three washing machines, wringers, ironing machines, etc., operated by a sixteen horse steam engine and boiler. Over 1,800 shirts are washed here weekly, in addition to large quantities of collars, cuffs and other goods too numerous to particularize. All work is executed in a most careful manner without injury to garments and fully equal to that of any similar concern in the country. Twenty-four skilled hands are employed, while the prices charged are extremely moderate. Three delivery wagons are constantly employed and goods are called for and delivered free in any part of the city.

Mr. Shealy has thirty-eight agencies in the city. He has obtained an excellent reputation with hotel keepers, families and individuals and makes a specialty of lace curtains and shirts. Mr. Shealy was born in Delphi, Ind., but has lived in Chicago for the past twenty-four years. He is an honorable and energetic business man, who is very popular with the general public. The telephone call of the laundry is 7152, and Mr. Shealy is a prominent member of the Chicago Laundry Men's Association.

GRANT BROTHERS.

As well equipped and as fashionable a tailoring establishment as can be found in the city of Chicago is that of the Grant Bros., at number 452 Ogden avenue. These gentlemen are natives of Scotland and have resided in Chicago about six years. They are both practical tailors and have had a long and careful training in the business. Mr. Aleck Grant was formerly with Alex. Dunlap, merchant tailor on Dearborn street, and Mr. John Grant learned his trade with one of the largest establishments of the kind in London, Eng. These gentlemen have become well known as experienced and painstaking artists, and as ones who give full satisfaction to their customers. Their store is 25x80 feet in dimensions, with work room in the rear. The store is elegantly furnished and contains a well-selected assortment of all the latest patterns of the best product of the weaver's art. The stock embraces the finest tweeds, cloths, cassimeres, serges, flannels worsteds and other fine goods. The business of the house is extensive, the patrons being from all sections of the city. The proprietors give personal attention to the perfection of all garments that leave the establishment, and the prices are remarkably low. Mr. Aleck Grant is a member of the Highland Association of Illinois, the Caledonian Society of Chicago and the Royal Arcanum. Mr. John Grant is a member of the Highland Association of Illinois and is prominent in social circles. These are young men of ability and the highest standing in the business world and are esteemed highly by all who know them.

F. WEINER.

Among the oldest established and most deservedly successful houses engaged in this important line of business on this thoroughfare is that of Mr. F. Weiner, wholesale and retail dealer in hams, shoulders, bacon, lard and all kinds of first-class fresh and salt meats, at No. 2359 Wentworth avenue, corner of Twenty-fourth street. This gentleman is of German birth and has been a respected citizen of Chicago for the past twenty-five years. Having acquired a thorough knowledge of the business by practical experience, he inaugurated his present enterprise in 1869, and at once became the center of a first-class and influential trade that has since steadily increased. Mr. Weiner occupies the ground floor of a two-story frame structure, having a frontage of twenty feet on Wentworth avenue and of sixty on Twenty-fourth street. These spacious premises are admirably appointed and fitted up with special reference to the trade, which involves the daily handling of large quantities of fresh and salt meats of all kinds, and which in quantity, excellence, quality and variety are unsurpassed by any similar house in this section of the city. The stock embraces the finest of everything in this line, and Mr. Weiner, having excellent cold storage facilities, is enabled to supply his patrons with the best of wholesome foods during all seasons of the year, and at lowest prices. The utmost neatness and cleanliness are observed, polite assistants attend promptly to customers, and orders are called for and delivered at residences free of charge. Being an expert judge of meats in the carcass or on the hoof, he selects only the very best from the most reliable sources, and his house holds a most enviable reputation for handling only first-class commodities and for fair, square dealings with patrons. Mr. Weiner is a pleasant, courteous gentleman and enjoys the fullest confidence of the trade and the community at large. In all his transactions he is accounted as an honorable enterprising and energetic man and customers can always count upon honest and honorable treatment.

THE BYRKIT HALL SHEATHING LATH COMPANY.

The march of improvement in the line of the architect and the builder had benefited almost every feature of the construction of buildings except that of the lathing, which remained at a standstill until the introduction of the Patent Byrkit and Hall Sheathing Lath, and which has proved the greatest boon to the builder, the plasterer, and the owner and occupants of all houses into which it has been introduced. The business of both the Byrkit and Hall interests were duly consolidated in 1887, and the "Byrkit-Hall Sheathing Lath Company" organized with an authorized capital of $500,000, of which $200,000 has been paid in, the company developing a trade national in extent, not in the

owners will consult their best interest by specifying it in all contracts, as the edifice into which it is introduced is stronger, handsomer and warmer than those with old style lath, while it will rent quicker, and sell at a better price. It is now in use in upward of 10,000 buildings – churches, schools, hotels, business blocks, dwellings and public buildings, and in all cases "fills a long felt want." Mr. Henry Colburn, the president of the company, is a lumber merchant and a prominent resident of Indianapolis, specially qualified to discharge the duties devolving upon him. Mr. A. A. Adair, the popular and energetic secretary and treasurer, is personally in charge of the office here. He is a well-known business man, for a number of years actively engaged in the book and stationery business, and whose excellent executive methods, specially benefit the interests of all customers. Mr. Adair is a native of Zanesville, O., and though still young, is a war veteran, having volunteered soon after the war of the Rebellion broke out, in the 78th Ohio Infantry. Those desiring full information, book of testimonials, and samples, should send to the company's offices in the Gaff building, 230 to 236 La Salle street. The Byrkit-Hall sheathing lath is a great step forward. It is fast displacing the old-time lath, and is one of the great staple modern improvements, bound to rapidly come into general use.

G. A. LIPPS.

A South side establishment that does the finest class of upholstering and decorating of furniture, is that of G. A. Lipps, at No. 124 Thirty-first street. Mr. Lipps is a young man, born and raised in Chicago, and is a practical upholsterer of the most artistic taste. He employs five assistants and his establishment occupies the ground floor and basement of the building, 25x110 feet. The store is in front and the workshop in the rear, while the basement is used for storage. The business was established in 1888 by the firm of Sues & Lipps, Mr. Lipps succeeding as sole proprietor in 1889. All kinds of upholstering and decorating is done, as well as everything connected with the repair and renovation of furniture, carpets, etc. Hair mattresses are also made to order and renovated. Furniture is cleaned, polished and packed and loose covers are cut, fitted and sewed. Carpets are taken up, cleaned by steam and relaid. A liberal patronage is enjoyed, which the quality of the work done and the reasonableness of the charges made, more than warrant.

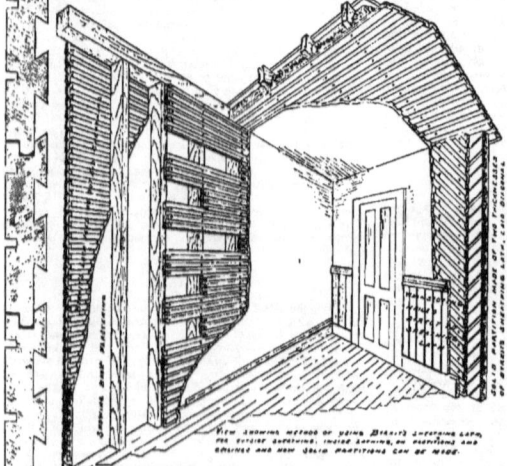

direct supply of this splendid lathing, but also in the sale of its special machines for making the lath. Already over 150 of the leading manufacturers of lumber and builders' woodwork are producing this improved lath, and it is kept in stock by the most enterprising dealers everywhere. *Once used*, no architect, builder or owner will ever leave it out of his specifications thereafter. The Byrkit lath is matched, or tongued and grooved, rendering it wind proof. It is dressed to an even thickness on the face side of the lath. When the plastering is applied it fills up the pores of the wood, and all danger of cracking is obviated, if the sheathing has been properly nailed. The great curse of and objection to the old style of lathing and plastering is, that it is not wind proof, and is very liable to crack—in fact does crack 90 times in a 100. The Byrkit sheathing lath are only 1⅝ inches wide on the face, with ⅜ inch spaces; between that are 5-16 of an inch deep, giving the plasterer a chance to work his thick mortar with the hair into the clinchers, cementing all solid together, and making a solid hard and smooth wall, the delight of all subsequent occupants of the premises. Architects and

G. MERZ.

Among the great representative houses in Chicago, which are devoted to the manufacture of cigar boxes, etc., the Northwestern Steam Cigar Box Manufactory, at 209 to 213 Superior street, of which Mr. G. Merz is the estimable proprietor, must be given the leading place. Mr. Merz began the business in 1867 on Kinzie street, and, although burned out by the great fire of 1871, immediately resumed operations, and eight years afterward built his present factory, a substantial three-story brick, with basement, measuring 80x130 feet, and exactly suited to the requirements of the industry. The motive force is steam, supplied by a fifty horse power engine, and every part of the great equipment is the most improved that is known to the trade. A staff of eighty expert assistants are constantly employed among whom are some of the most skilful designers of labels, etc., that are to be found. The line embraces cigar boxes and all kinds of cigarmakers' supplies, such as ribbons, labels, moulds, presses, boards and cutters, and it is a well substantiated fact that all goods turned out here are of the very best quality, and -pre-eminently adapted for their various uses. Boxes are also made for soaps, perfumery, confectionery, etc., and gotten up in the most attractive and convenient styles. The productions of this house deservedly bear the highest reputation throughout the Western states, and Mr. Merz is adding daily to the scores of city patrons, who invariably place their orders with him. This gentleman is a native of Switzerland, but has during his residence of upward of a quarter of a century in Chicago acquired a thorough knowledge of the wants of the best class of trade. He is an active Free Mason and a large capitalist, being one of the most prominent real estate owners in the city, and enjoys the respect and warm regard of all who have ever been thrown in contact with him..

EQUITABLE STORAGE WAREHOUSE.

We have great pleasure in bringing to the notice of our readers an establishment formed in 1887, and which under able management is rapidly coming into prominence, for the storage of merchandise, furniture, and valuables, namely, the Equitable Storage Warehouse, on the corner of W. Randolph and Ann streets, of which Mr. A. D. Daly is the popular proprietor. The building is a substantial three-story brick structure giving an area of no less than 55,000 square feet, and admirably adapted to the purposes for which it is used. Here the finest facilities exist for the storage of furniture, pianos, carriages and goods of all kinds, large steel safety vaults being provided for jewelry, silver, valuable records, etc. The building is absolutely fire and burglar-proof, and offers the most secure resting place for these precious articles. Mr. Daly moves goods, etc., to and from any part of the city, employing eight horses in this branch of industry, packs for shipment in the most careful manner, and makes liberal cash advances on all articles stored on his premises. Among his permanent patrons are numbered Messrs. F. C. Austin & Co., railroad grading and well machinery, and Mr. Geo. Schweinforth, flour, grain, etc. Inquiries are now pouring in from great firms in New York, and other leading centers of the Union, whose business requires the use of a reliable ware house such as this, and undoubtedly Mr. Daly has, in his growing connection with the East a fertile field of usefulness that will bring in a rich harvest in the near future. The rates charged here are lower than any other storage house in the city. Fifteen careful and experienced hands are constantly employed, and are always under the closest personal supervision of the practical and attentive proprietor. This gentleman came from Montreal, Canada, six years ago, and is to be heartily congratulated on his phenomenal success.

SMITH-OBERGFELL MFG. CO.

The extensive building enterprises that have made this city so great have given rise to many manufacturing plants that supply the demand for building materials. One of the leading companies, for reliability and extent of plant, is the Smith-Obergfell Manufacturing Company. This business was established in 1890, by Smith, Obergfell and Lanson, and was changed to the present form and incorporated in 1891, with a capitalization of $10,000. The officers of the company are prominent and well-known business men, who are thoroughly familiar with all the details of the business and have a business connection of high order with leading builders and contractors. The president is Mr. Ferd. Smith, and the secretary and treasurer is Mr. Fred. Obergfell. The business is conducted at Nos. 367, 369 and 371 Sedgwick street, near Schiller, where the company has a fine mill and complete plant. The factory is a three-story brick structure, 40x120 feet in dimensions, being thoroughly equipped with all the latest

improvements in woodworking machinery, including the finest planing, sawing, turning, grooving, mortising, dovetailing and moulding machines; the whole being driven by steam power supplied by a fifty horse-power engine. The entire premises cover an area of 75x204 feet, and the large yards are thoroughly stocked with great quantities of well seasoned lumber of all kinds, both pine and the finest hardwoods. This company has a reputation of high order for making a very superior grade of builders' supplies, consisting of sash, doors, blinds, etc., also frames, brackets, balusters and interior finish. Their work has very popular, and is in great demand everywhere. Thirty experienced workmen are employed, and the company has a large trade in the city and state, supplying many leading contractors and builders. The officers at the head of this concern are gentlemen of well-known ability and recognized business standing. Mr. Smith is a native of Denmark, and has resided in Chicago since childhood. Mr. Obergfell was born in this city, and has hosts of friends. Both are highly esteemed everywhere.

ALBERT NAFZIGER.

The drugstore of Mr. Albert Nafziger, at 296 W. Division street, has now come to be recognized as one of the prominent business institutions in this particular section of the city. It was founded in 1887 by Mr. R. Stangohl, and has been under the direction of the present proprietor since 1889. The situation of the store is a most eligible one, and with its handsome plate glass front, dark wood fixtures, and massive soda fountain, it has at all times a most attractive and pleasing appearance. Mr. Nafziger has at all times in stock a choice selection of pure drugs and chemicals, proprietary preparations, family medicines, toilet articles, perfumes, soaps, brushes, combs, sponges, surgical appliances, fancy goods, and the usual assemblage of goods that come under the head of druggists' sundries. Special attention is devoted to compounding physicians' prescriptions and family recipes, this department being in charge of a thoroughly competent graduate pharmacist, and under the direct supervision of the proprietor. The pharmacy and laboratory are carefully furnished with every necessary apparatus for the delicate responsibilities involved, and Mr. Nafziger manufactures all his own essences and extracts so as to secure purity in dispensing recipes. Born in Germany and a graduate of the University of Berlin, Mr. Nafziger, who is comparatively a young man, came to Chicago five years ago, and has already attained much popularity, as the policy upon which his business is conducted is characterized by a careful regard for the interests of his patrons.

CHAS. WIRTH & CO.

Among the prominent houses dealing in stoves, tin and hardware is that of Chas. Wirth & Co. The business of this house has been established fourteen years and has been remarkably successful. The founders were Leon & Freytag, who were succeeded in 1889 by Wirth & Newhouse. In January last Mr. A. O. Froebe purchased Mr. Newhouse's interest and the present style of firm name was adopted. Mr. Chas. Wirth is a native of Chicago, where he has always resided. He is a prominent member of the Royal League and the Order of the Iron Hall. Mr. A. O. Froebe was born in Germany, and came direct to Chicago in 1873. From 1883 to 1888 he lived in Kansas City, but returned to Chicago after being a member of the firm of Wolf & Co., furniture manufacturers, for five years, in the city by the Kan. This house is substantial and progressive. The firm occupy the ground floor and basement of the premises No. 827 Milwaukee avenue, and 165 West Division street, having a frontage of 25 feet no each street and a depth of 75 feet. Here they carry an immense stock of all kinds of stoves and ranges, tools, shelf hardware, furnishings for builders, cutlery and tinware. Jobbing is done at reasonable rates. The house enjoys an excellent reputation, and a most liberal patronage. The proprietors are well known in business circles and are everywhere held in the highest esteem.

11

RAYMOND BROS.

Among the prominent transfer and teaming establishments of Chicago a leading position is occupied by the Michigan Central Railroad Transfer Co., located at the foot of S. Water street, whose proprietors, H. V. & H. E. Raymond, are well-known as enterprising and reliable business men by the whole commercial community of the city. Mr. T. Raymond founded the house thirty years ago, conducting it in a systematic, well-balanced way, that secured the confidence of all and established it upon a firm and enduring basis. In 1889, the present proprietors succeeded, admitting Mr. Johnson in the following March, but dissolving again a few months later, and remaining as at present constituted ever since. They are the cartage agents for the Michigan Central Railway Company, and hold beside many contracts with the most important firms in the city, who find their orders carried out here with the greatest promptitude and care. They have every facility for the important work, occupying premises specially built for the purpose, and which afford the finest accommodation for both horses and vehicles. The business requires the constant services of fifteen experienced and careful hands and thirty horses, and is daily growing in magnitude and importance. The arrangements are perfect in every respect as regards stabling, wagon and buggy room, wash house, feed, storage, etc., and fifty stalls and two boxes are available for boarders, half of these being occupied at the present time. An elevator of 4,000 pounds' capacity runs to every floor, and, taken as a whole, it would be impossible to find premises which are more eminently suited to the business in any part of the city. The Messrs. Raymond are renowned for the care they exercise in moving the immense mass of goods passing through their hands, and having at command superior equipment and experienced help, they are prepared to execute all commissions in the most satisfactory and expeditious manner.

WEGNER & OLSEN.

A branch of industry of a very useful and important character in this section of Chicago is the manufacture of beer stills, railroad tanks, etc. In this connection special reference is made to the representative and progressive firm of Messrs. Wegner & Olsen, whose office is located at 44 W. Lake street. The firm's factories are at 43 to 45 W. Lake street and 12 to 16 Milwaukee avenue. The various departments of the works are fully equipped with the latest improved tools, machinery and appliances, operated by steam power. The area of the factories is 80x40 feet, and 35x150 feet. Messrs. Wegner & Olsen manufacture extensively beer stills, railroad tanks and all kinds of distiller's, brewers' and vinegar tubs, cisterns, milk vats, etc. Only the best and most carefully selected materials are utilized, and the articles turned out are unrivaled for strength, finish and workmanship. The firm carefully fills orders at the lowest possible prices, and their trade, which is steadily increasing extends throughout the Middle, Western and Northwestern States. The sales for the past year amounted to $70,000. This business was established in 1889 by Messrs. Wegner & Westerholm, who conducted it till March 1, 1891, when Mr. Westerholm retired and Mr. C. Olsen became a partner. They at first employed three men; now forty-five skilled workmen are employed. Both partners are thoroughly practical and expert workmen, fully conversant with every detail of this industry, and the requirements of the most exacting patrons. The firm has just completed contracts for the Illadovec Brewing Company and the Independent Brewing Company of this city, and are now constructing tubs for the Henn & Vabler Brewing Company of this city. They are also making tubs for the annex of Thieme & Wagner Brewing Company at La Fayette, Ind. Mr. Wegner was born in Germany, and Mr. Olsen in Norway. They have both resided in the United States the greater part of their lives, and are highly esteemed in trade circles for their integrity and energy, while their success in this business is as substantial as it is well deserved.

CHAS. F. ELMES.

The annually increasing demand for steam power machinery in the United States necessitates correspondingly extensive facilities for their production, hence the building of steam engines, boilers, etc, constitutes a very important branch of industry. Among the representative and reliable houses engaged in this trade in Chicago, special mention should be made of that of Mr. Chas. F. Elmes, engineer, founder and machinist, whose works are situated on Fulton and Jefferson streets. This business was founded in 1881 by Mr. C. D. Elmes. He was succeeded by his son, the present proprietor, who is a thoroughly practical and expert mechanical engineer and machinist, fully conversant with every detail of this industry and the requirements of patrons. He occupies and owns a substantial two-story building, 50x135 feet in area, fully supplied with modern tools and machinery, operated by a fifty horse power steam engine. Here he employs fifty skilled workmen and manufactures automatical and marine engines, hydraulic presses and pumps for all purposes, steam fire pumps and Willard's patent steam hammers. He also promptly rebuilds fire engines and makes to order all kinds of machinery. His steam engines, pumps, etc., are made of the best materials and are unsurpassed for efficiency, reliability and economy, while they are the embodiments of mechanical workmanship of the highest order of perfection. They are adapted for all kinds of service and have proved their superiority when brought into competition with those of other makers, while the prices quoted for them are exceedingly just and moderate. Mr. Elmes makes a specialty of fire boat machinery, having built machinery for both Chicago and Milwaukee fire boats. In consequence of a steadily increasing patronage Mr. Elmes soon intends to make a large addition to his works. His trade extends throughout all sections of Chicago and the state, and every effort is made to give entire satisfaction to patrons. Mr. Elmes was born in Maine, but has resided in Chicago for the last thirty years. He is highly esteemed in trade circles for his mechanical skill and integrity, and justly merits the liberal and influential patronage secured in this valuable industry.

ERHART & BERNARD.

The really most important business in a community is the family grocer. He it is who supplies us with that choice selection of edibles and condiments which, separate or combined in the quantities only known to the cook, become either the staff or sauce of life. It is our grocer who sells us the fruits of many climes, all properly prepared, and ready for household use; but it is necessary to healthfulness that these same groceries shall be pure, clean and fresh, and too much caution cannot be taken to guard against imposition in this important part of domestic life. The safest and best manner is to select as family grocers only those who are perfectly reliable, and understand their business that they themselves may not be imposed upon in buying, and unwittingly impose upon their trade. Such a firm as one can select with perfect confidence is that of Erhart & Bernard of 291 W. Twelfth street, near Halsted. This firm is composed of three young men, F. Erhart, A. and N. Bernard, all experienced in their line, and who, in their finely fitted and well-stocked store, carry a most complete line of staple and fancy groceries, including everything these comprehensive terms may imply, and making a specialty of the best brands of flour. Although in business for themselves but a short time, they employ a competent number of clerks, who keep two family delivery wagons busy distributing their orders in all parts of the city. One of their conveniences is they can take orders by their telephone, No. 4378, and deliver immediately. All of the members of the firm are natives of Chicago, have grown up with it, and take an active interest in everything pertaining to the city's welfare. They are also proprietors of a fine livery business on Blue Island avenue, and is one of the best in that locality. They also conduct an extensive carriage business at the rear of No. 291 W. Twelfth street, where the best line of buggies, carriages, phaetons, carts and other vehicles are kept in stock at all times.

W. D. MARTIN & SON.

The position of Chicago in the machinery trade of the western, northwestern and southwestern sections of the country is beyond question the leading one, and the rapid development of this interest greatly conduces to the permanent prosperity of the great metropolis of Illinois state. Among the leading manufacturing establishments, actively engaged in a special line of production in this connection, is that of Messrs. W. D. Martin & Son, whose well-appointed office and factory are located at No. 17 S. Canal street. This enterprise was established by Messrs. William D. and Thomas R. Martin, father and son, in 1887, and under their able and efficient management has enjoyed a continuously prosperous

career to date, the trading connections of the house annually increasing in volume and value. This firm manufacture improved woodworking machinery of every description for the use of car builders, planing mills, cabinet and carriage makers, railroad shops, house builders, sash, door and blind makers, etc., and they have arrangements with several large Eastern houses, which enable them to make estimates on complete outfits. As they carry these products in stock they are always ready to fill orders promptly. They are triumphs of inventive genius and mechanical skill, and have attained a widespread reputation throughout the Western and Southwestern states. The premises occupied comprise two spacious and commodious floors, 20x80 feet in dimensions, equipped with basement and factory in rear, 50x50 feet, with every facility for the expeditious prosecution of the business, a sample stock being carried, with a view to the prompt fulfillment of orders, valued at $20,000. Those interested will find it greatly to their advantage to make a factor of this house, and will obtain such marked concessions here as will fully sustain all that has been stated in this editorial article.

H. C. KERSTING.

The art of photography has made rapid strides in the last few years, and such great perfection has been attained that it is being utilized in all professions and sciences, as well as to represent the human features in portraits. One of the old established galleries of the city is that of Mr. H. C. Kersting, who has been located at 730 Milwaukee avenue for the past fourteen years. He has recently refitted his establishment, and furnished it in a handsome and artistic manner. He occupies two floors, 24x100 feet in dimensions, the first being fitted as a studio and office and the second as an operating room. Samples of work of the highest order are exposed on the walls and are meritorious specimens of high art photography. Mr. Kersting makes a specialty of crayon portraits and does superior work in this line. He gives especial care to the taking of children's pictures and has been remarkably successful in this line. His patronage is extensive and of the most desirable order, numbering many leading citizens among the customers. Mr. Kersting is a native of Germany and has resided in Chicago for forty

ears. He is a courteous, agreeable gentleman and an artist of undisputed ability. He has numerous friends and by all is held in the highest esteem. He employs four competent assistants and gives the business his close personal attention.

FRANK J. KNOWLES.

A popular and reliable pharmacy on the West side is that of Mr. Frank J. Knowles, at 475 Ogden avenue, northwest corner of Polk street. It is in all respects a first-class establishment and receives a very extensive patronage. The store is angle shaped, having a frontage of 50x37 feet, and is handsomely fitted up and furnished in a tasteful and elegant manner. It is provided with all the most modern improvements, including plate glass front, show cases and cabinets and a massive and attractive soda fountain. The laboratory is complete in all its appointments, and Mr. Knowles makes a specialty of Knowles' Cough Balsam, beef wine and iron and sarsaparilla, also the compounding of physicians' prescriptions, in which he is ably supported by a corps of experienced assistants. The ingredients used are absolutely pure, and the greatest care and accuracy is exercised, orders being filled by day or night. The stock carried is large and complete and includes carefully selected drugs, medicines and chemicals of every description, extracts, essences, spices, herbs and kindred products. All standard proprietary medicines, mineral waters, etc., also a full assortment of toilet articles, perfumery, cigars, etc. Born near Albion, Orleans County, N. Y., Mr. Knowles established himself fifteen years ago at Lockport, Ill., and in 1885 removed to Chicago.

GEORGE KARG.

A time-honored pharmacy on the West side is that of Mr. George Karg, at 952 Milwaukee avenue, at the corner of Paulina street, (telephone call 4707), and its history since its establishment is somewhat varied, for it dates its establishment back to 1876, when it was founded by Mr. Charles Hatterman. In 1885 the firm changed to Charles Hatterman & Son, in 1888 were duly succeeded by Mr. Albert Goetz, while in 1890 Mr. Karg assumed possession, and during the short time that he has had it under his control he has shown an adaptability which forebodes a successful future. The size of the store is 25x75 feet, and it is well ordered and appointed throughout, being fully equipped with everything requisite for the systematic carrying on of the business. A large and carefully selected stock is kept constantly on hand, including pure fresh drugs, chemicals and medicines of all kinds, standard proprietary remedies and sanitary preparations, pure medicinal wines, liquors and mineral waters, and a choice assortment of toilet articles, such as fancy soaps, perfumes, etc., and all druggists' sundries. A leading specialty is made of the compounding of physicians' prescriptions and family recipes from pure fresh ingredients, and all at the lowest rates. Two competent assistants are employed, and night bell calls receive immediate response. Mr. Karg is a native of Germany and has been in Chicago eight years, graduating with some distinction at the Chicago College of Pharmacy, class 1886-'87, gaining both the Alumni and Trustees' prize, and is now a member of the Alumni Association of his Alma Mater. He is also a registered member of the Illinois State Board of Pharmacy. He was formerly for five and a half years with Mr. Henry Schroeder at the corner of Milwaukee avenue and Chicago avenue.

SCHILLER & MAILANDER.

The trade of the florist has, amid the best and most refined circles of Chicago, become a profession, and the public are deeply indebted to those in the business, whose skill, taste and judgment unite so happily in providing floral decorations for events of every description. Among the most accomplished florists of the city are Messrs. Schiller & Mailander, whose great flower depot is so advantageously located at No. 730 W. Madison street, and who have a large and flourishing branch at Eckhardt's Fashionable Catering Co., No. 573 on the same street. The greenhouses of this enterprising company are situated at Niles' Center, Ill., and comprise four acres, half of which is covered with glass. These with the wholesale business have been in existence for twenty years, the founders being Messrs. Stielow & Kuske. On the lamented decease of the latter gentleman, in 1880, his nephew, the present senior partner, came from Germany to take his place, the old name however being retained until 1888. They are florists of great experience, gained in the best circle of trade, and are patronized by the leading society people of Chicago. They receive fresh cut flowers twice a day from their greenhouses, and make a specialty of wedding, parlor and funeral decorations. They also supply all kinds of house plants at reasonable prices, shrubs and plants for conservatories, etc., and attend in the season to the replenishing of hotel and dwelling floral embellishment. The retail trade was begun in November, 1889, in the convenient premises now occupied, and here a full stock of all the popular kinds of cut flowers, shrubs, bulb plants, etc., is always carried, giving a choice that is absolutely unexcelled elsewhere in the city. They employ a dozen experienced hands, and a wagon for the delivery of plants, allowing nothing to leave the premises that is not in the freshest possible condition, and that is not exactly the variety required. Orders are received by mail or telephone, branch call 7163, or main office 7056, and are promptly and accurately filled. They are to be heartily congratulated on achieving such an honored success in this important line of trade.

RABE & MEYER.

Prominent among the old established and most popular and reliable firms of Chicago devoted to fine merchant tailoring for gentlemen, youths and boys is that of Messrs. Rabe & Meyer, whose premises are centrally and advantageously located at No. 377 W. Chicago avenue, and who have a large and flourishing branch at No. 113 E. Adams street. This extensive business was founded seventeen years ago by Messrs. Gerard & Rabe, the change to the present style being effected in 1884. Both gentlemen bring to bear the widest range of practical experience, coupled with the best facilities, and influential connections. They keep in stock the choicest newly imported and domestic cloths, and suitings, including all the latest novelties in patterns, shades and textures, to suit all tastes. They also carry a full line of gents' furnishings, including everything in the way of shirts, hosiery, underwear of all kinds, neckwear, umbrellas, etc. They make a prominent specialty of uniforms, in any desired color and style, and enjoy a large trade in this branch. Messrs. Rabe & Meyer are masters of their profession, noted as tasteful designers, and skilful cutters, insuring a perfect fit to the most difficult figure. They require the constant services of ten competent assistants, and in every detail of the whole comprehensive and intricate business they practice invariably the best and most approved methods. Both gentlemen are Germans by birth, but have resided here for a great number of years. They are esteemed members of the Ancient Order of United Workmen, and of the Select Knights. Mr. Rabe is also on the roll of the Knights of Pythias, and Mr. Meyer on that of the Independent Order of Odd Fellows. They are able business men, and honorable private citizens, well deserving of the success which has attended their efforts.

WILLIAM SCHICK.

A leading headquarters in this city for artistic well made and thoroughly reliable furniture, as well as for carpets and kindred goods for the household, is the well-known and popular house of Mr. William Schick, at No. 184 W. Randolph street and 44 and 46 Clybourn avenue. This prosperous concern dates its inception back to 1866, when it was inaugurated by its present proprietor, at 184 W. Randolph street, where he is still doing a very active and increasing trade. In 1872 he purchased the property at No. 46 Clybourn avenue, on which he built a residence for his family, and a store, the latter being conducted as a branch of the W. Randolph street establishment. In 1890 he bought the property, No. 44, adjoining his building, No. 46 Clybourn avenue, and rebuilt both buildings for the accommodation of his furniture and carpet business only. Mr. Schick is a native of Germany, whence he removed to this country in 1863. He brings to bear a thorough and perfect knowledge of his industry in all its details, and an intimate acquaintance with the needs and requirements of the public. From its inauguration the record of this house has been one of continuous and uninterrupted success. The premises utilized by Mr. Schick are in an excellent and central location, well appointed throughout, and perfectly adapted for the purpose of the business. The salesrooms occupy two floors, each having an area of 22x152 feet, while a three-story building on Waldo place, in rear of Nos. 178 and 180 W. Randolph street, 40x60 feet in dimensions, is used as a warehouse. These are provided with all modern conveniences for the dispatch of business. The workshops are well equipped with all the latest improved machines, tools and appliances, employment being given to a sufficient force of skilled and experienced hands. In the salesrooms five assistants are employed. The store is very attractively fitted up and arranged; it is replete with an extensive and splendid stock of household furniture of every description in the finest upholstering, as well as of plainer appearance; carpets of all kinds, brussels, turkish, axminster, moquette, ingrain, 3-ply, etc., all representing the newest designs and patterns; rugs of all sizes, color and quality, etc. The facilities of the house enable Mr. Schick to offer these fine goods to his patrons at prices that defy competition, and his trade is large and profitable. He is one of our most successful business men, a result largely due to his superior qualifications, and honest and liberal methods.

A. READ.

The reliable cash grocery now so ably presided over by Mrs. A. Read, with Mr. James O. Read as manager, at No. 836 W. Madison street, is rightly regarded as one of the best of its kind in this section of the busy Western metropolis. It was primarily opened by Messrs. Read & Son, some three years ago, the ownership devolving upon the present proprietress in 1890, who has since conducted its affairs with a degree of success simply commensurate with the energy and ability she has exhibited in seeking such a result. The premises occupied comprise a commodious ground floor, 25x75 feet in dimensions, well ordered and systematized throughout. The business, which is chiefly of a local character, is conducted strictly upon a cash basis, and, as a consequence, the lowest prices prevail. Everything in the line of staple and fancy groceries is to be found here, and that of the finest quality—the stock embracing pure teas, coffees, sugars, spices, canned goods, sauces, condiments, choice brands of family flour, butter, cheese, eggs, bacon, ham, lard, laundry supplies, fruits, vegetables and other farm and garden produce. Three assistants and a delivery wagon are in constant service, and the establishment ranks A1 in every respect. Mr. Jas. O. Read was born in Stark County, Ill. He is a young, enterprising business man, popular alike in social and commercial circles, and a prominent member of the Patriotic Sons of America.

MRS. WM. GANSHOW.

The business at No. 534 Blue Island avenue, conducted by Mrs. Wm. Ganshow, was established in the same location several years ago by Henry Valk. In 1883 Mr. William Ganshow succeeded to the business. Under his management it continued to thrive for seven years. Ill health compelled Mr. Ganshow to retire in 1887, when Mrs. Ganshow assumed the management. She has conducted the business successfully to this time, to the eminent satisfaction of the trade and the profit of the proprietress. The business has been carried on at the present location for eight years, and has gradually increased in volume and extent, until now the firm employs five painters steadily. The store occupies a fine room, 25x82 feet, and basement. Here may be found a large and well assorted stock of paints, oils, varnishes and painters' supplies, window glass, window shades, wall paper, etc. The firm does all kinds of house and sign painting and interior decorating. Estimates are furnished on all work in the line of painting and decorating, and satisfaction guaranteed. The decorating of the homes of the people in tasteful tints has an elevating effect upon the occupants. Bright and cheerful surroundings have a direct effect upon the minds and hearts of people. Gloomy, dingy rooms and cheerless homes drive the children out into the streets, and the fathers to the saloons, and the mothers to despair. People seldom pause to reflect upon the effect of the surroundings upon the minds and habits of the people. Besides the habits of neatness and cleanliness that are inspired by neat and tasty home decorations, the family soon learn to cultivate finer tastes and fancies, and their minds are filled with brighter, loftier thoughts, and their whole nature is roused and changed. Chicago has made wonderful progress in the matter of cheerful, happy homes for the people within its gates. No city in the world has so many attractive, pretty, comfortable homes as Chicago. The West side is especially noted in this respect. There is an inexhaustible field of labor for painter and decorator. The demand for good work in this line increases every year. Mrs. Ganshow's business keeps pace with the times. By fair and honorable dealings she has gained a large patronage for her establishment, which happily increases year by year.

W. R. DENNIS.

Among the many great firms in Chicago devoted to the manufacture of mouldings, sash, doors, etc., that of Mr. W. R. Dennis, deserves prominent mention in a commercial and statistical review. This gentleman conducts a business whose ramifications extend to every part of the city, and to the most important centers of that great and progressive section of country which is tributary to the Western metropolis. His father, Mr. John Dennis, established the business in 1883, the style of Messrs. W. R. Dennis & Co. being adopted the following year, and on the lamented decease of the respected founder, in 1888, the present proprietor succeeded. His factory is centrally located at Nos. 243 and 245 Wells street, and is spacious and well equipped with all the latest improved machinery known to the trade. The line embraces the production of mouldings, pilasters, stairs, rails, doors, sashes, blinds, and such work as stair building, turning and band sawing, the material used and the workmanship being first-class in every respect. Mr. Dennis makes a specialty of screens for all purposes, and in every process the best methods are invariably practised, nothing being allowed to leave the premises which does not attain the highest standard in every particular. A large staff of skilled hands are constantly employed in this business, which often requires the exercise of great ingenuity and radical departures from the rule of thumb methods by which the operations of many industries are conducted. Mr. Dennis is a native of Oswego, N. Y., and during his residence here has earned the warm esteem of a large circle, not only in the trade, but throughout commercial and social circles generally. His surprising success is a notable example of what can be accomplished by enterprise, combined with discretion and an intimate knowledge of the wants of the trade.

C. F. SCHUMACHER, JR.

Chicago with its thousand new additions and plats, all of which are on the market, and, marvelous to say, are being bought as rapidly as the stakes can be driven, affords a fertile field for the real estate agent. However, this personage is one of the most important in the growth of our city, as upon him devolves the duty of affecting arrangements between buyer and seller that means the sale of a lot and the building of a home. There is no more popular, wide-awake and enterprising real estate man in the city than C. F. Schumacher, jr., who occupies handsome offices at the corner of Blue Island avenue and Twelfth street. Mr. Schumacher established his present business at the same location he now occupies in 1872, and has remained there ever since. He has been very successful and devotes himself to the buying and selling of real estate, managing of estates, collection of rents, effecting loans on real estate and to a general business in that line. He also places fire insurance in the most reliable companies, and is agent for the principal steamship lines between Europe and America. In addition to these Mr. Schumacher is a notary public, and attends to the making and acknowledging of deeds, mortgages and other legal papers. He is a native of Chicago, born in 1852, and has lived here all his life, hence is well posted on all the values of property in the market. As a successful business man, he has earned for himself a reputation that is truly enviable.

JOHN KLOFATH.

John Klofath, dealer in fine boots and shoes, at No. 629 Blue Island avenue, carries a full stock of everything in his line, in sizes and styles, and for ladies', misses', gents', and children's wear. None but the best Eastern made shoes are sold. A specialty is made of ladies' shoes, and in this line an assortment is carried that is not surpassed anywhere in that section of the city. Mr. Klofath was born in Germany, but has resided in Chicago for seventeen years. He opened his present establishment in 1884, and has built up a large trade and established a most enviable reputation for fair dealing and for the strictest integrity. He is a member of the Order of Knights and Ladies of Honor, and also of the Druids, and is a universally respected and esteemed citizen. His establishment occupies a storeroom 20x60, in an elegant three-story brick building, and is neatly and attractively fitted up. The show window is nicely decorated, and displays some fine goods. Three assistants are employed, and an excellent class of custom work is done. Repairing is also attended to, and is neatly executed at the shortest notice. In conclusion it may be said of this establishment that its reputation embraces the following three points: Best quality, latest styles and lowest prices.

O'BRIEN & PHELAN.

The wholesale meat markets of Chicago are the greatest in the world, and are among the most extensive and cleanly of any ever yet known. Prominent among the leaders are those of O'Brien & Phelan, at No. 11 Fulton street market, which are especially noted for their extensiveness and cleanliness. The business was originally established in 1882 by Messrs. P. Noonan & Co., of which firm Mr. O'Brien was a prominent member, and less than a year ago the present firm, composed of Mr. Dennis O'Brien and R. J. Phelan was organized. Thanks to their enterprise and energy, they have had an unexpected era of success and prosperity, and their already immense trade is rapidly increasing. They occupy handsome and well fitted rooms, 25 by 75 feet in size, fitted with large ice coolers and refrigerators, in which 100 head of cattle may be stored. They employ four experienced hands, who are each educated to their line of trade. Their specialty is dressed hogs, veal and poultry, in which they have a reputation second to none in the land. Mr. O'Brien is a native of the land of the Shamrock, and has resided in Chicago for more than twenty years. Mr. Phelan is a native Chicagoan, and well posted in his line of business. Both are genial, sociable and accomplished business men who merit their prosperity.

THE M. E. PAGE CONFECTIONERY CO.

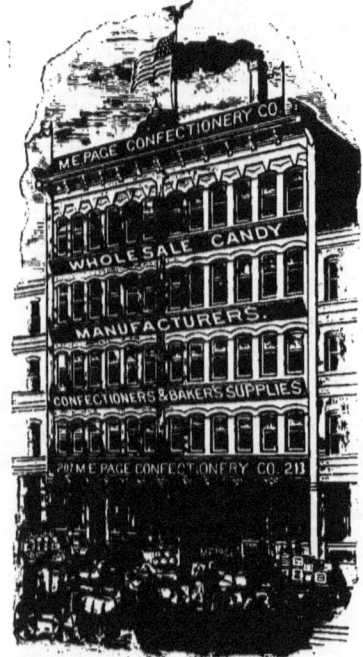

It is a pleasure to note in this bitter world there are a good quantity of "sweets," of which the M. E. Page Confectionery Company of this city are furnishing their share, not only to the people of our own favored land, but also to those of Peru, Guatamala, Australia, Mexico and other lands. This extensive business was virtually established thirty years ago by Mr. M. E. Page, the present president of the company. During the past year the business was incorporated under the laws of the state of Illinois, with the corporation name of the M. E. Page Confectionery Company. Mr. M. E. Page was chosen president; Mr. Josiah Cratty, vice-president and business manager; Mr. S. W. Davis, secretary; and Mr. E. A. Lyon treasurer. The company occupy the five-story and basement building at Nos. 211 and 213 Lake street and the two floors adjoining, 40x165 feet in size. Their sales are principally to jobbers of candy and confectioneries, and a happy indication of their business is that it is constantly increasing in all localities, foreign and domestic. Their present price lists include all kinds of candies and confectioneries, from the plain "stick" to the novelties and fancy box candies, cream work, glace fruits, licorice, pop corn and chewing gums, all of which are absolutely pure and of the best. The vice-president, Mr. Cratty, is a member of the law firm of Cratty Brothers, and all are representative and practical business men, who,

thoroughly understanding their business, are pushing it to even greater successes than it has sustained in the past. Chicago is proud of the concern and yields them a very liberal patronage.

THE CHICAGO SHORTHAND AND TELEGRAPH COLLEGE.

It has been said, and it is an unfailing criterion, that the best test of excellence of any school or college, is the feeling entertained towards it by its students, and, accepting this dictum unreservedly, the teacher of the Chicago Shorthand and Telegraph College, Mrs. Josephine G. Howser, may feel pardonably proud of the regard and esteem this institution is held in by the numbers of graduates it has turned out, since it was first established in the year 1875, and who by experimental comparison have been shown to compare favorably with the best operators and stenographers in the land. Mrs. Howser, who is a graduate of the Peoria High School, and an able teacher of telegraphy and stenography, opened this college seventeen years ago, since which period she has turned out some of the best operators in the country. The class rooms at 181 W. Madison street, corner Halsted, are completely equipped with all the latest-improved appliances, telegraph instruments, etc., and two first-class assistants are employed. This college has ample accommodations for sixty students, and the methods of teaching adopted embrace the most practical and well tested. Each student is taught the use, care and adjustment of the various telegraphic instruments, including the key, sounder, relay, switchboard, lightning arrester, cut-out, battery, etc. In stenography Mrs. Howser has adopted the Pernin system, which is without light and heavy shading and no word signs, while at the same time the first second and third positions are done away by it. This is the only system taught whereby students are free from the use of phrase books, arbitrary word signs or the dictionary. Everything is taught here practically, and carefully applied at each lesson. No additional fees are charged here for typewriting, and positions are furnished free of charge to pupils. Those interested should call or send for circular, the fees charged for instruction in telegraphy and shorthand being very moderate. The college is open day and evening. Mrs. Howser is a courteous and talented teacher, who has gained the entire confidence, not only of her present pupils, but also of those previously educated in her institution.

J. W. ASHBURY.

It is not often our pleasure to visit a more attractive and better appointed drug store than that kept by Mr. J. W. Ashbury, at 962 W. Twelfth boulevard, corner of Hoyne avenue. He established it five years ago and has since been amply repaid by the support which has been tendered to him, though it is no more than he deserves, as the place is conducted in so thoroughly first-class a manner. He always employs a full force of the necessary help to enable him to conduct his business. The store is 25x50 feet in dimensions and is well stocked with pure drugs, perfumes, toilet requisites, soaps, proprietary medicines and everything that may be usually looked for in a first-class drug store, and added to these a full line of very fine imported and domestic cigars, which Mr. Ashbury prides himself greatly are not to be excelled in this section of the city. Anybody requiring an excellent smoke should certainly pay him a visit. The pharmacy is in the rear, and in this connection we may say that Mr. Ashbury makes a specialty of and gives extreme care to the compounding of physicians' prescriptions, and manufactures his own tinctures and essences. His telephone call is 7,162, and a reference to the number of a prescription by telephone is all that is necessary to secure its repetition. He is a native of London, Ont., and was formerly in business in that city. He is a member of the Royal Ontario Pharmaceutical Association, and also of the Illinois State Board of Pharmacy.

THE D. W. BOSLEY CO.

The "comfortable householder," whose claim to be the backbone, the industry, the "bone and sinew" of the country, cannot be disputed, has, during his whole life, the privilege of combating two enemies, heat and cold. Mosquito screens keep out flies and other undesirable visitors in the summer, while in winter the winds would enter without a search warrant but for the cute devices of the weather strip. Of these latter the D. W. Bosley Co., at Nos. 208 and 210 W Washington street, manufacture a variety that keep up an impregnable barrier against the searching winds of winter, and the irrepressible dust of summer, and they have succeeded so well that the Bosley weather strip, like the Bosley window cleaner, are household necessities, the production of which make up the sum total of a fine business. The concern was established in 1869, at W. Madison and Jefferson streets, for the manufacture of picture frame mouldings. It was afterward moved to the corner of Madison and Market streets, where it remained for eight years. In 1890 it was incorporated under the present style with $50,000 capital. The corporation owns the spacious five-story building, 40x100 feet, and employs only the best skilled mechanics. It controls all patents on window cleaners and kindred articles, having the sole manufacture in the United States in its hands. The "Peerless" window cleaner, the rubber floor scrubber, the bar and counter cleaner, are widely known. The former, now being made with a sheet iron socket handle, is now considered a perfect window cleaner. Nearly all the large hardware, woodenware, drug, rubber, and brush houses in the United States are handling these goods. The flexible rubber weather strips of solid rubber, moulded into shape, all one piece, with no stitching or cementing, are the perfection of draught, snow, rain and dust excluders, and the trade is all over the United States. Mr. D. W. Bosley, the president of the corporation, is a native of Rochester, N. Y. He has been in Chicago since 1866. Mr. E. F. Bosley, his son, is the secretary of the corporation.

C. G. HINDBERG.

Among the most successful dental practitioners on the North side is Mr. C. G. Hindberg, 179 Elm street, at the corner of Sedgwick street. Mr. Hindberg is a native of Sweden, and is now a gentleman of middle age. He has been in Chicago eighteen years, and has practiced here in his profession during that period, having formerly graduated with distinguished honors at the Dental University of Sweden. He opened a branch office in the summer of 1891 at Lake View. His present premises comprise an elegantly furnished reception parlor, with operating room and laboratory leading from it, both the latter being equipped with every kind of modern apparatus which is known to the science of dentistry, and which will in any way tend to alleviate the sufferings of patients; and, as Mr Hindberg is a thorough master of his art, both in its mechanical and scientific features, and possesses an exceedingly light and gentle touch, the best possible results are obtained. He makes a specialty of and manufactures sets of artificial teeth in gold, platinum or composition, and will supply a single tooth if required. Teeth are extracted, filled and adjusted with the best skill and judgment, at prices which are always very moderate, and all kinds of affections or diseases of the gums are treated. Discolored teeth are also made white, and, in fact, Mr. Hindberg undertakes everything which falls to the lot of the dentists' art.

THOMAS O'MALLEY.

One of the best known and most respected representatives of that indispensable trade to a modern community, plumbing, is to be found in the person of Mr. Thomas O'Malley, whose handsome premises are centrally located at No. 317 Wells street. This practical and energetic business man has evinced a thorough mastery of his vocation in all its intricate details, and since the inception of the present business in 1875 he has executed some of the most important contracts that have been given out in the city of Chicago. Among these may be mentioned the plumbing and gasfitting for Mayor Washburne's residence; for the Weidemeyer block, on the corner of Burton place and N. Clark street; the McEwen block, on Wells street; the Lawson block, at No. 305 Wells street; the Crothers' building, on the corner of Schiller and Clark streets; the block of houses erected by Mr. Chas. Hinger, at the intersection of Wells and Oak streets, and scores of others, in all parts of the city, of equal size and importance. No one has a more intimate acquaintance with the requirements of the best class of Western trade, and no one performs his work more strictly in accordance with the principles upon which all really good sanitary work is based. In his elegant store a fine assortment of gas fixtures and plumbers' supplies is displayed, in such variety, and of such beauty of design and finish as to please even the most fastidious. Mr. O'Malley was born in Limerick, Ireland, but came here when so young that his whole training and education have been distinctly American. He is an esteemed member of the Catholic Order of Foresters, and several other societies, and holds an honored place among the directors of the Queen City Building and Loan Association. He is widely and most favorably known, both as a business man of great capacity and unquestioned standing and integrity, and as a public-spirited and honorable citizen.

C. J. LEIBACH.

To those who desire to be well dressed, they can at no place in the city find a finer or better line of patterns and styles to select from than at the merchant tailoring establishment of Mr. C. J. Leibach, No. 248 E. North avenue. Custom work being only done, he employs from eight to ten of the best skilled workmen to assist him in keeping up with his large and ever increasing trade. He keeps on hand a large stock of the very latest patterns in foreign and domestic goods, and has them displayed in fine style in his elegant store, so that the most fastidious can make their choice. Mr. Leibach is a practical cutter and tailor of experience and guarantees fit and workmanship on every garment. He is a young man and of German birth; has been in Chicago eight years, and has built up a splendid trade by his industry and fair dealing with all. He is a prominent member of different orders and societies and has hosts of friends which he has made by his generous and courteous manners, and by his thoroughly understanding his trade in every particular, and allowing nothing to leave his place that is not perfect in every way.

HENRY KAISER.

One who can claim more than his proportionate share of popularity among the clothiers on the West side is Mr. Henry Kaiser, dealer in clothing, hats, caps, gents' furnishing goods, trunks, umbrellas, etc., at 461 W. Chicago avenue, near Ashland avenue. Mr. Kaiser is a native of Germany, and has been in Chicago twenty-one years, during most of which time he has been honorably identified with the line of trade in which he is now engaged. He established himself in business at the present site in 1883, and the premises comprise a large store, 20x50 feet in dimensions. He makes a specialty of custom work, and in making suits to order, he employs only the very best materials and workmanship, his stock comprising some beautiful new importations of seasonable goods in the latest patterns and styles, whether it be in serges, tweeds, cassimeres or other coatings. His tables are loaded with a very large assortment of stylish ready made clothing for men, youths, boys and children, the latest fashions in hats and caps, and all the newly imported attractions in gents' furnishing goods and umbrellas, and while the goods cannot be excelled in quality, the prices are such as to draw the attention of the public and to lead to an ever-increasing business. Mr. Kaiser employs an accomplished cutter, and never fails to make a perfect fit or to please his patrons, and his styles may always be taken as a correct guide for those who desire to dress well.

THOMAS McDERMOTT.

An old established and most ably conducted concern is that of Mr. Thomas McDermott, dealer in imported and domestic wines, liquors and cigars, at No. 5536 Lake avenue, and which, for more than a score of years has maintained a prominent and honorable position in the trade. Mr. McDermott was born in Ireland, and founded his present enterprise in 1871, from the very start building up a widespread and influential trade. The premises utilized are of ample dimensions, and comprise a handsomely appointed hotel and beer garden, 50x120 feet in area, with spacious grounds in connection, the whole covering 50x270 feet of ground. These are very appropriately fitted up, and are furnished throughout with every modern convenience and facility that can promote the comfort and convenience of the patrons. A heavy, excellent and carefully selected stock is always carried, including all the choicest vintages of Europe and America, the finest French, Italian, Spanish and German wines, pure brandies, Holland, Plymouth and Old Tom gins, New England and Jamaica rums, liquors and cordials, bitters, case goods, beers, ales, porters, imported and domestic cigars, the best rye and Bourbon whiskies, and a general line of liquors, all celebrated for their purity and uniform excellence of quality. Mr. McDermott secures his supplies direct from the most reliable sources and on the most favorable terms, and is thereby enabled to place these excellent goods before the public at lowest prices. His establishment is very eligibly located immediately opposite South Park station. Cable cars pass by its doors, bringing it into direct connection with all parts of the city, and it is one of the most popular summer resorts in Chicago. The patronage is first-class in character, and it is a leading family resort. A numerous staff of polite and active assistants are in attendance, and orders are promptly filled, nothing being left undone to promote the comfort of the public. Mr. McDermott is a cordial and genial gentleman, and few men in this line of trade enjoy a greater, or better deserved, measure of public favor.

DOLESE & SHEPARD.

Chicago's leading firm of paving contractors is that of Messrs Dolese & Shepard, of 162 Washington street, whose long experience, ample resources, magnificent facilities and known honorable methods, worthily entitles them to the manifest preference shown for their work by the civic corporation contractors, property owners and builders everywhere. The business was established in 1868 by the present firm of Messrs. Dolese & Shepard, whose methods and progressive energy early secured to them a large and growing trade. They are now the principal paving contractors in Chicago for macadam streets, and leading manufacturers of and dealers in crushed stone, crushed granite, slag, cinders, and limestone for flux. They own and operate immense limestone quarries at Hawthorne, Ill., on the line of the Chicago, Burlington & Quincy Railroad, and C. & W. Indiana Belt R'y. These quarries are operated upon the most approved methods, and have complete outfits of the most powerful crushing machinery. Their broken stone is the standard for macadam paving and road building and is thus used in enormous quantities. They are also leading contractors for the supply of broken stone for foundations, for the granite blocks and for granite paving. They supply the quality of limestone needed for steel and iron fluxes, and are the contractors for this purpose to the North Chicago Rolling Mills, and the Union Rolling Mills. Contracts are taken by them for every description of paving, particular attention being given to the building of macadamized roads, boulevards and drives. They have had ample experience in this line, having constructed the principal macadam roads in Hyde Park and on the great boulevards; they always (during the season) have numbers of paving contracts under way, and keep 300 hands steadily employed in this way. Their immense yards are conveniently located at Wallace and Fortieth streets, also Grand boulevard and Fortieth street, and where is at all times carried enormous quantities of crushed stone, slag, cinders and crushed granite,

and those seeking materials in the above lines will do well to place their orders here, where prices and quality are guaranteed. Messrs. Dolese & Shepard are business men of sound judgment and sterling integrity, and have an honored record, ever devoting personal attention to all orders

NEW PRINCETON LAUNDRY.

Among the most active and enterprising firms engaged in the laundry business in this city, is that of Messrs. Loomis & Fitch. The copartners are both thorough going, live and wide awake, and, although they have only been established about a year, a well-merited success has rewarded their well-directed efforts. Their establishment is named the "New Princeton Laundry," and is located at 233 Sixtysecond street, corner La Salle. It is very complete in its appointments, no pains nor expense having been spared to make it one of the best equipped establishments of the kind in the city. The building is two stories in height, and is fitted up with the latest improved washing, ironing and other machines, and all the appurtenances necessary and requisite to do superior work quickly at moderate prices. Experienced hands, from twelve to fifteen in number, are employed in the different departments, and a thoroughly efficient system of organization is enforced. Messrs. Loomis & Fitch make a specialty of fine work, and pay particular attention to family laundry, and every care is taken so as not to injure the fabrics. Hotel work is done in the most expeditious manner, and satisfaction is always guaranteed and given. Laundry work is called for and delivered in all parts of the city, and the firm uses every honorable endeavor to please. They also make a specialty of carpet cleaning and renovating by a new process, which thoroughly removes dust, vermin stains, etc., without injury to the color or fabric. All orders receive immediate attention, and altogether the patronage of the establishment is of a most substantial character, and steadily grows apace. Mr. W. J. Loomis and Mr. A. B. Fitch, are well and favorably known in this city as progressive business men, and the admirable manner they conduct their laundry is at once an evidence that they are fully abreast of the times.

WM. LUEDEKA & SON.

It is with pleasure that we review the business of Wm. Luedeka & Son, manufacturers of double white wine and pure cider vinegar. This business was established in 1869 by Mr. N. Luedeka and continued by him alone until 1886, when he admitted his son, Mr. Emil Luedeka, to the business, and the firm name now in use was adopted. They employ from eighteen to twenty hands and conduct an important industry. The business is conducted at 566 and 568 N. Halsted street, where the firm occupy the two-story brick building, 50x120 feet in dimensions, for the manufacture of pure vinegars and fine compressed yeast. The manufactory is equipped with machinery used in the business, and has also a fine steam power plant for operating the same. The sales of the compressed yeast amount to 100,000 pounds per year, and it has become very popular, being used extensively in all parts of the city and suburbs. It is made of only the best and strictly pure ingredients, and is fully warranted. The company makes and sells over 10,000 barrels of vinegar each year and is sold to the trade throughout the Western states. It has a standard reputation and is in great demand. Mr. W. Luedeka is a native of Germany and has resided in Chicago thirty-seven years; he is prominent in business circles and has made the greatest success of his enterprise. He has numerous friends who hold him in high esteem. Mr. Emil Luedeka is a native of Chicago, and is a progressive business man; he is well-known in business and social circles and is held in high esteem. The house is strong, being rated well by the best commercial agencies, and as for the personal standing of the gentlemen, none have a better reputation for business ability.

W. W. SIMPSON.

Among the most widely and honorably known of the many dealers in pianos, organs and other musical merchandise in this city is Mr. W. W. Simpson, whose warerooms are eligibly located at No. 357 Milwaukee avenue. Mr. Simpson was born in the city of Buffalo, N. Y., 1847, whence he removed to Chicago with his parents in 1851, when but a child. He has had a long and varied experience in matters musical, having been identified with this line of business for

the past twenty-one years. For seventeen years he conducted the branch establishment at Effingham, Ill., of the celebrated piano manufacturing firm of W. W. Kimball & Co., a position which he relinquished in order to embark in business on his own account. He inaugurated his present enterprise in 1888, at No. 398 Chicago avenue, where he soon developed a very large and influential patronage, which increased to such an extent that in order to meet its demands he removed to his present quarters in 1889. His warerooms are of ample dimensions, having a floor area of 25x94 feet, and are handsomely, neatly and appropriately arranged. The stock carried embraces piano-fortes of all manufactures of any established reputation, and in all styles; also parlor organs, from the most elaborate in construction to those comparatively plain, all of the very best tone and excellence throughout. These are offered to the public at very lowest prices, for cash or on credit, the latter method enabling those of comparatively small means to obtain an excellent instrument upon the easiest of terms by paying weekly or monthly installments. A specialty is made of second-hand pianos of all makes, which are sold or exchanged upon most favorable conditions, while repairing and tuning receive special care and attention. Pianos are also rented for any length of time at low prices. Mr. Simpson also handles all other kinds of musical instruments, brass, string and reeds, and all other musical merchandise of every description at the lowest prices. The telephone call is 4730, and orders are promptly attended to. He is a prominent member of the I. O. O. F. and K. of P., and was clerk of Circuit Court and Recorder of Effingham County, which he filled with the greatest credit from 1880 to 1884.

J. P. GROSS & CO.

The trade in broom corn during the last few years has assumed extensive proportions in the city of Chicago. A representative and reliable firm, actively engaged in this important business, is that of Messrs. J. P. Gross & Co., whose offices and salesrooms are situated at Nos. 249 and 251 Kinzie street. This business was established in 1872 by Messrs. J. P. Gross and A. H. Grunewald, who conducted it till 1889, when Mr. Gross died after a successful career. Mr. Grunewald then became sole proprietor, and is now carrying on the business under the old firm name of "J. P. Gross & Co." He has had long experience, and possesses influential connections and perfect facilities. The premises occupied comprise a spacious and substantial six-story and basement building, 50x100 feet in area, fully equipped with every convenience, elevators, etc. Here a well selected and heavy stock of broom corn is always on hand, also full supplies of handles, wire, twines, tools and machinery. Only the best goods are handled, and the prices quoted necessarily attract the attention of careful buyers. A number of experienced buyers are employed in the best producing broom corn sections of the country, and the trade of the house now extends throughout the entire United States and Canada. Orders are carefully filled, and liberal advances are made when required on consignments of first-class broom corn. Mr. Grunewald was born in Chicago, where he is highly esteemed in trade circles for his business ability and strict integrity. This house is commended to the trade as one in every way worthy of confidence, and business relations entered into with it are certain to prove as pleasant, as they must be advantageous and profitable to all concerned.

JOSEPH G. HALL.

A representative and well-known wool merchant of Chicago is Mr. Joseph G. Hall, whose place of business is located at 190 and 192 E. Kinzie street. The business conducted by Mr. Hall is well known and of established reputation. It was founded by Wm. B. Hibbard & Co., in 1860, the partners being W. B. Hibbard and T. W. Hall and Jesse McAllister. The business was continued by this firm until 1862, when it was changed to McAllister, Hall & Livermore, with Jesse McAllister, T. W. Hall and Lewis Livermore as partners, and J. G. Hall, manager. From 1866-'69 the firm was Pixley, Hall and Kinsey. In 1869 the style was again changed to Pixley, Hall & Co., the partners being B. F. Pixley, T. W. Hall and J. G. Hall, and so continued till they were burned out during the great fire Oct. 9, 1871. From 1872 to 1876 the business was known as T. W. Hall & Sons, the members of the firm being T. W. Hall, J. G. Hall and H. R. Hall; and in 1876 Mr. J. G. Hall, the present proprietor, succeeded to the entire interest. Mr. Hall is a native of Ohio and has lived in Chicago since 1860; he has a large business, and occupies a fine three-story building for business purposes, being 40x100 feet in dimensions and thoroughly equipped with all conveniences. Mr. Hall does an extensive business, and in 1890 handled 500,000 pounds of wool; he expects to increase the amount to 1,000,000 pounds this present year. He receives wool on consignment from dealers and producers, and sells direct to the manufacturers. He is an active and progressive business man and keeps his patrons well posted with bulletins as to the condition of the markets' outlook. He quotes prices on request and furnishes sacks, tags, twine and needles to shippers. Fair advances are made on bills of lading and the wool is graded upon arrival and values reported promptly, each lot being sold upon its merits. Mr. Hall is well known in business and financial circles, and is everywhere held in high esteem.

TARRANT & RAMSAY CO.

In the manufacture of light and heavy castings of all kinds, a representative and progressive concern in Chicago is that 1884 by Messrs. Tarrant and Ramsay, who conducted it till 1891, when it was incorporated under the laws of Illinois, with known as the Tarrant & Ramsay Company, whose works are located at 46 to 66 Indiana street, and office at 52 Illinois street. This extensive industry was founded in a paid up capital of $35,000, and its trade now extends throughout the entire United States. The executive officers of the company are Mr. R. Tarrant, president, and Mr. C. J.

PHILIP RINN CO.

The indomitable pluck, energy and perseverance of the Chicago business man is in no case better shown than in that of the Philip Rinn Company, manufacturers and dealers in frames, sash, doors, blinds, mouldings and stair work, making a specialty of interior hardwood finish, at the S. W. corner of Crosby and Division streets. The firm was originally Kaeseberg & Rinn, established in 1865, and has twice been burned to the ground with total loss, and to-day is more prosperous than ever. The firm's business was always good since its opening, and their trade extends in all

De Berard, secretary and treasurer. The foundry is thirty feet high and 100x100 feet in dimensions, fully equipped with modern apparatus and appliances, operated by a fifty horse power steam engine, and is under the immediate supervision of Mr. John Ramsay, whose reputation as a practical foundryman is second to none. He is also vice-president of this company. The cupola has a capacity of melting thirty-six tons of iron daily, and from 150 to 200 workmen are constantly employed. They manufacture chiefly light and heavy castings of all descriptions, dry sand and loam work. Only carefully selected metal is utilized and the work produced is unrivaled for finish, smoothness and general excellence. Orders for castings up to twenty tons are promptly filled, at the lowest possible prices, and entire satisfaction guaranteed patrons. The yard is supplied with powerful cranes and derricks, and a specialty is made of castings for brickyard machinery, crushers, grate bars, etc. They likewise attend promptly to pattern making, and fully warrant all their work to be exactly as represented. The officers, Messrs. Tarrant and De Berard, are enterprising and honorable business men, who justly merit the abundant success secured in this important industry. Mr. Tarrant was born in Saratoga County, N. Y., and came to Chicago in 1856. He is a prominent Free Mason, Knight Templar and life member of the Cleveland Lodge of Freemasons. Mr. Tarrant is also treasurer of the Felt & Tarrant Manufacturing Company, 52 to 56 Illinois street, and proprietor of the Marine Engine Works, Illinois street. Mr. Ramsay is a Scotchman, but has resided in Chicago since 1868, and as a practical foundryman has no equal in the Northwest. He is a widely known Freemason, and one of the best foundrymen in the country. Mr. C. J. De Berard is a native of Wisconsin, and has been associated in business with Mr. Tarrant for many years, and he is secretary and treasurer of this company. He is also a prominent Freemason and Knight Templar, and is well known in commercial and social circles.

directions. In 1887 Mr. Kaeseberg dropped out of the business, which was continued as Philip Rinn & Company until in 1891, when they were incorporated under the laws of the State of Illinois as the Philip Rinn Company, Ph. Rinn, president; George P. Rinn, secretary and treasurer, and with a paid-up capital of $100,000. The old firm were victims of the great fire of October, 1871, they being then located at North Clark and Menominee streets, and, rebuilding much larger than before, were again burned out on the 1st of June, 1882, at their present location, with a total loss and no insurance. They rebuilt immediately with brick, in three, four and five story buildings, 172 by 195 feet in size, and have one of the most complete works of its kind in the country. They are operated by a 140 horse power engine, and are fitted with all the most modern and latest improved machinery, tools and appliances, necessary to facilitate their work. They employ 100 hands, and even then have a rush to supply their trade, which is constantly extending, not only in this city but in all parts of the state and country. Mr. Philip Rinn, the founder of the firm, and president of the present company, was born in Germany, but has been in Chicago since his infancy. He is a prominent Free Mason, and is well and favorably known in commercial and financial circles. Mr. Rinn is justly entitled to the plaudits of the business world for his pluck, perseverance and energy, and twice has arisen phœnix-like from the ashes of his business to make it still larger than before. Mr. George P. Rinn, the genial secretary and treasurer, could receive no higher praise than to say "He is the son of his father," and possesses the same excellent business qualifications that has made him a success. He was born and raised in Chicago, and is closely identified with all of its business interests, and under the able management of the present executive, the success of the Philip Rinn Company is bound to continue at a greater ratio than heretofore.

MURRAY & NICKELL MFG. CO.

The drug milling interests of Chicago and the West, are most ably and progressively represented by the famous Murray & Nickell Mfg. Company, whose immense establishment is so centrally located at Nos. 147 to 155 W. Polk street. The industry was established in 1865 by the old firm of Murray & Nickell. Both partners thoroughly understood the business in every detail, and early achieved an enviable reputation for the superiority of their product. Repeated enlargements of facilities were necessitated, until to-day the works are among the largest of the kind in the world, and the best equipped of any. The mills and warehouse are substantially constructed of brick, six stories in height, and 100 by 120 feet in dimensions, fronting on W. Polk street and Law avenue, and having a complete outfit of modern grinding mills and machinery, run by heavy steam power. The present company was duly organized in 1887, with a capital of $100,000 paid up Mr. A: F. Murray becoming president, Mr. F. B. Klock vice-president, and Mr. C. F. Lammert, secretary. They bring to bear the highest order of executive capacity, and the works are a model of thorough organization. The company employs from fifty to sixty hands in the grinding and preparation of all descriptions of drugs spices and chemicals, and are prepared to promptly fill the largest orders, guaranteeing quality and price. The leading jobbing druggists and grocers secure their supplies here, where such care is devoted to securing absolute purity, combined with the freshness of the drugs and spices as recently received from place of growth, so for all pharmaceutical or food purposes, drugs, spices and chemicals milled here, are preferred by the best class of trade. The company is doing an annually enlarging trade, developed solely on the basis of merit, and the city is to be congratulated upon the possession of such a nationally representative industrial establishment. Mr. Murray has all his business life been identified with the wholesale trade in drugs and chemicals, and is a recognized authority therein. He and his associates are sound and responsible business men, and are materially aiding in the development of Chicago's metropolitan supremacy.

J. FRED. WILCOX.

One of the recognized headquarters for the great and rapidly increasing cigar trade in this city is the office of Mr. J. Fred. Wilcox, general agent for Mr. Carl Upmann of New York, whose high class productions in this line are becoming universally popular throughout the United States, and for Messrs. H. Upmann & Co.'s Havana, Cuba, bankers and commission merchants, controlling the celebrated H. Upmann's factory; also representing the house of Mr. Cayetano Soria, Key West, Fla. Mr. Wilcox has represented these substantial houses here for the past fifteen years, his territory covering the whole of the Union and Canada, in every part of which he has established the most influential connections, and controls about one-half of the entire importation of cigars. Mr. Wilcox is a native of New York state, but came West when very young, his training and education being thoroughly Western, so that his qualifications are in every way perfect to exactly meet the requirements of the trade. The business is entirely confined to supplying the largest jobbers in all parts of the country, and no pains are spared to satisfy the wants of each particular customer, even to manufacturing special brands for his trade. His offices at suites No. 311 and 312 Insurance Exchange building, No. 218 La Salle street, are fitted up and arranged with all the modern improvements and facilities for the transaction of business. The trade is steadily growing and expanding upon the legitimate basis of supply and demand. It is the constant endeavor of Mr. Wilcox, and the celebrated houses he represents, to merit by the strictest principles of commercial probity and just dealing a continuance of the support they already enjoy. He is an honored member of the Union League, and his skill and capacity, coupled with his honorable record, render him deservedly popular and respected by all who know him either in a business or social way.

LOUIS KREBS.

As in all other trades or professions, there are in the undertakers' business both skilful and unskilful men, but it is rarely that the business has been brought to such a point of perfection as has been reached by Mr. Louis Krebs, whose place of business is at 216 Ninety-second street. Mr. Krebs is one of the oldest and most highly respected in the business in the whole of Chicago. He was established in South Chicago eight years ago, having been four years further south on this same street and four years at his present place and previous to his coming here he was in business in the city on Sherman street, also on Cottage Grove avenue. In all he has been established thirty years. He is a native of Chicago, and belongs to several of the leading orders, including the Catholic Foresters, Ancient Order of United Workmen, Society of St. Peter and St. Paul, and the National Undertakers' Union. Mr. Krebs attends the national conventions of undertakers, and, not only this, but is a graduate of the Oriental School of Embalming, whose headquarters are at Boston. He has made a close study of embalming from its scientific standpoint, and had to pass a very severe and strict examination before receiving his diploma, which may be seen at any time in his office. His store is a two-story frame building, about 60x20, and he resides on the premises. He carries an unusually fine selection of caskets and burial robes, and conducts everything connected with his business in a first-class manner. He also owns the large livery stable on Erie avenue, near the Illinois Central Depot. It is one of the largest in town and the only brick livery stable specially built for that purpose. He has twenty boarders, and about fifteen of his own horses, and a capacity for fifty, besides a very large assortment of buggies, hacks, surreys, phaetons and every kind of carriage.

T. WILCE & CO.

A representative and one of the most successful firms in Chicago, extensively engaged in the manufacture and sale of kiln dried hardwood flooring, lumber, etc., is that of Messrs. T. Wilce & Co., whose planing mills and yard are situated on Twenty-second and Throop streets. This extensive business was established in 1873 by Mr. Thos. Wilce, who eventually admitted Messrs. Geo. C. and E. H. Wilce into partnership. The partners bring great practical experience to bear, and possess superior connections and perfect facilities. They occupy a spacious and well-equipped yard, having a dock frontage of 1,600 feet by a depth of 250 feet, with railroad sidings, and every facility. Their planing mill, which is supplied with the latest improved woodworking machinery, tools and appliances is 260x260 feet in dimensions. Here they employ 200 skilled workmen, and the machinery is driven by a superior 50 horse power steam engine. The annual output of the mill is 35,000,000 feet of lumber. They produce largely flooring, doors, sashes, frames, mouldings, brackets, blinds; also all kinds of hardwood and interior finish, mantels, sideboards, office counters, store fixtures, pulpits and pew ends. A specialty is made of kiln dried hardwood flooring, bored for blind nailing, which is offered to the trade in carload lots, at extremely low prices. They have furnished their productions for many of the finest buildings erected in the last few years in Chicago and its vicinity, giving entire satisfaction to builders, contractors, architects and property owners. The sales of this firm now amount to over $1,000,000 per annum, and its trade extends throughout the entire United States and Europe. Only really first-class hardwood lumber is handled, and 100 teams are employed. Mr. T. Wilce, the founder of the business was born in Cornwall, England, and came to Chicago in 1848. With characteristic foresight he afterwards embarked in the lumber trade, and is one of the pioneers of this great industry in the western metropolis. All the partners are greatly respected by the community for their integrity and enterprise, and are very popular in trade circles, and all orders entrusted to this house will receive prompt and careful attention.

J. S. REEDER.

Mr. J. S. Reeder is a man with a history, and as he is by all odds the leading theatrical wig maker in Chicago it affords us great pleasure to have this opportunity of alluding to his business. His history is this; Born in Louisville, Ky., his ambition brought him on to Chicago, only to arrive here the night before the great fire, in 1871. His hotel fell a prey to the flames, and in it he had his trunk which contained all he then possessed, some two thousand dollars, and he lost every thing. This would have been enough to discourage most men, but with noble ambition he faced adversity and succeeded so well that nine years ago he established himself as a practical wig maker and manufacturer of all kinds of human hair goods, at 182 and 184 W. Madison street, and moved to his present store, 26 N. Clark street in March, 1891. He does a large theatrical business, and always has on hand, or makes to order, ladies' and gents' fine street wigs, theatrical wigs, beards, etc. He makes over old wigs to look like new, and as his terms are, of course, cash; his prices are very low, He makes large re- ductions to the trade and customers. He keeps every kind of paint, powder and cosmetiques for make-ups, and, in fact, everything that belongs to his trade.

WARNER BROS.

The associations of Chicago with Connecticut are manifold, for the western metropolis offers a rare field as a distributing center for the goods poured out like a flood by the busiest and most enterprising state in the Union. The Warner Corset Company of Bridgeport, Conn., saw the necessity of thoroughly utilizing the magnificent facilities afforded by Chicago as a dis-

tributing center, and in 1880 engaged Mr. J. A. Miner to open up a branch. He has succeeded in a remarkable degree, and has made a trade which extends all over the city, wholesale and retail, and reaches out in its greater development over the Northwest, the West and the Southwest. The "parent" firm is at Bridgeport, Conn., with the factory, a handsome quadrang- ular structure, in the beautiful little city of Bridgeport, nearly facing Long Island Sound. The head offices, however, are in New York, where one of the proprietors resides. They are wide-awake, enterprising men, who have fully realized the fact that when they have a good thing the printer and them- selves combined can get it before the public, and that the Warner corset is as widely known as the stars and stripes. In Chicago the firm of Warner Bros. (Lucien C. and I. De Ver Warner) own the handsome building they erected at 203 and 205 Jackson street, the ground floor of which, 90x125 feet, is used for their business. They employ a large staff of commercial travelers and clerks, and have a very large patronage. Mr. J. A. Miner, the wide-awake manager of this western branch,

has been identified with the corset business for over twenty-five years. Warner Bros. have a handsome store. The business is a typical one, illustrating in all its details the ingenuity, enterprise and business pluck inherent to the American mer- cantile character. It may be mentioned that the firm has made application for space during the Exhibition, and visitors to the World's Fair will have the best opportunity to inspect the wonderful designs of the firm.

J. P. DALEIDEN.

One of the handsomest and most artistic places of business on the North side, if not in the city, is that of Mr. John P. Daleiden. at Nos. 299 and 301 E. North avenue. Mr. Daleiden is a manufacturer and wholesale dealer in artificial flowers, leaves, wreaths, veiling, vases, etc., and also of all kinds of funeral designs. He also carries a complete line of books and stationery, school supplies, pictures and picture frames, and all kinds of church goods. Catholic goods a specialty. He occupies a handsome double store at the above number, 40x80 feet in size, one side of which is devoted entirely to artificial and wax flowers, and the other side to the book and stationery department. Mr. Daleiden established his present business nearly twenty years ago, and has been at his present location for about eight years. He is an energetic, industrious and courteous business man and has an immense trade, which is constantly increasing. Mr. Daleiden was born in Germany and has been in the city since 1869. He is a prominent member of the Catholic Order of Foresters and is forty-four years of age. He is very popular on the North side with all classes, and has a host of business and social friends.

BINDER & SEIFERT.

An important event in engineering circles last year was the formation of the firm of Messrs. Binder & Seifert, the well-known bridge designers and builders, and who are equally well prepared to contract for, and erect all descrip- tions of iron or steel roofs, buildings and foundation work. They have their office in room 803 Royal Insurance Building, 169 Jackson street. The copartners are of the highest professional standing. Mr. Carl Binder is a graduate of the Polytechnic Institute of Stutt- gart, Germany, and began the practice of his profes- sion in 1876. He has been a resident of the United States since 1883, and has made Chicago his perma- nent headquarters since 1888. Mr. Maurice Seifert is a native of Vienna, and a graduate of the Vienna Polytechnic Institute. He has been a resident of Chicago since 1879. The firm brings to bear special qualifications for the per- formance of every description of engineering work in its line, making a specialty of the designing and building of bridges, of any dimensions, of wood, iron, steel, or a combination of above materials. They enjoy superior facilities for the manufacture of all the iron or steel work from choicest pig iron, and under closest inspection. Their estimates are close and accurate, and they adhere rigidly to specifications. Their ripe experience and sound judgment, coupled with utilization of the most approved scientific methods, have enabled them to complete several of the finest specimens of bridge building and structural. iron work in the world, notably a viaduct 1,000 feet long, and 100 feet in height for the Pittsburgh, Akron & Western Railroad, iron dome for the agricultural building of the World's Columbian Exposi- tion; all the iron and steel work for the German Opera House, Chicago; Machinery Hall for World's Columbian Exposi- tion, largest iron contract ever let in Chicago, etc. The firm devotes close personal attention to the exe- cution of all contracts, and have invariably afforded the utmost satisfaction to their customers. They are progressive and keep abreast of the times, their bridges and iron work em- bracing all the improvements, and standing a permanent monument to their skill, ability and enterprise in this most arduous branch of civil engineering.

KAREL KVITEK.

We mention with pleasure the drug business of Karel Kvitek in this review of the business and commercial interests of this great city. Mr. Kvitek has only been in America a short time, but his ability and skill as a chemist has recommended him so favorably that he has already built for himself a most satisfactory business. He occupies for his store and laboratory the ground floor, 20x40, of the building 599 Throop street, near eighteenth. His store is thoroughly stocked with all the latest patent medicines, pharmaceutical preparations, toilet articles, physicians' and surgeons' supplies, perfumes, brushes, rubber goods, sponges, etc. The store is fitted up in excellent style, with large glass show cases, and every modern appliance. The stock is large, complete and of the highest class of goods. Special attention is given to the compounding of physicians' prescriptions, the greatest care being taken to insure accuracy. Mr. Kvitek is a graduate of the University of Prague, Bohemia, and is a competent analytical chemist and pharmacist, he has an established reputation of the highest order as an expert analyst of urine and victuals. He is a court chemist and has frequently been called upon to give expert testimony in most important legal cases. He has a large and very complete laboratory in the rear of his store, 20x20 feet in area. He has a number of preparations of merit of his own manufacture that have become known as specifics for the diseases and ailments they were compounded for, and we enumerate them with pleasure, hoping some of our readers may derive benefit from the knowledge of them gained through this medium. One of his leading preparations is K. Kvitek's lung balsam, for lung diseases, and others are capuchin drops, blood purifier, solution of albuminate of iron, Dr. Kromphelz's stomach bitters, David's tea, Dr. Klestow's essence of life and K. Kvitek's headache cure. These remedies are all recommended as being very meritorious and are compounded under the direction of Mr. Kvitek personally. Mr. Kvitek is making a great success and his learning and skill are fully appreciated by his friends and many patrons who hold him in the highest esteem.

THE BARTHOLOMAE & ROESING BREWING AND MALTING CO.

At the present day lager beer is rapidly becoming the national beverage of the American people. When pure, manufactured only of the best materials, and by the most improved processes, beer is acknowledged by leading physicians and medical authorities to have excellent tonic and strengthening properties, while it is also a well-known fact, that our people are notably less intemperate since the introduction of lager beer. In this connection, we desire to make prominent mention in this commercial review of Chicago, to the representative and reliable Bartholomae & Roesing Brewing and Malting Company, whose brewery offices, etc., are located at the corner of Twelfth and Brown streets. This brewery was first opened in 1865 by Rehm & Bartholomae, who were succeeded in 1872 by the firm of Messrs. Bartholomae & Roesing. Eventually in 1890, it was incorporated under the laws of Illinois with ample capital, Mr. F. Bartholomae being the president, treasurer and general manager. The brewery, malt house and adjacent buildings are spacious and are constructed in a most substantial and durable manner, while the greatest care is exercised by Mr. Bartholomae to secure absolute cleanliness in all operations. The brewery is five stories high and the malt house seven stories, and the capacity of the brewery is 100,000 barrels of lager annually. There are two first-class ice machines of fifty and twenty-five tons daily, and the storage capacity is equal to 25,000 barrels. The brewery contains every modern improvement. The large fermenting vats, mash tubs, settling tanks, kettles, boilers, pumps, etc., all bespeak the large capital invested, and the perfection of the arrangements. The company's lager beer is preferred by thousands to that of any other brand, and is unrivaled for purity, flavor and excellence. The demand for it is steadily

increasing, and it is a general favorite with retailers and the public wherever introduced. One hundred men and sixteen teams are employed, the trade extending throughout all sections of Chicago and its vicinity. The prime quality of the company's lager is due, not only to purity and quality of ingredients and the skill in manufacture, but also to the ample facilities of the establishment for keeping in stock large quantities, which are allowed to mature previous to being entered for consumption. Mr. Bartholomae and Roesing are honorable and able business men, who are very popular in trade circles. Mr. Bartholomae was born in Germany but has resided in Chicago the greater part of his life. He is also largely interested in the United States Brewing Company, and is one of Chicago's public spirited and influential citizens.

BRENNAN'S GROCERY AND FISH MARKET.

Any of the residents of this neighborhood will bear high testimony to the exemplary manner in which Mr. Patrick Brennan has conducted a grocery and meatmarket for the last twelve years. He has been all the time on W. Twenty-second street, but moved to his present store, No. 690, at the corner of Paulina street, four years ago. His store occupies the whole of the ground floor, and is about 25x40 feet and is at all times well stocked with a full supply and variety of staple and fancy groceries and also fresh and salt meats, which he receives daily from the stock yards, buying none but the very best qualities. He also has the various kinds of fish that come to the market. His prices throughout, are exceedingly low, and he gives special rates for hotel, boarding house and ship supplies. In canned goods he always carries an immense variety and all of the latest manufacture. Mr. Brennan is a native of Ireland and has been in Chicago for forty years, being almost one of the pioneers of the place.

FRED SCHOLER.

"How much fairer jewels make one!"

With these simple words the heroine of Goethe's Faust expresses her delight, when presented with the tempting golden trinkets, and though the mind conceiving this expression is but a childish one, and a model of innocence, her words contain a beautiful truth. Since ages, jewelry has been regarded as giving an evidence of a country's wealth, or prosperity of its ruler, and even to-day, the greater the proportion of the jewelry trade, the more prosperous and creditable the community. Chicago is well represented in this class of work, combining art and skill, and has many first-class establishments in this line. One of no little prominence in the southwest portion of the city is the one owned by Mr. Fred Scholer, and located at 286 W. Twelfth street, southeast corner of Halsted street. It has been in existence since 1869, when it was established by its present proprietor. The store occupies the ground floor of a 20x40 two-story building, and it is, the least to say, highly attractive. Mr. Scholer, like many of Chicago's pioneer jewelers, is a native of Germany, and has been a resident of the World's Fair city for over twenty-two years. He is a thorough watchmaker and jeweler, and well versed in even the most difficult details of his vocation. He has with him three clerks and assistants, who are kept busy in attending to the wants of the public in general. His patronage is, not only in the neighborhood, but comprises a large number of men throughout the city; for those who have once traded with him, are bound to realize the reliability of his work, and so remain his customers. The store is well equipped, and the display of fine gold and silver watches, beautiful silverware, jewelry and spectacles, as arranged in shining show cases, a worthy representative of the fine work which can be procured in this establishment. Everything is first-class and worthy of closest inspection. Special attention given to repairing fine watches and jewelry, and all work done in this house is guaranteed to be as perfect as it is possible to make it. The visitor to Fred Scholer's jewelry store will find it to be deserving of much credit, and an honor to the community.

TURNBULL & CULLERTON.

The necessity of good roofing material, in a climate liable to extremes of heat and cold, is imperative, and this desideratum is found in Turnbull & Cullerton's "Gypsumineral" Cement Roofing, an invention of the utmost value used by men of the most practical type, who have known all the disadvantages of other roofing, and who in this compound have conquered all such difficulties. "Gypsumineral" has had

GYPSUMINERAL CEMENT ROOF

TRADE MARK

twenty-three years' test; is practically fireproof; can be walked over with less injury than any other; contracts and expands in sudden changes without injury to roof; contains no injurious matter; does not run in the hottest, nor crack in the coldest weather; is the only cement which can be applied successfully to pitched roofs; will last thirty years, and last, but not least, can be laid on old felt roofing, and be as good as new, and much better than a new resin composition roof. With this as their specialty Messrs. Turn-

G. A. TURNBULL.

bull & Cullerton have made a success of their business. It was established in 1868 by Messrs. Freutel & Turnbull.

In January, 1890, Mr. Freutel retired, and for a short time the firm was known as Turnbull & Co. In March, 1890, Messrs. Turnbull & Cullerton joined their interests, the latter gentleman having been for some time a silent partner. He is an alderman from the ninth ward, and has represented that section of the city in the City Council since 1871, in fact, he is the premier of the Chicago City Council, having been elected twelve consecutive times from three different wards; has been twice acting mayor and ten years the Chairman of

HON. E. F. CULLERTON.

Finance Committee, which is really one of the most important offices in the city government. He was also a member of the House of Representatives of the Twenty-eighth General Assembly of the State of Illinois. He is a native of Chicago. Mr. Cullerton was formerly connected with the car heating and sidewalk ventilation business, and the many who know him give him the credit of being a genial whole-souled business man. Mr. Turnbull is a native of Scotland, but has made his home in Chicago for about a quarter of a century, and is an unassuming hardworking and successful business man. He is, we are told, a relation of Pittsburg's most successful and enterprising iron master, who is also a Scotchman, an author and a public benefactor. The factory of the "Gypsumineral" is at Sixteenth street and Blue Island avenue, and about fifty people are employed, the works covering a large area of ground. They are general manufacturers of corrugated iron and sheet steel roofing, as well, Turnbull's Patent Spring-Cap Sheet Steel Roofing and Corrugated Iron being the specialty, under control of the Chicago Metallic Roofing & Corrugating Co., of which the genial and popular Col. Egerton Adams (president of Chicago Forge and Bolt Co.), is president, G. A. Turnbull vice-president, and E. F. Cullerton secretary and treasurer. Their success is shown in the wide adoption of their roofs and the unvarying testimony to the worth of the material, so that the motto of the company can well be quoted here, and fitly conclude this brief notice of its commercial success: "Build not thine house upon a sandy foundation, and keep the waters from intruding into thy dwelling by putting on a Gypsumineral cement roof, then when the floods come thou wilt surely be glad." Among the numerous works in hand or executed by this progressive and prosperous company may be mentioned the roofing of the Frazer & Chalmers Mining Machinery Plant in this city, and which covers an area of over half a million square feet, the roofing of the Grant Locomotive Works, covering an area of 250,000 square feet, besides many other large contracts in and out of Chicago. They roofed J. M. Smyth's new Town Market, and have been working half the summer on the large engine houses and machine shops of the Chicago & Northwestern Railroad Co. along their different lines, in fact, almost wherever large concerns of any class require permanent roofing they call upon Turnbull & Cullerton.

F. & WM. F. YOTT.

Unquestionably the leading livery business of Chicago is that conducted by F. Yott & Son, at 532 and 534 N Clark street This business was established in 1850 by Mr. F. Yott, who continued it alone until 1876, when he admitted his son, Mr. W. F Yott, to the business, and moved to the present location. Here they occupy the ground floor and basement of the large

three-story brick building, 45x150 feet in size. The office is on the ground floor, as are also the carriage rooms, the basement being used as a stable room for the horses. The place is well lighted and ventilated and everything done to add to the convenience and comfort of the horses. The carriages here embrace every variety of landau, phaeton, carriage, buggy, carts, etc. An immense trade is had and conveyances are supplied at the shortest notice for weddings, funerals, or, in fact any occasion calling for vehicles. The horses are selected for their reliability, beauty and traveling qualities. Seventy-five horses are kept on hand constantly, and ten workmen are employed. The owners of this business are also proprietors of the Union Riding Academy, at 527, 529 and 531 N. Clark street, being directly opposite the stables. This place was built by the Union Riding Club, in 1883, and was leased by the Yotts in 1884. It is the only riding school in the city conducted especially for that purpose. The building is of pressed brick, with white stone trimmings, and is 75x200 feet in dimensions. There are two floors in front, one in the center and three in the rear. The place is elegantly and conveniently fitted up, having handsome parlors for ladies, dressing and toilet rooms. The "rink" is placed in the center of the building, and is 75x125 in area ; it is well lighted and well ventilated, and has a delightful packing of two feet of tan bark on the floor. In the rear there is a two-story stable where the saddle horses are kept for riding and park service. During the winter season this academy is the resort of the various riding clubs of the city, as well as of the novices in this art. From November 1 to April 1 lessons in riding are given, and as it will no doubt be of great interest to our readers, we append the rates charged: $40 for the season is the rate for three lessons a week; while a club of eight or more have two lessons per week at $30 each. Fifteen private lessons are given for $25. The price

for a single private lesson is $2.50; lessons in leaping are given for $2.50 each, and road lessons of two hours each for $5. A set of twenty tickets is issued for $25, or forty tickets for $45, which somewhat reduces the above prices. Horses are let on the road for $3 for the first two hours, and $1 each succeeding hour. Horses are boarded for $25 per month, and the owner has the privilege of using the academy on hours set for exercise riding. Horses are purchased on commission, and trained for the saddle for ladies and gentlemen. Horses are always to be had for military purposes. Mr. F. Yott is a native of Kingston, Ont., and Mr. W. F. Yott was born in Chicago; they are well known and highly respected, being held in the highest esteem by numerous patrons and friends.

E. M. NEWMAN.

It would be difficult for an architect in Chicago to open his professional career under greater promise than has Mr. E. M. Newman, whose handsome and commodious offices are at rooms 906-907 in the Insurance Exchange building, at 218 La Salle street. Mr. Newman established himself here in 1891, prior to which he had been for five years in some of the leading architect's offices in the city, as, for instance, Adler & Sullivan, Edbrooke & Burnham and N. D. Little; and during this time he displayed a talent and aptitude which foreboded great things for his future. Since his establishment he has designed a large apartment building on Madison avenue and Sixty-first street, and is now preparing plans for a handsome residence for the Rev. C. G. Truesdell, of Lake Bluff, Illinois, while he has several other important works on hand. Mr. Newman is a native of Indiana, and a member of the Independent Order of Odd Fellows and of the Patriarchal Circle. In the ranks of his profession he has won an enviable place that he fully merits, and he has gained the confidence and esteem of all who know him.

E. H. ROCHE.

One of the most reliable and old-established wholesale wine and liquor houses in this section of Chicago is that of Mr. E. H. Roche, distiller and importer, whose office and salesrooms are at 226 and 228 Kinzie street. This business was established in 1864 by Messrs. Enright & Kelly, who conducted it till 1890, when Mr. E. H. Roche became sole proprietor. Mr. Roche is a recognized authority on the qualities and values of wines and liquors, and possesses influential connections and superior facilities. He controls the sale of the whiskies of the widely known New Haven E. H. Roche Distilling Company, and handles 5,000 barrels of these liquors annually. The premises occupied comprise a spacious four-story and basement building, 50x100 feet in area, fully fitted up with every convenience for the accommodation of the choice and valuable stock. The assortment includes ports, sherries, clarets, champagnes, Irish and Scotch whiskies, brandies, rum, gin, case goods, cordials, etc. A specialty is made of the finest Kentucky whiskies, the principal brands being "Woodford", "Home Ruler", "Red Cloud", "World's Fair" etc., which are admirably suited for a first-class bar, club and drug trade, being unrivaled for quality, purity and excellence. Mr. Roche's Glenville hand-made sour mash whisky is singled and doubled over open wood fires. This whisky possesses rare tonic and strengthening qualities, and is sold under a guarantee to give perfect satisfaction. Orders are carefully filled at the lowest possible prices, and the trade extends throughout Chicago and the principal cities of the Western and Northwestern States. Mr. Roche was formerly a traveling salesman for Messrs. Enright & Kelly, and is a popular member of the National Protection Association. He is an honorable, able and enterprising business man, who has won success by honestly deserving it. Mr. Roche has always a heavy stock of whiskies on hand, and has a bonded warehouse in New Haven, Ky. We would recommend dealers and critical buyers to sample some of the leading specialties of this house, as they positively are not to be duplicated elsewhere.

THE FULLER WATCHMAN'S ELECTRICAL DETECTOR COMPANY.

One of the most substantial and reliable firms in the city of Chicago is the Fuller Watchman's Electrical Detector Company, who manufacture the Fuller Watchman's Electrical Detector. This excellent company was incorporated November 25, 1890, with $200,000 capital stock, and is one the best in Chicago, as regards the excellence of its manufactured goods, and the immense sales of its specialty. The Fuller Watchman's Electrical Detector is the most complete and perfect watchman's detector ever offered to the public, and is the result of many years of practical experiments on the part of the inventor, whose experience and skill as an electrician is second to none in the United States, and whose inventive genius was demonstrated by his invention of the electric battery jar and method of insulating the same, and is now used by all telegraph and other companies requiring gravity batteries. The detector is the best in existence, it alone gives an unalterable recoil, which is of great importance, and it owes its birth to the necessities of the times and the genius of a progressive American. It is an impregnable device to be used where watchmen are employed, to guard against loss by fire

or burglars. It reports the faithful or unfaithful performance of duty of the one in charge, and is the only detector made that cannot be tampered with, without detection. It is a great and truly wonderful invention, and merchants and manufacturers should avail themselves of the advantages this device alone affords. It is an established fact that two-thirds of all the factories and extensive business houses that are destroyed by fire are destroyed in the night time, and ninety per cent. of these do not have reliable watchmen's electrical detectors. It is reasonable to suppose, if your watchman is kept moving through the entire factory, knowing that our detector is a mute, but truthful sentinel over him, a fire cannot get the start. The detector is often placed in combination with a large regulator or office clock, and thus it forms a handsome, desirable and useful fixture. They make special systems of the Fuller Detector for banks and police patrol service for towns, villages and cities. This company in all cases guarantees its work, and will take back their machine and refund the money paid if it does not do all that is claimed for it. They solicit your careful consideration and correspondence. Call upon them or direct them to call upon you, should you at any time consider the advantages this **improvement alone affords.** They occupy suite 416 and 418 Rookery as offices.

C. BUNGE.

One of the most important factors in the rapid development of the commercial and manufacturing interests of Chicago is the coal trade. Prominent among the old established and reliable houses actively engaged in this important trade is that of Mr. C. Bunge, whose yards are located at 616 to 622 W. Lake street. This business was established thirty years ago by Mr. C. Bunge, who conducted it till 1890, when he died after a successful and honorable career. He was succeeded by his sons, Messrs. A. J. and G. Bunge, who are now carrying on the business under the old name of "C. Bunge." They occupy two commodious yards, each being 100x125 feet in area. Here they have superior sawing and splitting machinery, operated by a twenty-five horse power steam engine, and deal largely, not only in the best grades of anthracite and bituminous coal and wood of all kinds, but also in hay, grain and feed. The business is both wholesale and retail, and chiefly local, while thirteen men and ten teams are constantly employed in filling orders at the lowest possible prices. They always keep a large supply on hand, including the best Lehigh and Lackawanna anthracite. All coal purchased of this responsible house is guaranteed to maintain in every respect the highest standard of excellence, coming as it does from some of the most famous collieries in America. Messrs. A. J. and G. Bunge are natives of Chicago. They have influential connections, and their high character is a sufficient assurance that all orders will receive prompt and faithful attention. The telephone call of the house is 7090.

GEO. SCHWITZNER.

The successor to Clement & Co., One Price Clothing House, established in 1875, is Mr. Geo. Schwitzner. He is the proprietor of the double numbered building at 577 and 579 Blue Island avenue, where the store is located. The commodious establishment occupies the ground floor and basement of the three-story building, and covers an area of 4,000 square feet, soon to be increased by an additional extension of 1,000 square feet, making it one of the largest establishments on Blue Island avenue. The store is gorgeously fitted up in hardwood finish, and is stocked to its utmost capacity with A1 goods, including clothing, gents' furnishing goods, hosiery, neckwear, gloves, hats and caps, trunks and valises and all the other sundry commodities which go to make up a fully equipped clothing emporium. The handsome French plate glass windows display in artistic style the magnificent assortment of the above mentioned goods. Mr. Geo. Schwitzner employes, on an average, all the year round about ten experienced clerks; during busy seasons this number is swelled more than half. He carries a very large line of imported and domestic suitings, and in conjunction therewith operates a custom work department, a branch of which is now located at 583 Blue Island avenue. Mr. Schwitzner has been identified with the clothing business for the past twenty years; he is a German by birth, and a resident of Chicago since 1870. Mr. Schwitzner is a prominent member of the Ancient Order of Foresters. His trade is very extensive, and still growing.

A. KAEMPFER.

For strictly A1 goods in the line of diamonds, watches, jewelry and silverware, or for fine workmanship, promptness and reliability, few, if any, in the business in this section of the city, enjoy a more substantial measure of recognition than Mr. A. Kaempfer, whose elegant establishment is located at No. 336 W. Madison street. He is, in fact, one of the leading exponents of the watchmakers' and jewelers' art on the West side, and his patronage is at once large and substantial. Mr. Kaempfer, who is a gentleman in the prime of life, is a thoroughly practical watchmaker himself. and, migrating to this country from Germany, settled in Chicago in 1866, five years later opening an emporium on the same thoroughfare between Halsted and Union streets. This, however, was destroyed by fire, and the present premises have been in occupation since April of the current year. The store is large and commodious, and very handsomely appointed, a superb display being made of fine gold and silver watches of all kinds, magnificent diamonds and other precious stones, novelties in earrings, pendants, brooches, scarf pins, finger, wedding and engagement rings, etc., also sterling silver and plated ware, French and American clocks, and kindred articles. The very lowest consistent prices are quoted here, and every article sold is fully warranted, while all work executed is guaranteed first class,—repairing of every description being done in a prompt superior manner.

THORNBURGH & GLESSNER.

A representative and one of the most successful firms in Chicago engaged in the manufacture of mill and elevator supplies is that of Messrs. Thornburgh & Glessner, whose office and factory are situated at 110 and 112 S. Jefferson street. This extensive business was established in 1881 by Messrs. Thornburgh & Glessner, who have since built up a liberal and influential patronage, not only in all sections of the United States and Canada, but also abroad. In June 1890 a stock company was formed with $50,000 capital, fully paid in. They occupy a spacious and substantial six-story building, 70x125 feet in dimensions. The various departments are fully equipped with modern tools, machinery and appliances, operated by a fifty horse power steam engine. Here over sixty skilled workmen are employed, who turn out all kinds of mill and elevator supplies, including the "Excelsior" Mill Buckets, corn buckets, special buckets, also the famous Salem Steel Elevator Buckets. They likewise manufacture and deal in elevator bolts, clinch bolts, conveyor fixtures, hangers, excelsior wrought iron elevator boots, take-up boxes, belt tighteners, cast iron turn heads, with hopper, crane spouts and tunnels, dump gates, elevator and main drive belts, etc. Their facilities for placing mill and elevator supplies on the market are unexceled, if equaled, by any other house in existence, while their prices in all cases are extremely just and reasonable. The firm issues a superior Illustrated Catalogue. Mr. Thornburgh was born in Macomb, Ill., and Mr. Glessner in Galena, Ill. They are honorable and enterprising business men, who have been very successful in this useful industry. The telephone call is 4245.

GEO. B. BARWIG.

The avocation of the druggist is one of the most important and responsible of the many that contribute to swell the industrial activities of any given community, and the public expect to find in him a man specially trained and educated for the onerous duties he undertakes to discharge. In Mr. George B. Barwig the citizens of Chicago have just such a man, and the liberal share of patronage he has come to control since he embarked in the drug business here in 1891 is ample evidence of their appreciation of him. At his handsomely appointed store, No. 3659 South Halsted street, he has every facility for the transaction of a continually augmenting business, and carries a complete and comprehensive assortment of medicines, drugs, proprietary remedies of all the most approved kinds, a very choice selection of elegant toilet articles and fancy goods, and a general line of physicians' supplies. Only the freshest and purest goods of their kind and of the best quality are to be found in this stock, as Mr. Barwig takes a just pride in keeping it up to the highest standard of excellence. A special feature of this well-known establishment is its prescription department, over which he presides in person. A regular graduate in pharmacy, Mr. Barwig has supplemented his technical training by years of practical experience, and the skill and care which characterize his compounding of physicians' prescriptions have won him a reputation for accuracy and reliability with the medical profession and the general public, second to that of no other druggist in this section of the Western metropolis.

12

TRADE MARK

pies an entire ground floor, having a frontage of 20 by a depth of 60 feet. The salesrooms are very tastefully and attractively fitted up and furnished, while the tailoring department is well equipped with all necessary appliances and devices for the prompt execution of orders and the prosecution of the business on the most satisfactory basis. Two skilled tailors are employed and Mr. Slater, who is a practical and experienced master of his art in all its branches, gives his close personal attention to the making of every garment that leaves his establishment. He at all times carries full and complete lines of the finest productions of English, Scotch, French and American looms, and here are always displayed the latest and most stylish patterns and textures, such as broadcloths, worsteds, serges, flannels, cheviots, meltons, kerseys, tweeds, suitings, overcoatings, etc. The assortment has been very carefully selected and from it the most critical and fastidious cannot but be suited. As a cutter and tailor, Mr. Slater has no superior in this section of the city, and all goods made by him are unsurpassed for the excellence of their fit, as well as for the beauty and quality of material. Moderate and reasonable prices prevail, and the utmost attention is paid to the wishes and desires of patrons, among whom are many of our most stylishly dressed citizens.

CUBAN CIGAR FACTORY.

The establishment of a new cigar factory should be an event of interest to all smokers, especially when the firm give promise of building up a large trade, and of occupying a prominent place in that widely extended industry. We, therefore, have great pleasure in bringing to the notice of our readers the Cuban Cigar Factory, founded a year ago by Messrs. W. B. Smith & Co., at No 176 to 180 Michigan street. The capacity of this factory amounts to no less than 2,000 daily, and some of the special brands produced are becoming recognized as among the very best in the market. His five cent line embraces "Homespun," "La Gratitude," "Cuban Queen" and "Clear Havana," the latter a really wonderful cigar for the price. Among his ten cent productions "El Saroni" deserves special mention, and "Las Skogofinas" a fifteen cent cigar, is one of the most fragrant, cool and sweet smokes that could be desired by the most fastidious lover of the weed. Mr. Smith has had twelve years' experience in this interesting avocation, is recognized as a good judge of a cigar, and as one who has a thorough knowledge of American tastes and requirements in this important line. He employs on an average fourteen skilled assistants, and has every appliance necessary to the business installed in his spacious premises. He is a native of Albany, N. Y., and during his eight years' residence here has become widely known and greatly esteemed by an extensive circle among the community generally for his many high qualities of heart and mind.

WILL C. SLATER.

A widely known and successful exponent of the difficult art of the fashionable tailor in the southern district of Chicago, and whose patronage has from the start been large and influential, is Mr. Will C. Slater, whose handsome establishment is located at No. 506 Sixty-third street, in the Opera House block. This business was founded by him in 1890, and from its inception it has been very brisk and active, and still continues to grow and develop at a very rapid rate. Mr. Slater's establishment occu-

H. C. SPEER.

The importance of Chicago as a commercial center is conceded and recognized on every hand, and this naturally brings vast amounts of money here for investment, which, with the local wealth of many millions, creates an opportunity for the best and largest banking enterprises. One of the leading houses in its line in the city is the well-known and highly honored house of H. C. Speer, at 237 La Salle street. The business of this house has been established since 1885, prior to which Mr. Speer was the investing officer of the state of Kansas for four years, purchasing nearly 10,000,000 of municipal and school bonds, every dollar of which has a good history in the state treasurer's hands for the prompt payment of interest and principal. With such an experience and with such personal standing his success in the business of investment banking was not a matter of chance. To-day he has well-appointed offices in Chicago, Boston and Topeka, necessitated by the rule of personal investigation given to securities before they are offered to the large patronage of clients of the house all over the country. Mr. Speer does a general investment business, dealing in all kinds of first-class investment securities. He handles high-class stocks, municipal and corporation bonds and municipal warrants; has a large clientage who purchase city bonds, township bonds, school bonds and water bonds, also commercial paper, local securities and bank stocks. Loans are negotiated on approved collateral. Whole issues of city, town and county bonds are purchased and placed with investors in sums to suit purchasers. The offices of this house are elegantly fitted up in bank style, and employment is given to a large and competent force of clerks and accountants. Mr. Speer is one of the leading financiers of the city, and his high standing, coupled with his ability and sterling worth, has brought to him a clientage that is of the best character and of the most desirable kind. He numbers among his patrons some of the leading and best known capitalists and investors in the city. The houses at Boston and Topeka are closely connected in all business transactions, and by these means a large and satisfactory business is transacted.

E. L. MANSURE & CO.

Chicago presents the most desirable and profitable center for the carrying on of any branch of industry, due to its vast trade relations and splendid transportation facilities. Among the newly organized firms who have chosen Chicago as headquarters is that of Messrs. E. L. Mansure & Co., manufacturers of the newest and most popular lines of upholstery and drapery trimmings. Mr. Mansure was born in Philadelphia, and though a young man, is old-experienced in this difficult branch of skilled industry. He settled in Chicago seven years ago, and was formerly the manager for Messrs. J. H. Stevenson & Co., in the same line. For seven years he was a traveling salesman in the lines of trimmings and achieved a deserved success, besides creating warm friends, and establishing influential connections throughout the trade. In January, 1890, he started in business upon his own account, locating his factory and salesrooms on the five floors of Nos. 45, 47, and 49 Randolph street, a most central location between State street and Wabash avenue. The premises are 70x192 in dimensions, and very completely equipped with latest improved machinery and appliances. Upward of 150 hands are here employed in the manufacture of full lines of upholstery and drapery trimmings, including many novelties and specialties in rich effects, much sought after and preferred by the best class of trade. These high grade trimmings give perfect satisfaction, and their popularity is evinced by the fact that during its first year's operations the firm did a business of $150,000. Quality and artistic designs have ever been Mr. Mansure's first consideration, and his prompt, honorable mercantile methods, coupled with his splendid facilities, insure to him prospects of the most favorable character. Mr. Mansure is universally popular, both in business and social circles. He is an active Freemason and a Knight Templar, and has been honored with election to important offices, while he is an active member of the Chicago Athletic Club, Farragut Boating Club, and Hamilton Republican Club, and worthily retains the confidence of leading commercial and financial circles, as a manufacturer of ability and integrity, whose firm name is becoming a veritable trademark as regards all their products of upholstery and drapery trimmings.

D. B. FULLER.

Among the prominent and representative florists in Chicago is that of Mr. D. B. Fuller, located at No. 3801 Cottage Grove avenue. He is in all respects a leader in this interesting line of trade, and his patronage is derived from the most fashionable parts of the city and suburbs. Mr. Fuller has for many years been engaged in the business, having established it in 1878, and a year ago last fall he purchased ten acres at Downer's Grove, twenty-one miles from the city, on the line of the Chicago, Burlington & Quincy R. R. Here he owns a large florist's plant, the greenhouse covering twenty thousand square feet under glass, with large gardens attached, all of which are perfectly arranged as far as the skill of the floriculturist can make them. Almost every species of cut flower is here found that is esteemed and valued. In 1890 Mr. Fuller removed his greenhouses to Downer's Grove, retaining his salesrooms in this city, at his present address, in order to more effectually meet the requirements of his numerous patrons. His salesrooms are of ample dimensions, and are in one of the most eligible and desirable locations. They are handsomely appointed and elegantly fitted up with every modern convenience, including the electric light, etc., and contain at all times a choice assortment of greenhouse and bedding plants, bouquets, baskets, wreaths, crosses and all the most beautiful and popular flowers, while a specialty is made of novelties in choice cut flowers, decorative plants and floral designs. Six skilled assistants are employed, and all their skill and care are directed toward obtaining the best results. Mr Fuller is at all times prepared to furnish plants and flowers for funerals, banquets, balls, weddings and entertainments, and to decorate halls, churches and private residences, guaranteeing low prices and the best service. He has always on hand all kinds of rustic

work, wire and earthenware, and possesses unequaled facilities for successfully meeting the most exacting demands. He is a prominent member of the American Florists' Association and of the Chicago Florists' Club. Born in New Hampshire, he has resided in this city for the past thirty-five years, and is highly esteemed for his ability and honorable business methods.

WM. HOOD.

The rapid displacement of gas as an illuminating medium and the substitution of electricity have called into play during the last few years a new branch of industry, which is rapidly assuming gigantic proportions. Among those intimately and prominently connected in Chicago with that branch of electrical science which has to do with the great problem of economic illumination is Mr William Hood, whose office and warerooms are located at 239 La Salle street under the Grand Pacific Hotel. For the past three years Mr. Hood has devoted himself assiduously to his business in this city, and in the face of great opposition has demonstrated the practicability of the storage battery system for electric lighting. Among the many heavy contracts for furnishing isolated plants, which Mr. Hood has filled during the last two years, we desire to mention a few of the more prominent ones, notably that of the large plant placed in the magnificent residence of Potter Palmer, Esq., and as this is one of the largest private plants in the world, a somewhat detailed description will not be out of place. The engine is of the well-known Otto type, rated at twenty actual horse power. The dynamo is 125-light machine. The engine, countershafting and dynamo are all mounted on substantial foundations. The battery room contains 112 cells of the accumulator company's fifteen-light type. These cells when fully charged have a normal capacity of 100 lamps for ten hours, or 130 lamps for six hours, or a joint capacity of 250 sixteen candle power lamps when the dynamo and accumulators are working together. These cells are placed upon substantial shelving, the supports of which rest upon glazed tiling, and in order to still further improve the insulation each cell stands on an insulated tray. The switchboard upon which are grouped the various devices used in manipulating the plant is one of the most complete in existence. The current is conveyed from the storage battery plant to the house, about 200 feet distant, by means of an underground cable laid in a wooden conduit which is filled with a mixture of pitch and gravel. The capacity of this plant has been tested several times, and has been found to do almost double the work it was guaranteed to do. Mr. Hood has just closed a contract for furnishing an isolated plant for the residence of J. J. Hill, Esq., of St. Paul, Minn., the millionaire president of the Great Northern Pacific. This will be by far the largest plant in the world. It will have a capacity of 650 sixteen candle power lamps, running ten hours, from the accumulators alone. In the spring of 1889 Mr. Palmer contracted with Mr. Hood to place the accumulator system in the Palmer House with a capacity sufficient to light the barber shop, ladies' and gentlemen's Turkish baths, halls, elevators, etc., and a brief quotation from a letter written by Mr. Tanner to Mr. Hood under date of August 18, 1890, is sufficient evidence of the unqualified success of the system. In this letter Mr. Palmer says: "The plant at the Palmer House, installed by you April last, does all that you claim, and I have no reason to doubt that it will continue to do good work." Besides furnishing storage battery plants for lighting, Mr. Hood carries a full and complete assortment of electrical supplies, including storage batteries for medical and scientific purposes, also dynamos, motors, incandescent and arc lamps, etc. In the office will be seen the complete workings of the accumulator system. Mr. Hood is a gentleman in the prime of life, whose honorable, upright business methods have secured for him the respect and esteem of a wide circle of business acquaintances, including many of the wealthiest and most prominent business men of the country. By his untiring energy and persistent effort he has placed himself among the successful business men of this city, and is now reaping the reward of his efforts, and we predict for him a brilliant future.

L. WILMER KENDALL.

Unquestionably one of the finest drug stores of this city is that of Mr. L., Wilmer Kendall, located at the corner of Clark and Center streets. Mr. Kendall brings all the advantages of the highest education and long practical experience to bear in catering to the demands of patrons, and strives to serve them with intelligence and in a satisfactory manner. That he has succeeded his large and constantly increasing patronage attests. The business now conducted by Mr. Kendall dates its establishment back to 1860, when Mr. Anton Hottinger founded it. He was afterward succeeded by his son, who in time formed a partnership with a Mr. Weihe, and later with Mr. Kendall. Since April last Mr. Kendall has conducted the business alone and has the finest store and best stock, with the most liberal patronage in the district. The fixtures are of solid oak, the show cases and windows of plate glass, while the floor is of an exquisite design in tiles. The arrangement of the store is perfect, and the decorations are such as would satisfy the most fastidious. A large soda fountain graces the establishment, and an immense business is done in that line as the store is directly opposite Lincoln park. The syrups and novel drinks prepared by Mr. Kendall have become famous. A full line of pure drugs and chemicals is carried, also everything in the line of druggists' sundries, physicians' supplies, toilet articles, perfumes, soaps, patent medicines, and all the requirements of the sick room or nursery. Fine brandies, whiskies and wines, both domestic and imported, are carried in stock, for medicinal use. The prescription department is under the direct supervision of the proprietor, and all prescriptions are compounded accurately, special care being taken with those prescriptions whose medicinal value depends upon the quality of the materials used, and the care exercised in their combination. The services of the proprietor or assistants may be had at any hour of the day or night, and the telephone, 3201, is always at the disposal of patrons, free of charge. Many proprietary articles are manufactured and for sale by Mr. Kendall, and on the whole, his business interests are extensive and constantly increasing. Mr. Kendall is a native of Boston, Mass., and has resided in Chicago about two years. He graduated from the Chicago College of Pharmacy and the Massachusetts College of Pharmacy, and is a duly registered pharmacist in this state. He was graduated from the Harvard University with the degree of A. B. and A. M. and is a popular, enterprising and skilled gentleman, and has succeeded in building up a very successful business.

O. F. Harms.

Es giebt keinen Industrie-Zweig, in welchem in den letzten Jahren solch' rasche Fortschritte und Verbesserungen anzutreffen sind, wie in der Anfertigung von kunstvollem Hausstattungs-Mobiliar, und keines der an längsten etablirten Geschäftshäuser auf der Nordseite, das mit dem Zeitgeiste Schritt hält, ist das Geschäft des Herrn O. F. Harms, 105 Clybourn Avenue und 202 Larrabee Straße. Diese Firma wurde vor achtzehn Jahren in derselben Straße gegründet und benutzt sein jetziges Geschäftslokal seit zehn Jahren. Er errichtete und eignet das Anwesen, welches aus einem hübschen dreistöckigen Backstein-Gebäude mit Basement, 33x140 Fuß, besteht. Er benutzt die untere Etage und das Basement für seinen Laden, und hier findet man jederzeit eine umfassende Auswahl von Parlor-, Bibliothek-, Speisezimmer-, Schlafzimmer-, Hallen- und Küchen-Mobilien, Teppichen, Spiegeln, Bettzeug, Polsterwaaren, Oeltuchen u. f. w. Die von der Firma geforderten Preise sind ungemein niedrig und verlauft für Baar oder nach dem Abzahlungs-System, welch' letztere Methode die weniger Bemittelten in den Stand setzt, ihre Haushaltungs-Bedürfnisse leicht und sicher zu bekommen. Herr Harms ist aus Deutschland gebürtig und dreiundzwanzig Jahre in Chicago. Er ist allerseits geachtet wegen seines Unternehmungsgeistes und aufrichtigen Methoden, und ist ein beliebtes Mitglied der Pythias-Ritter, der Rothmänner, des Turnvereins und der Ehren-Ritter und Ehren-Damen. Er steht im mittleren Lebensalter.

LOUIS BRODHAG.

At no period in the history of Chicago are the services of an architect in greater demand than the present, and no time when it is more important to choose the best in that line. Mr. Louis Brodhag whose office is at No. 385 Wells street, near Division street, has as wide an experience in this line as any in the city and is second to none in his reputation for doing good work in all cases, as the Winkleman flat on Oakdale avenue, Berg's flats on Wells street, and countless other flats and dwellings will show. He also was the architect of that handsome structure, the Bethseda home and training school on Belden place. Mr. Brodhag was born in Germany and has been in Chicago nine years. He is a graduate of the Stuttgart Polytechnical Institute of Architecture, the acknowledged authority of Germany, if not of all Europe.

THE COREY CAR AND MANUFACTURING COMPANY.

The use of specially constructed cars for all descriptions of contracting on public works, where earth, rock or gravel have to be speedily and economically removed, has become a special feature, since the famous Corey Car and Manufacturing Company of No. 55 Fifth avenue this city began operations. Both as regards design, build, durability and practical working capacity, the Corey Dumping Platform and Mining cars are far ahead of all attempted competition. It was in 1873 that the firm of Francis W. Corey & Co. was formed and began the manufacture of dumping and mining cars at La Porte, Ind. Mr. Corey's model cars achieved such celebrity, and came into such enormous demand, that in 1885 he removed to Chicago, where the present company was duly organized and incorporated with a paid up capital of $75,000, Mr. Francis W. Corey becoming the president and manager, and Mr. W. A. Hooker, E. M. of New York, vice-president, and Mr. James B Riely, lately a prominent merchant of Louisville, secretary and treasurer. New works were constructed at North Ashland and Carroll avenues, and the company, with greatly enlarged facilities is still driven to fill its numerous orders. The factory is 100 by 150 feet in dimensions, and is fully equipped with the latest improved machinery and appliances. Upward of fifty hands are there employed in the manufacture of a variety of different styles of side, end, rotary and bottom dumping cars, of any required capacity, for use in grading railroads, parkways, etc., in moving material in brickyards, stone quarries to and from lime kilns, gravel pits, and mines of every sort. Also lighter cars for agricultural and plantation works, levee building, coal and ore docks, tunnel work, logging and narrow gauge railroads. The best of seasoned oak, iron or all steel are the materials used, while these cars solely embody Peters', Greggs' and Corey's patents (all owned by the company) while it is exclusively licensee under Healey's patents. The company also builds the popular Corey engine, the best upon the market, and full lines of hoisters, motors, turn tables and steam traction gear, hand cars for inspection and section work, portable tracks, frogs, switches, etc. Both as to price and quality most substantial inducements are offered, and a trade has been developed, covering every section of the United States and Canada, with a lively export trade to Cuba, Mexico, Australia, South America, etc. Mr. Corey is a practical mechanical engineer of the highest standing in his profession; one who has made a close study of contractors' and miners' requirements, and can save them large sums by the use of these cars in preference to wagons or barrows. Those interested should send for the companys' illustrated descriptive catalogue, and which also contains hosts of testimonials from leading firms of contractors all over the United States. Mr. Corey is universally popular and respected in business and professional circles, and the company bearing his surname, is a worthy and invaluable addition to the skilled industries of Chicago.

CHICAGO SCHOOL AT ARMS AND BOXING.

The useful and elegant arts of boxing, fencing and swimming have a distinguished representative in Chicago in the person of Colonel Thomas H. Monstery, whose school at arms is located in the Fidelity Bank Building, at No. 143 Randolph street. Colonel Monstery is a graduate of the leading institutions of Europe, devoted to giving instruction in these manly

exercises, and has had a varied and distinguished career in the services of Russia, Spain, Central and South America and the Mexican Republic, as well as the United States, being wounded in the Mexican war of 1847, while in the American navy. The colonel is one of the most brilliant swordsmen of modern times. From the year 1855 to 1876, he met and defeated nearly every master of the art in America, and several of the most distinguished in the world. Among the more celebrated of these may be mentioned his encounter with the famous Senor Colon, at Columbia, S. A., in 1855, whom he defeated with ease. Three years later he vanquished General Bracamonta, and shortly afterward the highly reputed Angenau, a Belgian by birth, who stood seven feet in height, and who had acquired, in Peru, a great reputation for his skill with all weapons from the foil to the bayonet. Captain Perrier was his next opponent, a highly reputed Parisian swordsman, but who met with defeat at the hands of the invincible colonel. Two years later he won easily against Professor Chauvel, who was then residing at Virginia City, Nev., notwithstanding the fact that he had to use his left hand, his right having been disabled through an accident. On the first of March 1868, he won an assault at arms in the City of Mexico against the famous Professor Ponpard, and on the 9th of April, 1876, he met Professor Senac of Paris in Tammany Hall, New York. This contest was decided in favor of Senac because of the colonel retiring in disgust, owing to the incapacity of the referee, who, according to the Army and Navy Journal, "kept giving his decisions at random, first to one and then the other, while the audience began to shout and groan at each new count, which seemed to be decided on the principle of chance." The only dignified course open to Colonel Monstery was to record his protest in the most marked manner possible by withdrawing, although up to that stage he had really scored twenty-one points out of the twenty-seven contested. Such has been the brilliant record of one of the greatest masters of all kinds of gymnastic exercises that America has produced. The colonel is a native of Baltimore, Md., and, in addition to his wide experience in North and South America, he has made several extended trips through Europe, visiting the leading Salles DeArmes at the principal centers for the purpose of acquiring all the latest "points" etc., and is now prepared to give full instruction in fencing with foils, rapiers, infantry and cavalry sabre, knife, bayonet and cane, and boxing and swimming, in a manner that is absolutely unexcelled by any other institution in the country. His school is in a thriving condition, the average number of pupils being 40, and the annual business amounting to nearly $5,000. His premises in the Fidelity Bank building, at No. 143 Randolph street, are spacious and admirably well adapted to his purposes. Colonel Monstery is an honored member of the Masonic order, being on the roll of the Hope Chapter, New York, the Warren Blue Lodge, Baltimore, Md., and the Columbia encampment at San Salvador. He is a warm advocate of these manly arts, not only as a means of acquiring agility and strength, but as a preventive and even a cure for many diseases and forms of debility. Personally the colonel is a gentleman of the most distinguished appearance, and is highly respected for his unsurpassed record, his professional skill, and his honorable and straightforward methods. Colonel Monstery, a graduate of the Central Gymnastic Institute, of Stockholm, for fencing, calisthenics and Swedish movement cure, also of the Royal Military Institute of Gymnastic and Arms of Denmark and the leading schools at arms of France and Germany. The Colonel has had among his gentlemen and lady pupils the champions of America, both in fencing and boxing, among whom were: Chas. Bennet, California, "boxing;" Dolly Davenport, "foil;" Junius Brutus Booth, "foil and sabre;" and Francis Wilson, "foil, sabre and boxing," New York; Miss Ada Isaac Mencken, "sabre," and Miss Jacquerina, "sabre." The Manvils, Dr. Chas Rich, "foil, sabre and boxing," and Miss Mildred Holland, "foil and sabre," Chicago. Of his pupil teachers there are two in Chicago.

FRANK DIESEL.

An important industry that has had a rapid development from small beginnings is the manufacture of fruit, meat and oyster cans by Mr. Frank Diesel. This business is to-day one of the representative manufacturing enterprises of the city, giving employment to about one hundred and twenty five workmen, and turning out an average of 50,000 cans, of all kinds, each day. The business of the house dates back to 1877, when Mr. Diesel began business in a humble way with a gentleman named Folz, at 425 Larrabee street. In 1884 Mr. Folz retired and Mr. Diesel removed to 415 and 417 Larrabee street, continuing the business on an increased scale. The business began to develop rapidly, and in 1885 Mr. Diesel built the two-story building and basement he now occupies at 701 to 705 N. Halsted street. Here he has every appliance for manufacturing cans of all kinds for fruits, meats, oysters, vegetables, fish, etc., and also manufactures all kinds of tin and sheet iron wares, doing an immense business. Mr. Diesel has purchased the ground adjoining his premises and will soon erect a splendid four-story factory, 60x100 feet in dimensions, at 701 to 707 N. Halsted street. The business has grown to exceed his most sanguine expectations, and constantly demands increased facilities. The trade is with all parts of the West and Northwest, and is being constantly widened in scope. The manufactures of this house have a popular reputation, and are reliable, and of the most pleasing style for use by packers, having a superior shape and finish. Mr. Diesel is well known in Chicago, having resided here for the past thirty years, and being a leader in business and G. A. R. circles. He fought honorably in the late war, in the 59th Illinois Volunteers, and was wounded at Murfreesboro, Tenn. He was born in Germany, but came to America when a mere lad. His parents located in Cincinnati, O., where Mr. Diesel spent his youth. He is now one of Chicago's prominent and respected business men and manufacturers, and has every prospect of an increased business from year to year. Mr. Diesel has also four sons, who are connected with this business in the various departments: Their names are Louis Diesel, who is acting as manager, assisted by his three younger brothers, Conrad Diesel being in the machinery department, John A. Diesel attending the outside duties, and Lambert, also assisting in the office duties.

GEO. F. RIEL.

The progress that has been made within recent years in the art of photography is nothing less than marvelous. The methods, the apparatus and the manner of posing, all are virtually revolutionized by the march of progress, and modern ideas and improvements have marked the transition from the clumsy appliances of Daguerre to the unique Kodak camera of to-day. In no photographic establishment on the West side is this more strikingly demonstrated than in the elegantly appointed studio of Mr. Geo. P. Riel, located at No. 330 W. Madison street. Mr Riel has made a study of photog-

raphy since boyhood, and after eight years' association in a subordinate position with Hartley, the celebrated photo artist of this city, in 1874 engaged in business on his own account on S. Canal street, removing thence to his present commodious quarters January 1st of the current year. Here he executes, in the highest style of the art, every description of photography, including copying and enlarging, the finishing of portraits in pastel, crayon, india ink and oils, a special feature being made of the portraiture of children. The high order of work done, the uniform satisfaction rendered to patrons, coupled with the courtesy and uniformly reasonable charges of this artist, have been the chief features contributing to the position and permanent success he to-day enjoys. Mr. Riel is a native of Chicago, a man of keen intelligence, courteous and gentlemanly manners, and in all respects an artist of the highest order of ability and progressiveness.

CHICAGO FOUNDRY CO.

For many years the manufacture of iron castings has constituted one of the most important American industries. It is an industry that requires the investment of a large amount of capital, while at the same time it is a source of employment to numbers of skilled workmen. Among the prosperous and representative concerns extensively engaged in this line in the Western metropolis is that known as the Chicago Foundry Company, manufacturers of dry sand rolls, ingot moulds, rolling mill and machinery castings, whose office and works are situated on Redfield and Stein streets. This business was established in 1870 by Dyer, Lamb & Co., who conducted it till 1877, when it was incorporated under the laws of Illinois, with ample capital, the executive officers being at the present time, Mr. W. W. Flinn, president and treasurer; Mr. H. A. Keith, vice-president and Mr. W. M. Downs, secretary. The works and yards have an area of three acres, and have excellent railway and water facilities. The foundries are substantial brick structures, 60x160 feet and 30x100 feet in area, and there are also other brick buildings utilized by the company. The various departments are fully equipped with modern appliances and machinery, operated by a powerful steam engine, also several large steam cranes. Here 150 skilled workmen are employed, and 20,000 tons of first-class pig iron are used annually. Orders are carefully filled at the lowest possible prices, and the trade of the company extends throughout Chicago and the adjacent cities. The various castings produced here are unsurpassed for quality, finish and uniform excellence, and have no

superiors in this country. They likewise cheerfully furnish estimates for any descriptions of castings, and attend promptly to designing and pattern making. This concern has done a large amount of work for the North Chicago Rolling Mills, now the Illinois Steel Co., and adopts promptly every invention and improvement that gives any promise of perfecting their castings. The officers are active competitors for business, and are widely known in trade circles for their integrity and enterprise. The telephone call of the company is 4300.

HOTEL MIDLAND.

There is no more valuable or necessary public convenience in a city than a well-regulated, comfortable homelike hotel. Chicago is well provided with these conveniences, and there is no better one conducted on the European plan than the "Hotel Midland," 133 and 135 E. Adams street, opposite the Rookery. This hotel was opened in 1873 by the present propr'etress, Mrs. F. H. Thompson, who has since built up a liberal and influential patronage. The premises which have just been remodeled and renovated, comprise a spacious and substantial five-story and basement building, 60x150 feet in dimensions. The offices and handsome parlors are on the second floor, and the hotel is fully supplied with all modern appliances, gas, hot and cold water, steam heat, elevator, electric call bells, and all other conveniences, while the means of escape in case of fire are perfect. The hotel contains 100 elegant rooms and can easily accommodate 175 persons. One of the finest restaurants in the city is across the street, and the "Midland" is admirably located near the railroad depots, theaters, post-office and the leading business houses. Street cars constantly pass the door to all parts of Chicago, and the terms are only $1.00 per day, with reductions for permanent guests. The hotel is a model of neatness, cleanliness and order, and it would be well for the city if there were more like it. Mrs. Thompson is a native of New York. She is highly esteemed by guests for her kind and courteous manners and strict integrity, and visitors having once stopped here are sure to return when again coming to Chicago.

D. W. RYAN.

The enormous quantity of cooperage required in the United States for the transportation and preservation of liquors, beer and other goods renders the item of barrels and kegs of the greatest importance to the community. Prominent among the principal manufacturers of cooperage, barrels, kegs, etc., in Chicago is Mr. D. W. Ryan, whose works are located at Nos. 17 to 29 Coventry street. This extensive industry was established in 1874 by Mr. Ryan, who has since built up a liberal and permanent patronage, not only in the Western but also in the Eastern and Middle states. The plant covers an area of 200x250 feet, the main building being a two-story brick structure, 175x90 feet in dimensions, while the dry kilns are 100x100 feet in size. The various departments are fully equipped with modern tools, machinery and appliances operated by steam power. Here from seventy-five to 100 skilled operatives are employed, who turn out 4,000 barrels and packages weekly. Mr. Ryan receives his oak lumber from Indiana, Wisconsin, Arkansas and Tennessee, and his iron work from Pittsburgh, Pa., and Youngstown, O. He manufactures all descriptions of cooperage, but makes a specialty of whisky and beer kegs, half barrels and barrels, which are made of the best materials, and have no superiors in the country for finish, durability and strength. Orders are filled at the lowest possible prices, and all packages are fully warranted to be exactly as represented. Mr. Ryan was born in Ireland, but has resided in Chicago for the last thirty years, where he is greatly respected in trade circles for his promptness and strict integrity. During the Civil War he served in Battery M, 1st Illinois Artillery, for three years. Mr. Ryan was present at the principal Western battles, being at different times under the command of Generals Sherman, Thomas and Sheridan, and was one of the severest engag'ments which took place under these distinguished commanders. The telephone call of the house is 4324.

LIBBY PRISON WAR MUSEUM.

The great and famous Richmond Libby Prison was removed to Chicago and opened September 21, 1889, on Wabash avenue, between Fourteenth and Sixteenth streets. It has been converted into a great museum illustrating the civil war and African slavery in America. This famous old structure is too well known to require any repetition of its history, and during the late war held more than 40,000 Union officers and soldiers. It is now filled with thousands of genuine relics of the war, such as scenes, views, portraits, arms, guns, etc., and original orders and manuscripts of prominent officers, both north and south. The Libby Prison War Museum Association, which carried out this enterprise, was incorporated with a paid-up capital of $100,000, the

following gentlemen being the officers and directors, viz. : C. F. Gunther, president ; A. G. Spalding, vice-president ; C. E. Kremer, secretary and treasurer ; Chas. R. Macloon, manager ; directors, L. Manasse, S. H. Woodbury, Irving L. Gould, W. H. Gray, Fred S. Eames, The prison is now lighted by electricity, and is exactly the same as it was at Richmond, Virginia. It is surrounded by a massive stone wall of artesian stone, quarried within the city limits. Notwithstanding that the prison is now filled with thousands of relics, new ones are being added every day, and in the near future this museum will be second to none in the country. Captains Matt Boyd and Eli Foster who escaped from the prison through the Yankee tunnel, are employed by the association as guides, and are assisted by twelve other veterans. The complete exhibit of war relics is owned by Mr. C. F. Gunther, the esteemed and popular president. No sectional animosity is intended, no north, no south, but a fair representation of the great civil war from both northern and southern standpoints. The museum is open daily, Sunday included, from 9 A. M. to 10 P. M., admission being 50 cents, adults, and 25 cents, children. The Libby Prison War Museum Association is to be warmly congratulated on the success of its novel and massive enterprise, and every family should be taken to see the museum, while no stranger in the city should fail to pay it a visit.

WILCOX, SHAW & CO.

There is no feature of progress in Chicago of equal importance to that of real estate, which long has been and ever will continue to be the principal feature of permanent and absolutely secure investment. The fact is made most palpably apparent by the constant establishment of new houses devoted to this interest, each month seeing an acquisition to the roll of real estate traders in the western metropolis. In such connection we make due reference to the newly-formed firm of Messrs. Wilcox, Shaw & Co., whose

business offices are No. 905 Royal Insurance building, Jackson street. This house was opened during the current year, the individual members of the copartnery being Messrs. James L. Wilcox (a native of Illinois, formerly connected with the commission business) and Frank Shaw, (of Toledo and twenty years connected with Chicago's dry goods commission trade. While the firm attend to every branch of the real estate business, buying, selling, exchanging and renting property, they make a feature of handling subdivisional realty, the specialty being Whiting and Harvey acreage, both of which places, especially the latter, rank among the youngest yet most important of Chicago's manufacturing suburbs. Personally, the members of the firm are live, energetic and reliable business men, favorably known in financial and commercial circles, and are justly entitled to the confidence and respect of the general public.

CHARLES M. HEWITT.

Chicago is recognized as the metropolitan headquarters for the trade in railroad materials and supplies of all kinds, and the largest contracts ever made in these lines are here entered into. The importance of this branch of trade to Chicago cannot be over-estimated, and one of the leading representatives thereof is Mr. Charles M. Hewitt, of 607 Phenix Building, an active and respected young business man, whose qualifications as a salesman are generally recognized, and whose valuable experience in the trade, enables him to satisfactorily meet the most advanced requirements. He was for some years the representative here of the St. Charles Car Company, of St. Charles, Mo. In 1891 he became general agent here for several prominent companies engaged in the manufacture of railroad material, rolling stock supplies, equipments, etc. These include the Middleton Car Spring Company, Fort Madison, Iron Works Co., Hewitt Manufacturing Co. and the Buda Foundry and Manufacturing Co. The Fort Madison Iron Works Co. owns and operates large works at Fort Madison, Iowa, engaged in the manufacture of car wheels of superior quality, and all kinds of railroad forgings and castings. The Middleton Car Spring Company is located at Harvey, Ill., and is devoted to the manufacture of the famous bolster springs, producing them upon an extensive scale. The Hewitt Manufacturing Company makes a specialty of improved self-fitting, head-lined journal bearings, locomotive bells and brasses. Its large works are located at 21 Ontario street. The Buda Foundry Company has large works at Harvey, Ill., devoted to the manufacture of wood wheels, hand and push cars, railway castings and forgings,, switch stands and track supplies in general. Mr. Hewitt is thus prepared to offer the most substantial inducements to railroad companies, both as to price and quality. Many of the leading railroads centered in Chicago and other large cities, secure their supplies through him, as he devotes the closest personal attention to the filling of all orders ; inspecting material, and rigidly keeping it up to sample and terms of specification. He also furnishes material to car builders, and is rapidly enlarging his volume of trade, making his customers' interests the same as his own and pursuing a prompt, honorable policy that insures him permanent success in this branch of trade. Indeed, herein lies the secret of Mr. Hewitt's success in the past, and the future is, in his case, full of bright and encouraging prospects. Orders placed in his hands are at once given his close personal supervision, and these are attended to with a desire to return the confidence which has been so liberally accorded him.

CHAPMAN VALVE MANUFACTURING CO.

This is the largest and most successful concern of the kind in America, and its trade extends, not only throughout the entire United States and Canada, but also to all parts of the world. The Chapman Valve Manufacturing Company was incorporated in 1875 under the laws of Massachusetts, with a

COMPOSITION VALVE, SCREWED END, FOR STEAM OR WATER.   IRON BODY, BOLTED TOP, FLANGED END, FOR STEAM OR WATER.

paid-up capital of $400,000, its executive officers being Mr. S. R. Payson, president; Mr. C. J. Goodwin, treasurer, and Mr. Jason Giles, general manager. The Chicago branch, at 24 W. Lake street, was opened in 1888, under the efficient

IRON BODY, BOLTED TOP, SCREWED END, FOR STEAM OR WATER.   BELL END VALVE, FOR WATER OR GAS.

management of Mr. Edmund W. Buss, for the purpose of supplying the Western trade. The works, which have an area of six acres, are located at Indian Orchard, Mass. The various departments of these extensive works are fully equipped with the latest improved tools, machinery and ap-

pliances, operated by two splendid 150-horse power steam engines. Here 300 skilled workmen are employed, who turn out valves varying in size from a quarter inch, weighing one and a quarter pounds, to one of forty-eight inches, weighing 16,000 pounds. The Chapman Valve Manufacturing Company manufactures largely gate steam valves, gate water valves, gate ammonia valves, gate radiator valves, gate bibb valves, and fire hydrants. The Chapman valves have straight-way passages the full diameter of the connecting pipe. The body and cap or main parts of shell are of two pieces, forged or bolted together with screw, flange, hub or spigot connections, as may be desired, of heavy proportions, to withstand any extraordinary strain that may occur. The seats of the Chapman valves and gates are composed of alloys, which are almost similar to babbitt metal, but are not what is commonly used for lining boxes or similar work. The company guarantees its seats not to melt under a less heat than 430 degrees Fahrenheit. These unrivaled valves are now taking the place of globe valves in many establishments, owing to the fact that there is no loss of pressure, except the loss by fric-

ANGLE VALVE, FLANGED OR SCREWED ENDS, FOR STEAM OR WATER.   ALL IRON VALVE, FOR AMMONIA.

tion. They wear longer, and are not so liable to injury by rough handling, and are much tighter. In fact, the Chapman valves are unsurpassed for efficiency, durability and workmanship, and have no superiors in the United States or Europe, while the prices quoted for them are extremely reasonable and moderate. Mr. Buss, the western manager, was born in Boston. During the Civil war he served in company A, 45th Massachusetts Volunteers, and was present at several important battles. He was at one time P. C. of Post 70, Pennsylvania Department, G. A. R. Mr. Buss is descended from a famous old family, his grandfather serving with honor in the Revolutionary war. He has in his possession, his grandfather's diary and correspondence, when stationed at West Point and Valley Forge, from 1776 to 1778.

THE CARL ANDERSON CO.

In all the various branches of activity connected with the profession of engineering the central headquarters are always to be found in the great Western metropolis, especially in the line of mechanical skill. Among those prominent in this class, a conspicuous place belongs to The Carl Anderson Co., whose works are situated at Nos. 74 and 76 W. Lake street. The business was established in 1889, at No. 20 N. Canal street, but on the incorporation in March, 1891, the headquarters were removed to the present spacious and convenient location. Here they have greatly increased facilities for contracting for stationary and marine engines, boilers, pumps, and all kinds of well-boring machinery, and for carrying out the most extensive and thorough repairs to the complete satisfaction of all who favor them with their patronage. They have abundant resources, the capital of the company being $10,000, influential connections, and are continually developing added elements of prosperity. The Carl Anderson Co., being expert machinists and mechanical engineers, have been able to fit their premises with every suitable appliance containing the latest results of modern inventive genius, and as a consequence they perform their work with the greatest promptitude and skill, and are able to fix their rates as low as is consistent with first-class work. A large staff of skilful employes are constantly at work, and every process of manufacture and repair is carefully supervised by the practical heads of the firm. Their trade in the great departments of contracting, repairing and jobbing is coextensive with the United States, and is rapidly increasing in all the principal centers, from ocean to ocean. The officers are Mr. Carl Anderson, president, treasurer and manager, and Mr. Edward Johnson, secretary; both gentlemen of high standing and reputation in the business circles of the city. They are natives of Sweden, and are esteemed members of the Knights of Pythias and of the Order of United Workmen. Directors of the company are Carl Anderson, Geo. Goodfellow and Nelson Anderson, all practical mechanics who give close attention to the business.

O. LARSON & SON.

Of those engaged in the manufacture of furniture, and as dealers in household goods, it is very safe to say that none have so high a reputation for superior goods at low prices as Messrs. O. Larson & Son, whose spacious double warerooms are at 179-181 W. Indiana street. The foundation of this house dates from 1880 and from its inception has always been admirably conducted and managed, and a name for fair, honorable dealing acquired, which greatly redounds to the credit of the firm. The warerooms are 60x70 feet in area and arranged with an especial adaptability for the display of the goods and, convenience of customers. The Messrs. Larson manufacture a general line of furniture, and pay particular attention to orders for fine richly upholstered parlor suits in any of the styles made popular by the decrees of fashion. Besides a full and general line of furniture, a large assortment of stoves and ranges are kept in stock, also carpets in new beautiful flower and figure patterns, and curtains, window shades, oilcloths and lamps in many and varied designs. Competent salesmen are always in attendance and goods are delivered to any part of the city or environs without extra charge. Every honorable endeavor is made by the firm to please customers, and as a consequence business is brisk and active. Mr. O. Larson, who is sixty-two years of age, was born in Norway. He has lived in Chicago since 1871, enjoyed prosperity, made many friends and is held in high esteem as a business man and citizen. His son and copartner was born in the same country thirty-seven years ago. He is active, thoroughgoing, live and wide awake and is popular with all having dealings with the house.

KNAUER BROS.

No firm in the city of Chicago can lay claim to a larger establishment than Messrs. Knauer Bros., real estate and loan brokers, whose office is on the corner of Kinzie and Clark streets, for they were founded in 1855, and are entitled to an important page in the history of the annals of the city. Born in Germany they came to Chicago in 1848, when the place was but a small settlement, without a vestige of a dream of its present magnificence; and by close attention to business and adopting throughout an honorable course, which is, alas, too uncommon in these rushing times, they stand to-day without a stain upon their business career, and a bright example to the younger generation of what honesty can do for men. They largely handle their own property, have extensive interests in sub-divisions and acreage property at Kenwood, Ill. They have the handling of large estates, and manage a fine class of property for non-residents, paying taxes and receiving rents and superintending repairs. They also have at all times on their lists houses, stores and factories for sale or rent, besides acres and sub-divisions in all parts of the city and suburbs, and those wishing a desirable investment of any nature would do well to correspond with this firm. Mr. Wm. Kath takes charge of all the real estate business of this firm, and may be consulted in regard to investments at any time.

BRAUN ILLUSTRATING CO.

There is no single particular about a firm's business that is so indicative of their business methods as their style of stationery and job work. Probably one of the largest and most extensive of this kind of decorators' or engravers' is the well-known Braun Illustrating Company of Nos. 328 to 334 Dearborn street. This splendid establishment has been many years in existence and has earned a most enviable reputation in its special line. They do a general engraving business in wood, wax and half tone, also zinc-etching and the finest quality of work, making a specialty, however, of half tone work. The officers of the company are H. A. Braun, president, E. L. Braun, vice-president, and Louis Braun, treasurer, all of whom are practical and experienced engravers with established reputations in their line of business, and under their talented management of the same, thoroughly understanding its every detail, they are making their way in the illustrating line in this city that bids soon to reach vast proportions.

JAMES A. MILLER & CO.

In 1875 Mr. William G. McCormack established the fire insurance business which, since 1880, has been carried on by his former associates and successors, James A. Miller, John T. Sweetland, and P. J. Kerwin, under the style of James A. Miller & Co. Under their able direction, the business has increased to a gratifying extent, which is not to be wondered at, when the experience of the gentlemen composing the firm is taken into account. On matters of fire insurance Mr. James A. Miller is facile princeps, one of the ablest, at least, of fire underwriters in the city. Mr. Sweetland and Mr. Kerwin have each had twenty-one years of experience, both having been connected with Mr. McCormack as employes. In all matters, therefore, relating to fire insurance it is obvious that the most implicit confidence can be placed in James A. Miller & Co., whose experience and technical knowledge reaches that of experts. The agency employs eleven persons, and is located at Nos. 169 to 171 La Salle street, Chicago, the offices being well fitted and arranged for its purposes. Messrs. James A. Miller & Co. represent the following insurance companies, all of which are of the first rank: Liverpool & London & Globe; Western Insurance Co. of Pittsburgh; Peoples' Insurance Co. of Pittsburgh; Phenix Insurance Co. of Brooklyn; New Hampshire Insurance Co. of Manchester, N. H., etc. These companies, which have literally been "tried as by fire," represent that due conservatism of management which bears the best of fruit in times of stress, and are always ready to meet their obligations promptly. The firm have represented the Liverpool & London since 1879, the Western and People's for ten years, the Phenix of Brooklyn for four years, and the New Hampshire since 1879. Mr. James A. Miller is a member of the Board of Trade and of the Fire Underwriters' Association, and the firm have a reputation for honorable dealing and special skill that have made an excellent business, the effect of which is a benefit alike to insurer and agent.

R. WALLACE & SONS' MFG. CO.

This is the Chicago branch of the famous R. Wallace & Sons' Mfg. Co., manufacturers of sterling silver and nickel silver tableware and fine table cutlery, whose factories are located in Wallingford, Conn., and salesrooms in this city at 86 Wabash avenue. In their factories they employ 500 skilled workmen, and turn out tableware and cutlery that are

absolutely unsurpassed for quality, elegance of design, and workmanship. This industry was established in Wallingford in 1855, and Mr. Wallace, the founder, was the first manufacturer in the United States to make spoons of hard metal, known as German silver. The Chicago branch is under the careful management of Mr. Geo. M. Wallace, who promptly fills orders at the lowest possible prices. The premises occupied here are commodious and are fully stocked with velvet and morocco cases of spoons, knives and forks, salts, peppers, tea and coffee sets, trays, butter dishes, fruit stands, cake baskets, etc., which are general favorites with the trade, owing to their great salability and intrinsic merits. The business is wholesale, and the trade of this branch extends throughout the Western and Northwestern states. A specialty is made of sterling silver tableware, coffee spoons, tea, dessert and tablespoons, dessert and medium forks, and silver handle medium and dessert knives, peppers, salts, napkin rings, etc., made up in numberless combinations. In plush or leatherette cases, for wedding and other presents. Polished oakwood trunks, with silver combinations, consisting of any number of pieces up to two hundred and fifty, are also made.

JAMES C. GAFFNEY & CO.

A prominent and representative house engaged in the real estate business in this city is that of Messrs. James C. Gaffney & Co., of 84 and 86 La Salle street. This house was established in February, 1890, and has been conducting important business transactions ever since. Mr. Gaffney, the proprietor, is one of the most prominent and influential citizens, and is recognized as a representative business man of enterprise, and a most worthy citizen. A general real estate business is carried on in all the various branches, making a specialty of acreage and subdivision property at Tolleston, Lake county, Ind., consisting of a hundred and twenty acres, which he subdivides to suit purchaser. This is a new town, lately settled, and the subdivisions he has laid out are some of the finest in the neighborhood, both as to location and accessibility, and the most eligible sites for homeseekers and investors. Every inducement is offered to customers; abstracts furnished free of charge. He also buys and sells outright, manages estates, takes entire charge of non-resident property, and negotiates loans on bond and first mortgage at favorable rates. Upon his books are full descriptions of the most eligible bargains available in lots, and also country property, and conservative investors, who act on his advice and sound judgment can in all cases rely on securing a steady income, with a prospective increase of values. The proprietor is a recognized authority as regards both present and prospective values of the residential and business property of Chicago and its vicinity, while his extensive connections afford excellent facilities for the immediate disposal of any real estate placed in his hands. He has an influential and liberal clientage, numbering among his patrons many wealthy investors and active operators. Mr. Gaffney is a native of Rochester, N. Y., formerly resided in Kansas City six years, and has been in Chicago only about fifteen months, building up this extensive patronage in so short a time, which alone speaks for itself. He is a thoroughgoing exponent of those enduring principles of equity and honor, and well merits the success attained in his active and enterprising career.

ROBERT R. HESS.

This gentleman is a native of the good old Empire state, and established himself in Chicago in the business of wood engraving in 1886, and is now so closely identified in the progress of art, and with the business interests of Chicago, that it is safe to predict that here he will cast anchor. Mr. Hess followed his chosen calling in the city of 'Brotherly Love" for several years before coming to the great West. Like many another pilgrim that has sought the "Fair City" by the shores of Lake Michigan in search of better prospects and wealth galore. Mr. Hess has met with gratifying success. His efforts find ready appreciation and sale, and the demand is for more. The modern wood-cut has gained for itself a proud place in art. In spite of the innumerable cheap and flashy substitutes that have been thrust upon the market of late years, for true and faithful presentation of outline and shade with that living, speaking fidelity to nature which constitutes true art, the wood-cut is still the choice of the connoisseur. The highest ambition of the imitator is to approach in perfection the real. Thus the lithograph, photo-gravures and innumerable other pretenders may imitate, but never can equal the product of the wood engraver. The subject of this sketch is an enthusiast in his art, and has given it the best years of his life. He has traveled all over the world to acquaint himself with the works of the old masters, and to study nature in all its phases, the great educator and unfailing source of inspiration to the true artist. He thus brings to his work the gift of genius, enthusiasm inspired by success, and that practical knowledge, acquired only by travel, so essential to the success of an artist. Mr. Hess' specialty is landscape drawing, and he has a fine collection of views and plates of real merit. He is favored with a very liberal patronage from the better class of trade. His office is at 126 Washington street, and he will be pleased at all times to estimate on any and all work in his line, and would recommend him as a gentleman with whom satisfactory dealings are always assured.

GREGSON & FISCHER.

The importance of Chicago as the great wholesale center of the West for the produce commission trade is forcibly illustrated by a review of several of the leading concerns in business here. Prominent among the number thus referred to is the progressive and reliable house of Messrs. Gregson & Fischer, whose office and salesroom are situated at 134 W. Randolph street. This business was established three years ago by Messrs. Geo. Gregson and H. F. Fischer, who possess widespread and influential connections and an intimate knowledge of the wants of the trade. They occupy a commodious store, and

deal extensively in butter, cheese, eggs, poultry, game, veal, fruits, vegetables, etc. The firm are regular receivers of large consignments of produce from the best producing sections of the country, and their trade extends throughout the Southern, Western and Northwestern states. Sales are made in wholesale lots only at the lowest ruling market prices, while all orders are filled with dispatch, and goods are shipped direct from producers on orders. Liberal advances are made on consignments of first-class produce and quick sales and immediate returns are the characteristics of this responsible house. Mr. Gregson was born in Canada, but has resided in Chicago for the last twelve years, while Mr. Fischer is a native of Iowa. They are commended to shippers and dealers alike, as well worthy of every trust and confidence. Messrs. Gregson & Fischer refer, by permission, to the Prairie State National Bank, and First National Bank of Englewood. They have a branch at Englewood.

I. FRANKENSTEIN.

Fine tailoring is an indispensable requisite to the genteel well-dressed man. No art of modern times has made such remarkable development and progress as the tailors' art. The variety and beauty of fabrics now produced and the refined tastes of his patrons give him inspiration and encourage him to greater efforts in the production of neatly fitting, becomingly chosen and well-made garments. Chicagoans are rapidly and certainly coming to the front as good dressers. In the period of her adolescence, when the "Garden City" was being developed from the swamps and sand hills that skirted the western shores of Lake Michigan, and during the trying period of regeneration after the great fires of 1871 and 1873, her people were too busy to dress well, anything in the way of garments that gave shelter and protection from the

elements, with a decent regard for appearances was, then good enough for the hustling Chicago business man. But now in the zenith of success, with the bright glowing prospects of future achievements, he can afford to, and does, pay due attention to the amenities of dress and style, nothwithstanding the sallies of the Eastern press to the contrary. This happy change in our conditions has called into existence a great number of establishments for the production of fine artistic clothing. Prominent among these is the fine custom tailoring establishment of Isidor Frankenstein at 860 W. Madison street, Mr. Frankenstein has an experience of several years in the tailoring business, and was connected with the house of Messrs. Kuh, Nathan & Fisher, importers and dealers in fine cloths, on Fifth avenue, where he became thoroughly familiar with the trade and its requirements. His practical knowledge of the tailoring business is extensive, and he has in his employ a force of skilled and experienced workmen for the production of fine goods. Mr. Frankenstein has been engaged in his present enterprise five years, and has built up a fine trade. His close attention to the business and his careful study of the wants and interests of his patrons have served to attract the confidence and patronage of a large and respectable custom. Mr. Frankenstein is an active man socially. He is a member of the Royal Arcanum and also of the Independent Order of Foresters, Independent Order of Odd Fellows, and Patriotic Order of Sons of America. He is a popular man personally and enjoys the confidence and regard of a large following of warm friends, who guarantee his work to be first-class, both in fit and workmanship. His trade is spreading rapidly, the public seeing that his work and fit are not to be surpassed by any house in his line in the city.

F. G. BUCKELY & BRO.

Any one walking through the residential localities of Chicago in an evening, and peeping in at the gaslit parlors, cannot fail to be impressed with the taste and culture of interior decorations, and it is to such firms as that of Messrs. F. G. Buckely & Bro. that we are indebted for guiding our ideas in this refined direction. Their handsome double store is located at 671 and 673 Larrabee street, and comprises ground floor and basement, 45x125 feet in dimensions. The basement is devoted to storage and to the paint shop, while a handsome office fitted up in bank style is on the ground floor; and in No. 671 will be found a stock of paints, oils, colors, varnishes, shellac, enamels, brushes, glass, sandpaper and artists' materials, while 673 contains a magnificent display of wallpapers. The place is fully equipped with every convenience and appliance necessary for the attractive display of the large and handsome stock of goods on hand. The business was established sixteen years ago by Mr. F. G. Buckely, and in 1882 was continued as Buckely & Schumacher. In 1888 a dissolution took place, Mr. Schumacher retiring, and Mr. J. A. Buckely was admitted to partnership under the present style. They undertake all kinds of interior decorations and house and sign painting, and the demands of the business find employment for thirty skilled hands. Estimates are furnished and jobbing punctually attended to. The assortment of wallpapers, friezes, dados and ceiling decorations embraces a line that ranks as high in the estimation of art critics and interior decorators as any goods in the same line of industry in any portion of the world, and the trade is derived principally from the leading and most distinguished citizens, while the prices are unusually low, and patrons of the firm can rest assured that any and all representations that are made will be strictly carried out.

THE ROYAL REMEDY & EXTRACT CO.

The above house, with laboratory at Dayton, O., and branch office at 51 Wabash avenue, Chicago, was founded in 1876 by the present president of the company, Mr. Irvin C. Souders, who is the originator of Souders' Elegant Flavoring Extracts. This was continued till 1888, when it was formed into a stock company and again the inventive genius of Mr. Souders produced the now famous Souders' "Sweet Wheat" chewing gum. It was a success from the start and became known throughout the United States and part of Europe. Under his supervision the company continued putting out new brands until they now make twelve different kinds. Prominent among them are "Merry Bell", which became so popular that millions of children were made glad by "Merry Bell" chewing gum. "Tolu" sugar plums is also a favorite gum and is known from lake to gulf. We cannot help calling your attention to their advertisment on inside front cover. It shows the originality of their packages and the neatness with which they put up goods. Their flavoring extracts are absolutely pure and it is conceded that for the money there is nothing to excel them anywhere on the market. Their Chicago office was not opened till May, 1891, when there became such a demand for these goods that it was impossible to supply the trade without an office in Chicago. Mr. J. A. Ulrich is manager of the Chicago office and he has been very successful in building up this part of the business. Mr. Ulrich was traveling salesman for the firm several years and subsequently became a stockholder in the enterprise. He is a native of Ohio.

C. A. STORER & CO.

Unquestionably the finest drug store in Chicago is that of C. A. Storer & Co., at the corner of Rush and Ohio streets. This business was established in 1890 by Messrs. C. A. Storer and A. Obermann, both well known and reputable pharmacists. The location is one of the most desirable to be had in the city, being under the magnificent, new, Virginia hotel. Everything that could be done to make this a beautiful and attractive pharmacy, has been done faithfully, The fronts and cases are of the finest plate glass; the fixtures, counters and all woodwork are of solid mahogany. The decorations are rare novelties and everything is harmoniously and tastefully blended. One of the finest soda fountains in Chicago is in the store, and the entire apparatus cost over $3,000, Everything in the line of drugs and chemicals is carried in stock, also fine toilet necessities, fancy articles, supplies for the sick-room, physicians' and surgeons' supplies; braces, trusses and rubber goods. Perfumes, sachet powders and proprietary articles may be had in all kinds and varieties. A specialty is made of compounding physicians' prescriptions, and great care is taken to insure accuracy and purity. The store is open at all hours, and orders by telephone are given prompt attention and delivery. The patronage of this pharmacy is deservedly large, and the proprietors stand in the highest social and business circles. Mr. C. A. Storer is a native of Watertown, Wis., and has resided in Chicago for five years; he is a registered member of the Illinois State Board of Pharmacy and is prominent in leading social circles. Mr. A. Obermann has resided in Chicago for eleven years and is the proprietor of the popular North side pharmacy; he is well known and highly respected in leading professional and business circles.

H. P. BRUELL.

A popular and reliable place to have carriage and wagon painting done is at the establishment of H. P. Bruell, 521 and 523 Throop street, near Blue Island avenue. Mr. Bruell is a practical painter and has an excellent reputation as a painter of merit. He uses only the best materials in his work, and is assisted by thoroughly competent and experienced hands. He has been established at the above address for four years, and has built up an extensive and appreciative patronage. He confines himself to carriage and wagon painting, letter-ing and varnishing, and gives all his talent and energy to so perform his labor as to make it a lasting advertisement of his ability, hence his success. Mr. Bruell has built up a good city trade, and has at the present writing, four assistants employed steadily, with prospect of an increased business. The demands of the business are such that two floors, each 40x60 feet in area, of a large brick building are used for office and workshop, and these are usually filled with work in all stages. Mr. Bruell is a native of Germany, and is a young man of genius and ability, he is active and industrious and of the highest business reputation. He believes in faithfulness to detail and close application, and his work is thus always highly satisfactory. The business is growing steadily and will continue to prosper as only honorable methods and just dealing are known to this house.

KASPAR & KAREL.

The most popular banking institution on the West side, is unquestionably that of Messrs. Kaspar & Karel. This is a private banking concern of high financial standing. It was established in 1888 by Mr. W. Kaspar and John Karel, with a capital of $100,000, and has had a most successful and prosperous business career. Messrs. Kaspar & Karel are active, progressive and energetic business men, and have displayed every fitness for the highest business connections. They are able real estate managers, thoroughly posted on values, and conservative in their appraisements. They do a general banking business, draw drafts on all principal cities of this and foreign countries, receive deposits subject to check, buy and sell sterling exchange in all parts of Europe, having correspondents in all the leading cities of the United States, Canada and Europe. They also buy and sell real estate securities, and act as agents for all the leading European steamship lines. Many tickets are sold for passage each year and the house has a reputation of the most flattering character throughout Europe. In the placing of insurance Messrs. Kaspar & Karel have many advantages, being the representatives of the leading and strongest companies of this country and England. They are prepared to negotiate loans of any magnitude, having the control of great amounts of capital from eastern and foreign investors, waiting for use in good securities. The house has magnificent offices at 623 to 627 Blue Island avenue, these being fitted up handsomely and furnished with every modern convenience. Messrs. Kaspar & Karel are both natives of Bohemia and have resided in Chicago for twenty-seven years.

ERRICO BROTHERS.

In consequence of the rapid advance made in the last few years in the United States in wealth, culture, and refinement, there has arisen a demand for objects of elegance and works of art, and to supply these the principal countries of Europe are diligently searched, and their most artistic goods imported by our merchants. One of the most reliable and successful concerns in this line in Chicago is that of Messrs. Errico Brothers, importers of Italian works of art, jewelry and fancy goods, whose store is located at No. 170 Wabash avenue. The firm's headquarters in America are at No. 862 Broadway, New York, and they likewise have branches in Newport, R. I., and Saratoga Springs, N. Y. They occupy a spacious and handsomely equipped store, 20x100 feet in dimensions, fully stocked with all kinds of Italian works of art, jewelry, stationery and fancy goods. The firm handle only really superior goods, and quote prices that necessarily attract the attention of close and careful buyers. Messrs. Errico Brothers import direct from the most celebrated Italian houses, and their trade, which is retail, extends throughout Chicago and the adjacent cities. This business was established in 1859 in New York by Messrs. Errico Brothers, the present proprietors. The Chicago branch was opened in 1890 and is under the able and energetic management of Mr. Louis Errico, who is widely known in business circles for his promptness and integrity.

THE FECKER BREWING CO.

One of the latest and most important additions to the great brewing interests of the city is the organization of the Fecker Brewing Co., whose fine new establishment, built only last year at Nos. 871 to 897 Dudley street, on the corner of Bloomingdale road, is equipped with all the modern appliances required for the business. Mr. Fecker, the esteemed president, is a typical American, and brings to bear a wide experience, having been for many years foreman of the M. Brane Brewing Co., so favorably known in the business. Mr. Fecker presides over a corporate body, whose resources are ample, and whose facilities are as nearly perfect as possible. The brewery is of brick, and is arranged on a most convenient plan, which secures the greatest economy, both of time and labor. The malthouse contains five stories and the brewhouse three, each giving a floor space of no less than 7,500 square feet. A fine steam engine of 100 horse power runs the machinery, and everything is on a par with the great business done and the brilliant prospects of this prosperous company. A thirty-five ton ice machine has been installed, and the capacity of this well-equipped establishment amounts to no less than 40,000 barrels every year. They give constant employment to upwards of thirty men and fifteen horses, and number among their permanent patrons many of the largest hotels, saloons, etc., in the city and suburbs. They are brewers of the famous Western brands, "Chicago Bräu," and "Garden City Bräu," and have a high reputation for their pure, sparkling and generally superior beer. Mr. Fecker offers every facility to customers in the way of business, and receives orders by telephone (call No. 7586), as well as by mail and orally, the most prompt and careful attention being paid to them all, and their requirements at once attended to. This company invariably practices the best methods in every detail of the business, and has already built up a large trade upon a solid and enduring basis.

ACME BAG CO.

The manufacture of bags for flour is an industry requiring considerable skill and experience. It is one in which the Acme Bag Company find full scope for their energies, and one in which they hold the leading position throughout this great section of the Union. The factory is located at No. 220 to 224 E. Kinzie street, with ample accomodation for a large force of skilled hands, and for the machines, appliances and general equipment of the most improved kind, necessary to the successful prosecution of this industry. The company number among their customers all the great millers in the Western and Northwestern states. The capital of the company is $50,000. The increasing demand for bags in preference to barrels taxes this company to its utmost, so much so that during the last six months it has doubled its capacity.

E. HILL TURNOCK.

Among the new school and generation of architects, whose work is exciting great interest, may be mentioned Mr. E. Hill Turnock, of Nos. 21 and 23 Kent building, and Nos. 151 and 153 Monroe street. Eight years of training, preparation and experience in the office of that renowned architect, Mr. W. L. B. Jenney, added to a thorough course in Art Schools, both in London and Chicago, preceded his establishment in June, 1890, and his conspicuous success, and already wide and growing reputation, abundantly prove the great advantage of a thorough professional training before attempting the duties and responsibilities of an architect's work. Mr. Turnock entertains only the highest ideal of the functions of his profession, and practices the best methods in all the details of his work. He has designed and erected many large buildings since establishing his office, among them the Methodist church on the corner of Dearborn and Thirty-first streets, a building of which any firm might be proud. His other commissions include many large buildings, flats, banks, etc., not only in Chicago, but in the outlying suburban towns and other States. Mr. Turnock combines the profession of an engineer with that of an architect, and is equally skilled in both. He occupies commodious offices, and has every facility at command for executing the largest contracts in either of his departments. He is a native of London, England, but has resided in this country during the past eighteen years, winning high encomiums for his conspicuous talents and honorable methods. His business is a large one and constantly increasing, as building after building eloquently proclaims his skill; and we have no hesitaon in expressing the well-founded conviction that Mr. Turnock will yet rival the most distinguished architects and engineers in this Western metropolis.

J. W. SALLADAY & CO.

A prominent house engaged in the commission business is that of Mr. J. W. Salladay trading as J. W. Salladay & Co.), whose office and warehouse are centrally located at No. 199 South Water street. This business was established fourteen years ago by its present proprietor. He was born in Michigan, has now been a respected resident of this city for the past eighteen years, and is a recognized authority on the value and quality of foreign and domestic fruit products. The premises

occupied by him comprise the east half of the four story structure at the address indicated, being equipped with elevator and every accommodation for the proper storage of stock, and the general advantageous prosecution of the business. He handles on commission every description of fruits and general produce, making a prominent specialty of apples. An inspection of the large stock at all times stored, and an investigation of the manner in which the trade is conducted, point at once to a system of order and method that pervade every department, which must in the nature of things result in permanent advantages to patrons.

T. A. PETERSON & CO.

Among the best known and most responsible firms engaged in the real estate business on the North side is that of T. A. Peterson & Co. of 319 E. Division street. Established several years ago by Mr. C, O. Olsen, this popular and reliable firm has from its inception steadily won its way to public favor and confidence, and numbers among its clientele some of the staunchest citizens in the community. Mr. Peterson assumed control of the business a year and a half ago, and has since conducted it in a manner befitting the reputation of his predecessor. The firm transacts a general real estate business, buying, selling, letting, exchanging city and suburban property of every description, also collecting rents, paying taxes, superintending repairs and assuming the general supervision and management of estates, for residents and non-residents. Loans are procured on bonds and mortgages while investments of all kinds are desirably placed, and insurance risks effected with all the first-class companies. Mr. Peterson always has on his lists some choice city and suburban corner lots and invites correspondence. His office is roomy and nicely fitted and is centrally located in the Division Street Bank building. Mr. Peterson is a native of Sweden and has been in Chicago twenty-five years. He is a man of strict probity in his dealings, and shows absolute impartiality to his numerous clients.

NATIONAL SILK MFG. CO.

In Chicago there are many reliable and responsible houses engaged in the manufacture and handling of silk goods, and prominent among them is that known as the National Silk Manufacturing Company. It was founded in February, 1891, and although but a limited space of time has elapsed since the business was inaugurated, it has under its present efficient management built up a business connection which places the house in a prominent position in the ranks of the trade. The company is made up of several of the leading and influential business men of this city, and its management is in the hands of Mr. William M. Provines. This gentleman was formerly engaged in business in this city on his own account, and brings to bear an extensive experience on the requirements of the trade. The offices of the company are centrally located in room 9 of the building at Nos. 221 and 223 Fifth avenue. They are neatly fitted up and furnished. The company handle all kinds of dress silks, either in the piece or made up, which they offer to their patrons on the popular plan of payments by installments. They purchase direct at first hand from the most reliable manufacturers, and their excellent facilities enable them to offer the finest goods to the public at prices that defy competition. They make a specialty of ladies' cloaks, sacques, hosiery, underwear and other silk goods, and their trade is rapidly extending to all parts of the state. Several traveling salesmen are employed, and it is the intention of the company to establish agencies throughout all parts of the Union. Mr. Provines is an energetic business man, and under his able management the success of the company is well assured.

H. ZIMMERMANN & SON.

An old established and well-known cigar manufactory is that of H. Zimmermann & Son. This house has been in continuous business for over twenty years and has a reputation second to none in Chicago. It was founded by Mr. H. Zimmermann, and in 1881 the firm name was changed by the admission of Mr. Julius Zimmermann, the son of the founder. The house occupies an important place among the business enterprises of the city; its long and successful career has been due to the superiority of the goods manufactured, which have never been for a day allowed to deteriorate in quality. This house manufactures the celebrated "Fancy Shaped" cigars, making over two hundred kinds in all. Among their best known brands of five and ten cent cigars are the "Volonta," "La Radosa," "Partigas," "Principes," etc. In these the house has an immense trade in all parts of the city and surrounding country. The factory is located at 196 Ontario street, and is a large building, 25x100 feet in dimensions. The second floor is used as an office and packing room, and the third and fourth floors as a factory. Here forty skilled cigar makers are kept constantly employed, with ten strippers and two clerks; the capacity of the factory being 50,000 cigars a week. The workmen are all paid the highest rates of wages current, and thus the house secures the best workmanship possible. The tobacco is all purchased by Mr. Zimmermann, who has it carefully selected and brings his long experience and superior skill to bear in procuring the finest grades. The best of Havana leaf is used and no inferior stock handled for any grade of goods. The store is located at 189 N. Clark street, and is beautifully fitted up and stocked with everything calculated to cheer the heart of the smoker; cigars, tobacco, pipes, pouches and everything of the kind are to be had at reasonable rates, and the selection of cigars is not excelled by any house in Chicago. A specialty is made of box trade, which is extensive. Mr. H. Zimmermann is a native of Germany and a Chicago resident for thirty years. He is a prominent and active business man of the highest standing. Mr. Julius Zimmermann is a native of Chicago, and is well and favorably known as an enterprising man of business and a delightful social companion and the firm are increasing its business each year brought about by its careful management.

F. L. LADE.

There has never been a time, perhaps, when greater attention was given to the proper care of horses and other valuable animals, than is done to-day, and the progress in the veterinary profession keeps fully abreast of that of the medical practitioner. A leading representative veterinary surgeon and dentist in Chicago is the gentleman whose name forms the caption of this sketch, and whose office is located at No. 361 W. Randolph street. Dr. Frank L. Lade, was born in the state of New York, and pursued a thorough course of study, theoretical and practical, at the Ontario Veterinary College, one of the most famous institutions of the kind on the American continent. He graduated as a member of the class of 1888-'89, and removed to Chicago in 1890. Shortly afterwards he opened his office and embarked in the practice of his profession. His ability soon became widely recognized, and his practice has rapidly developed, so that to-day he stands in a prominent rank. Dr Lade does a call and consulting business only, not having as yet established a hospital or stables. His office premises are centrally located, easy of access, and are in direct telephone connection with all parts of the city and vicinity. They are of ample dimensions, neatly appointed and well equipped with all necessary appliances for the prosecution of the business on a satisfactory footing. A full stock of drugs, lotions, liniments, etc., is always on hand, and animals are carefully attended to at the shortest notice, while the fees charged are very moderate. Dentistry is made a leading specialty and satisfaction is guaranteed. All calls, either night or day, receive prompt attention. Dr. Lade is a gentleman of great promise, and his well-deserved success is a source of gratification to his numerous friends and well-wishers, who include all who know him.

MOORE BROS.

This firm are extensive dealers in furniture, carpets and household goods, and everything that is necessary for the furnishing of a house from top to bottom. The business was founded in 1881, by the present firm, at 455 West Madison street, and in 1885 moved to larger quarters, at 281-283 same street, and in 1886 moved to present location, 287-289 West Madison street. Their establishment is one of the largest and finest in the city, comprising seven floors, 50x100 feet in dimensions, each floor being well stocked with goods. The furniture department is stocked to repletion with everything that can be desired in fine and modern furniture, art goods, bric-a-brac, statuary and fine household decorations, including parlor suits, chamber sets, and dining room, hall and library furniture, besides innumerable special pieces in wood, silk, brocades and plushes. They manufacture all kinds of artistic furniture to order, and the most elegant fabrics are used in the upholstering. And all the work is done by skilled artisans and upholsterers. It has always been the aim of this house to produce goods which should rank superior in the trade, not only in the quality of material, but in the equally important matters of tasteful designs and artistic workmanship. The stock of goods is large and valuable, amounting to $65,000 to $70,000, and are sold either for cash, or on the popular installment plan. Sixty-five hands are employed in the establishment, as well as 10 teams for delivering goods to all parts of the city. The trade is large, first-class and influential throughout the city and the entire state. The proprietors are both young men and were born in New York, but have been residents of Chicago since 1863.

BERGER BROS.

A remarkable example of what industry, thrift and fair dealing may do, is exemplified in the case of Berger Brothers, one of the leading wholesale and retail firms dealing in charcoal. They started in business in this city eight years ago, on a very limited scale, selling but 4,000 bushels of their coal. It has grown since, until the past year their sales exceeded 70,000 bushels. They handle charcoal, wholesale and retail, and make a specialty of carload lots, having railroad yards on the Michigan Central and the Wabash roads, from which they are prepared to fill all orders in the Northwest. In charcoal they sell in carloads and casks to any part of the Northwest. Their city offices are at Nos. 170 and 172 Michigan street, where they employ a full corps of men and a sufficient number of teams to take care of their retail trade, which is constantly increasing, both at home and abroad. The senior member of the firm, Mr. William G. Berger, was born in Jefferson, Wis., and has been a resident of Chicago since 1872. He had been in the employ of several leading coal houses in this city before engaging in business for himself. The junior member of the firm, Mr. Robert Berger, is also a native of Wisconsin, and was formerly in the employ of J. G. Spaulding & Co. Both are members of the Independent Order of Foresters, are popular in social and business circles, and merit the prosperity their energetic methods have earned them.

WM. DAVIDSON & CO.

One of the old established and thoroughly reliable meat and vegetable markets of the North side is that of William Davidson & Co. This business was established twelve years ago by William Davidson, under the present firm name. The house has become well known and is recognized as being a reliable place in which to trade, the proprietors having a reputation for honesty and fair treatment of the first order. The company occupies the ground floor and basement of Nos. 78 and 80 N. State street, having here a floor space, 20x80 feet in dimensions. All kinds of fresh, salt and smoked meat are sold, the fresh meats being had from the abbatoirs daily, and embrace the finest cuts of beef, pork, mutton and veal. Poultry, fish, game and fruits are handled in season, and vegetables, fresh from the growers, are always to be had of the finest assortments. The business done by this house is representative; four assistants are employed and three teams are utilized for delivering purposes. The telephone call is 3305, and all orders received by telephone meet with prompt attention and free delivery. The gentlemen who compose this firm are well-known, upright and popular business men. Mr. Wm. Davidson is a native of Glasgow, Scotland, and a resident of Chicago for eighteen years, he is well known and highly respected. Mr. Gus Hopp is a native of Quiney, Ill., and is manager of the Crown Creamery Co; he is also popular and trustworthy. The business of the house is of the most stable character and reflects great credit upon the proprietors.

J. O. ALLARD.

Among those who have acquired a wide reputation for manufacturing a superior quality of confectionery and ice-cream must be named Mr. Joseph O. Allard, who is located at No. 3647 Wentworth avenue. Mr. Allard has had a long practical experience in this business, and brings to bear upon it a full knowledge of its every detail. He commenced operations on his own account several months ago, and although a short time has elapsed since then, owing to the superiority of his goods he has built up a fine trade. This business he has ample premises and is well provided with every convenience for filling orders promptly. He manufactures a general line of fine candies and confectionery and ice cream of all flavors, and supplies a wide spread demand. The best materials only are used, and every care is exercised to render satisfaction to customers. In the store and in the parlor adjoining icecream and ices are served at popular prices. Mr. Allard is a German by birth. He came to Chicago fourteen years ago and is a wideawake pushing business man, well deserving the success he has won and enjoyed.

MADLUNQ, EIDMANN & McCORTNEY.

There is in the city of Chicago, the metropolis of the West, no feature of progress of equal importance with that of real estate. Among those occupying a leading position in the business who are eminently well qualified by long experience and practical ability for rendering service of the most valuable character is the firm of Madlunq, Eidmann & McCortney, whose office is 420 Chamber of Commerce building, with branch at 6857 Halsted street, Englewood. This firm makes a specialty of handling South side property in such desirable sections as Englewood, Hyde Park and Town of Lake, where they have subdivision holdings of upward of one hundred acres, which are being disposed of in building lots at the very lowest prices, and which offer opportunities for industrious men to procure a home, or those seeking investment for speculation. They also handle all manner of city and suburban real property, and possess unsurpassed facilities for the prompt negotiation of loans on bond and mortgage. The trio of co-partners are all natives of this city. Mr. Wm. Madlunq was for a period of ten years engaged in the dry goods business. Mr. H. F. Eidmann was formerly connected with the Northern Pacific railroad for five years, and Mr. J. H. McCortney was for five years with E. A. Cummings & Co., in the real estate business. They are all well and favorably known in financial and real estate circles, and their reputation as business men is of the highest character. The firm sells South side property on a plan, and in this way alone have during the past year disposed of many hundred acres divided up into building lots.

HANS FEHR & CO.

A widely known business house in this section of the city is that of H. Fehr & Co., dealers in stoves, tin and hardware and all kinds of tools, table and pocket cutlery, etc. This business was founded five years ago by Mr. H. Fehr, who conducted it successfully alone until last year, when the firm became Fehr & Co., and the house maintains a high reputation for reliable goods and excellent work. The building occupied is owned by Mr. Fehr. It is a 24x60 foot structure, located at 249 North avenue, most admirably arranged and appointed for the successful operation of trade. A large and first-class assortment of stoves, tinware, shelf hardware, hollow-ware, wood and willow ware, and house furnishing goods of every description is kept constantly on hand, and also tin, copper, sheet and galvanized iron, and metal work is executed with promptness and dispatch in the most excellent manner, and jobbing of every description is reliably attended to. Several skilled workmen are regularly employed, estimates are furnished and contracts made, while all charges are as low as consistent with fair dealing. The patronage which this house enjoys is of a widespread and permanent character, the proprietor leaving no effort untried to please every customer. He is a practical, experienced man, thoroughly conversant with the business in all its branches, his establishment being a most desirable one with which to enter into commercial relations. Mr. Fehr was born in Switzerland, but has resided in Chicago eleven years, and is a prominent member of the Schweyzer Club, while the Co., Mr. Jurgenson, is a Chicagoan by birth, and sustains a high reputation in the community.

GREGORY BROTHERS.

Every day creates new uses and demands for the printers' work. As a result of its great importance to man it is the most progressive of all arts, displaying wonderful ingenuity in its startling developments. Chicago has long been recognized as the great center for the printers' and publishers' art. Block after block of colossal structures are devoted to the different branches of "the art preservative." Mountains of capital and armies of men are employed in this monster industry. One of the most enterprising firms in this great trade in Chicago is the well-known printing house of Gregory Brothers, 788 W. Madison street. The firm com-

prises three brothers, C. D. Gregory, W. E. Gregory and E. L. Gregory, all practical printers and experienced business men of excellent standing. This establishment is complete in every detail, embracing all the best machinery and latest improvments for the production of first-class work. Their outfit includes two fine job presses and an improved cylinder press, and other machinery of the latest and best design, a gas engine, etc. Their product includes everything in the book and job printing line, for which they enjoy special facilities. They give special attention to society work and commercial job printing. Estimates furnished on all kinds of fine job printing. Their work is guaranteed to be equal to the best and their prices and terms are always reasonable. Gregorys Bros. are natives of Chicago. Their present establishment was opened two years ago and has been very successful from the start. Their trade is rapidly increasing. By close attention to business and a faithful devotion to the interests of their patrons they hope to merit and receive a liberal share of the public favor in the future.

I. TOMLINSON & CO.

A newly established and one of the most reliable firms in this section of Chicago, actively engaged in the manufacture and sale of hardwood lumber of all kinds, is that of Messrs. I. Tomlinson & Co., whose office and yard are situated at Twenty-second and Laflin streets. This business was established in 1891 by Messrs. I. Tomlinson, E. Heath and K. T. Witbeck, all of whom have had long experience and possess an accurate knowledge of all details of the lumber trade, and the requirements of contractors and manufacturers. Their yard is 1,000x500 feet in area, and has excellent railroad and dock facilities, 1,000 feet track, and 1,000 feet dockage. Here they keep a heavy, choice and well-seasoned stock of hardwoods, including plain and quartered oak flooring, walnut, cherry, ash, hickory, whitewood, etc. They make a specialty of car lots and special bills cut to order, and promptly fill orders at the lowest possible prices. Messrs. I. Tomlinson & Co. own and operate five well equipped mills in Arkansas, and one in Michigan, and employ there 200 workmen. Only really first-class hardwood is handled, and the trade of the firm now extends throughout the entire United States. Messrs. Tomlinson, Heath and Witbeck are all natives of Chicago. They are highly esteemed in trade circles for their enterprise, promptness and just methods, and fully merit the liberal and influential patronage secured in this important industry.

E. W. KEMPTER.

There is an immense business done in Chicago in copper and sheet iron working, one of the most responsible houses in this line being that of E. W. Kempter, whose place of business is at 32 N. State street. The business was started in this city in 1890 by Mr. Phil Kempter, and he was succeeded in July, 1891, by the present proprietor, his brother. Mr. Kempter is a native of Galena, Ill., where he learned his trade with his father, Mr. Frank Kempter, who has conducted the same kind of business in Galena for many years. Since coming to Chicago he has made many friends, and has already established a reputation for superior work and honest dealing. He occupies the ground floor of the above mentioned premises, and employs eight experienced workmen. All kinds of tin, copper and sheet iron work is done to order, and the house makes ventilators, chimney tops, conductor pipes, stove and furnace repairs, and does all kinds of roofing and repairing. Mr. Kempter is the owner and patentee of the Kempter Rockford Safety Elevator, introducing the safety elevator brake and self-closing door, a model of which he has in his store. When the door is open the elevator cannot move. He also manufactures the Daniels' Window Ventilator. Estimates are cheerfully furnished, and prices are as low as is consistent with good business management. The house has a liberal patronage and Mr. Kempter is reported favorably upon by the highest commercial authorities, and has a reputation as excellent socially as that in trade circles.

F. W. SEELOW.

Without doubt one of the leading carriage and wagon manufacturers of this section is Mr. F. W. Seelow. He has a representative and well equipped establishment at 461, 465, 467 and 471 W, Twenty-second street, where he has been established since 1880, when he began business. The business has grown

phenomenally and now assumes large proportions, having many orders from all portions of the city, as well as from various parts of this and neighboring states. Mr. Seelow is a native of Germany and came to Chicago fifteen years ago. He began the manufacture of wagons and buggies in a small way, and increased his plant yearly to meet the demands of his business, until he now has a large three-story brick manufactory, thoroughly equipped with every appliance for turning out the best work in the most satisfactory manner. Here Mr. Seelow manufactures all kinds of buggies, express, farm, lumber 'and delivery wagons. He has every facility for obtaining the best materials and employs only skilled and competent help. His manufactory is of large capacity and he keeps eighteen hands constantly employed. All kinds of repairing, painting and general jobbing is promptly attended to and the workmen are kept busy the year around building and repairing vehicles. The painting and trimming department of this establishment is one of the finest we have ever visited, and the facilities for turning out work in all of the departments are unsurpassed. Mr. Seelow is a gentleman of wide experience and a thoroughly practical mechanic as well as a business man of acknowledged ability.

J. HILGENDORF

The art of house building has been completely revolutionized by the introduction of modern machinery. In olden times the preparation of the lumber and material for the construction and finishing of an ordinary family dwelling or store building was the work of months, requiring the hard work of a large force of men; now the preliminary work of dressing and shaping the lumber and material for all parts of the building is done by machinery. The work is speedily and satisfactorily accomplished and at greatly reduced cost. Buildings are planned, staked off, framed, inclosed, plastered, plumbed, painted, finished and occupied in less time than it used to require to dress out the flooring or make the shingles. With all the saving of time, labor and money, a superior class of buildings are erected of far better style and finish, and more comfortable and convenient, than was ever dreamed of in the good old times of "hand work." The planing mill and sash factory has worked wonders for the carpenter and builders' trade. Mr. J. Hilgendorf's wood-turning and scroll-sawing establishment, at 465 and 467 W. Twenty-second street, occupies the second floor of a spacious and substantial three-story brick building, supplied with ample steam power and equipped with a vast array of the most modern wood working machinery. His specialty is wood-

turning, scroll-sawing, band-sawing and shaping, including all manner of trimming, finishing and decorating wood work, such as scrolls, brackets, columns, moldings, verandas, balconies, stair cases, cornices, etc. The business was established in 1885 and has steadily grown and increased, until it now assumes large and important proportions. Mr. Hilgendorf is a practical mechanic and has a thorough knowledge of his business. This together with his close application to his work and his good business abilities will ensure the success of his undertaking. Mr. Hilgendorf is a German by birth and has lived in Chicago for about twenty-five years.

THE HOME NATIONAL BANK.

One of the soundest and most conservatively conducted financial institutions of Chicago is "The Home National Bank," which was duly organized and incorporated under the National Banking Act in 1872, with a paid up capital of $250,-000. It has total resources of $1,765,000, and judiciously carries large amounts available in specie and legal tender notes to meet the current calls of its customers, the amounts thus held amounting to nearly half a million, while $770,000 are invested in loans and discounts. The bank has accumulated the handsome surplus fund of $100,000, besides undivided profits amounting to $125,392. The deposits average over half a million dollars, representing the active accounts of many of the leading firms and corporations of Chicago. The bank transacts a general business; discounting approved commercial paper-making collections on all points through its chain of correspondents; buying and selling foreign and domestic exchange and issuing drafts and letters of credit. The Board of Directors is composed of prominent capitalists and business men. Mr. A. M. Billings, the president, is one of Chicago's ablest financiers and one of wide range of practical experience, whose policy has ever retained the confidence of the public. In Mr. H. H. Blake the bank has a cashier of great experience and correct financial methods. The banking house is very centrally located at 184 W. Washington street and is of commodious proportions, handsomely fitted up, and in every respect convenient for the transaction of business. The bank has ever retained the confidence of the public in the highest degree and is in every respect a model financial institution.

JAMES CONLAN, JR., & CO.

In no branch of industrial activity is the demand for artistic excellence greater than in that of fine tailoring, modern clothing having to be, not only comfortable and suited to the season of the year, but also elegant and perfect in fit. A house which has done much in the creation of this improved taste is that of Messrs. James Conlan, Jr., & Co., of No, 25 N. Clark street. It was started in 1878 by Mr. H. T. Mullen, and conducted by him with conspicuous success until his lamented decease in 1888, when it passed into the hands of Mr. Conlan. This gentleman inaugurated a new era of prosperity by a complete reorganization of the business, and has now placed it in an enviable position among the successful establishments in the trade. He carries a superior stock of woolens and suitings, in all the choicest and newest patterns, shades, and textures, the best products of both foreign and domestic looms. He is a master of his trade, and employs a dozen hands, each selected for his skill in the special branch for which he is required, and he is thus enabled to guarantee an accurate fit and perfect satisfaction in every instance. There are abundant indications on all hands of the high appreciation in which Mr. Conlan is held by the most fashionable residents of the city, his patrons being found chiefly among the bankers, brokers and influential business men. He is a native of Chicago, and is an honored member of many the most select clubs, among them being the Shendon, Bournique's, and Art Institute, and he also stands high on the roll of the Catholic Order of Foresters. Mr. Conlan is a popular business man, and is abundantly worthy of the large measure of success attending his efforts.

13

THE NEWBERRY WAREHOUSE AND STORAGE COMPANY.

Prominent among the substantial firms in this city is the Newberry Warehouse and Storage Company at 79 to 83 Kinzie street. The Company was incorporated under the state laws in 1888, with a paid-up capital of $50,000. The executive board is composed of the following well-known gentlemen, viz., General Walter C. Newberry, president; Mr. Walter F. Newberry, vice-president and general manager, and Mr. Alex. H. Gunn, secretary. The premises occupied embrace a substantial brick structure, containing five stories, and provided with elevators and other accessories for the rapid and convenient handling of large quantities of non-hazardous merchandise, etc., the capacity for which is on an extensive scale, the dimensions of the building being 44x107 feet. Employment is given to an adequate force of hands to meet the demands of the liberal patronage received. The president, General Newberry, who is an active member of the Produce Exchange, was for many years at the head of the firm of W. C. Newberry & Co., one of the largest brewery supplies manufacturing concerns in Chicago, severing his connection therewith in 1890. The General is a member of Congress from the Fourth Illinois district, and late postmaster of Chicago. He was born in Waterville, N. Y. He served with great distinction during the war of the rebellion. Enlisting in the early commencement of that memorable struggle as private in the Eighty-first New York Infantry, under command of Gen. B. McClellan, he was promoted to the captaincy of his company in the place of Captain L. M. Kingman, who was killed at the battle of Seven Pines. Later, he was still further advanced, and at Gettysburg, in 1863, served on the staff of General H. M. Nagle, and, in recognition of his personal bravery in that terrible engagement, received the appointment of Major of the Twenty-fourth New York Cavalry, was advanced to Lieutenant-Colonel during the same year, and in 1864 was placed first in command of the same regiment. In 1865 he was breveted Brigadier General, which office he held at the close of the war.

F. & O. STENICKA.

Among the thoroughly qualified druggists in this city is the firm of F. & O. Stenicka, whose well-equipped pharmacy is at 4132 Wentworth avenue. The business they are now conducting with such success and ability was originally established by Mr. H. Schmidt, from whom Mr. Frank G. Stenicka bought it, and during the present year he was joined by his brother, Mr. Otto Stenicka. The firm have made many improvements about the store and recently put in a stock of pure fresh drugs and all the various articles belonging to the business. The store is one of ample dimensions, neatly and tastefully appointed and supplied with every modern convenience. The prescription laboratory is under the immediate supervision of the firm, and medicines are compounded and dispensed at all hours of the day or night. Besides the usual line of drugs and chemicals the firm have a full stock of proprietary preparations, pharmaceutical, toilet and fancy articles, supplies for the sick room and physicians' and surgeons' requisites. The store is a model of neatness, and is made attractive by handsome show windows. The Messrs. Stenicka are from Wisconsin originally, and are gentlemen of courteous manners and strict probity. They are fully alive to the requirements of the public in their line of business, and the able manner they conduct it proves at once that they are fully abreast of the times.

BEIERSDORF & LOHSAND.

The hardware trade necessarily forms a very important feature in the commerce of Chicago but there are few, if any, firms whose efforts cover so wide a compass as Messrs. Beiersdorf & Lohsand, of 154 North Wells street, near Erie street, indeed, this is the representative house of the North side. Established in 1868 by Chivill & Lenox on the present site, the business

passed into the hands of the present proprietors in 1882. They occupy commodious premises, comprising the ground floor and basement, each 20x110 feet in dimension. These are admirably fitted up and arranged, and are provided with all modern conveniences for the handling of stock and facilitating the rapid fulfillment of orders. A very large and comprehensive stock is constantly carried, embracing shelf and heavy hardware of every description, cutlery, mechanics' and carpenters' tools, as well as a large assortment of heating stoves and ranges of all prices and styles, and tin ware, enameled ware and household goods generally. But their general jobbing forms a large branch of their trade, and embraces the erection of iron smoke stacks, ventilaors, tanks, guttering and spouting as well as the execution of all work in copper, tin and sheet iron. Furnaces are also cleaned and repaired with dispatch. They make a specialty of manufacturing a variety of patented articles. The firm is ably assisted by a competent staff of clerks. The hands employed in the various branches of shop work are selected for their experience, and the central position and facilities enjoyed by the house enables it to offer inducements to customers that cannot be duplicated elsewhere. Mr. Beiersdorf has been in Chicago for twenty-two years, while Mr. Lohsand has been in this city nineteen years and takes an active interest in the order of the Odd Fellows. Both partners are practical men, and have won success by close attention to business.

FENNO & SMITH.

It was scarcely necessary for a firm whose members are as well known in insurance circles as are Mr. H. C. Fenno and Mr. W. B. Smith, of Fenno & Smith, to give a reference as to their reliability, but when they started together in partnership in the present year they were anxious to commence with an absolutely clean sheet and so they give as references The Globe National Bank, Messrs. Walker & Lowden, attorneys, and Bradstreet's Commercial Agency. Their offices are at room 513, in the Insurance Exchange, 218 La Salle street, and they employ an efficient staff of clerks for the conduct of their business. They carry on the business of Fire Insurance Brokers only, and have had many years' experience in this line, having been active in local insurance circles on a commission basis, and now they represent the largest and leading home and foreign insurance companies in the world. They have facilities for obtaining special rates and so wide is their range of connection that they can place any fire risk, however large, and of whatever nature.

JOHN SUCHY.

As everybody in civilized countries knows, the science of photography has been developed to a wonderful degree, and many new processes have been introduced by means of which we are enabled to produce works of art unknown to our forefathers. It is therefore reasonable that the advocates of the new school of photography should become more popular in a comparatively short time than older concerns, and as one of the former we are pleased to give special mention to the house of John Suchy. It was established early in the spring of this year. Mr. Suchy was born in Bohemia and has resided in the World's Fair city since 1881. The house was organized with the object of making large groups of photographs a specialty. Fine and large premises are occupied at No. 3510 No. Halsted street. The gallery is in the rear, and is nicely carpeted with fancy matting. Altogether, the reception rooms, parlors, studio, etc., are elegant and attractive, and are evidence of the refined and educated class of patrons who favor this concern. There are five skilled assistants and operators, who work under the supervision of the proprietor. A visit to his beautiful studio would amply repay the visitor, as it is the eye that is appealed to, not altogether the intellect. The bare mention in a printed article of this concern would only convey a very inadequate idea. Such care is exercised in the production of fine portraits that they are as nearly faultless as lies within the power of man.

RITCHIE CARPET CO.

Among the reputable business concerns of Chicago none stand higher for honest dealing and business integrity than the Ritchie Carpet Co., of which Mr. Thos. Ritchie is the proprietor. This business was established twenty years ago by Mr. Ritchie and has been continued with the most flattering success uninterruptedly. He has been located at the present site for the past fifteen years in the building he erected at that time. This consists of a handsome four-story brick building, 22x150 feet in dimensions, the whole being occupied by the firm. It is located at 347 E. Division street, in one of the most favorable localities in the city. The basement is used for the oilcloth, spring, mattress and stove and range departments. On the first floor may be found the carpet and rug department; on the second the parlor furniture; the third is used for chamber furniture, suites, etc., and the fourth floor is devoted to the carpet sewing rooms and making-up department. The building is supplied with a fine elevator running from basement to the top floor. Mr. Ritchie carries an immense stock of goods, consisting of carpets, stoves, oil cloths, bedroom furniture, parlor, dining room and kitchen furniture, and household goods of all kinds, the stock being valued at over $70,000. Mr. Ritchie is a native of Scotland, and has resided in Chicago for over thirty-eight years. He is well-known as an active, upright and progressive business man, and he well deserves the large competency he has acquired by honest methods and strict business integrity.

HEITMANN & WILEY.

It is with decided pleasure that we note the business of Messrs. Heitmann & Wiley in this business review, inasmuch as the firm is one of the leading factors in the real estate business on the north side. The business was founded six years ago by Mr. John Heitmann and continued by him alone until June last, when Mr. O. G. Wiley was admitted, and the present style adopted. This house has a liberal patronage and an established reputation. Mr. Heitmann has been for a long time identified with north side property and has become well-known as an appraiser of ability, and the firm has a large business in handling property of all kinds. They occupy the first floor of 385 Wells street, near Division street, for office purposes, and do a general real estate business. They buy and sell on commission, collect rents, pay taxes, negotiate loans, manage estates, place insurance, and act as agents for non-residents. Their indorsements are of the highest character, and the business increases steadily. This house makes a specialty of North shore and Wilmetta property, which they sub-divide and sell on commission. They have cheap lots for sale in all sections. This house is recommended highly, and the proprietors are energetic and progressive in their methods. Mr. Heitmann was born in Hamburg, Germany, and Mr. Wiley is a native of this city.

F. W. PUSHECK.

There is no line of business so important, or of such great convenience, as a well conducted grocery and provision house, nor one that is appreciated by the community more. A veteran in this line is Mr. F. W. Pusheck, of No. 225 Evanston ave., the pioneer grocery and provision man of the north side. More than a quarter of a century ago Mr. Pusheck established his business, which he has continued uninterrupted only for the time in 1871 when he was a victim of the great fire. The past season he has erected the handsome brick building now occupied by him, and which is 25x70 feet in size. Mr. Pusheck deals in all kinds of staple and fancy groceries, provisions, teas, coffees, spices, canned goods, fruits, table delicacies and vegetables in season. He employs a force of six clerks and two delivery teams, calling for orders and delivering goods to all parts of the city. By his industry, thrift and fair dealing Mr.

Pusheck has had a prosperous career and owns considerable real estate and property in different localities of the city. He is a German by birth, and for the past thirty years has been a resident of Chicago, where he has made a host of friends and business acquaintances, who rejoice in his well-merited success.

MADISON HOUSE.

All the great hotels of Chicago are distinguished for the sterling spirit of enterprise which characterizes their management. The Madison House, which is centrally located on the corner of West Madison and Clinton streets, is not deficient in this essential factor of success, and has become a favorite resort of a numerous class of business men and others who find the situation most convenient, and the accommodation unexcelled in the city, at rates that bring it within the reach of all. Special attention is given to cleanliness, the most scrupulous regard being paid to this important requisite by the large staff of assistants, in whom this is considered the chief qualification. The rooms, which will accommodate about 60 guests, are light, well ventilated, and comfortably furnished, and no pains are spared to cater to every requirement of those who partake of the warm hospitality here offered. Mrs. F. M. Roundy, well known for her former connection with a similar business on the corner of State and Jackson streets, fills the position of hostess to the complete satisfaction of her multitude of patrons, and during the four years of her installation at this popular hotel has developed its resources and brought it to an advanced stage of usefulness. Rooms can be obtained here at from 50c. to $1.00 per diem, or from $1.50 to $7.00 per week, prices that, considering the high-class accommodation offered, are not to be duplicated elsewhere. Mrs. Roundy has proved her executive capacity by a long and successful career in this responsible position, and many who have experienced her liberality and anxious regard for their welfare will ever retain the most pleasurable recollections of this excellent house. She is remodeling the hotel all through, and has just built a new addition of 18 rooms, which give accommodations for about 100 guests.

HENRY G. EMMEL.

Chicago contains no more firmly established or thoroughly representative firm, than that of Mr. Henry G. Emmel, whose elegant premises are located at No. 500 Wells street. The father of the above gentleman, Mr. Peter Emmel, founded the business as long ago as the year 1855, and for thirty-five years, conducted it upon those sound business principles, which are the only firm foundation of enduring success. In 1875, the three-story brick building which is now occupied was constructed, affording superior facilities for the active prosecution of the work, and exhibiting in what is acknowledged to be one of the most richly and artistically decorated showrooms in the West, a striking illustration of the superior work that this company is capable of executing. The business was incorporated with a capital of $50,000 in August 1891, and the company are about to enter upon the manufacture of paints, oils, colors, etc., of the best quality, a branch of industry for which they are peculiarly fitted by reason of vast experience and perfected facilities. All the latest styles of wall paper and paper hangings, both imported and domestic, are here kept in stock in immense variety of any desired shade or tone, and Mr. Emmel is prepared to furnish estimates, and to execute the most important contracts for the decoration of interiors, in the highest style of the art. The business now amounts to no less than $150,000 in annual value, and requires the constant services of sixty-five skilled workmen. Mr. Henry G. Emmel occupies the position of president and treasurer, bringing to bear a wide range of experience, and giving his large circle of fashionable customers the most perfect satisfaction. The secretary, Mr. Geo. Schuler, is a gentleman of great capacity and sterling integrity.

J. C. NIXON & CO.

It is a fact not generally known outside of those immediately interested that the labor market of Chicago is the largest in the world. Not only is the great West supplied from this source, but the South, Southwest, Northwest and many portions from the East even look to Chicago for the labor that is needed to develop their resources. When it is known that over 20,000 men annually leave this city to put their brawn and muscle at the

service of railroad construction alone the importance of this market can be correctly estimated. Railroad construction is naturally governed, like all other branches of industry, by fixed rules and quantities, and its prosecution depends to a very appreciable extent upon net earnings or surplus. Notwithstanding this fact the figures given above can be safely considered as representative of the average annual supply furnished from this point. Such an extensive field of operation is naturally worked by several lreliable and responsible firms, and by many more who are thoroughly unreliable and perfectly irresponsible, Italian padrones and others. It is, therefore, a pleasant task to be able to refer in this review to a firm whose reputation for upright and honorable methods have gained for it the confidence and respect of the entire community. We refer to that of Messrs, J. C. Nixon & Co., railroad labor agents, whose headquarters are at No. 79 Canal street, with branch offices at the corner of South Water and Lake streets, and at No. 105 Canal street. This business was established in 1879 by Messrs, Nixon & Reed, the latter withdrawing in 1886, when he was succeeded by Mr. F. Asping, the present firm name being then assumed. Mr. Nixon, who is a native of Steuben Co., N. Y., has resided in Chicago for the past twenty-seven years. Mr. Asping was born in Sweden, coming here in 1881. Both are able and enterprising business men, and their honorable record is too well known to need any further commendation.

WELLER MANUFACTURING CO.

A manufacturing concern worthy of mention in this review of the business and manufacturing interests of Chicago is the Weller Manufacturing Co., founders, machinists and manufacturers of mill and grain elevator supplies. This business was established in 1880 by the Weller Brothers, and was duly incorporated in 1890, with a capitalization of $70,000; and Mr. Felix J. Weller, president, and B. H. Weller, secretary and treasurer. They occupy the premises located at 113 and 120 East North avenue, which are 75x100 feet in dimensions, and consist of a fine brick building. Here they manufacture all kinds of mill and elevator supplies and specialties, power grain shovels, car pullers, elevator buckets, turn spouts, belt conveyors, elevator boots, pulleys, shafting, hangers, etc. They employ twenty-five to thirty-five experienced workmen, and

have every improvement in machinery to facilitate the work done. They are the sole manufacturers of the Chase Patent Steel Conveyor. Their employes are all skilled, and quality is a first consideration in the articles of their manufacture, while the prices are as low as those of any competitor, quality considered. The plant is operated by a forty-five horse-power engine. The trade of this house extends to all portions of the United States, and increases from year to year. The Weller brothers are well known and highly respected, and as business men and citizens are of unquestioned integrity. Their success is well merited.

JAS. JOHNSON & SON.

One of the leading grocery houses of the West side is that conducted by Messrs. Jas. Johnson & Son. These gentlemen have built up a business that is very important in character and has a liberal patronage. They occupy the ground floor and basement of the two story brick building, 25x75 feet in dimensions, located at 776 West North avenue, and have a very attractive store. They have been established in business for five years and over, being formerly located at 681 W. Indiana street; and have occupied the present location for eighteen months. The stock of groceries carried is very large and well selected. It includes all kinds of staple and fancy groceries, canned meats, fruits and vegetables, fresh fruits, flour, sugar, preserves, vinegar, oil, molasses, table luxuries of all kinds and fine butter and fresh eggs. The house is liberally patronized, many of the foremost citizens and business men of the district being regular customers. Three experienced and courteous clerks are employed, and goods are delivered to any part of the city free of charge, a team being used for that purpose exclusively. The members of the firm are Jas. Johnson and C. W. Johnson, father and son. These gentlemen were born in Denmark, and came to Chicago twenty-eight years ago; they are well known and most highly respected, and are active business men of strict integrity. They have numerous friends and have achieved their success by close application to business and honest methods. Mr. James Johnson was a valued employe for fifteen years with the Northwestern Car Company, where he made many friends and was highly esteemed by his employers and those working with him.

G. F. KIMBALL.

There is no profession meeting the popular needs more than that of the dentist. He confers a positive boon on humanity, and supplies that which is either deficient or destroyed in nature, to complete the appearance and invite the comfort of his clients. One of the well established and responsible dentists of this city is Mr. G. F. Kimball. He has been practicing dentistry for the past eleven years, and has an established reputation for ability and skill. He was located at 306 West Indiana street for about three and one-half years, and has recently removed to an elegant suite of dental parlors of seven rooms in the new building, on West Indiana street, cor. Center avenue, which are without doubt the finest for the purposes intended in the city. They are supplied with steam heat, hot and cold water, etc. Every modern appliance used in the profession is had by the doctor, and his rooms suggest ease and comfort to his patients. He administers gas, and extracts teeth without pain to the patient. All kinds of dental work is done, and artificial teeth are inserted in any of the modern forms; one of these, the movable bridge, is a most wonderful discovery in dentistry, and should be investigated by all who are unfortunate enough to need artificial teeth. Dr. Kimball is a skilled and experienced dentist, a graduate of the University of Michigan, and is well known as a master of his profession. He is a representative man in professional and social circles, and enjoys the confidence and esteem of the leading professional, business and social leaders of the city. He has an extensive practice, and employs a skilled assistant.

E. J. PERRY, D. D. S.

E. J. Perry, D. D. S., occupies an elegant suite of three rooms in the Tacoma Building, No. 1212, consisting of reception and visiting parlor, operating room and laboratory. The rooms are not only most elegantly furnished, but are fitted up with all modern improvements and the most costly appliances. All branches of dentistry are practiced, and a high order of crown and bridge work is done, while none but the best Philadelphia and Chicago white teeth are used. A specialty is made, however, of operating, and anæsthetics are administered to sensitive patients when required. All operations are performed by Dr. Perry himself, and he has the highest reputation for skill as an operator and thoroughness of work. He was born in Chester county, Pennsylvania, and is now in the prime of life. He graduated at the Philadelphia Dental College with the class of 1871, and practiced at Sycamore, Pennsylvania, from that year until 1877, when he came west and located at Rockford, Illinois. In 1884 he came to Chicago, and by his ability has since gained a splendid reputation and acquired a large practice. He is a member of the Illinois State Dental Association and of the American Dental Association, and for one year was on the clinical staff of the Chicago College of Dental Surgery. No member of the profession has a higher standing among his fellow practitioners, or a better reputation with the public.

O. P. EMERSON & CO.

In the commission business in this city there are none better known than Messrs. O. P. Emerson & Co., whose house is one of the oldest in the city. The foundation of this house dates from 1860, when it was established by Mr. O. P. Emerson and continued until 1873 when he was joined by his son, Mr. F. Emerson, and in 1877 by Mr. D. J. Maxon. The firm has secured first-class connections throughout all the producing sections of the country, and, besides its correspondents, employs a number of solicitors whose duty it is to secure the choicest products of the farm, garden, dairy and orchard. Messrs. Emerson & Co., as wholesale commission merchants, handle the finest and best qualities of butter, cheese, poultry, fresh eggs, etc., and also every variety of fruits and vegetables and game when in season. The premises utilized for business purposes are located at 213 and 215 South Water street, and are 30x100 feet in area, and every convenience is provided to facilitate operations. Mr. O. P. Emerson, the founder of the house, is a native of New Hampshire. He has been in this city many years, and is one of the oldest and best known members of the Produce Exchange. His son, Mr. F. Emerson, was born in Illinois, and has been in this city most of his lifetime. Mr. Maxon is a New Yorker by birth. The firm belong to the Produce Exchange. This house has always stood high in commercial and financial circles, and among its references is the Hide and Leather National Bank.

W. E. BLAIR.

Sign-making has been developed to the highest plane of perfection, and among the leading and most reliable houses engaged in this city in this line of trade is that of Mr. W. E. Blair, at Nos. 171 and 173 Madison street. It was founded in 1873 by Mr, W. E. Blair, who conducted the business with much success, building up a large and widespread connection. In January, 1891, in order to better cope with its rapidly-increasing requirements, he formed the present stock company, which was at that time incorporated under the laws of Illinois, with a capital of $5,000. The president is Mr. A. H. Blair, the office of secretary and treasurer being assumed by Mr. W. E. Blair, who also manages the business. The factory is located on Oakley street, on the West Side, and is well equipped with all the latest improved appliances, apparatus, and time and labor-saving devices, a force of fourteen skilled hands being steadily employed. The salesrooms, on Madison street, comprise the second floor of a building, 30x85 feet in dimensions, and are replete with a heavy stock of board and glass signs, etc., etc. This house was the first to manufacture wire-screen signs, of which they control the patent and sale in the west. They are the sole manufacturers of the W. E. Blair patent wire signs, and their trade in this line covers all the States and Canada, as well as Mexico. These signs form the best advertising medium of the age ; the banner, being composed of wire, affords escapement to the wind ; the letters are made of metal, and when the sign is suspended in the air the wire is invisible, giving the letters the appearance of hanging in the air without support. All orders are promptly and satisfactorily filled, while the lowest prices are quoted. Mr. W. E. Blair, the founder, is a native of New Jersey, and is numbered among Chicago's representative business men. His son, Mr. A. H. Blair, who is president of the company, was born in this city, and is an able assistant in his father's well directed and successful efforts.

MAUTNER BROTHERS & CO.

One of the most progressive and reliable firms in this section of Chicago engaged in the manufacture of pocketbooks and fancy leather goods is that of Messrs. Mautner Brothers & Co., whose salesroom and factory are located at 27 East Washington street. This business was established in 1889 by Messrs. S. and Chas. Mautner, both of whom are thoroughly practical and expert leather workers. They occupy a spacious floor, 30x120 feet in area, where they manufacture all kinds of pocketbooks, card and leather cases, belts, medical instrument and bankers' cases, and fancy leather goods. Messrs. Mautner Brothers & Co. exercise great care in the selection of their skins and other materials, trimmings, etc., and maintain in all their goods a high standard of excellence for workmanship and finish, while they are widely known for the originality and artistic beauty of their various styles and designs of leather goods. Both Messrs. S. and Chas. Mautner were born in Austria, but have resided in Chicago for the past eight years. They are highly regarded in business circles for their enterprise and strict integrity, and are members of the Royal Arcanum and several other societies.

OLSON BROS.

In the whole range of commercial enterprise no interest is of more importance than that representing the sale of groceries. This fact is recognized and appreciated by all intelligent and thoughtful people, and therefore, the matter of the selection of a dealer from whom to purchase our supplies calls for careful consideration and discriminating judgment. In this connection we take genuine pleasure in calling the attention of our readers to the well-known and reliable house of Messrs. Olson Bros., located at No. 5203 Wentworth avenue. The business of this establishment was inaugurated by its present proprietors, Messrs. Anton F. and Julius J. Olson, in 1887. Being conducted on sound mercantile principles, and its management characterized by energy and ability, Messrs. Olson have from the start enjoyed a large and prosperous trade, the unequivocal excellence of the goods handled, coupled with upright and honorable dealing, being among the special features contributing to the positive and permanent success that has attended the enterprise from its inception. The spacious well-appointed premises comprise a commodious ground floor 25x85 feet in dimensions, and a choice A1 stock is carried, embracing the choicest foreign and domestic staple and fancy groceries of every description. The Messrs. Olson are natives of Sweden, now resident in Chicago for the past ten years, where the success they have achieved is simply the result of well-directed and intelligent business effort. The Messrs. Olson Bros. make a specialty of "Golden Key" brand of flour, also one of their greatest efforts is in the finest grade of creamery butter which is the best the market affords ; also special mention may be made of their teas and coffees which are simply "par excellence," and all desiring to trust a reliable house we can safely mention the above-named firm.

H. A. EVERETT.

The making of saddles is one of the most ancient of trades, and one which ranks of first importance in all countries. Chicago is noted for the extent of numerous enterprises identified with this trade, and among those establishments located on the South Side there is none better known, and none which meets a more substantial patronage, than that conducted by Mr. H. A. Everett, at No. 2948 Cottage Grove avenue. Mr. Everett is a gentleman of middle age, familiar with every detail of the trade, and his productions in the saddlery line have a standard reputation among horse owners generally. He opened his present establishment in January, 1888, and the patronage accorded sufficiently demonstrates that the venture is a wise one. For the purposes of his business he occupies the ground floor and basement of the building at the address indicated, and these are severally 25x100 feet in dimensions. The salesroom is very tastefully fitted up and stocked to repletion with light and heavy harness, collars, saddles and horse goods generally of a superior quality, and in the rear of this is a well equipped workshop, furnished with all the best modern appliances, tools, etc., and giving employment constantly to from four to six hands, skilled and experienced in the trade. Mr. Everett makes a specialty of manufacturing the well known fine Kay saddles, which, for excellence of material, substantiality of workmanship and durability, have not their equals. Light and heavy harness, collars, coats, and everything requisite for the caparisoning of steeds are made to order at short notice at low prices and guaranteed to give perfect satisfaction. A splendid show is made of fine saddlery of all kinds, whips, blankets, curry combs and everything belonging to horse garniture. The house is one worthy of its name and has a bright future before it. Mr. Everett, who is a native of Michigan, has been a resident of Chicago for the past fifteen years, and during his business career has earned the good will and esteem of all who have come in contact with him.

JULIUS MEYHOEFER.

The trade in fine furs is an important factor of the commercial and industrial activity of this city. A leading representative and reliable house engaged in it is that of Messrs. Julius Meyhoefer & Co., manufacturers of fine furs, repairers and refitters of seal garments, at Nos. 150 and 152 La Salle street. This business was established in 1889 by Mr. Julius Meyhoefer. He orought to bear a thorough knowledge of the business in all its details, and an intimate acquaintance with the latest fashions and styles, as well as the requirements of the most fastidious. He occupies rooms 29 and 30, and these ample and commodious premises are neatly appointed and well equipped with all the best machines and appliances, while steady employment is given to nine skilled operators. The range of work embraces the production of fine fur garments and other articles, such as coats, cloaks, sacques, dolmans, muffs, caps, gauntlets, also fur lined goods, as well as general repairing and refitting. The concern manufacture largely for the leading houses in the trade, as well as to order for private parties. Mr. Meyhoefer was born in Germany, and has been a resident of Chicago since 1887. He is a member of the Knights of Pythias, and of the Order of Chosen Friends.

KNIGHT & LINDERMAN.

The inhabitants of this great metropolis are well aware that in all branches of science, art, trade and commerce, and the professions, women have gained and ably retain a prominent position. The latest firm composed of women to enter into successful competition with the old time school of real estate brokers and agents is that of Knight & Linderman, of 142 Dearborn street. It is composed of Miss Margaret Knight and Miss Mary A. Linderman, both business women of remarkable ability. Although the venture was only entered into in the present year, the most influential connections have been established, and many important transactions have been carried through to a successful issue. The offices are in room 14 of

the Hawley building, at the corner of Madison and Dearborn streets. They have an area of 20x40 feet, are handsomely fitted up and furnished, and two assistants are employed. A general real estate and loan brokerage business is carried on; property of all kinds is bought, sold, exchanged, loaned, etc. The firm also negotiate loans on bond and mortgage at lowest rates, and undertake the general management of estates for absent and other owners, secure desirable tenants, collect rents regularly and punctually, pay taxes and insurance premiums, and disburse for necessary repairs. Both partners have a thorough knowledge of values, both present and prospective, of city and suburban realty. Miss Knight is a native of Canada, and has resided in Los Angeles, Cal., being prominently identified with the real estate boom there for several years. Miss Linderman was born in Ohio, removing to this city in 1886. These ladies have shown great pluck, energy and enterprise, and are to be congratulated on the success they have achieved.

AMERICAN SUGAR REFINING CO.

Chicago has long been the distributing center of the sugar trade of the western and northwestern states, and the business in this important staple is now so vast that it necessarily involves consideration of the greatest importance. A representative concern in this city actively engaged in this trade is that of Wm. A. Havemeyer & Co., whose offices are located at 31 Lake street. This business was established in 1874, and this firm has ever since held a leading position in the sugar business of this city and the west. Messrs. W. A. Havemeyer & Co. represent the various interests of the American Sugar Refining Co. This company was formed by a consolidation of the leading sugar refineries of this country into a joint stock concern, and this combination has resulted in an economy of management and a consequent reduction in the cost of production that has been felt and appreciated by consumers In the hands of Messrs. Havemeyer & Co, the business of the company is rapidly increasing, and, carrying the large stock that they do, and possessed as they are of every facility for the prompt execution of orders, jobbers have long recognized this firm as the leader of the sugar business in the west. Messrs. W. A. Havemeyer and Norris W. Mundy, the partners of the firm, have long been identified with the interest they represent. , They are natives of New York, and have won popularity and success in their business by justly deserving it.

LOUIS LEOPOLD.

The livery business of Chicago is represented by many active business houses doing a large business, but none are better known or more liberally patronized than Louis Leopold & Sons. The business of this house has been established for seven years, and has been from the first a decided success. They occupy the premises located at 415 and 417 North Wells street, which have recently been remodeled and rebuilt. Here they have a fine business place with accommodations for thirty-five horses. The house has eighteen horses and accommodates about twelve boarders. All kinds of carriages, hacks, phaetons, coupes, etc., are kept on hand for the convenience of patrons at any time, and the horses let for livery are selected for their style, speed and trustworthiness. The business done by this house is extensive, the patronage being very large. Ten persons are employed and everything is kept in first-class order. This house is well and favorably known and the proprietors are prominent in business and social circles. Mr. Louis Leopold was born in Germany and has lived in Chicago for twenty-seven years, he is an active Free Mason, and is also a member of the Select Knights, Chicago Union, No. 4. Mr. Lesser Leopold was born in Germany, Mr. Samuel Leopold in this city and both have numerous friends. The telephone call is 3402, and the rates charged are as moderate as may be obtained at any other first-class house in the city.

R. D. WHEATON & CO.

The triumphs of civil engineering science in America are many, and the results which have astonished the world are due in no small degree to the daring and skill of the contractor and builder, as well as to the designer. In their career of nearly fifteen years Messrs. R. D. Wheaton & Co., whose Chicago office is in room 358 Rookery Building, have done much to merit the reputation of daring and successful contractors in building bridges, viaducts, roofs and other structural work. The business was established in 1879 in Michigan, and removed to Chicago in 1886. The firm contracts for building, all kinds of iron work, especially bridges. They have just finished a three-span bridge at Joliet, Ill., seven spans at Lockport, Ill., and a 200 feet span bridge at Martin, Wis., and numerous others. The bulk of operations are done in the states of Illinois, Iowa, Indiana, Michigan and Wisconsin. The works are at the Wisconsin Bridge & Iron Co., of Milwaukee, Wis., and these are kept busy in producing the many forms of structural iron that go to make up the complement of the modern bridge, modified indefinitely in form, if not in principle, by the taste and skill of the designer. In all these requirements the firm of R. D. Wheaton & Co. will be found more than equal to the task at all times. Mr. Wheaton is a gentleman of middle age, a native of Michigan. He has reaped the reward of a life of rare industry and unremitting toil in a demand for his services that is of the most flattering character.

UNION FURNACE CO.

Modern architecture calls for a more satisfactory method of heating residences and stores than the old way of using stoves. It is doubtful if there be any method superior to that of furnishing heated air, by furnace, to an establishment. This method insures ventilation, or the introduction of pure heated air, and is in many ways superior to steam heating. One of the leading furnace manufacturing companies of this city, and very popular, is the Union Furnace Company. This company was incorporated in 1890 under Illinois state laws, with a paid up capital of $5,000, and the following officers: James Sayre, president; W. P. Jenks, vice-president; S. A. Jenks, secretary and treasurer. These gentlemen are competent business men, and are prominent in their business lines. Mr. Sayre was born in Utica, N. Y., and at present resides in Minnesota. Mr. S. A. Jenks was born in Providence, R. I., and is well known in Chicago business circles. In addition to his interests in the Furnace Company, he conducts an express and delivery business and coal business. Mr. W. P. Jenks is the son of Mr. S. A. Jenks, and is a young man of excellent business qualifications. The general salesman is Mr. W. C. Knight. The business is conducted at 65 Dearborn avenue, where the company occupies the ground floor and basement of the premises, 26x80 feet in dimensions. Here they manufacture warm air furnaces in six different sizes, of superior merit. They also manufacture and deal in heating pipes, registers, galvanized guttering and spouting, roofing, iron and tin work. They employ twelve experienced workmen, and have a large trade in Chicago and suburbs. The business done is both wholesale and retail, and the heaters especially have a reputation of the highest order.

SMITH CORRUGATING CO.

One of the most reliable and prosperous concerns in this section of Chicago, engaged in sheet metal and corrugated iron work is that known as the Smith Corrugating Company, whose office and factory are situated at 198 South Desplaines street. This business was established in 1890 by Messrs. Smith & Cade, and afterwards was incorporated under the laws of Illinois with a paid up capital of $30,000, its executive officers being Mr. John Smith, president and treasurer, and Mr. J. H.

Perkinson secretary, Both Messrs. Smith and Perkinson, bring great practical experience to bear, coupled with an accurate knowledge of every detail of this important industry and the requirements of patrons. They occupy a spacious ground floor, 25x160 feet in area, fully equipped with modern tools machinery and appliances, driven by steam power. Here forty skilled hands are employed, and the trade of the company extends throughout all sections of the city and state. They manufacture to order all kinds of sheet metal and corrugated iron work, including cornices, window caps, skylights, etc. A specialty is made of packing house work and of Smith's Patent Ventilators, which last have received several awards at various expositions for their efficiency and utility. The Smith Corrugating Company uses only the best materials, and turns out work that is unrivalled for quality, durability and workmanship. Orders are promptly filled at the lowest possible figures, and complete satisfaction is guaranteed customers. Mr. Smith is a native of Boston, Mass., and for many years was successfuly engaged in business in Kansas City, Mo., while Mr. Perkinson was born in Wisconsin. They are widely known in trade circles for their energy and integrity, and have won success by honestly deserving it. The telephone call of the house is 5127. This Company has handled many large contracts in their line, including the City Pumping works, the Illinois Steel Co., Fraser & Chalmer, the Grant Locomotive Works and the Transportation Building of World's Columbian Exposition. We here-

with insert a cut of the "Smith Patent Ventilator" which is used on the U. S. Capitol Building at Washington, D. C., and below we insert a copy of a letter written to Mr. Smith by the U. S. government architect.

WASHINGTON, March 21, 1887.

MR. JOHN SMITH.

The six ventilators that we have placed on the U. S. Capitol at Washington have stood the most severe test and done better service than we have been able to get for the past twenty years.

U. S. ARCHITECT.

JOHN N. HUBBARD.

The character and magnitude of the broom corn trade in Chicago is apparent by reference to the prosperity of the exchange devoted to its interests, with its influential membership, and perfected facilities. Among the leading wholesale houses closely identified with this exchange is that of Mr. John N. Hubbard, the widely and favorably known commission merchant and wholesale dealer in broom corn and broom manufacturer's supplies of all kinds, located at 125 and 127 Kinzie street. The business was founded in 1865 by Mr. W. L. Hubbard, the present proprietor being admitted a partner in 1881, and succeeding to the sole charge three years later. He occupies the whole of a fine six-story brick building with basement, and carries an immense stock of these staples, receiving large shipments direct from the producers in Illinois, Kansas, Nebraska and Iowa. He transacts a wholesale business of vast proportions in all parts of the United States, Canada and Australia, having the most influential correspondents in every important center throughout these countries. He handles an enormous amount of broom corn annually, a fact which practically demonstrates the high position which he has achieved. Mr. Hubbard is a native of Massachusetts, and has resided in Chicago since 1879, enjoying the respect and esteem of all for his conspicuous ability, expert knowledge and sterling integrity,

7

LAUREL BAKERY LUNCH ROOM.

One of the best located and most neatly fitted up lunch rooms among the many popular establishments in this line, is the Laurel Bakery Lunch Room, in the basement at the northwest corner of Clark and Madison streets, under Atwood's clothing store, presided over by Mr. E. T. Olson. Everybody is invited to visit this convenient and popular resort. The rooms are spacious and airy, capable of seating over two hundred persons. There are special tables reserved for ladies, and the service is strictly first-class. Mr. Olson prides himself on the quality of the eatables he places before his patrons. He fearlessly claims to serve the best tea and coffee in Chicago, and thus far his claim has not been controverted. The bread and pastry are all of Kohlsaat's celebrated make, and there are no better in the whole world. Everything offered the patrons of this place is strictly first-class and strictly pure, and free from adulteration or dilution. In the important matter of price the Laurel Bakery Lunch Room is on the popular side. The scale of prices is made as low as is compatible with good service and first-class fare. The excellent location of this establishment, its neat and airy appearance, and the most courteous treatment accorded its patrons, added to the excellence of the service and fare, will certainly make it one of the leading eating houses in Chicago. The proprietor, Mr. E. T. Olson, is a native of far off Norway, a young man of good business faculties and excellent character. He came to this country when but a boy, and located in Minneapolis, where he afterward engaged in the dry goods business. He removed to Chicago about seven years ago, following the dry goods trade, and opened his present venture in June, 1891. His establishment enjoys an excellent patronage, and the prospects for the future success of the venture are certainly very flattering.

ALONZO VANAMAN & CO.

Mr. Vanaman is one of the best known cigar men in the city, or indeed in this district, and, though he does not manufacture cigars, he controls the products of some of the best factories and also has special brands of which he is the sole proprietor. His is a western distributing house for New York and Pennsylvania cigars. He also imports largely Havana cigars, and is a heavy jobber in Key West and domestic cigars. He has been established in business six years, and occupies the ground floor and basement of the three story brick store at 94 Van Buren street; he also uses the next basement which extends to Dearborn street, for storage purposes. His store is about 40x30 feet in dimensions, and is heavily stocked with the finest brands of cigars. His own special brands are all well known and are the "Pure Leaf," "Partidos" and "Parrot," all nickel cigars, but honestly better than the average ten cent cigar. His trade is mostly in the city, and be employs six traveling men. Mr. Alonzo Vanaman is a native of Philadelphia, and is highly respected in the trade; indeed no man has done more than he to endeavor to keep up the standard of the cigar trade, and to rid it of all objectionable features and unscrupulous methods.

J. NEUBERGER & CO.

Few houses are so well equipped for successful and satisfactory service as that of Mr. J. Neuberger (trading as J. Neuberger & Co.), the well known commission merchant in butter, eggs, cheese, poultry, etc., at No. 195 South Water street. Mr. Neuberger has been engaged in this business for the past seventeen years, and has deservedly enjoyed a continuously prosperous career to date. He is, therefore, a thoroughly experienced merchant, commands a wide and valuable acquaintance in trade circles, and is active, enterprising and capable to a marked degree. He has developed an extensive and important trade broadly distributed over the western and northwestern states. The business premises comprise four commodious floors and basement, 20x150 feet in dimensions, admirably arranged and provided with every convenience for the handling and proper preservation of the choice

stock here carried. The advantages possessed by Mr. Neuberger are of the best possible character, and his transactions are marked by prompt attention to every detail. The facilities and resources of the house are admirable for reaching a desirable class of buyers, and the distinguishing policy of the establishment is the activity displayed in placing its consignments on the market, and making prompt and satisfactory returns. The finest quality of creamery and dairy butter, fresh eggs and prime cheese are handled, a leading specialty being made of live and dressed poultry and game in season. Mr. Neuberger is a native of Germany, and has been a resident of Chicago since 1866, and is as well and favorably known in mercantile circles, as he is earnestly devoted to the interests of his patrons. He is a prominent member of Chicago Lodge No. 37 of the Order of Free and Accepted Masons.

H. L. BEST.

Mr. H. L. Best is a gentleman who can boast an extended experience in his business, and there is no house in Chicago in the same line that possesses better facilities for handling it than he does. He is a dealer and shipper of all kinds of poultry and game, and receives consignments from the principal raisers in Illinois, Indiana, Wisconsin and Ohio, making advances on same when desired, and always effecting quick sales and rapid returns, according to the ruling prices of the day. Poultry, turkeys, chickens, ducks, geese, prairie fowls, partridges, quail, jacksnipe and woodcock, can all be found in their choicest variety at his store, according to their season. His store, at 176 South Water street, possesses every possible convenience for the careful handling of consignments, and he employs an ample force of skilled help under the able management of Mr. William Oram. Mr. Best is a native of Brunswick, Maine, and in 1883 came west to Dakota and interested himself in the live stock business, dealing largely in Texas and Montana cattle. In 1890 he went into his present business, and as results have shown, he has more than justified his most sanguine expectations. His methods have from the commencement been unvarying, and have been characterized by all that is honorable and fair. Mr. Best belongs to the Independent Order of Odd Fellows, and has a very wide circle of influential friends.

THOMAS BALL.

There is no more popular and well-patronized enterprise in Chicago than the well-known Bee Hive Laundry and Lace Curtain Cleaning Works. This establishment is located at 741, 743 and 745 Wells street and 2, 4 and 6 Lincoln avenue. The premises are 77x80 feet in dimensions. Three floors are occupied for the purposes of the business and this is one of the most complete laundries in the country. It is equipped with all the latest and most approved machinery. The motive power is supplied by a fifteen horse-power engine, and the engineer is a lady, the only licensed lady engineer in the city, and one who is thoroughly competent. The machinery consists of four complete steam washing machines, five ironing machines, twelve dry closets, run on pulleys, four starchers, and two starching machines and every other kind of improvement in laundry machinery. The capacity of the laundry is 4,000 shirts weekly. The building is admirably arranged for the purpose, the basement being used for washing and machinery, the first floor for office and finishing room, second floor assorting and bundling room, etc. There are from twenty-eight to thirty agencies; four delivery wagons are used, and thirty-five persons are employed. All kinds of laundry work is done. Lace curtains are renovated and made equal to new. The prices charged are extremely moderate and all work fully guaranteed. Mr. Thomas Ball, the proprietor, is a progressive business man who is well liked by his numerous friends and patrons. He was born in London, Eng., but reared in Chicago, coming here when a boy in 1850. He has been established in this business for ten years and has achieved a great success. He is a member of the Mystic Circle.

UNION PARK HOTEL.

We have great pleasure in bringing to the notice of our thousands of readers one of the very recent additions to the great facilities of Chicago for accommodating strangers, namely, the Union Park Hotel, situated in a most salubrious and select portion of the city, at No. 521 West Madison street. Mr. L. Burk, the proprietor, has had a long experience in the art of catering to the traveling public in Kansas City, having been for eighteen years the popular head of the Union Park Hotel of that place, which has long been known as most comfortable and homelike in its accommodations. He has just completed the rebuilding of his premises in Chicago, and has entirely renovated and remodeled it to suit the purposes of a first-class house. New decorations and furniture of the most artistic kind has been everywhere introduced, and neither expense nor pains have been spared to make guests comfortable and contented. The building as it now stands is a four story stone with basement, the lower portions being occupied by stores, etc.,and the three top floors, containing forty rooms, are now in the most perfect condition possible for either permanent residence or transient visits. , The first floor contains the office, ladies' and gents' parlors, reading room, smoking room, etc., while above are the well furnished and comfortable chambers. Every modern convenience is found here, including baths, electric calls, etc., and the whole is well lighted by gas in every room. Transport facilities are at hand, street cars pass the door, and in a very short time any part of the city may be reached. The rates are seventy-five cents and $1 per night, or $2 to $5 per week, and must certainly be considered most reasonable taking into account the high class accommodationafforded. An excellent feature of this house is that there is no bar with its disagreeable accompaniments to offend the eye or ear, and we strongly recommend those who intend visiting the World's Columbian Exposition with their wives and families to secure rooms here in advance, and be assured of rest and quietness after the weariness of the day. No meals are served, the object of the enterprising proprietor being to avoid everything that would interfere with his one great—aim, to secure the greatest comfort and offer the warmest hospitality to all.

WM. TRAUTWEIN.

Chicago has become a great manufacturing center and has numerous enterprises of great magnitude in operation, with negotiations pending for new lines each day. The wool business, always an important industry, has become one of the most prominent features in Chicago, and already extensive factories are in active operation, making superior grades of goods. In this connection the dyeing of woolen yarns is a most important business, and the most important establishment of the kind is that of Mr. William Trautwein, 361 Clybourn avenue. Mr. Trautwein has been established in the business at this address for the past two years, and has been very successful. He occupies the ground floor and basement for the business, having the dye room in the basement and the packing and drying room on the first floor. His premises are 40x75 feet in dimensions, and thoroughly equipped for the business; the boiler is sixteen horse power and the engine eight horse power. Mr. Trautwein does an extensive business in dyeing cotton and woolen yarns all colors. He is a native of Germany and has resided in Chicago three years; he is well known in business circles and is a Knight of the Golden Eagle. His factory has a capacity of 400 pounds of wool daily, and the business increases constantly.

F. H. EDLER.

Mr. F. H. Edler, who is a shareholder in the World's Fair, has been established for many years in the harness and saddlery business in this city, and has become known as one of the most reliable and progressive dealers in that line to whom the public may go for supplies with every assurance of honorable and fair dealing. In 1869 Mr. Edler began business at 125 Wells street. He continued at that location until the increase in volume of business necessitated his removal to more commodious quarters at 205 N. Wells street. In May last, he again removed to his present location,207 N. Wells street. Here he has a fine store and factory, the store being 25x60 feet and the factory in the rear 25x50 feet in dimensions. He employes from 10 to 15 skilled harness makers and manufactures as a specialty fine coach, coupe and buggy harness, and also all kinds of single and double harness, saddles, bridles, collars and heavy and light harness of all descriptions. He also deals in all kinds of horse, turf and stable goods, blankets, whips, robes, etc. The quality of the goods manufactured by Mr. Edler is equal to that to be obtained anywhere in America. The leather used is all carefully selected and inspected, and is the best oak tanned stock to be obtained. Mr. Edler uses almost entirely the well-known Moffatt stock. The house does a representative business, patrons holding it as the *best place* to deal in the city. Mr. Edler was born in Germany and has lived in Chicago since 1868. He is prominent in business circles, a leading Odd Fellow, and is regarded with the greatest respect by all who know him.

THE COLUMBIAN PORTRAIT CO.

The citizens of Chicago always have a keen appreciation for art, and enjoy that which is beautiful. The Columbian Portrait Co. has come into prominence as one of the leading institutions producing a high class of art work in portraiture. The business was established in 1889 by Mr. P. A. Burns, and in 1891 the company was formed and duly incorporated under the state laws with a capital of $8,000. Mr. P. A. Burns is the president, and Mr. C. J. Quinn manager. The company occupies the ground floor and basement of the premises 179 Wells street, and have floor space 25x60 feet in dimensions. They carry a fine stock of picture frames, oil, water and crayon portraits and landscapes; also pictures of all kinds in the finest form and most beautiful subjects. They make a specialty of portraits and employ eight artists who are skilled and stand high in their profession. The company has a large local and suburban trade, the patrons being many of the most prominent and best known citizens. The work turned out is highly appreciated and very meritorious. The officers of the company are well known as business men, artists, and connoisseurs, and are held high in public estimation. Mr. Burns is a native of Michigan, and Mr. Quinn was born in England and has resided in Chicago a number of years.

KIKKEBUSCH BROS.

One of the most popular among the representative groceries in the section in which it is located, is that of Kikkebusch Bros., located at 128 West Indiana street. The co-partners, Mr. V. and Mr. P. Kikkebusch established themselves in their present location in 1887, since when they have been doing a first-class permanent business, and enjoyed a success as deserved as it is merited. The spacious store, which has dimensions of 20x60 feet, is excellently well fitted up and arranged for business purposes, and is filled with an extensive assortment of staple and fancy groceries of every kind, also provisions, and when in season a specialty is made of choice fruits, fresh vegetables, poultry and game. Pure fresh teas, fragrant coffees, family flour, canned goods and creamery and dairy butter can always be obtained at the establishment, of unsurpassed quality, and all goods sold are freely warranted as represented. Several clerks and two delivery teams are employed and all orders are filled promptly and satisfactorily. Popular prices prevail and business is always active and brisk. The Messrs. Kikkebusch are both young men, and have had quite an extended experience in the grocery trade. They make it their aim to deal in the finest and best staple and fancy groceries, provisions and the products of the farm, garden, orchard and dairy, and are unremitting in their attention to patrons. They are natives of Denmark, but since 1879 have been residents of this city.

T. F. DUNTON.

Down among the grim towering warehouses and hustling markets of the North side, at 186 E. Kinzie street, Mr. T. F. Dunton, commission merchant and dealer in broom corn and broom materials, has his headquarters. Mr. Dunton has been engaged in the commission business for over twenty-five years. The present business was first established in 1865 by Messrs. Wight, Dunton & Co. Three years later Mr. Dunton succeeded to the business of the firm, and has since conducted it successfully and to the entire satisfaction of an extensive and widely scattered patronage. The present location is a very eligible one for the business and comprises a fine brick building, 30x80 feet, four stories and basement, thoroughly equipped with hydraulic elevators and all the necessary facilities for the prosecution of the heavy and bulky business. The stock includes every thing in the broommakers' line, broom corn of the best grades, wire, twine, etc., and all the necessary tools and machinery for the manufacture of brooms. Mr. Dunton receives consignments of broom corn from all the best known sources of supply. Liberal advances are made on consignments, when required, on the most reasonable terms. His trade in this staple is very large, averaging 2,000 tons annually, or about 15,000 pounds daily, and extends over the entire Union and even across the border into Canada. The rule of this well-known house is prompt returns and instant attention to orders. By strict attention to the markets and every detail of the business, Mr. Dunton has built up a magnificent trade, which is a fine testimonial to his business ability and integrity of character. Such concerns are a credit to the community and form the solid foundation for the future growth and development of the metropolis of the West.

GARDEN CITY STOVE CO.

An establishment which stands in the front rank of the city's furniture and stove trade, is that above named. The business was established one year ago by Mr. E. D. Porter. He occupies five floors, each 25x135 feet in dimensions, and two floors, each 75x125 feet, at 71 West Washington street, which are fully equipped with every convenience, including an extensive, choice and well-selected stock of parlor, chamber, hall, dining and drawing room and kitchen furniture, the parlor sets being obtainable in all the latest styles of upholstery. Here also can be obtained carpets, rugs, oil-cloths, mattresses, lace curtains, baby carriages, refrigerators and stoves of every description, all quoted at extremely low prices. Mr. E. D. Porter is agent for many of the leading manufacturing companies, among

which are the Buckwalter Stove Co., Royersford, Pa.; Le-

high Stove & Mfg. Co., Lehighton, Pa.; The Perry Stove Co., Albany, N. Y.; Pittston Stove Co., Pittston, Pa.;

Conrey & Birely Table Co., Shelbyville, Ind.; Goshen Furniture Co., Goshen, Ind.; Hodell Furniture Co., Shelbyville, Ind. Mr. Porter handles only really superior goods, and employs in his warehouse several salesmen and one traveling salesman. He was born in Marshall, Mich., and came to Chicago some ten years ago. Mr. Porter is highly regarded for his integrity and enterprise by the community, and his establishment is an in-

teresting feature of Chicago's industry and activity. The Buckwalter Stove Co., Lehigh Stove and Manufacturing Co. and the Perry Stove Co. belong to the leading manufacturers in their line in the country. They manufacture only superior goods and command an enviable reputation as to integrity and fairness of dealing.

BENEDICT LUDER.

One of the reliable houses doing a general plumbing and gasfitting business, is that of Mr. Benedict Luder, whose establishment is at 451 W. Chicago avenue. This business was established eight years ago by O'Brien & Luder, and was continued in this form until August 1 of the present year, when Mr. O'Brien retired and Mr. Luder succeeded to the entire interest. The business carried on by this house is of the most important and extensive character. The fifteen employes are all experienced and practical men. The materials used are selected with special reference to their strength and quality, and the prices charged for work are always as reasonable as maintained elsewhere. The business is conducted from the large store, 25x50 feet, on the ground floor of the four-story building, 451 W. Chicago avenue, and the basement of the premises is used as a workshop and store room. All kinds of plumbers' supplies, gas and steam fixtures, chandeliers, globes, hose, pipe, lamps, brackets, etc., are carried in stock. Jobbing is promptly attended to; sewers contracted for, and houses completely furnished with sanitary plumbing of the highest order. Mr. Benedict Luder was born in Switzerland, and has resided in Chicago for forty-two years; he is a prominent member of the Knights of Pythias and the G. A. R., and served in the Ninth Illinois regiment during the late war with honor and distinction,

WILLIAM R. GIBB.

With the increase of population, refinement and wealth in the principal centers of the United States, has arisen a growing demand for the blending of the artistic with the utilitarian in modern architecture. Among those who have acquired a wide reputation for great skill and artistic conceptions as an architect in this city is Mr. William R. Gibb, who occupies spacious and eligible office quarters in the Royal Insurance building, No. 169 Jackson street. Mr. Gibb is a native of Chicago, and early in life acquired a thorough, practical, as well as theoretical knowledge of the science of architecture. He engaged in business on his own account during the current year, and enjoys every modern facility for designing, draughting, making computations etc , and gives employment to a corps of three talented assistants. He attends faithfully to details, his plans are well digested and studied, and his architectural efforts have tended greatly to beautify the urban characteristics of this city and state. Mr. Gibb is constantly engaged in planning and supervising the erection of the most advanced classes of public and private buildings, and is prepared to execute all commissions not only promptly, but with that intelligent apprehension of design which has served to make his efforts so highly appreciated. Mr. Gibb is recognized as a young man of marked professional attainments and great promise. He is a prominent and popular charter member of the order of Sons of America.

BURKE & DELAP.

A leading and exceedingly popular North side house, is the butcher and grocery business of Burke & Delap. This business has been established at the present location for the past eight years, and has had a steady development in popularity until it has become recognized as the leading store in the district handling fine meats, vegetables and groceries. The business is conducted at 819 North Clark street, and 1, 3, 5 and 7 Wisconsin street, the premises being 30x110 feet in dimension. Here all the finest fancy and staple groceries are carried, teas, coffees and spices of the best grades, flour, preserves and all kinds of table delicacies are to be had at popular prices. In the meat department, the finest fresh pork, beef, mutton, veal or lamb can be had, fresh daily, and in season every variety of poultry, game and fish are to be found on the counters. Early vegetables and fine fruits are made a specialty, and are received early by special consignment in first-class order. The business done by this house is immense and is constantly increasing, it amounting to from $75,000 to $100,000 per annum, and is with the best citizens of the North side as patrons. Five attendants are employed, and four teams are used in the delivery department, goods being sent to all parts of the city free of charge. Messrs. Burke & Delap import all their fancy groceries direct, and have such commercial relations that they cannot be outpriced in competition. They are young men of pronounced ability and integrity and deserve the greatest credit for their business character and success. Mr. Burke was born in Argyle, Ill , and raised in Chicago, he is a leader in social circles, and an energetic and reliable man of business. Mr. Delap is a native of Detroit, and has resided in Chicago thirty years. He is a Royal Arch Mason, a member of the Royal Arcanum, the Royal League and Knights of Honor, in all of which he is very popular.

MRS. C. WASKOW.

The oldest among the many first-class and reliable grocery houses in this city, and of Mrs. C. Waskow is especially worthy of mention in this review, on account of the successful career it has experienced for quarter of a century. This house was founded by the husband of the present owner, and the business has always been conducted on the same street; being located for the past twenty-one years at the present place, 1476 and 1478 Milwaukee street. The store is very large and is neatly furnished and completely stocked with a fine assortment of staple groceries, canned goods, flour, teas, coffees, spices, pickles, preserves, condiments, etc., also the best of dairy products, butter, cheese and eggs. The house has an established reputation for fair dealing and superior goods; and the patronage is large and appreciative, most of the customers having done their trading with the house for years. Two clerks are employed, who are courteous 'and attentive and fully alert to meet the wishes of the patrons. Goods are delivered to all parts of the city free of charge, by team owned by the house. Mrs. Waskow was born in Germany and has resided in Chicago for the past twenty-five years. She has conducted the business alone' for the past four years, and has shown rare executive and business ability. She is regarded with respect and esteem in all business circles, and is popular with her many patrons.

J. M. PETTERSEN.

It is but right that the important business interests of Mr. J. M. Pettersen should be noticed in this review of the business and commercial interests of Chicago. Mr. Pettersen conducts two fine drugstores at 1741 Milwaukee avenue and 439 Fullerton avenue. He established his business about twelve years ago, occupying the Milwaukee avenue store for the last nine years, and the Fullerton avenue branch two years. His stores are splendidly fitted up, and furnished in modern, complete and elegant style. The drugs carried in stock are strictly pure, and many preparations are manufactured on the premises under the direction of Mr. Pettersen, who is an experienced and practical chemist. In addition to the drugs a full line of oils, toilet articles, patent medicines, soaps, fancy articles, brushes, physicians' and surgeons' supplies, rubber goods, etc., are carried, and sold at reasonable prices. Three experienced registered pharmacists are employed and prescriptions are given most careful attention, being compounded accurately and of pure and unadulterated drugs. Mr. Pettersen is a native of Denmark, where he graduated. He is a regular licensed druggist and is a Free Mason and a member of the I. O. O. F., Royal Arcanum, and Iron Hall. He has a liberal patronage and is prominent in social and professional circles. The leading physicians in this section of the city send their prescriptions to Mr. Pettersen to be filled, and this fact is in itself sufficient evidence of the confidence reposed in his ability and accuracy as a pharmacist.

ROBERT H. GIVEN, JR.

Mr. Robert H. Given, Jr., the well-known real estate investor, handles a large amount of property during a year, and among his clients are many of the best citizens of Chicago. Mr. Given is a gentleman of experience in the real estate market and his advice is sought by investors in real property as well as those who wish to dispose to advantage of their holdings. He handles lots in the subdivision at New Humboldt Park and has some of the most desirable sites in that section to sell on terms that cannot prove otherwise than satisfactory to purchasers. He also has property for sale and to rent in all sections of the city and suburbs. He makes a specialty of down town improved real estate and always has splendid opportunities to offer those seeking good paying permanent investments. Careful and expert attention is given to the negotiations of loans on bond and mortgage, making collections and looking after and taking charge of estates. Mr. Given, who was born in Cincinnati, O., is a young man, and was for some years engaged in a manufacturing business. He has resided in Chicago eighteen years and since 1888 devoted his attention to handling and dealing in real estate. He has acquired a well deserved reputation as a shrewd real estate dealer, and those contemplating investments for business, residence or speculative purposes will find it to their advantage to call upon Mr. Given, as superior bargains are constantly being offered by him and all transactions are placed upon the most satisfactory basis. Mr. Given makes a specialty of down town property and renting valuable property on a 99 year lease. His office is room 608 Chamber of Commerce.

THE ILLINOIS SEED CO.

This business, originally that of Messrs. Hiram Sibley & Co., was purchased by the present proprietors in 1889, the company being incorporated at the same time, under the laws of Illinois, with a paid up capital of $25,000. The trade embraces all kinds of field seeds, such as timothy, clover, millet, red top, orchard grass, Hungarian, blue grass and buckwheat. The connections of this company are influential and wide-spread, their trade extending throughout the United States, Canada and Europe, where large shipments are continually being sent. They conduct an extensive jobbing trade in the states tributary to Chicago, as far east as Pennsylvania, but outside of this home district they sell to the largest jobbers only, their reputation for high class and reliable seeds causing a steadily increasing demand. The premises are spacious, and are fitted and equipped with every convenience requisite to the successful prosecution of the industry. All orders receive prompt attention. The officers of the company are: Mr. T. H. Gault, president; Mr. Chas W. Morris, secretary; and Mr. Alexander Rodgers, treasurer and general manager; all gentlemen of high standing and ripe experience, Mr. Rodgers being intimately acquainted with every phase and feature of the business, and supervising his large staff of assistants with conspicuous ability. The whole business is conducted in an honorable, well-balanced way, a credit alike to themselves and to the mercantile community of the Western metropolis.

GEO. PIEPER & CO.

In the growth of Chicago trade during the last few years the increase of the demand for fine hardware has necessitated the opening of many new establishments, but there is none that is more representative of a first-class store than that of Messrs. George Pieper & Co., at 283 Clybourn avenue, and running through to 149-151 Weed street. The business was established three months since by Mr. Pieper and a silent partner. The store is ample and capacious, and fitted with every modern convenience for the successful carrying on of the business. The stock is large, well selected and displayed in a manner that reflects the greatest credit upon the good taste of Mr. Pieper. The dimensions of the store are 25x100 feet. The store comprises a large assortment of builders' and mechanics' tools, stoves and ranges, builders' and shelf hardware, pocket and table cutlery, hollow-ware, tinware, enamel ware, copper goods, wooden ware, and general house furnishing goods, besides a large display of fine stoves and ranges, and the whole is sold at prices which are as low as can be found anywhere. A force of polite and efficient salesmen are always on hand to look after the wants of customers. Mr. Pieper is a young man and a native of Germany. His large trade is due to the reputation which he has always enjoyed for integrity and fair dealing. He is a popular member of the Odd Fellows, Knights fr Pythias and Foresters.

J. P. CARUTHERS & CO.

The metropolitan character of Chicago is conceded on all sides, and here are to be found many of the most ably conducted and extensive mercantile establishments in the United States, such for example, as that of the widely and favorably known house of Messrs. J. P. Caruthers & Co., wholesale dealers in, and importers of carriage and heavy hardware, wheels, etc. Mr. J. P. Caruthers is most favorably known in business circles. He is a native of Memphis, Tenn., coming to Chicago fifteen years ago, and has been during the intervening period, actively identified with the hardware and iron trade, acquiring invaluable experience, having been connected with two of the leading wholesale iron houses in Chicago, while he has special qualifications as a live and progressive business man, and since opening the present establishment in 1887, has developed a trade of great magnitude, numbering among his customers, leading carriage manufacturers, hardware dealers, etc., here and all over the North and West He has had to enlarge his facilities, and now occupies the two substantial

five story brick buildings, Nos. 136 and 138 East Kinzie street, 25 feet by 100 each in dimensions. Here is an enormous and most comprehensive stock of carriage and heavy hardware, including merchant and bar iron and steel of all shapes and dimensions, with special line of Swedes' iron for carriage work, horse shoes, anvils, forges, vises, blacksmith's tools, etc. Carriage hardware in complete assortment, wood material for carriage builders', including tops, bodies, and a specialty of the Sarven and other patent wheels, furnished in the white. Quality has ever been the first consideration with Mr. Caruthers and he gives the closest personal attention to the selection of his stock in its every detail. He has an established reputation for giving the best for the value, of any house in the trade, and his progressive methods and energy are proverbial. The trade and manufacturers should place orders here, where all goods shown are reliable, and of newest styles, inclusive of improvements as they come out. The North side can well feel pride in this fine establishment, which is in every respect representative, and has retained to Chicago such an extensive line of out of town trade.

L. A. GORDON.

An enterprising firm, and one that takes a front rank in the line of the manufacture of stove repairs, firebrick, stove cement, etc., is that of L. A. Gordon of No. 131 N. Wells street, successor to P. Callahan, who established the business in 1872 at the above stand, and who was succeeded by the present proprietor the 1st of May, 1891. Mr. Gordon is a young man and was formerly with W. C. Metzner Stove Repair Company for three years, and three years ago purchased their branch house at St. Paul, Minn., where he remained from 1886 to 1889. He employs four men and occupies the ground floor and basement of No. 131 N. Wells street and the basement of No. 129 N. Wells street, 20x60 feet in size. He has established a splendid local trade and furnishes his own patterns. He carries an immense stock of stove repairs, and is prepared to do work on all kinds of stoves. Since Mr. Gordon assumed control of this enterprise he has revolutionized the business, and has not only retained the old customers of the house, but by sheer ability has extended his business connections over a wide area. Mr. Gordon is a prominent member of the Knights of Pythias, and is popular in social and commercial circles. He is a native of Chicago and possessed of all the push and enterprise characteristic of the Chicagoan.

DEAHL BROS.

Among the many superior retail establishments, which are to be found in the southern part of the city, who deal in fine groceries, one of the most prominent is that of Messrs. Deahl Bros. of No. 638 Sixty-third street. The premises are particularly well suited to the requirements of the trade, and have been fitted up in an elegant manner, and one which displays to the best advantage, both outside and inside, the excellent stock always carried here. Messrs. Deahl Bros. have on hand a very superior and varied line of staple groceries, besides canned goods, condiments, cured meats, dried fruits, and all the multifarious incidentals of the business, at prices that are as reasonable as will be found in any similar establishment in the city. The practical and experienced proprietors have satisfied themselves that it is always the best to keep none but first class articles, and by a strict adherence to this rule they have secured, during the twelve months that have elapsed since their inception, a large and influential connection among some of the best families of the city. The firm are natives of Iowa, but have resided in this city for a number of years. They bring to bear great experience, and a thorough comprehension of the wants of the Western trade in all its details. Their resources are ample, their facilities perfect, and their management economical without being penuri ous, and all the factors of a great and lasting prosperity are present in their popular establishment.

C. T. BOAL STOVE CO.

The enterprising dealer naturally seeks the best, and finding it makes a leader of it. One of the most important firms in this city is that of the C. T. Boal Stove Co., with offices and salesroom at Nos. 245 and 247 Kinzie street, near the State street bridge. This firm was established in 1863 under the firm name of Austin & Boal, and so continued until 1868, when Mr. Austin retired. In 1872 he built the Chicago Stove Works, and in 1880 Mr. Boal became a member of the firm of Cribben, Sexton & Co., stove manufacturers. In 1885 Mr. Boal withdrew from the firm and the concern was incorporated under the laws of the state of Illinois with a capital of $100,000, all paid up, and it adopted the present style of firm name, C. T. Boal Stove Co. They at present represent the following stove companies: Orr Painter & Co., of Reading, Pa., the largest stove works in Pennsylvania, with a capital of $500,000, employing over

250 men; also the Highland Foundry Co. of Boston, Mass. Their own special line is the "Henrietta," made at their own foundry on the West side, which employs fifty men. Their line of stoves, ranges and furnaces are the largest and best sold in this section, and their warerooms the most extensive. At Nos. 245 and 247 Kinzie street they occupy the splendid five-story brick block, 40x100 feet in size, which is crowded with their own work, and their trade, extending from the Ohio river to the Pacific slope, is all supplied from this central depot. Their special lines are the "Sunshine," "Othello" and "Torrid" of the Orr, Painter Foundry of Reading, Pa.; the "Henrietta" line of the Chicago foundry and the "Highland" and "Good News" lines of the Highland Foundry Co. of Boston, Mass. Their trade is immense and is constantly increasing. The past year they exceeded $200,-000 in their business, while the increase is continuously greater. Mr. Boal is a native of Ohio, but has been in Chicago since 1854, all of which time he has been identified with the stove business. The officers of the company are: Jesse Orr, president; C. T. Boal, vice-president and treasurer, and Harry Kuhl, secretary; all of whom are practical stove men and understand the details of their business thoroughly. Their offices at Nos. 245 and 247 Kinzie street are handsomely furnished, and the salesroom is equipped with samples of the different lines they sell.

THE UNION LIVERY CO.

One of the popular and very largely patronized livery establishments of the city is the Union Livery Co., of 333, 335 and 337 N. Clark street. This company was incorporated under the Illinois State laws in 1885, with a paid up capital of $25,000. The premises occupied were built especially for the purpose by Mr. Geo. M. Clark, and the company has taken a long lease on them; the building consists of a fine structure of three stories, built of brick and 75x125 feet in dimensions. The first floor is divided into a ladies' waiting room, office, carriage rooms and wash rooms, all completely furnished and neatly arranged. The second floor is used exclusively for horses and is divided off with 100 stalls and eight box stalls. The third floor has accommodations for more horses, and is also used as a feed storeroom. The whole establishment is well lighted and ventilated, and is supplied with every convenience, elevators, etc. The office is splendidly fitted up in bank style, and is never closed. Carriages may be had at all hours of the day or night and all kinds are kept at hand; landaus, hacks, buggies, carts, victorias, broughams, etc. The equipment is perfect, the rigs are as fine as may be had anywhere, the harness the best obtainable, the animals selected for their good driving qualities and reliability, and the drivers and liveried coachmen careful and well trained. The manager is Mr. J. M. Henry, who was formerly manager for Leroy Payne, of the Southern Hotel stables; he is an experienced and capable business manager of the strictest integrity. The president and treasurer of the company is Mr. John M. Tarble, who is a native of Pensacola, Florida, and conducted a livery business there for nine years, and served with honor during the late war. He is well-known and highly respected, and is eminently fitted for the superior business position he occupies. About sixty horses are boarded regularly and thirtyeight or more owned by the company. Every care is taken to supply the demands of patrons in a satisfactory manner. The telephone call is 3349.

ALOIS M. KAPSA.

The hardware establishment of Alois M. Kapsa, at No. 441 S. Canal street, corner Taylor, occupies the entire ground floor of the building, 40x40. A large stock is carried and an excellent trade commanded. Four assistants are employed and Mr. Kapsa also gives his own undivided attention to the business. The stock includes all kinds of shelf and builders' hardware, tools and cutlery, stoves and ranges, gas stoves, tinware, refrigerators, wash wringers, sewing machines and sewing machine supplies, etc. The workshop is in the rear of the store, and the most competent mechanics are employed in this department. A specialty is made of the manufacture of smoke stacks and guttering, and these are of the best class produced in the city. The most careful and prompt attention is also given to repairing of all descriptions, and charges are most reasonable. Mr. Alois M. Kapsa, the proprietor, was born in Bohemia, but has resided in Chicago for ten years. He opened his present establishment in 1889, and by close attention to business and superior qualifications in his line has made it a leading one in that section of the city. He has a reputation for fair dealing that is highly creditable, and is personally a most excellent gentleman who deserves the prosperity he enjoys, and merits the confidence and patronage of the public. Securing his supplies direct from the manufacturers on the most advantageous terms, he is always in a position to offer corresponding liberal terms to his customers. Thus his prices are always the lowest, while his goods are the equal of any of a like character put upon the market.

RIEGERT & KNORR.

The city of Chicago is characterized as the first city of America in architecture. The gentlemen who have originated the designs and planned the great structures of this city are the foremost in architectural skill and engineering ability in the country and worthy of the highest praise. One of the leading and best known firms of engineers and architects is that of Riegert & Knorr, 291-293 North avenue. This house has only been established for five years, but the ability of the gentlemen has been so potent and their designs so original and meritorious that they have become among the most prominent in their line in the city. They have originated the plans for some of the best foundries, residences and stores on the North side and have given satisfaction to all who have engaged them to design or construct buildings. The architectural department is presided over by Mr. Chas. Knorr, who is a graduate of the Polytechnic University of Munich, Germany, and is a skilled architect, familiar with the latest departures, and a resident of Chicago since 1885, being identified with her interests closely, and one of the most advanced and progressive in his profession. The engineering department is conducted under Mr. Emil Riegert, who was born in Germany and graduated from the Polytechnic University of Stuttgart. He has been in America twenty years, and has become one of the best known and most popular engineers in this city. He superintends the construction of buildings, and does the general engineering work of the house. This house has planned and superintended the construction of several very large and important buildings, also some very fine residences, among the accepted work being the four story store and flat building at the southeast corner of Ninth avenue and Wieland street for John Jauch; the residence of Mr. L. Lowenschein, and that of Mr. A. L. Kraus on Freeman street; also the store and flats at southwest corner Center and Bissell streets, and the boiler factory of John Moore & Son, 32-42 Illinois street. The firm stand as the head of the profession in this city and is well patronized. The gentlemen of the firm are of unquestioned ability and integrity.

F. A. OSWALD & CO.

It is a pleasure to record in this commercial review of Chicago the character and enterprises of houses whose existence is emphatic evidence of the honorable position they occupy, and the long course of just dealing they have pursued. Such a house is that of Messrs. F. A. Oswald & Co., dealers in hardware, tools, etc., whose store is located at 139 and 141 Milwaukee avenue. This business was established in 1850 by Mr. F. A. Oswald, who conducted it till 1873, when Mr. Theo. Krueger became a partner. They occupy a spacious double store, 50x80 feet in dimensions, conveniently arranged and equipped and fully stocked with an extensive and choice assortment of hardware. The stock includes all kinds of supplies for builders, cabinet-makers, carpenters and blacksmiths, also coopers' tools, truss hoops, stoves, ranges and tinware. Only really reliable and first-class goods are handled, and the prices quoted necessarily attract careful buyers. The partners, Messrs. Oswald & Krueger, have had long experience in the hardware trade, and spare no efforts to give general satisfaction to their numerous patrons. They employ five clerks and assistants, and their trade extends throughout all sections of the city and its vicinity. Messrs. Oswald & Krueger were both born in Germany, the former of whom has resided in Chicago since boyhood. They are honorable and able business men, who are very popular with all classes of the community.

PETER OKONIEWSKI.

Among the most prominent and successful business men on the West side who have been closely identified with the rapid growth of Chicago is Mr. Peter Okoniewski, dealer in diamonds, jewelry and silverware, located at 695 Milwaukee avenue. Mr. Okoniewski is a Polander by birth, and came to Chicago eighteen years ago, establishing in business in 1879 previously, however, having taken a thorough business and classical training at

Calvary College, Wisconsin, graduating with honors in the class of 1879. He is a gentleman in the prime of life, a deep scholar and an accomplished linguist, speaking five languages with fluency. He is one of the most expert jewelers and watchmakers in the city, having learned his trade in Danzig, Prussia, and devoted eighteen years in the pursuit of his chosen calling. By his superior education and exceptional executive abilities Mr. Okoniewski is to a large extent a leader among the many thousands of his countrymen who have made Chicago their home, and in matters of finance and politics he is looked to for advice and instruction by his countrymen. He is the only expert jeweler and watchmaker of the Polish nationality in Chicago, and as such controls this entire trade, besides acting as agent for all the trans-Atlantic steamship lines and issuing foreign exchange for the Polish people. Mr. Okoniewski is undoubtedly the most conspicuous and influential figure among the many thousand Polish residents of Chicago to-day, and by his rare business and executive abilities he is fully competent to be the adviser and guide of his fellow countrymen who make this Western metropolis their home. His store is handsomely fitted up and well adapted for the transaction of the extensive business which he carries on, and here will be found a choice line of watches, diamonds and jewelry, as well as an extensive assortment of silverware.

F. W. WAGNER.

In these days of public improvements no trade holds a higher position than that of the painter and decorator, and none in this line is better known than Mr. F. W. Wagner of No. 673 Wells street. Mr. Wagner established his business five years ago at No. 546 North Wells street, and his business growing and increasing, he was compelled two years ago to remove to his present commodious quarters, where he occupies the main floor and basement, each 22 by 75 feet in size, and carries a full and complete line of wall paper, dry and mixed paints, oils, glass, window shades and decorating goods, and does a general business in the line of painting, decorating, graining, glazing, kalsomining, room moulding, etc., employing from fifteen to twenty hands in his work. Mr. Wagner is a native Chicagoan, and, possessed of the vim and energy of the city, he does a thriving and prosperous business. He is a member of the A. O. U. W., and personally is popular and well liked by every one.

GROVES & COMPANY.

Twenty years ago George and Isaac Groves came to the city of Chicago from the interior of the state, and two years later established the well-known firm of Groves Brothers, and as such conducted the busines until August, 1891, when the firm was reorganized. Mr. George Groves retiring, and Messrs. B. W. Brockway, F. P. Field, D. A. Mitchell and J. D. Clark entering. Mr. Brockway is the only one of the new members at the Chicago office, the other gentlemen being extensive breeders and shippers of cattle. The offices of the company are located in suite 81 in the Exchange building, at the Union Stock Yards. Mr. Isaac Groves is a thoroughly experienced live stock-salesman and understands every detail of the business. In his long years of experience, he has made the acquaintance of all the leading cattle men of the country, and is better known in the West and Southwest than any one doing business in the yards. Mr. Groves looks after the cattle sales exclusively, while Mr. B. W. Brockway attends to that of the sheep and hogs; and consignments in any line receive prompt attention. The firm do an extensive business in all of these lines, and make liberal advances on consignments. They have an established reputation for the zeal they display in furthering the best interests of their patrons, and in the prompt returns they make for all consignments received. Their financial standing is of the highest, and their responsibility and reliability as dealers beyond question, as reference to any of the mercantile agencies will assure. Both Messrs. Groves & Brockway are cordial, genial gentlemen whom it is a pleasure to have business dealings with.

STRASBURGER & VAN METER.

No one can doubt the influence of the real estate fraternity in developing Chicago, and to them the credit is cheerfully given for bringing the advantages of the city so before the world as to have brought the best manufactories and the most liberal investors into her precincts. A firm doing an immense business in real estate, loans, etc., is that of Strasburger & Van Meter, who are located at the northwest corner of Clark street and Chicago avenue. The business of this house was established about seven years ago, by Mr. John B. Strasburger and continued by him until 1890, when Mr. Absalom J. Van Meter was admitted to partnership and the present style of firm name was adopted. The house does a general real estate business, buys and sells property on commission, handles property for non-residents, collects rents, negotiates loans and places insurance in reliable companies. The business done by this house is of an extensive character, and the heads of the concern are well posted in values in all parts of the city, especially those of the North side, and are often referred to for appraisement. Mr. Strasburger is a Chicagoan by birth and is an attorney of prominence, and has a separate legal office at room 23 in the Reaper block. In 1882 Mr. Strasburger went to Milwaukee, but remained only about a year, and was spoken of as a desirable candidate for representative in the State Legislature, but his vast interests in Chicago would not permit of his remaining away and he returned the following year. Mr. Strasburger was for ten years closely connected with the South Chicago schools, being the principal of the South Chicago schools and high school. He is also a leading member of several of the larger singing societies and of the North side Mannerchor. He graduated in thorough bass, under the instructions of Professor Rehm of Peoria over twenty-five years ago. He was born at Napierville, thirty miles west of Chicago, his father being the Rev. William Strasburger, then considered one of the ablest ministers in the Evangelical Association. His mother, Mrs. Abbie Strasburger, is still living at the old homestead on the North side. Mr. Van Meter is a native of Columbus, O., and has resided in Chicago since 1886. He gives his undivided attention to the real estate business, and is an acknowledged authority in that line. He is held in the highest esteem in business and social circles and is a prominent member of the Knights of Pythias.

BERNARD ROZIENE.

A first-class pharmacy on this important thoroughfare is that conducted under the style of Bernard Roziene, located at No. 2901 Wentworth avenue, at the corner of Twenty-ninth street. This business was originally established by Mr. Bernard Roziene, who obtained his professional training as a chemist and druggist under the most experienced masters of the science and graduated from the College of Pharmacy in Sweden with signal honor, after a long and successful course of study. In 1865 he embarked in his present enterprise and from the start secured a large and influential patronage, which has since steadily developed and increased. The store occupies the ground floor of a three-story stone building, 20x60 feet in dimensions, located in a central situation and admirably adapted for the purposes of the business. The pharmacy is one of the most attractive establishments in this part of the city. It is fitted up with large plate glass show windows, cases and cabinets; the floors are of marble and the fixtures of black walnut; the whole combining to form a rich and tasteful interior. The stock carried is full and complete, the assortment embracing everything in the line of pure fresh drugs, chemicals and medicines, acids, extracts, essences, tinctures, etc.; herbs, barks, roots and kindred botanical products; standard proprietary remedies of acknowledged merit and efficiency; pharmaceutical specialties, physicians' and surgeons' supplies; also fancy and toilet articles in great variety, fancy and medicated soaps, perfumery, brushes, combs, sponges, chamois skins and other druggists' sundries. Physicians' prescriptions and family recipes are here compounded from pure fresh ingredients and in the most careful manner, every precaution being taken to avoid even the possibility of error. The business is now superintended by Mrs. Roziene, who is proprietress. She employs two qualified and experienced assistants, and in all branches popular prices prevail. Mrs. Roziene is the recipient of a widespread and first-class patronage, and is highly esteemed and deservedly popular in business and social circles. Among the many specialties above mentioned we can here find all the different kinds of Swedish remedies known to science. Mr. B. Roziene was one of the very few who graduated from the College of Pharmacy in Sweden and established business in this country. Mr. Roziene was in business in this country about fifteen years before his demise, which occurred in 1888, when but thirty-six years of age, and since then the business has been ably continued by his ever faithful wife, Helga, and still continues to increase in proportions.

ANTON BOENERT.

One great advantage in dealing with a general passage agent like Mr. Anton Boenert of No. 92 La Salle street is that tickets may be obtained by any line of steamships whatever, and not merely one or two, as is the case with agents who represent particular companies. Mr. Boenert began business in 1876, having formerly held a responsible position in the Austrian Consul's office here, from the date of his arrival from Germany, in 1871, until the establishment of his present agency. He conducts an immense trade in the convenient modern way, which offers such great advantages to those desirous of 'sending for their friends, or of transacting business in Europe, most of whom are entirely ignorant of the methods of procedure, rates of exchange and other matters with which Mr. Boenert keeps thoroughly conversant. He issues passage tickets from any point in the United States to any point in Europe, or vice versa, at the lowest rates, and by any railroads or steamships available, effects all transactions in the department of foreign exchange, obtains United States passports, handles American Express money orders, and makes European collections, bringing to bear a sound judgment and wide experience that peculiarly fit him for the business in which he is engaged. He makes a prominent specialty of transfers of money to foreign countries, offering facilities in this branch of the work that cannot be duplicated elsewhere. He deals extensively in real estate at Lake View, West Hammond and other equally desirable locations, which, being his own property, he is able to suit the wants of customers much more effectively than those who are tied down by the instructions they have received. Personally, Mr. Boenert is a gentleman of great ability, and enjoys the esteem of a wide circle, both in social and commercial life for his integrity, probity and many sterling qualities.

BALLARD & PERRY.

The hay, grain and feed house of Messrs. Ballard & Perry, at 5224 Lake avenue, is one of the largest and most important in its line in this section of the city. The business was established about five years ago by Mr. C. Large, from whom Messrs. Ballard & Perry purchased it in the spring of the present year, since when they have made many needed improvements and have materially extended the trade. The building occupied is 20x100 feet in area, two stories in height, and well-equipped throughout with every convenience for the accommodation of the stock. The firm deal in baled hay, grain of all kinds, meal, feed, etc., and can quote the lowest prices to all favoring the house with patronage. Mr. Frederick Ballard is from England originally and Mr. Wm. H. Perry was born in this country. They are live, wide-awake business men of unquestioned reputation, and are doing a splendid flourishing business, well deserving the success which has crowned their ably directed efforts. Their trade is steadily increasing and about the premises there is always a scene of busy activity. Telephone call 10042. In all their business relations the firm are noted for their promptitude and reliability, and in commercial circles they are spoken of in the highest terms of commendation.

NATIONAL DISTILLING CO.'S RED STAR COMPRESSED YEAST.

The need for an absolutely pure and wholesome yeast has been fully met by the National Distilling Company of Milwaukee, Wis., manufacturers of the famous "Red Star" Compressed Yeast, whose branch house in Chicago is at 268 Sedgwick street. This extensive business was established in Milwaukee in 1870 by Wm. Bergenthal & Co., who conducted it till 1887, when it was incorporated under the laws

of Wisconsin, with a capital of $200,000, the executive officers being Mr. A. M, Graw, president, and Aug. Bergenthal, secretary and treasurer. The Chicago branch was opened in 1879, and is under the energetic and careful management of Mr. Ad. Seidel, who is highly regarded in trade circles for his promptness and integrity. They occupy in Chicago a commodious basement, 25x60 feet in area, and employ twelve men and seven teams. The company's factory in Milwaukee is fully equipped with special apparatus and machinery, operated by steam power. In Chicago, last year they sold 200,000 pounds of their famous "Red Star" Compressed Yeast, and from this branch operate thirty-five sub-agencies throughout Illinois, Iowa and Indiana, supplying the principal bakers and grocers. The "Red Star" Yeast is pronounced by competent experts to be the best and most economical in the market, while it is a general favorite with retailers, owing to its great salability, purity and uniform excellence. The prudent housewife, baker, hotel and restaurant proprietor, and indeed all who need a pure substance for aerating bread, and have given this yeast a trial, are unanimous that it accomplishes its work in a re. markable satisfactory manner. Orders are promptly filled at extremely low prices, and complete satisfaction is guaranteed patrons. Mr. Seidel was born in Germany, but has resided in Chicago since 1871. He is a prominent member of the Chosen Friends and Knights of Honor, and has greatly developed and increased the company's business in the city and its vicinity.

B. C. ERNST.

The manufacturers' agent plays an important part in business operations, and is the direct connecting link between the jobber, wholesale dealer and the producer. There are quite a number of these active business men in this city, among whom is Mr. B. C. Ernst, located at 132 La Salle street, who represents leading manufacturers of window glass in the states of Ohio, Indiana, Pennsylvania and New Jersey. Mr. Ernst has been handling and dealing in window glass upwards of twenty years in this city, and in that time has built up a widely diffused through the West and Northwest, and each succeeding year his operations are becoming extended. He can supply any kind or size of window glass

required at manufacturers' prices, and ships orders direct from the factories. His business is of a wholesale character and orders are filled in carload lots. Mr. Ernst, who was raised in Covington Ky., is a gentleman in the prime of life and well known as a business man of unquestioned integrity. He has a wide circle of friends and acquaintances in commercial circles, and altogether is very popular as a business man and citizen.

SUMNER FAULEY ART CO.

The last decade has noted rapid strides in improved picture moldings and the production of art specialties. One of the leading houses devoted to the manufacture of the highest grade of picture frames, mouldings and art novelties is that of Mr. Sumner Fauley, known as the Sumner Fauley Art Company. This business was established about thirteen years ago at Zanesville, O., by the Fauley Brothers, under the same title as now used. In 1883 the partnership was dissolved and the business removed to this city in 1890 and continued by Mr. Sumner Fauley. Mr. Fauley is a native of Zanesville, O., and is one of the leading art critics of the West. He has numerous friends and acquaintances, and is well known in business and trade circles. He is a prominent member of the Knights of Honor and is progressive and liberal in his business. He occupies two stores and one large basement, each 20x60 feet in dimensions, at 835 and 839 West Harrison street; the store at 839 is used as a show room and office, and here is carried a first-class and complete stock of fine frames, in gilt, hardwoods, bronze, relief, enamel, plush, etc., all of taking patterns, and unique designs. A full line of moldings and art specialties are carried, and oil paintings are made a specialty. The room at 835 and basement is used for the manufacture of picture frames, moldings, etc., and here are employed from seven to ten workmen, who are experienced and skilled in their line. The house does a large business in Chicago and neighboring cities, and is regarded as reliable and highly representative. Mr. Fauley also has in connection large portrait studios, where from seven to ten artists are employed making portraits from small pictures and painting pictures of all descriptions. In all instances satisfaction is guaranteed.

STRAUS & SMITH.

Among the principal firms, whose energies are devoted to the trade in furniture, carpets, stoves, etc., that of Messrs. Straus & Smith, whose great warerooms are located at Nos. 279 and 281 W. Madison street, directly central to their large and influential connection, deserves prominent mention. These enterprising gentlemen purchased the business of Mr. Woodhull in October, 1889, and at once infused such energy and life into the trade, that it began a steady development, which has continued to the present, abundantly testifying to the wisdom of the management. The store contains no less than 10,000 square feet of floor space, every inch of which is occupied by the immense stock. This is of such a varied and complete nature that they are prepared to thoroughly equip houses from top to bottom with every article required, and to supply suites for the various apartments that will harmonize in shade, style and tone with its decorations. They sell on the easy payment system when desired, and offer every facility for the transaction of business, orders being received by telephone (call No. 4371), and as promptly and accurately executed as those orally delivered. The quality of the stock carried here is first-class in every branch, only the best manufacturers being dealt with, and the articles being selected with the greatest care. Mr. David Straus is a native of Texas, and Mr. S. H. Smith of Baltimore, Md., both being young energetic business men of great capacity, respected and esteemed by all who know them, and well worthy of their conspicuous success.

GANIERE & LAYTON.

A notable and popular establishment devoted to the photographic art in this section of the city, is that of Messrs. Ganiere & Layton at No. 3140 State street. Few studios in Chicago so evidently illustrate the remarkable improvements that have of late been made in the practice of the art. The business was established six years ago. The firm is composed of Mr G. E. Ganiere and Mrs. L. C. Layton, both artists of the highest professional standing and superior artistic attainments. From the time they assumed control their gallery has attracted very great interest by the unmistakable excellence of its work, and as a result, a very extensive patronage has been built up. The premises occupied comprise a single story brick building, 25x60 feet in dimensions. The parlors and reception rooms are elegantly and tastefully fitted up and furnished, and present a most attractive and inviting appearance, while the operating rooms are equipped with all the latest improved appliances and instruments known to the art. Photography in all its branches, portraiture and landscape, interior and commercial, is here executed under the most advantageous conditions, and the eminent satisfaction rendered to patrons, who are among the most discriminating classes in the city, is the best tribute that need be offered to the artistic excellence of the work. Pastel, water color, crayon and India ink work are made a prominent specialty and executed in the most artistic manner that science and skill can accomplish. Four competent assistants are employed, and the most popular prices prevail. Mr. Ganiere is a native of Chicago, and has been in pursuit of the art since his early youth. Mrs. Layton was born in Buffalo, N. Y., and is a thoroughly skilled exponent of the profession. They are personally popular and reliable in their business methods, and are highly esteemed and respected.

G. A. GRUONER.

Some men are possessed of such remarkable energy and activity that they are not content to do business in as extensive a manner as their competitors, but strive onward with restless zeal to excel them all and place their own establishment foremost in the ranks of industry. Men of this kind are valuable citizens, and are always foremost in advancing the public welfare. Mr. Gustave A. Gruoner is a representative man of this class. He conducts a first-class drug business at 2801 Archer avenue, where he occupies the entire ground floor of the handsome two story building, 20x50. This establishment was founded in 1890, and, though yet in its youth, is a worthy example of what energy and ambition can perform. Mr. Gruoner is a native of the state of Illinois, and has always resided in Chicago. His entire business is city trade, and it has of late grown to very large proportions. His store contains a full line of drugs, medicines, perfumery and beautiful toilet articles. The handsome show windows display an immense variety of carefully selected and assorted goods of the class which we generally find in apothecaries' shops. The shelves and counters are finely decorated. The show cases are filled with all kinds of drugs and chemicals, sundries, etc., and are calculated to attract the visitor's attention, thereby gaining his patronage. As Mr. Gruoner also carries a full line of cigars of the most tempting brands, He makes a specialty of compounding physicians' prescriptions carefully and accurately. His establishment is connected by telephone, 9049 Mr. Gruoner is a man of prominence in his community, and his transactions are characterized by zeal, sound judgment and discretion, qualifications essential to success.

THE LEVER SPIRAL SPRING CO.

A representative, and one of the most noted and enterprising of those manufacturing concerns which, having their works established outside of this state, have been led to open branch houses in Chicago in order to participate in the numerous advantages to be derived from the trade that flows into this market from all sections of the great west, is The Lever Spiral Spring Company, manufacturers of Spiral King and

Spiral Queen Springs, Spiral groove sand collar axles and Crown fifth wheels. This responsible company was organized at Oshkosh, Wis., in 1887, and duly incorporated, its officers at present being Mr. H. C. Swan president, and Miss M. E. Dickinson secretary. An office was opened in this city in 1889, and its management intrusted to Miss Dickinson, a lady of exceptional business abilities, and in whose hands the trade of the company from here has attained a remarkable development. The premises at first occupied were at No. 375 Wabash avenue, but lately the office and salesroom were removed to room 302 in the Boylston building, Nos. 265-269 Dearborn street. They have an area of 15x20 feet, and are neatly fitted up and appointed, and provided with every facility for the prompt execution of all business. One traveling salesman is kept constantly on the road, and the trade extends over all the west, northwest and southwest. The goods of the company are well introduced, and are favorites alike with the carriage manufacturer as well as the consumer. Their "Crown" fifth wheel is a perfect anti rattler. All its parts are absolutely interchangeable, and the company have the most complete line on the market, and can fit anything that runs on wheels. The spiral groove sand collar is simple but effectual, and is the only axle ever invented that will exclude sand; it will last twice as long as any other axle. The "Spiral" spring is the easiest riding spring in the world. These goods are all first-class, and are offered to the trade at the lowest figures. Orders are promptly filled, and fair dealing is the motto of this reliable company, while their products justly merit the commendations bestowed upon them by the trade and public in general.

JOHN A. BONGARD.

Mr. John A. Bongard is destined to make his mark in Chicago as an architect of special attainments. His handsomely fitted office is at room 30, 169 La Salle street, where he recently removed from the Ashland block. He is prepared to make designs for and estimate on all classes of proposed new buildings for public and private use, preparing all sketches and plans for same, and studiously embodying every wish and suggestion of his clients. His plans are both practical and economical ; modern ideas are noticeable features, coupled alike with symmetry and architectural beauty. His estimates and computations are always accurate and not exceeded in actual construction, while under his careful and personal supervision of builders and contractors the specifications are most rigidly adhered to. Mr. Bongard is a native of Wisconsin, and received his education in Chicago. He is exceedingly popular, both professionally and personally, and has the most favorable prospects before him.

THE RASCHER MAP PUBLISHING CO.

If history should be correct and true how much more important is it than maps of cities and countries should be accurate, as upon these history is founded and explained. A map publishing firm, with an established reputation for accuracy and exactness is the Rascher Map Publishing Company, whose main office is at room 42, No. 164 La Salle street. This business was established seventeen years ago by Mr. Charles Rascher, the manager of the present company, which was incorporated with ample capital some years later, and of which Mr. Louis V. Silenberg is secretary, and W. L. Niehorster is general agent. The company employs a large staff of reliable draughtsmen and assistants, and publishes maps of all the cities in the United States from accurate surveys made by its own staff of engineers. Their work is always the most finished and complete in details, being used where accuracy is most essential by the fire insurance companies. Each of the members of the company is a practical civil engineer and draughtsman, and is thorough in his line. Their reputation is second to none in the land, and they enjoy an excellent patronage all over the world where their reputation is known The same firm publishes the most reliable real estate maps of the city as well as of the county, and these are acknowledged by the real estate men in this city to be the best yet put on the market.

PRINCE'S EUROPEAN HOTEL.

Chicago is favored with the benefits and advantages derived from having in her midst some of the best American hotels in existence, pronounced by competent authorities as best illustrating in their management the modern art of hotel-keeping. One of the most popular on the South side is Prince's European hotel, located at Nos. 277 and 279 S. Clark street, corner of Van Buren street. This house (formerly the Van Buren House) has been under the management of its present well-known proprietor, Mr. Simeon D. Prince, since 1889, and has enjoyed an enviable reputation with all who ever experienced its hospitality. Management is the keynote to success in the record of any hotel, and so with Prince's. The proprietor has made hotel-keeping a life study; he early took his share of its cares and responsibilities, an experience which fully accounts for the smoothness with which everything connected with his present hostelry is conducted. It constitutes the third and fourth floors of the four story stone building at the address indicated, and contains 110 rooms, and can accomodate 150 guests. The furnishings are all strictly first class; the beds and bedding new and of the best quality, the rooms large, light and airy, and a thorough system of organization is enforced by Mr. Prince, who personally sees after the comfort of all guests. He is a native of Massachusetts, and has been a highly respected resident of Chicago for the past twenty-six years. Prince's hotel is run exclusively on the European plan, the following being the modest tariff: Single rooms 25c to 50c per day; $1.25 to $1.75 per week.

J. A. McCONNELL.

One of the largest and most popular establishments in that progressive section of the city known as Englewood is that of Mr. J. A. McConnell, of No. 646 Sixty-third street. This enterprising merchant has developed a business of very considerable proportions during the few months that have elapsed since his opening, and now controls a first-class patronage in all parts of the city. The firm name was at first Messrs. McConnell & Holmes, but, on the retirement of the latter gentleman in May last, the senior partner became sole proprietor. The business consists of a wholesale and retail trade in butter and cheese from some of the most celebrated dairies and creameries in the West, eggs, poultry, game, fruit, canned goods; and on the 18th of June last, Mr. McConnell opened a first-class meat market on the premises, and is now fully prepared to give the most perfect satisfaction to his customers in each department. He carries full lines of fresh, salt and smoked meats as well as fish and game in season, and has been so fortunate as to secure Mr. C. L. Thomas the well-known manager of Messrs. J. Bredin & Co.'s market, as his foreman. The reputation of this house for high class goods is extending to all parts of the city, and many of the most desirable retailers and private families are becoming its permanent patrons. Mr. McConnell has a very handsome and convenient store, kept in the neatest manner, and has perfected his facilities for the preservaton of perishable goods in the finest condition, large and elegant ice chests being provided in rear of the store for this purpose. He is a native of Illinois, and is deservedly popular and respected by all who know him. He constantly endeavors to merit by the strictest principles of commercial probity and just dealing a continuance of the support he already enjoys.

CHICAGO POP CORN FACTORY.

A novel business of large dimensions and immense popularity is that of the Chicago Pop Corn Factory, of which Mr. J. T. Dalton is the proprietor. This gentleman established the business five years ago, at 248 F. Randolph street. On the first of May last he moved to 184 East Indiana street, where he has every facility for prosecuting the business. It seems almost incredible that so much of this popular article should be sold, but Mr. Dalton manufactures over forty barrels of pop corn daily, using for this purpose three furnaces and employing eight hands. He manufactures all kinds of pop corn and sweet parched corn, dealing in the product, both wholesale and retail. His factory at 184 Indiana street, near Clark street, is 25x60 feet in dimensions, occupying ground floor and basement. The packing room is in the rear and the factory in basement, the front being used for store purposes. The trade extends all over Illinois, Iowa, Michigan, Minnesota, Texas, Missouri, Mississippi and Tennessee. The corn is purchased direct from producers in large quantities, and the weekly sales average over $600. Mr. Dalton is an active and progressive business man. He was born in Shelby Co., Tennessee, and has resided in Chicago for six years. He is well known in business circles, where he is held in high esteem.

F. PRUSSING.

The North side is in no way deficient in its first-class establishments in every branch of trade. In fact, many of them rival in size and conveniences the more pretentious houses of the city proper. Prominent among these is F. Prussing, dealer in foreign and domestic groceries, at Nos. 51 and 53 North State street. This house was established by the present proprietor twelve years ago, and occupies the ground floor and basement of the handsome block at the above number, 40 by 65 feet in dimensions. His stock, consisting of a large and carefully selected stock of foreign and domestic, staple and fancy groceries, wines, liquors and cordials for family trade, and in fact, an elegant assortment of everything in that line, is the largest on the North side. Mr. Prussing imports all of his own French, English and German goods, hence can compete with any house in the city, in price or quality. His lines of teas and coffees are the very best, and his large family trade is due to the excellence of all his goods. He employs ten assistants and four delivery wagons, and all orders are promptly and correctly attended to. To accommodate his immense trade he receives orders by his telephone, numbered 3131. Mr. Prussing is a native of Germany, and he has been in Chicago since 1874. He is popular in social and business circles, and is an honored member of Dearborn Council No. 1105 Royal Arcanum.

HEINZE BROS.

Few firms on the North side are better qualified to serve the interests of the public than Messrs. Heinze Bros., dealers in staple and fancy groceries, at 198 Wells street, corner of Superior street. The firm is composed of Messrs. W. G., G. A. & H. H. Heinze, three young able and enterprising men, who founded this concern three years ago, and from the start have, by their close attention to business, built up a large and remunerative trade. The premises are provided with every modern convenience and comprise the ground floor and basement, each having dimensions of 25x60 feet. The store is handsomely fitted up and furnished, and is replete with a large, comprehensive and carefully selected stock. The assortment embraces full lines of staple and fancy groceries, such as fresh crop China, Japan and Ceylon teas, Mocha, Java, Rio and Maracaibo coffees, pure spices, ground or whole, flavors, extracts, pickles, sauces, condiments, and all kinds of table luxuries, sugars, syrups, the best brands of family flour and prepared cereals, baking powders, bakers and laundry supplies, etc., etc.; also fruits in season; nor must we forget to include fresh butter, daily from the farms, and which is carefully kept in a large and well-equipped refrigerator for the purpose. Messrs. Heinze adopt a free delivery system and have an ample force of help so that customers are not kept waiting, and orders are at all times sent out with quick dispatch. They are all natives of Chicago, are enterprising young business men, and have gained success at the expense of hard work and close application to business. It is to such enterprising firms as Messrs. Heinze Bros. that the rapid growth of this city is largely due.

N. GROSS.

A tailor who has established a reputation for the manufacture of the highest class of goods, and the latest styles is Mr. N. Gross, whose establishment is located at 578 Milwaukee avenue. Mr. Gross has been established at his present location since the beginning of 1889, and has built a reputation of the highest order. He is thoroughly practical, having served his apprenticeship abroad, and having also followed his trade in Chicago for nineteen years. His customers unite in their praise for the excellence of the goods used, first class fit always obtained, and the superiority of the workmanship. Mr. Gross occupies a neatly fitted store on the ground floor, 25 x40 feet in dimensions. This is stocked with goods of all kinds pertaining to the business, including suitings of tweed, cheviot, cassimeres, worsted, broadcloth and other desirable fabrics. Two practical cutters are constantly employed, and the work is all done under the personal supervision of the proprietor, thus securing the best and most satisfactory results. Mr. Gross was born in Germany and came to the United States when but fourteen years of age. He has resided in Chicago for twenty-two years, and is known as a business man of sterling worth and unquestionable integrity. Mr. Gross is a prominent member of the Knights of Pythias, Knights of Honor, I. O. B. B., I. O. S. B. and Sons of Israel. His friends are numerous and his trade extensive.

H. LANGE.

One of the most practical and responsible carriage trimmers in Chicago is Mr. H. Lange, who is located in business at 61 Wendell street. Mr. Lange has been established in business for fifteen years. He was first located at Green Bay, Wisconsin, but came to Chicago about thirteen years ago and located in business at 262 Michigan street. He occupied the present premises about five years ago, and has since had a large and growing business connection. His establishment is provided with everything necessary to carrying on the business successfully and properly, and he employs only experienced and competent help. Mr. Lange was born in Germany, and learned his trade in the old country. He is a practical carriage trimmer and repairer, and carries on this business with great success. He does all his work with promptness and dispatch, and in the most practical manner. Mr. Lange has had a wide experience, and is a skilled and thorough mechanic. He has numerous friends and acquaintances who hold him in the highest esteem, and his business connections are of the finest and most flattering character. He has many patrons, who are pleased to continue to patronize him on account of his excellent work and unquestioned integrity.

ADOLPH SCHWARTZ & CO.

The meat and provision trade is well represented in this city. The business has fortunately fallen into the hands of men who take pride in securing for their patrons the best that can be obtained at the abattoirs and wholesale markets. One of the best meat and provision stores on the West side of the city is that of Adolph Schwartz & Co., 373 Loomis street. These gentlemen have been established in the present location for two years, and have succeeded in establishing a leading and very substantial business. The firm is composed of Mr. Adolph Schwartz, who was born in Germany, and learned the butcher trade thoroughly in all its branches; in fact it might almost be said he was reared in the business. He came to America in 1880, and after a year's residence in Milwaukee settled in Chicago, with whose interest he has been identified ever since. Mr. Jacob Cohn, his partner, is also a German who has lived in America for two and a half years, and all of this time in Chicago. These gentlemen are very cordial and popular; they have hosts of friends, and are considered thoroughly reliable by all who know or have dealings with them. Their business is quite extensive, they have a large store, 25x50 feet, splendidly fitted up and stocked with the best the markets afford.

They carry the finest beef, mutton, veal, pork and poultry that can be had, and in season game and fish are always on hand. They also handle vegetables, fruits, berries, melons, etc. Their selected hams, bacon and sausages are the best to be found in the city, and every customer's interest is studied carefully. They have a splendid ice chest, with a capacity of one and a half tons, where all supplies are kept in the most perfect manner during the hot season. They own their own delivery wagon, and goods are delivered promptly to all parts of the city.

W. F. BACH.

There are very few articles which have occupied the attention of inventors to such a degree as washing machines. The field is a tempting one, because of the universal demand, and because of the great reward that is to be gained by the production of a really good article, at a reasonable price. In this connection, we have to call the attention of our readers to a new invention in this line by Mr. W. F.

Bach of No. 103 S. Canal street, and which possesses such advantages that it is sure to become the household washer of the future. Some of these are: the ease with which it can be worked, the thorough manner in which it operates, the reduction of wear and tear, its compactness, its lightness, its imperviousness to rust, rot or leakage, and its durability,—qualities which at once commend themselves to the anxious housekeeper, as of the utmost importance in articles so constantly in use as these. Every part is interchangeable, and if fractured can be replaced at a small cost. Mr. Bach is an expert machinist, and has given his special attention to the production of a washer that will meet the requirements of all. Although his letters patent are but of recent issue, he has already many testimonials from the most desirable quarters as to the efficiency of his invention. He is a German by birth, and emigrated to Chicago in 1884, establishing his present business six years later. He is an esteemed member of the Masonic order, as well as of the Foresters, and has won the sincere respect of all classes of the community for his originality, urbanity and integrity.

C. F. RITTERSHAUS.

The North part of the city is well supplied with first-class markets, and one of the most popular is located at No. 907 Clybourn avenue, the splendid appointed meat market of Mr. C. F. Rittershaus, who deals in all kinds of fresh, salt and smoked meats, sausages, etc., and handles all kinds of poultry in season. Mr. Rittershaus established his present business five years ago, and in 1890 built his present handsome building at the above number, 30x75 feet in size. He occupies the ground floor and basement. The store is handsomely fitted and finished in ash, with marble top counters, large coolers and every convenience. Mr. Rittershaus' trade is very extensive and increasing, he now employing four assistants, who are kept busy. He was born in Germany and has resided in Chicago for fifteen years, where he has made many friends by his honesty and industry.

OTTO N. HARDEKOPF.

Mr. Otto N. Hardekopf is one of the oldest established and most favorably known undertakers and embalmers in the city. He has been established in the business for fifteen years, and has a record for honorable dealing and courteous treatment. Mr. Hardekopf is a native of Germany, and has resided in Chicago since 1865. He has a large patronage, and is most highly esteemed by all who know him. He conducts a first-class undertaking business, having the best selection of caskets, coffins and cases to be obtained, together with all necessary supplies for the funeral. His place of business is on Milwaukee avenue from No. 1479 to 1481, and here he has a splendid building divided to suit the needs of his business. The dimensions are 50x100 feet, part being used as a wareroom and office, and the balance as a livery and boarding stable. Mr. Hardekopf has sixteen horses and some very fine carriages, also a magnificent hearse, which cost over $2,000. He has also a number of horses taken to board at his stable. He employs regularly an assistant undertaker, six men, and does a thriving business. His stables are finely fitted up, and he has a great many regular customers. Mr. Hardekopf is a practical embalmer and funeral director, and conducts his business in a gentlemanly and sympathetic manner. His treatment of his patrons is both liberal and courteous, and in everything he is a business man and gentleman of the most exalted character.

HEALEY & KEATS.

One of the neatest and most popular drugstores on the north side, is that of Healey & Keats, at No. 44 Wells street, near the Northwestern depot. The business of this house has been established for nine years, being founded by Mr. H. J. Bates, the former proprietor. About four months ago Mr. Bates disposed of his interest to the present proprietors, who have taken hold energetically and with every possible omen of success. They are young men of business ability and social standing. They have been educated in the best school of the kind in the country, the Chicago College of Pharmacy; and they bring special fitness to bear on their venture. They are members of the Illidois State Pharmaceutical Society, and the Illinois Pharmaceutical Association. The store is 20x40 feet in dimensions, and is elegantly fitted up with plate glass windows, show cases and large marble soda fountain of the finest make. Their stock is fresh and well selected, consisting of all kinds of pure drugs and chemicals, toilet articles, brushes, fancy articles, perfumes, physicians' and surgeons' supplies, proprietary articles and druggists' sundries of all kinds. They are the proprietors of a compound that has already gained considerable prominence as being of great merit—the Healey & Keats' Wild Cherry Balsam. They make a specialty of compounding physicians' prescriptions, giving personal attention to the matter, and guaranteeing the use of pure drugs. Two competent assistants are employed, and the patronage is large and is making a steady increase. The proprietors are worthy every confidence, and merit the richest success.

JOHN C. RICE.

In all localities the convenience of a well stocked hardware, tin and stove store is appreciated, and the more extensive the stock to select from the greater convenience. A splendid establishment of this kind is that of Mr. John C. Rice of No. 494 Wells street, who carries a large line of the best makes of stoves, heaters, ranges, shelf and builders' hardware, house furnishing goods, etc., and is also manufacturer of everything in the line of tin, copper and sheet iron ware, does jobbing of all kinds, cleans and repairs furnaces, and in fact everything pertaining to his line of business. Mr. Rice opened in business ten years ago, and his trade increased so rapidly that five years ago he

moved to his present quarters, which he owns, and occupies the main floor and basement, each 25 by 60 feet in size, for his business. The main floor is used for his office and show rooms, and are neatly and conveniently arranged for the line of goods handled. The basement serves as his extensive workshop, where six men are employed in the manufacturing line, making a specialty of roofing, spouting, guttering and jobbing of all kinds. Mr. Rice is a Pennsylvanian by birth, and has resided in Chicago for twenty years, where he has built up an extensive trade and made hosts of friends.

GEORGE FRASER.

This city has many business houses that have had a long and successful career and stand in the front rank in their respective localities. Among these there is notably worthy of mention the old established and reliable confectionery and bakery establishment of Mr. George Fraser. This business was established twenty-six years ago by Mr. Fraser, who began the business and was doing well when the great fire came, devouring everything in 1871. After this he erected the neat two-story brick structure he now occupies at 409 Division street, where he has ample accommodations and every convenience in his splendid establishment which is 50x100 feet in dimensions. Mr. Frazer occupies for business purposes the ground floor and basement of this building, having his bakery in the basement and rear and the store on the ground floor front. This he has stocked with the finest cakes, pies, buns, rolls and pastry of all kinds, also confectionery, etc. Mr. Fraser uses only the finest materials in his work ,and is thus enabled to guarantee satisfaction. He has a large patronage, and his goods are well known for their superiority in all parts of the north side. He employs ten experienced bakers and helpers and everything is in every way first-class. Mr. Fraser was born in Scotland, and came to this city thirty years ago. He is well known in business circles, and is a heavy holder of real estate. His business is popular and constantly increasing.

EDWARD MALAM.

The well appointed, handsome, attractive establishment of Mr. Edward Malam, wholesale and retail grocer, is one of the largest and most prominent on Milwaukee avenue. The premises, two stores adjoining each other, have a combined area of 40x100 feet, well equipped with every facility for meeting all the demands of the large and growing trade with which it is favored. Mr. Malam established the splendid business he is now conducting at 274 Blue Island avenue in 1873, and six years later secured and removed to the very desirable double building now occupied at 250 and 252 Milwaukee avenue. An immense stock of goods is carried, embracing everything in the line of imported and domestic fancy and staple groceries of a superior quality, and which has been selected expressly for a first-class custom. A specialty is made of choice China and Japan teas and Mocha, Java and South American coffees, family and pastry flour, hermetically sealed goods in tin and glass, table luxuries, preserves, condiments, pure spices, and creamery and dairy butter, fresh eggs, etc. The wholesale trade comes from the city and the state, and also Michigan, Indiana and Wisconsin, while the flourishing retail trade is of the most substantial character, and is growing in importance and magnitude. Mr. Malam, who was born in England, is a gentleman in the prime of life. He has lived in this city since 1872, and during his business career always enjoyed the unbounded confidence of all having dealings with his house. He selects his stock of goods with care, and patrons are always assured of receiving the finest and best at the lowest price. Six clerks are employed, and three teams call for and deliver goods in any part of the city, steamboat docks and railroad depots, without extra charge.

SCHNIEDEWEND & LEE COMPANY.

There is no branch of mechanical industry in which the march of progress has been more apparent than in that devoted to the manufacture of printing presses. In this connection we desire to here make special reference to the old established and reliable house of Schniedewend & Lee Company, 303 and 305 Dearborn street, and whose factory is located at Nos. 2529 to 2547 Leo street. It was founded twenty-one years ago, and has always maintained a leading and foremost position in the ranks of the trade. The Challenge Machine Works, which were completed in 1890, are 100 by 200 feet, with an ell 35x60 feet for blacksmith shop and power; the floor space occupied is over 60,000 square feet. They are fully equipped with all the latest improved machinery and appliances, including a complete electric light plant, and Sturtevant system of heating, which is also arranged for cooling in summer, so that the works can be kept at an even temperature the year round. A force of 150 skilled workmen are employed in the manufacture of printing presses, paper cutters, electrotype and stereotype machinery, shafting, pulleys, engines and boilers, and, in fact, nearly every machine required by printers, electrotypers, photoengravers and their kindred trades. Among the machines which have given Schniedewend & Lee Company a world wide reputation, we may mention the celebrated Challenge job presses, the Schniedewend & Lee Gordon job presses, Challenge lever and power paper cutters and Advance paper cutters. A notable feature of the job presses manufactured by Schniedewend & Lee Company is the high speed at which they may be run without injury or undue work. It is no uncommon thing to see their eight medium presses running at 3,500 per hour, while other sizes may be safely run at as high speeds as the sheets can be handled. Every machine is fully tested in ac-

tual use before being shipped, and is guaranteed as to quality of material and workmanship. The product of the Challenge Press Works is about a quarter million dollars per annum, and it is expected to reach twice this amount the coming year. Their trade extends all over the United States and Canada, Brazil, Australia and some parts of Europe, and Schniedewend & Lee Company are deservedly looked upon as among the leaders in this important line of industry.

H. BUTT & CO.

The firm, H. Butt & Co., has been long enough established to inspire their patrons with confidence that they will still continue to serve them in the same faithful, conscientious way that they have adopted since they opened their doors at 102 La Salle street, three years ago. But recently they moved to larger and more commodious premises at 205 Wells street, and here they have an ample store on the ground floor, 25x60 feet in dimensions, with a large yard and stables in the rear. In addition to carrying a large stock of hay, grain and mill feed, they also have all kinds of anthracite and bituminous coal from the best Lehigh, Lackawanna and other leading mines, all thoroughly screened; and also wood by the cord or basket, cut or sawed to any desired size. Their business is wholesale and retail, and prices are reduced for large quantities, though the retail prices are considerably lower than those charged in some sections of the city. They deliver all goods free, and their coal always weighs 2,000 pounds to the ton. They also do a large express business, employing several teams and careful hands in the removal of furniture or breakable articles. Their stables for this purpose are at the rear of 101 Wells street. The firm consists of Mr. H. Butt and Mr. Wm. Driscoll, both young men and both natives of this state, and their close attention to business has secured for them a long list of influential friends.

L. F. REMBOLD.

Thanks to the prosperity of our great America, it is no longer the very wealthy who are enabled to indulge in the convenience of a good watch, and it is few persons we meet who are not supplied with one. Necessarily the manufacture and sale of watches form no inconsiderable part of the business of the day, and in that line none better are known

in the city than Mr. L. F. Rembold, practical watchmaker, at No. 225 Dearborn street, in the Temple Court building, opposite the Post Office, who makes a specialty of fine watch repairing. Mr. Rembold is a practical mechanic, has had years of experience and his work at all times is known to be perfectly reliable. He carries an immense stock of optical goods of all kinds, and which he sells at most reasonable prices and absolutely guarantees. He is a courteous gentleman and visitors are cordially invited to give him a call. He makes a specialty of fine repairing, and his references are unexceptionable, among which may be mentioned some of our most prominent citizens. Mr. L. F. Rembold was born and raised in Switzerland, the home of watchmaking. He has spent a life time in acquiring his valuable experience in this industry.

GRACE VARNISH COMPANY.

The importance of Chicago as a manufacturing center is becoming recognized the world over, and its houses doing a manufacturing business, in various lines, have become leaders in trade circles occupying the foremost rank for superior goods and moderate prices. One of the best known and well-established companies of the city is the Grace Varnish Company, manufacturers of fine varnishes, whose establishment is located at 119 and 127 Larrabee street. This business was established by Grace & Co. about ten years ago. In 1890 the business had so increased that it was thought advisable to incorporate, to more readily handle the business. This was done and Mr. Parker Grace was made president and Wm. Mr. Swannell secretary and treasurer. The premises occupied for business are ample in all respects and thoroughly equipped with all necessary machinery for the manufacture of fine varnishes, a specialty being made of coach, agricultural and furniture varnishes. Of these the company manufacture great quantities and do a thriving business, having a large city and country trade. They keep on the road a number of traveling salesmen who visit the trade and sell to the dealers of the West and Northwest many hundreds of gallons of the superior manufactures of this company. This house has a reputation of manufacturing an extra fine and reliable varnish much in use by our leading carriage-makers. The gentlemen at the head of this enterprise have a high reputation for ability and standing.

They are well known in business and general trade circles, and are held in the highest esteem. Mr. Parker Grace is a native of Cincinnati, Ohio, and has resided in Chicago twenty years. Mr. Wm. Swannell was born at Kankakee, and is well and favorably known in this city.

E. A. ROSENE.

It is a good many years now since Mr. E. A. Rosene established a pharmacy on the North side. In 1885 he died and his estate decided to continue the business, which they have since done under the very able management of Mr. Axel E. Th. Letzler, who is pharmacist in charge. The store is situated at 318 E. Division street, at the corner of Sedgwick street, and is one of the most attractive in the neighborhood, being 22x50 feet in dimensions and fitted up in the most approved style with every possible convenience for the successful prosecution of the business. Special attention is paid to the compounding of physicians' prescriptions and a well-appointed pharmacy is set apart for the purpose, but more than this, Mr. Letzler manufactures all his own tinctures, essences and extracts, so that there can be no possibility of impurity or inaccuracy. The stock is very comprehensive and embraces a full line of pure drugs and chemicals, toilet requisites, perfumes, soaps, brushes, combs, and sponges, chamois, powders and cosmetiques, mineral waters, pure wines and liquors for medicinal purposes, sick room necessaries, surgical appliances and everything that is to be found in a first-class drug store. Mr. Letzler is a native of Sweden and in 1884 came to this country. He was formerly in business in Rockford, Ill., having left there three and a half years ago to come to this city. He is a gentleman who has always been conspicuous for his courteous manners and has made himself deservedly popular in the community, being regarded as one of the most reliable men in his profession. Two polite and skilled assistants are in the store to attend to customers at all hours and devote their undivided attention to their duties. The trade is continually increasing and the class of patrons is of the best.

L. E. NELSON & CO.

A leading hardware firm on the North side is L. E. Nelson & Co. of 70 N. Clark street, which has now been in existence for ten years, having been originally established by 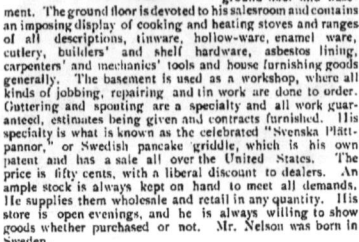 Nelson & Bellhorn, but in 1885 Mr. Nelson succeeded and has since continued it alone. In that year he moved to his present location, having previously been at 231 N. Clark street. His store is 20x100 feet and comprises the ground floor and basement. The ground floor is devoted to his salesroom and contains an imposing display of cooking and heating stoves and ranges of all descriptions, tinware, hollow-ware, enamel ware, cutlery, builders' and shelf hardware, asbestos lining, carpenters' and mechanics' tools and house furnishing goods generally. The basement is used as a workshop, where all kinds of jobbing, repairing and tin work are done to order. Guttering and spouting are a specialty and all work guaranteed, estimates being given and contracts furnished. His specialty is what is known as the celebrated "Svenska Plättpannor," or Swedish pancake griddle, which is his own patent and has a sale all over the United States. The price is fifty cents, with a liberal discount to dealers. An ample stock is always kept on hand to supply all demands. He supplies them wholesale and retail in any quantity. His store is open evenings, and he is always willing to show goods whether purchased or not. Mr. Nelson was born in Sweden.

MRS. J. F. SER VIS.

One of the best known confectioners in the city is Mrs. J. F. Ser Vis, whose confections are much sought after. The business was established in 1881 by Mr. J. F. Ser Vis and continued by him until his death in 1891, when his widow, Mrs. J F. Ser Vis, continued the business to the intense satisfaction of the many patrons of the house. Mrs. Ser Vis is a lady of charming manner and excellent business tact and judgment, and she manages the affairs of the house in the most creditable manner, and is rapidly extending the trade. The main store is at 65 N. Clark street, and a popular branch store is conducted at Eighteenth and Wabash avenue, Havlin's Theater. The store on Clark street is neatly fitted up, has glass wall and counter show cases and a fine ice cream parlor. From five to seven practical and experienced confectioners are employed, and the house enjoys a reputation for the superior excellence of its products. As none but the finest and best materials are used, satisfaction is in every way guaranteed. Candies are made every day, and a full assortment of all kinds of ice cream and ices are kept constantly on hand. The prices are moderate, and there is constantly a liberal demand for the goods. All orders are promptly filled and delivered to any part of the city. The success achieved by Mrs. Ser Vis is substantial and well deserved.

B. GRIMM.

The needs of a large city are so varied and many that they are best supplied by those who give their attention to some specialty. Among all the various lines of business there is none that gives more satisfaction than a first-class butter, dairy produce and cheese depot. Such an one is that of Mr. B. Grimm, whose place of business is at 521 W. Twelfth street. Here Mr. Grimm has a large and neatly fitted store, where he carries a select stock of butter, eggs and cheese, together with other dairy products. He receives his goods fresh daily, and keeps them in the best manner in large and conveniently arranged refrigerators. The butter is from the best creamery, a specialty being made of the finest grade of Wisconsin butter, sold in larger or small pails. Mr. Grimm has a large local patronage of the most desirable character, and also retails to many customers all over the city. He has quite a reputation for his goods and his business is growing daily. He has his own delivery team and attends strictly to his own business, thus giving assurance to his customers of the continued standard and excellence of his goods. Mr. Grimm is a native of Germany, who has resided in Chicago only three years; in that time he has made numerous friends and acquaintances, who hold him in the highest esteem. He has an established reputation with both business men and customers for the strictest honesty and integrity.

ANDREW SCHERER.

It belongs to Mr. Andrew Scherer to boast of one of the leading and best equipped pharmacies on the North side. The store which is neat and well ordered is located at the corner of State and Division streets, and has been occupied by Mr. Scherer for five years, though he has been established since 1875. The size of the store is 25x50 feet, and it is situated on a busy corner, doing a large trade and maintaining a good class of patronage. Physicians' prescriptions and family recipes are here compounded in the most careful and accurate manner, in every instance from absolutely pure ingredients, while bottom prices always prevail. Mr. Scherer himself presides over the prescription department and laboratory, and two experienced assistants are also employed at all hours. A large and carefully selected stock is constantly carried embracing, besides pure drugs and chemicals, standard proprietary medicines of all kinds, also acids, extracts, herbs, roots, barks, medicinal liquors, mineral waters, pharmaceutical specialties in great variety, also a full and fine assortment of toilet articles, perfumes, fancy soaps, sponges, chamois, and choice cigars and everything that comes under the head of druggists' sundries. Mr. Scherer is a middle-aged gentleman, and a native of this city. In his early days he graduated from the Chicago College of Pharmacy, class 1875. He fully merits the large measure of popular favor he enjoys, being at all times courteous and ever anxious to please.

JOHN A. BONGARD.

Mr. John A. Bongard is destined to make his mark in Chicago as an architect of special attainments. His handsomely fitted office is at room 30, 169 La Salle street, where he recently removed from the Ashland block. He is prepared to make designs for and estimate on all classes of proposed new buildings for public and private use, preparing all sketches and plans for same, and studiously embodying every wish and suggestion of his client. His plans are both practical and economical; modern ideas are noticeable features, coupled alike with symmetry and architectural beauty. His estimates and computations are always accurate and not exceeded in actual construction, while under his careful and personal supervision of builders and contractors the specifications are most rigidly adhered to. Mr. Bongard is a native of Wisconsin, and received his education in Chicago. He is exceedingly popular, both professionally and personally, and has the most favorable prospects before him.

R. B. HAAKER.

A very prosperous and enterprising establishment on the North side is the "Eagle" Boot and Shoe Store of Mr. R. B. Haaker, at the corner of Wells and Oak streets. This business was originally opened in 1878, and was removed to the present location in May, 1891, being previously at 307 and 309 Wells street. Business had increased to such an extent that more commodious quarters were imperative, hence the removal to the handsomely fitted "Eagle" boot and shoe store now occupied. The premises comprise the ground floor and basement, 40x60 feet in size, at the above number, with the work room in the rear. Mr. Haaker carries an immense stock at all times of the best footwear in ladies', gents' and children's sizes, and makes a specialty of fine custom work and repairing, using the invisible patch. Mr. Haaker is German by birth, has been in Chicago twenty-two years, is very popular and a member of the National Union, the Turners and Mutual Aid Protective Association.

JOHN BUCKLEY.

In few branches of trade has the march of progress wrought such a veritable revolution of late years as in the stove and kindred lines of business. What with invention, improvement and the development of skill, something closely akin to perfection has been reached in this department of industrial activity. A popular and prosperous West side establishment in this line is that of Mr. John Buckley, dealer in hardware, tinware, stoves, house furnishing goods, etc., and manufacturer of sheet metal goods, at No. 308 W. Madison street, than whom none engaged in the business in this division of the city has been more fortunate in establishing and maintaining a high reputation, both as to the superiority of the goods made and handled and the excellence of the work executed. This well and favorably known concern was established here in 1869, at the corner of Halsted and Madison streets, removal being made to the present more commodious quarters in 1871. These premises consist of store and workshop, 25x115 feet in dimensions, and a heavy and excellent stock is carried, comprising the latest and best cooking ranges and heating stoves in the market, general hardware, tinware and house furnishing goods, special attention being given to every description of tin, copper and sheet iron work. Mr. Buckley is a native of Ireland, and prior to settling in Chicago, was for nineteen years favorably identified with this branch of trade in Canada, an experience which has been used to advantage in the purchase of his present stock, which ranks A1 in every respect.

SANGER, MOODY & STEEL STONE CO.

The Sanger, Moody & Steel Stone Company, dealers in Joliet limestone, and leaders in their line of building material, bear a very important relation to the building industry of this city. Their extensive yards are placed at points in the city for convenient access and delivery, and their immense trade is fully shown in their facilities for the transportation and hauling of the product of their quarries. The firm originated in 1865 as L. R. Sanger & Son, which was afterward Sanger & Moody. The business was incorporated in 1880 under its present style, with a capital of $80,000, under the laws of Illinois. The officers are H. A. Sanger, president, C. C. Moody, vice-president and secretary, and Sanger Steel, treasurer. The offices are located at 139 La Salle street, room 7. The stone is found in Joliet, Ill., just north of the Penitentiary and is of peculiar value. It is the best limestone in the United States. It will not crumble or crack, and is used in all United States locks on the Illinois river, United States arsenals in the country, the principal court and state houses. The quarries at Joliet cover an area of 230 acres, and have exceptionally good canal and railway facilities. The Sanger, Moody & Steel Stone Company have a fleet of five steamboats. Their yards are well located for facility of distribution. The west yard is at Harrison and Rockwell streets; the Central yard at Twelfth and State streets; the North side yard at North avenue bridge, and the South side yards at the Stock Yards Slip. Thirty-ninth and Halsted streets. They employ 300 workmen, and their trade extends over the West and Northwest, their splendid facilities of transportation being fully taxed to meet the growing demand for the product of their quarries.

R. LINKE.

One of the most useful and deservedly popular business agencies in Chicago is that of Mr. R. Linke, at No. 79 W. Madison street, corner of Jefferson. It was inaugurated in 1862 by Mr. Linke. Energetic and honorable in all his transactions, and possessed of a keen appreciation of values, this gentleman at once secured a large share of public patronage, and built up a prosperous and thriving business, which time has greatly increased and developed. His offices are of ample dimensions, located in the heart of the business district, and are neatly and appropriately appointed, every facility being at hand for the prompt transaction of the large business done. The firm buy, sell and exchange, on commission, business places of every description, saloons, restaurants, hotels, cafes, laundries, stores, etc. Mr. Linke has established widespread and influential connections, and has unusual opportunities for direct and profitable dealings and quick turning over of money. His connections are of a strictly first-class character, and he has perfect facilities for the receipt of early information as to the probable fluctuation of the market. He is also a notary public, and makes a prominent specialty of conveyancing and the drafting of all kinds of legal papers, deeds, leases, agreements, contracts, etc. His extensive knowledge with business in all sections of the city renders his advice particularly valuable to all preparing to embark in commercial enterprises, while his fees are always fair and equitable. Mr. Linke numbers among his regular customers many leading business men and real estate owners, and has carried through to a successful issue many important transactions.

BJERKE BROS.' PHARMACY.

The business of the pharmacist and dispensing chemist is always a subject of interest to members of the community, and in this work we desire to refer more particularly to such establishments as are thoroughly representative of this important and difficult profession. Prominent among these is that of Messrs. Bjerke Brothers, which is located at No. 5727 Wentworth avenue. Few among the leading representatives of the profession in this section of the city sustain a higher reputation for skill and reliability than do these gentlemen, Messrs. J. C. and H. K. Bjerke. They are natives of Norway, and have been residents of Chicago, the former since 1888, and the latter since 1889. In the latter year they founded their present business, and bringing to bear a thorough practical and scientific knowledge of the profession in all its branches, they at once built up a brisk and active trade, which time has since greatly extended and developed. They occupy the ground floor of a two-story frame building, 15x40 feet in area, where they have every facility and convenience for prosecuting their calling with satisfaction and success. The pharmacy is handsomely fitted up with large plate glass show windows and cases, and cabinets, and all its arrangements and appointments bear evidence to the excellent taste and sound judgment of the proprietors. The stock carried is at all times full and complete, the carefully selected assortment embracing everything in the line of pure fresh drugs and chemicals, fancy and toilet articles and other druggists' sundries. Special attention is given to the compounding of physicians' prescriptions and family recipes, which is done at all hours of the day and night, and at lowest prices. Night bell calls receive prompt response, while the telephone call is 95. The Messrs. Bjerke Bros. are the only ones in their line of business who are twin brothers, a case which is very rare in any part of this country. Mr. J. C. Bjerke is a graduate of Christiana University of Norway, also of the Northwestern University. Mr. H. K. Bjerke is a gentleman who took the full course in all branches of the Royal University of Norway.

LEFFMANN & TIMM.

In the whole range of commercial enterprise no interest is of more importance than that representing the sale of groceries. This fact is recognized and appreciated by all thoughtful and intelligent persons. In this connection we take pleasure in calling attention to a house which, though only established in 1889, has already proved itself to be indispensable to the locality. This business was inaugurated by Mr. C. Leffmann, and in 1891 he admitted Mr. L. J. Timm into partnership under the style of Leffmann & Timm. Their store is at 552 W. Lake street, and is 25x75 feet, with meat market in the rear. The store is attractively fitted up in accordance with the most improved ideas of modern taste, and the meat market is equipped with large ice boxes, having a capacity of several tons. An A1 stock is constantly carried, embracing the choicest staple and fancy groceries of every description, specialties being made of fine grade teas and coffees, pure spices, canned goods and bottled goods of every description, also fruits and vegetables in their season. They get their supplies of fresh meats daily from the stock yards, and always have very choice cuts at their disposal. Mr. Leffmann is a native of New York City, and Mr. Timm of Chicago. The former has been in Chicago for twenty-five years and is first lieutenant of the Select Knights of America. The latter is a prominent member of the Masonic Order, having taken his 3rd degree.

JOHN J. HILTY.

The trite old saying that a "genius must be born" is especially in place with regard to Mr. John J. Hilty, who follows the profession of an architect, at rooms 3 and 4 in the Commercial Block, on the west side of Commercial avenue. Mr. Hilty has been established in South Chicago since 1875, and the best evidence of his success and popularity is that he has been entrusted with the superintendence of the erection of many of the leading structures in town. His residence is on the corner of 103rd street and Avenue F, Colehour, Ill., a suburb or outlying district of South Chicago, but has now permanently settled his location here. His office was at one time in the Winnipeg Block, across the street. Among some of his chief works of recent date are the splendid Polish church of this city and Turner Hall, City Hall at Hammond, near South Chicago, Huehn and Miller Block, besides very many large blocks in South Chicago; also one for Mr. Henry Heidenrich, with 236x136 feet frontage. He is the oldest architect who has settled in South Chicago, and a master of every detail of his business. Mr. Hilty is a native of Switzerland, and is associated with several of the German and other societies here.

J. B. JONES MANUFACTURING COMPANY.

This firm are the sole manufacturers of the Eureka Folding Woven Wire Mattresses and cots, which are becoming known throughout the United States as the most comfortable, the most easily transported and the best in the market. They have so many obvious advantages over others that they have only to be seen to be appreciated. They also manufacture a full line of plain and supported woven wire mattresses, hospital beds, folding beds, cots, child's cribs, etc. Their office

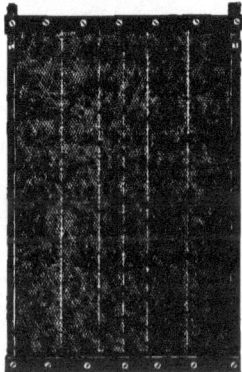

and factory, covering an area of 50x160 feet, is centrally located at Nos. 14 and 16 Ann street, corner of Randolph. Mr. J. B. Jones, who has designed so many useful improvements in this line, is at the present time engaged in the perfection of other new and useful designs in spring beds, which will add materially to his already great reputation in this line. The prominent features of his inventions always are to combine comfort and durability with cheapness. The establishment was first located at Kalamazoo, Mich., prior to its removal to this city, four years ago. At present the active members are Mr. J. B. Jones, president; Mr. F. C. Jones, vice-president, and Mr. Geo. M. Illingworth, secretary and treasurer. Mr. Jones, senior, was born in New York, and has resided in Michigan thirty-two years and in Chicago the past four. He has shown high inventive genius and great originality, besides other superior qualities which have won him the esteem of all classes of the community. His son is a native of Michigan, and is a young man full of true American enterprise and possesses qualities that have made him popular and respected in every part.

BARRON BROS.

A prominent and reliable firm in Chicago, actively engaged in the sale of coal, coke, wood, hay and grain, is that of Messrs. Barron Brothers, whose yards are located at 875 and 878 West Lake street, and 1 to 5 Flournoy street. This flourishing business was established eight years ago by Mr. T. R. Barron, who conducted it till 1884, when his brother, Mr. Joseph Barron, became a partner, the firm being known by the title of Barron Brothers. Their yards are commodious and are fully equipped with every facility for the handling and storage of coal, coke, etc. Here they keep a heavy stock of the best grades of anthracite and bituminous coals, which are received direct from the most famous collieries of Pennsylvania, Ohio and Illinois. The coal handled is thoroughly freed from culm and slate, and is in every instance carefully screened

before being loaded for delivery. They also handle the finest qualities of Connellsville coke, and deal largely in wood, grain and hay. Twelve men and six delivery wagons are employed, and orders for either a ton or a car load lot of coal or coke are promptly filled at the lowest possible prices. The trade is local, and is steadily increasing Messrs. Jos. and T. R. Barron were born in England, but have resided in Chicago several years, where they have made many friends, owing to their sound business principles and strict integrity. They are popular members of the British American Association, and their telephone call is 7618.

FALK, WORMSER & CO.

No careful review of the progress of the hop and malt trade of Chicago would be complete without special reference to the widely known and reliable house of Messrs. Falk, Wormser & Co., hop merchants and dealers in barley, malt and brewers' supplies, whose offices and salesrooms are situated corner Kinzie and N. State street. The firm's malt house, which is located at 335 Larrabee street, is fully supplied with modern apparatus, appliances and machinery. Last year they sold 300,000 bushels of malt and 8,000 bales of hops, and their trade extends throughout all sections of the Western states. This business was established in 1871 by Messrs. H. B. Falk & Brother, who conducted it till 1889, when Mr. H. B. Falk died, after a successful career. He was succeeded by the present firm of Messrs. Falk, Wormser & Co., the co-partners being Messrs. M. L. Falk, D. Wormser and C. W. Oker. They have had long experience and possess superior connections and perfect facilities. Their salesroom is 75x150 feet in area, fully fitted up with every convenience. A large stock of foreign and domestic hops and brewers' supplies is always on hand, and orders are promptly filled at the lowest ruling market prices. The firm's malt is highly appreciated by our brewers, and is unrivalled for quality and uniform excellence. Messrs Falk and Wormser were born in Ger many, but have resided in Chicago many years, while Mr. Oker is a southerner. They are honorable and enterprising merchants, who justly merit the high reputation they have permanently attained in the malt and hop trade of the Western metropolis.

S. V. BRUNDAGE & SONS.

The manufacture of carriages and wagons is a prominent industry in the city of Chicago, and one of the oldest and most reliable houses in the business is that of S. V. Brundage & Sons. This business was established in 1877 by Mr. S. V. Brundage and continued by him alone until 1888, when he admitted his sons, Messrs. F.L. Brundage and N. A. Brundage. The business developed rapidly from small beginnings, and is to-day one of the representative industries of the city. The proprietors of the business are well known and highly respected in business and commercial circles, and have become known as leaders in their profession. They occupy as office, warerooms, and factory the large and substantial three-story brick building at 511 to 515 W. Twenty-second street. This building is 75x125 feet in dimensions, and is owned by the firm, having been built to meet the demands of the business. It is thoroughly equipped with all the latest improvements in machinery for woodworking purposes. The motive power is steam, the establishment being supplied by a large fifty horse power boiler and engine. Twenty-five hands are given steady employment and the factory is taxed to its full capacity to keep ahead of the orders. The firm manufacture and keep in stock all kinds of express and lumber wagons, lumber carts, buggies, etc., also side and end door rollers for cars, dolleys, cart hooks, chains, etc. They have a department devoted to repairing, and do all kinds of work satisfactorily and in a first-class manner. A specialty is made of the manufacture of lumber wagons and hand carts. The house has a large trade all over the United States, and the proprietors are progressive business men and highly esteemed for their sound principles and integrity.

THE CHAMPION TABLE SLIDE CO.

Among the various interests which diversify the industries of Chicago none deserve more prominent mention in this review of the commercial and manufacturing interests than that devoted to furnishing wood table slides and cabinet makers' tables. In this connection we desire to bring before our readers the Champion Table Slide Company, the leading manufacturers in this line. This enterprise was founded in 1883 by T. B. Hennessey & Co., and was continued by that firm until 1885, when the present style was adopted, the proprietors being August Heuer & Sons. These gentlemen are noted in business and commercial circles for their enterprise and progressive ideas, and are foremost in pushing the business and extending the trade. The office of the company is located at No. 173 Randolph street, and the factory is at the corner of Blackhawk and Hawthorne avenues. Here they have a splendid building that cost $25,000, including the ground, and is owned by the company. The factory consists of a two-story brick structure, 60x100 feet in dimensions, and equipped with all the latest and best woodworking machinery, put in at a cost of $5,000. Here they manufacture the "Champion" table slide, cabinet clamps, iron bench stops, cabinet-makers' work benches, and carvers' benches. These articles are made from the best materials obtainable, and have a reputation established of the highest order. This house is the only one in Chicago manufacturing these supplies exclusively, and is the largest one in the United States. It has an immense trade in all parts of the country, and ships many thousands of dollars' worth of benches, etc., each year, and has a constantly increasing trade. The factory is about as complete as can be conceived of, and is well managed. It has a fifty-five horse power engine in addition to the other machinery. Twenty-five skilled workmen are given employment. Mr. August Heuer was born in Germany, and has lived in Chicago over forty years, and is everywhere known as a gentleman of the greatest integrity and soundest business principles. His sons, Mr. H. F. Heuer and Aug. Heuer, jr., are young men, held in the highest regard by all who know them, and prominent as business men of the greatest abilities.

CASE & COMPANY.

This work would be incomplete without mention of the old and well-known firm of Case & Company, Fire Insurance Underwriters. This house is the largest of its kind in the city and does an immense volume of business. It has been established since 1867, when Mr. Chas. H. Case, the senior member of the firm, began business. Afterward Mr. Ed. B. Case, nephew of Charles H., was admitted to the firm, and the style was changed to C. H. Case & Company; and in 1891 the firm name was again changed to Case & Co., its present style. Mr. Chas. H. Case is a native of Vermont, has been identified with insurance interests for thirty-five years, and with those of Chicago for the past thirty-two years. He is president of the Chicago Safety Trust Co., and is connected with the Royal Trust Co. of this city. He is also president of the Washingtonian Inebriate Asylum, and is a prominent and honored member of the Union League Club. Mr. Edward B. Case is a native of Massachusetts, and has lived here a number of years; he is well known in the social and business world, where he is regarded with the highest esteem. He is vice-president of the Board of Fire Underwriters' Association of Chicago, and has been engaged in the fire insurance business for thirty years. He is a prominent member of the Hyde Park and Athletic Clubs. The offices of this firm are the largest and most elegantly fitted insurance offices in the city, occupying the east half of the ground floor of the Royal Insurance building, 169 Jackson street. The counters and fixtures are all of solid mahogany, and the walls frescoed in the highest style of art. This house does a large business, having an extensive patronage for commercial insurance; they write many important risks on grain stored in leading railway and private elevators, some forty in number. They have a large staff of clerks and assistants constantly employed. Case & Co. represent the well-known Insurance Co. of

North America of Philadelphia, Pa., which is now in its ninety-ninth year of active business, being the oldest stock insurance company in America. Its assets, cash value, are $8,951,518,- 83, and its surplus, as regards policyholders, $5,451,961,04. They also represent the popular and well known Royal Insurance Company of Liverpool, England. This company has as total assets in the United States, $5,973,780,32. Case & Co. enjoy the largest patronage of the kind in the city and are thoroughly reliable in every sense.

FRED KAEHLER.

One of the most important factors in the rapid development of the commercial and manufacturing interests of Chicago is the coal trade. Prominent among the reliable and old established houses actively engaged in this important business is that of Mr. Fred Kaehler, shipper and dealer, whose offices are located at 845 and 847 Clybourn avenue, and dock and railyard on Clybourn avenue, near Fullerton avenue. This extensive business was established in 1838 by Mr. Kaehler, who has also branches corner Lincoln and Fullerton avenues, and at 1322 Lincoln street. His yards have excellent railway and water facilities, and the stock on hand always amounts to over 35,000 tons of the choicest anthracite and bituminous coal. He also deals heavily in maple, beech and slabs, carrying constantly 17,000 loads. He employs fifty men and a number of teams, filling orders in all parts of the city and its vicinity, at the lowest possible prices. All coal purchased of Mr. Kaehler is guaranteed to maintain in every respect the highest standard of excellence as regards the care in its preparation for the market, coming as it does from some of the best equipped collieries in America. The business is both wholesale and retail, and customers can be supplied with a ton or a carload lot. Last year Mr. Kaehler sold 100,000 tons of coal, and his trade is steadily increasing. He was born in Germany, but has resided in Chicago for the last forty years His experience and systematic conduct of his coal business gives him excellent advantages, while his high character is a sufficient guarantee that all orders will receive prompt and faithful attention. The telephone call of the house is 3578. He has another yard at Clark street and Addison avenue.

S. W. EDWARDS & SON.

A popular and prosperous commission house is that of S. W. Edwards & Son, who deal in grain, hay and feed. This house has been established in the business for twenty-one years. The business was founded by Mr S. W. Edwards in 1869, and in 1886 he admitted his son, Mr. S. T. Edwards, to a partnership with him. For many years the business was conducted on Clinton street, but they found their quarters inadequate to the demands of the business, and removed to their present location, Nos. 373 and 375 Carroll avenue. Here they have a large storeroom, 169x86 feet, and carry a large stock of feed of all kinds. The warehouse is located alongside of the St. Paul, Northwestern and Pan Handle railroad tracks, and offers the best facilities for receiving and shipping the products grown in the territories traversed by these railroads. They do a wholesale and retail business, and employ twelve assistants and helpers, and have five double and two single teams at work all the time in handling local business. They act as shippers and receivers of grain and feed, making a specialty of car lots. The trade of the house is very large, extending through the leading Eastern and Western states. Mr. S. W. Edwards is well known in leading business and financial circles. He was born in Ashtabula County, O., and has resided in Chicago for the past twenty-one years. He has been a prominent member of the Board of Trade for the past fifteen years. Mr. S. T. Edwards is a young man of ability and energy; he has been in Chicago twenty-one years and has an excellent reputation as a business man. He is a member of the Patriotic Order Sons of America, and is a leader in social circles. The house is well known to the trade and enjoys the highest reputation.

KIMBALL & LA GRAVE.

Messrs. Kimball & La Grave, are deservedly prominent as the proprietors of the Empire Carpet Cleaning Co., and their works and salesrooms are eligibly located at Nos. 39, 41 and 43 Washington street. There is no establishment in the city that will better repay the patronage of the careful housewife. The foundation of this business was laid in 1872 by Mr. C. N. Hamilton, at Nos. 54 to 60 S. Canal street. In 1890 Mr. C. L. Kimball became his partner, and the business was removed to the present address. Shortly afterwards Mr. Kimball purchased Mr. Hamilton's interest, and associating with him Mr. W. E. La Grave formed the present firm. The premises now utilized are of spacious dimensions, and give ample accommodations for supplying the most extensive demands. They are supplied with automatic carpet cleaning machines of the most modern make and pattern, and have the capacity for cleaning 1,500 yards of carpet per day. Carpets are cleaned thoroughly, quickly and cheaply, and the process adopted is such as to remove all dust, to completely disinfect them, to destroy all moths, moth eggs and vermin, and to raise and brighten the nap. Carpets are taken up, cleaned and relaid, refitted and made over, and all work is done honestly, expeditiously, and at low prices. Window shades of all kinds are made to order, and in all branches the business has grown immensely, owing to the perfect satisfaction given to customers. Eight experienced hands are employed, while ten wagons call for and deliver all goods free of charge. Both partners were born in Michigan and have resided for the past ten years in this city, where they are much esteemed for their ability, industry, and sterling personal worth. The telephone call of the office is 519. Messrs. Kimball & La Grave are also purchasing agents for all kinds of merchandise and carpets and make a specialty of furniture. Their facilities in this line are unsurpassed, their connections with the most prominent wholesale dealers in the city enabling them to save their patrons fifteen to twenty-five per cent, on all goods purchased through them.

CONSOLIDATED COPYING COMPANY.

Few branches of industry have had so marked an effect in contributing to domestic refinement as that which has busied itself with the production of picture frames in which to encase the beautiful work of the painter, engraver and artist. In this connection we desire to make special reference in this commercial review of Chicago to the representative and progressive Consolidated Copying Company, manufacturers of picture frames, picture mats, solar prints, albumen prints, etc., whose offices and factory are situated at 154 and 156 W. Van Buren street. This company was incorporated under the laws of Illinois in 1890, all the stockholders being practical men in this line of business, and nearly all of them occupy positions in the various departments of the house. The trade of the company, which is rapidly increasing, extends throughout all sections of the United States, Canada and Mexico. They occupy a spacious and substantial five-story brick building, 60x120 feet in area. The various departments are fully equipped with special machinery and appliances, operated by a forty-five horse power steam engine. Here 140 skilled hands are employed, who turn out daily vast quantities of the finest picture frames and mats, solar prints, etc. Their goods are unrivaled for beauty, finish and originality of design by those of any other house in the country, while the prices quoted in all cases necessarily attract the attention of close and prudent buyers. The following gentlemen, widely and favorably known in business circles for their enterprise, executive ability and just methods are the officers, viz: C. P. Whetston, president, H. M. Little, secretary. This is the largest concern of the kind in the world, and fifteen clerks are employed in the elegant and well-equipped offices. Orders are carefully filled and several traveling salesmen represent the company on the road. This concern is the most responsible and successful in its line in the country, and its trade is an important feature of the manufacturing resources of the great western metropolis.

JAMES I. LYONS.

It is seldom that one man's misfortune proves so beneficial to his fellow-beings as in the case of Mr. James I. Lyons, manufacturer of artificial limbs at 78 Fifth avenue. Mr. Lyons is a native of Wisconsin, but has resided in Chicago since boyhood. At the age of twenty he learned his trade in, one of the largest in this city. He founded his present enterprise and his eminent skill and proficiency in the art have secured for him a patronage derived from all parts of the United States, and his manufactures are even used in Europe. The premises are perfectly equipped with all the necessary and most perfect tools and appliances, and he offers to the maimed artificial legs that not only possess a natural motion, combined with ease and comfort in walking, but a degree of strength, elasticity and lightness never before attained. He can give to the wearer not only a reasonably graceful step but a perfect form, and a leg that for reliance, stability, firmness and durability has no superior. Entire satisfaction is by him guaranteed, or no sale. His prices are merely nominal, and hundreds of testimonials can be furnished as to the perfection of his wares, which fact ought to be the best proof of the superiority of his goods and the reliability of his transactions. Leading surgeons in Chicago recommend these goods very highly and are glad to testify to this effect. Mr. Lyons is a gentleman of integrity and has much feeling and sympathy for his patrons. Directions for measuring and blanks to be filled out by the patient at his own home are cheerfully sent to any address. Mr. Lyons is a pleasant, able and courteous gentleman, very popular with all with whom he has dealings.

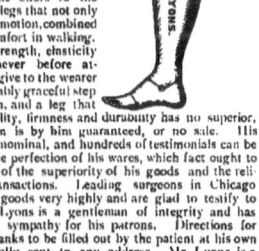

M. VAN GELDER.

A representative house in this city having a wide reputation for the excellence of its goods is the well-known mattress and bedding factory and store of M. Van Gelder, 212 Blue Island avenue. This house has been established since 1889 and has a large and appreciative patronage. Its reputation for the manufacture of superior goods is of the first order, and the trade is most extensive, goods being sold to dealers all over the city and in surrounding towns. All kinds of mattresses are made to order and renovated; and a specialty is made of the manufacture of hair mattresses, of which this house makes a very superior grade. The store is well stocked with excelsior, husk, patent, wool and hair mattresses; and in addition to supplying the trade, a large retail business is done. Many of the residents in various parts of the city have their work done by this house, and there is not any in the city with a better reputation for first-class work. Employment is given to six hands and these are kept steadily employed. The store is 30x75 feet and is well arranged for displaying the goods kept in stock. Mr. Van Gelder is a native of Holland, and learned his trade, there. He has been in Chicago some years and stands well with the leading business houses; his goods being considered in every way first-class, and his house worthy of patronage. He is a first-class business man, has ability and close application and is very successful and now commands a very lucrative trade through his energy and ability.

LINDSTROM, MALMSTED & CO.

One of the most prominent among the many occupations engaging the attention of the city of Chicago is buying and selling and exchanging realty, and among those most active in this direction is the firm of Lindstrom, Malmstedt & Co., whose main office is at 68 La Salle street, and branches at the most desirable locations in the city and suburbs. The copartners, Mr. C. O. Lindstrom and Mr. F. L. Malmstedt, have been associated and established in business since 1885, and have always enjoyed the esteem and confidence of the public, and shown their adaptability to the needs of patrons, and acquired a name and reputation for promptness, uprightness and fairness greatly redounding to their credit. They occupy handsomely fitted up offices, employ a number of clerks and sub-agents, and pay particular attention to transacting all business pertaining to the purchase, sale and exchange of realty, negotiating loans, etc. The firm handle and deal in all kinds of city and suburban property, and are well prepared to offer special inducements to those seeking investments. The properties handled are absolutely perfect as regards title, and no real estate is dealt in except that which is thoroughly safe to investors. Besides buying and selling real estate, the firm effect loans and negotiate contracts for building houses and families. Both members of the firm are from Sweden originally. Mr. Lindstrom, who is a gentleman in middle life, has been in Chicago many years, while Mr. Malmstedt, a gentleman a few years older, came here in 1881. They have risen to their present position as business men by strict devotion to the interests of patrons, and in all cases endeavoring to give the limit of satisfaction. They are both owners of considerable real estate.

HOWARD, TERRELL & CO.

The plumber's is perhaps the most indispensable of all trades in the modern community, and while there are many who carry on this industry in Chicago, there are but few who can conscientiously be called thoroughly representative. Such, however, are Messrs. Howard, Terrell & Co. of No. 10 Centre avenue, the members of the firm being practical plumbers of great experience and ability. The business was commenced by Mr. William Howard and Mr. W. F. Terrell, in January, 1886, on the corner of Centre avenue and Madison street, with a branch at Loomis and Van Buren streets. On January 1st, 1891, Mr. M. Terrell was admitted, and the style altered to that as at present known. The capital of this house on its inception was $360 only, yet within four years and a half they had secured such a fine trade that a removal to larger quarters was absolutely necessary, the branch referred to being now absorbed in the main establishment. Their success is an excellent example of the results of energy and perseverance, and should encourage all who are endeavoring to struggle through the difficulties that surround the starting of a new business. In their fine premises at No. 10 Centre avenue, they have every appliance necessary to the trade, of the latest patterns, and carry a full line of supplies for gas fitting, ventilation and sanitary work, and the staple duties of the business. Messrs. Howard, Terrell & Co. have a great reputation for the thoroughness of their plumbing and the intimate knowledge they possess of the scientific principals which govern their trade, and have carried out the largest contracts in a highly satisfactory manner. Mr Howard is a native of New York, and the Messrs. Terrell of Kendal County, Ill. They are all young, energetic business men, who personally attend to every detail of the industry, and fully merit the great success they have achieved.

CURREY MANUFACTURING COMPANY.

In the manufacture and sale of paints and varnishes, etc., a representative and successful concern in Chicago is that known as the Currey Manufacturing Company, whose factory and salesrooms are situated at 211 and 213 S. Clinton street. This business was established in 1887 by Mr. J. S. Currey. Mr. W. Phillipson is president, and Mr. S. E. K. Harrington manager. They occupy two spacious floors and basement, the manufacturing department being fully equipped with the latest improved apparatus and machinery known to the trade. They manufacture all kinds of mixed paints and varnishes and keep in stock full supplies of white lead, zinc, putty, priming, ochre, colors, wood fillers, wall sizing, brushes, bronze powders and general painters' supplies, which are offered to the trade at the lowest possible prices. A specialty is made of the company's best mixed paints, gem liquid paints, liquid carriage paints, liquid oil stains, durable mineral paints, tinted paints etc., which are unrivaled for purity, quality and uniform excellence. Only really first-class goods are handled, and the trade of the house extends throughout the Middle, Western and Northwestern states. Orders are carefully filled and all goods are fully warranted. Mr. Phillipson was born in Lyons, Ia., and Mr. Harrington in Detroit, Mich. Mr. Harrington has formerly for many years in the paint business in Detroit, while Mr. Phillipson is president of the Phillipson Decorating Company, 251 Wabash avenue, to whom has been awarded large contracts for the exterior decoration of the Columbian Exposition. Both Messrs. Phillipson and Harrington are honorable and energetic business men, who are very popular in trade circles.

THOS. JACKSON & SON.

One of the representative firms of this city, and one controlling a vast business is that of Thomas Jackson & Son, general contractors for sewers, subways and electric underground conduits, at 177 La Salle street, and we may say without fear of contradiction that the firm is the oldest and most highly respected in this line of business in Chicago, for it was established as far back as 1862. The copartners are

Mr. Thomas Jackson, the founder, and his son, Mr. G. W. Jackson, who was admitted in 1883, when the present style of firm was adopted. Mr. Thomas Jackson was born in England, and is now 58 years of age. He came to Chicago thirty-nine years ago. His son is a native of this city. As we have already hinted, the capacity of their work is simply enormous, giving employment to from one hundred and fifty to three hundred men. Their yards at 19 and 21 Sacramento avenue cover an area of several acres. They furnish estimates from architects' and engineers' drawings and specifications and undertake all kinds of mason work. They are members of the Contractors' and Sewer Builders' Association. The following items will enable the reader to form some idea of the extent of the work accomplished by this firm. They carried 32,000 feet of sewerage through Douglas park. They constructed sewers for the Tremont House, the Board of Trade building and the Calumet and Goff buildings. They also built sewers in Garfield park, Union park, the Morrison block, the Otis block, and twenty-five public schools. They constructed ten miles of cable road for the North Side Cable Company, and twenty miles of underground cable conduits for the Chicago Telephone Company, at East Chicago, Ind. Also several miles of underground conduits for arc lights and Western Union Telegraph Company. One of their great works is three miles of seven-foot sewer for the city of Chicago, on Belmont avenue, and several miles of pavement underground conduits for the city. Also subway underground conduits for the Chicago Telephone Company, on Franklin street, from Madison street to Randolph street.

H. C. T. BORRMANN.

Those living on the West side may feel perfectly happy in being able to secure a good suit of clothes at a reasonable figure, for we have in the store of Mr. H. C. T. Borrmann, at 832 and 834 W. Twenty-first street, an emporium for clothing, tailoring and gentlemen's furnishing goods which is equal to any store of its size down town. When we say that Mr. Borrmann has been established for twelve years it is a pretty fair indication that he has made a success of his business, which indeed he has, but only by dint of selling the very best articles at the very lowest prices. The store is a large double one, 50x90 feet in dimensions, and half is devoted exclusively to clothing and tailoring, while the other half is devoted to gentlemen's furnishings. In clothing he carries a full assortment of the latest styles and patterns suited to every season, and can in every instance guarantee a perfect fit, while in his tailoring department he always has the newest things in English and Scotch tweeds and suitings, getting them almost directly after they land in New York. His gents' furnishing goods are particularly well selected, and here we find styles equal in taste to anything we can get in the city, and not only the style but the quality is also there. Thus Mr. Borrmann's $1.50 shirt is equal in value to what many a store would ask $2.50 for, and so, by comparison, we find the majority of goods are of equally good value. He employs as a rule about twelve or fifteen hands, all of whom are thoroughly competent, and the salespeople are particularly courteous to their customers. In a word the business is conducted in a thoroughly first-class manner, and everything denotes that Mr. Borrmann understands every department of it. He is a native of Germany and has been in Chicago for twenty-five years. A branch store devoted exclusively to dry goods, conducted under the style of H. C. T. Borrmann, at 931 Twenty-second street, and 1041 Hoyne avenue, is managed by the wife and daughter of Mr. Borrmann. This store was established in 1891, and is centrally located in Durkee's elegant brick block, recently constructed, having 3,000 feet of floor space and a frontage of twenty-five feet on Twenty-second street, and twenty-five feet on Hoyne avenue, with a depth of seventy-five feet. Here a large and comprehensive line of first-class dry goods is to be found in imported and domestic woolens, dress goods and silks; and eight courteous lady clerks are employed.

C. H. SCOTT.

Prominent among the leading grocers in this section of the city is Mr. Clarence Scott, whose popular establishment is located at the corner of 79th and Dickey streets. Mr. Scott, who was born in Illinois, has been a resident of Chicago since 1885. In 1890 he founded his present business, and has from the start made his house the center of a large and flourishing trade. The premises he occupies comprise the ground floor of a three-story stone building, 20x60 feet in dimensions. The store is handsomely fitted up, and is one of the most attractive establishments on 79th street, and, in fact, in all Auburn park. Every facility has been provided for the storage and handling of the heavy and comprehensive stock always carried, as well as for its effective display and close inspection. Mr. Scott has always for sale full and complete lines of fancy and staple groceries of every description, including choice fresh crop teas, coffees, spices, sauces, pickles, catsups, condiments and relishes; olives, olive oil, truffles, capers, mushrooms; jams, jellies, preserved fruits in glass, and other table relishes; canned goods in great variety, the best brands of family flour, prepared cereals and farinaceous goods, sugars, syrups and molasses, bakers' and laundry supplies, soaps, starch, cornstarch, brushes, brooms, mop handles, fancy creamery and dairy butter, cheese, fresh eggs, dried fruits, vegetables, bacon, lard, hams, etc., etc. The patronage is large and first-class, and gives every promise of a steady increase. Mr. Scott is a popular and successful merchant, and is held in high esteem by all with whom he has dealings.

FIDELITY MORTGAGE LOAN COMPANY.

The enlargement of the loan market, so as to cover the wants and necessities of the vast classes of the public who are not owners of real estate, was one of the most necessary innovations of recent years. When prudently and honorably conducted, the business is of importance and value to the community, as it gives relief from pressing claims at the very time when most essential. The Fidelity Mortgage Loan Company, of No. 153 E. Monroe street, is one of the leading representative concerns engaged in the business. The company was incorporated in July, 1890, and occupies large offices, neatly fitted up, and well suited to the avocation, giving every privacy to ladies and gentlemen in need of temporary assistance. These can promptly obtain loans on chattel security, as well as on lands and houses, their furniture, etc., being left in use as before, and every care being taken to secure the confidential character of the negotiations. The policy pursued by this company is most honorable and equitable, and they loan to the fullest extent on all tangible securities. Payments can be made in as easy installments as required, and at intervals which are most convenient to the borrower. They are well known for their just and honest treatment of customers, and have in consequence a large and influential patronage throughout the city and the tributary states. We can heartily recommend those of our readers in want of a loan to make application to the Fidelity Mortgage Loan Company, from whom they will receive the most agreeable courtesy, and the most prompt and business like treatment.

MRS. J. BATY.

Perhaps in no other line of productive industry are manipulators so controlled by the vagaries of fickle fashion as in the production of fine millinery. The number of new shapes in bonnets and hats it is absolutely necessary to invent each season is almost illimitable, and requires a skill in designing quite unthought of by the ordinary observer. A prominent West side house engaged in this business is that of Mrs. J. Baty, No. 740 W. Madison street, which she established some three years ago. Anything that adds to the personal appearance of the fairer sex is always of the greatest value, and at the above establishment all that may be included in the term fashionable millinery may here be found, of the finest quality and greatest variety, having been purchased through the lead-

ing New York importing houses. The prices charged are very moderate, considering the superior character of the goods offered, and naturally Mrs. Baty's emporium is very popular among the ladies, who are well aware that they can always find here something new, beautiful and useful at a fair and reasonable price. The premises occupied, consisting of a store and workroom, are very handsome and commodious, the stock embracing the latest novelties in Parisian bonnets and hats, trimmed and untrimmed, silks, satins, velvets, plushes, flowers, feathers, pompons, passementerie and kindred millinery goods. Mrs. Baty was born in La Salle, Ill., and brought up in Chicago. She is a lady of exquisite taste and good judgment, and prior to engaging in business on her own account, was head milliner in the fashionable emporium of Mme. Jacobson, on Wabash avenue.

MAHLUM & JOHNSON.

One of the most complete and excellent grocery houses in the section in which it is located is that of Messrs. Mahlum & Johnson. The situation, 201 W. Erie street, corner May, is very central and desirable and a splendid flourishing business is being carried on. The foundation of the business dates from 1884, when it was established by Mr. K. Mahlum & Co., and continued until February 1 of the present year, when the firm was changed to Mahlum & Johnson. Both partners are thoroughly practical experienced men and have put in a new fresh stock of goods in the store, and are conducting operations in a manner greatly redounding to their credit. Besides a first-class assortment of staple and fancy and imported and domestic groceries, including choice teas, coffees, pure spices, sugar, syrups, canned goods, dried fruits, table luxuries, condiments, the best brands of family flour and a full line of sugar cured hams, salt and smoked meats will be found, and prime creamery and dairy butter, cheese and fresh eggs. Several clerks are employed and three wagons owned by the firm are used expressly for calling for and delivering orders. The business premises have an area of 25x75 feet, and every modern convenience is at hand and prompt attention is paid to customers. The copartners are both natives of Norway. They have resided in Chicago for some years, and are gentlemen of strict integrity in their dealings as well as experience and splendid business qualifications. Trade is steadily growing and increasing, and about the premises there is always a scene of busy activity.

SHALEK & LINTZ.

A tailoring establishment with an excellent reputation is that of Shalek & Lintz, 445 S. Halsted street. This house has been established since 1889 and enjoys a reputation of the highest character for superior workmanship and highest grade of goods. The premises are well stocked with a fine line of imported and domestic suitings of leading designs in cloths of all kinds, tweeds, serges, cashmeres, worsteds, broadcloths and corkscrews. The goods manufactured by the house are of the finest grade, and cut in the latest styles, all garments being made by competent hands under the direct supervision of the heads of the house. A large staff of competent help is employed and the house enjoys a most liberal patronage. The goods manufactured by this house have a standard reputation in the district in which they do business, and their name to a garment is a guarantee of its character. Their patrons are fulsome in their praise and advertise the house in the most acceptable manner. The firm is composed of Mr. Frank Shalek and Frank Lintz, both gentlemen being natives of Bohemia, practical tailors and residents of the United States since boyhood. They stand very high among friends and patrons, are considered everywhere to be business men of character and ability, and are leaders in the social circle in which they move. The store has a large cutting room in the rear, and the facilities for turning out the finest work at moderate prices is unexceled by any house in the city.

SMYTH CROOKS.

The North side is signally fortunate in having such representative business houses of all kinds, and in none is this so apparent as in the boot and shoe trade, custom made and shop work. One of the oldest and best established is that of Smyth Crooks, at No. 450 N. Clark street, who twenty-three years ago opened this business at No. 516½ Division street, but which grew so rapidly that eighteen years ago he was compelled to remove to his present extensive and

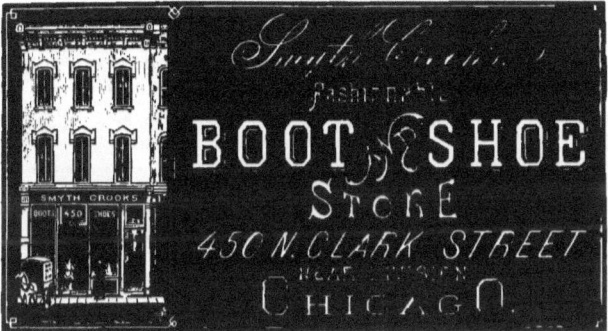

well-fitted store, 25x60 feet in size, with shop in the rear, 25x50 feet, fitted with all the appliances for modern and first-class shoe making. In addition to his extensive stock of ladies', gents' and children's shoes, footwear, rubbers and slippers, including the most reliable makes, Lilly Brackett & Co., of Boston; Pingree & Smith of Detroit; G. W. Ludlow of Chicago, and Jno. Foster and Co., of Beloit, Wis.; he employs six men in the manufacture of the finest and best custom work, for ladies' and gents' wear. Mr. Crooks is a native of Ireland, and has resided in Chicago for twenty-four years. He is a live, energetic and prosperous business man, who has a well-earned reputation for his many excellent qualities, and hosts of friends, socially and commercially.

ERNST STOCK.

The real estate men of Chicago may justly claim the honor of making the city the great place it has become. They undiminished faith in times of adversity and indomitable energy at all times has made it possible for this to become America's metropolis. One of the most active and responsible agents on the North side is Mr. Ernst Stock, who is located at 374 E. Division street. Mr. Stock was born in Germany and came to Chicago in 1865. He engaged in the grocery business and was very successful, acquiring much real estate and property of various kinds, so that he was induced to embark in the business of real estate and loans in 1887. He has been extraordinarily successful and has built up a liberal patronage of the most desirable character. His office is neatly fitted up, and he handles a large amount of property for non-residents; he also makes loans, having superior connections for money; deals in first mortgages, collects rents, etc. He does an extensive business, and buys and sells much real estate on commission, having always a fine list of bargains. Mr. Stock is a progressive and active business man, and has made a pronounced success in his business. He is well known in real estate business and financial circles, being highly respected. The telephone call is 3656.

R. E. OBERG & CO.

The number of cereal foods that have of late years been produced and brought into the market is legion. Almost all the known grains have been operated upon to furnish new delicacies, or health-giving dishes for impaired digestions, and it is really marvelous what results have been attained. Messrs. R. E. Oberg & Co. of No. 213 W. Lake street, contribute their share to these favorite articles of diet by manufacturing the well-known "Excelsior" Buckwheat and Rolled Oats, for which there is a great and growing demand. Mr. Oberg began the business in the year 1885 and conducted it with such energy, producing pure and easily digested foods, that his name soon became famous in this line of trade. His resources are ample and his facilities unexcelled. He occupies a very large floor, fitted with a full set of packing machinery, driven by steam power, and transacts a very extensive business, mainly in Chicago and its environs, in goods done up in convenient packages intended to preserve their freshness and their nutritive qualities. Messrs. Oberg & Co., in addition to manufacturing, are large jobbers in these excellent foods of the best known varieties. Mr. Oberg is sole proprietor and manager of the business and has a large and successful trade. He is a native of this city and is highly respected and esteemed in both trade and social circles, being justly ranked among the most enterprising and upright business men of the city.

EDWARDS & FITZGERALD.

There is no business in a neighborhood so well appreciated as a good meat market, one where you can always be sure of getting fresh, clean meats, and have the different kinds to select from. Such a one in fact as is that of Edwards & Fitzgerald, at No. 55 N. State street, the most popular market on the North side. This business was established eight years ago by S. Edwards & J. B. Fitzgerald, and has been a success since its opening. They keep constantly on hand a splendid stock of the best fresh, salt and smoked meats, poultry, game, fish, oysters, vegetables and fruit in season, and employing four assistants with three wagons are always ready to deliver all orders promptly to any part of the city. They make a specialty of family trade, and number the best families of the North side among their customers. Mr. Edwards is a native of the South of England and has been in Chicago for twenty years. He was brought up to the butchering business, and is very thorough in his management. Mr. Fitzgerald was born in Ireland, but was raised in Chicago, and has been eight years in his present business. They are members of the Retail Butchers' Association, are live, enterprising and energetic, and merit the splendid trade the people of the North side favor them with. Their market is neatly arranged and fitted with refrigerators, coolers and all appurtenances that go to make up a first-class place and in every arrangement and detail patrons will find this market as near perfection as the wants of the present times demand.

THE KNAUS & GREEN MFG. CO.

The manufacture of furniture is one of the most important industries of the city of Chicago, as well as one of the most progressive, engaging the attention of some of the most substantial firms, and a large army of skillful workmen. One of the most promising of these firms, who confine themselves to the production of parlor furniture frames, is that of the Knaus & Green Manufacturing Co., whose extensive factory is centrally located at Nos. 51, 53 and 55 W. Pearson street. Although incorporated as recently as July, 1890, under the laws of the State of Illinois, with a paid up capital of $10,000, this enterprising company already transact a business whose annual value amounts to $50,000. Their premises are splendidly equipped with the most improved machinery, driven by steam power, and afford unexceled facilities for the manufacture of their well-known frames. The greatest care is exercised in every detail of the work, from the selection of the material to the final making up, and the result is seen in the great demand that is rapidly springing up in all parts of the United States for these superior articles. The officers of the company are: Mr. N. M. Green, president, Mr. Joseph Pregenzer, vice-president, and Mr. Wm. J. Knaus, secretary and treasurer, the latter gentleman being also general manager. These practical business men were all previously connected with the well-known Zengerle Manufacturing Company, also in the furniture business, and bring to bear vast experience and the highest qualifications, both natural and acquired, for the successful management of this industry. They occupy honored positions on the rolls of membership of some of our large societies, and have ever secured the esteem and respect of all who have been thrown into contact with them. Their business has been established upon sound commercial principles, and gives great promise of a long and brilliant career of usefulness.

NIESEN BROS.

Mr. Frank Niesen has for many years been known as the leading manufacturer of fine vinegars and cider in this city. In the early part of the present year he retired in favor of his sons, Messrs. Fred A. Niesen and Frank L. Niesen. Mr. F. Niesen has been identified with the trade since 1854, and in 1865 he founded this business, which has steadily grown until to-day immense quantities of this acid seasoning are made, the qualities being warranted strictly pure. The premises occupied by the Niesen Bros. are located at 752 N. Halsted street, and consist of a two-story building, 20x100 feet in dimensions, which is owned by their father. Here pure white wine, cider, pickle and double vinegars are manufactured, as well as pure apple cider. Only the best and pure materials are used and every care is taken to secure high quality and sustain the reputation of the house. The cellar of the adjoining building is utilized for storage purposes, and the rapid increase in business will soon necessitate more commodious quarters. The manufactory is equipped with every facility for the successful conduct of the business, and has six tanks with a capacity of fourteen barrels each, two of sixteen barrels, and one of ten barrels. Four persons are employed and two teams are used for delivery purposes. The business done by this house is extensive and increases steadily. The members of the firm are gentlemen of business ability and social standing; they are capable and reliable and worthy of the greatest confidence. They are both members of the Catholic Order of Foresters, and are esteemed by all who know them.

H. L. WALLACH.

Prominent among the leading business houses in the city that have built up a widespread reputation is that of Mr H. L. Wallach, the hatter, shirt-maker and furnisher, at 188-190 N. Clark street. The establishment of the business dates back as far as 1876, when it was founded by Radzyunski Bros. and in 1886 Mr. Wallach, who had for years been their managing clerk, purchased the business and adopted the present style. It was then at 184 N. Clark street, and he has been in the present location since 1890. The premises are large, fronting fifty feet on N. Clark street and 110 feet on Huron street, and the store is very handsomely fitted up with plate glass front and nickel show cases and antique oak. Mr. Wallach is a native of Poland, and has been in Chicago eighteen years. He is a comparatively young man, and an ex-member of the National Union and an ex-member of the National Guards. He has endeared himself to a large number of business and other friends through his close attention to business and honorable business methods. He is justly conceded to be the leading representative in his various lines on the North side, and always has the newest styles and fashions as soon as brought out in London or New York. His stock comprises all qualities of hats, shirts, collars and cuffs, including the leading brands; elegant neckwear, silk and woolen underwear, hosiery, gloves and all that goes to complete a gentleman's costume. He makes fine shirts to order, all of which are cut on scientific principles and warranted to give the best fit and satisfaction. College and lawn tennis, boating and outing shirts, form another specialty, also silk and flannel suits for sleeping in. Mr. Wallach controls a large business, employing ten salesmen and shirt cutters, and his store is always identified with thorough respectability.

THE HURON PHARMACY CO.

Among the well-known and centrally located pharmacies on the North side is that of the Huron Pharmacy Co., at 192 N. Clark street. This pharmacy was established immediately after the great fire, and from its inception to the present time has met with universal favor and a large patronage from the best classes. A large and carefully selected stock of drugs and chemicals, as well as toilet and fancy articles, is constantly kept on hand and a competent corps of gentlemanly pharmacists will always be found to attend to the wants of customers. The manager, Dr. Ambrose Breese, has been connected with this business for fifteen years, and is a graduate in medicine, doing, however, only an office-practice. He also attends to the correspondence of his patients, who, having left the city, still desire his services. Dr. Breese, however, is scrupulously careful to respect the rights of other members of his profession. Great care is taken in the compounding of all prescriptions. Dr. Breese is a native of Peoria County, Ill., and has been a resident of Chicago seven years. He is a member of the Illinois State Board of Pharmacy, and graduated from the Bennett Medical College in the class of 1887. He is an active Free Mason, and a member of the Order of Knights of Pythias.

THE CRESCENT.

The trade of appareling mankind grows more extensive with the lapse of years, and each department becomes separate, the better to include all of the minor details of each. The line of hats, caps, gloves, gents' furnishing goods and shirts has long been the acknowledged important one, and no firm in the city is more representative in this line than the "Crescent" at No. 129 N. Clark street, under the management of the enterprising proprietors, Mr. I. Rogats and Mr. L. Silverman. The "Crescent," although but a year in existence, already commands an immense trade, due to the splendid stock the customer may select from and the courteous treatment everyone receives who visits this handsome store. They carry a complete and carefully selected stock of hats, caps, gloves, gents' furnishing goods, and make a specialty of custom made shirts, all of which are of the very best quality and sold at remarkably low prices. Messrs. Rogats and Silverman are both natives of Germany, and have resided in this city a number of years. Both are young men, live, industrious and enterprising and are rapidly making their mark in commercial circles.

M. SCHOMMER.

A deservedly prosperous and liberally patronized establishment in this section of the city is that of Mr. Matthew Schommer, dealer in fine boots and shoes, at No. 2405 Wentworth avenue. Mr. Schommer was born in Germany, whence he removed to Chicago in 1882. Having acquired a thorough, practical knowledge of this important line of trade, and gained valuable experience in all its branches, he established his present enterprise in 1888, from the start securing a large and influential patronage, which has steadily grown and developed to its present gratifying proportions. Mr. Schommer occupies the ground floor of a two-story frame building, having a frontage of 20 by a depth of 60 feet. These spacious and commodious premises are neatly appointed and handsomely furnished, and are fitted up with every modern convenience that can add to the attractiveness of the display of fine goods, or promote the comfort of patrons. The stock carried is large and comprehensive, the assortment embracing full lines of footwear for both sexes and all ages, only the products of the most reliable manufacturers being handled. The house is leading headquarters for fine boots and shoes for men, youths and boys, and for ladies, misses and children. Several assistants are employed, and all the needs of the public in this direction are promptly attended to. His goods are unrivaled for their excellent quality of material, their elegance, easy fit, and stylish appearance, as well as their great durability. Repairing is also executed at short notice in the most workmanlike manner. Mr. Schommer is a popular merchant, and is held in high esteem by all with whom he comes in contact.

H. G. SCHRAMM.

A reliable and responsible house devoted to the importation and sale of watches, silverware, diamonds, jewelry, etc., in the southern part of the city, is that of Mr. H. G. Schramm, at No. 3915 Cottage Grove avenue, Oakland Square. This business was established in 1875 by Mr. E. R. Williams, to whom Mr. Schramm succeeded in March, 1890. From its inception the house has been a leading and influential one, and since it has come under the enterprising management of its present proprietor the limits of its trade have been greatly extended, and its patronage has been largely increased in volume and importance. He has had great experience, and is considered one of the best judges of diamonds and jewelry in the city, while at the same time he has influential connections in all the leading sources of supply. His store has a frontage of 25 by a depth of 60 feet; it is elegantly equipped, handsomely furnished, and is fitted up with large plate glass front, nickeled show cases and cabinets, the whole combining with the magnificent stock to form one of the most attractive establishments on Cottage Grove avenue. Mr. Schramm keeps constantly on hand all kinds of diamond jewelry, watches, clocks, bronzes, sterling silverware, chains, bracelets, ear rings, finger rings, brooches, pins, charms, lockets, etc., also optical goods of every description. These goods are all purchased at first hand from the most reliable sources. Three courteous assistants are employed, and all goods are fully warranted to be exactly as represented. Mr. Schramm was born in New York. He is an enterprising gentleman, and is highly esteemed by the community for his ability and sterling integrity.

E. LINDLEY.

The popular and enterprising news depot, located at No. 3456 State street, of which Mr. E. Lindley is the efficient proprietor, has become a favorite resort in this section of Chicago for the majority of its leading citizens. Mr. Lindley deals in the most fragrant brands of foreign and domestic cigars, chewing and smoking tobacco of the finest quality, the freshest and choicest confectionery of all kinds, stationery of every description, magazines, periodicals, etc., while here will also be found all the daily papers which are published in the city. The foundation of this business dates back ten years, when it was established by Mr. J. Hurd, who was succeeded by A. M. Marbaker, and he in turn by the present proprietor, who has had sole control for the past two years. The store occupied is 25x30 feet in dimensions, handsomely appointed and perfect in convenience of arrangement for the handling of the large and varied stock of goods at all times carried. Prices are placed at the lowest point of moderation, and an able assistant is in constant attendance. Mr. Lindley, who is a man in the prime of life, a native of this state, has been a widely and favorably known citizen of Chicago since 1882, and is the recipient of a large, liberal and permanent patronage. Mr. Lindley has also a finely fitted ice cream parlor in conjunction with his store, as well as a handsome soda fountain. He manufactures his own ice cream, and his establishment is fast becoming popular in this section of the city.

GARDEN CITY BAKERY.

In this section of the city there is no more popular establishment than the Garden City Bakery at Nos. 2927 and 2929 Wentworth avenue. It was established in 1883, by Mrs. E. Ramseyer, and from its inception, owing to the excellence of its products and the enterprising and liberal methods that have at all times characterized its management, a large and prosperous trade was established. The premises utilized are in a central location, and comprise the ground floor and basement of a two-story brick building, 20x60 feet in dimensions, perfectly adapted in every respect for the successful prosecution of the business on a satisfactory basis. The store is handsomely fitted up and well furnished, and, with its elegant showcases and fine counters, presents a most attractive appearance. The bakery adjoining is of ample dimensions, and is well equipped with all the latest improved machinery, tools and appliances known to the trade, including several perfected ovens of modern make and pattern. Sixteen skilled bakers and pastry cooks are employed, and the output is very large. It embraces all kinds of plain and fancy bread, Garden City Graham and Vienna loaves, cakes, buns, crumpets, rolls, crullers, doughnuts, pies and other domestic and fancy goods. Wedding cakes are made a specialty, also rich pound, fruit and sponge cakes. A heavy stock is always carried, and is daily renewed with fresh supplies. Mrs. E. Ramseyer transacts a wholesale and retail business, supplying hotels, clubs, restaurants, cafés, grocery stores and families with anything in these lines at lowest prices She specially attends to catering for balls, weddings, parties, etc., is prepared to enter into contracts of any magnitude, and has earned an enviable reputation by the reliable manner in which she fulfils all her undertakings. This establishment is under the able management of Mr. L. Ramseyer, whose extended business experience amply fits him for the duties of this position.

LEWISSON, BOICE & SMITH.

A business which has been singularly successful here, since its incorporation in 1890 (December 27), is that of Lewisson, Boice & Smith (incorporated), manufacturers of umbrellas and walking-sticks, at Nos. 220 and 222 Madison street. The corporation consists of W. N. Lewisson, president; W. H. Boice, treasurer; and C. Smith, secretary. Mr. Lewisson is a resident of Boston, Mass., and is the special partner of the concern. He is in the same line of business in New England's capital. Messrs. Boice and Smith attend to the business here. They were formerly interested in the same line of manufacture in New York, and, though young men, have had a rare experience in the details of the business, which under their excellent management has extended its influence over all the country west of the Ohio river. Both gentlemen are natives of New York. Here the firm occupies the ground floor, an apartment 60x100 feet in extent, where they carry a large stock of all grades of umbrellas and canes. About thirty-five people are employed in the manufacture of the specialties of the company, besides four traveling salesmen. Messrs. Boice & Smith are devoting themselves to the interests of the trade in a manner that is a presage of a magnificent success.

THE PLANO MFG. CO.

There is no line of business carried on to-day in the United States that so perfectly illustrates the progressive influence of modern methods, and the boundless enterprise of American manufacturers, as the manufacture of agricultural and harvesting machinery. One of the most noted and successful houses in the United States, actively engaged in this important in-

THE PLANO MANUFACTURING CO.'S WORKS AT PLANO, ILL.

dustry is that known as the Plano Manufacturing Company, manufacturers of harvesting machinery, whose office in Chicago is located at 81 and 83 W. Monroe street. The company's works, which have an area of ten acres, are situated at Plano, Ill. The various departments of the works are fully equipped with special machinery and appliances, operated by a superior 300-horse power steam engine. Here 600 skilled workmen are employed, and the trade of the company extends, not only throughout the entire United States and Canada, but also to Central and South America, Europe, India, Australia and New Zealand. The company manufactures the famous new Plano Mowers, the Jones' Chain Drive Mowers, the Plano Twine Binders, etc., which for utility, efficiency, durability and general excellence are absolutely unsurpassed in America or Europe. Only the best materials are utilized, and the result is that the Plano harvesting machinery and mowers produced are the embodiments of mechanical workmanship of the highest order of perfection. In competition with other harvesting machinery those of this company have frequently manifested their superiority, and the demand for them is rapidly increasing. There are no machines that can approach their record in the way of economical work, while there are no delays from breakage or other causes. The company points with pride to its "chain drive" improvement on its harvesters and binders. It never was an experiment with them; they knew the principal was right and did not fear the result. It turned out as they expected in a popular demand, resulting in enormous sales. The company employs 150 traveling salesmen and last year sold over 20,000 machines. The Plano Manufacturing Company was incorporated under the laws of Illinois in 1881, with a paid up capital of $500,000, and the following gentlemen who are widely known in trade circles for their executive ability, enterprise and honorable methods are the officers, viz: Wm. H. Jones, president; J. P. Prindler, vice-president; L. B. Wood, secretary and treasurer; A. J. McCormick, superintendent of agencies. The distributing points for the company's machines, twines and extras are as follows: Chicago, Ill.; Council Bluffs, Ia.; Jackson, Mich.; Minneapolis, Minn.; Rochester, N. Y.; Portland, Ore.; Tacoma, Wash.; New Orleans, La.;

Kansas City, Mo.; St. Louis, Mo.; Indianapolis, Ind.; Fargo, N. Dak., Harrisburgh, Pa.; Peoria, Ill.; Fort Worth, Tex.; Columbus, O.; Foreign: Milan, Italy; Buenos Ayres, S. A., Montevideo, S. A. The offices are elegantly fitted up and equipped, and all orders are promptly filled at extremely low prices. The standing of the Plano Manufacturing Company is high in financial and business circles, and both as regards business capacity and true American enterprise it justly merits the representative position it has attained in this important industry.

LOUIS STAUBER

The hardware business is one of the best represented mercantile pursuits in Chicago. A leading house in this line is that of Louis Stauber, who has been established in the business since 1873, and is one of the leading and best known dealers in the trade. Mr. Stauber is a native of Germany, and has resided in Chicago since 1869. He is well known as an upright, responsible business man, and has numerous friends and patrons who hold him in the highest esteem. He occupies the ground floor and basement of 360 W. Chicago avenue, and has them thoroughly stocked with a fine line of stoves and hardware, including shelf goods of all kinds, screws, nails, wire, tools, builders' hardware, etc., also a fine assortment of house furnishing goods of all kinds. A specialty is made of all kinds of tinware, and the house does a large tin jobbing trade. Castings and bricks are furnished for all kinds of stoves. The patronage of this house is very large and continues to increase steadily. Every attention is shown customers and the reputation for fair and honorable dealing is not exceeded by any like house in the city. Two competent clerks are employed, and patrons are promptly supplied with their needs.

CONRAD KAPP.

This popular and well patronized bakery and confectionery was established by its present proprietor, Mr. Conrad Kapp, in 1889, and under his able management, it has deservedly enjoyed a continuously prosperous career to date, the patronage of the house annually increasing in volume and value. The premises, No. 3212 Wentworth avenue, consist of an eligible store, with bakery and manufacturing department in the rear. The latter is supplied with every facility known to the trade, while the former is fitted up with a special view to the satisfactory prosecution of the extensive counter trade enjoyed. The large show window is always beautifully arranged with specimens of fancy cakes, confectionery and other delicacies, all of which goods are manufactured on the premises. All kinds of plain and fancy cakes, including rich fruit and pound cakes, lady fingers, crullers, jumbles, macaroons, etc., are baked fresh every day, and the regular family trade is always large and constant. A specialty is made of supplying weddings, parties, etc., and every convenience is at hand for frosting cakes, making pyramids, chocolate and other sweet material. Only the very purest ingredients are used, and Mr. Kapp takes every pains to fully merit the increasing patronage he to-day enjoys.

G. W. VARNEY.

An artist of high standing in his profession is Mr. G. W. Varney, the photographer. Mr. Varney has had many years' practical experience, and has achieved a wide-spread popularity. For about four years he was in business with a partner at Thirty-eighth street and Cottage Grove avenue, and in 1887 commenced operations on his own account at No. 189 Wabash avenue, where he remained until three years ago, when he secured and removed to the very desirable premises now occupied at 3915 Cottage Grove avenue. The facilities enjoyed by Mr. Varney for executing the best class of work are perfect and complete, his equipment comprising the latest improved apparatus and all the appurtenances for obtaining superior results. Nine artists assist Mr. Varney, and photography in all branches is executed, particular attention being paid to finishing pictures in pastel, India ink, oil and water colors. Mr. Varney's splendid portraits and groups are highly commended, and all his work is brilliant, highly finished and lasting. He makes a specialty of fine cabinet pictures, which are furnished at the low price of $4 per dozen. Mr. Varney is a young man, a native of Maine, but for many years has been in the city where he has become well known as one of the most distinguished and successful photographers. He is moderate in his prices, and as a consequence is doing a splendid business. The premises occupied are spacious, commodious and neatly and tastefully fitted up. The parlors, reception rooms and operating department are on the second floor, and have an area of 25x75 feet. The third floor is the finishing department.

K. G. DEKKER.

The establishment of Mr. K. G. Dekker, 216 South Water street, is noteworthy as being prominently engaged in handling Holland produce in this city. It was founded in 1884 by Mr. Dekker, its present sole proprietor, who imports largely from Holland, and wholesales to the trade only. The premises, consisting of a store 20x75 feet in dimensions, afford ample accommodation for the receipt of his goods, employment being furnished to two assistants. Mr. Dekker keeps a very choice stock, which is highly appreciated by Chicago people coming direct from Holland. He handles Holland plants, such as roses, bulbs, etc., cheese, herrings, beans and many other things, the quality of which is not obtainable in this country, and a trade is transacted which extends throughout the whole city and surrounding states. Mr. Dekker is a native of Holland, and has been for eight years a resident of Chicago, where he began business, and, as may be inferred from his enterprise, has identified himself with the commercial advancement of this community. The characteristics which regulate his business policy are such as to entitle the house to the success it has attained, while its resources enable the proprietor to extend unusual advantages to his patrons. He is a young man, and the position which his house occupies in this city is clearly indicative of an energy and liberality that has been justly rewarded in the brilliant success achieved, and the high esteem with which he is regarded.

THE WESTERN FIREMAN AND JOURNAL OF PUBLIC WORKS.

Journals which devote their pages to the interest of some special organization, business or sect, are rightfully growing in importance, and the reason is obvious that the function of the general newspaper is too diffuse. Hence some of the greatest successes in the newspaper world are found in organs of special interests, such as the grocers, boot and shoe, etc. One of the most marked illustrations of this specialized newspaper work is the Western Fireman and Journal of Public Works, which is now in its fourteenth volume, and has made a success. It was established in 1878 by Dr. Bloomister, and is devoted to fire protection and allied branches of the public service, water supply, electrical science and general municipal affairs. It is the official organ of the National Association of

Fire Engineers, and of the S ate Firemen's Association of the Western States. Mr. T. E. Smith, Jr . is the proprietor, and during his energetic management the paper has taken a decided boom. Its columns contain not only the latest news of interest to firemen, and well illustrated sketches of firemen's conventions, etc., but it also has the latest possible information on the newest devices for extinguishing fires or saving life from fire, of electrical lifting devices or any other distinguishing feature of municipal control in harmony with the aims of the paper. The paper is well edited, has marks of careful typography, and a show of advertisements that gives the paper a really comfortable appearance, suggestive of place, a clear conscience and an ordinarily fat pocket book. The Western Fireman and Journal of Public Works has been so conducted as to make no one but the enemy of the public interest its enemy, and that is the best word to say of a paper. The office of the paper is at room 85 Calumet building, 187 La Salle street, where advertising rates are furnished on application. The subscription price is $2 per annum.

RICHARD EHRHARDT.

The expert sanitary plumber fills a niche in the long list of skilled mechanics which combine to constitute the world of labor unapproached by any of his peers, for on his efforts oftentimes depend the health and life of the community in the provisions he makes against the generation of sewer gas, and which is only to be accomplished through the sanitary condition of our dwellings. A leading exponent of this important industry is Mr. Richard Ehrhardt, whose well-appointed establishment is located at No. 2338 Wentworth avenue. He has been engaged in the business on his own account since 1865, and to-day deservedly enjoys a large share of the local trade. The premises occupied comprise a spacious and commodious store, 20x100 feet in dimensions, and handsomely and appropriately fitted with a view to the expeditious conduct of the business. Mr. Ehrhardt furnishes estimates and completes contracts for the complete plumbing and gas fitting of buildings, and pays particular attention to sewer work, jobbing and repairing. He likewise deals extensively in fine gas fixtures, his stock of these commodities being without question the finest displayed in this section of the city. Six skilled assistants are employed; all orders receive prompt attention, and charges are invariably based on a scale of moderation. Mr. Ehrhardt bears the reputation of being one of the most skilled exponents of his highly important craft in Chicago; he, as an expert sanitary plumber, having few equals and no superiors, in this section and is now doing business that is well repaying him for this the energy and push he has put forth.

FELIX AUERBACH.

Chicago, the great central metropolis, is one of the most extensive markets for musical instruments in America, and has many worthy representatives of this industry. Among these, Mr. Felix Auerbach is well deserving of special mention. He is the proprietor and manager of a finely equipped music store, located on the ground floor of the building No. 2823 Archer avenue. Mr. Auerbach is a native of Germany and has only resided in Chicago for a term of six years. He has shown himself however a man of rare ambition, a highly cultivated musician and an upright and well principled business man. He is agent for the celebrated Hartman pianos and carries a fine line of other musical instruments, which make a fine display. The instruments offered by him are unequaled, and the delight of the devotees of "Terpsichore." Mr. Auerbach also carries a line of sewing machines, the treasures of every household, and a large assortment of sheet music. His trade is entirely city trade, but has expanded to great proportions; in these times of competition only the most strenuous efforts for advancement are crowned with success, and great credit is due to Mr. Auerbach for accomplishing his aim in making himself popular with the music loving public of Chicago. Such institutions as his are always welcome, and cannot fail to be a blessing to the community.

W. GUTHRIE & CO.

Among the most active of those engaged in the real estate business in this city we find W. Guthrie & Co., a comparatively new firm in the business arena, having been established only since May, 1890. Yet previous to this, Mr. Guthrie had been connected with the real estate business for the past thirty years, and, owing to an experience of this length of time, he has succeeded in acquiring an influential line of patronage. He occupies offices in the Methodist Church block, room 12, where all the various branches of real estate business are carried on by him, such as negotiating bonds, mortgages, loans, insurance, collecting rents, taking entire charge of estates, leasing and renting property, etc., etc. Mr. Guthrie, who is a native of Sackett's Harbor, New York, has been a resident of Chicago for forty-five years. His long experience in real estate has qualified him as an expert, and in respect to disputes over real estate questions he is frequently called as such, and he has been the recipient of a very flattering and remunerative support. He is a member of the "Sons of New York."

MYRON H. CHURCH.

The rapid and substantial development of Chicago has been favorable to the construction of handsome private and public edifices. While no recognized style of architecture has been strictly followed, the beauties and advantages of the Grecian, Roman Corinthian and Gothic have been adopted by our architects and blended with our modern ideas, varied occasionally with suggestions originating with themselves. In connection with these remarks, special attention is directed to the office of Mr. Myron H. Church, Royal Insurance building, who has acquired a substantial reputation for the beauty and originality of his plans and designs. Proofs of Mr. Church's skill and ability are numerous, as embodied in the many large edifices erected in the business portion of the city, while he is draughtsman for some of the leading firms of the city. Mr. Church devotes all his energies to his favorite profession, and conscientiously discharges his duties to all favoring him with commissions. He was formerly employed at a very high salary as head draughtsman to Messrs. Burnham & Root, and also to Mr. S. S. Beeman. Prior to this he held a high position in the house of Mr. W. W. Boyington, and is employed at the present time as architect for the Chicago and South Side Rapid Transit R. R. Co., which is one of the best proofs of his standing and ability. His office, No. 711 Royal Insurance building, is conveniently located and arranged. Mr. Church is a native of Detroit, Michigan, and has resided in Chicago for the last eighteen years. He is a young man of the highest ability, and is worthy of special mention as one of Chicago's prominent architects and as one of its representative men.

GARDEN CITY CIGAR MANUFACTURING CO.

All the world smokes in these days, and the greatest harm from the habit arises from the poor quality of the tobacco most people use. There is no excuse for this in Chicago, as any one can obtain a first-class smoke of the best tobacco by buying cigars made at the Garden City Cigar Manufacturing Company, Richard Bradel, proprietor, No. 609 North Wells street. Mr. Bradel organized his business in Racine Wis., twenty years ago and removed to Chicago ten years later. He has long had the reputation of making the best cigar in the world for a good smoke, and will always sustain it. His specialty is the celebrated "Grip" cigar and the "El Faro" all strictly pure, handmade Habanas and of the highest grade. In his manufactory Mr. Bradel employs eight skilled cigarmakers who are taxed to their utmost to keep peace with his immense, and constantly increasing trade, which the excellence of his goods has created. Mr. Bradel is a veteran of the late war, having served in the Wisconsin Turner Volunteer infantry with distinction. He is a genial sociable gentleman as well as a first-class business man and merits his splendid patronage.

BOGUE & MILLS MANUFACTURING CO.

The dangers attendant upon crossings at grades are becoming more patent every day, and any device that will lessen the danger is a positive boon to the community. In this connection it is a pleasure to speak of the Mills' system of air lever and cable gates for railroad crossings. This system has had a thorough test, and has met all the requirements of the most exacting, and is now being introduced extensively. It is manufactured by the Bogue & Mills Manufacturing Company, whose office and factory are located at 31 and 33 East Indiana street. This company was incorporated in 1888 with ample capital, and the following well known business men as officers: Geo. M. Bogue, president; M. B. Mills, vice-president; O. A. Bogue, secretary and treasurer. The factory is equipped with all the modern appliances and machinery necessary to the proper manufacture of the devices handled, and the whole plant is as complete as could be desired. The company occupies the ground floor and basement of the premises here mentioned, which are 50x150 feet in dimensions, and afford ample and commodious quarters for the business. About thirty workmen are employed in the manufacture of the specialty of the company, and in other railroad appliances. The trade is scattered all over the United States; and is extensive in character. The company has an excellent reputation, and the utility of the device and the integrity of the manufacturers is unquestioned.

H. M. SMITH.

It is nearly ten years ago since H. M. Smith started the business of dealer in stoves, furnaces, ranges, tinware and all kinds of hardware, and his success has been of the most gratifying kind. He occupies for the purpose of his rapidly growing business the ground floor and basement, 25x75 feet, of the building 141 Thirty-ninth street, with a workshop in the rear, and manufactures tinware, sheet iron and copper ware, blowers and ash pans, in addition to which he carries a large stock of general hardware, and attends to general jobbing, to the repairing of gas and gasoline stoves, to the full equipment of kitchens, and to all the duties which are comprised in the range of the business in which he has been so successful. Seven people are employed, and Mr. H. M. Smith, who is still a young man, has a rare prospect of more remarkable success than that which has so far attended his efforts. He is a native of Chicago, is a member of the Masonic fraternity, and is universally respected, not only in his business, but in his social relations.

WILSON P. CONOVER.

Among the sound and prosperous houses engaged in the realty field of activity is that of Mr. Wilson P. Conover, whose offices are located in the Chicago Opera House building, where he occupies suite No. 718. This gentleman was born in the state of Ohio, and has been a resident of this city since 1885. In 1886 he established his present business, and the development it has acquired in the short space of time it has been prominently in the front of the market in realty is conclusive of the great practical knowledge he possesses of the values and their fluctuations of real estate. His offices are spacious and commodious, handsomely fitted up and elegantly furnished, and are provided with every facility and convenience for the prompt transaction of his large business. The experience he has acquired in this field of usefulness has been of inestimable value to his patrons, and few real estate brokers have had more important trusts committed to their care. Special attention is given to the sale, letting, purchase and exchange of realty, of which a large and important list, both city and suburban, is always to be found on his books. Estates of absentees are also carefully looked after, rents collected, taxes paid and the utmost care given to their management, the whole at very moderate rates. Loans on bonds and mortgages, are negotiated and put through without any delay, his financial connections being of the most influential character. He is a respected citizen, and commands the confidence and esteem of all classes of the community.

FRED. F. BISCHOFF & CO.

One of the most successful and progressive firms in Chicago, actively engaged in the manufacture of architectural ornaments in sheet, zinc, brass or copper for interior and exterior decorations for buildings, is that of Messrs. Fred. F. Bischoff & Company, whose statuary and metal ornament works are located at 83 and 85 W. North avenue, while their office and salesrooms are at 24 and 26 W. Lake street. This business was established in 1884 by Messrs. Spiers & Bischoff, who first commenced the manufacture of cornices. In 1888 Mr. Spiers retired, and Mr. Wm. Rauen became a partner, the firm being known by the title of Fred. F. Bischoff & Co. Then they gave up the manufacturing of cornices and turned

their attention solely to the manufacture of metal ornaments, sheet steel ceilings, statuary, etc. Their factory is 83x85 feet in dimensions, fully equipped with the latest improved appliances and machinery, operated by a forty horse power steam engine. Here they employ some expert designers and modelers, together with thirty skilled workmen, enabling them to guarantee perfect workmanship, and the prompt shipment of all orders placed in their care. They manufacture largely all kinds of sheet zinc, brass and copper ornaments, which are unrivaled for elegance, finish and durability, and have no superiors in the market, while the prices quoted in all cases are exceedingly moderate. The firm's sheet metal ceilings are susceptible of the most artistic ornamentation, their capability in this respect being limited only by the skill of the designer, while finer effects can be produced than are possible when the painting is done on a flat surface. As the metal ceiling can be made of any size, it is admirably adapted for large buildings,

churches, schoolhouses, stores, factories and dwellings. This metal ceiling is fire and waterproof and will not shrink, burn, warp, crack or fall like plaster or wood ceilings; its durability is unquestionable. It is easily handled and can be placed in position by any mechanic with little labor. The firm carefully fills orders, and its trade extends throughout the entire United States and Canada. Mr. Christian W. Minnich, the manager, has had long experience in the manufacture of the firm's goods, and is widely known for his skill and ability. Messrs. Bischoff & Rauen were both born in Germany, but have resided in the United States many years. They are enterprising and honorable business men, who have secured a liberal and permanent patronage, owing to the superiority of their productions. The firm issues superior illustrated catalogues, and most of the article shown in them are always in stock.

J. LAZENBY.

The interesting and delicate industry of manufacturing color cards for mixed paints was begun by Mr. Lazenby ten years ago, and has gradually expanded and prospered year by year, until it now numbers among its patrons many of the largest manufacturers in the United States. Mr. Lazenby occupies extensive and convenient premises at 39 Dearborn ave., and a factory across the street, over 203 W. Kinzie street. He employs on an acrage thirty - five work people, superintending carefully every process of the work. He manufactures a full line of cards for mixed paints, many of which are of elegant design, and all give an accurate idea of the shades and tints which each paint will produce. In addition to this the striking and attractive appearance of these cards arrests the attention and pleases the eye in a manner well calculated to give the greatest popularity and the largest sale to paints which are advertised by this means. Every facility is at hand for the production of these beautiful articles in the highest style of the art, and in all the details of the work the best methods are invariably practiced. Mr. Lazenby is intimately acquainted with every phase and feature of the business, and is prepared to execute the most important commissions in color work, with promptitude and accuracy. He was born in Clifton Springs, N. Y., and served during the war in the 148th New York Infantry, under General Ben Butler, with faithfulness and credit. He is an esteemed member of the Grand Army of the Republic, and a talented business man, favorably known to the trade.

DU VIVIER & CO.

The recognized overshadowing importance of Chicago as a great center of the wine and liquor trade renders it of importance to give due prominence to those representative houses whose enterprise has developed the industry, and maintained it in its present high state of efficiency. One of these, whose operations are of national importance is that of Messrs. Du Vivier & Co., of New York, a name which has become a household word in every part of the United States and Canada, and whose Chicago establishment is in room 7, Sibley Warehouses. They are large importers of the finest Perrier Jouet champagne, also the finest table clarets, Chateau wines, Sauternes, Burgundies, Rhine wines, ports and sherries of the best vintages, besides brandies, whiskies, gins and rums of the highest grades. Their splendid cellars, which have a capacity of 300,000 bottles, are modelled after those of France and Spain. Large and flourishing branches have been opened in Montreal, Canada, as well in the Hiram Sibley Warehouse building, at Clark street bridge, Chicago, and these have proved sources of great prosperity, and tend greatly to facilitate trade in their respective sections of the country. The proprietors have shown characteristic wisdom in the selection of Mr. Henry McKay as the general manager of the western department, this gentleman having acquired a wide experience during his twenty-five years' acquaintance with this influential house, and shown himself possessed of great energy, and high executive ability. He has sole charge of the important Western and Northwestern business, and since the inception in 1890 has developed his connections among the most desirable trade in a rapid and promising manner.

JOHN SIMMETH.

Mr. John Simmeth's store at 516 Twenty-ninth street is just our idea of what a neat bakery and confectionery store should be like. The business was established by him in 1883, since that time has progressed and developed into a very comfortable and first-class connection. But this was only to be expected, for Mr. Simmeth is a thoroughly practical man, and is blessed with a high sense of his duty to others and therefore in every instance uses the best materials he can buy for the purposes of his business. Besides bread, bakerstuffs and the ordinary staple articles of pastry and confectionery he makes wedding cakes and other fancy cakes to order, and his fancy sugar work and frosting cannot be surpassed in the city for artistic skill. Mr. Simmeth has attached to his store very handsome and attractive ice cream parlors, and also sells candies in great variety. He is a native of Germany, and has been in Chicago for twelve years.

W. T. MASON.

The greatest benefactor to suffering humanity is, undoubtedly, the dispensing druggist. He it is who deals directly with the people, and is their healer and physician. The most popular place on the West side, where all the minor ailments are attended to and physicians' prescriptions promptly filled, is that of W. T. Mason, dispensing druggist, at No. 525 Van Buren street, northeast corner of Laflin street. This store was opened by Dr. C. L. Clancy ten years ago, and the present proprietor assumed the proprietorship in 1890, after serving eight years with Messrs. Buck & Rayner, and is a practical druggist. He is a graduate of the Chicago College of Pharmacy, and manufactures all of his own extracts, tinctures and essences, besides making the celebrated Chicago tooth paste, Chicago Dentifrice, the Floral Lotion, Lightning Corn Salve, Lightning Hair Grower, and Beef, Iron and Wine, Mason's Cough Syrup and other household remedies that have earned a reputation in the community. Mr. Mason's store is one of the handsomest and best equipped in the city, the laboratory being furnished with the latest improved and best chemical appliances. The success of Mr. Mason is due simply and solely to his abilities, perseverance, energy and industry.

FERDINAND FRITZ.

One of the best and most popular grocery houses of the West side is that conducted by Mr. Ferdinand Fritz at 1769 Milwaukee avenue. Mr. Fritz established this business two years ago and has met with success beyond his most sanguine expectations. He has the patronage of the best people in the district, and finds his trade increasing steadily. His store is large and attractive, and has one of the most favorable locations possible to be secured, being the principal thoroughfare of the district. He occupies the ground floor and basement of the premises, which are 25x60 feet in dimensions, and here he carries a complete and very fine stock of staple and fancy groceries of all kinds, imported and domestic, also fine teas, coffees and spices selected especially for his trade, flour of fine brands and feed; also preserves, condiments, pickles, wooden ware, brooms and grocers' sundries, canned goods, sauces and vegetables, also the finest dairy products. The stock is kept up and is always fresh and clean. Two experienced assistants are employed to attend to the needs of customers, and goods are delivered to all parts of the city free of charge. The trade is very large, and Mr. Fritz is one of the most popular and agreeable grocers in Chicago. He is a native of Germany, and has lived in Chicago twelve years; he attends closely to business and thus has achieved his telling success.

H. H. MARTINDALE.

Mr. H. H. Martindale is perhaps as well known among horsemen as any man in Chicago. He established himself in business in 1850 at Peterboro, N. Y., and in 1872 removed to Chicago, where he has since continued the business. He built his present premises at 432 W. Lake street and removed thereto in 1882. They consist of a three story brick building, 75x30 feet, which he uses as a horseshoeing establishment, and at the rear is a barn, also of brick, 95x30 feet, which he uses as a strictly first class light livery and boarding stable, having about dozen horses of his own and fifteen boarders. He employs a large staff of specially skilled men, and his shoeing is all done on the most scientific principles. He thoroughly understands the horse's foot, and receives and treats horses for diseases of the feet, boarding them if required, during treatment. He has had many hundreds of cases under his care, and it is rarely that he does not effect a complete cure; and his charges are at all times moderate. Mr. Martindale was born in Madison County, N. Y., and is a member of the Masonic order. His straightforward honorable business methods have won for him the confidence and esteem of the public.

E. L. VOGNILD.

In former times a watch or clock was considered a luxury to be indulged in only by the wealthy, but now no home is considered complete without one or more, as no lady's or gentleman's toilet is complete without a watch. As a consequence there is a greater demand for watchmakers and jewelers, and no part of the city can boast of one more thorough and capable than Mr. E. L. Vognild, of 1144 Milwaukee avenue, at the corner of Fontenoy court, who at all times carries a large and carefully selected stock of diamonds, watches, clocks and jewelry, and employs experienced men in making repairs on all kinds of watches, clocks and jewelry, which work is all guaranteed to be first-class and moderate in price. Mr Vognild established his business in Chicago about ten years ago, and has been very successful in his business enterprises. He is a native of Norway, and came to Chicago more than twenty years ago. Mr. Vognild is a practical watchmaker, learning his trade in the old country, commencing at the bench when only thirteen years of age. He has worked for the leading jewelry houses in this city, and is a most skilful workman. He is a member of the Jewelers' League, also an honored member of the Chosen Friends. He is popular, energetic and industrious, and has hosts of friends who rejoice in his prosperity.

THE SCANDIA FURNITURE COMPANY.

One of the most popular and progressive houses in its special line is that of the Scandia Furniture Co., located in the spacious, commodious double building, Nos. 235-237, W. Indiana street. The company was organized and incorporated Jan. 1st of the present year, with Mr. B. C. Bjornstad as president, and Mr. T. C. Peterson as secretary-treasurer. Although but a short time has elapsed since the organization of the company, by the enterprise and ability of the officers a flourishing business has been built up, and is steadily growing in volume and importance. The company manufacture parlor suites in all the new fashionable styles, and in the warerooms carry a full and complete assortment of all kinds, household furniture of every description, also stoves and ranges of the newest designs, and a general line of carpets in flower and figure patterns. The company fully guarantee all goods made and sold, and, having every facility and convenience for conducting business, can always name the very lowest prices and give the best satisfaction. Mr. Bjornstad, the president, has had a long experience in the furniture trade, and, previous to becoming connected with the company, carried on business on his own account for a period of eight years. Mr. Peterson, the secretary-treasurer, is an experienced, practical business man, and was for some years engaged in the dry goods trade at Stewart, Wis. These gentlemen are both natives of Norway. They have been in this country many years, and have always enjoyed a high reputation for probity and integrity. Mr. Petersen, the Secretary-treasurer, is an experienced practical business man, and has had several years' experience in general merchandise at Stewart, Wis.

PHOENIX CHEMICAL WORKS.

A representative business, connected intimately with that of the grocer's business, is that of the Phoenix Chemical Works, manufacturers of grocers' sundries. The business was established in 1870 by Mr. C. O. Strutz, the present proprietor. The business done is very extensive and highly representative. The large four-story building, 25x100 feet in dimensions, is used as a manufactory and storeroom, and here are made all kinds of grocers' sundries, consisting of baking powder, washing compound, scouring soaps, flavoring extracts, stove polish, borax, etc. Bird seed is packed for retail trade in an attractive manner, and all the specialties are put up in a taking and saleable form. The business done is very extensive, the trade being in the city and in all parts of the country. Fourteen hands are employed in the laboratory and works, and two teams are utilized for the delivery of goods. The business is conducted at 194 Kinzie street, and is in a convenient and prominent location. Mr. Strutz is a native of Germany, and has been in the United States since 1862, and has resided in Chicago for the past twenty-two years. He first established himself as a dealer in grocers' supplies, and in 1881 adopted the present style of business. He is a leading and well-known business man, having the highest standing commercially and financially. He gives the business personal direction, and has a reputation for ability and integrity of the highest order.

BOWMAN DAIRY CO.

Chicago is noted throughout the West for her fine dairy establishments, which in all desirable qualifications are unsurpassed by those of any other great center in the Union. One of the chief of these is the Bowman Dairy Co., of Nos. 68 and 70 N. State street, and which was established thirty-five years ago by Mr. M. A. Devine, and which is among the most reliable distributors of pure country milk in the city. The business was incorporated under its present style in 1885, with a capital of $150,000, and at once began a new era of prosperity, which has culminated in its present enviable proportions. They buy direct from the farmers, thereby securing the purest article in the freshest possible condition, and handle no less than 2,400 gallons per day, their fine premises affording accommodation for 350 cans in the large ice safes, to which they are immediately consigned on arrival. In addition to the headquarters on N. State street, they conduct a flourishing branch on Stanton avenue, in a substantial and roomy three-story brick building just being completed by them. This fine business requires the services of forty employes and thirty teams, and the routes lie among the most desirable families in all parts of the city. We cannot be too careful where we obtain milk for our households, and should invariably deal with an establishment such as the Bowman Dairy Co., who are experts in the handling of this product, and who have an intimate knowledge of the sanitary conditions to be observed. The officers are: president, Mr. R. Bowman; vice-president, Mr. G. E. Peck; secretary, Mr. J. R. Bowman; assistant secretary, Mr. E. M. Bowman; and treasurer, Mr. R. A. Bowman, all gentlemen of the highest reputation and standing in commercial circles.

L. STOCK.

Few people know the value to them of clothes and garments which they have cast off, as worn out or faded, as in many instances the expenditure of a dollar or so will restore a garment equal to new, and which the owner had decided was only fit for the rag bag. W. L. Stock, whose Fancy Steam Dye Works are at 459 Ogden avenue, makes a specialty of restoring old clothing, also of scouring, dyeing and dry cleaning. Mr. Stock is a native of Germany and came to Chicago seven years ago, and five years ago established this business. His place is equipped with every modern convenience for his business, and he has a ten horse-power engine to supply the necessary power. The greatest care is taken of goods, even the most delicate textures not being injured, and all colors are warranted not to fade or to remove from the surface. W. Stock cleans, dyes and finishes all kinds of ladies' and gentlemen's garments, and goods, including silk, satin and poplin dresses, cloaks, ulsters, jackets, wraps, shawls, etc., also gents' coats, suits and uniforms without shrinking, and these latter he repairs and presses equal to new. Ostrich plumes are cleaned, dyed and curled in the latest style, and a specialty is made of cleaning kid gloves. All work is done promptly and delivered to any part of the city. Mr. Stock himself supervises every detail of his business and enjoys the confidence of a large patronage.

GEO. ROUNSAVELL.

One of the oldest established and most successful concerns in Chicago extensively engaged in the manufacture of all kinds of cooperage is that of Mr. Geo. Rounsavell, whose office and factory are situated at 68 to 76 Clybourn place. Mr. Rounsavell, who is a thoroughly practical and expert cooper, first commenced business in a small way in 1858, employing only three hands. By energy, skill and industry he made great progress, and now employs 70 to 80 skilled workmen. He owns and occupies a substantial three-story brick building, 60x110 feet in dimensions, with dry-kilns attached, fully supplied with modern tools, appliances and machinery, operated by a forty horse-power steam engine. Mr. Rounsavell manufactures largely lead, cider, vinegar and pickle kegs, and makes a specialty of patent white barrels. He also produces barrels, half-barrels and kegs for brewers and distillers, and turns out annually over 200,000 packages. His barrels, kegs, etc., have always been noted for their strength, finish and durability, while the prices quoted for them are extremely moderate. Only carefully selected and seasoned oak is utilized, which is received direct from Indiana, Tennessee and Arkansas. His facilities are so complete that barrels can be put together in a minute, and yet be equal in every respect in strength and finish to any in the market. Orders are promptly and carefully filled, and every effort is made to satisfy customers. The factory has excellent railway and water facilities, and the trade of the house extends throughout the Middle, Western and Northwestern states. Mr. Rounsavell was born in New Jersey, but has resided in Chicago since 1858. He is an honorable, able and hard working manufacturer, who is promoting the commerce of the city with skill and success.

W. H. GRAY & BRO.

An important branch of skilled industry is that of the boring of artesian wells, and the manufacture of drills and other machinery, with the supplies necessary to carry on this difficult line of work. In this line, as well as in so many others, Chicago leads all America, being made the permanent headquarters of the large establishment of Messrs. W. H. Gray & Bro., the leading artesian well contractors of the United States, who have bored several of the deepest in the world; and where contractors of less experience, and with inferior facilities would fail, they will guarantee to sink a well

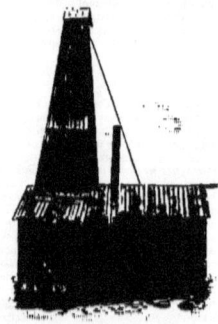

to any depth, thus securing an abundant supply of pure, fresh water for all purposes. The business was established in 1871, by Messrs. John F. Gray & Co., succeeded in 1879 by the firm of Messrs. W. H. Gray & Co., thus continuing until January 24, 1891, when the present firm was formed, Mr. W. A. Gray coming into co-partnership. The firm have an extensive factory at Nos. 4 to 12 Michigan street, where upward of 75 hands find employment in the manufacture of well boring and mill machinery tools and supplies. The premises are of brick, two stories in height, and are fully equipped with a complete line of machine tools, run by 13 engines and boilers. The firm have achieved an enviable reputation for introducing invaluable improvements in this line, including special machinery for rapid boring and thorough tubing of deep wells. They are prepared to contract for the sinking of wells to any depth, through the most difficult strata, and refer to hundreds of powerful flowing wells here and all over the Western and Middle states. They always keep full lines of supplies on hand and can promptly fill orders at most reasonable prices. Mr. W. H. Gray is a native of Franklin county, New York, and came to Chicago in 1855. Here he has had a lengthy and honorable business career, and has won the esteem and the confidence of the community at large. He is a member of the Oriental Consistory, and is thus a 32 degree Mason, while socially he is deservedly popular. Mr. W. A. Gray is equally respected, well known in the trade, and the firm stands preeminent in its line, the most successful contractor, for artesian wells in America, fully prepared and thoroughly responsible to engage in any work of the kind, and give entire satisfaction.

JOHN E. FOWLER.

Fowler's West Side Fashion Bazaar and Sewing Machine Rooms occupy ample premises at No. 253 W. Madison street, corner of Sangamon. A branch establishment is also run at No. 623 S. Ashland avenue, corner of Hastings street. Mr. John E. Fowler, the proprietor, is the West side agent for McCall's Bazaar Patterns, and a full line of celebrated domestic patterns is also carried. Patterns are sent to any address on receipt of the number, size and price. Mr. Fowler is also the Chicago agent for Hall's Bazaar Forms. All makes of sewing machines, including the celebrated Singer, Domestic and New Home machines, are carried, and sold on easy monthly payments. A large stock of second-hand machines is also kept on hand and sold cheap—from $5 up. Machines are also rented at the lowest figures. All kinds of sewing machines are skilfully repaired at the most reasonable rates. Supplies for all makes of machines are sold, including repairs, attachments, needles, oils, etc. Pleating of all kinds is done to order, including accordion, kilt, knife and box pleating. Stitching, shirring, fringing and pinking are also done in the best style and on the shortest notice. Buttonholes, including silk, are made for a cent and a half each, and buttons are covered with any kind of goods desired. Mr. Fowler was born in Manchester, England, fifty-three years ago, and has resided in Chicago since 1867. He has had sixteen years' experience in the business. For twelve years he was with the Singer Sewing Machine Company. Since he opened his present establishment in 1888 he has built up an excellent patronage.

HENRY L. OHLENDORF.

There is no establishment in a community more necessary and convenient than a well-regulated pharmacy and drug store. One of the most popular and best in the city is that of Mr. Henry L. Ohlendorf of No. 315 N. Wells street, at the corner of Oak street. This splendid business was established in 1883, and has been a success and prospered ever since. The proprietor is a graduate of the Chicago College of Pharmacy, a member of the Alumni and registered by the State Board of Pharmacy of Illinois. He is a studious and well-read chemist, and manufactures all of his own tinctures, extracts, essences and syrups, and makes a specialty of compounding prescriptions, at which business he has earned a splendid reputation. His store is 23x50 feet in size, and is conveniently located and handsomely fitted with rich cherry furniture and dazzling cases for the immense stock of pure, fresh drugs, chemicals, patent medicines, toilet articles and druggists' sundries, and he has also a large marble soda fountain that is useful as well as ornamental. Mr. Ohlendorf is a Chicagoan by birth, and has, by his industrious and honorable conduct, made a large circle of friends.

NORDAHL & OLSON.

One of the oldest and best known reputable jewelry establishments on Milwaukee avenue is that of Nordahl & Olson, located at 213 on that thoroughfare, extending through to 194 N. Halsted street. The copartners, Mr. Hans Nordahl and Mr. O. E. Olson, are both practical watchmakers and jewelers, and well versed in all the details of the business. They are gentlemen in middle life, coming to this country from Norway in 1866, and three years later laid the foundation of the splendid business they are now conducting with such marked success. The store is handsomely and attractively fitted up with ornamental show cases and wall cabinets, and everything about it is in perfect keeping with the character of the business. The plate glass show windows always present a handsome appearance and contain many beautiful specimens of the goods to be found on sale in the store, comprising rich, elegant jewelry of every description, in all the new fashionable styles, diamonds and other gems in various mountings, solid silver and plated ware, gold and silver watches, optical goods, clocks and a wide range of useful and ornamental articles eminently suitable for wedding presents and gifts for all occasions. The firm make a specialty of gems representing each month in the year, which are mounted in an appropriate manner for birthday presents, on rings or in any style desired. They also repair watches, clocks and jewelry and fully warrant all their work. They are doing a fine business, and, as they never make misrepresentations to effect sales, and can always name the lowest prices, they are recognized as the most reputable watchmakers and jewelers on the West side.

GARRATT'S DREXEL STEAM LAUNDRY.

Unquestionably the best known and most popular establishment of its kind in the section in which it is located is Garratt's Drexel Steam Laundry, located at Nos. 3853 and 3855 Vincennes avenue. It was established in 1887 by Mr. Thos. Garratt, who has conducted it with ability and acquired a reputation for promptness, reliability and excellent service, and is enjoying a positive and substantial success. The work he turns out is of a superior character, while extremely low prices prevail. The premises occupied comprise the ground floor and basement of the double building, having an area of 50x75 feet, which are equipped with the latest improved appliances and general appurtenances, including steam power, three washing, several centrifugal, starching and ironing machines, and lucrative employment is given to from thirty to forty competent hands in the different departments, while four teams call for and deliver orders in any part of the city and suburbs. Family and hotel laundry work is done in the most expeditious manner, and every care is taken so that the most delicate fabrics are not injured. Fine shirts, collars, cuffs and linen and transient work is a specialty, and every care and attention is given by Mr. Garratt to render satisfaction. He is a young man, a native of England, came to Chicago in 1881 and has since been identified with the laundry business. He is a member of the Chicago Laundrymen's Association, and throughout his business career has ever maintained a high reputation for probity and integrity. He is very popular and his well-conducted laundry is commended by all who patronize it. The ring-up on the "phone" is 9843. Business is active and the patronage continues to steadily grow, and is becoming more widely extended each succeeding year.

J. HART.

In the manufacture and sale of room and cove moldings, picture frames, etc., a representative and one of the most successful concerns in this section of Chicago is that of Mr. J Hart, whose office and salesroom are situated at 430 West Lake street, and factory at 375 W. Lake street. This business was established nine years ago by Mr. Hart, who has built up a liberal and influential patronage in the city and its vicinity. Mr. Hart has had long experience in this artistic industry, and possesses excellent good taste and judgment. He occupies for salesroom, etc., a commodious ground floor and basement, each being 25x60 feet in area, and employs eleven persons. Mr. Hart manufactures largely ornamental, gilt, walnut, oak, cherry and pine finished or imitation room and cove moldings, and makes a specialty of putting up moldings for hanging pictures. He also gilds and makes hardwood and gold leaf picture frames in any style or size, and promptly attends to repairing or regilding. All goods are warranted not to tarnish or discolor, while the prices quoted by him are exceedingly just and moderate. A large and choice stock of moldings, picture frames, etc., is always on hand, and the business is both wholesale and retail. Mr. Hart was born in Germany, but has resided in Chicago for the last twenty years. He is an honorable and energetic business man, who is richly deserving of the abundant success achieved in this artistic industry. Mr. Hart is a popular member of the I. O. Foresters and Masons. Telephone call is 4626.

W. H. EMERY.

There is, perhaps, no commodity that we could as ill spare in these modern days as leather, and when we attempt to consider its important uses, whether in shoes, harness, belting, satchels, or what not, we ought to feel a debt of gratitude to those who are engaged in any business that will bring it more easily into our markets and our factories. There is no man in Chicago who is better acquainted with the hide business than Mr. W. H. Emery, of No. 143 Kinzie street. He established himself twenty-five years ago in the business and continued it on a large scale until 1883, when he abandoned the business of hide merchant for that of hide broker, and this latter he now successfully follows. He does a very large business. It is claimed for Mr. Emery that he is one of the best judges of hides in the trade, and one thing is certain, namely, that his long experience in this line, and his watchfulness of the market enables him at all times, to secure the very best results to the tanner. At the time of the great fire in 1871 he was completely burned out, but was in no way discouraged, and with a spirit of true Yankee energy he was soon on his feet again. Mr. Emery is a native of Kennebec County, Me., and comes from a very old New England family. He has resided in Chicago for twenty-five years.

THE ATLAS FOUNDRY CO.

One of the most prominent concerns in Chicago, in the fundamental line of iron and machinery castings, is that of the Atlas Foundry Co., whose large and well-equipped works are located at Nos. 32 and 36 Erie street, on the corner of Kingsbury. The business is one of long standing, having been founded in 1866 by Messrs. Fife & Anderson, who established and developed it upon sound and enduring principles. In 1888, Messrs. Webster & Comstock succeeded, handing it over the following year to Messrs. Barton & Needham, and in 1891 the firm of Needham & Cleveland assumed charge. Recently the business was reorganized under the style of the Atlas Foundry Co. The foundry occupies a substantial stone building, 50x100 feet in dimensions, which was erected in 1886, and which, with the large shed in the rear, affords ample facilities for the heavy work carried on. Here are to be found all modern appliances and tools known to the trade, a staff of twenty-five competent employes constantly at work, and a large and varied stock of heavy and light castings for all purposes, made of the best material, and in the most approved style. These castings are in demand over the city and surrounding district, where their great strength, superior finish and perfect adaptability to the requirements of the trade are fully recognized. This company makes a specialty of large pulleys, and in every process of manufacture invariably practice the best methods. Messrs. R. J. Cleveland, W. H. Brett, G. Wright and O. C. Bramow, are proprietors of this concern, and are thoroughly practical mechanics, and give their whole attention to business, conducting it in a meritorious way which secures the confidence and support of the trade. Mr. Cleveland was born in La Mont, Cook Co., Ill., having resided here for a number of years, enjoying the respect and esteem of a large class, in both social and commercial circles.

J. & A. BOSKOWITZ.

A representative house established for many years in this city, and well known all over the country and in Europe, is that of J. & A. Boskowitz, dealers in raw furs and robes. This house was established in this city thirty-five years ago. Headquarters were afterward made at New York, about thirty years ago, and have since been maintained at that point, the Chicago business being done entirely through the office. The manager of the concern here is Mr. H. Leaman, who has resided in Chicago for the past thirty-five years. He is a cultured gentleman of wide experience and travel, a native of Germany, who settled in this city when twenty-two years of age. He was formerly an active and prominent member of the Board of Trade, and is well-known in business, social and financial circles, where he is highly respected and courted for his genial manner and unquestioned integrity. The heads of the house reside in New York, where the storehouses are located, and the business done is extensive and important. An immense export trade is carried on, and the house favorably known abroad. Mr. Leaman buys throughout the West and Northwest and ships to New York direct. All kinds of raw furs are dealt in, seal, beaver, mink, otter, bear, coon and other skins are handled in large and valuable packages and the finest robes are purchased. The business is conducted at 196 E. Kinzie street, and the house is representative and responsible in the highest degree.

AUG. N. STONE.

There is no line of business better patronized in Chicago than that of the watchmaker and jeweler, and one of the most popular and progressive of the dealers in this line on the North side is Mr. Aug. N. Stone, who has been located for over four years at 385 E. Division street, opposite Franklin street. This business was conducted for five years by Mr. John Wiht, who was succeeded by Mr. Stone. The business has developed rapidly, and Mr. Stone is now favored with one of the best trades on the North side. He is a practical and experienced watchmaker and jeweler, does his work in a careful and skilled manner and at reasonable rates, and is courteous and obliging in his dealings. He occupies the ground floor of the premises and has an elegantly furnished store, well stocked with watches, clocks, silverware, all kinds of jewelry, spectacles and optical goods. A specialty is made of the celebrated Rockford watches, which are carried in all styles, and in fine gold and silver cases. Mr. Stone has a reputation of the highest order, and, in addition to a liberal patronage, has numerous friends who are pleased with his success, and hold him in the highest esteem. He employs two competent assistants and has a great quantity of work always on hand. Mr. Stone is a native of Sweden and has resided in Chicago for eleven years. He is a prominent member of the I. O. O. F., and is well known in leading business and social circles.

LINCOLN BICYCLE EXCHANGE.

Within the past few years the bicycle has become almost a necessity in the line of vehicles and travel. Its many excellent points for health, exercise and economy is acknowledged. Its popularity is ever on the increase, and thus has sprung up a new industry. A leading house in this line is known as the Lincoln Bicycle Exchange at No. 857 N. Clark street. Mr. Gus Thiele, that well-known wheelman, being proprietor. Mr. Thiele is a native Chicagoan, and was formerly with A. G. Spalding & Co., and later with the Pope Manufacturing Company for three years before establishing his present business. He handles all kinds of bicycles of the leading manufacturers, buys, sells, rents and repairs them, employing a force of eight assistants to accommodate his large and increasing trade. He rents bicycles by the hour, day or week, also children's carriages, and has an excellent line of goods on hand. Mr. Thiele is a member of the Lake View 'Cycling Club, also of the American League of Wheelmen, and is popular with all who ride the wheel. He occupies commodious quarters at the above number, and can accommodate any one desiring anything in the line of bicycles or repairs, or bicycle sundries.

ERICKSON & LARSON.

The large, handsomely fitted up boot and shoe establishment of Erickson & Larson, No. 211 West Indiana street, is one of the most important in its line in the section of the city in which it is located. Mr. J. Erickson and Mr. N. Larson are thorough practical men, and have been associated and established in business since 1886. Their store has dimensions of 25x65 feet, and as regards appointment and convenience is perfect in every respect. An extensive stock of boot wear is carried, embracing everything that is new, fashionable and stylish in fine and medium calf boots, shoes and gaiters for men and boys, and elegant kid, morocco and other footwear for ladies, misses and children, also rubbers and slippers in great variety. Only the very best and most reliable goods are dealt in by the firm, while the prices in all cases are extremely moderate. A splendid business has rewarded the well-directed efforts of Messrs. Erickson & Larson, and throughout their career they have always enjoyed the unbounded confidence of all having dealings with them. Particular attention is given to making boots and shoes to order, and repairs are promptly and neatly executed. Both members of the firm are natives of Norway. They are progressive business men of unquestioned reputation and very popular as fine custom boot and shoe makers and dealers. Business is active and brisk, and each succeeding year is steadily increasing

JOS. DORTSCH.

Chicago can boast of being the headquarters of an art which is very rare in this country, namely, the manufacture of artificial flowers and leaves, a prominent specialty being funeral flowers and wreaths, conducted at Nos. 1488 to 1490 Milwaukee avenue, by Mr. Jos. Dortsch. This gentleman, who is a native of Hungary, learned his difficult and intricate profession in France, after several years of careful study, and is now an expert in all its branches. He began business nine years ago, being then located on Chicago avenue and Commercial street, prior to removing to his present eligible premises in April, 1891. These are ample in size, giving a floor space of 3,000 square feet, and afford abundant room for the large staff of skilled assistants, averaging sixty-five, which are required in the industry. Mr. Dortsch manufactures artificial flowers and leaves having such a striking resemblance to the original in the most minute details as to completely deceive the eye and sense, and to please by the tasteful commingling of form and color. He supplies flowers, wreaths, crosses, anchors, stars and pillows to the largest undertakers in every part of the Union, his specialty being bridal and confirmation wreaths. Mr. Dortsch possesses qualifications that fit him in a pre-eminent degree to exactly meet the requirements of the American trade, and his expert knowledge, ripe judgment, and artistic taste have given him a high position in the estimation of both professional and social circles. Mr. Dortsch is a specialist in this line of business, and was the first to introduce it in Chicago. His designs are strictly original, and far ahead of all Eastern competitors.

ROBERT McEWEN.

Modern civilization demands more than four walls for the home, and the decorator is now an important personage in the body politic. One of the most enterprising of decorators is Robert McEwen of No. 457 Ogden avenue, dealer in wallpaper, paints, oil, glass, etc., and who does a general business in the line of painting, paper hanging, sign writing and decorating. Mr. McEwen opened in business two years ago at the corner of Robey and Harrison streets, and, finding his trade increasing so rapidly, was compelled to remove to his present location in May last. He occupies at the above number the large room 25x67 feet in size, where he carries a large and well-selected stock of everything in his line. He gives steady employment to five men, and by his excellent work has built up a splendid lucrative trade, which is constantly increasing. Mr. McEwen is a native of Scotland, coming from the classic town of Glasgow. He was raised, however, in Toronto, Canada, and learned his trade there. He is a young man, twenty-five years of age, a member of the I. O. G. T., and has a host of friends in social and busines circles.

THE GARDEN CITY SAND CO.

The Garden City Sand Co. was incorporated eight years ago, under the laws of Illinois, with a capital of $25,000. To-day it has a clear surplus of $58,000, or, including capital, of $83,000. They are dealers in standard brands of fire brick, fire clay, foundry facings and supplies, building, moulding and white sand, "Savage," "Black Diamond," and all other standard grades of fire brick. They have gravel pits on five different railway lines, employ at times on their various works as many as five hundred people, and do the largest business in their line of any concern in the city, aggregating some $350,000 per annum. Their trade extends all over the west and northwest, and they ship a very superior quality of sand used for glassware to all the glassworks in the country. The Garden City Sand Co. are also the agent of the "Black Diamond Fire Brick Co.," foreign and domestic cements, and are the owners of the Fox River Sand Co. of Wedron, Ill. Mr. C. B. Shefler is president and manager; Mr. N. C. Fisher, secretary and treasurer. The output for 1890 was 315,000 tons, a testimony to the far reaching volume of business done. The office of the company is at 159 La Salle street.

G. H. FOSTER & CO.

For more than a quarter of a century the house of G. H. Foster & Co. has held high rank as one of the leading importing establishments in the city. To be exact, it was twenty-six years ago since Mr. G. H. Foster opened his office in this city, and he has long since made a reputation and built up a business which will be a monument to his great administrative abilities for many years to come. The firm are sole agents for the following domestic and foreign manufactures: J. N. Leonard & Co. silk threads of Northampton, Mass.; the Crawford linen threads of Leith, Scotland; the crescent brand elastic ducks of Belfast, Ireland; also of the Fostra and ex-

celsior roll braids, pure dye silk and mohair bindings, "Royal" brands of plain and fancy silesias and sateen. The firm consists of Mr. G. H. Foster, a native of England, who has been in the United States for fifty years, and his son, G. A. Foster, born in Chicago, who is now the manager of the business in this city, Mr. Foster, Sr., having gone to New York, where a branch house was established four years ago. Fifty people find employment at the Chicago house, where the firm occupies three floors of the building, 228 and 230 Fifth avenue, corner of Quincy street. They carry here an immense stock of their specialties, beside which should have been mentioned the products of the Rhode Island Braid and Button Company, Pawtucket, R. I. The trade from the Chicago house is through the West and Northwest, while from the New York establishment, 100 Green street, all the business east of the Ohio river is cared for.

O. G. HALLER.

One of the handsomest and best appointed drug stores on the West side is that of Mr. O. G. Haller, at the corner of Milwaukee and North avenues. The business at this location was established in 1870 by Mr. John A. Mayer, the premises at that time consisting of a frame building.

Several years ago Mr. C. H. Plautz, now city treasurer, bought out the establishment, and three years ago the present proprietor, Mr. Haller, purchased the same from Mr. Plautz, and Omar H. Allen erected the present handsome and commodious building upon the site. Mr. Haller has one of the handsomest drug stores in the city, and is justly proud of his achievement; it is finished in solid oak, with beautiful counters, shelves and show cases to match. The walls and ceilings are splendidly frescoed, and the windows and show cases are of heavy, selected plate glass. The store occupies a space 20x35 feet and is completely stocked with a carefully selected line of the best and purest drugs obtainable; also elegant toilet articles, powders, soaps, perfumes, etc. A complete assortment of druggists' sundries and 'physicians' and surgeons' supplies is carried, and attention is given to the compounding of prescriptions with the greatest care. Mr. Haller is a native of Chicago, a graduate of the Chicago College of Pharmacy and a young man of ability and skill. His patronage is deservedly large and his success marked with pleasure by his numerous friends. He employs three skilled assistants and attends to his customers' needs with care and courtesy.

C. M. CLARK.

Prominent among the old-established and reliable real estate dealers of the western metropolis ranks Mr. C. M. Clark, whose office is centrally and eligibly located in the Tacoma building (room No. 410), at the northeast corner of Madison and La Salle streets. Mr. Clark originally engaged in the business in 1870 on Washington street, corner of Clark, combining the handling of his own realty with that of his extensive interest as a dealer in tailors' trimmings. Burned out in the great fire he closed out the latter interest in 1874, and has since devoted himself assiduously to the purchase, sale and exchange of improved and unimproved real property. Mr. Clark is owner of extensive improved and subdivision realty, notably three hundred valuable South Englewood lots. His connections are of a superior character, including, as he does, many of our leading merchants, capitalists and operators among his permanent customers, and he has carried through to a successful issue many heavy transactions. Mr. Clark was born in Tully, Onondaga County, N. Y., and has been a highly respected resident of Chicago for the past twenty-one years. The characteristics that have ever regulated the business policy of his house, and the extent of its operations have made it a leading one in the city.

JOHN HAZARD.

When Mr. John Hazard came to this country nine years ago he little dreamed that to-day he would be the proprietor of one of the best hardware businesses in South Chicago, but such are the vagaries of fate that his store at 140 Ninety-second street is one of the most complete of its kind and for its size in South Chicago. He occupies the ground floor of a two-and-a-half story frame building and established the business here in 1890, though for some years previously he had been managing a similar business for a relative in Rochester, N. Y. It would be difficult to say what he does not keep in the hardware line. He carries all kinds of builders' and shelf hardware, locks, imported cutlery, tinware, gasoline stoves and cooking ranges and general household articles, besides dealing largely in bricks and castings. The firm repairs all kinds of stoves, and strictly attends to all jobbing. They have a large country business and give close attention to mail orders. Three experienced hands are employed and one delivery wagon. They make a specialty of window and door fly screens. Mr. Hazard is a native of Belfast, Ire., and is a prominent man in business circles. He is very highly respected both in and out of his business, and there are few who have brighter prospects. He attends closely to his business, and is trustworthy in all he says or undertakes.

CHICAGO OF TO DAY THE METROPOLIS OF THE WEST.

MRS. V. ROLFE.

What has now come to be looked upon as a leading medium of fashion on the North side is the millinery store of Mrs. V. Rolfe, at 480 North Clark street, and although only established in March, 1891, it has taken such a hold upon the residents of this neighborhood as to make promise for a very large and increasing as well as select patronage. The store is 25x60 feet in dimensions, and is elegantly fitted up with plate glass cases and costly furnishings, and the window is always a center of envious attraction on the part of hundreds of the gentler sex. The stock, much of which is imported from Paris, comprises bonnets and hats trimmed and untrimmed, ribbons, velvets, plush, feathers, plumes, aigrettes, pompons, flowers, ornaments, gold and silver lace, veiling, and everything that is usually kept in a first-class millinery store. Mrs. Rolfe possesses a rare artistic ability and seems almost to foreshadow the coming fashions. She employs a full force of young ladies as milliners and trimmers, and special attention is paid to the prompt completion of mourning and wedding orders. Hats and bonnets are also trimmed to match costumes in any shade. The prices charged throughout are most reasonable, while the class of patrons which the business commands numbers in its ranks some of the very best residents of the North side. Mrs. Rolfe is a native of Milwaukee, Wis., and has been in Chicago some years.

BEIER & WYBURN.

There are few classes of business that are of more real benefit to the community than the furniture business, and when Messrs. Beier & Wyburn opened their doors at 203 North Wells street to the public on May 1st, 1891, they conferred a benefit which cannot at first sight be estimated. They occupy the ground floor and their store is very commodious and well adapted for successful handling of their business. Being both young men, they possess an amount of energy and enterprise which is a certain fore runner of success. Their stock comprises a large and varied assortment of parlor and bedroom sets, extension tables, rockers, lounges, sideboards, folding cabinet and mantel beds, chairs, baby carriages, lamps, cabinets, bookcases, kitchen furniture and stoves. And in order to accommodate those customers who feel that they cannot comfortably afford new furniture, they will take their old in exchange and charge a very moderate difference. They also buy, sell and exchange all kinds of household goods. Their trade has already assumed large proportions, and this is in great measure accounted for by the fact that they can always be depended upon in selling goods exactly as they are represented, and their prices throughout are very reasonable. Mr. C Beier and Mr. H. Wyburn are both natives of this city and all having business relations with them will meet with fair and upright treatment.

DIETHELM & ROY.

In a newly developing town, and especially one which is making such rapid strides as South Chicago, there is always a wide field for the conceptive brain of an architect. In one of Herrick's aphorisms there is a line which runs, "Nothing is new; we walk where others creep." But we cannot fully admit the truth of this in view of some of the beautiful buildings which have been erected in South Chicago from the designs of the well-known architects, Messrs. Diethelm & Roy, whose offices are at rooms 12, 13 and 14 Winnipeg Block, on the northeast corner of Commercial avenue and Ninety-second street. Mr. Titus Diethelm established the business three years ago, and Mr. Franz Roy joined him in 1891, when the firm became Diethelm & Roy. Among their most praiseworthy masterpieces is the Bowen schoolhouse, which has been styled by some a "poem" in architecture, and beside this they have designed many of the large handsome blocks on Ninety-second street. Mr. Diethelm is a native of St. Gallen, in Switzerland, and Mr. Roy was born in Berlin, Germany. Both gentlemen possess the advantage (envied by so many) of having studied in the finest European schools, and their refinement of architectural education manifests itself in everything they turn out.

MISS L. MALCHER.

The cultivation of flowers and plants is one of the most beautiful ideas of nature, and the great convenience of florists, and their pretty stock, is every day more apparent. There is no nicer floral establishment in the city than that of L. Malcher of 385 Wells street, near Division street. The finest display of flowers and plants may be seen here every day, also a complete line of shrubs and bulbs which are received from the green houses daily. Special attention is paid to the designing of all kinds of floral work, in every conceivable design for weddings, parties, banquets, house, table and funeral decorations. Miss L. Malcher is a native of Austria, and has been in Chicago six years. This establishment has built up a splendid trade, which is increasing rapidly, owing to the excellence of its work.

EUREKA DIGGER CO.

A novelty of any kind, that will reduce labor on the farm is always hailed with delight, and if it be a good one, meets with a ready sale; but exceeding all expectations in this line the "Eureka Digger" has become famous, and is meeting with phenomenal sales. It is manufactured by the Eureka Digger Company, an organization incorporated under the laws of Illinois, with a capitalization of $10,000, and the following officers: President, A. Bauer; secretary and treasurer, F. Bauer. These gentlemen are well known in business circles and have a reputation of high order for ability and strict business integrity. They are energetic, reliable and progressive, and calculated to make a success of any business venture. The Eureka digger is an excellent device for digging post holes, etc., and works in the most excellent manner. With it a great number of post or pole holes can be dug with the minimum expenditure of labor. The company occupies the ground floor of the premises, 25x100 feet in dimensions, at 178 East Huron street, and employ here fifteen workmen in the manufacture of the diggers. The company takes contracts for digging post holes or will contract to dig the holes for an entire line of telegraph poles. The Bauer brothers are young men of great ability and are fair samples of the energy and push that have characterized Chicago from the beginning, they being worthy sons of this great city and interested in all things that tend to advance her welfare.

GEO. STRAUSS.

Since Mr. George Strauss engaged in the hardware business his record has been one of unbroken prosperity. In 1874 he commenced as Strauss & Wendsler, but they dissolved in 1885 and he has since conducted the business alone. In 1887 he built his present commodious premises at 1085 Milwaukee avenue, opposite Evergreen avenue. The building is a handsome four story and basement structure, 25x80 feet in dimensions, and cost Mr. Strauss upwards of sixteen thousand dollars. He occupies for his store the ground floor and basement, and has his stable at the back, which is two-story brick, 20x32 feet. So it will be seen that with such commodious premises he possesses unusual facilities for his business, and his modern arrangements in the store enable him to fulfil orders promptly. His stock comprises a large and well-selected assortment of stoves and ranges (including the Garland stoves, for which he has the West side agency), builders' and shelf hardware, pocket and table cutlery, carpenters' and mechanics' tools, machinists' supplies, and an extensive variety of house-furnishing goods generally. The store, on the whole, has a most attractive appearance, and indicates at a glance that Mr. Strauss is a thorough master of his business. The basement is devoted to a very completely fitted workshop, and here all kinds of tin and sheet iron work is executed, but especially galvanized iron work for builders, and in all branches Mr. Strauss will only employ the most skilled help. Mr. Strauss is a native of Germany, and during his long residence in this city has won the esteem of his patrons and in fact the entire community and has succeeded in building up a trade that many older houses in his line might well envy.

CHAS. E. SIMON.

Though only established two years ago, Mr. Charles E. Simon has taken a firm stand in the long line of general produce commission merchants in the city, and in soliciting further consignments he does so with the confident pleasure of knowing that the prices he has hitherto been able to obtain for his customers have in every case been higher than the average prices of the day. He receives consignments of vegetables of all kinds from the principal farming sections of Ohio, Indiana, Illinois and Wisconsin, and will in all cases make the fullest advances on consignments, and make prompt returns. He established himself at 160 South Water street, but in February, 1891, he moved to 172½ on the same street, where he has the best possible accommodation for the display and rapid handling of the consignments intrusted to his care. He employs a full force of help, and keeps a large double and single team, so that goods are never allowed to remain at the railroads, but are instantly transferred on arrival. He supplies hotels and restaurants with vegetables, and can always find a good market and good prices for any quantity. Mr. Simon is a native of Chicago, and can boast of a very comprehensive business experience. He has always been careful to adopt the most scrupulously honorable methods at any sacrifice to himself, and his continued success is assured.

KRAMER BROS. & CO.

The constantly increasing demand from all circles of the public for the most artistic effects in the painting and decoration of interiors has rendered this branch of trade of the highest importance. A representative house in this line is that of Messrs. Kramer Bros. & Co., at 2314 Cottage Grove avenue. They take contracts for the painting, decorating and papering of houses, etc., in all styles of the art. They are prepared to furnish elegant paper hangings and wall paper, also special designs to harmonize with the hangings and the style of the apartment whether it be ancient or modern. All kinds of painting, graining and calcimining are embraced in the business, and novel interior decorations whether plastic, carved, painted or of any other class. The premises occupied are very commodious, 25x100 feet, consisting of the ground floor and basement, and contain a very large stock of all the newest and most fashionable paper hangings, together with paints, varnishes, etc., of every description. The business was first established in 1884, and came into possession of the present proprietors in 1886. The firm require the constant services of upward of twenty-five skilled workmen. Messrs. J. D. and J. W. Kramer are natives of Pennsylvania, and have resided here for a number of years, winning the esteem and respect of all classes of the community.

CLARK & POTTINGER.

It is not surprising that so many of our ablest business men devote their time and attention to the development of the real estate interests of this city. Among the most reliable of those thus engaged are Messrs. Clark & Pottinger, the well-known real estate brokers, whose offices are in room 26 of No. 116 La Salle street. This business was established in 1889 by the then firm of Clute & Pottinger, which was dissolved the following year. Mr. Ed. S. Clark and George E. Pottinger at once formed the present partnership, and from the start were the recipients of a patronage which they have since ably retained and greatly enlarged. The firm transact a general real estate business in all its branches, buying, selling, exchanging and leasing property in all parts of the city. They give particular attention to suburban subdivisions and residential property. They also possess unsurpassed facilities for the prompt negotiation of loans, at low rates and on easy terms. They undertake the total management of estates, securing tenants, collecting rents and making all necessary disbursements, while their fees are always moderate. They are highly respected members of the business community, and their success is as gratifying as it has been well deserved.

YOUNGDAHL & LILJA.

An establishment that never fails to attract the attention of passers-by is the large and elegant store of Youngdahl & Lilja, dealers in fine diamonds, watches, jewelry and silverware, at No. 273 West Madison street, corner of Morgan. The store is fitted up with a costly and handsome plate glass front, and elegant showcases that run the whole length of the building. A complete stock of the finest goods in all the lines carried is kept on hand at all times, and is tastefully displayed for the inspection of patrons. The members of the firm, Mr. A. J. Youngdahl and Mr. J. R. Lilja, are both natives of Sweden, but have resided in Chicago 10 and 25 years respectively. They are both accomplished gentlemen and business men of the brightest order of ability and the most sterling integrity. Mr. Youngdahl is thirty years of age, and Mr. Lilja fifty. They employ four assistants and do a very large business, which is fully merited in every sense of the word. A specialty is made of fine repairing and diamond setting, and the very best class of work is done in this line. The business was established on the 25th of March, 1889, and probably no concern of like character in the city has met with such marked success in so short a time.

DR. H. C. WAACK.

Dr. H. C. Waack is a young dentist who has a bright future before him. He is a native of Germany, but has been in this country for some time, having lived at Quincy, Ill., before coming to Chicago. He is a graduate of the American College of Dentistry of this city, where he completed his course with the highest honors. Personally he has a fine presence, and his attainments and ability as a dentist are spoken of in the highest terms of praise by his professors and by numerous patrons who have had opportunity to test his work since he established himself in his present quarters, in April, 1891. His office is located in the Brown building, at the northeast corner of State and Forty-seventh streets, over C. E. Brown's drygoods store, where he occupies two rooms 20x30. These are reached by one flight of stairs, and the cable cars pass the door. The locality is a good one, and an excellent practice has already commenced to establish itself. The doctor is thoroughly qualified in all branches of his profession, as diplomas attest, and coming fresh from college, is thoroughly versed in all the latest discoveries and improvements, while his practice there as a student was sufficient to make him proficient in their practical application.

M. A. FOUNTAIN & CO.

Modern invention has contributed greatly to the improvement and development of printing, and at the present time its price has been so reduced by labor-saving machinery, that books, pamphlets and that great educator, the newspaper, and indeed, all printed matter is within the reach of all. One of the most complete and reliable printing establishments in Chicago is that conducted by Mr. M. A. Fountain (trading as M. A. Fountain & Co.) in the Standard Oil building, No. 5 Wabash avenue. This enterprise was originally established by Mr. Fountain, at Waterloo, Iowa, in 1879, and some brief period later removal was made to Rockford, Ill, permanent headquarters being secured in Chicago in 1887, when Mr. J. E. Reeves became an interested party in the concern and the present firm style was adopted. In 1889 Mr. Reeves retired, and Mr. Fountain has since conducted the house alone retaining the original trading title of M. A. Fountain & Co. The premises occupied comprise a portion of the fifth floor of the Standard Oil building, fully equipped with all kinds of the latest improved machinery, the motive power for fine printing presses being furnished by electricity, and constant employment being provided a force of thirteen skilled and experienced operatives. Every description of printing is here executed, from a business card to a book of any dimensions, a specialty being made of fine commercial work, while Mr. Fountain's prices will be found to be reasonable in the extreme.

F. ZABEL.

A great convenience in any locality is a clean and well-conducted meat market, which permits householders to get their meats in just the quantity desired and to at all times have it fresh. There is no better establishment in the city of this kind than that of Mr. F. Zabel, dealer in fresh, salt and smoked meats, poultry, sausages, lard, etc., at No. 230 Larrabee

street, at the corner of Vedder street. Mr. Zabel established his business at the same location six years ago, and occupies the handsome corner room in the elegant corner block, 30x50 feet in size, which is neatly and conveniently fitted in light and dark woods, counters, shelving and wainscoting, and which contains an immense ice cooler that will hold five tons of meat. Mr. Zabel employs three assistants, has a delivery team to attend to his rapidly increasing trade, and carries the freshest and nicest stock of all kinds of meats at all times. Mr. Zabel was born in Germany and has resided in Chicago for the past seventeen years, where he has made many friends.

S. KRAUSZ.

In no department of the fine arts has there been such marked improvement made within the past quarter century as in photography, and the exquisite productions of the modern exponent present a strong contrast to the crude pictures and likenesses of an earlier period. A leading and representative establishment in this section of the Western metropolis is that so ably presided over by Mr. S. Krausz at No. 2030 Cottage Grove avenue. After years of study in the principal art centers of Europe, Mr. Krausz settled in Chicago in 1883, here opening his studio and meeting with a success simply commensurate with the energy and ability he has since exhibited in its management. The premises occupied comprise a commodious ground floor, 30x100 feet in dimensions, with finishing department on the upper floor, the whole replete with every modern convenience and appliance known to photography and having a bearing on the reproduction of perfect portraiture. Every branch of the art is here prosecuted, including enlargements in oils, water colors, pastels, crayons, etc., and the skill and taste displayed in these productions, coupled with the fair and equitable dealing of the establishment, have given it a popularity from which accrues a large, extensive and most desirable patronage. Mr. Krausz is the only photographer who has made a specialty of presenting to the public photographic specimens of the many nationalities to be found in Chicago, and his "character studies," upon which he has spent much time and money, are well worthy of careful attention. As before hinted, Mr Krausz is a native of Hungary, a graduate of the celebrated Academy of Munich, and a thoroughly skilled exponent of photography in all its branches.

H. M. TINDALL.

There is no more popular place of business in the city than than the fish and canned goods, butter, cheese and egg store of Mr. H. M. Tindall of No. 114 N. Wells street. The business was established three years ago, and has proved a success ever since the present proprietor assumed the management. He deals in fresh, salt and smoked fish, fancy delicacies, imported and domestic canned goods, preserves, jellies, butter, eggs and cheese of every description, and makes it a principle to deal in nothing but strictly first class goods in his various lines. His store is handsomely and conveniently fitted for the management of his business, and on the counters and shelves is as fine an array of goods as can be seen in any hous. in the city. Mr. Tindall has greatly improved the business and now commands a splendid trade, not only on the North side, but in all parts of the city, where buyers look for an excellent quality of his line of goods. He was born in Sodus, N. Y., is yet a young man, and has resided a number of years in Chicago, where he has gained a practical experience in his line. The specialties handled are oysters, fresh lake and sea fish in season, pickles, sauces and condiments.

HUBERT THE TAILOR.

This work would be incomplete were mention not made of the popular and extensive tailoring business of Mr. Hubert Altenhofen, who is so well-known to the leading merchants, business men and gentlemen generally of the North side. The business is most popularly known as that of "Hubert the Tailor," and has been conducted for the past six years at the junction of Clybourn avenue and Halsted street. Here Mr. Altenhofen occupies the ground floor of the magnificent, ornamental building having a frontage on both streets and facing the intersection. It has a frontage on Clybourn avenue of seventy-five feet and the same on Halsted street. The store has magnificent plate-glass fronts, and the windows are always attractively arranged with the latest novelties in suitings. An immense stock is carried, consisting of the finest imported and domestic tailoring supplies, woolens, cloths, worsteds, cheviots, tweeds, serges, flannels, cassimeres and vestings. Everything is selected especially to meet the demands of the excellent patronage enjoyed by this house, and all goods are purchased by Mr. Altenhofen personally, who brings long experience and great practical skill to bear. The proprietor of this establishment caters to the finest patronage of the city, and has the most fastidious and stylish customers of the city as patrons. He employs thirty-five skilled workmen, and guarantees entire satisfaction. Mr. Altenhofen was born in Germany and came to Chicago ten years ago. He is a popular member of the Knights of Pythias, I. O. Foresters and Iron Hall, and is a progressive business man who is held in high esteem by all who know him

NIC KRONENBURGER.

The magnificent stores, offices and public buildings of this city speak volumes for the skill and ability of the architects who have made Chicago the most beautiful of America's leading cities. An architect of skill and decided ability, who has given his life to his profession, is Mr. Nic Kronenburger, who is located at the Northwest corner of Chicago avenue and Clark street, rooms 16, 17, 18. Mr. Kronenburger is a native of Germany, and came to Chicago nine years ago. He is a graduate of a German school of architecture and has spent his life in the study of his profession. He is a careful and competent designer, giving the closest attention to the minutest details; and yet his conceptions are often bold and novel. He has made a special study of residence architecture and has planned some of the finest houses in the city. He employs three competent draughtsmen and has a liberal patronage, which increases steadily. Mr. Kronenburger has many friends who hold him in high esteem, and regard him as a genius and artist of the greatest ability. In all his plans he aims at securing the maximum of convenience in the minimum of space, and gives the closest attention to the interests of his patrons.

H. P. STIMSON.

Mr. H. P. Stimson, the proprietor of the Hoyd Patent Hoisting Machine and Mason Material Elevator, represents the feature of the world's industrial progress, so' marked during the present century, of substituting machinery for unskilled labor, and which is ultimately destined to become universal in its application. The Hoyd Patent Hoisting Machine and Mason Material Elevator, as its name shows, is a machine for the purpose of carrying material to the tops of buildings, releasing the "tender" or bricklayers' laborer from the unmitigated drudgery of hod carrying, and thus giving a man a chance to use a man as a thinking machine rather than as a mere beast of burden. Mr. Stimson was for four years manager for Mr. James Boyd, who established the business six years ago. In 1889, Mr. Stimson purchased the business, and has since continued it. The hoisting machines are made by the American Manufacturing Company of Minnesota. Among the companies and parties handling the machines, are the Philadelphia Bridge Company, George A. Fuller & Co., Chicago. Geo. C. Pressing, Herrman Bossler, E, Ernshaw & Co., Amgress & Gindle, W, A, & A. E. Wells, storehouse, Lake and Robey streets—all in Chicago. The hoisting machines are chiefly rented for the season in Chicago and vicinity, but sold outright to outside parties. There are over sixty in use in the city. Mr H. P. Stimson, the proprietor, is a native of Watertown, New York. He was raised in Syracuse, in the same state, and came to Chicago twelve years ago. He is a member of the G. A. R., having served in the 185th N. Y. Vols. during the war, and had the misfortune of being five times made a prisoner and three times wounded. He is a member of the Builders' and Traders' Exchange, having box 479. Office telephone No. is 2800; residence telephone No. is 7098. Mr. Stimson's office is in room 7, 159 and 161 La Salle, and his house is at 183 Walnut street.

THE NATIONAL LINSEED OIL CO.

The National Linseed Oil Company was organized in January, 1887, with a paid-up capital of $18,000,000. This is the largest syndicate in the world. It has special facilities, the most widespread, influential connections, and the most complete manufacturing system in existence. · It owns and operates fifty linseed oil mills in various sections of the United States, with storage tanks in convenient localities for direct transportation. The company's mills are fully equipped with the latest improved machinery and appliances, and in them are manufactured the purest and finest grade of linseed oil known to the trade. It is the staple everywhere, and the consumption is enormous. The company annually exports thousands of tons of oil cake to Europe, and in every way greatly conduces to the better filling of orders, maintaining a higher standard of excellence and securing the lowest possible range of prices to the consumer. Thus the company is a public benefactor. It has wisely chosen Chicago as its headquarters, and here it has offices in rooms 955 to 975 in the Rookery building. The president of the company, Mr. Alexander Euston, is a prominent linseed oil manufacturer of St. Louis, and an influential resident of that city. Mr. T. G. McCulloch, the secretary and treasurer, is personally in charge of the executive offices here. The company is noted for its sound and equitable policy, and for the uniform excellence of its product.

A. M. WILSON.

The furniture establishment of Andrew M. Wilson, at Nos. 65 and 67 Thirty-first street, corner of Rhodes avenue, occupies the ground floor and basement of the building, 50x125 feet. A full line of fine furniture, carpets, stoves, crockery, etc., is carried on, and a specialty is made of complete house furnishing. The establishment was opened January 1, 1891, but the proprietor, though a young man, has been raised in the business, having been formerly connected with Wilson Brothers, 823 Broadway, New York. A retail business only is done, but a large stock is carried, embracing all that is new and attractive in the several lines. Fine upholstered furniture of new and elegant designs is manufactured to order. Mr. Wilson was born and raised in Chicago, and added to his experience in the business he has all the push and vim for which Chicago young men are noted. He has built up a large patronage already, in the few months since he began business. He is prepared to furnish his patrons with the very best of household goods of all descriptions, and enjoys advantages that enable him to do so at the lowest prices.

DR. A. FAHNESTOCK.

Perhaps no public servant deserves more grateful recognition at our hands than a dentist. The practice of Dr. Fahnestock is one of the oldest established in the city, having been established at the present offices, 1802 State street, since 1865 by Dr. Fahnestock, but for some time he has had as a partner, Dr. David J. Smith, D. D. S., who is a very skillful operator, and holds his diploma as a licentiate of the Ontario Royal College of Dental Surgeons, where he graduated with high honors. The offices at 1802 State street, have operating rooms both back and front with elegantly furnished reception rooms, the whole dimensions of the floor being about 80x254 feet. Dr. Fahnestock is a native of Pennsylvania, and has seen nearly threescore years of service. He served an honorable career through the war, and was captain of his company. Dr, Smith is a native of Kingston, Ont , and has been in Chicago for ten years. He is somewhat the junior of his partner, but equally skilful. He is a faithful adherent of the Free Masons. The firm does all kinds of dental work, and gives special attention to the preservation of the natural teeth. Drs. Fahnestock & Smith control a large practice, and number among their patients some of the most influential citizens of Chicago.

SAMUEL R. EMMETT.

Among the more recently established, yet none the less progressive and proficient, job printers in his section of the city, ranks Mr. Samuel R. Emmett, of No. 73 Thirty-seventh street. This enterprise was established in May, 1890, by Mr. Will McCormack, the present proprietor succeeding him during . the current year. The premises occupied comprise a commodious ground floor, equipped with three improved presses, a full supply of types, borders and kindred accessories, employment being provided for a force of from six to eight skilled journeymen. Mr. Emmett is prepared to execute all kinds of composition and press work, but makes a specialty of fine jobbing and newspaper printing, having every facility for the production of work of the most artistic and intricate character. He prints the South Side World and Hyde Park Times, and enjoys a liberal patronage of a general character, which is daily increasing in volume and value. Mr. Emmett is a native of Ohio, a young, energetic business man, and a thorough master of his craft in all its branches and has made a name and standing in the trade.

BRADBROOK'S ICE CREAM PARLORS.

Bakers have always been noted for making the choicest ice cream, and if the article manufactured by Mr. Charles Bradbrook, at No. 2957 Wallace street, is to be considered a criterion, popular opinion is correct in this matter. Mr. Bradbrook's establishment occupies the ground floor, 20x40, of a two-story brick building. The ice cream parlor is very elegantly furnished and fitted up, and genuine lace curtains drape the entrance, which is through the store, in front. A fine line of confectionery and of cigars and tobacco is also carried. Two assistants are employed, Mr. Bradbrook is a native of England and came to Chicago in 1890. Early in 1891 he opened his present establishment, and has been successful from the start. He is also the proprietor of a tinsmithing and repairing shop which is attached to the other establishment, and does the best class of work at the most reasonable prices and on the shortest notice.

KEMPER BROS.

The wholesale fruit and produce interest constitutes a very substantial and important factor in the trade and commerce of this city. The business is ably represented by the Messrs. Kemper Bros., who, as buyers and shippers of foreign and domestic fruits, vegetables, etc., control a widespread trade. The co-partners, E. H. and R. G. Kemper, are young men, natives of this city. Their parents are old settlers of Chicago, coming here in 1837, and always residing here. Their business has been established since 1886, and in that time they have founded a first class business connection with importers in the seaboard cities and producers throughout the country, and are well prepared and equipped to fill orders from jobbers and the trade generally. While the firm's operations extend throughout the east, south and west, they are doing an immense business in the northwest, to which section, when in season, they make heavy shipments of the choicest and best fruits and vegetables to be obtained on the market. The Messrs. Kemper's reputation as business men is unquestioned, and is one not only indorsed but highly recommended by all having dealings with them. Their establishment is at No. 144 South Water street.

S. C. LOOMIS & CO.

Among the leading exponents of artistic photography is the firm of S. C. Loomis & Co. These gentlemen have brought to bear upon this enterprise extended experience, wide acquaintance and undisputed ability. Their handsomely fitted gallery is located at No. 2867 Archer avenue, and is most complete in all its furnishings, from the dark room for developing the plates to the magnificent waiting rooms with their excellent art collection, beautiful carpets, luxurious couches and oak fittings. This business was established in 1888 by the present proprietors, and has a deservedly large patronage. The senior member of the firm is Mr. Samuel C. Loomis, a native of Illinois, and for the past nine years a resident of Chicago A good photograph is not the result of a purely mechanical operation, but is the combination of chemical knowledge and artistic skill. The large trade of this firm shows the high appreciation in which its members are held in the city, and their honorable and prompt business methods, together with their undisputed skill, have secured, for them the esteem and confidence of all who know them. Noticeable among the many branches in which Loomis & Co. excel is that of photographing children, and this most difficult task is by them executed in the finest and most satisfactory manner.

R. C. RADTKE.

This gentleman, although still a young man, has been prominently identified with the wholesale fruit and produce commission business in this city for over twelve years, and in that time his record has been of the highest. He is a native of Wisconsin, removing to this city in 1879, when but twenty-one years of age. The two succeeding years he was in the employment of Mr. G. H. Nieman, in the same line, as a salesman, and there acquired a thorough knowledge of the business in all its details. In 1881 he embarked in his present enterprise, and in the ten years that have since intervened, while handling tons of products as the intermediary between the producer and the trade, he has shown the best results for his customers at both ends of the line, establishing on a sure foundation a most enviable reputation for business ability of a high order and strict commercial integrity. The premises occupied by him comprise the ground floor and basement of a building located at No. 180 South Water street, and having an area of 20x50 feet, giving him a fine chance to display the varied products which he handles, comprising all kinds of foreign and domestic fruits, vegetables, etc He is in daily receipt of heavy consignments from southern and western points, He makes liberal advances on consignments, when it is so desired, immediately accounts for all sales, and promptly makes returns. His trade is exclusively wholesale, and is mainly local. Three assistants and one delivery wagon are employed.

RAMSEY & LOWE.

The transactions of the commission business are conducted upon an enormous scale, and engage the attention of some of our most active, enterprising business men, among whom is Mr. George F. Ramsey and Mr. Adolph Lowe, who, under the style of Ramsey & Lowe, located at 272 South Water street, are doing a splendid business. As commission merchants, they handle and deal in choice butter and cheese from the dairies and creameries, fresh eggs, poultry, veal, potatoes, apples, and, when in season, game, dressed hogs, etc., also seeds, hides, pelts, tallow, etc. Messrs. Ramsey & Lowe's business connections, which are of a most substantial and gratifying character, extend to all parts of the west and throughout the adjoining states, and a brisk trade is carried on. Unsurpassed facilities are possessed by the firm for conducting large operations, and ample accommodations are provided for storage purposes for the preservation of perishable articles. Mr. Ramsey is from New Jersey originally, and Mr. Lowe from Wisconsin. They are well known in commercial circles, and enjoy the esteem and unbounded confidence of all having dealings with their house. They are prompt and correct in rendering accounts of sales to shippers, and devote their entire attention to the interests of all intrusting consignments to their care.

H. C. WILEY.

In the neat and nicely-arranged store building, No. 6803 South Halsted street, Mr. H C. Wiley has established a first-class ice cream, fruit, confectionery, stationery and news stand. Mr. Wiley is a native of New York, and has only resided in Chicago for the past four years, but has established at the place mentioned, a good business with a liberal patronage. A complete assortment of foreign and domestic fruits is always kept in season, and sold at prices as moderate as their excellence will allow. In addition to these, there may always be found a complete assortment of pecans, walnuts, almonds, butternuts, and such other luxuries as are usually found in the best stores of this character. Mr. Wiley gives especial attention to supplying his customers with ice cream, selling only the best that can be made, in all flavors, and serving it, together with the most delicious soda, at his establishment. Everything handled by Mr. Wiley is first-class in every respect. The very complete stock of confections is particularly attractive, while the supplies of stationery are all that can be desired for home, office or school needs. Mr. Wiley is an authorized agent for the "Morning News," and orders left with him are sure of prompt delivery. The proprietor of this establishment is to be congratulated upon his success, and it is to be hoped his business may continue to increase, as it certainly must when every attention is given to caring for the needs and meeting the wishes of patrons.

W. E. SCHOFIELD.

One of the most reliable among the representative real estate dealers in this city is Mr. W. E. Schofield, a gentleman of sagacity, sound judgment and business ability of a high order. The business Mr. Schofield is now conducting with such marked success was originally established by J. S. Robinson & Co., and continued until 1888, when he became a partner. In May, 1891, the firm was dissolved. Since then Mr. Schofield has conducted operations on his own account. He is doing a general real estate business, buying, selling and exchanging city and suburban vacant and improved property, negotiating mortgages and procuring loans on first-class securities, placing investments judiciously, leasing houses and lands, collecting rents and interest, taking charge of and managing estates for resident and non-resident owners. He makes repairs, secures good permanent tenants and attends to all matters that legitimately belong to the business. He is a gentleman in whom the most implicit confidence may be placed. He is a native of Michigan, but for the past seven years has resided in this city. For a long time the business was carried on at 161 La Salle street, and two years ago removed to the very desirable office now occupied, suite 614, in the Tacoma building.

ECKSTEIN BROS.

The name of "Eckstein" has justly attained a widespread local celebrity in connection with the famous "Ermine" Washing Compound, which has, solely upon its merits, come into universal consumption, and since its introduction to the public has never had a competitor worthy of the name.

It stands alone to-day as the "Wonder of the Age" in its line, the best that talent and capital can produce, and the only one that ever maintains its original standard of excellence. The business of its manufacture was established by its present proprietors, Messrs. William, Herrman and Christopher Eckstein in 1876, and it has steadily developed in volume, until now it has attained proportions of the greatest magnitude. The office and salesroom of the concern are eligibly located at No. 849 S. Halsted street, and comprise a commodious ground floor, 25x75 feet in dimensions, giving ample accommodation for the manipulation and display of a large sample stock, and the general advantageous prosecution of the business. "Ermine" is purely and simply a clothes and labor saving washing compound, and may be used in such capacity upon the most delicate fabric without injury to the same, and is yet equally as efficacious as a dirt remover in all the rougher branches of scrubbing and housecleaning. Messrs. Eckstein, the sole manufacturers of "Ermine," are natives of Wisconsin, known far and wide for their honorable methods and sterling integrity, and well merit the large measure of success which has attended their exertions in this department of industrial activity.

R. E. RHODE.

Mr. R. E. Rhode, the well-known druggist and pharmacist of No. 504 N. Clark street, corner of Goethe street, took possession of his business in 1883 (though it had been established since 1874), and has developed an influential and extensive patronage, not only with the general public, but also with the medical profession at large and with whom no house stands in better favor. His store is the handsomest on the North side, being elegantly fitted up with oak fixtures and handsome druggists' bottles, etc. The various departments are under the personal supervision of the experienced proprietor, and the stock displayed embraces the purest drugs and chemicals, standard family medicines, essences and extracts, surgical appliances, perfumery, toilet articles and druggists' sundries generally. The goods are selected with special reference to their strength and freshness. The patronage, while always influential and of the best, has had a continuous steady growth, and in consequence of the ever increasing demand for his goods, Mr. Rhode found it incumbent upon him to have more room for his business, and he opened at No. 566 N. Clark street a pharmaceutical laboratory, equipped with the best appliances and apparatus known to the profession, where he compounds all of his finest chemical and pharmaceutical preparations. Mr. Rhode is a native of Germany and has been in Chicago for sixteen years. He is a graduate of the Chicago College of Pharmacy, a licensed druggist of the State of Illinois, and a member of the American Pharmaceutical Association. He is held in high esteem generally in the city. He prepares a number of pharmaceutical specialties and toilet

requisites of high merit; and also supplies pure vaccine virus, kumyss, eau de quinine, a superior hair tonic and many elixirs of rare qualities.

COWLEY, YATES & CO.

The metropolis of the West is the great headquarters of the trade in every kind of goods and second to no other city in the Union in enterprise, business, push, vim and dash, and her merchants are all live, wide-awake, sagacious and ever ready to attract buyers by offering the best inducements. Among those quite conspicuous as importers and jobbers in fine cigars in the city is the firm of Cowley, Yates & Co., whose office and salesroom are at 2 and 4 Wabash avenue. Mr. Joe W. Cowley and Mr. Ralph T. Yates, the active co-partners, although young men, have had quite an extended experience in the trade, and are well and favorably known to dealers in all the commercial centers in the West and Northwest, having for sometime previous to embarking in their present enterprise traveled "on the road" as salesmen for I. Z. Farwell of Freeport, Ill. They have been associated and established in their present location since 1889, and formed first-class business connections and built up a trade which keeps growing and increasing with each succeeding year. They are straightforward and upright in their dealings and assiduous in their attentions to the trade, and can always recommend and guarantee all goods they handle and sell. They carry a full stock of all the leading and most popular brands of fine Havana goods, and are the representative agents for such well known reputable manufacturers as Seidenberg & Co., Geo. P. Lies & Co. and Bondy & Lederer of the city of New York, and many others of like character and standing. The firm can always name the very lowest prices, and their goods will be found of a uniform quality and unrivaled excellence. Mr. Cowley is from Massachusetts originally, and has been in the West many years, while Mr. Yates is a native of Freeport, this state. They are public spirited business men of unquestioned reputation, and take an active interest in promoting every enterprise that has for its object the welfare of the community.

E. J. W. FOSS.

The growth and development of photography are among the most striking results of this century's progress. A perfection of result has been attained which marks the highest type of artistic development, yet scarcely has an admiring public ceased to wonder at the latest improvement than a fresh one is thrust upon their view. Photography has in truth become one of the fine arts, and the successful photographer must needs be an artist in the truest sense of the word. Chicago has photographers who will compare with those in any part of the world, and among them none ranks higher, in either the esteem of the general public, or of his professional associates, than Mr. E. J. W. Foss, whose handsomely appointed studio is conveniently located at No. 302 Milwaukee avenue. Mr. Foss is a native of Denmark and has been a resident of Chicago for the past ten years. This business was established sixteen years ago and has from the start occupied a foremost rank. Always abreast of the march of development, Mr. Foss is constantly adopting new devices for producing superior work. His establishment is one of the best in the city, with the most admirable facilities for business. His studio is on the ground floor, thereby avoiding the necessity of climbing stairs, and his parlor, reception room and office are very tasteful and pleasing in their furnishings. In the operating room are in use all the latest appliances and devices known to the art, including the best of light, accessories, plain and landscape, and other properties for back grounds and effects. Photography in all its branches is here executed, Mr. Foss producing in all his work the best and most beautiful effects. Pictures are taken by the new instantaneous and flash process, and patrons are thus enabled to secure accurate and perfect portraits. Three first-class artists assist him, and his prices are extremely low,

G. W. MAERKLIN.

To the inhabitants of the West side we take pleasure in recommending the drug business of Mr. G. W. Maerklin, 570 and 572 Blue Island avenue, corner of Loomis. Mr. Maerklin has a large and elegantly appointed store, with fine plate glass front, with entrances both on Blue Island avenue and Loomis street. The walls are splendidly decorated and the furnishings are all in solid cherry wood. The show cases are of the latest and most taking patterns and are well stocked with the finest toilet articles, brushes, perfumes, toilet soaps, powder, bottles, etc. A full line of the finest and carefully selected drugs is carried, also all the leading patent medicines, rubber goods, and druggists' sundries. Special attention is also given to the compounding of physicians' prescriptions, care being given to secure accuracy and purity. Mr. Maerklin has a large local trade and increases his patronage from week to week. He is a graduate of the Wisconsin State Pharmaceutical Society, and is a duly registered druggist and pharmacist. He is a careful and painstaking gentleman and a thorough chemist. He has prepared and offers for sale some excellent remedies that have become quite popular, and are highly recommended by physicians, notably his sarsaparilla and belladonna and capsicum plasters. The most attractive object in the store is a handsome soda fountain, one of the most costly and beautiful in the city. Mr. Maerklin is a young man, a native of Wisconsin, and a professional gentleman of ability. He is held in the highest esteem by all who know him, and has a wide circle of friends.

COOK & SHANNON.

Being in a measure a collateral branch of the brewing industry, the manufacture of beer pumps, faucets, spigots and kindred articles has grown to be a business of no inconsiderable importance in this country within comparatively recent years. The extraordinary increase in the consumption of malt liquors has, as a matter of course, imparted to this branch of industry an interest and importance entirely unknown some thirty or forty years ago. A recently opened concern in Chicago engaged in this line, is that of Messrs. Cook & Shannon, dealers in beer pumps and supplies, No. 577 S. Halsted street. This popular house was founded during the current year, and the trade already enjoyed furnishes an ample forecast of pronounced and permanent future prosperity. The premises occupied comprise the ground floor of the eligible two-story frame building at the address indicated, having dimensions of 20x40 feet, and in every respect admirably adapted for the advantageous prosecution of the business. The stock embraces a full line of all kinds of pumps, faucets, spigots, conveyors and general brewery and saloon supplies in such line. The individual members of this enterprising firm are Messrs. P. J. Cook (a native of Ohio), and Henry T. Shannon (born in England), both active competitors for legitimate trade in their line and well worthy of the success that has so far attended their ably directed efforts.

R. WUNDERLICH.

Among the most enterprising and interesting West side establishments is that so ably presided over by Mr. R. Wunderlich, manufacturer of brass instruments and importer of musical instruments of all descriptions, whose business premises are located at No. 226 Blue Island avenue. Here can be found a magnificent stock of German accordions, mouth harmonicas, violins, guitars, mandolins, banjos, flutes, fifes, zithers, cavalry trumpets, bugles, clarionets, and all kinds of instruments that are to be found in a strictly first-class and thoroughly equipped establishment of this kind. The house was established by Mr. Wunderlich in 1888, and has ever since maintained a high reputation for the superior class of goods handled, and has enjoyed a large and prosperous patronage. The premises occupied comprise a commodious salesroom with workshop in the rear, a special feature being made of repairing of all kinds, gold, silver and nickel plating, etc., reasonable charges prevailing in all departments. Mr. Wunderlich was born in Germany, where he acquired a thorough knowledge of this trade in all its branches. He is a prominent member of the I. O. O. F. Associated with Mr. Wunderlich is Mr. Louis Rischar, violinist, who has traveled extensively in this country as a soloist. Mr. Rischar was born in Munich, Bavaria, and has been a resident of the United States eight years. He is prepared to give instructions on the violin, and his numerous pupils will gladly testify to his superior ability as a teacher and to his conscientious devotion to his profession. Mr. Rischar studied for several years in Europe, and was a pupil of some of the most noted teachers of violin, among them Carl Hess of Leipsic.

J. O. SEABORG.

One of the largest and most popular stores on this leading thoroughfare is that of Mr. J. O. Seaborg, dealer in staple and fancy, groceries at No 3159 Wentworth avenue. Mr. Seaborg is a native of Sweden and has been a resident of Chicago for the past ten years. In 1889 he founded this business, and has since conducted it with unvarying success. Active and energetic, he brings to bear a perfect knowlege of the business in all its branches. He occupies the ground floor of a three-story brick building having a frontage of twenty, by a depth of 60 feet. His spacious store is handsomely fitted up and neatly furnished. A large, well-selected and complete stock, comprising everything pertaining to the family grocery trade is carried, the assortment embracing full and complete lines of pure, fresh crop Oolong, Hyson, Young Hyson, Gunpowder, Souchong and other China, Japan and India teas; fragrant coffees from Mocha, Java and South and Central America; ground and whole spices; the most popular brands of family flour; prepared cereals and farinaceous goods, pickles, sauces, preserves, jams, jellies, canned goods in great quantity; sugars, soaps, molasses, bakers' and laundry supplies and grocers' sundries of every description. Two assistants are employed and patrons are waited upon promptly and courteously their orders satisfactorily filled and delivered at residences free of charge.

WM. H. SCHIMPFERMAN & SON.

Among the great houses of Chicago who now import their supplies direct from the best manufactories of the world may be mentioned that of Wm. H. Schimpferman & Son, who have such a wide reputation for the superiority of their wines, liquors, ales, porters, groceries and cigars. This reputation is the direct result of an intimate acquaintance with the finest foreign products, and a sound and unerring judgment in the selection of those qualities that best meet the large demand for these articles in this country. In fact, this house which is so centrally located in fine premises, 35x200 feet, at 172 Madison street, is the headquarters for the choicest vintages and brands of champagnes, sherries, ports and all other imported wines, brandies, liquors, etc., as well as the finest canned goods in tin and glass, condiments, table delicacies and luxuries, and the best brands of foreign cigars. Their trade, both wholesale and retail, extends to all parts of the United States and Canada, and every where they have formed connections of the most influential character. Mr. Schimpferman is a native of Germany, and has resided in this country since 1842. He established the present business nearly thirty years ago, and in 1876 admitted his son, Wm. H. Schimpferman, as junior partner. On the lamented decease of the latter in 1880, the sole charge again devolved upon the father, who, however, made no change in the name. His premises on Lake street were swept away by the terrible fire of 1871, and after occupying temporary quarters for a few months he, with characteristic energy, reopened in his present commodious location in 1873. The standing and reputation of this house is national in its extent, and as regards business capacity and true American enterprise it justly merits the excellent name it has permanently maintained during a long and honored career.

SHERMAN HALL & CO.

One of those old established and representative houses that have contributed so largely to the building up of Chicago's commercial interests to their present extensive proportions is that of Messrs. Sherman Hall & Co., wool commission merchants, whose warehouse is eligibly located at Nos. 122 to 128 Michigan street and Nos. 45 to 53 La Salle street. This

..ESTABLISHED 1856.. ..INCORPORATED 1885..

business was established in 1856 by Mr. J. Sherman Hall. Mr. Hall became owner of all the stock, and at his death, August 7, 1888, the corporation was dissolved, and was succeeded by his son, Mr. E. Sherman Hall, as sole proprietor, who conducted the business under the name of Sherman Hall & Co. Mr. Hall is possessed of a wide range of experience, and is a recognized authority on the wool market, while his connections are both influential and widespread. The premises occupied comprise a spacious and substantial six-story

and basement brick building, 80x100 feet in area, which is fully equipped with all modern conveniences, elevators, etc. Here an immense stock of desirable wool in great variety is always on hand, while orders from manufacturers are promptly and are fully filled at the lowest ruling market prices. The trade of the house, which is steadily increasing, now extends throughout the entire United States and Canada. Liberal advances are made on consignments by Mr. Hall, while prompt sales and immediate returns have ever been a leading characteristic with this responsible house, and wool growers and shippers can always implicitly rely on his judgment with regard to the value and quality of any kind of wool. Mr. Hall is very popular in trade circles for his sterling integrity, and is one of Chicago's influential and public-spirited citizens.

CHAS. T. MESSENGER.

The lumber interests of Chicago are second to none in the world, and being the metropolis of the West and North, with

the very best distributing facilities, cannot help but grow is extent yearly. One of the leading houses of the city, and whose reputation is national in this line, is that of Mr. Charles T. Messinger, manufacturer of, and dealer in hardwood lumber, whose yards are at Blackhawk street and Hawthorne avenue, and at the foot of "B" street. Mr. Messinger has been in the lumber and manufacturing business for the past thirty-six years, and runs mills at Marrianna, Ark., and in Cross and St. Francis counties. He was formerly in the same business in Logansport, Ind., where he was one of that city's foremost citizens. In 1876 he removed his lumber business to Chicago, still retaining his mills at the above places. In 1879 the business style was changed to Messinger, Hubbard & Granger, and afterward to Messinger & Granger, and in 1889 to Messinger Hardwood Lumber Company, and the past year back to the present and old reliable firm of Charles T. Messinger. His yards at Hawthorne avenue and Blackhawk street are 400x225 feet in area, with 400 feet of railway tracks from the Milwaukee & St. Paul railroad. The yards at the foot of "B" street, on Dominick, have 350 feet of dock frontage, and are 225 feet deep, and two yards having an area of 750x350 feet, employing from thirty to fifty men, and several heavy teams to do the business of the firm. Mr. Messinger makes a specialty of walnut, ash, oak, beech, birch, cypress, maple, cherry and elm lumber, and his business exceeds $250,000 per annum. He handles 10,000,000 feet of lumber annually, and unloads over 700 cars during the season. Mr. Messinger is a native of Long Island, N. Y., and has been nearly forty years in the West. He came directly to Logansport, Ind., and from there to Chicago, where he has had an opportunity of more extensive operations, and facilities for handling lumber than he could possibly have in a less favorably located city. Mr. Messinger is an energetic and live business man, well-known in commercial and financial circles, and has an immense and constantly increasing business

F. KONAPASKE.

Among the business men on Wentworth avenue, there are none better known than Mr. Frederick Konapaske, proprietor of the popular C. O. D. dry goods house located at No. 4518 on that thoroughfare. Mr. Konapaske, who was born in Germany, came to this city in 1884, and a year later established his present thriving house. From the start through his fine business ability and the superior quality of his goods, he secured a firm footing, and has ever enjoyed the unbounded confidence of his many patrons. The premises he occupies are of ample dimensions, admirably arranged and fitted up with a special adaptability for the display of the stock and convenience of customers. Here are always to be found a large and varied line of staple and fancy dry goods, dress fabrics, notions, ladies' and gentlemen's furnishing goods, a general assortment of oilcloths in new patterns, and everything belonging to the business. Low prices always prevail and the utmost courtesy and attention are paid to patrons by Mr. Konapaske and his assistants. He is a close buyer on the market, and all goods handled and dealt in by him are first-class in every respect, and fully warranted as represented. He is an honorable, upright business man of unquestioned reputation and well deserves the success he has won and enjoyed.

THE IMPORTERS' WAREHOUSES A & B.

The extensive business of Waken & McLaughlin, at 504 to 528 N. Water street, was established in 1886 by Messrs. J. Wallace Waken and George D. McLaughlin at 169 to 175 N. Water street. In September of the same year, in consequence of the collapse of their building on account of overstorage, the firm lost $10,000 for damage claims, which they immediately paid. In May, 1887, they removed to their present premises, which were designed and built under the supervision of Mr. Waken, and are admirably adapted for the warehouse business. Their warehouses, A & B, are each five-stories high and 125x100 feet in dimensions. They are constructed in a most substantial and durable manner and are

absolutely fireproof, while they are fitted up with all modern appliances, elevators, electric lights, etc. The dynamos, engines, etc., are of the latest type, and the warehouses are connected with the fire department by wire and fire alarm annunciators. The goods in storage are valued at $3,500,000, and the premises have superior track and water facilities. They number among their permanent patrons the leading mercantile houses of Chicago and its vicinity. They store goods largely for such houses as Hibbard, Spencer & Bartlett, Franklin McVeagh & Co., Reid, Murdoch & Co., and many others. On account of this responsible firm promptly paying all claims in full, owing to the collapse of their old building, they have retained all their old customers and have secured a host of new ones. Mr. Waken was born in Liverpool, England, while Mr. McLaughlin is a native of Illinois. Mr. Waken is the active manager of the firm's business, and Mr. McLaughlin attends only to the finances. They are honorable, enterprising and energetic business men, justly meriting the liberal patronage secured in this important industry.

STREET, YOUNG & KENT MFG. CO.

In the manufacture of plumbers' brass goods and hose trimmings, one of the most successful concerns in Chicago is that known as the Street, Young & Kent Manufacturing Company, whose factory and office are situated at the southwest corner of Monroe and Jefferson streets. This company was incorporated under the laws of Illinois in 1888, with a paid up capital of $35,000, its executive officers being Mr. S. E. Young, president; Mr. T. M. Kent, vice-president; and Mr. C. D. Street, secretary and treasurer. Mr. Kent, the

vice-president, attends personally to the manufacture of the company's goods, and is widely known for his mechanical skill and ability. The premises occupied comprise two spacious floors, each being 25x125 feet in area, fully equipped with modern appliances, tools and machinery operated by steam power. Here sixty skilled workmen are employed and turn out all kinds of plumbers' brass goods and hose trimmings, also sanitary specialties. The company's goods are unrivaled for quality, reliability and general excellence. Orders are promptly filled and the trade of this company extends throughout the entire United States, the sales for the past year amounting to $80,000. The officers are honorable business men, and are worthy of the success that has rewarded their efforts. Messrs. Young and Street are large Chicago real estate owners, and are among our public spirited and influential citizens.

LOUIS HAAKE.

Nearly as old as the city's charter is the old reliable grocery firm of Louis Haake, now of No. 74 Wells street. The business was originally established on State street in 1847 and from there removed to Water street. In 1854 the present site was purchased and improved and upon it a three-story building erected. In 1877 the son of the original proprietor, John H. Haake, took charge of the establishment, and in 1888 the present proprietor, Louis Haake, succeeded to his grandfather's business. In the great fire of 1871 the firm suffered with the rest, and their immense establishment crumbled to ashes, but in the succeeding year the present splendid three-story brick edifice was erected, 30x100 feet in dimensions, with a handsome plate glass front, making one of the best stores on the street. In the meantime the excellent reputation, established by the original founder more than forty years ago, has been maintained, and the various proprietors, keeping abreast of the times, have made Haake's grocery an established institution of the city. The present proprietor is a practical grocer, born and bred to the business, and carries one of the most extensive stocks in the city of staple and fancy groceries, fruits, table delicacies, canned goods and, in fact, everything that goes to make up a first-class grocery house. He is a young man, born and raised in Chicago, energetic and pushing, having hosts of friends who rejoice in his prosperity.

ROBERT SMALE.

The trade in meats and provisions is one of the most important branches of business engaging the attention of the citizens of Chicago. It is ably conducted by men of capital, and foremost among the West side traders, in such connection, ranks Mr. Robert Smale, whose well-appointed market is located at No. 342 W. Madison street. Mr. Smale, who is one of the pioneer settlers of this division, and well remembers when the West side was a mere barren prairie, primarily engaged in this business at the corner of Randolph and Sangamon streets in 1861, securing the present premises in 1872. He rested from business for some seven years and subsequently, about three years since, associated with him his eldest son, Wm. R. Smale, who has since taken an active part in the conduct of the business, which is on a most prosperous basis, showing every evidence of capable management. The premises occupied are commodious as to dimensions, admirably appointed throughout and in every respect peculiarly well adapted for the advantageous prosecution of the business. The stock embraces prime fresh beef, veal, mutton, lamb, pork, salt and smoked meats, bacon, ham, lard, sausages, and shoulders; likewise poultry and game in their respective seasons. Prices are based on ruling market rates. Polite assistants serve customers intelligently and promptly. All orders are delivered to any part of the city free of extra charge, and no effort on the part of the proprietor is spared to please and satisfy each and every one of his numerous patrons. Mr. Smale was born in Devonshire, in the west of England, sixty years ago. He carries his years well, however, and does not seem to have lost any of the oldtime snap and business vim of twenty years ago.

E. V. ADKINS & SONS.

One of the most successful and reliable concerns in this section of Chicago, engaged in handling steam and hot water heaters, is that of Messrs. E. V. Adkins & Sons, whose offices and salesroom are located at 236 and 238 East Lake street,

and warm air combination heaters, admirably adapted to warming residences, churches, educational institutions, hotels, banks, stores, etc., manufactured under United States patents, by Mr. E. V. Adkins of Chicago, Ill. Messrs. E. V. Adkins & Sons are also the western agents for the Superior Warm Air Furnace. Adkins improved steam and warm air combination is one of the most perfect, practical and easily operated heaters of the kind in the market, while the price quoted for it is extremely moderate. Hundreds of these splendid heaters are now in successful operation in all parts of the country, giving the best satisfaction at less expense than the loudly advertised patent hot water heaters, the only important features of which are the intricacy and difficulties of their mechanism. Messrs 'E. V. Adkins & Sons promptly furnish estimates for all kinds of heaters, and their patronage is steadily increasing, owing to the superiority, efficacy and reliability of their heaters, which are general favorites wherever introduced. Too much care cannot be taken in all matters connected with laying and setting a furnace, and the cutting down of a few dollars on the original cost often results in regret and expense thereafter. Messrs. E. V. Adkins & Sons are highly regarded in trade circles for their integrity, while at the same time they offer advantages in heaters very difficult to be duplicated elsewhere in this country.

AUGUST TORPE.

No part of the city shows greater activity in real estate circles than the North side, and the wonderful growth and prosperity of this favored section is due in no small measure to the energetic action of the real estate broker. A firm which has been unusually prosperous and confines itself exclusively to North side property is that of Mr. August Torpe, at No. 227 East North avenue. The business was originally opened as Hoefer & Torpe, some years ago, but owing to ill health Mr. Hoefer retired, and Mr. Torpe now continues the business alone. In addition to doing a general real estate business, buying and selling on commission, he effects loans on first mortgage and real estate securities, places fire insurance in reliable companies, is a notary public, attends to non-residents' property, pays taxes, collects rents, and does a general business in this line. Mr. Torpe's offices are neatly arranged for his

This business was established in 1888 by the present firm, who have since built up a liberal and influential patronage, in the western and northwestern states. They occupy a commodious floor 30x60 feet in area, handsomely equipped and fitted up with every convenience. Here they display all kinds of steam and hot water heaters, also steam and warm air and hot water

work, and fitted up with an idea to their convenience. He is a German by birth, and has been in Chicago many years. He is prominent in society circles, being a Free Mason, Odd Fellow, Knight of Pythias, and a member of other organizations. He is also secretary of Cook County Building and Loan Association

THE UNION NUT COMPANY.

The largest, best known, and most prosperous concern in the country engaged in the manufacture of nuts, bolts and washers, rivets, etc., is unquestionably The Upson Nut Company, of Unionville, Conn., and Cleveland, Ohio, the Union Nut Company being a branch house of this corporation. The foundation of the business dates from 1854, when operations were begun in Unionville, Conn. In 1872 the Cleveland branch came into existence, and in 1880 a house for the supplying of the trade in the West was established in Chicago,

UNIONVILLE WORKS, ESTABLISHED 1854.

now known as the Union Nut Company. In July, 1891, the parent house purchased the business, machinery, good-will and copyrighted label of the assigned estate of Welch & Lea, Philadelphia, and under the rights of this purchase are now prepared to furnish the celebrated J. M. Coleman Eagle Nut on short notice. That they maintain the standard of quality

CLEVELAND WORKS, ESTABLISHED 1872.

of these goods, which characterized the product of their predecessors, goes without saying, and they invite correspondence in regard to this bolt, and also to their line of different grades of bolts, nuts, clips, washers, carriage hardware, rules, iron and wood bottom planes, and carpenters' tools, all of which for many years have held a prominent place in the market. The parent house in Unionville, Conn., started in 1854 with twenty hands, in 1890 the plants gave employment to 900 men, the majority of whom were connected with the Cleveland factory. Their output finds a ready market in every section of the country, and their trade extends outside to the continents of South America and Australia. The products of the company are recognized by consumers, as invariably first-class, and this high standard is rigidly maintained. The special lines of goods produced by the house include a great variety of hot forged, hot and cold pressed nuts, wrought and cast iron washers, common carriage bolts, Philadelphia Eagle carriage bolts, Norway iron and common tire bolts, stove bolts, shaft bolts, spring bolts, whiffletree bolts, elevator bolts, regular and lock-nut track bolts, stud bolts, bridge bolts, plow bolts, machine bolts, bolt ends, coach screws, hanger screws, set screws, boiler and bridge rivets, Norway rivets, axle clips, saddle clips, felloe plates, boxwood and ivory rules, try squares and,

tee bevels, plumbs and levels, iron and wood bottom planes belt fasteners, steel pliers, etc., etc. The Cleveland Works are fitted up with special machinery, which turns out an immense and varied product in an incredibly short space of time. As an indication of the amount of raw material used, it may be stated that over thirty thousand tons of iron and steel are consumed by the company in the manufacture of their goods in the course of a year. Large quantities of brass and German silver are also used, a vast quantity of boxwood, rosewood, and other hardwoods, most of the latter material being turned into mechanics' tools, of which the Unionville factory makes a specialty. The company also have a branch house at 99 Chambers street, New York City, as well as at 232 Lake street, Chicago, Ill. The Chicago house is under the direct supervision and management of Mr. A. C. Hooke, formerly of the New York house, and a native of New York City, who has been a resident here for the past four years. A heavy stock is always carried in Chicago and a brisk business done. Mr. A. S. Upson is president, and Mr. Samuel Frisbie, treasurer of the company.

N. Y. SIGN AND SHOW CARD WORKS.

A representative of one of the most noted concerns in the country actively engaged in the production of artistic show cards, etc., is the N. Y. Sign & Show Card Works, of which Mr. J. Weiner is proprietor. The business was founded in 1879 by this gentleman, and the all-round excellence of the work done here secures for the house a large and influential trade. Mr. Weiner brings to bear an intimate and accurate acquaintance with every feature of the business and a full knowledge of the requirements of the most critical customers. The premises utilized are centrally located at No. 136 Clark street, at the corner of Madison, over Atwood's clothing store. They are of ample dimensions, and the various departments are admirably equipped with the latest improvements. Steady employment is furnished to a number of skilled hands. The range of work includes the manufacture of all kinds of signs, show cards, and other attractive advertising novelties for all classes of business, and the trade is very large, covering all the United States. All the work turned out is by the best artists in the profession, and is unrivaled for quality, beauty of finish and general excellence by that of any other concern, while the prices are extremely moderate. This is the only house in the business in the country that issues a catalogue. This gives valuable information, and will be sent free of charge on application. Mr. Weiner was born in Philadelphia, and has been a resident of this city since 1879. He is widely and favorably known in trade circles as an honorable business man, fully meriting the abundant success he has achieved in this useful and artistic industry.

LEOPOLD & AUERBACH.

The leading cigar store of Chicago, both as regards fine wholesale and retail trade, is unquestionably that of Messrs. Leopold & Auerbach, so desirably located in the elegant Rand-McNally Building on Adams street. Mr. H. Leopold and Mr. J. C. Auerbach formed the existing copartnership in 1886, both gentlemen bringing to bear special qualifications, including a wide range of practical experience in the fine cigar trade. They have achieved a great and deserved success, having from the start made it their undeviating rule to handle only the *finest goods* in every grade. Their establishment is noted as headquarters both with wholesale and retail trade, for strictly first-class, reliable cigars, which are preferred in the future after one trial. The firm have the handsomest fitted up store in town. It is a model in every way. They were the first tenants to locate in the new Rand-McNally Building, and have invested large capital in this beautiful store, with the finest hardwood fixtures, elegant show cases, French plate mirrors, electric lights, and all conveniences. They are direct importers of fine Havana cigars, and also are leading wholesale dealers in the best brands of Key West cigars, handling, as they do, Seidenberg & Co.'s cigars; Elmo Delo Cigar Mfg. Co's goods; D. Hirsch & Co.'s cigars; Julius Ellinger's; all the above Key West and Arguelles; also Lopez & Bros., cigars. New York. The above lines cover all the choicest brands in the market. All goods are hand made by experienced men. The firm make a specialty of box trade, and hundreds of our leading citizens purchase all their cigars here. They also deal generally in full lines of tobaccos, pipes and smokers' articles.

NEW YORK INSTALLMENT COMPANY.

C. F. Thayer, doing business as the New York Installment Company, deals in house furnishing specialties on the installment or time payment plan. This plan of selling goods is very much in vogue at present, and extends to every branch of trade that enters into the domestic economy, except the supplies of food and fuel, which branches of trade still insist upon the old-fashioned cash plan. The New York Installment Company is located at 132 Lake street, and carries a full line of house furnishing specialties, including carpets, rugs, lace curtains, draperies, pictures, mirrors, lamps of all kinds, banquet, piano and library, albums, Bibles, clocks, watches and jewelry, silverware of all kinds, both plated and solid, statuary, sewing machines,

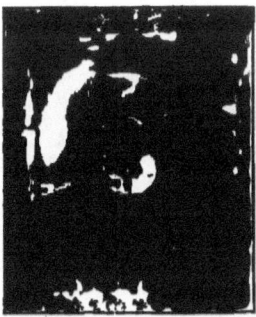

clothes wringers, and other household articles too numerous to mention. These are sold on the most liberal and accommodating terms—a small payment being made on the delivery of the goods, the balance being paid in monthly, semi-monthly, or weekly payments, to suit the convenience of the purchaser. This excellent system enables people of moderate means and small incomes to beautify their homes and enjoy the comfort of pleasant household surroundings without depriving themselves of the necessaries of life. Another good feature of the installment purchase is that the money thus expended in the purchase of some useful article or household ornament is thus saved to the purchaser. The same principle holds good in the purchase of a home on payments. Many a family now happily gathered around its own hearthstone would never have known the luxury of owning their own home but for the beneficent help of building and loan associations. The operation of the installment business is more or less

familiar to all. This firm employs from one hundred and fifty to two hundred traveling agents or solicitors in Indiana and Illinois, in which territory there are fifteen branch houses or distributing depots. The firm have a reputation for selling first-class goods on most favorable terms, and are noted far and wide for their fair and honorable treatment of their patrons. That they have a large and satisfactory business under such circumstances goes without saying. Mr. Thayer is thoroughly posted in his line of business, having spent many years acquiring the necessary experience. He is a native of New York, and has been in his present business in Chicago four years. Mr. Thayer is also doing an extensive wholesale business, controlling several factories, and buying in such large quantities puts him in a position to sell to the largest jobbers in the country. He is a young man of fine business ability.

RICHARD R. TRENCH.

Although but a comparatively short time established in Chicago, the talented organist, music teacher, and dealer in pianos and organs, Mr. Richard R. Trench, has secured a hold on public favor, and achieved a success that fully attests his ability as an instructor and upright, reliable business man. He is a native of Dublin, Ireland, came to the city in 1876, and two years ago established the music room now occupied by him in the building No. 271 Wabash avenue, corner of Van Buren street. The premises are neatly and tastefully appointed, and every convenience is provided for the accommodation of patrons. Mr. Trench has a full and complete assortment of all the various makes of standard pianos and organs, and is agent for the unexcelled Ahlstrom pianos, which, for the low price for which they are sold, are not surpassed by any other in the country. Pianos and organs are sold at moderate prices, and if credit is wanted, Mr. Trench will make as liberal terms as any others in the city, and fully guarantees every instrument to be as represented. He is prominent in church, social, and Masonic circles, is organist of Immanuel Baptist Church, Chicago, and of Apollo and Mount Joy Commanderies Knights Templar, Fair View and Lafayette Chapter, and W. B. Warren and Home Lodges, Free and Accepted Masons. He is a composer of the highest ability of music for lodges and societies, and as an accomplished organist ranks foremost in his profession. Mr. Trench gives instructions on the piano and organ, and his classes are made up of the best representatives of the leading families and citizens. He is a practical teacher of music, and is a business man and citizen of entire probity and integrity. The tuning and repairing of pianos and organs receives Mr. Trench's personal attention.

LATTA & RAFF.

Much attention of late years has been given to the decorative and beautifying of our public buildings and dwellings, and artists of acknowledged ability are constantly employed furnishing new and attractive designs. In this section of the city of Chicago, Messrs Latta & Raff, located at 5741 Wentworth avenue, makes specialty of this branch of business, and have already achieved an enviable reputation for the artistic character of their workmanship. These gentlemen engaged in this business during the current year, and the existing widespread character of the patronage they to-day enjoy is a sufficient voucher for the character of the goods they handle and the superiority of the work they perform. They conduct a large trade as house, sign and fresco painters, and also deal in paints, oils, glass and wall papers. Messrs. Latta & Raff are thorough artists, and are noted for the skill they display in combining shades and colors so as to produce the most pleasing effects. The individual members of this enterprising firm are Messrs. Ernst W. Latta and E. W. Raff, respectively natives of Ohio and Indiana, and residents of Chicago for the past ten years. Operating at low expense, all exorbitant charges are avoided, and the public and those interested will realize the advantages and benefits by giving their custom and support to this progressive and popular establishment.

EXCELSIOR IRON WORKS.

This enterprise was started in 1850 by Mason & McArthur as iron workers, doing sheet iron and boiler work, and gradually extending their business to machinery. In 1859 their entire plant was destroyed by fire, and no insurance. The partnership was soon after dissolved and the business again started by Mr. Carlile Mason. In 1866 his oldest son, Mr. Geo. Mason, who had established a foundry business, joined forces, and the firm became Carlile Mason & Son. In 1869 the foreman of the boiler department was admitted to partnership and the firm

name was changed to Carlile Mason & Co. Some years later Mr. Jas. A. Mason was admitted to the firm, and became junior partner. In 1878 the business was reorganized and incorporated as a stock company under the name of the Excelsior Iron Works, and they are now located at 100 N. Clinton street. Their plant now consists of machine and pattern shops, blacksmith shop and boiler works. Their machine shops and offices occupy a five story and basement building, with a frontage of 75 feet and a depth of 150 feet. The building is a model of its kind, all principal columns and girders are of iron and steel; floors and beams are

of the type known as slow combustion walls, and are faced with pressed brick and stone. Their equipment is modern, most of their tools having been purchased within the last three or four years, and the very best of their several kinds. The boiler shops and forges occupy an equal space of ground, viz.: 75x150 feet, are of brick and stone, two stories and basement, and as thoroughly equipped as the machine shops. These are the oldest iron works in Chicago, and their work is a part of the growth of Chicago. Their boilers and boiler works are found in the largest and best of the public buildings and public enterprises of the city. The wrought iron and plate work, boilers, stoves and furnaces for the Illinois Steel Co. at South Chicago, for Pullman's works, and a host of other great enterprises, came from their works. In machinery their specialty is in dredge and pile driving machinery, swinging engines for bridges, reduction works for precious metals. Their stamp mills and reduction works have been shipped to the mining centers of the United States; to Canada, Mexico and South America, and have been of the highest class in workmanship, design and material, eliciting well merited testimonials everywhere. In machinery for public works they have world wide celebrity for the superiority of their engines, machinery and boilers. They have executed many of the most important contracts ever let for dredges, steam and friction pile drivers, wrought iron cranes, truss work, derricks, swinging and hoisting engines, steel dippers, clamshells, and generally everything for the efficient execution of public works. Both as to the design, build and outfit of their dredges, the leading contractors prefer them to all others, and the company has supplied fleets of them for harbor excavations and channel deepening at all the principal ports on the lakes. In repair work they are especially active and painstaking, and solicit inquiries for machine and boiler work of any description.

M. FRIEDERANG ART PUBLISHING HOUSE.

The rare qualities of artistic genius when displayed evoke instant recognition, and when with them is happily combined the practical and the utilitarian the results are at once as magnificent and complete as they are inspiring and elevating. These remarks have been elicited by a visit recently paid to the studio of that internationally famous art designer, etcher, painter and engraver, Mr. M. Friederang, with headquarters in the Oxford block, 84 and 86 La Salle street. Here can be seen beautiful specimens of his elaborate and strangely fascinating art work. Mr. Friederang is a native of Baden, Germany, who early in life manifested a predilection for art, and achieved a well-deserved celebrity by his achievements in Rome and other old world cities. He executed important contracts in Rome for church and palace frescoes of large proportions, and embodying elaborate studies of figures, flowers, fruits; also in Heilingenberg. He did the illuminating for the "Book of the Donators," deposited in the Vatican, the Papal residence in Rome. Work of a similar high character occupied his attention in Europe until he came to America, where his talents at once received due recognition. Mr. Friederang came to Chicago in 1886, wisely deciding to make this metropolitan center his permanent place of abode. He has here developed an extensive business connection, and his art publishing house is nationally famous. Mr. Friederang is prepared to promptly exe-

cute, in the highest style of art, all orders for designing, engraving and press work. Among the examples of his pen and brush are the illustrating and drawings for the memorial of the twenty-fifth anniversary of Archbishop Feehan; also the publishing of the richly ornate book commemorating the event. Illustrations in the "Herboblaetter" (Autumn Leaves) a volume of poems by Dietz of this city. In 1890 Mr. Friederang was appointed chief artist for the Chicago *Graphic*. He also drew the sketches for the decoration of the Holy Name Cathedral, and is driven with orders of all kinds from publishers, societies, ecclesiastical and social bodies, etc. Mr. Friederang loves his work and is master of his art; his work elicits the commendation of expert critics, and the admiration of the public, and those having anything difficult or intricate in the line of designing or illustrating should come to him. As a sample of his original and appropriate ideas, we refer to his handsome letterheads, giving an allegorical scene, showing the Goddess of Bounty, in the guise of a mermaid, making an offering to the Worlds' Fair in 1893. The buildings are given detail in the background, and the effect is striking and artistic. He will design "World's Fair" letterheads and cards for firms at low rates, and those wanting something bound to arrest attention, and beautiful and original, should secure the services of Mr. Friederang, whose studio and offices are so centrally located in the Oxford building, 84 and 86 La Salle street.

WIRTH, GUTMAN & CO.

The trade in tobaccos, cigars and smokers' articles has assumed extensive proportions in the city of Chicago. A representative and prominent house actively engaged in this steadily growing trade is that of Messrs. Wirth, Gutman & Co., importers and manufacturers' agents for cigars and jobbers of tobacco and smokers' goods, whose salesrooms and office are located at 78 Wabash avenue. This business was founded in 1880 by Wirth, Dickie & Co., who conducted it till 1886, when the present firm assumed the management. The copartners, Messrs. H. Wirth and N. S. Gutman have

had long experience, superior connections and perfect facilities, enabling them to fill orders with first-class goods at the lowest ruling market prices. They occupy two spacious floors, each being 30x175 feet in area, where they keep an extensive, well-selected and choice stock of chewing and smoking tobaccos, domestic and imported cigars, snuff, pipes, and smokers' articles generally. Messrs. Wirth, Gutman & Co. have control of the factories whose cigars they handle, and employ in their salesrooms twenty persons and ten traveling salesmen on the road. Their goods are widely known in the trade for their quality, reliability and uniform excellence, and their patronage extends throughout the principal cities and towns of the Western and Northwestern states. Mr. Wirth is a native of New York, while Mr. Gutman was born in Germany, but has resided many years in Chicago. They are honorable and enterprising business men, who are very popular in trade circles. This house makes a specialty of the superior brand of cigars known as "La Flor de Nectar," manufactured from pure Havanna tobacco and guaranteed to be of the finest quality. There is a large demand for this cigar by the leading stores and prominent hotels of the city. For fine quality and flavor this cigar excels anything in the market, and the demand, now large, is constantly increasing.

SANGER, MOODY & STEEL STONE CO.

The Sanger, Moody & Steel Stone Company, dealers in Joliet limestone, and leaders in their line of building material, bear a very important relation to the building industry of this city. Their extensive yards are placed at points in the city for convenient access and delivery, and their immense trade is fully shown in their facilities for the transportation and hauling of the product of their quarries. The firm originated in 1865 as L. P. Sanger & Son, which was afterward Sanger & Steel, then Sanger & Moody. The business was incorporated in 1888, under its present style, with a capital of $80,000, under the laws of Illinois. The officers are H. A. Sanger, president, C. C. Moody, vice-president and secretary, and Sanger Steel, treasurer. The offices are located at 159 La Salle street, room 7. The stone is found in Joliet, Ill., just north of the penitentiary, and is of peculiar value. It is the best limestone in the United States. It will not crumble or crack, and is used in all United States locks on the Illinois river, United States arsenals in the country, the principal court and state houses. The quarries of Joliet cover an area of 230 acres, and have exceptionally good canal and railway facilities. The Sanger, Moody & Steel Stone Company have a fleet of five steamboats. Their yards are well located for facility of distribution. The west yard is at Harrison and Rockwell streets; the central yard at Twelfth and State streets; the North side yard at North avenue bridge, and the South side yards at the South Stock Yards slip, Thirty-ninth and Halsted streets. They employ 300 workmen, and their trade extends over the west and northwest, their splendid facilities of transportation being fully taxed to meet the growing demand for the product of their quarries.

J. H. STEVENSON & CO.

Chicago is rapidly becoming the manufacturing center, not only for the heavy machinery, millstuffs, etc., but also for the articles that have for years been confined to the Atlantic States for manufacture, or have been imported from Europe. In 1881 Mr. J. H. Stevenson established a manufactory for making fine fringes, upholstery trimmings and art decorations, at No. 15 E. Washington street. In 1889 he sold out to Mr. A. Lotz, who has since conducted the business under the old firm name (J. H. Stevenson & Co.). In July last, Mr. Lotz removed the business to his present commodious quarters at 125 to 137 Rees street. Here Mr. Lotz has a fine plant of

machinery of all kinds used in his business, including thirty looms and spinning machines. The premises occupied are well located, and offer every advantage for the successful conduct of the business. Mr. Lotz occupies the third floor, where he has space, 120x135 feet in area, giving him ample room for all needs. The machinery is operated by steam power, and he employs about eighty skilled hands in the manufacture of the goods he handles. These goods consist of fine silk and woolen fringes, in all the leading designs and patterns, upholstery and drapery trimmings, and art decorations. A specialty is made of fine art work, for which the house has an established reputation. The business done by Mr. Lotz is of great importance, the trade being from all over the United States and territories. Many thousands of yards of fine materials are worked each year, and the business is increasing rapidly, having every prospect for a much larger scope. Mr. Lotz was born in Germany, and came to Chicago twenty years ago. He is thoroughly conversant with the business in all its details, having been connected with other houses for many years before going into business for himself. He has developed a large business, and his familiarity with all branches in this line enables him to conduct his enterprise in the best manner for success and profit. He is prominent in business circles, and is of the highest respsibonility and integrity.

A. OBERMANN.

The position of druggist and chemist is one requiring special fitness and ability in the persons who engage in the business. One of the most capable gentleman engaged in this business in Chicago is Mr. A. Obermann, whose establishment is at the corner of Clark and Kinzie streets, McCormick hall building. Mr. Obermann has been established in the business for eleven years, and has met with the most pleasing success. He was born in Burlington, Ia., and came to Chicago about eleven years ago. He occupies the ground floor of the building for business purposes, 25x50 feet in dimensions. This he has fitted up and furnished in an elegant manner. The counters and fixtures are of fine hardwood, the windows and showcases of plate glass, and a magnificent soda fountain of the most approved style is an attraction of the most important kind. A complete, fresh and well arranged stock of drugs and chemicals is carried; also a complete line of toilet and fancy goods, soaps, perfumes, brushes, rubber goods, physicians' supplies, trusses, shoulder-braces, cutlery, etc. This store is kept open at all hours of the day or night, and six competent assistants are employed. Orders for medicines and physicians' prescriptions can be telephoned for at night, as well as during the day, and receive prompt attention and delivery to any part of the city. The telephone call is 3182. Mr. Obermann is a genial, obliging gentleman, who is held in high esteem by all with whom he has dealings.

FELIX LANG.

Many and many a mile of moulding does Mr. Felix Lang turn out of his factory in the course of a year, and it would be interesting to know how many years it would take him to make moulding enough to reach around the world. Mr. Lang's business can boast of an establishment of twenty-four years, standing, for it was then that he founded it, and has since continued it with the greatest success. His factory is at the corner of Loomis and Twenty-first streets, and occupies the ground floor of a two-story brick building, 100x200 feet in dimensions. He manufactures and deals in all kinds of mouldings, and his factory is thoroughly furnished with the most improved woodworking machinery, and if ever a new machine is introduced, which he can apply to his business, he at once adopts it. He has a 250 horse power engine to control his works. His trade extends all over the United States. "He has purchased the right to manufacture the Allen compound balance piston valve and automatic governor, for the state of Illinois, and is now prepared to attach same to old or new engines on a guarantee to produce from twenty to forty-five per cent. economy in fuel or power over any ordinary class of engines, or equal to the Corliss or any other best make, of automatic engines. He guarantees such results even on many old, abandoned engines deemed worthless except for scrap iron. Having had experience with this valve before purchasing said right he had the utmost confidence that such phenomenal merit exists in it and also that it is destined to revolutionize steam power. We would advise all owners of either old or new slide valve engines not to sell or exchange them for other high priced (and less valuable) engines before investigating the Era." Mr. Lang usually employs sixty hands. He is a middle-aged man, and a native of Chicago, and has long enjoyed the reputation among business men as being perfectly straightforward in all his dealings. In his moulding work, and, indeed, in his valve work, he uses only the best materials and workmanship, and he adopts machinery where others have in many instances to use hand work.

HENRY SCHEIB.

The business of Henry Scheib, which was established in 1888, is the outgrowth of an experience which precedes that establishment by over seventeen years. It follows therefore that there is pretty nearly a quarter-century of ripe artistic skill and experience coming out of a time when art has thoroughly taken possession of the workshop, and the people's taste has been educated to the highest point. Mr. Scheib has had no old fogy ways to discard, nor no stereotyped methods to be alienated from, but in his line is

energy and business enterprise keep the wheels of the home department humming. Mr. Scheib is a native of Ottawa, Ill., and was raised in Iowa. At fourteen years of age he came to Chicago, and his subsequent career is a proof of the reward which waits upon industry and success in this city, whose fierce business competition emphasizes the law of the survival of the fittest. Business success amid mercantile giants and huge capacities shows the possession of these qualities, and Mr. Scheib is therefore to be congratulated on the present growth and steadily increasing proportions of his enterprise.

prepared to meet the demands for the highest artistic forms and the best material. The prices are worthy of the same careful comparison as the workmanship which distinguishes the goods manufactured and jobbed by Mr. Scheib. They comprise pier, mantel, cheval and bar mirrors, and looking-glass plates of every description. The catalogue for 1891-2, a handsomely illustrated quarto, contains many admirable designs, sound in artistic taste and finished with rare skill. They comprise mirrors of all kinds, toilet, cabinet, mantel, sideboard, hall-stand and bar mirrors, in all varieties of setting, if the term may be used, the framework in all cases being of a high degree of finish and in all woods. Special designs are furnished, and those who in the city fail to call on this firm for anything in the mirror line make a mistake. The business of the firm is carried on at 46 and 48 South Canal street, formerly at 27 East Lake. The premises consist of one floor for salesroom and offices, 50x150 feet in area. The factory is located in another building, and Mr. Scheib has all he can do to find room for the development of his rapidly increasing business. He employs twenty people, and his trade extends all over the United States, at wholesale only. He employs five traveling salesmen, whose

M. WALKER & CO.

There are none among Chicago's dealers in realty that enjoy a larger measure of public confidence than Mr. M. Walker, the head and active co-partner of the firm of M. Walker & Co., licensed real estate and loan brokers, whose admirable offices are en suite 918 Chamber of Commerce building. Mr. Walker, although a young man, has had quite an extended experience in handling and dealing in real property and negotiating loans, and brings to bear upon the business a full knowledge of its every detail. Acreage and subdivision property is handled, the firm having under their control large blocks situated at Stony Island and Jackson Park and which are being disposed of at low prices and satisfactory terms. When desired, houses will be erected to suit purchasers of lots, and terms made for payment in monthly or other stated installments. The firm also takes charge of estates for non-resident owners and does a general real estate business, buying, selling and exchanging city and rural property on commission. Mortgages are negotiated, loans made on approved collateral, investments desirably placed, and real estate appraised for owners and intending purchasers. Mr. Walker is a native of this city and has always resided here.

A. F. WITHE.

Chicago possesses some very handsome pharmacies indeed. We do not know of any city that can boast of so large a number of what we would term thoroughly first-class drug stores. One of the most notable of these is that of Mr. A. F. Withe, which is known as the Leland Hotel Pharmacy, at the corner of Michigan avenue and Jackson street, and though only established in June of the present year Mr. Withe has imported into it an atmosphere of respectability which will before long secure for him the position of one of the leading pharma-

cists of Chicago. The store is very large and very luxuriously fitted up, and being in the very center of the aristocratic hotels, controls a class of trade which will do credit to such an establishment. Mr. Withe makes a specialty of compounding physicians' prescriptions, and his laboratory, which is a distinct department, is equipped with every modern convenience and apparatus for this delicate work, and as an extra precaution toward accuracy he makes all his own tinctures so as to secure absolute purity. He carries a very extensive stock of toilet requisites and fancy articles such as are demanded by the class of customers who chiefly patronize his store. He also has specially imported French perfumes and soaps. The store contains an unusually handsome soda fountain, which is patronized by all the best residents of the neighborhood. Mr. Withe is a thorough chemist and graduate. He is registered in the Illinois State Board of Pharmacy. He is a native of Mt. Clemens, Michigan, and is a gentleman of much refinement and high attainments. He employs an efficient staff to assist him in his store.

WILLIAM GREEN & CO.

The firm of William Green & Co., whose office is 1169 Rookery building, and whose store is at Nos. 544 and 554 North Water street, was established in 1891 (March), in order to bring to the attention of builders and others the value of the special brand of Portland cement imported by Mr. Green. To the development of this business Mr. Green brought the experience of many years in England in the business, and a thorough knowledge of his subject, combined with a firm belief

in the virtues of the "Hog" brand. The proof of this quality is attested by severe tests to which it has been subjected in London, under the direction of A. E. Casey, Esq., member of the Institute of Civil Engineering, and F. C. S. In addition to this brand, Messrs. Green & Co. import other varieties, and also sell cements of domestic production. He has built up already a fine trade, and supplies some of the leading builders of the city. Mr. Wm. Green and Mr. H. J. Rodgers comprise the firm. Mr. Rodgers is a resident of Appleton, Wis., and is a director of the First National Bank of that town. At the dock or stores of the firm, at Nos. 544 to 554 North Water street, can be found for sale imported and domestic cement in any quantity desired. Mr. Green has, however, the sole control of the "Log" brand, which is making rapid strides in the favor of master builders and others, on account of its ability to resist any frost, however severe. The firm are storage and general warehousemen, and their warehouse contains 90,000 feet flooring in a five-story brick building. The building is perfectly dry, and the location is free from dust and smoke.

E. G. MINNICK.

Of late years no form of investment has become so popular with the conservative public as judiciously selected real estate. Just now the market is active, and among those conspicuous in the operations that are now going on is Mr E. G. Minnick, general real estate dealer and subdivider of city and suburban property, whose office is suite 615, Chamber of Commerce building. He has been thus employed since 1885, and the benefits conferred upon the city through his agency are many and valuable. A broad gauge man of comprehensive views, identified with Chicago in the best sense, he is extremely liberal toward all who will invest in the soil in this vicinity, and thus become permanently attached to this section. Mr. Minnick owns considerable tracts of real estate within a few miles of the city, comprising valuable and desirable lots at Englewood, where he has 21½ acres ; at Rogers' Park, 10 acres ; Oaklawn, 173 acres ; Windsor Park, 20 acres : Pleasant Hill, 80 acres ; Cheltenham, 21 acres, and Auburn, 7 acres. The situation of these subdivisions are unquestionably the most delightful spots within a short distance from the Court House. Lots are now being sold at the very lowest prices, on easy terms, and, when desired, houses will be erected to suit purchasers, and arrangements can be made for payment by monthly or other stated installments. This is indeed a rare opportunity for procuring a profitable and charming home which no industrious man can afford to neglect; many have already in proved the chance and are well pleased with their investments, and we would advise those who are thinking of purchasing not to delay it long as the lots are rapidly selling, and ere long none will be left. Mr. Minnick, who was born in Indiana and raised in Iowa, is a graduate of the Rush Medical College class, '71 and for a time was in the active practice of his profession. He has resided in this city since 1885, and is well and widely known as a staunch business man and capitalist. He has always enjoyed a high reputation and the esteem and unbounded confidence of all having dealings with him. Mr Minnick is a member of the Odd-Fellows and Knights of Pythias, and has a large circle of friends and acquaintances, and all who come in contact with him either socially or in a business way pronounce him a gentleman in every respect, and patrons can depend upon any and all representations made by him, and that their interests will always be protected.

K. B. OLSON & CO.

In reviewing the leading industries of the great city of Chicago, the clothing interests naturally claim special attention. For many years the whole suit of clothes was made in one establishment, but latterly the demand for pants has increased faster than that for whole suits, thus causing the establishment of numerous pants factories throughout all sections of the United States. In this connection, we desire to make special reference, in this mercantile review of Chicago, to the representative and enterprising firm of Messrs. K. B. Olson & Co., manufacturers of pants exclusivsly, whose factory and office are situated at 741 to 745 Elk Grove avenue. This extensive business was established in 1863 by Mr. K. B. Olson, who conducted it till 1867, when Mr. K. C. Bolstad became a partner, the firm being known by the title of "K. B. Olson & Co." Eventually in 1887 Mr. J.

B. Nordhem was admitted into partnership. All the partners are thoroughly practical and expert manufacturers, and possess an intimate knowledge of every detail of the trade and the requirements of jobbers, dealers and a critical public. They employ constantly about 100 skilled hands, and removed to their present factory in March, 1891, which is owned by them. The factory is a spacious four-story building, 125x52 feet in dimensions, fitted up with modern machinery and appliances, operated by an improved Baxter steam engine. The capacity of the factory is 2,000 pairs of pants weekly. They employ only the best talent in their cutting rooms. Their pants have earned an excellent reputation on their merits as being among the best made, most stylish and reliable in the market. The partners were all born in Norway, but have resided in Chicago the greater part of their lives, where they are greatly respected in trade circles for their energy and integrity. During the Civil War Mr. J. B. Nordhem served for three years in the 16th United States Infantry. He was present at several important battles for the cause of the Union.

A. C. DE PODE & CO.

There can be but little question but that the introduction of what are known as "patent specialty" houses has proved a boon to many a housekeeper of limited means. A house of this character and one that has a solid and substantial standing, is the well-known concern of Mr. A. C. De Podé (trading as A. C. De Podé & Co.), whose headquarters are located at No. 221 Fifth avenue. This enterprise was established some four years ago by its present proprietors, who have since met with a success that is the reward of energy, ability, liberal and honorable business methods. Mr. De Podé handles hardware specialties, clothing, boots, shoes, woodenware, patent medicines, watches, clocks, jewelry, no-

tions and fancy goods too numerous for particularization in these columns. All these goods are warranted the best the markets produce and are sold both at wholesale and retail upon a basis of easy payments such as can hardly embarrass either retailer or consumer of the most limited capital. Some idea of Mr. De Podé's business may be inferred from the statement that he has already established thirty agencies, and his trade is still annually growing in volume and value. Mr. De Podé is of French nationality, and has been a highly respected resident of Chicago for the past four years. Price lists are sent to applicants and agents are wanted.

ANDERSON & HANSON.

Among the practical expert painters and decorators in the Hyde Park section of the city is the firm of Anderson & Hanson, 273 Fifty-fifth street, who have had many years experience in the business, and bring to bear a full knowledge of everything pertaining to it. The business they are now conducting with such marked ability and success was originally established about seventeen years ago by Mr. C. M. Anderson, from whom the present firm bought it some months ago. They have since made many improvements in the premises occupied, put in a new stock, and are conducting operations in a manner greatly redounding to their credit, and besides the old patrons left them by their predecessors are adding many new ones. A large stock of goods is carried by the firm, embracing paints, oils, glass, brushes, painters' supplies, and materials generally; also wallpapers, dados, friezes, and handsome centerpieces in all the new beautiful styles and designs. Employing a force of ten skilled workmen, Messrs. Anderson & Hanson are prepared to enter into contracts for the execution of paperhanging, general interior decorating and house painting, doing the very best work in the most expeditious manner at prices always based upon the principles of equity and fairness. Mr. Axel Anderson and Mr. Chas. L. Hanson were both born in Sweden. They have been in Chicago many years, and have a wide reputation as expert skilled painters, paperhangers and decorators.

C. J. LARSON.

In that growing and ambitious suburb of the Western metropolis, Auburn Park, the passerby can hardly fail to be attracted and pleased by the energy and enterprise exhibited by Mr. C. J. Larson, at the corner of Seventy-ninth and Sherman streets, in his most advantageous display of groceries, meats, fruits and vegetables. Mr. Larson's premises are large and convenient, and offer superior facilities for the disposal and arrangement of his fine stock, facilities which have been considerably improved by the appliances and valuable methods he has introduced. As a consequence, everything here may be relied on as being in prime condition, as well as of high class quality. He carries a full stock of staple articles, canned goods in tin and glass, condiments, and table delicacies and luxuries, besides meats, fruits and vegetables in great variety. The latter are neatly arranged in front of the store, and form a very attractive feature in their fresh color and crisp condition. Mr. Larson opened this store in 1889, and has now the finest establishment of the kind in all parts. He is a native of New York, but came here in 1881. His knowledge of his chosen avocation is perfect, and with his abundant resources, influential connections and superior organization, he would appear to be but entering upon a career whose future contains promise of the most brilliant character. Mr. Larson is widely known and greatly esteemed, not alone within the lines of this important trade, but by a wide circle among the community generally.

BLUE ISLAND AVENUE CLOTHING HOUSE.

The novel location and the well-known business of the Blue Island avenue clothing house, makes it proper that it be mentioned here. It occupies the best business site in the section of the city in which it is located, being at the junction of Blue Island avenue, Loomis and Eighteenth streets. This business has been established eighteen years, and is one of the most popular in the West side district. The store has been at the present location three years, in which time the business has been greatly augmented. The proprietor is Mr. A. Silha, and he has made a great success of his enterprise, and is worthy of the congratulations of his numerous friends. He carries a very large and complete stock of clothing for men's and boy's wear, including everything in this line; the stock consists of ready made suits of tweed, woolen, cashmere, cheviot, worsted and other fine goods, also a complete line of furnishing goods, neckwear, shirts, collars, cuffs, etc. In addition to these he has a fine assortment of trunks, valises, etc. He makes a specialty of fine custom work, and carries a very select line of patterns of the latest importation. The store is very large and attractive, and has a frontage of 75 feet on Blue Island avenue, and 100 feet on Eighteenth street. It has a beautiful plate glass front, and substantial and artistic furnishings. Mr. Silha employs three clerks, and has a large and appreciative patronage. Mr. Silha was born in Bohemia, Austria, and has lived in Chicago twenty-five years. He is an active, progressive business man, and is making a great success. He has numerous friends, and is regarded in the highest esteem by all who know him. His business methods are above question, and his customers not only continue to come to him, but consider it a pleasure to recommend the house to their friends.

ROBT. ROBERTSON.

In the mechanic arts there is no branch of more importance than sanitary plumbing and gasfitting. This work has to be performed in almost every house erected in our city, and for the health and comfort it is more than important that this feature in the construction of a building should be both carefully and well performed. Health and happiness, nay, sometimes life and death depend in a great measure on how this work is executed, and too much care cannot be exercised in selecting those to be intrusted with your sanitary plumbing contract. Among the more recently established, yet none the less reliable, West side houses devoted to this industry may be named that of Mr. Robert Robertson, plumber, gasfitter and sewer builder, No. 844 W. Harrison street. This business was founded in 1891, and almost from the establishment of the business the present proprietor has ably conducted the affairs of the enterprise alone. His business now demands the employment of several skilled assistants, who are selected with care as to their ability and knowledge of the trade. Estimates are furnished and contracts completed for the fitting up of dwellings and public buildings in all that pertains of sanitary plumbing and practical gasfitting, satisfaction being guaranteed in every instance. Mr. Robertson is a native of Dundee, Scotland, and has resided in Chicago for the past eleven years, prior to engaging in business on his own account, being favorably identified with the well-known Chicago plumbing house of Messrs. Hamblin & McDonald. He is a regular licensed plumber, and a member of the Journeymen Plumbers' Association and Scottish Clans of America.

BUSHNELL LUMBER & MILL CO.

In the manufacture of sash, doors, blinds. etc., Chicago has better facilities than any other city in the United States. In this connection we desire to refer especially to the reliable and successful Bushnell Lumber & Mill Company, whose yard and plaining mill are situated on Clyboorn place bridge. This business was established originally by Mr. H. O. Sherman, who was succeeded by H. O. Sherman & Sons, and in 1889 by the Sherman & Bushnell Company. Eventually the present Bush-

nell Lumber & Mill Company was organized in 1890, the proprietors being Messrs. Jas. F. Bushnell, A. T. Bushnell and E. A. Lord. The partners are thoroughly practical manufacturers and lumber men, fully conversant with every detail of the trade, and the requirements of builders and contractors They occupy a spacious yard, and their mill is a commodious two-story brick structure, 40x75 feet in dimensions. The planing mill is fully supplied with the latest improved wood working machinery and appliances, operated by a 100-horse power steam engine Seventy-five skilled workmen are employed, who turn out extensively, lath, shingles, sash, doors, blinds, mouldings, frames and all kinds of mill work. Everything in the way of dimension lumber, dressed lumber, flooring, sidings, etc , is executed to order, and every facility is at hand for turning out work promptly and in the best manner. They promptly furnish estimates for all kinds of inside woodwork. The trade is chiefly local, and they have furnished their materials for several of the finest buildings latterly erected in Chicago. The partners are all natives of Chicago. They are highly esteemed in trade circles. The telephone call of the house is 4725.

J. I. SCHIMEK.

The popular pharmacy now owned and controlled by Mr. J. I. Schimek, at 547 Blue Island avenue, has always maintained a high reputation for pure drugs and fresh medicines. It was established thirteen years ago by Mr. R. Schiffbauer, in whose employ Mr. Schimek acquired the sound, practical rudiments of his profession, and his ultimate purchase of the pharmacy he now presides over, was in 1885. Mr. Schimek is a young man, born in this city, a regular graduate of the Chicago College of Pharmacy, and a thoroughly educated druggist and apothecary. The store is attractive, and in its fittings and furnishings very complete. In size it is 15x30 feet in dimensions, and the stock carried embraces pure, fresh drugs, chemicals, pharmaceuticals, all the requisites for the toilet, the standard proprietary remedies of known merit, surgical appliances, trusses, etc. The strictest attention is paid to compounding of physicians' prescriptions, which are always prepared in the most accurate and prompt manner, under the immediate supervision of Mr. Schimek. The patronage of the establishment is of the most substantial character, and each succeeding year is steadily growing.

A. ARENSON.

Mr. A. Arenson dealer in hardware, tinware, carpenters' tools and stoves, has been established at No. 427 W. Harrison street since 1890. The store, which is stocked with an A1 grade of goods, occupies the ground floor of a two-story brick building and covers an area of 2,000 square feet, having a frontage on Harrison street of 25 feet. Mr. A. Arenson, the present genial proprietor, is sole agent on the West side for the world renowned Garland stoves manufactured by the Michigan Stove Co. This well-known make has never been eclipsed and is, considering its many advantages over inferior manufactures, the very cheapest in the market. This brand cannot be recommended too highly—and the satisfaction it has given to so many housewives will bear out all that has been said in its behalf. Mr. Arenson employs four able assistants, who are accommodating and courteous. He is a native of the former Kingdom of Poland, and has resided in the Garden City of the West about ten years. The success which he has attained as merchant is directly attributable to his close attention to business, to his ever ready courtesy and affability and to the pleasant methods which he employs to win friends and patrons. He advertises his goods very largely and believes in sharing the profits, which he nets through the agency of others, with them. In other words he invests a certain percentage of his net profit, accrued to him by advertising, in advertising. That he is decidedly awake to the exigency of the hour is further proven by the great esteem that all his rivals and competitors hold for him, and they constantly praise his methods.

THE E. JENNINGS CO.

Among Chicago's varied branches of industry must be specially mentioned the large establishment of The E. Jennings Co., leading manufacturers in the world of sleeping, parlor and dining car furnishings. Chicago is the great natural center of the principal railroads of the United States and Canada; it is the best shipping point on the continent, and decidedly the best place to locate such an important manufactory as is this. The business was started in 1865 by Mr. E. Jennings, who was originally located at 92 W. Madison street. As the trade developed, repeated enlargements of facilities were necessitated, and in 1882 the present

extensive premises were erected by McMillan Bros. a cost of over $100,000. They are palatial in outfit and appointments, and present the handsomest architectural appearance of any building on W. Madison street. The present company was formed in 1886, and has a paid up capital of $400,000. Mr. E. Jennings is the president and treasurer, and Mr. Goerge A. Follansbee, the secretary. Mr. Jennings is a respected and popular business man, noted for his sound judgment and marked executive abilities, and is the recognized leading authority in these branches of skilled industry. The premises are at 399 to 405 W. Madison street, six stories and basement in height, and 100x200 feet in dimensions. They are constructed in the most substantial manner of pressed brick. All the modern improvements have been introduced, including elevators, speaking tubes, electric light, steam heat, telephone, etc. Upwards of 125 skilled hands are employed in the various departments, engaged in the manufacture of such specialties as berth curtains, lambrequins, mattresses, window curtains with embossed leather trimmings, and spring rollers, chair covers, pillow covers, pillow slips, sheets and napkins, tablecloths, waiters' jackets, aprons and caps, etc. The company's goods are all of the choicest materials and best workmanship, and of the most popular and approved patterns, meeting the most advanced requirements of the

Pullman, Wagner and other palace sleeping and dining car companies. The company also are proprietors of the "Oriental Laundry," splendidly equipped with all the latest laundry machinery, including many improved appliances. Here is headquarters for all the laundry business of the great Pullman Palace Car Co., as also for the leading hotels, the principal steamer lines, restaurants, shirt factories, etc. The office and the delivery room are on the ground floor, and are 100x100 feet in dimensions. A visit here will reveal the magnitude of the Oriental's business. The wash houses are in the rear, and this is emphatically the finest and best organized laundry in the city, doing the finest and most elaborate work, all linen being rendered absolutely pure, clean and sweet. The company has branch laundries and offices in Kansas City, Mo., and Louisville, Ky., owning its premises in those cities. It is progressive and vigorous, having the benefit of such able and judicious guidance as that of President Jennings, whose success is well deserved, being based on the sure foundation of merit, and the keen insight as to what is best adapted to and most needed by the modern and palatial American vestibule trains and dining, sleeping, and parlor cars

THE MORSE CHOCOLATE CO.

Prominent among the new, but promising institutions of our great city, is The Morse Chocolate Company, manufacturers of liquid chocolates at Nos. 80 and 82 Illinois street. The company is composed of some of the most substantial business men in the city, with C. F. Pasdeloup, president; W. W. Wyatt vice-president and treasurer; Newton Morganroth, secretary and manager; Artie Brucker, superintendent. They were incorporated this year with a capital stock of $100,000, and occupy a factory 50x100 feet at the above numbers. The delicious beverage made from chocolate and the many other uses it is put to, in ½ pound and 1 pound jars, needs no cooking or grating, and is ready for use at a moment's notice, makes it an important industry, and one which is rapidly increasing. The Morse Chocolate Company is composed of live, energetic business men who are pushing their goods to a front rank in the market, and under the superintendence of so experienced a man as Artie Brucker, they cannot help but succeed. At present they manufacture four chocolate syrups, and are fitting their manufactory for more extensive operations. The excellence of their goods is attested by the already large and constantly increasing trade, extending rapidly over this section and various parts of the United States. It is the intention of the company to use nothing but the purest ingredients, and with the facilities at their command they are sure to succeed.

HENRY J. AFF.

This city has a great many houses engaged in the manufacture of wagons, carriages, etc., and many of them are representative and do a thriving business. One of the old established and reliable houses of this kind is that conducted by Mr. Henry J. Aff, at 682 to 686 Clybourn avenue. Mr. Aff established this business sixteen years ago, and by close application and persistent effort has succeeded in building up a business that is meritorious and extensive. He owns the building he occupies for business purposes, which is a two-story brick structure, 25x100 feet in dimensions. Here he manufactures all kinds of carriages, wagons and trucks for all uses. Mr. Aff has had a long and practical experience in this business, and brings his skill to bear in producing vehicles of the best grade, using only the best seasoned materials in their construction, and employing only skilled workmen for all branches of the trade. He employs a number of first-class workmen and personally superintends the work. The patronage of this house is large, although mostly local in character, many of the customers being leading business houses in various quarters of the city. Mr. Aff is well known in this city as a careful painstaking business man of rare energy and integrity, and he has numerous friends in all sections. He was born and reared here and in character is above reproach.

D. W. BURROWS.

Mr. D. W. Burrows, the efficient and popular general agent for the Pennsylvania Fire Insurance Company and the Insurance Company of North America, has had a most successful career in this city, culminating in his appointment as general agent of the two companies mentioned, for Cook county. The fact that these immense interests are placed entirely in his hands by the management of these companies, speaks eloquently for the business tact and energy displayed by Mr. Burrows in the conduct of his busi

ness, Mr. Burrows' experience has, however, been of the most complete character. He successfully acted as agent for these companies in other states, and is perfectly conversant with all the details of their management. Besides this fact, it should be noted that Mr. Burrows represents two of the most prominent, as well as the most successful companies. The Pennsylvania, which was established in 1825, has become a proverb for its security and strength, while the Insurance Co. of North America, with its "hoary antiquity" of nearly a century—it was founded in 1792—has become a synonym for strength and conservative government. Mr. Burrows is a member of the Board of Fire Underwriters, and all the principal clubs of the city. He is also the secretary of, and a large stockholder in the Chicago & Naperville Stone Co. He is a native of Plymouth, N. H., and has been in Chicago for a number of years. Mr. Burrows gives the most careful attention to the details of the business, all the agents for Cook county reporting to him, he having the sole control of that territory for both companies. Such prominent firms as Case & Co., Geo. C. Clarke & Co., and Geo. M. Harvey & Co., represent, locally, the above named sterling companies. Of the Western department, with offices at Erie, Pa., it may be noted that J. F. Downing & Co., are the general managers, with whom are associated George Talcott and Charles H. Harry.

JAC. ELIAN.

Although a comparatively young firm, having only been established a year, the hardware store of Mr. Jac. Elian is one deserving our special attention. Located as it is, at 149 Clybourn avenue, in the midst of a populous section of the North Side, it has, from the start, enjoyed a very liberal and substantial patronage. Mr. Elian has always believed that what is worth doing at all is worth doing well, and it is on this motto that he has been rewarded by the success which has fallen to his lot. The store is 25x60 feet in dimensions, and very handsome and fitted with every modern convenience and appliance

for the successful prosecution of the trade. The stock is well kept and thoroughly well selected. It is displayed on the first floor, while the basement consists of a workshop. This stock comprises a fine assortment of stoves and ranges, builders' and and shelf hardware, carpenters' and mechanics' tools, pocket and table cutlery, bird cages, tinware, hollowware, enamel ware, general house furnishing goods and everything that is kept in a first-class hardware store. A specialty is made of the order trade, in the way of all kinds of galvanized iron work, tin and copper work, gutters, spouts, ventilators and copper work for bar rooms, as well as drip pans, sinks, etc. Estimates are furnished for all work if desired, and contracts taken, and the prices charged for all work and jobbing and repairs are very reasonable. Mr. Elian is a gentleman of middle age, and a native of Germany.

ROBERT MAURER.

The leading importer of and dealer in musical merchandise on the North side, is unquestionably Mr. Robert Maurer, whose place of business is at 384 E. Division street, corner Franklin street. Mr. Maurer has been established in this business since 1884, and is well known as one of the best informed dealers in music and musical merchandise. He has occupied his present beautiful store since 1890, being formerly located at 425 E. Division street. Mr. Maurer carries a full stock of all kinds of wooden musical instruments and small string instruments, zithers, violins, flutes, guitars, mandolins, accordions, harmonicas, etc., making a specialty of zithers and zither music, which he imports, having the finest instruments that have ever come to Chicago. Mr Maurer carries in stock genuine Italian and German strings for all

kinds of string instruments, making his leader fine zither strings. All kinds of music is carried, but it is as an importer of zither music that Mr. Maurer most excels, and is best known. He is a player of this most delicate and sympathetic instrument, of great skill and ability. His catalogues of zither music are the finest ever published in the United States, containing about 150 pages, and special care is given to selecting music for customers. The patronage of this house is extensive, patrons from all over the country sending many orders to Chicago by mail. The store is elegantly fitted up and arranged, and is well patronized by the music loving public. Mr. Maurer is a native of Germany, and has resided in Chicago for seven years, being engaged in business ever since coming to the city.

THE MIDLAND DESK MANUFACTURING CO.

A progressive and one of the most reliable houses in this section of Chicago, actively engaged in the manufacture of desks and office furniture, is that of The Midland Desk Manufacturing Co., whose factory and office are at 82 to 88 Fulton street. This business was established in 1889 by Messrs. Anton and Julius Clemetsen, and Charles Miller, the two former being practical and expert cabinet makers, fully acquainted with every detail of this useful industry, and the requirements of the most critical patrons. They occupy for manufacturing purposes 15,000 feet of floor space, fully equipped with the latest improved wood-working machinery, tools and appliances, operated by steam power. Here 35 to 40 skilled hands are employed, and the trade of the firm extends throughout the entire United States. They manufacture exclusively desks and office furniture to order. Carefully selected lumber and fittings are utilized, and the goods turned out are unrivaled for elegance of design, workmanship and finish. Their roll-top desks are general favorites wherever introduced, and the prices quoted for all goods are extremely moderate. Messrs. Anton and Julius Clemetsen and Charles Miller were born in Norway. They are honorable and enterprising business men, who have secured a liberal and influential patronage in this valuable industry, and the demand for the firm's goods is steadily increasing owing to the excellence of the product and the honorable and straightforward method of the proprietors under whose able and experienced management the trade is bound to increase.

LORANG, ANDERSON CO.

One of the manufacturing concerns especially worthy of mention is the Lorang, Anderson Co., manufacturers of musical instruments. The business to which this company has succeeded was established in 1889 by Lorang & Anderson. In 1890 the company was duly incorporated with an ample cash capital, and with Mr. G. Nelson as president and treasurer, and A. Wecen secretary. The company manufactures guitars and mandolins exclusively, being the only firm manufacturing these instruments exclusively. In the city. The company does an extensive business; they employ a large force of skilled workmen, and have a capacity of about 800 instruments per month. The heads of the company are practical and skilled instrument makers, and bring to bear the results of many years' experience on their work. They occupy the top floor of the building at 145 Ontario street as a factory, and have the room equipped with all needful machinery. They have a floor space, 25x125 feet. This company make a specialty of the manufacture of a bridge and string adjuster the patent for which is owned by the firm, and which is coming into extensive use. This house is well patronized and is favorably known in the business world. The officers are gentlemen of sterling worth, and are appreciated in leading trade circles. They are both natives of Sweden.

J. SIDNEY VILLERE & CO.

Mr. Villeré established himself in business as an architect in Chicago three years ago in the Major block on La Salle street, and in May, 1891, moved to his present well lighted and capacious offices on the sixth floor of the McCormick block at southeast corner of Randolph and Dearborn streets. He has mostly devoted himself to residential architecture of all kinds A little book published by him in 1891, is called "Villere's Model Homes." By possessing this book, every man may be his own architect, as it gives to each design, a complete first and chamber floor plan besides the elevation plan, as well as the cost of each. In fact, it will pay any one to communicate with him before building a suburban residence. The book in question is practically a standard work, and a sort of encyclopedia of new residences, as it embraces every possible arrangement of rooms. Mr. Villere is himself a native of New Orleans, his family being the oldest in that city and one of his ancestors, General Villere, having rendered conspicuous service in the war of 1814.

17

McDONOUGH & WALKER.

The above firm established their business in 1889. Both are young men, and are thoroughly practical and conversant with all the details of the printing business in its every department, and by their energy and enterprise have built up a large and flourishing trade. The establishment is located at 236 South Water street and is well equipped with everything requisite for doing all kinds of printing, and besides new fonts of type and all the necessary appliances there are several printing presses, while skilled workmen are regularly employed in the different departments. All kinds of book and job printing is done, while a specialty is made of illustrated catalogues and grocers' billheads. Messrs. McDonough and Walker are very popular, have many influential friends, and enjoy a very liberal patronage. Business continues to grow and increase, and about the establishment there is always a scene of busy activity.

S. S. BORDEN.

A representative commission house in this city is the one owned by the above-named gentleman, at 228 South Water street. It was originally established by Foster & Borden November, 1879 In January, 1891, Mr. S. S. Borden succeeded to the business, and the house has since its establishment won the highest rating in mercantile circles. Mr. Borden solicits consignments of country produce, especially of butter, eggs and poultry, foreign and domestic fruits, while ample facilities are at hand for receiving and shipping the products dealt in, eight able clerks and three delivery wagons being constantly employed. Mr. Borden, being well informed as to the needs of the public, has won his success and prosperity through his commendable efforts to supply the wholesale trade with the most satisfactory goods. He is a gentleman of middle age, a native of New York, and a prominent member of the Produce Exchange.

JEROME PLANKINTON.

Among the surveyors in this city it is very safe to say that none have become more prominent or achieved greater distinction in the profession than Mr. Jerome Plankinton, who occupies a suite of offices, 23 and 24, in the building, 88 La Salle street. Mr. Plankinton is a gentleman in the prime of life, and was born, brought up and educated in Philadelphia. He has had a valuable experience in his profession, and during the twenty-two years he has been in the city has done considerable work as a city and county surveyor, and in every instance the best satisfaction has been expressed. While he gives his attention to surveying in the country, he makes a specialty of city lots and suburban tracts, and of the laying out of building lots in the subdivisions. In his business Mr. Plankinton displays remarkable energy and ability, and his services are always in demand. He has a large circle of acquaintances in the city, and is held in high esteem as a useful business man and citizen, and is liked by all who come in contact with him in any way.

B. CURTIS & CO.

There are no more prominent and reliable business houses in the city of Chicago than the enterprising commission house of Messrs. B. Curtis & Co. of Room 8, No. 226 La Salle street. This firm although comparatively young is doing an immense business, which is constantly increasing. They do a general commission business, making a specialty of grain and provisions, and are members of the Chicago Board of Trade, employing two assistants in their regular business. The firm is composed of Mr. B. Curtis and Mr. W. D. Goverus, both of whom are live, energetic young men who pay strict and close attention to all business entrusted to them and have splendid reputations in all commercial and financial circles. Their offices are handsomely fitted and arranged for the convenience of their rapidly increasing business.

FRED SEEGER & CO.

The lovers of a good cigar in Chicago are particularly fond of the brands manufactured by Mr. Fred Seeger & Co., whose establishment is located at 79 N. Clark street. This business was established twelve years ago by the Laubenheimer Bros., who sold their interest to Mr. Fred Seeger, now the sole proprietor, some years ago. Mr. Seeger is a progressive and popular business man. He does not wait for something to turn up, but is always on the alert, and accomplishes results that speak well for his future. He has a large retail store and employs twenty-three skilled cigarmakers in his factory. The store is large and elegantly fitted up, and is stocked with a superior line of cigars, tobacco, pipes, cigarettes, smokers' supplies, etc. The factory, in the rear, is large and commodious; every arrangement for convenience is made; and the celebrated brands of cigars made by Mr. Seeger are manufactured from carefully selected tobacco. His ten cent brands are as follows: "Reconstruction," "Flor De Nelson," "Principes," "La Corona" and "Hilda." The five cent brands are, "Sensation," "Louisa" and "Henry Clay". Mr. Seeger makes a specialty of the wholesale box trade, in which he has a large custom. This gentleman is a native of Milwaukee, Wis.; he has resided in Chicago a number of years and is held in high esteem, both socially and among business men.

MINER & LOWE.

There is no more popular hay, grain and feed house on the North side than that of Messrs. Miner & Lowe, whose establishment is located at the corner of Clybourn and Webster avenues. The business of this house was established twelve years ago by Chas. Grevenor, and was later changed to Grevenor and Icefield, then to E. B. Chapman & Co., who were succeeded in 1891 by the present firm. The premises occupied are 25x60 feet in dimensions and are admirably adapted to the business; they are fitted with every appliance for convenience and utility. All kinds of hay, grain, feed and flour are handled, both wholesale and retail, and a general commission business is also done. The stock carried is very complete, the oats, corn, shorts, etc., being the finest obtainable; while the shipments on consignment are very large. The business done is extensive, the house having many patrons, both among producers and consumers. The proprietors of this establishment are young men of pronounced business ability, and have made a reputation of a high order for themselves as business men and merchants. Mr. R. L. Miner was born at Arlington Heights, Ill., and Mr. E. E. Lowe at Kankakee, this state; both are well-known and highly respected in leading business and social circles.

R. P. BRAUN.

The vocation of the pharmacist is unquestionably a highly important one in any and every community, for upon his care and skill, almost as much as upon that displayed by the medical profession, oftentimes depends the physical welfare, nay, the life or death of the sick and ailing. Among the favorably known druggists in this section of the Western metropolis may be mentioned the name of Mr. R. P. Braun, whose elegant and attractive store is located at the Southwest corner of Wentworth avenue and Thirty-first street. He established this pharmacy in 1881, and has since been deservedly accorded the recognition of the medical profession and the liberal patronage of the general public. The store is spacious and commodious, and is made attractive by its unique imitation marble floor, neat show cases and ornamental counters, and, in fact, is fitted up with every convenience, especially as regards its prescription department. The stock of drugs includes everything usually needed in the trade, consisting of pharmaceutical preparations, patent medicines, physicians' supplies, and fine perfumery and such fancy articles as are usually found in a first-class pharmacy. Mr. Braun is an expert, conscientious, thorough pharmacist, who thoroughly understands the business, and, being duly qualified and registered, he may be relied on for the exact, scientific compounding of physicians' prescriptions and family recipes, while his charges are moderate. Mr. Braun was born in Illinois, has been a lifelong resident of Chicago, and is regarded as an honorable member of the useful fraternity to which he belongs.

LARSON BROS.

A novel and most useful industry is the manufacture of rugs, by a weaving process, using new or old material from carpets at the discretion of the buyer. Larson Brothers, at No. 283 Wells street, are the sole manufacturers of the celebrated Universal rugs and mats and have a very extensive establishment at the above number, occupying three rooms, each 20x30 feet in size, on the ground floor. They have in constant operation five weaving machines, and employ eight experienced hands to care for their large and increasing trade. They make a specialty of manufacturing rugs to order in any desired width from one-half a yard up to four yards and in any desired length. The firm is composed of Mr. E. C. Larson and Mr. C. M. Larson, the latter being the manager and a practical workman of many years' experience. Born in Chicago, they possess all that energy which makes their business such a popular success.

GUNDERSON BROS.

An enterprising and energetic firm, in the line of hay, grain, coal, coke and wood, is that of Gunderson Bros., of Nos. 554 and 556 W. Lake street. This firm was established three years ago by the present proprietors, E. S. & G. C. Gunderson, at the corner of Erie and Ashland avenue, but their trade increased to such an extent that they were compelled to move to their present commodious quarters, about two years ago. They carry a large stock of everything in their line, and do a wholesale and retail business. Their yards are 50x150 feet in size, and are well covered with coal, wood and hay sheds. They employ three yard men, and have three teams for the prompt delivery of orders. Their office, 20x15 feet in size, is conveniently fitted, and arranged for the management of their immense trade. Both of the Messrs. Gunderson are young men, born in Chicago and possessed of all the enterprise characteristic of the city. They are honest, industrious and entitled to their liberal patronage.

E. E. JOHNSON.

Among those of our carpenters and builders who are well acquainted with Western methods,—a very necessary knowledge in this industry,—Mr. E. E. Johnson occupies a very prominent place, his experience dating back to 1863. It was not, however, until 1876 that he began his present business, on the corner of May and Randolph streets, and which succeeded so well that he purchased the spacious premises, 311 W. Lake street, where he is now located, and transferred his plant in 1887. These in turn grew too small for the prosecution of his rapidly expanding trade, and he has been compelled to erect an addition this season, to accommodate new plant and more employes. Mr. Johnson builds residences on contract, manufactures doors and window screens to order, takes contracts and furnishes estimates for repairs of all kinds, shingles houses, barns, etc., and performs the work of a general jobber in the carpentering and house building line with promptness and accuracy. He employs a dozen skilled workmen and personally supervises every detail of the business with the eye of an experienced and practical tradesman. He is a native of New York city, and when but eighteen years of age removed West to Joliet, Ill., where he was engaged in the same avocation for some years, prior to coming to this city. Mr. Johnson is a middle aged gentleman, with that pleasing presence that denotes the successful business man, and is a thoroughly accomplished builder, who is held in the warmest respect for his sturdy integrity and goodness of heart, as well as for his ability and mechanical acquirements.

T. W. & C. B. SHERIDAN.

Printing of all kinds continues to increase beyond all comparison with the progress in other industries, and in its particular line is one of the greatest industries of the age. Necessarily the supplies for the different branches of the art form an important part, and none more so than the supplies for book binderies. One of the oldest firms in this line in the country is that of T. W. & C. B. Sheridan, established

in 1835 as manufacturers of paper cutters' and book binders' machinery, making a specialty of binders' wire. Although the headquarters of the firm are in the East, they long since appreciated the fact that Chicago was the great central metropolis of the West, and established a branch agency at No. 413 Dearborn street. The line of goods manufactured and carried by this concern are absolutely standard and of the best made. They include everything in the line of book binders' machinery and supplies, and the firm can quote prices favorable to any one desiring anything in their line that will call upon them or address them.

THOMAS BLAKE.

There is nothing which add so much to the metropolitan character of a city as her well stocked, thoroughly appointed and ably managed livery stables. In such connection we make due reference to the livery and undertaking establishment of Mr. Thomas Blake, located at 229 W. North avenue, and which is one of the most popular and well patronized in this section of the city. This house has been in existence six years and Mr. Blake is a practical, experienced gentleman in this important line of business, and can furnish the latest and most artistic designs in caskets and funeral furniture of every description. He is at all times prepared to take charge of funerals, from the moment of death until interment, and no house is better prepared to conduct funerals in an efficient manner and at such low prices. The offices are connected by telephone No. 4774 and all orders are promptly attended to day or night. The stable is nearly new and well arranged, in which accomodation is afforded for some thirty or forty horses, and here are some of the most stylish equipages for rent and hire, for business or pleasure. Horses are boarded by the day, week or month. Mr. Blake is a young man, born and raised in the city and a straightforward reliable business man and a highly popular citizen.

A. A. CAMPBELL.

A good reliable practical plumber is one of the most useful business men that a great center can possess, as on the faithful execution of every detail of his work depends the sanitary condition of many of its buildings. Mr. A. A. Campbell, whose fine premises are well located at No. 842 W. Madison street, is one of these experienced and skillful tradesmen, whose past successes and whose present reputation equally attest the superiority of his work. The business

was begun six years ago by Messrs. Campbell & Co., the style being changed to Messrs. Jacobs & Campbell in 1886, and in August, 1888, the proprietorship devolved solely upon the present head of the establishment. He is of Scotch descent, but born in the United States, and has an intimate knowledge of the requirements of the best class of the western trade. He employs a staff, which averages twenty in number, all carefully selected for their superiority in the branches of the industry for which they are engaged, and over every process of the work Mr. Campbell keeps a watchful eye, thereby insuring the accurate and faithful completion of every contract. He carries a large stock of the finest gas fixtures and sanitary plumbing materials, including every article in various styles that can be required in the comprehensive business. Mr. Campbell pays particular attention to ventilating, and has a great advantage over his confreres in thoroughly understanding the laws which govern this scientific branch, his advice being considered of the highest value in the solution of vexed problems arising where a supply of pure air has to be obtained under the most difficult conditions. Mr. Campbell has secured and retained the warm esteem of a large circle in all classes of society. Mr. Campbell has filled contracts for plumbing some of the largest buildings in the city, among them are 100 buildings on Hickey avenue, for H. C. Van Schaack & Co., forty-eight buildings corner Kedzie avenue and Central Park boulevard for Anderson Bros., and an apartment building of forty-three flats at the corner of Cottage Grove and Bowen avenues.

J. TRIGGS & CO.

The oyster and fish market of J. Triggs & Co., occupies the entire ground floor and basement, 30x70, of the two-story brick building at No. 102 W. Adams street. The market is fitted up with marble-topped counters of oak finish. Everything is kept scrupulously neat and clean and the establishment presents a most attractive appearance. Oysters of all kinds are kept on hand in season, and the largest variety of fish and shell fish can be found there at all times. Game of every description is also kept on hand in season. This market has the reputation of keeping the best and freshest on hand at all times, as well as the largest variety, and prices are as low as can be found in the city. Mr. John Triggs, the sole proprietor, was born in England, but has resided in Chicago for the last twenty-five years. He opened the market early in 1867, and has gained an excellent patronage of the best class. Eleven assistants are constantly employed and four teams. The promptest and most courteous attention is paid to customers. A branch establishment is also run at No. 785 S. Halsted street, and those living in that vicinity will find it fully equal in every respect to the main market.

S. M. RANDOLPH.

Chicago, with its many elegant public and private structures, whose towering tops rise skyward, is the home of some of the best architects that live to-day; and of all of these none take precedence over that veteran, Mr. S. M. Randolph, who nearly forty years ago united his destinies with that of the great metropolis of the West. Mr. Randolph has too wide a reputation to need mention in this article, suffice it to say, he has superior facilities for furnishing designs plans and specifications for every description of work. His office at room 38 in the Marine building, corner of Lake and La Salle streets, are handsomely furnished and equipped with all conveniences for his staff of draughtsmen and assistants. Mr. Randolph enjoys a very liberal patronage, not only in Chicago, but in all parts of the West. He designed many of the leading buildings in the city and enjoys the confidence of the builders and public at large. Mr. Randolph is a native of New Jersey, but has been a resident of Chicago, with slight intermission. since 1854. He served with gallantry in the Board of Trade battery during the war, and is popular, both in commercial and social circles.

EMIL LAITSCH.

The business of the undertaker has during past twenty years received such advancements in its methods that from a trade it has become a profession, exacting from those who would be successful in its practice qualifications and acquirements little dreamed of before. Among the numerous exponents of this science in Chicago none take precedence over Mr. Emil Laitsch, undertaker and embalmer at No. 171 North avenue, near Halsted street. A quarter of a century ago the present proprietor's father established this enterprise, and, keeping abreast of the times, did a very large business. He handed it over to his son in May of 1889, changing the firm name from George to Emil Laitsch. At his quarters Mr. Laitsch carries a complete line of coffins, caskets, burial cases, shrouds, grave clothes, etc., and furnishes carriages and everything in connection with a funeral. He is a practical embalmer, a graduate of the Industrial Embalming school of the class of 1883, and is also a member of the Illinois and the Chicago Undertakers' Association, also of the Chicago Mutual Aid and Benefit Society. Mr. Laitsch is a native of Chicago, well and favorably known, and possessed of that tact and discretion so essential in a funeral director. He has a large business, which is increasing, and no one envies him the success his efforts have earned.

W. P. ALLRICH.

This excellently conducted business house first opened its doors to the public under the management of Mr. Allrich some three years ago, and constitutes to-day the best establishment of the kind in this section of the city. The finely equipped store occupied, at No. 446 West Harrison street has an area of 25x125 feet, provided with a large refrigerator for the preservation of meats and is fitted up in the most approved style with every convenience and appliance. He deals in all kinds of fresh, salt and smoked meats, beef, veal, mutton, lamb, pork, hams, bacon, lard, sausage, fish, oysters, poultry, etc., and is enabled to guarantee that all meat products purchased over his counters are in every instance fresh and in a wholesome condition. The stock in all departments is at all times ample to meet all demands, and Mr. Allrich is zealously engaged in maintaining the high reputation his goods have gained in the community. Several competent assistants are employed, a steady active trade is enjoyed, derived from the best classes of customers, and two delivery wagons are kept busy in filling orders. He is a young man, a native of New York state and highly regarded in mercantile circles; and under his able management his widely known and progressive establishment remains permanently prosperous and successful, and is steadily growing in volume and importance.

F. S. BROWN & CO.

One of the most successful and active firms in Chicago, engaged in the construction of bridge, masonry and foundations, is that of Messrs. F. S. Brown & Co., whose office is located in the Counselman Building, room 92. The co-partners, Messrs. F. S Brown and Frank Ericksen, first commenced business in Milwaukee, Wis., in 1887. In 1888 they removed to Chicago, where they have since built up a liberal and influential patronage, principally with railroad companies. They make a specialty of the construction of railroad bridges, masonry and heavy foundations, and also deal largely in rough and dressed stone Their quarries, which are well equipped with all modern appliances, and have an area of 40 acres, are situated at Stone City, Iowa. They employ from 60 to 100 men at their quarries, and from 50 to 100 men on their contract work. They have done a large amount of work for the following companies to the entire satisfaction of the officials, viz.: Illinois Central R. R., Chicago, Madison & Northern, Chicago & Eastern Illinois, Chicago, Milwaukee & St. Paul, Chicago & Western Indiana R. R., Belt Railway of Chicago, Calumet Terminal Railway, and other Western railroads. Estimates and plans are promptly furnished for all kinds of

masonry and railroad work at the lowest possible prices, consistent with the best material and superior workmanship. Their work is highly indorsed by eminent civil engineers and experts, and is unrivaled for strength, solidity and reliability. Their specialty is masonry constructed of "Anamosa" stone from their famous quarries at Stone City, Iowa, which has been indorsed by the U. S. Govt. engineers as unexcelled for qualities required in building stone. This stone has been in use about thirty years. F. S. Brown & Co. opened their Gold Hill Quarry in 1887. Their output has been as follows: 1887, 593 carloads; 1888, 1644 car oads; 1889, 1920 carloads; 1890, 2248 carloads. Their business is increasing from year to year and has compelled them to open a second and still more extensive quarry (Crescent Quarry), which will be in full operation in the spring of 1892. Mr. Brown was born in Bangor, Maine, while Mr. Ericksen is a native of Norway, and resides at Anamosa, Iowa, four miles from the quarries. They are honorable and energetic business men who undertake the construction of the most difficult masonry foundations, and no more reliable contractors and engineers can be found in the ranks of the profession. Mr. Brown was formerly engaged as civil engineer on the Chicago, Milwaukee & St. Paul railway, and is a popular member of the Western Society of Civil Engineers. He is also a prominent Royal Arch-mason and Knight Templar and is connected with other philanthropic societies in the city.

A. HENSEL.

Prominent among the houses on the North side, successfully engaged in the wallpaper and painting business, is W. A. Hensel's, 135 Clybourn avenue, with residence at 1651 Melrose street (Lake View). His store has long been a popular center for purchase of wall paper among the residents of this district. It is now twelve years since he established himself on this street, and he has occupied the present site for six years. The premises are centrally located and comprise the ground floor and basement, 25x60 feet in dimensions, of a three-story brick building. The place is neatly fitted up with every possible convenience for the successful carrying on of the business, and the stock is large and comprehensive, showing excellent judgment in its selection. It comprises the latest patterns and styles of imported and domestic wall papers, also paints, oils, glass, putty, colors, artists' materials and everything that is usually to be found in a first-class store of this kind. He is a middle-aged gentleman and a native of Germany, having been in Chicago twenty years, and now enjoys the reputation of being one of the most straightforward men in his line of business.

HENRY CORRELL.

A shoe store on the West side that has attracted much notice of late is that of Mr. Henry Correll, of 379 W. Indiana street, and too much cannot be said in favor of the very estimable and straightforward manner in which Mr. Correll has conducted his business during the five years since he has been established. He gives an honest value for a moderate price and will not sell anything that he cannot absolutely guarantee. His store contains everything from fine to medium grades of footwear, and is so complete and comfortable in its appointments that it is a pleasure to have any dealings there Men's, women's, misses' and children's boots and shoes are here to be found in all sizes, as well as slippers and rubbers, from the daintiest satin ball slipper to the more substantial article, which contributes so much to man's domestic comfort. Mr. Correll lays himself out especially for custom work, and has always given satisfaction, as he employs only the most skilled help and uses only the very best materials. In every case he acts on the principle that he wants to see a customer a second time, and so his conscience always travels side by side with his business. He is a native of Ireland and lived some years in Toronto, and since his residence in Chicago has made many valued friends in the community.

J. CHILDS.

There is no line of trade so important to the public generally as is that which provides us with what we eat, and the most important of these is the one that supplies us with meat. It is a gratifying fact to say that Chicago is favored with one of the finest markets in the land. We refer to that of Mr. J. Child of Nos. 25 and 27 Rush street. This market was established in 1868 by William Hoalch, and the present proprietor purchased it twelve years ago, since which time it has been the foremost market in that part of the city. It occupies handsome plate glass fronted store 40x90 feet in dimensions, and is elegantly fitted with handsome marble topped counters, costing alone $4,300. Two ten-ton refrigerators are in the rear, and a handsome fountain is in front to preserve the freshness of the vegetables. Mr. Childs keeps constantly on hand a large and well-selected stock of fresh and smoked meats, fish, poultry and game; also a choice line of green vegetables, and the very best line of canned goods in the market. To accommodate his immense trade, Mr. Childs employs eight assistants and four teams, all being kept constantly engaged in supplying the trade. He is a native of England, and a citizen of the United States, having been in Chicago for the past twenty years, where he has made a host of business and social friends, who rejoice in his prosperity. A visit to Mr. Child's meat market will be a revelation to patrons of smaller concerns.

HENRY J. BATE.

Mr. Henry J. Bate can boast of an experience as a Pharmacist of which many might be proud, for he has been thirteen years in the employ of Gale & Blocki, the well-known Chicago druggists, and was mostly engaged as head clerk at their main store and afterwards was chief clerk at their Palmer House store for four years. His present store, at 126 N. Clark street, corner of Ohio street, was one of Gale & Blocki's branch stores, and had been for ten years until he purchased it in 1889. The store is 25x75 feet in dimensions, and is handsomely finished with dark wood fixtures, tiled floor and a massive and costly soda fountain. He carries a very full line of drugs, toilet articles, etc., and also every proprietary medicine of any importance. He also makes a specialty of compounding physicians' prescriptions, which he does with accuracy and dispatch, and in reordering a prescription it is only necessary to telephone the number of it, his telephone call being 3045. Mr. Bate carries a very full line of imported and domestic cigars and is also agent for the celebrated White Rock Waukesha Water. He is a native of Ontario, Canada, and has been in Chicago for twenty-one years. He graduated from the Illinois College of Pharmacy, and is a member of the Illinois State Board of Pharmacy, and few men in the city in his profession are more deservedly popular than he is.

JACOB PICKEL & BRO.

The development of Chicago has been so rapid as to be almost startling. The buildings are as handsome and as substantial as those of cities centuries in building, and all this has been done in less than a half century. The business of cutting stone for the beautiful residences and office buildings is one that is highly representative and growing steadily, and one of the most prominent and popular houses in this line is the subject of this sketch—that of Jacob Pickel & Brother, cut stone contractors, 297 and 299 W. North avenue, corner Paulina street. This yard was established about two years ago and business begun by the brothers, Jacob and William Pickel, both experienced and practical stone cutters. They selected the location for their office and yards with great care, and have fitted them up with every appliance and convenience for the business; and the business has been a success from the outstart. The yards are 75x125 feet, and have a fine office and sheds for the convenience of the workmen and business.

Twenty-five workmen are given steady employment, and much work has been done in contracting for the stone work for first-class residence and store buildings. This yard cuts all kinds of building stone to order, but the business has mostly been in handling blue Warrensburg stone. They have now several large contracts for the stone work for fine private residences. The business is growing very rapidly and reflects great credit upon these two bright young native Chicagoans, who have shown such rare business ability and far outstripped older competitors.

LAKE SHORE SAND COMPANY.

The Lake Shore Sand Company, as its name implies, was organized and incorporated four years ago for the purpose of dealing in sand, gravel and building materials of all kinds. Its capital was $30,000, and controlled by men of first-class ability and experience. The company has been successful, and done its full share in the development of the city's building interests. Its sources of supply are of the best, and each of them is so near the railroad or other means of effective transportation as to give the greatest facilities. The stone quarries are on the Chicago & Alton railway; gravel pits are on the Baltimore & Ohio, the Lake Shore & Michigan Central, the Pittsburgh, Fort Wayne & Chicago, Chicago & Eastern Illinois, the Chicago & St. Paul, Chicago & Northwestern railroad and also available to ship and boat. The company deals also in brick, handling on commission the finest qualities of faced, as well as all the grades of ordinary brick. A very fine quality of white sand handled by the Lake Shore Sand Company comes from pits on the line of the Chicago & Rock Island railway. The company deal in all kind of street paving material. They have yards in all sections of the city. They represent in themselves an important adjunct to the building trades, keeping twenty-five teams and employing about 100 men. In the winter they cut ice, selling it at wholesale to dealers exclusively. The company has a membership in the Builders' and Traders' Exchange, and is composed of men foremost in industrial enterprises and above the average in point of business ability and commercial experience. The officers of the Lake Shore Sand Company are Charles H. Stebbins, president; J. S. Putney, secretary and C. R. Fogg. treasurer. The office at room 9, 157 La Salle treet, is neatly furnished and has telephone No. 5233.

LAMPRECHT & BYRNES.

There is no part of the city that shows greater growth and improvement than the West side.' Nor is this growth alone in the extension of suburbs and additions, but there is evidenced a general air of improvement in every locality, in handsome buildings. Prominent among the best stores is that of Lamprecht & Byrnes of No. 990 W. Madison street, dealers in dry goods, notions, underwear and gents' furnishing goods. This establishment, occupying the ground floor and basement of the building, fronting twenty-five feet on Madison, and extending back 125 feet, was opened by Messrs T. H. Lamprecht and P. J. Byrnes, two years ago, and since the first day the doors were opened this enterprising firm has met with unusual success. The store is one of the most convenient in the city, heated by furnace, has the railway cash system and every facility to enable the ten salesmen to accomodate the rapidly increasing trade. Mr. Lamprecht is a native of Brooklyn, N. Y., but has resided in Chicago the past ten years and is well posted in the dry goods business, having been connected with one of the large Chicago wholesale dry goods houses for over eight years. Mr. Byrnes is a native of Cleveland, O., and has also resided in Chicago for ten years. He has been raised in the dry goods business, entering it when fourteen years old, and is at present the representative of one of the largest Eastern wholesale dry goods houses for the states of Illinois and Wisconsin. With the experience these gentlemen ave had, their courteous treatment of their customers, and the splendid class of goods they carry, it is small wonder they have been favored with so large a patronage.

BATTLE OF GETTYSBURG PANORAMA.

One of the most famous battles in the world's history is that of Gettysburg. This tremendous contest is admirably depicted and portrayed in Chicago by the magnificent Panorama of the Battle of Gettysburg located at the corner of Wabash avenue and Hubbard Court. This panorama was painted in 1883 by Paul Philopoteaux, the eminent French artist, and is a splendid triumph of perspective drawing The visitor, though aware that he is looking at a building 134 feet in diameter and ninety-six feet high, finds himself ascending

the narrow stairs in an open country, stretching many miles in every direction toward the horizon. The panorama is accurate in every detail of the landscape, and the spectator looks down upon the dreadful scenes of destruction, carnage and death of the battlefield of Gettysburg. The real snake fences and stone walls are skilfully depicted, and one can almost hear the agonizing cry of the rebel General Armistead, as he falls in the moment of temporary victory. The dead and dying strew the fatal field, and as a whole and in every particular the panorama fills the onlookers with awe and admiration. The panorama is the property of an incorporated company that originally had a capital of $180,000, which has been increased to $360,000 It has already paid dividends of $430,-000, and the business is under the careful and energetic management of Mr. A. Henrotin. The building is heated by steam, and is fitted with every convenience for the comfort of patrons, and includes electric lights, ladies' parlors, etc. Lectures are given every hour on the picture of the battle. The panorama is open daily, Sundays included, from 8 A. M. to 11 P. M., the prices being, .sadults 50 cents, and children 25 cents.

EVANS' ART GALLERY.

There are many fine photographic studio's in this city that are worthy extended notice in our pages, and prominent among these the establishment so popularly known as Evans' art gallery deserves more than passing mention at our hands. This business was founded some six years ago, and though young in comparison to many of its contemporaries, enjoys a reputation few, if any of its competitors in this section can boast of. This is due entirely to the artistic character of the work produced. Mr. Evans is a thorough artist, and some specimens of his handiwork that were shown us on the occasion of our visit were gems of photographic art. He takes all kinds of pictures, and that his prices are low is demonstrated by the following excerpt from his business card, viz.; "twelve cabinets and one panel $1.50; twelve panels $2.00." All his other work is executed at a correspondingly low rate, and for fine photographs at reasonable prices, we unhesitatingly commend all needing such to go to Evans' at No. 188 S. Halsted street. The attractive studio occupies the second floor of the building at the address indicated, and

is supplied with every necessary appurtenance pertaining to the production of artistic photography. Mr. Evans executes portraits in oil, pastel, crayon, India ink, and water colors, and gives particular attention to copying and enlarging old pictures. He is a Canadian by birth, a resident of Chicago for the past nine years, and an authority on all matters pertaining to photography in all its branches. Mr. Evans is a prominent member of the order of F. and A. M.

O. F. HARMS.

There is no branch of industry in which such rapid progress and improvement have been made in recent years as in the production of artistic household furniture and one of the oldest established houses on the North side that keeps pace with the times is that of Mr. O. F. Harms, 105 Clybourn avenue and at 262 Larrabee street. This business was established eighteen years ago by Mr. Harms on the same street, and he has occupied his present store for ten years. He built and owns the premises, which consist of a handsome three-story and basement brick building, 33x140 feet He occupies the ground floor and basement for his store, and here may be found at all times a most comprehensive stock of parlor, library, dining room, bedroom, hall and kitchen furniture, carpets, mirrors, bedding, upholstery goods, etc.; carpets, oilcloth, etc. The prices charged by the firm are all exceedingly low, and he sells either for cash or on the installment plan, which latter method permits those of moderate circumstances to obtain what they want for housekeeping both safely and easily. Mr. Harms is a native of Germany and has been in Chicago twenty-three years. He is esteemed on all sides for his enterprise and just methods, and is a popular member of the Knights of Pythias, the Red Men, the Turner's Society and the Knights and Ladies of Honor. He is a gentleman of middle age, and respected by all who know him either socially or in a business way.

S. KLEIN.

One of the finest stocks of dry goods in the western part of the city is to be found in the splendid store of Mr. Simon Klein, at Nos. 379, 381 and 383 Blue Island avenue, near Fourteenth street. It is an old stand, in fact, the oldest dry goods establishment on the street, Mr. Klein having begun the business in the year 1873, and is a place of resort for all who require first-class goods at fair and reasonable prices. The store is spacious, having a depth of forty-two feet, and its interior arrangements are of the most perfect description, everything being displayed in the most advantageous manner, and so conveniently distributed that the customer has no difficulty whatever in obtaining exactly what he wants. Dry goods form the bulk of the large and varied stock, and in this great branch will be found all the newest shades and patterns, showing a wise discrimination in their choice, the knowledge of which goes far to make this one of the most popular houses in the city. The carpet department in the rear is full of the productions of the best looms in the world, offering a choice, both as to quality, pattern and price that it would be extremely difficult to duplicate elsewhere. Mr. Klein also carries a full line of shoes and boys' clothing of the most fashionable kinds, from the most reputed makers and at reasonable prices considering the quality. Those who have not visited this first-class store would do well to call at the first opportunity. They will find every one of the thirty-five assistants most attentive and polite, and may rely on the statements made by them as exactly describing the goods they sell. Mr. Klein has been a resident of Chicago for twenty-five years, and is honored and respected on every hand.

M. N. SMITH.

Few establishments attract so much attention at the hands of the general public as a handsomely kept, well stocked and brilliant jewelry store. None deserve this title more than the prosperous house of Mr. M. N. Smith, dealer in watches and jewelry, at No. 147 N. Clark street. Mr. Smith is considered one of the finest and best practical jewelers and watch-makers in the city, where he has resided for the past seven years, and a year ago he started in business for himself at the above location. He carries an elegant and well selected stock of watches, clocks, jewelry, precious stones, chains, charms, vases, silverware and other novelties found in first-class jewelry houses. He makes a specialty of gold and silver watches, which he sells upon the payment of $1 per week. He also makes a specialty of fine repairing of all kinds, and has two able assistants to enable him to handle his rapidly increasing trade. His store is elegantly furnished, and fitted with all the conveniences and luxuries of a modern first-class jewelry palace, where dazzling gems and highly polished jewels make a rich and handsome display. The store is kept open until 9:30 o'clock every evening. Mr. Smith was born in Denmark and has been a resident of Chicago for seven years. He is industrious, honest, reliable and energetic and merits the splendid trade he is having.

WEST, ANDRESS & CO.

The populous and fertile section of which this city is the natural center gives her great importance as a point of distribution for grain and country produce, while the commission merchant is the recognized medium through which such goods are placed on the market. A prominent and popular house thus engaged is that of Messrs. West, Andress & Co., whose business offices are centrally and eligibly located in the Royal Insurance building, No. 169 Jackson street. The firm are extensive commission merchants in grain, seeds, hay, produce and provisions, transacting business through the medium of the Board of Trade. They are thoroughly posted in all the needs and requirements of the commission interest, and among the most active and efficient trade representatives in Chicago. The business was established by Messrs. John West and M. S. Andress in 1872, ten years later Mr. H. Higgins being admitted to an interest, when the present firm style was adopted. They are esteemed members of the Board of Trade, active and influential in promoting every movement calculated to advance the well-being of that organization, and always exercise that policy of integrity and enterprise, fairness in dealing and promptitude in closing transactions that render the firm so deservedly popular in leading business circles.

ALEX. H. GUNN.

The rapid development of the real estate market of Chicago, and the rapidly enhancing values of choice property, render the financial interests involved of paramount importance. Some of our most prominent business men are actively engaged as real estate agents and operators, prominent among whom is Mr. Alex. H. Gunn, whose office is in the Newberry Warehouse and Storage Company's building at 79 Kinzie street. Mr. Gunn began business in 1865 and continued therein until 1876, when he engaged in various other lines. In 1880 he was elected assistant secretary of the Board of Trade, which office he filled until 1885. He then resumed his former business, in which he is still actively engaged, being also secretary of the Newberry Warehouse and Storage Company, and having in his charge the property divided among the heirs of the Newberry estate. He transacts all business connected with real estate, such as collecting rents, paying taxes, superintending repairs and taking general charge of the property of non-residents and others. He also buys and sells on commission and negotiates loans on first mortgages. His insurance facilities, too, are considerable, as he is in touch with many of the leading companies, and can place risks of all kinds at the most

favorable rates. Mr. Gunn is a native of New York, but has resided in this city twenty-nine years, and is one of the oldest established real estate men in Chicago. His long experience in the business, coupled with his intimate knowledge of values present and prospective, enables him to offer superior facilities to investors, as well as to those having property for sale. Mr. Gunn is well and favorably known in financial circles and enjoys the confidence and esteem of all having dealings with him.

C. N. P. NIELSEN.

The citizens of the West side can be safely relied on to know what constitutes a good cigar, and they can always get just what suits them at the store of Mr. C. N. P. Nielsen, manufacturer of fine cigars, and dealer in tobacco and stationery, at 335 West Indiana street. Mr. Nielsen established himself in business as a cigar manufacturer at 190 N. Carpenter street in 1883 and moved to his present store three years ago. His store is 20x40 feet in dimensions and is well stocked with a full line of domestic and imported cigars, also tobaccos, pipes, smokers' articles and stationery, etc. Among his own make of cigars the favorite brands are "La Mata" and "Imperial" for 10 cent cigars and "Our Special" for a 5 cent cigar. These he sells largely at retail and also jobs a great number of them, his manufacturing capacity being 2,500 cigars per week. His jobbing trade is for the most part local, but he always has a good stock on hand and can usually fill outside orders promptly and without delay. Mr. Nielsen is a native of Denmark and has been in Chicago for twenty-one years. He is a member of the Knights of Pythias, the Free Masons, the Ancient Order of United Workmen and the Independent Order of Foresters.

BONESTEEL & CO.

The firm of Bonesteel & Co., though only established a year at 9153 Commercial avenue, has come to stay. They deal in all kinds of men's, women's, misses' and children's boots and shoes, and always manage to secure the choicest makes and styles. The store is in charge of Mr. Ernst Grubel, who assumes the complete management. It is in the Winnipeg block, and is about 50x25 feet in dimensions. It is well stocked and presents an exceedingly neat appearance. Mr. Grubel is a thoroughly practical man and has been brought up in the business. Since he came here he has formed a large German connection and built up quite a nice trade. He himself was born in Germany, and belongs to the order of the Knights of Pythias here. Three hands are employed and special attention is given to repairing, which is done at the back of the store. In low-priced shoes Messrs. Bonesteel & Co., supply an article of extra value and well adapted for use in the mills, and will last equally as long for that purpose as those costing double the money. The firm is thoroughly conscientious and will at all times exchange any articles that are not what they represent them to be.

WAMSUTTA SHIRT CO.

One of the most promising and rising institutions of the city is that of the Wamsutta Shirt Company, at No. 151 Washington street, which carries a complete and elegant line of men's furnishings at popular prices, and makes a specialty of manufacturing shirts to order of all sizes and styles. The firm is composed of Mr. W. H. Myer and Mr. F. J. Rossbach. It was established in May of 1891 and has since done a large and constantly increasing business. Mr. Myer is a native of Jeffersonville, Ind., and has resided in Chicago some time. He is a prominent member of the Masonic Fraternity, also of the Knights of Pythias. Mr. Rossbach is a native of Indianapolis and has been in Chicago for ten years. He is a member of the Royal Arcanum. Both young men are popular and have hosts of friends.

CHICAGO OF TODAY THE METROPOLIS OF THE WEST.

KLEIN & SAWYER.

A well-ordered, perfectly equipped pharmacy is a *sine qua non* in any and every community, and in such connection we desire to direct attention to the ably conducted establishment of Messrs. Klein & Sawyer, located at No. 322 W. Madison street, which is in all respects one of the finest and best in this vicinity. It is an old established concern, indeed the oldest west of Halsted street, having been devoted to the purposes of the pharmacy since 1860. Its founders, as far as our reporter could learn, were Messrs. Clacius & Co., to whom succeeded Messrs. Vaughn & Sawyer, who were the immediate predecessors of the present proprietors. The premises present an ample area, and in all appointments are simply perfect and complete. They are elegantly fitted up with plate glass show windows and show cases, ornamental counters and shelving, and a splendid soda fountain of unique design, and contain all the necessary conveniences for preparing and dispensing medicines. The patronage is large and fully commensurate with the character and high reputation of the establishment for pure, fresh drugs, chemicals, proprietary remedies of standard reputation, toilet articles, druggists' sundries, also imported and domestic cigars. All orders by mail, telegraph, telephone (call No. 4521) or in person, are promptly attended to, and no effort on the part of the proprietors is spared to please and satisfy their numerous patrons, both of the medical profession and the public at large.

CHAS. T. MESSINGER.

The lumber interests of Chicago are second to none in the world, being the metropolis of the West and North and with the very best distributing facilities, cannot help but grow in extent yearly. One of the leading houses of the city, and whose reputation is national in this line, is that of Mr. Charles T. Messinger, manufacturer of, and dealer in hardwood lumber, whose yards are at Blackhawk street and Hawthorne avenue, and at the foot of "D" street. Mr. Messinger has been in the lumber and manufacturing business for the past thirty-six years, and runs mills at Marrianna, Ark., and in Lee Cross and St. Francis counties. He was formerly in the same business in Logansport, Ind., where he was one of that city's foremost citizens. In 1876 he removed his lumber business to Chicago, still retaining his mills at the above places. In 1879 the business style was changed to Messinger & Granger, and afterward to Messinger, Hubbard, Granger & Gray, and in 1889 to Messinger Hardwood Lumber Company, and the past year back to the present name. His yards at Hawthorne avenue and Blackhawk street are 400 by 225 feet in area, with 400 feet of railway tracks from the Milwaukee & St. Paul railroad. The yards at the foot of "B" street, have 350 feet of dock frontage, and are 225 feet deep, the two yards having an area of 750 by 250 feet, employing from thirty to fifty men, and four heavy teams to do the business of the firm. Mr. Messinger makes a specialty of walnut, ash, oak, beech, birch, cypress, maple, cherry and elm lumber, and handles 7,000,000 feet of lumber annually, and unloads over 700 cars during the season. Mr. Messinger is a native of New Jersey, and has been nearly forty years in the West. He was at first located at Logansport, Ind., and from there came to Chicago, where he has had an opportunity of more extensive operations, and facilities for handling lumber than he could possibly have in a less favorably located city. Mr. Messinger is an energetic and live business man, well known in commercial and financial circles, and has an immense and constantly increasing business.

R. JUNGKAUS & SON.

The firm, R. Jungkaus & Son, located at 920 Twenty-first street, is composed of R. Jungkaus and Henry Jungkaus. They carry a general dry goods store, having in addition special departments. The copartnership was formed in 1885. Prior to that time Mr. R. Jungkaus, the senior member of the firm, was connected with one of the largest lumber concerns in the country, with which business he had been identified for twenty-five years. Mr. Henry Jungkaus is the active partner

and manager of the present establishment, while his father is more particularly the financier and capitalist. Their commodious and handsomely decorated store occupies the ground floor and basement of a two-story brick building and covers an area of 1,500 square feet, having a frontage of twenty-five feet on Twenty-first street. It might be very appropriately called a palace of trade, for the store contains every imaginable article which chronic shoppers could expect to find. Their stock of trimmed and untrimmed bonnets and hats is very large and contains all the latest European styles. This department is in charge of an experienced milliner. Suede, dressed and undressed kid, silk and mousquetaire gloves are found in great variety here. Messrs. Jungkaus import them directly from Paris and retail them at the same prices as they are offered for sale at the world renowned Bon Marché. They have connections with modistes and tailors in all the European markets, and are apprised of new innovations as quickly as the steamboats can travel. They command a very large trade and are certainly entitled to the credit of making heavy inroads upon the vantage ground of their rivals. Both gentlemen and their five assistants are courteous, obliging and affable. Their goods are all one price and strictly as represented.

CHAS. HAUSSNER.

An old established and popular real estate business is that of Mr. Chas. Haussner, who has been in the business, and occupied the premises at 409 Clybourn avenue, for the past twenty-two years. He is one of the best known and most highly respected real estate men on the North side. He is thoroughly familiar with the property of the district and is well posted on values, being called upon for appraisements almost daily. He has two offices, 20x25 feet in dimensions, neatly fitted up and furnished with every convenience. He does a general real estate business, buys and sells on commission, negotiates loans, pays taxes and acts as agent for non-residents, collects rents, appraises values, and places insurance risks, being agent for several first-class companies, notably the North British Mercantile, and Germania of New York; also the Fireman's Fund of California, and the London Assurance Corporation. Mr. Haussner is also the agent for the Hamburg-American Packet line and sells many passage tickets, to and from Europe, annually. The business of Mr. Haussner is one of the best on the North side and he has a numerous clientage and does a thriving business. He is a gentleman of strict integrity and responsibility; he has numerous friends and is held in high esteem in business and social circles in which he is prominent. He is a native of Saxony and came to Chicago in 1855. The telephone call is 3799.

JOHN VASUMPAUR.

A very encouraging fact, noticeable in Chicago, is that when any young man starts in business with a knowledge of what he intends to pursue, and follows out his ideas with energy and industry, he is sure to succeed. Especially is this true of one who knows a trade and connects it with his business. This has been the history of Mr. John Vasumpaur of No. 728 W. Eighteenth street, who, three years ago, opened at the above number a hardware and stove store, including tools, lamps, cutlery, woodenware, tinware, and general house furnishing goods. He also is a manufacturer of tin, copper and sheet iron ware, making any and everything these useful metals are capable of being turned into. Mr. Vasumpaur understands his business thoroughly, and has prospered beyond his most sanguine expectations, until now in his store alone he finds constant employment for four competent mechanics, who do the work under his own personal supervision, including all sorts of repairing. His store and shop occupy the three floors of a brick building, 20x60 feet, and is among the neatest fitted and best equipped in the city, where he has all the latest improved appliances for the facility of his work. All orders for work of any kind entrusted to him are carefully attended to, and promptly executed.

WASHINGTON WIRE WORKS.

The use of wire has of late years been introduced into many diverse industries, and into the manufacture of many useful articles, and so great has been the demand that has arisen for these popular goods that large firms devote their energies solely to the making of wire window guards, wire work for signs, church guards, flower stands, coal screens, elevator inclosures, and goods of a similar character. One of the most prominent of these, who occupy the field most efficiently, is that denominated the Washington Wire Works, whose premises are situated at Nos. 51 and 53 N. Jefferson street, corner Lake street. These works were established at No. 106

W. Randolph street, in 1887, but soon outgrew the factory there, the concern being from its very inception, a conspicuous success. The proprietors are Messrs. F. J. Hearnshaw, and B. Nelson, both young and enterprising gentlemen, who fully merit the large connection that they have permanently secured. They employ a full staff of skilled wire workers, and turn out articles of the greatest beauty, as well as service, and are in constant demand in every part of the United States. Mr. Hearnshaw was born in England, and Mr. Nelson in Norway, but of English parents, and both have resided here for several years, becoming popular and esteemed by all classes of the community. Their telephone number is 4391. All orders by telephone are promptly attended to.

C. C. & F. COFFINBERRY.

A well-equipped establishment in this portion of the city, devoted to fine commercial printing, artistic designing, etc., is that located at No. 1461 Milwaukee avenue, and known as the branch office of C. C. & F. Coffinberry. Mr. Coffinberry, Jr., was born in St. Louis, Mo., and has been established in business with his father some years. The main offices are located in the government building on Adams street, where they have had a contract with the government for the United States railroad mail service for about twelve years. The branch establishment, which was opened in December last, is fully provided with all the requisites necessary for the business, where a general commercial job printing business is done, and they are prepared to execute all kinds of work in that line in the very best and most artistic style of workmanship known to the art. A specialty is made of society work, also of executing fine bill, letter and note heads, envelope printing, blank receipts and bills of lading, plain and ornamental business and visiting cards, ball, social and picnic invitations, programmes, etc. They are practical and experienced printers, familiar with every detail, and employ twelve first-class operatives on Adams street, and three at the Milwaukee avenue branch. In mechanical execution their printing cannot be excelled, and a very extensive supply of new type is always on hand, com-

prising all of the latest styles, while the prices are very reasonable. These gentlemen are well known in commercial circles, and although this house is comparatively a new beginner, their credit stands as high as any of the oldest houses, while their work is conceded by their patrons to be unsurpassed in excellence.

W. J. O'MALLEY.

Thanks to American prosperity which allows every one to have many of the good things of life, and few are so poor that they cannot afford meat on their table. The dealer in meat, from the wholesaler to the retailer, is consequently a person of importance, and none more so than the wholesale commission merchant, who buys direct from the breeder, and sells to the market or consigns his goods to the reliable middleman, who places the stock on the market to the best advantage. One of the most reliable houses in Chicago is that of W. J. O'Malley, which was established a quarter of a century ago by John O'Malley, Sr., and has since been one of the most prosperous concerns in the city. Latterly, the firm became that of O'Malley Brothers, and for the last few years the present proprietor son of the founder, has assumed the proprietorship. He occupies the full market space, 25 by 75 feet in Fulton market, and employs five assistants to conduct his immense and rapidly increasing trade. The market is furnished with immense cooling rooms and refrigerators, which will accommodate 100 head of cattle, and are fitted up with every convenience for the business. Mr. O'Malley is a native Chicagoan, progressive and enterprising; he buys and sells on commission all kinds of fresh meats, and commands an extensive trade in the city. His honest, square dealings have made him a host of friends, who rejoice in his prosperity and success.

CHICAGO COTTON MILL CO.

In 1869, Messrs. Grubbs & Grow established a cotton batting factory at Nos. 92 and 94 Illinois street, which passed into the experienced hands of Mr. P. Peterson in the year 1880. This gentleman inaugurated a new era of prosperity, by the erection in that year of a substantial brick mill, at Nos. 21 to 29 E. Wabansia avenue, 50x150 feet in dimensions, and perfectly adapted to the work for which it was designed. At the same time the style was changed to the Chicago Cotton Mill Company, and appliances of the most improved kind were installed, giving unsurpassed facilities for the active prosecution of the industry. A steam engine of forty horse power drives the machinery, and a full staff of experienced hands is constantly engaged in the production of the superior goods which have made these mills famous in all parts of the country. The line embraces the manufacture of all grades of wool shoddy for mattresses of all kinds, carpet linings, and stair pads, and a specialty is made of picked and prepared cotton for bedding purposes. Mr. Peterson buys the raw material in the South by the carload, and ships direct to his factory, being thereby enabled to effect a considerable saving. He is a native of Sweden, but an old resident of this city. His name occupies an honored place on the roll of the Knights of Pythias and he enjoys the respect and esteem of all with whom he is thrown into contact both, in a business and social way, and patrons can always rest assured that all representations made by him will be carried out.

D. P. REED.

The keen, intelligent public of Chicago are quick to perceive and prompt to patronize that tradesman who, by skilled experience, sound judgment and untiring industry facilitates the securing of the choicest honestly made goods at the lowest prices. To this fact is due the success which has marked the business career of Mr. D. P. Reed, dealer in household goods at No. 434 W. Madison street. This gentleman has had a wide experience in this branch of commerce, and since he established himself in the business here, some two years ago, has shown his eminent fitness to conduct the affairs of the same with profit to himself and the most complete satisfaction to the trading public. He occupies a commodious, well-arranged ground floor and basement, 20x50 feet in dimensions, and carries a splendid stock of parlor, dining room, kitchen, and chamber furniture in all the latest and most fashionable designs, carpets, rugs, beds and bedding, stoves, ranges and general house furnishings. This is one of the leading houses of its type on the West side, and is the center of a large, substantial and influential trade. Anything in the line of household goods can here be supplied, of the best material and workmanship, while the prices ruling will be found to compare favorably with those of any other house in the trade. Mr. Reed is a native of Goshen, Ind., and has been a resident of Chicago for the past five years.

JNO. J. DVORAK & CO.

Mr. John J. Dvorak has shown a public spirit which does him great credit and for which the citizens in his locality ought to be grateful, for on the 22d of October, 1886, he established a business as clothier and merchant tailor under the style of John J. Dvorak & Co., and it has since developed into one of the finest stores in this part of Chicago. It is located at 604 and 606 Blue Island avenue, where he moved to in 1887, having formerly opened at 594 on the same avenue; but his business soon outgrew his capacity and that is why he moved to his present large double store, which has a frontage of fifty feet and runs back eighty-five feet. He carries a very fine stock of ready made clothing of all kinds, and in all the latest fashions and styles. He also does a considerable business in custom work and has on hand throughout the year a very large stock of imported and domestic suitings and overcoatings, including some especially fine Scotch cheviots and tweeds. A part of his store is also devoted to gents' furnishing goods, and hats and caps. In these, as in his clothing, he buys the very latest styles and gets them from the finest New York importing and jobbing houses, always buying the best qualities. Mr. Dvorak is a native of Bohemia and has been in Chicago for twenty-six years. He is a member of several Bohemian and church societies. Such is the extent of his trade that he requires the services of no less than fifteen tailors, and in his store he also has a full force of courteous and polite salesmen. It is always a pleasure to deal with Mr. Dvorak, as no trouble is spared to satisfy the wants of customers, and while the prices are really low, the quality is always of the very best.

CAPITOL MANUFACTURING CO.

An extensive and enterprising concern is that of the Capitol Manufacturing Co., which is located at Nos 125 to 137 Rees street, near Halsted. This company was incorporated a number of years ago, with ample capital to conduct their extensive business, and has had a very prosperous career. Their special line of manufacture is automatic bolt, and pipe threading, and nut tapping machinery, wrenches, screwdrivers, handscrews, bung bushes, and other specialties to order and by pattern. Their works occupy a substantial four-story and basement brick building, 125x150 feet in size, and employ about fifty skilled mechanics in the manufacture of their goods. Their trade extends to all portions of the United States, and many European countries, and the first prize medal of the great Paris Exposition of 1889, and also at the Jamaica Exposition of 1891, was awarded to them for the novelty and excellence of their manufactures. The officers of this enterprising company are Mr. L. Schlesinger, president, and Mr. C. H. Gurney, secretary and treasurer, both gentlemen being well-known in commercial circles as enterprising, reliable and energetic gentlemen, who are pushing the interests of their company to the front in the business world.

J. H. F. RUETER.

There is no better equipped and stocked wholesale and retail grocery house on the North side than that of Mr. J. H. F. Rueter of No. 404 Clybourn avenue, who, five years ago, established his business at this stand. Mr. Rueter's store occupies the main floor, 25x60 feet, at the above number, and is at all times well stocked with A No. 1 goods in his line, consisting of foreign and domestic, staple and fancy groceries, the best brands of flour, choice creamery and dairy butter, teas, coffees, spices, canned goods and country produce of all kinds. Mr. Rueter's trade, already large, is constantly increasing, and his energetic manner of doing business, with straight, reliable treatment of his customers, is sure to succeed. He is a native of Germany, and has been in Chicago for ten years, where he has made many friends.

THOMAS CASEY.

The boot and shoe establishment of Thomas Casey occupies a storeroom, 20x40 feet, at No. 843 Root street, in Christman's block, a two story brick edifice, that is one of the handsomest in that portion of the city. The store is filled with a large and complete stock of A No. 1 goods, including boots and shoes, slippers, rubbers, and everything usually carried in a first-class establishment of this kind. The workshop is in the rear of the store, and an excellent reputation is enjoyed for custom made work. A fine business in this line is done, and repairing is also attended to in the best and promptest manner. Mr. Thomas Casey, the proprietor, is a native of Ireland, and has resided in Chicago for twenty years. He established his present business in 1889, and has met with splendid success. The street cars pass the door making the establishment easy to reach for patrons who live at a distance.

J. S. LOW.

A thriving young industry, and one that has met with a very liberal patronage on the North side, is that of Mr. J. S. Low, manufacturer of fine upholstering and mattress maker, at No. 403 N. Clark street. Mr. Low has had ten years' practical experience in the work and is, without exception, one of the most artistic upholsterers. He also pays especial attention to artistic and fine work, and the hanging of shades and draperies. His business occupies the main floor and basement at the above number, and has an elegant office and store room on the main floor, for the proper display of his work, which is all guaranteed to be first-class in every particular. Mr. Low is a native of Chicago, a young man of energy and ability, and is having an excellent trade.

A. NOREN.

A first-class and enterprising firm on the North side, and one of the greatest convenience to the community, is that of Mr. A. Noren, dealer in flour, feed, pressed hay, corn and mill feeds of all kinds at No. 292 North Wells street. Mr. Noren established his business in 1883, and has seen it increase and grow to such proportions that he now employs three assistants and two teams to take proper care of his immense trade. He is a member of the Feed Dealers' Association and was railroading in the Chicago & St. Louis Railroad before establishing his present business. He is an immensely popular young man in commercial and social circles and has established a good reputation for honesty, industry and enterprise.

LOUIS ROMAN.

A house in the gents' furnishing business that has made a good reputation among its patrons is that of Mr. Louis Roman, at 214 N. Clark street, and when we think of the discouragement which Mr. Roman encountered at the commencement of his business career, we cannot help expressing our admiration for the energy and strength of purpose which he has since displayed. He established the business twenty years ago, and was completely burned out by the big fire, and lost everything. He then started afresh on Blue Island avenue, on the West side, and later at Wells street, on the North side, and has been in his present store since 1890. It is large and commodious, being 18x75 feet in dimensions. Here he carries a full line of staple dry goods and also gents' furnishing goods, having the new styles and fashions in each as soon as they reach the American market. He makes a specialty of his dollar shirts, which are worth a dollar and a half elsewhere. College and regatta, lawn tennis and outing shirts form another specialty, and his stock of underwear cannot be exceled either in price or quality. Hosiery, gloves and neckwear also form an important part of his stock, and are here in great variety. With regard to his dry goods we can only say that his prices are about half of those charged in some of the expensive stores. Mr. Roman is a native of Germany, and has been in Chicago for thirty years, having previously been in Wisconsin. He is a gentleman in the prime of life, and an active Freemason.

H. REISS & CO.

The above named house is one of the leading and most responsible houses in this line of business in the city. The business was established in 1889 and has had a phenomenal growth from the very first. H. Reiss & Co. are well known to the trade and business men generally; they are considered in every way representative, and have a large business all over the country, employing several competent representatives who meet the trade most acceptably. They do a wholesale business only, manufacturing fine picture frames of all kinds and moldings. They also produce and collect oil paintings, steel engravings, etc , and make special sizes of frames to order. They sell direct to dealers and have a liberal and appreciative patronage. They occupy as office and manufactory the ground floor and basement of the building at No. 218 Blue Island avenue, the same being 25x110 feet in area. Here they carry a fine stock of all the latest designs in frames and mouldings, including fine effects in natural woods, enamel, gilt, bronze, plush and other fine materials. They employ from seven to ten experienced hands, and all goods are manufactured under the direct supervision of the proprietors. Mr. Reiss is a native of Germany, and has resided in Chicago a number of years. He is well known in business and financial circles and is a representative exponent of his profession

F. VISCONTI.

Of the marked improvement on the culture and general good taste of the public no more convincing proof is to be found in this quarter of the Western metropolis than by a visit to the establishment of Mr. F. Visconti the well-known dealer in antique furniture, etc., at No. 2920 Cottage Grove avenue. This enterprise was established by the present proprietor in 1888, and under his able and efficient management has enjoyed a deservedly prosperous career to date. The premises occupied comprise a commodious ground floor, suitably arranged for sales and work purposes, his workshop being fully supplied with all the necessary tools and appliances, and employment is afforded four first-class experienced workmen. While carrying in general stock a choice line of antique furniture, Mr. Visconti makes a specialty of executing all kinds of fine cabinet work to order, which is substantially and artistically completed in thoroughly seasoned, flawless woods, while none but the finest quality of goods and conscientious workmanship are permitted in his upholstered wares. Repairing, varnishing and polishing of furniture also receive prompt attention. Mr. Visconti is a

native of Italy, where he acquired a thorough knowledge of the cabinet-maker's craft, and has been a highly respected resident of Chicago for several years past.

THE CHICAGO GLOVE AND MITTEN CO.

A representative prosperous concern in its special line in this city, is that of the Chicago Glove and Mitten Co., located at No. 170 N. Halsted street. The business has been in successful operation since 1871, and was established in 1877 at W. Lake street, and in 1884 removed to Van Buren street. In 1888 the premises now occupied were secured and specially fitted up and provided with every facility and all the necessary appliances, knitting machines, etc., for conducting the business on a large scale. The building is 23x 90 feet in dimensions, and from twelve to twenty skilled hands are employed in the different departments. The goods manufactured comprise kid, dogskin and cotton and woolen mittens of fine and medium grades, and are always in active demand by the trade. Mr. C. Wiltshire, the manager, is a practical man in every department of the business, and was born in England. He has resided in Chicago since 1870, and is well and popularly known as a business man and a citizen. The selling agent for the company is Mr. J. B. Henderson, whose store is at 236 Fifth avenue.

HENRY BORNSTEIN.

Among the establishments on the West side worthy of note is the mattress and bedding factory of Mr. Henry Bornstein, located at 531 W. Twelfth street, Mr Bornstein has had many years practical experience in this special line of manufacture, and although only established in business on his own account about a year has achieved an enviable reputation, for the superior quality of his goods. He has built up a large trade, which is steadily growing in importance and volume. The premises occupied are quite commodious and have a depth of fifty feet. Every facility and convenience is at hand, and the range of production embraces the manufacture of wool, flock, hair and excelsior mattresses, also feather beds, pillows, bolsters and cushions. Mr. Bornstein manufactures for the trade and fills orders from families and pays particular attention to executing all kinds of work in his special line at the shortest notice satisfactorily. Mr. Bornstein is a native of Germany, but for the past nine years has resided in this city, where he is well and favorably known as an upright business man and a member of the A. O. U. W.

JOSEPH L. BRYAN.

At the popular establishment of Joseph L. Bryan, "the Hatter," can always be found a fine assortment of hats and caps in every style and variety, from the dignified and becoming silk hat to the natty and attractive derby, of all shades and grades, all kinds of soft and felt hats, caps in infinite variety, and a specialty is made of the Bryan hat. This business was originally founded twenty-one years ago. Mr. J. L. Bryan purchased the business in 1885. The store is at 91 Madison street, and is under the efficient management of Mr. Con. H. Tafe, a native of Ohio, who has been a resident of Chicago five years. He is not only thoroughly conversant with the details of the business, but equally so with the demands of the public, whom he zealously and successfully strives to serve to their best mutual advantage, and under his keen, careful supervision this house has attained a position in the foreground in its line and has secured a hold on public favor accorded to few houses of the kind in the city. The store is neat and commodious, with a very attractive display which the closest examination only serves to increase. Mr. Tafe has become so popular with the firm that he has not seen them for a long time. This alone speaks for itself, and his activity and enterprise have met with the liveliest appreciation since the beginning. We predict for him a prosperous and extensive business career, and one which is well deserved.

TEN EYCK PORTRAIT CO.

In no branch of art has there been such progress during the last twenty years as in that of portrait making. Particularly is this true of the art of making enlarged portraits from small originals. This has, as every one knows, become a regular business in itself and many establishments to-day devote their

entire attention to it. The pioneer house in this line is the Ten Eyck Portrait Company, established in 1870 and reorganized in 1886. The show rooms and studios of the company are at No. 261 W. Madison street. Their apartments there are finely fitted up and elegantly furnished, and contain one of the choicest assortments of specimen portraits in crayon, oil, water colors and pastel, to be found in the country. The manager of the company is Mr. J. G. Staats, a gentleman of great business and executive ability. He is a native of New York state, but has resided in Chicago for the last ten years. The patronage of the company extends throughout the entire country, and it is represented in all sections by local and traveling agents. During the past few years it has placed over 500,000 portraits in American homes, and these speak for themselves, being the best of testimonials.

THE CHICAGO RAWHIDE MFG. CO.

The Chicago Rawhide Manufacturing Company was duly incorporated in 1878, with a paid up capital of $150,000, originally locating at 38 and 40 Monroe street. Enlarged facilities were early necessitated, and in 1882 a portion of the present magnificent factory was erected as a substantial brick building, four stories and basement, and two years ago two stories were added, the dimension being 50x100 feet in area. The works are fully equipped with machinery of special construction for this industry as conducted under the ten patents of Mr. Krueger, Mr. W. H. Prebles and others. They are inventors of ability and have perfected peculiar processes, fully protected, which are solely and exclusively, the company's property. Between 150 and 200 hands are employed in the various departments, manufacturing enormous quantities of rawhide belting, lace leather, and also such specialties as rope, lariats, fly nets, picket leather, stock and farm whips, washers, hame straps, hame strings, halters, pinions for electric motors and other purposes, and other rawhide goods of all kinds. They manufacture strictly from the best native hides obtainable, and all lace leather is produced from the finest green salt hides. The choicest hides are carefully prepared here for machinery, artificial limbs, blocks, etc. The pure rawhide is hard as a horn and admirable for such purposes. The company received a medal at the National Exposition of Railway Appliances, held in Chicago in 1883, for the excellency and superiority of its belting and lace leather. The company have executed hundreds of the most important contracts, among them the round rawhide belting that runs the ventilator shafting in the new Board of Trade building. For the transmission of power these rawhide belts are pronounced by experts to be far superior to any other belting made, and are especially adapted

to paper mills, breweries, chemical works, electric lights, gas works, laundries, shoe factories etc. The trade relations developed, cover every section of the United States, Canada, Mexico, South America and Australia; also all over Europe. Mr. W. H. Emery is the president, and is favorably known in Chicago business circles and is prominent in the Masonic Order. Mr. W. H. Preble, secretary and treasurer, is a native of Maine; has been with the company fifteen years, and under his guidance the company has been remarkably prosperous. He is a noted Freemason ; has held several of the most important offices in his native state and was a member of the Maine State Legislature in 1870. Mr. A. B. Spurling, vice-president, is a native of Maine, and has been a very highly esteemed resident of Chicago since 1876.

HELMER A. HAGENSON.

Among those engaged in the retail trade in cigars, tobaccos, pipes and smokers' articles generally, there are none who have become known and more generally popular in a brief period on the West side, than Helmer A, Hagenson of No. 212 West Indiana street. This business was established by Mr. A. Thompson, in 1890, and was purchased by the present proprietor in October, 1891, and has always enjoyed a liberal and substantial patronage. The store is of fair dimensions and is admirably fitted up and arranged with elegant show cases, shelves, etc., for the display of the fine stock. The aim of the proprietor from the start has been to carry a reliable cigar, worthy of the good opinion of smokers, and that he has been successful in this direction is amply evidenced by the annually increasing demand for his goods. He has constantly on hand a general line of imported and domestic cigars of the best quality, and also all the leading brands of smoking and chewing tobaccos, snuffs, cigarettes, pipes and every variety of smokers' articles, supplemented by a choice assortment of pure confectionery, toys, fancy goods, notions and small wares. Mr. Hagenson, who is a young man, is of Norwegian nationality, and during a five-years' residence in the western metropolis, has ever enjoyed the respect of all who know him.

THE PARK ONE PRICE SHOE HOUSE.

A popular shoe house of the West side is that known as the Park shoe house, of which Mr. L. F. Shanovski is the proprietor. This business was established fourteen years ago on Milwaukee avenue by Mr. Shanovski, and was moved to the present location, 782 W. North avenue, about one year ago, Mr. Shanovski having built the store to meet the requirements of his ever increasing trade. The premises occupied for business purposes are 20x60 feet in dimensions, and the store is well arranged and conveniently furnished. The stock is very complete and consists of a full line of leading makes of ladies', gents' and children's footwear; all styles of boots, shoes, slippers, gaiters, and overshoes are carried in stock, and prices will be found to be as reasonable as may be obtained elsewhere. The house has a large local trade, many of the patrons having dealt with Mr. Shanovski for a number of years. He has always maintained a high reputation and increases his business each year. Fair dealing, low prices and quick sales are his maxims, and his success is evidence of the excellence of his methods. Mr. Shanovski was born in Germany, and has lived in Chicago for about twenty years.

S. J. FISHER.

One of the oldest and most reliable jewelry emporiums in this division of the Western metropolis is that now so ably presided over by Mr. S. J. Fisher, at No. 144 South Halsted street. This time-honored establishment dates its existence back thirty-five years, when it was founded by Mr. C. T. Fisher, the father of the present proprietor, who retired in favor of his son some twelve months ago. The premises occupied are of ample dimensions, and the tasteful distribution of the exceptionally fine lines of goods carried reflects the utmost credit on Mr. Fisher's good judgment. The stock embraces gold and silver watches of the best American and foreign manufacture; also jewelry of the latest designs and patterns, selected with cultivated taste, and a view to beauty and utility; diamonds and other precious stones, clocks, silver and plated-ware, optical goods, and the usual complement of the first-class jewelry store. Repairing receives prompt attention, and all goods are guaranteed to be exactly as represented, while charges in all departments are based on uniformly moderate scale. Mr. Fisher is an accomplished watchmaker and jeweler, was born in Chicago in 1867, and is ably maintaining the popularity and prestige this establishment so long enjoyed under the management of his respected father.

NORTH SIDE NATATORIUM.

One of the most convenient and healthful institutions in Chicago is the North Side Natatorium at Nos. 408 and 410 N. Clark street, the finest, largest and best equipped swimming school in America, under the management of Professor Fritz Mayer, whose reputation as an expert swimmer and teacher is world wide, and who has been connected with this institution as an instructor since its inception eight years ago. It is superfluous to say anything here in favor of swimming as a useful, healthful, pleasant art and recreation, as that is admitted by all classes of society. The Natatorium occupies a two story brick building, and is 50x100 feet in dimensions, the swimming bath being 115 feet long, thirty feet wide and varies in depth from two to eleven feet. The water is kept at a temperature of seventy-eight degrees and the hall at eighty degrees. Eight bath rooms, supplied with hot and cold showers, are provided, and an imperative rule obliges every person to bathe before entering the swimming bath, which is constantly supplied with a steady flow of fresh water from the lake. Persons with cutaneous diseases, or of objectional appearance, will not be admitted under any circumstance. There are 112 dressing rooms provided with every convenience, and all arrangements are absolutely first-class in every particular.

WM. SCHRAMM.

No line of business is more essential to a community than a good grocery store, where the wants of the neighborhood may be supplied with all they need in the line of staple and fancy groceries and family supplies. No better or more representative store in this line can be found than the splendid grocery of Mr. William Schramm, at No. 126 Wells street. This popular business was established by Mr. Schramm in 1885, at the present location, and occupies the ground floor and basement, 30x60 feet in dimensions. The store is handsomely fitted with all conveniences for the conducting of his present large and first-class business. Mr. Schramm carries a large and well-selected stock of staple and fancy groceries, teas, coffees, vegetables and general family supplies, making a specialty of the best brands of flour, of which he always carries a large and carefully selected stock of the best brands. Mr. Schramm is a prosperous, energetic business man, who has prospered in his business, solely owing to his fair dealings with his customers and a general desire to please his patrons at any sacrifice consistent with sound business principles. Mr. Schramm is a member of the Loyal League, popular with his trade and has a host of business and social friends and acquaintances.

FRANK PYATT.

The peculiar responsibility which attaches to the compounding and dispensing of prescriptions and kindred functions imparts to the calling of the druggist an interest and importance somewhat unique in this respect among the arts and sciences, and therefore it is that accuracy and vigilance become elements closely akin to knowledge and skill in the laboratory. In such connection we make due reference to Mr. Frank Pyatt, whose neat and popular pharmacy is located at No. 438 W. Madison street, corner of Throop, and who sustains such an excellent reputation for reliability in preparing prescriptions and family recipes, as well as ability in the general exercise of his profession. This establishment was opened by Mr. Pyatt in 1879, and under his judicious and capable management has been continually prosperous to date. The store, which is 20x40 feet in dimensions, is handsomely fitted up and admirably kept, an elegant soda fountain, beautiful show cases, and attractive appointments tendering a very inviting display. A carefully selected stock is constantly carried, embracing pure, fresh drugs and chemicals, proprietary remedies of standard reputation, perfumery, toilet articles, fancy goods, cigars, druggists' sundries and the usual complement of the first-class pharmacy. Mr. Pyatt is a New Yorker by birth, a resident of this city for some years past and a regular graduate of the Chicago College of Pharmacy and Licentiate of the State Board.

PHILIPP JAEGER.

No industry in the great city of Chicago is worthier of attention than that of the wholesale meat dealer. He it is who buys the cattle from the dealer in the country, has it killed, and sells it at wholesale to the retail dealer, from whom the family is supplied. Probably no firm in the city enjoys a higher reputation than that of Philipp Jaeger, general commission merchant, who occupies stalls Nos. 1 and 3 Fulton street wholesale market. Mr. Jaeger occupies a space in the market, 40x75 feet, which is conveniently fitted and equipped with ice coolers, refrigerators, and other appliances for the handling of his immense trade. Mr. Jaeger is the oldest dealer in the market. He employs a force of nine men, all experienced in this line, and who pay prompt attention to all orders received. Mr. Jaeger pays special attention to the sale of dressed hogs and country produce, and remits proceeds of all consignments promptly to the shippers. Mr. Jaeger is a native of Germany, and has resided thirty-five years in Chicago. His trade has been rapidly increasing since its foundation in 1869, and his capacity is over 500 head of calves and 600 sheep weekly, while his sales exceed $75,000 per month.

PATRICK HAMILL.

Among those dealers who have attained prominence and popularity in the meat trade on the West side of this city is Mr. Patrick Hamill, the popular proprietor of the market at 456 W. Twelfth street. This gentleman has been established in the business since 1888, and has built up a large trade as a dealer in all kinds of fresh, salt and smoked meats. Mr. Hamill commands all the advantages accumulated by experience in a special line of business, and possesses the best facilities for conducting all operations under the most favorable auspices. The stock is complete, including shoulders, hams, lard, poultry, etc., and he is prepared to supply hotels, restaurants and private families in quantities to suit at prices which defy competition, and having always been unremitting in his endeavor to please his customers he has developed a patronage of gratifying proportions. Three assistants are employed and all communications by telephone, etc., receive immediate attention. Mr. Hamill was born in Ireland, but has been a resident of this city for the past thirty years, and his reputation as a man of business as well as that of a public-spirited citizen has made him a host of friends.

R. VALENTINI.

An establishment that has gained great favor in catering for fashionable parties, picnics, etc., is that of Mr. R. Valentini, manufacturer and wholesale and retail dealer in ice cream, at No. 208 W. Madison street. The product of this establishment is of the very best class. Pure cream is used and the most skilful care is exercised in mixing the ingredients and in the freezing process, the result being a most delicious article. The best flavors are used, and they include a large variety. Fancy ices of all descriptions are also made. The business was established in 1863, at 117 W. Randolph street, and was moved to the present location in 1867. Here neat, spacious premises are occupied, and a first-class stock of confectionery cigars and tobacco, etc., is carried. An attractive ice cream parlor is run in connection, and cleanliness and taste are features of the whole establishment. Mr. R. Valentini, the proprietor, was born in Tuscany, came to Chicago in 1859, and is now fifty-one years of age. He is a leader in his line of business, a polite and courteous gentleman, and an honored and esteemed citizen, and it is with pleasure that we commend his establishment to the public.

W. M. MOORE.

A striking example of what patient industry and energy will do in a progressive city is shown in the case of Mr. W. M. Moore, the extensive druggist, at No. 351 N. Clark street, at the corner of Oak street. Mr. Moore was an employe of L. Burlingham & Co. in the drug business at his present location, and about three years ago was enabled to purchase their store, which he conducts as only a first-class pharmacist can. He carries an excellent line of drugs, chemicals, patent medicines and toilet articles, and has a large soda fountain in the front of his handsomely furnished store. He employs two assistants, and makes a specialty of filling physicians' prescriptions carefully and conscientiously. Mr. Moore was born in London, Ont., and has been in Chicago for ten years. He is a graduate of the Ontario College of Pharmacy at Toronto, Canada. He is a popular young gentleman, who by his own efforts has amassed a competency and has a wide circle of friends.

G. W. DOWDELL.

A nice business in general real estate brokerage is done by Mr. G. W. Dowdell, whose office is in room 10, No. 196 La Salle street. A specialty is made of acre property, and a large amount is handled. Loans are negotiated on real estate. Mr. Dowdell is a native of St. Lawrence County, N. Y., and is now in the prime of life. In 1874 he went to Sacramento, Cal., where he engaged in the building and contracting business. When the Black Hills' excitement broke out, shortly after, he went to Mitchell, Dak., and engaged in the same business there. From 1877 to 1879 he was traveling salesman for the Fairbanks, Morse & Co. Scale Works of this city. In September, 1889, he located permanently in Chicago, and established his present business, opening an office in the Inter Ocean building. There he remained until May, 1891, when he removed to his present location. The office he now occupies is neatly fitted up and nicely arranged.

WM. WRIGLEY, JR., & CO.

Acknowledging the fact, that cleanliness is next to Godliness, the manufacturers of Wrigley's Mineral Scouring Soap have established their Western agency in Chicago under the style of William Wrigley, Jr., & Company, at No. 157 Kinzie street, in the Puhl and Webb building. The original firm was established in Philadelphia about twenty-one years ago, and the excellence of their manufactures has increased the trade, east and west, north and south, until all the world acknowledges the wonderful properties of the best scouring soap in the world, "Wrigley's Mineral." The firm representing the manufacturers here, composed of William Wrigley, jr., and William Scatchard, jr., opened in the early spring of 1890, and have since built up a trade in this section that is the wonder and envy of their competitors. At their warerooms, No. 157 Kinzie street, they carry a large stock of the now celebrated Mineral Scouring Soap and occupy the entire floor 25x100 feet, at the above number. Mr. Wrigley, jr., and Mr. Scatchard, jr., are both native Philadelphians, are live, energetic and are pushing the interests of the home house in such a manner as to make older men in the business look "queer."

E. L. WUNDERLE.

A well-stocked and thoroughly equipped drug store is a great convenience in any community, and the North side is favored with one of the best at No. 278 Wells street, being that of E. L. Wunderle's prescription drug store, which was established in 1876 by H. Reinharden, the present proprietor taking charge in 1890. He carries a full and complete line of the purest and best drugs and chemicals, patent medicines, toilet articles, notions and druggists' sundries, also has a handsome soda fountain. Mr. Wunderle is a graduate of the Chicago College of Pharmacy, a member of the Alumni, and a registered member of the Illinois State Board of Pharmacy. His store occupies the main floor at the above number with pharmacy in the rear, and he employs two assistants. He manufactures all of his own tinctures, essences, extracts and syrups, and remains open until eleven o'clock each evening. He is a native Chicagoan, is immensely popular and has a splendid trade.

A. C. SCHIEWE.

No more convenient institution exists in any community than the dry goods and notion houses, well stocked and ably conducted. The West side is particularly fortunate in this line, and no firm takes precedence over the well-known house of A. C. Schiewe of No. 959 Milwaukee avenue. The business was originally established under the firm name of Schiewe & Maas, eight years ago, and upon the death of Mr. Maas in 1887, the present proprietor conducted the business alone, and has been in his present splendid location for nearly three years. Mr. Schiewe carries at all times a handsome line of staple and fancy dry goods, ladies' and gents' furnishing goods, notions, and that comprehensive line of notions known only to first-class dry goods houses. Mr. Schiewe is a native of Germany, and has been in Chicago for nearly twenty years, although still a young man. He is live, energetic and progressive, and is doing a splendid business, which is constantly increasing.

BAVARIA LAUNDRY.

There is no laundry of higher standing or doing a more satisfactory business than the Bavaria Laundry, owned and operated by Mr. Andrew Sedlmayer. This business has been established for six years, and has come into its present prominence through the diligent efforts and close application to business of its proprietor. He occupies the ground floor and basement of numbers 313 Larrabee street and 138½ Wells street, and has a very complete plant. The premises are 25x75 feet in dimensions, and the washing machinery is in the basement. This consists of all the latest improvements for washing, bleaching, starching, drying, etc. The power is supplied by a twelve horse power engine. The first floor is used as office and delivery room, and in the rear the ironing department, where the latest mangles and ironing machines are in operation. Everything is of the best character and the work is all done in the best possible manner. The laundry gives employment from twelve to fifteen hands and two teams are kept busy attending to the delivery of the goods. Branch agencies have been established in all parts of the city for receiving and delivering goods. The prices charged are popular and moderate. Mr. Sedlmayer is a native of Germany and has resided in Chicago a number of years.

UNION SPECIAL SEWING MACHINE CO.

In the manufacture of sewing machines for all purposes the United States is greatly ahead of all other nations. In this connection we desire to make special reference in this commercial review of Chicago to the representative and successful Union Special Sewing Machine Co., manufacturers of Elastic Stitch Sewing Machines, whose office and factory are situated at 60 Michigan street. This industry was established in 1881 by the Union Bag Machine Company, which was succeeded in 1884 by the present corporation, with ample capital, the execu-

tive officers being Mr. W. S. North, president and treasurer; Mr. W. H. Hoyer, secretary and Mr. L. Muther, superintendent. The company's "Union" Elastic Stitch Sewing Machines were invented and patented by Messrs. L. Muther and R. G. Woodward, who are in the employment of the company as superintendent and expert respectively. These machines are the best yet offered to the public for seaming and ornamental work on knit fabrics, shoes, mitts and gloves, shirts and drawers, burlap and bag sewing, jerseys, cloaks and suits, corsets, sails and awnings, umbrella sewing and hemming, etc. These machines can be run at double the speed of others, besides always insuring a strong, durable, double thread elastic seam. They have a guaranteed speed in every day work of 2,500 stitches per minute, and have no shuttles to thread or bobbin to wind, but take the thread directly from the spool. In the construction of these splendid power machines only the best materials and the highest mechanical skill are employed, making them unsurpassed for durability and efficiency, while the prices quoted for them are exceedingly moderate. Already 12,000 of these machines have been sold, and the trade of the company is by no means confined to the United States and Canada, but extends to Europe, Mexico, Central and South America, India, South Africa and Australia. The company's factory is fully equipped with special machinery and appliances, operated by a sixty-horse power steam engine. Here seventy-five skilled workmen are employed, and they also manufacture White's improved bag folding and cutting machines, Lockwood's bag turning machines, etc., which are general favorites wherever introduced, owing to their superiority and utility. They are owners of the Dewees' famous fabric trimmer, which is an admirable device for trimming knit fabrics and other materials simultaneously with their being sewed upon a sewing machine.

The company promptly fills orders, and furnishes references and samples on application. Absolute protection from hostile litigation from patentees of other trimmers is likewise guaranteed by the Union Special Sewing Machine Co. to all who use it. The Union Special Sewing Machine Co. has also branches in New York, Philadelphia, Boston, London, Amsterdam and Berlin. Their latest and most valuable production is a machine for sewing carpets, which is operated by electricity and does the work of forty hand sewers. Two of these plants are in operation in the stores of Marshall Field & Co., and the company are about starting a complete plant of their own in New York City. The company, in connection with Mr. Franklin Ames, owns a large number of patents which control the sewing of carpet by electricity. The officers are able, energetic and honorable business men, under whose guidance the prospects of the company are of the most favorable character.

UNION TAILORING CO.

Chicago's numerous merchants and business men have the reputation of being the best dressed citizens of any city in America. This is due to the superiority of the skill and ability of the merchant tailors, who do business here and never spare expense nor labor to attain the highest perfection in their art. The leading establishment of the district in which it is located is unquestionably the Union Tailoring Co. This establishment has been in the field of popular favor for five years, and is patronized by the leading merchants and citizens of the North side. The proprietor is Mr. Harry M. Brown, a gentleman well-known and highly respected for his skill and social qualities. He occupies the elegant store located at 30 Clybourn avenue, which is 20x60 feet in dimensions, and neatly fitted up, having a superior stock well displayed. All the latest novelties and designs in woolens, cloths, cassimeres, serges, cheviots, tweeds, flannels, worsteds, etc., are carried, and received as soon as produced by the leading manufacturers of this country and Europe. Only the finest custom work is done and twenty skilled workmen are kept constantly employed, producing the best effects in suits, overcoats, etc. The patronage of this house has grown steadily from the first, the customers recognizing the fact that they were obtaining the highest results in the tailor's art at the minimum price by dealing with Mr. Brown. This gentleman has always catered to only the first-class trade, and has had an extended experience in many of the largest European cities before coming to America. He was born in Germany, and came to Chicago twelve years ago, and since his coming here has built up a business that but a few older concerns can lay claim to and is brought about by his untiring energy, and careful and constant attention to patrons. He is in the prime of life and is an active, energetic business man of the utmost skill and irreproachable character. Mr. Brown has numerous friends, who are ardent in their admiration and never neglect an opportunity to speak well of him and his business, which has been brought about by his honorable and honest methods of conducting his affairs, and fair treatment to all.

L. SCHMIDT.

Those whom the sad surroundings of death have brought into professional contact with Mr. L. Schmidt, of 869 W. Twenty-first street, near Hoyne avenue, are all of one opinion, and that is, that his manner of conducting funerals is all that can be required in the way of thorough respectability and decency. He always has on hand every style of coffins, caskets, shrouds and necessary funeral appurtenances. He also takes charge of remains at any hour of the day or night and prepares them for burial in a very superior manner, embalming being performed when desired according to the most approved process. Carriages and hearses are supplied, and interment obtained in any of the city cemeteries or those in the surrounding locality. All funerals are personally directed by Mr. Schmidt, and he employs assistants of well-tried experience, so that there is no room left for any possible kind of mistake. His telephone call is 9002, and all messages, whether by day or night, receive instant attention. In the matter of charges Mr. Schmidt is very reasonable, and does not take advantage of the helpless surroundings of relatives in the time of bereavment, as so many do. He is of German nationality, and has been established in this business for the last seven years.

THE FIRST COLUMBIAN EXPOSITION TOWER.

It was reserved for T. W. Slattery & Co., a real estate firm, doing business at No. 115 Dearborn street, Chicago, to construct the first observatory tower adjacent to the World's Fair grounds at Jackson park. A number of such projects had been discussed, many elaborate plans had been drawn, and a score of corporations organized for this purpose. Even M. Eiffel, the originator of the wonderful Paris tower, had submitted a proposition to the directors of the Columbian Exposition to erect a similar structure here; but this, like all the other projects, got no farther than the architect's hands, and was finally abandoned altogether. A high board fence surrounding Jackson park effectually shuts out from view the exceedingly interesting work of constructing the many imposing and novel edifices which are destined to amaze the world in 1893. What object could be worthier than to afford the public a comprehensive bird's-eye view of this panorama? This was the thought that occurred to Mr. Maurice G. O'Brien, the junior member of the firm, and with characteristic energy he lost no time in putting the idea in tangible shape. The tower stands at the corner of Stony Island avenue and Sixty-fourth street, and commands a magnificent view of the exposition grounds, as well as the many beautiful suburbs surrounding Jackson park. The firm has established a branch office at the base of the tower, where the usual features of their business will be transacted, viz.: Buying and selling real estate on commission, negotiating loans, placing insurance, etc. They will pay special attention to the negotiation of leases and the collection of rents in the district adjacent to Jackson park.

T. E. COPELIN.

The North side boasts of as fine stores as there are in the city, and among them is that of T. E. Copelin of Nos. 35 and 37 N. State street. Mr. Copelin carries a full, complete and well selected stock of stoves, tinware and builders' hardware, also house furnishing goods, and manufactures all kinds of work in tin, copper, sheet and galvanized iron, paying especial attention to stove and furnace repairing. He opened this store five years ago at the above location, using the handsome room, No. 37. as the office and storeroom and No. 35 as the workshop. The shop is fitted with all the modern appliances for the manufacture of his wares, and five men are employed in manufacturing and jobbing. Mr. Copelin was born in New York city, but was raised in Chicago, and is thoroughly identified with its interests. He is industrious, energetic, courteous and attentive to business, meriting the immense trade he has been favored with.

FRANK J. BERGER.

Since the inception of this enterprise in 1885, this store has become one of the leading centers of trade in this section of the city. The premises occupied are located at 1486 Milwaukee avenue, and are fitted up with every improved convenience to be found in a first class store of this kind, and has handsomely fitted plate glass show cases, etc., etc. The stock carried embraces a full line of pure and fresh drugs and chemicals, reputable patent medicines, druggists' sundries, fancy and toilet articles, physicians' supplies, etc., all of which have been selected with great care. A specialty is made of compounding physicians' prescriptions and family recipes, in an accurate, prompt and careful manner, and nothing is wanting to render the establishment in every respect a model of its type. Mr. Berger employs none but competent assistants, who are graduates of the Chicago College of Pharmacy. Mr. Berger has earned an enviable reputation in professional circles as a thorough, reliable pharmacist, and a large and liberal patronage is the result. He is a native of Wisconsin, but Chicago has been his home for the last fifteen years, and previous to his venture in business, was a drug clerk here several years. He is about thirty-three years of age. The prescription department is under the supervision of the proprietor, or his wife, who is also a pharmacist.

A. WEISSKOPF.

One of the best known and oldest established dry goods houses on the West side is that of A. Weisskopf, 610, 612 and 614 Blue Island avenue. Mr. Weisskopf has an elegant store at this place, and has it stocked with a fine line of imported and domestic dry goods. He carries everything in the line, finest silks, satins, brocades, velvets, together with cashmeres, cloths, woolens, ginghams, sheetings, embroideries and, in fact, everything of this nature. His stock is very complete and select, all the goods being of superior grades. The business was established in 1873 by A. L. Klein & Co., and continued in this style until 1880, when the parenership was dissolved, Mr. Weisskopf succeeding to the business and continuing it ever since. The patronage of this house is very large, the many years it has been in the business, and the honorable methods employed, all combine to establish it in public favor. Five persons are employed and the business has not by any means reached its maximum. Mr. Weisskopf gives the business his personal attention and selects his goods with the greatest care. He is a well-known business man, standing very high in commercial and financial circles, and is also a prominent member of a number of fraternal orders, notably among which are the following: Royal Arcanum, Knights of Honor, Free Sons of Israel, D. B. Society, the latter an Austrian society, Mr. Weisskopf was born in Austria and came to Chicago in 1871. His business relations have been of the most pleasant character and his success is due to his straightforward methods and fair dealing. He resides at 608 Blue Island avenue, adjoining the stores, in his own property.

G. W. BOALCH.

One of the greatest and most important businesses to have established in a community is a first-class family drug store and prescription pharmacy. Such, in fact, as is that of Mr. G. W. Boalch, at the corners of Fullerton and Clybourn, and Webster and Southport avenues. This reliable house was opened twelve years ago by Ripke & Weber, and was purchased by the present proprietor within the past year. The room is elegantly furnished with glass wall and counter show cases, which contain a splendid line of pure, fresh drugs, chemicals, patent medicines, toilet articles, and druggists' sundries. Mr. Boalch is a native Chicagoan, a graduate of the Chicago College of Pharmacy, a licensed druggist, and registered by the Illinois State Board of Pharmacy. He is a young man of ability, energy and character, and has established a large trade, which is constantly increasing.

CHICAGO UNION LIME WORKS.

An old-established business is that now so ably and thoroughly represented by the Chicago Union Lime Company, manufacturers of Chicago quick lime and Macadam and concrete stone, for which F. E. Spooner is the agent. It was originated in 1859 by Mr. T. W. Phinney under the style of the Chicago Union Lime Works. Mr. Phinney is a resident of Newport, R. I. A capitalist of rare business capacity, he saw the need of such an enterprise in Chicago, and his sagacity has been more than justified by the magnificent success of the undertaking. Mr. F. E. Spooner has been the agent for the past twenty-seven years, the whole of the time he has been in Chicago. In his efficient management is found the success which has attended the enterprise, which now keeps 250 hands fully employed, and has left its impress on this and many another city in the broad west. The capacity of the Chicago Union Lime Works is 50,000 barrels of lime monthly. Besides this the firm manufactures Macadam and concrete stone. The works are on Nineteenth and Lincoln streets, covering an area of seventeen acres of land. The trade is largely local. The stone-crushing works at the same place, on Nineteenth and Lincoln, is fitted with all the best machinery for the crushing of stone for macadamizing purposes, and the trade for this specialty is very widely diffused. Mr. Spooner, who can always be found in the spacious and neatly appointed offices at room 5, 159 La Salle street, is a gentleman of the most complete experience in the business, in which his name and that of the works are standard and almost above comparison. He is a native of Massachusetts.

THE McCLOUD IRON AND STEEL COMPANY.

The prominence of Chicago as a commercial center, together with its proximity to the iron-producing districts, makes it a natural center for the iron trade. The many railroads running into the city and recognizing it as their chief headquarters also give prominence to the business of dealing in iron ores and the manufacaure of articles of steel. One of the foremost establishments doing business in this line is the McCloud Iron and Steel Co., whose offices are in the Rookery building, room 653. This enterprise was incorporated in June, 1890, and is establishing plants in different parts of the country for the manufacture of wrapped bars, both iron and steel, and the reduction of old steel rails to steel plates, by a new process, and the manufacture of links and pins, in the reducing of old rails a patent process is used by this company which puts the bars together without welding, by a process of wrapping and pressing. The company will in the near future build a large plant in this city, and give employment to many artisans. In the manufacture of wrapped steel bars many thousands of old rails will be used annually, being reduced by this company's process into all kinds of shapes. The officers of the company are all residents of the city, and gentlemen of ability and known business integrity. Mr. J. C. Fortiner is the president, and is very well known in leading financial circles. Mr. F. G. Holton, the vice-president, is also president of the Chicago Battery and Traction Co. Mr. Sidney McCloud superintends the entire work and brings long experience and technical knowledge to bear in producing a most valuable commercial product. Mr. H. L. Norton, the treasurer, is also secretary of the Traction Co. The secretary of the company is Mr. W. D. Crossman. Its rating is high and its output constantly increasing with the demand.

CHICAGO BATTERY AND TRACTION CO.

The adoption of electricity for motive power has brought many inventions into the market of the greatest commercial value and interest. One of the principal parts of the mechanism of independent electric motors, and that of greatest importance, is the battery. To manufacture these the Chicago Battery and Traction Company was organized in 1890. The

officers of the company are F. G. Holton, president, H. B. Meech, vice-president, G. E. Farley, treasurer, H. L. Norton, secretary; all progressive and representative business men. Mr. Holton is also vice-president of the McCloud Iron and Steel Co., and gives his personal attention to the business. Mr. H. L. Norton, the secretary of the company, is also treasurer of the McCloud Iron and Steel Company. The factory of the company is in Chicago, where a force of workmen are employed in the manufacture of the various styles of batteries used by the company. They manufacture storage batteries for car systems, which method of street car propulsion is daily growing in favor. They also make stationary storage and primary batteries for various uses. The trade of this company extends all over the United States, and the demand for their product increases daily. The batteries manufactured by them have many points of excellence, for which they are preferred by those needing such machinery, and the workmanship is all that knowledge and skill can bring together in production. The office of the company is in the Rookery building, number 653, and here may be found models, drawings and designs that show the productions of the company. The company are bringing their products into the greatest prominence, and it is rapidly coming into competition with the oldest and most extensive manufactories in the country, with credit to the management.

BIRKIN & PHILPOTT.

With the rapid and immense growth of Chicago, and the ever increasing demand for residences and manufacturing and commercial buildings, the real estate interests has naturally come to form one of the chief investments for capital with the well-to-do and thrifty portion of the populace. The large trade now done in realty of every description has naturally drawn to this branch of enterprise many of our leading capitalists and go-ahead citizens, and among this number are Messrs. Birkin & Philpott of No. 195 Wabash avenue, who have built up an extensive and influential connection among speculators, investors, and those seeking homes for themselves. This is a live, progressive firm, and has made its mark in other commercial fields. Messrs. Birkin & Philpott in their realty department make a specialty of handling South Side property, and of dealing in lots in the subdivisions in this section of the city, and also of handling several tracts contiguous to the Illinois Central railroad and in close proximity to the manufacturing centers of Pullman, Harvey and Hyde Park. This business was established by the present firm in 1889, and from that time on they have been steadily building up a trade of such importance as it now presents itself. The members of this firm have a thorough and complete knowledge of the present and prospective value of realty of all kinds in and out of the city, and are at all times prepared to offer building lots and other investments on terms that merit the attention of investors and thrifty artisans and others who seek to acquire homes which they can call their own. At Homewood, a growing suburb of this great city, the firm have for sale many nice residences and business lots situated on the high ridge. This is a most desirable district in which to dwell, and here is offered a most ample security for investments, for the place is rapidly growing, and with this growth comes an announcement of building lots which now can be had from the firm at very low figures, while three years hence they will command much higher prices than they do to-day. Exceptionally low prices that now prevailare sure to be enhanced ere long, and parties with an eye to business and to an increase of their wealth will do well to consult Messrs. Birkin & Philpott as to location of properties they have for sale, and for prices. In all their dealings they will be found prompt, reliable and straightforward. Messrs. R. H. Birkin and T. W. Philpott are both natives of England and old residents in Chicago, familiar with the need of the city and with the increasing wants of the populace. Both were formerly in the service of the Pullman Palace Car Co., which they left to embark in their present commercial enterprise. Mr. Philpott is a member of the Sons of St. George and numerous other societies.

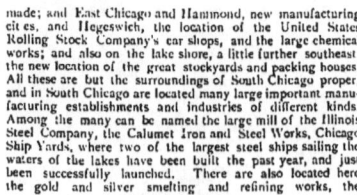

KRIMBILL & FUCHS.

Chicago has no financial interest of more paramount importance than that of real estate, and at the present time, when the securities of the money market are so depressed, coupled with their diminished earning power, the investing public has turned its attention to the city real estate market, as one absolutely secure, and where, if judicious purchases are made, not only is a steady source of income assured, but likewise increase of values. Prominent among the active and enterprising houses which have so greatly aided in the permanent development of South Side Chicago property is that now conducted by Messrs. Krimbill & Fuchs of room No. 23, Reaper Block, 95 Clark street, and rooms Nos. 4 and 5, Winnipeg Block, South Chicago. The business was established by Mr. A. Krimbill in 1873 at the latter location, he being quick to perceive the prospective values of South Side

made; and East Chicago and Hammond, new manufacturing cities, and Hegeswich, the location of the United States Rolling Stock Company's car shops, and the large chemical works; and also on the lake shore, a little further southeast, the new location of the great stockyards and packing houses. All these are but the surroundings of South Chicago proper, and in South Chicago are located many large important manufacturing establishments and industries of different kinds. Among the many can be named the large mill of the Illinois Steel Company, the Calumet Iron and Steel Works, Chicago Ship Yards, where two of the largest steel ships sailing the waters of the lakes have been built the past year, and just been successfully launched. There are also located here the gold and silver smelting and refining works, the

property, and during the current year he admitted Mr. G. Fuchs as a partner in the city office, who has also had many years' experience in handling South Side property. They transact every branch of the real estate business, buying, selling and renting property, placing insurance, loaning money on bond and mortgage, and making a specialty of taking entire charge of estates. The firm are also notaries public, having made a complete study of the law of real estate, and can be consulted with implicit confidence on all matters pertaining thereto. In the matter of South Side property no one is better qualified than Mr. Krimbill to give a reliable opinion on actual and prospective values, and to render full information as to titles and the incumbrances thereon (if any). He accordingly takes charge of the South Side office, Mr. Fuchs attending to the affairs of the city branch. Both are prominent members of the Real Estate Exchange, and we confidently recommend this house as one with which property investors can enter into satisfactory business relations. Mr. Krimbill, who is the veteran real estate dealer at South Chicago, in the Calumet region, gives the following short description of that wonderful and important industrial center: It is located on both sides of the Calumet River, has one of the finest and best harbors on the chain of lakes, and is the coming manufacturing and industrial center of the World's Fair City, bounded on the east by Lake Michigan, and entrance of the famous Calumet harbor, on the west by Calumet Lake, on the west shore of which is located the wonderful City of Brick (Pullman) and Stony Island Boulevard, extending from this beautiful inland lake to Jackson Park, the location of the World's Fair; on the north by the World's Fair site, and on the south and southeast by the Phœnix like establishments of the Standard Oil Company at Whiting. Five million dollars of improvements are being

steam forge works, large iron boiler works (not yet completed), iron foundry, the large frog and crossing works, large planing mills and wood working establishments. There are several large lumber yards, both wholesale and retail, two large wholesale coal yards, shops of the Baltimore & Ohio Railroad Co., the shops of the Pittsburgh, St. Louis & Chicago Railroad Co., the Fowler Car Wheel Works, grain elevator and eight railroads, besides the Belt Line system, connecting every railroad that enters the city of Chicago. Eight miles of Chicago streets are supplied with street cars, both electric and horse power. Eight large brick public schoolhouses are now accommodating thousands of school children. Twenty-two religious societies have good and substantial church buildings. About twenty-five secret societies have well furnished lodge rooms. South Chicago has two banks, one daily and several weekly newspapers, and contains many stores and business houses that will compare with any business houses of the large cities. Sewers, water pipes and electric lights are being placed in most of our streets. The government of the United States is spending from seventy-five to one hundred thousand dollars yearly for the improvement and extending of Calumet harbor and river. Now, to sum up all these wonderful improvements which have mostly been brought about within ten years, a careful observer would naturally suppose that the price of real estate has already reached a point that the poor man could not touch, or that it has reached a point beyond speculation, which is not the fact. South Chicago has had no boom. Its growth has been steady and healthy, and the price within the reach of most any one, and there is no place in the United States to-day where so sure and profitable investments can be made for the same amount of money as in South Chicago. But it is impossible for any one to comprehend the importance of this locality without inspecting it, and any one who wishes to make investments, either in lots, acres or improved property, or locations for manufacturing purposes, either on river docks or on railroads, or both, or business lots or residence lots for immediate use, should correspond with the old veteran real estate dealer, Andrew Krimbill.

EAST SIDE—SOUTH CHICAGO.

The East side is the beautiful ridge of land formerly called Indian Ridge, and derives its name from an old Indian trail leading from the hunting grounds of the upper Calumet region to the mouth of the river (now the Calumet harbor). This ridge contains the finest residence property in the vicinity of South Chicago. It is located between the Calumet river and the beautiful beach of Lake Michigan, and contains about 6,000 inhabitants, with a fair proportion of business of most all kinds, and this desirable locality is laid out in several thousand very desirable lots for both business and residence, convenient to railroad depots, street cars, and well supplied with churches and schools, water, sidewalks and several paved streets, with many important improvements in contemplation.

THE ILLINOIS TYPE FOUNDING CO.

The importance of Chicago as a great center of the trade in printers' materials is forcibly demonstrated by reference to the well-known establishment of the Illinois Type Founding Company, whose product is preferred by reason of its excellence and artistic elegance, and whose prices are the most moderate, quality considered. The company was incorporated in June, 1871, with a paid up capital of $20,000, and early developed a flourishing trade. In 1885, Mr. F. M. Powell's business was consolidated with it, and he became the president. The company continue to do a flourishing business in its line, and secures to Chicago the supremacy in this branch of trade in the West. The company has had to greatly enlarge its facilities, and in February, 1891, increased its capital to $100,000 paid up. Mr. Powell has the valued support of Mr. C. S. Conner of New York, as secretary, and Mr. David W. Bruce of New York, as treasurer. These gentlemen are prominent type-founders, heads of the oldest established concerns in the East; Mr. Conner is western agent for Geo. Bruce's Son & Co. of New York, and James Conner's Sons, of New York. The company occupies extensive premises at Nos. 200 and 202 Clark street, and carries a very complete and extensive stock of type and materials as can be found in Chicago. This is, in fact, *recognized headquarters* for everything in type used in a printing office, from "Pearl" up to "60-point" size, all of most modern improved workmanship, and made from the best metal in the market. The stock includes all styles and sizes of cases, cabinets, stands imposing stones, galleys, sticks, rules, quoins, etc.; job inks, news inks, mailers and mitering machines, roller composition, engravers' wood, etc. The company also carries full lines of the best makes of job and news presses, including many good second-hand presses, cheap for cash. Mr. Powell brings to bear all the qualifications for the discharge of the onerous duties devolving upon him, and is a business man of good judgment and executive capacity, who controls one of the largest and most desirable trades in printers' materials in America.

GEORGE E. BROWN & CO.

This business was originally established some years ago by the present proprietors, and two years ago a removal was made from the old stand at 60 Wabash avenue to the premises now occupied at No. 116 Randolph street. The copartners are Mr. George E. Brown & Son, who are thoroughly practical printers, conversant with all the details of the business in every department, and by their energy and enterprise have built up a large and flourishing trade. Throughout the establishment is well equipped with everything requisite for doing all kinds of printing, and all the latest improved machinery which is operated by electric power. Mr. Brown brings to bear a wide range of experience, and executes work for elegance equal to

any in the city, and all work executed here bears the unmistakable stamp of excellence, in both design, neatness and finish, every care being exercised to render the best satisfaction. A specialty is made of fine job and commercial work. Mr. Brown came to Chicago in 1837 on a stage coach, when the place where the city nowstands was a vast prairie. He has watched the steady, rapid growth of the great metropolis, and is one of its prominent time-honored citizens. He is the oldest printer in Chicago, and to-day works actively at his business. Previous to this venture, he was connected with the "Chicago Journal" twenty-five years and is very popular and has many influential friends. His son, Mr. F. D. Brown, was born and raised in this city, is well and favorably known, and the ripe experience of the father, combined with the vigor, ability and business talents of the son, form a business of commanding influence, eminent popularity and solid worth.

DEAN & REYNOLDS.

There are few features of metropolitan enterprise which contribute a larger quota to the convenience of the residential and transient public than the well-appointed livery stable, and a recent valuable acquisition to the many located in Chicago is that of Messrs. Dean & Reynolds, occupying the site Nos. 329, 331 and 333 Thirty-fourth street, with smaller branch at No. 268 Thirty-third street. The latter concern was the first to be opened by Mr. T. A. Dean some eighteen months ago, he in June, 1890, forming a copartnership with Mr. C. N. Reynolds, and adding the Thirty-fourth street stables to the original plant. The stabling capacity of the latter is seventy horses, while accommodation at the Thirty-third street establishment provides for thirty-six equine guests. With regard to complete appointments, the same remarks apply to both concerns, and parties desiring superior accommodations for their stock and equipages would do well to note the advantages these stables possess. The water is pure and abundant, the stalls are well ventilated, drained and lighted, and the grooms and stallmen are careful and experienced. A special feature is made of buying and selling horses on commission, this department receiving Mr. Dean's exclusive attention, whose long experience as a horseman is a sufficient guarantee that he understands everything pertaining to the business. He is a native of Rockford, this state, and was favorably identified with the livery business in his native town prior to engaging in this enterprise here. His partner, Mr. Reynolds, hails from Wisconsin, and thoroughly understands every phase of the business. The offices are connected by telephone (calls Nos. 8115 and 8599), and all orders, day or night, receive prompt attention.

H. J. MOORE.

Chicago is the recognized center of fashion in the Western states, her leading business men exercising the same sway here as do those of Paris and London, in France and England. In the line of the finest ladies' tailor-made garments, a prominent and influential house in the city is that of Messrs. H. J. Moore & Co., No. 188 Wabash avenue. This business was established in 1884 by Mr. H. J. Moore, who is sole proprietor. Mr. Moore is a thoroughly practical and artistic cutter of ladies' suits, riding-habits, robes, jackets, etc., and has developed a liberal and first-class trade in the city and its vicinity. He always is the first in Chicago to introduce the latest Paris and London styles, importing all the choicest fabrics and novelties. Consequently buyers can always make selections here with confidence, being assured that they are getting the most fashionable goods in the western market. Mr. Moore, although a young man, and established but a comparatively short time, has placed himself among the leading importers of foreign fabrics and novelties, and has made the firm of H. J. Moore & Co. an authority throughout the West in the matter of style and material. The warerooms are handsomely furnished, and here may be found as complete and choice a line of ladies' suits, robes, riding habits, cloaks and garments, as are to be found in the warerooms of the celebrated eastern importers.

STRAUSS, YONDORF & ROSE,

WHOLESALE CLOTHIERS, MARKET AND QUINCY STREETS.

The above firm are the successors of the business of manufacturing clothing established by Meyer, Strauss, Goodman & Co. in the year 1870, and the splendid results which have attended the enterprise are seen in the establishment of which Messrs. Strauss, Yondorf & Rose are to-day the proprietors. It is one of the most thoroughly equipped and extensive clothing houses in the United States, and is a magnificent monument to the energy and enterprise of its managers. From 1886

know how to appreciate this in preference to the most approved artificial lights. This tenth story sample room is a feature of the establishment, having a vaulted ceiling sixteen feet high, and beautifully decorated and fitted up. Throughout the building are elevators and speaking tubes connecting all the floors. The place is heated by steam, and has electrical alarms. The cutting is all done on the premises. They employ 100 people in the house, while an army of men and

to 1890 the firm was known as Strauss, Goodman, Yondorf & Co., and in January, 1891, the present style was adopted, the firm consisting of Abr. Strauss, Simon Yondorf and Edward Rose. They occupy a handsome structure on the corner of Market and Quincy streets, ten stories and basement, being the first actual fire-proof building in the city erected and used for commercial purposes. This building is fitted up with rare taste and judgment for the extensive business of the firm; the basement is used for packing purposes; the ground floor for offices; the second, third, fourth, fifth and sixth for the storage of their immense stock; the seventh and eighth floors for cutting, receiving and examining the work; the ninth and tenth stories are used for sample rooms, thus securing on these floors at all times of day an unobstructed natural light. Buyers of textile fabrics of delicate shades of colors will

women are engaged in the manufacture of the goods in the various tailor shops in the northern and western part of the city. The trade extends all over the United States, competing easily with the best houses in the country, and in the West especially commanding a trade unparalleled in its extent. Messrs. Strauss, Yondorf & Rose make a specialty of putting good trimmings and good workmanship in the low-priced goods, as well as the more expensive grades, fully believing that the man of small means is as well entitled to good workmanship as his more fortunate neighbor. The goods supplied by this house are "cheap" only in the legitimate sense of that much-abused word, and are by no means inferior. The proprietors of this fine establishment all give their full attention to the business, each having a separate department under his control.

WEIR & CRAIG MANUFACTURING COMPANY.

IT is only reasonable that in Chicago, which is the center of so many packing houses, there should be a manufactory of packing house machinery, and a firm which makes a speciality of this is the Weir & Craig Manufacturing Co., at 2421 to 2439 Wallace Street, on the corner of Twenty-fourth place. The business was established by this company as a machine shop and brass foundry in 1865, and incorporated in 1889, with a capital of seventy-five thousand dollars, and Mr. John A. Kley is President, while Mr. Robert Craig is vice-president, and Mr. Robert Weir fulfils the equally important duties of secretary and treasurer. They own and occupy the whole of the building as per cut herewith, and which

is 150x200 feet in dimensions, and fitted with all the latest improved machinery that it is possible to get for the conduct of their business. They usually employ about one hundred and twenty-five skilled hands, and turn out some of the finest work in the country, giving estimates of every kind of machine work, and they are also manufacturers and dealers in plumbers' steam and gas-fitters' supplies. The trade extends all over the United States, and there seems to be no limit to it, provided their goods continue in the same demand as they are at present. Everything is thoroughly tested before leaving the works, and it is hardly necessary to say that the firm in all cases uses the very best material they can buy. Their productive capacity is very large, and they possess the best possible facilities for shipping their goods by any of the roads out of Chicago. Under the able management of its present directorate, the business has experienced a prosperous and reassuring growth, and is looked upon as one of the best conducted and most reliable of its kind in the country.

HOFFMANN DECORATIVE MOULDING CO.

THE superiority of the finish and decoration of the business blocks and private residences of Chicago is a source of comment from all who visit the city. Every novelty and improvement in design receives careful attention and consideration from builders and decorators, and the houses handling these decorations have had a steady increase in their business from year to year, while new manufactories have been started to meet the increasing demand. Among the thoroughly reliable enterprises manufacturing artistic interior decorations is notably that known as the Hoffman Decorative Moulding Company. The business conducted by this house was first established in 1888 by Hoffman, Roth & Co. In 1890 Mr. Roth retired and the firm name was changed to L. Hoffman & Co. In June, 1891, the Hoffman Decorative Moulding Company was incorporated under Illinois laws, with a capital of $13,000, and Augustus Sparr, president, and Louis Hoffmann, secretary and treasurer. The business is conducted, at present, at 125 and 127 E. Indiana street, where they temporarily occupy the fourth floor of a large four-story brick building, 150x60 feet in dimensions. Here they have all kinds of woodworking machinery and

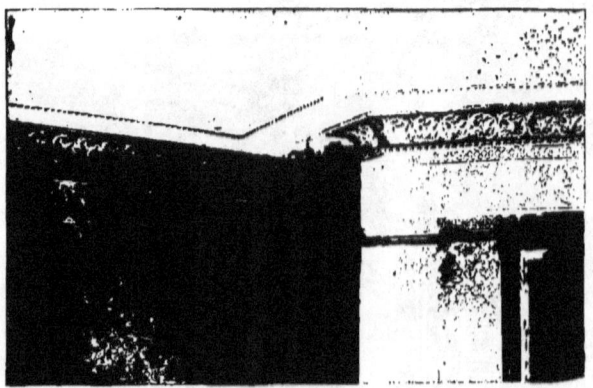

The above Cut taken from a Photograph showing the corner of room in the residence of K. T. Martin, Esq., Michigan avenue.

tools for making all kinds of decorative mouldings, the machinery being operated by steam power. But the quarters are much too small for the constantly increasing demands of the business, and the company is now erecting a fine six-story building, to be complete in every feature, and constructed to meet the needs of the business, to be situated on Ohio and Union streets, where they will remove to about June 1st, 1892. This company manufactures fine and artistic interior ornamental mouldings, in composition and wood. All kinds of oak, ash, cherry, maple, walnut and other woods are used, and the designs are characterized by novelty and beauty, with many original departures and exquisites effects. Twenty-five skilled workmen are employed by the company, the highest wages being paid them, that the best results may be attained, consequently the trade increases steadily. The goods manufactured by this company are sold all over the United States, and are having a steady demand. The members of the company are experienced and well-known business men, who are thoroughly representative. Mr. Sparr was born in Germany, and has resided in Chicago twenty-four years. He is thoroughly familiar with the business and is an energetic manager. Mr. Hoffmann, who founded the business, is a native of Germany, and came to Chicago about five years ago, being formerly located in Syracuse, N. Y., where he was engaged in business for thirty-five years. His success is his best indorsement. This is one of the few firms who make a specialty of designing and cutting their own dies, a feature of the business which fails to Mr. L. E. Hoffmann, in which he has attained eminent success.

C. O. SETHNESS & CO.,
Manufacturing - Chemists,

262, 264 & 266 N. CURTIS STREET,

TELEPHONE 7465. CHICAGO.

Acid C. P.
Acid Commercial.
Ammonia
Ethers.
Solution Muriate Iron.
Solution Nitrate Iron.

Fruit Flavors.
Liquor Flavors.
Essential Oils.
Sugar Coloring.

AMONG the prominent and enterprising concerns in its special line of production is that of C. O. Sethness & Company, Manufacturing Chemists, whose office and laboratory are at 262, 264 and 266 N. Curtis street. This business was founded by Mr. C. O. Sethness in 1884, who established himself in the retail drug business on Milwaukee avenue. In 1887 Mr. A. E. Thompson purchased an interest in the business and the firm style became C. O. Sethness & Co. The following year Mr. Sethness sold his interest in the retail drug business to Mr. Thompson and founded the present successful and growing enterprise, at 1201 Milwaukee ave. The rapid development of the business soon necessitated larger quarters and in January, 1890, Mr. Sethness transferred his plant to the present commodious quarters. On April 1, 1890, Mr. Conrad Hogenson became a partner in the concern, the firm style remaining as before C. O. Sethness & Co. The premises occupied are eminently suitable for the requirements of the business, consisting of a fine three-story building, giving ample accommodation for the extensive plant and appliances. Here the firm have the finest facilities for the manufacturing and distilling of ammonia, ethers and C. P. acids, sulphurous acid, butter of antimony, solution muriate iron, solution nitrate iron, and also manufacture a full line of C. P. chemicals. The company make a specialty of the above named chemicals and their products have no superior in the market. A full line of flavoring extracts are manufactured for rectifiers, confectioners, the soda water trade, etc. ; also essential oils, sugar coloring (the latter being a specialty), full lines of fruit juices, extract of malt, etc. Every appliance that experience and modern discovery has approved is to be found applied here, enabling the company to produce goods of the highest class and at prices, which, considering the quality, are extremely reasonable. They employ a full staff of experienced hands, and command an extensive and influential patronage in every part of the United States, besides a very important connection in Chicago and Illinois. Mr. Sethness as well as Mr. Hogenson, are Norwegians by birth, both being thoroughly American by training and education. They are gentlemen of integrity and keen business ability, who are abundantly worthy of the large measure of success attending their ably directed efforts.

LANSING & McGARIGLE.

THERE is no more accurate test of the refinement of a community, than the character of its hotels and restaurants. In this respect Chicago may justly claim the precedence over many older, but less progressive cities, her fame in this respect having circled the globe. This reputation has recently been materially enhanced, by the opening in May, 1890, of what is to all intents and purposes a new restaurant-cafe, at Nos. 122 to 126 Clark street, by Messrs. Lansing & McGarigle. Ever since the great fire, a small establishment of this kind has existed on the premises, the original proprietor being Mr. Julius Kirchoff. In 1881 Messrs. Lansing and Sickler succeeded, the latter gentleman giving way to Mr. McGarigle in 1889. It was then resolved to enlarge, redecorate and refurnish the premises throughout, at a cost of no less than $20,000, and the result is the most magnificent restaurant-cafe west of the Alleghany mountains. The highest skill, and the most distinguished talent, have been employed in the work of decorating, each of the four floors being treated in an entirely distinct way, the furniture, the floor, the walls and the ceiling of each, being made to harmonize perfectly, producing effects that are truly marvelous and incredible to those who have not seen them. These effects are greatly enhanced when the well-placed electric lights shed their mellow radiance on mirror and panel and cornice, turning one's thoughts involuntarily to the fairy palaces so vividly described in the "Arabian Nights" Entertainment. On going through this wonderful place, we are no longer astonished that the average number of customers here is 2,250 per diem, or that visitors to Chicago are instructed on no account to miss this unique sight. The main restaurant is situated on the ground floor, the second is for ladies and gentlemen, while the third and fourth are prepared for the larger private dining parties and club meetings, each floor being divided into two equal apartments. The stairway is one of the features of the place, harmonizing in splendor and design with the various floors which it connects, and partaking successively of the character of each. The basement is devoted to the cafe, which is unquestionably the finest in Chicago. The tiled floor, the large mirrors, the paneled ceiling and the unique circular bar in the center about which upward of one hundred electric lights are fixed, all displaying marvelous elegance and taste, and a clear insight into the requirements of the best class of trade. The cuisine of this unrivaled establishment is the talk of the city, and has acquired a great reputation far beyond its limits. Messrs. Lansing, and McGarigle, are natives of Saratoga, N. Y., and both gentlemen are reckoned among the most popular caterers in the West. We strongly advise our out-of-town readers, who intend visiting the great Columbian Exposition, to obtain their meals here if possible, or at the least, to inspect this perfect specimen of decorative art, as otherwise they will miss one of the marvels of the western metropolis, and one of the finest interiors in the United States.

ÆTNA COMPANY.

A MONG the enterprises established to supply the people's necessities, there is none more popular in Chicago than the Ætna Company, dealers in all kinds of coal and wood. This business was established by P. J. Quinn & Co. in 1877, and was continued by them with great success until Mr. F. Millerschin purchased the stock of the concern, and succeeded to the business in 1889. Mr. Millerschin had been for twelve years previous in the employ of the Company, and was familiar with the business and trade. Since his accession to the business it has increased remarkably, and is being augmented rapidly. The office and yards are located at 174 and 176 N. Clark street, and are large and well stocked with all kinds of hard and soft coal from the best mines and in convenient sizes. Pittston hard coal is a specialty, and soft coal from the following well-known mines may be had at any time, viz.: Erie, Briar Hill, B. & O., Hocking Valley, Gartsherrie, Indiana and Wilmington. The supply of hardwood and pine kindlings is complete and well selected. All kinds of slabs may be had, at 25 cents per cord below market prices. Maple, beech and pine woods are always carried in stock. The business done by the Company is extensive and of the most satisfactory character. Six teams are kept constantly in use, and the annual sales of coal exceeds 7,000 tons. Expressing is done to order, and trunks are promptly conveyed to and from all depots at moderate prices. Mr. Millerschin is a young man of pronounced business ability and unquestioned integrity. He is a member of the Independent Order of Foresters, also Royal League and has been remarkably successful, and has the brightest prospects for his career in the future.

C. F. GILLMANN & CO.
JEWELERS.

PROMINENT among the leading jewelry houses of Chicago, and one that is reliable and responsible, is that of C. F. Gillmann & Co. The business of this house was established in 1889.
Mr. Gillmann is well known in business and social circles, and is a young man of skill and ability.
He was born at Mineral Point, Wis., and has resided in Chicago for the past eight years. He has special qualifications for the business he is engaged in, and by his courteous manner and thorough
knowledge of the business has developed a large and representative trade. They occupy as a store,
the ground floor, 20x60 feet in dimensions of the building on the corner of N. Clark and Ohio
streets. This they have fitted up in elegant style, and stocked with fine watches of American and
foreign makes, in gold, silver and jeweled cases; also fine diamonds and other precious stones, beautiful jewelry of all kinds, including earrings, finger rings, bracelets and charms. They are also
importers of musical boxes of which they carry a large and well selected stock. A specialty is made
of resetting diamonds, which is done with skill and in the best manner. Watches, jewelry and
musical boxes are carefully repaired, and engraving neatly done. Mr. Gillmann is the agent of the
Western Clock Manufacturing Co., and sells many of these well-known clocks. The patronage of the
house is large and representative. Nine skilled persons are employed and every attention is paid
to the customer's request. Mr. Gillmann is a member of the Knights of Pythias, and is highly
respected.

W. P. SPALDING.

A MONG the leading houses in his section of the city engaged in his line of trade is that of Mr. W. P. Spalding, dealer in books, stationery, periodicals, etc., at No. 3733 Cottage Grove avenue. Mr. Spalding is a native of the State of Massachusetts, and has for several years been a resident of this city. He founded his present enterprise in 1886, and by his thorough knowledge of the business, coupled with well-directed efforts to meet the popular taste, he has built up a large and remunerative trade, which is rapidly and steadily increasing. His store is handsomely appointed and furnished, and is fitted up with every modern convenience and facility for the display of the heavy stock always on hand, and the successful prosecution of the business. The stock reflects in a creditable manner the good taste and enterprise of the proprietor, the walls, counters and floors being crowded with books in every branch of literature, ancient and modern. The house is leading headquarters for all the latest productions of the press, the newest books being found here as soon as published; likewise those whose variety commands the admiration of the scholar and man of letters. Periodicals, monthlies, magazines, etc., are always to be obtained here, and subscriptions are received for all publications. The assortment of stationery embraces full lines of plain and fancy goods, paper, envelopes, pens, pencils, inks, mucilage, rulers, erasers, blank books, journals, ledgers, diaries, etc., and all school and office supplies. Competent assistants are employed, and courteous and prompt service is accorded to all patrons. The lowest prices prevail, and the trade is very brisk. A large and handsome soda fountain is also in the store, which is altogether one of the most attractive on the avenue. Mr. Spalding has made hosts of friends by his courteous manner and sterling integrity, while his standing in commercial circles is in every respect of the highest. Mr. Spalding served with distinction in the late war in Company D, Fifth Regiment, for three years, where he was severely wounded. He was born in Lowell, Mass., where his father, W. P. Spalding, died only a few months ago, and who was one of the most esteemed and best known men, having filled the position of paymaster on the Northern Pacific Railroad for several years, and having completed his term as Judge of Probate.

CHARLES GARBEN.

THERE is no better Bakery and Ice Cream parlor on the North Side than that of Charles Garben, 176 North Clark Street. Mr. Garben established this business in 1883 at 181 North Clark Street, The business became popular and increased with phenomenal rapidity until it necessitated removal to the present commodious and convenient quarters at 176.

Mr. Garben is a native of Germany, and came to Chicago in 1872. He was formerly manager for Mr. Ed. Lary, on the North Side, and since he has been in business for himself has been very successful He has special qualifications for the business, being practical and experienced in all branches of the business besides having the most desirable business and social connections.

He occupies the ground floor and basement of the above mentioned premises, as store, icecream parlor and bakery. The floor has dimensions of 25x100 feet, and the parlor has a seating capacity of ninety. All kinds of fine cakes and confections are made fresh daily and exposed for sale in the store Sponge cake, wedding cake, fruit, jelly and all fancy cakes are always carried and sold at popular prices The confections are of the finest manufacture, and the bakery is furnished with every appliance for the making of the best class of goods. One hundred and fifty gallons of ice cream is the amount made for the parlor sales each day. The store and parlors are elegantly finished in hard wood, and have tile floors and elegant furnishings. Mr. Garben is a leading and representative business man; he is a prominent member of the Legion of Honor, and is held in the highest esteem by all who know him.

A. S. COWAN.

THERE is no more reputable Druggist and Chemist in Chicago than Mr. A. S. Cowan, who has been established in the business in this city for the past ten years. Mr. Cowan is a native of Dublin, Ireland, and graduated from Apothecaries' Hall, Dublin, in the class of 1878, was also assistant at the Carmichael College there, and for two years at the Queen's College, at Belfast, after which he came to Chicago and established his drug business at Clark and Division Streets. He remained in this location for six years, when he removed to his present location, corner State and Ohio Streets. In 1890 he opened a branch store, on the corner of Clark and Maple Streets. In all of these locations Mr. Cowan has had a liberal patronage. He employs four competent and experienced assistants at each place, and does a large and representative business. His stores are well stocked with fresh drugs, carefully selected by the proprietor; also druggists' sundries, perfumes, toilet articles, brushes, rubber goods, surgeons' supplies, proprietary articles, chemicals, etc. The stores are large and splendidly arranged, the showcases are fine plate glass, the woodwork and fixtures are all in oak, the soda fountain is one of the finest in the city, being inlaid in the most beautiful manner ; having a canopy top and fine silver trimmings. Everything is complete and beautiful. Mr. Cowan makes a specialty of compounding physicians' prescriptions to which he gives special care to insure accuracy, and also manufactures several proprietary articles of high order; his Beef, Iron and Wine Extract having an excellent reputation, and his tinctures being of the purest and most reliable character. Mr. Cowan is a successful and reliable druggist, and is worthy of the confidence and regard reposed in him.

EDWARD BEEH, JR.

THERE is no better representative of the art preservative in the city than the job printing offices and among them none takes precedence over that of Edward Beeh, Jr., at No. 59 Clybourn Avenue. Mr. Beeh established his business at the above location in 1877, and has prospered to such an extent that he now employs fifteen regular compositors, an indefinite number of " subs," and keeps six first-class printing presses in motion to accommodate his large and ever increasing trade.

Being a practical mechanic himself, he knows good work when he sees it, and will employ none but the best workmen, hence his work is always clean, neat and artistic. His "sorts" are of the latest and finest, and he does work in all of the modern languages in Commercial, Book and Job lines, making a specialty of newspaper and society work. Also furnishes Lodge seals, badges, and does bookbinding and engraving.

His power is a gas engine and his commodious offices are most conveniently furnished with all modern improvements.

Mr. Beeh is a German by birth, coming from Berlin in 1871. He is a prominent member of the Knights of Pythias, Foresters, Harugari, Order of Mutual Protection and Red Men, and is popular in business and social circles.

A MAN

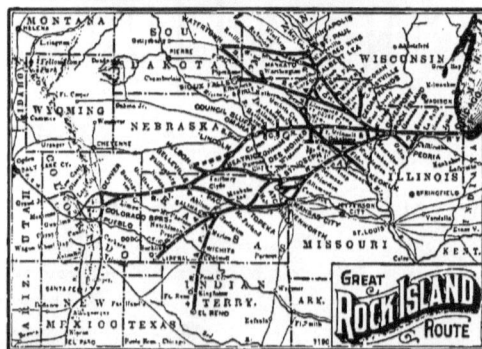

THE CHICAGO, ROCK ISLAND & PACIFIC RAILWAY,

The Direct Route to and from Chicago, Joliet, Ottawa, Peoria, La Salle, Moline, Rock Island, in ILLINOIS – Davenport, Muscatine, Ottumwa, Oskaloosa, Des Moines, Winterset, Audubon, Harlan and Council Bluffs, in IOWA – Minneapolis and St. Paul, in MINNESOTA – Watertown and Sioux Falls, in DAKOTA – Cameron, St. Joseph and Kansas City, in MISSOURI – Omaha, Lincoln, Fairbury and Nelson, in NEBRASKA – Atchison, Leavenworth, Horton, Topeka, Hutchinson, Wichita, Belleville, Salina, Dodge City, Caldwell, in KANSAS – Kingfisher, El Reno and Minco, in the INDIAN TERRITORY – Denver, Colorado Springs and Pueblo, in COLORADO. Traverses new areas of rich farming and grazing lands, affording the best facilities of intercommunication to all towns and cities east and west, northwest and southwest of Chicago, and to Pacific and trans-oceanic Seaports.

MAGNIFICENT VESTIBULE EXPRESS TRAINS,

Leading all competitors in splendor of equipment, between CHICAGO and DES MOINES, COUNCIL BLUFFS and OMAHA, and between CHICAGO and DENVER, COLORADO SPRINGS and PUEBLO, via KANSAS CITY and TOPEKA and via ST. JOSEPH. First-Class Day Coaches, FREE RECLINING CHAIR CARS and Palace Sleepers, with Dining Car Service. Close connections at Denver and Colorado Springs with diverging railway lines, now forming the new and picturesque

STANDARD GAUGE, TRANS-ROCKY MOUNTAIN ROUTE,

Over which superbly equipped trains run daily THROUGH WITHOUT CHANGE to and from Salt Lake City, Ogden and San Francisco. The Direct and Favorite Line to and from Manitou, Pike's Peak and all other sanitary and scenic resorts and cities and mining districts of Colorado.

DAILY FAST EXPRESS TRAINS

From St. Joseph and Kansas City to and from all important towns, cities and sections in Southern Nebraska, Kansas and the Indian Territory. Also via ALBERT LEA ROUTE from Kansas City and Chicago to Watertown, Sioux Falls, MINNEAPOLIS and ST. PAUL, connecting for all points North and Northwest, between the Lakes and the Pacific Coast.

For Tickets, Maps, Folders, or desired information, apply to any Coupon Ticket Office in the United States or Canada, or address

E. ST. JOHN,
General Manager.

CHICAGO, ILL.

JOHN SEBASTIAN,
Gen'l Ticket and Pass'r Agent.

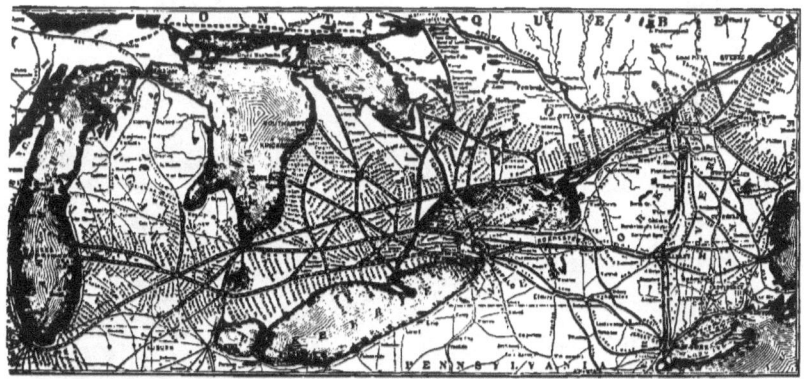